JULIUS LEVALLON

When John Mason first meets Juli[
feels an immediate connection. The
before—not in this lifetime, but m[
LeVallon introduces his young friend to a much larger
world, the world of *feeling-with*, of communing with the
Forces of Nature, even directing them. As Mason is pulled
into LeVallon's peculiar world, he discovers that not only
had they known each other before, but they had to correct
a mistake they had made with *another* in the days of pre-history, when they had loosed an elemental on the world. The
forbidden experiment needs to be recreated to set things
right. After college, Mason loses track of LeVallon. But destiny must be fulfilled, and many years later Mason is contacted by his old friend with portentous news—he has
found the *other!* It is time to set things right.

THE BRIGHT MESSENGER

Edward Fillery and Paul Devonham have a new patient at
their Spiritual Clinique, a young man raised in the Juru
mountains by an eccentric mentor. He seems to be suffering
from a split personality. One part of him manifests as a simple country lad by the name of Julian LeVallon, but there is
another force within him that Dr. Fillery quickly names
"N.H." and seeks to develop. Dr. Devonham, on the other
hand, is convinced that "N.H." is the unhealthy side, that
LeVallon is the true personality and must be encouraged to
become the dominant one. But the young man is more than
he seems, for he is not entirely human. And when "N.H."
does take control, no one is prepared for the results. Everyone is changed—by the bright messenger.

ALSO BY ALGERNON BLACKWOOD

NOVELS:
Jimbo: A Fantasy (1909)
The Education of Uncle Paul (1909)
The Human Chord (1910)
The Centaur (1911)
A Prisoner in Fairyland (1913)
The Extra Day (1916)
Julius Le Vallon: An Episode (1916)
The Wave: An Egyptian Aftermath (1916)
The Promise of Air (1918)
The Garden of Survival (1918)
The Bright Messenger (1921)

CHILDREN'S BOOKS:
Sambo and Snitch (1927)
Mr. Cupboard (1928)
Dudley and Gilderoy: A Nonsense (1929)
By Underground (1930)
The Parrot and the ‑ Cat (1931)
The Italian Conjuror (1932)
Maria (of England) in the Rain (1933)
Sergeant Poppett and Policeman James (1934)
The Fruit Stoners (1934)
How the Circus Came to Tea (1936)
The Adventures of Dudley and Gilderoy (1941)

AUTOBIOGRAPHY:
Episodes Before Thirty (1923)

ORIGINAL SHORT STORY
COLLECTIONS:
The Empty House and Other Ghost Stories (1906)

The Listener and Other Stories (1907)
John Silence —
    Physician Extraordinary (1908)
The Lost Valley and Other Stories (1910)
Pan's Garden: A Volume of Nature Stories (1912)
Incredible Adventures (1914)
Ten Minute Stories (1914)
Day and Night Stories (1917)
The Wolves of God and Other Fey Stories, w/Wildred Wilson (1921)
Tongues of Fire and Other Sketches (1924)
Full Circle (1929) [single story]
Shocks (1935)
The Doll and One Other (1946)
The Mysterious House (1987) [single story]
The Magic Mirror: Lost Supernatural and Mystery Stories (1989)

PLAYS:
Karma: A Reincarnation Play, w/Violet Pearn (1918)
Through the Crack w/Violet Pearn (1925)

Julius Le Vallon: An Episode

The Bright Messenger

BY ALGERNON BLACKWOOD

STARK HOUSE

Stark House Press • Eureka California

JULIUS LEVALLON / THE BRIGHT MESSENGER

Published by Stark House Press
1315 H Street
Eureka, CA 95501, USA
griffinskye3@sbcglobal.net
www.starkhousepress.com

JULIUS LEVALLON
Copyright © Algernon Blackwood, 1916

THE BRIGHT MESSENGER
Copyright © Algernon Blackwood, 1921

Introduction copyright © 2005 by Mike Ashley

ISBN: 0-9749438-7-8
ISBN 13: 978-0-9749438-7-9

Cover design and layout by Mark Shepard, www.SHEPGRAPHICS.COM
Cover art by Cynthia Bryn Williams

Note: Rather than tamper with Blackwood's prose, we have kept in all cases to the
spelling from the original hardback editions.

First Stark House Press Edition: June 2005

Reprint Edition

Contents

A Life's Work

BY MIKE ASHLEY

How great it would have been if this volume had been available thirty years ago. It was in 1978 that I started my researches for a biography of Algernon Blackwood, little knowing then that it would take me over twenty years to complete it. One of the problems—surprisingly greater than I anticipated—was acquiring all of Blackwood's books. Thanks to Richard Dalby I was able to purchase a copy of *Julius LeVallon* early on, but *The Bright Messenger* eluded me for several years—this was, of course, pre-internet days. As a result, when I did find it and eventually read it, it was some way removed from my reading of *Julius* and I lost the continuity. It was not until I came to write the biography, during which time I re-read all of Blackwood's books, that I came to read the two together and suddenly the inner light of *The Bright Messenger*, which had escaped me on first reading, shone forth.

It was then that I realised just how significant *The Bright Messenger* was. It wasn't simply a sequel to *Julius LeVallon*— and as I'll explain in a moment it wasn't really that anyway—but it was a culmination to most of Blackwood's work up to that point. It placed the period, perhaps even an exclamation mark, on a whole sequence of stories and novels which had started perhaps with "The Willows" and included most of the content of *Pan's Garden* and *Incredible Adventures* and novels such as *The Centaur* and *The Promise of Air*. It was effectively tracing the evolution of an entirely new form of existence.

I'd better explain, though I need two starting points, rather like tackling Everest from either Nepal or Tibet. Alas, we can't take the easy route first, as we have several foothills to traverse.

Anyone who has read sufficient of Blackwood's work beyond his early ghost and occult stories will know that he had a passion for Nature. It was something he shared with his father and the two liked nothing better than, with the first hint of spring, to set off into the countryside and commune with the wild. Blackwood never stopped doing it. He became such a Nature Boy that friends believed there was something almost non-human about him. He could sense things no one else could, because our senses have become far too dulled by so-called civilization. On travels in more remote parts of the world Blackwood would be overcome by the sense of place and time. You have only to read "A Descent Into Egypt" in *Incredible Adventures* to experience how the vast expanse of desert and Egypt's history absorbs your soul.

Blackwood became a nature mystic and through his extensive reading, exploration and experimentation, he came to believe that there was another form of existence with which we shared this planet. Possibly more than one, depending on how you interpret their manifestation. In *The Centaur* they took the form of primeval beings that were manifestations of the Earth-Soul. In "The Wendigo" they were the spirits of Nature itself, a manifestation of the "call of the wild". In *The Bright Messenger* they were the *Devas*. In fact we learn that the *Devas* are an all-encompassing spiritual evolution which incorporates all of these other entities from fairies and elementals to gods and demi-gods.

Throughout the peak of Blackwood's productivity he was striving to explore the world of the *deva*, though the concept was almost too vast to grasp. Instead he gave us glimpses of them in various forms. In "The Willows" they are the strange forces beyond our world but where we can unintentionally stray if we are not careful. In "The Sea Fit" they are the gods of old. In "The Glamour of the Snow" it is an ice elemental. In most of Blackwood's nature stories you will find some aspect of these spiritual beings. What you don't get a chance to see are these beings in their entire angelic form. Except, that is, in *The Bright Messenger*.

Back as early as 1908, after finishing the stories that make up *John Silence*, Blackwood struggled with the idea of how he could portray these nature beings. The idea that took hold was to have one such *deva* in human form so that it could be explained through human perspective.

But how to get the spirit in human form ... ??

On to our second starting point.

Blackwood was a student of the occult. He had migrated from theosophy to hermetical and alchemical studies as had so many others of his day, not least W. B. Yeats, George 'æ' Russell and Arthur E. Waite. As a member of the Order of the Golden Dawn Blackwood studied Hebrew magic and the Kabbala. Several of his stories, including "With Intent to Steal", "Smith: An Episode in a Lodging House", the John Silence series and especially the novel *The Human Chord*, arose out of these studies. But the most intense re-creation of his hermetical knowledge will be found in *Julius LeVallon*.

Julius LeVallon is intensely autobiographical. The narrator, John Mason, is Blackwood. You follow through his experiences—embellished for the sake of the story—at both private school and Edinburgh University. In his autobiography, *Episodes Before Thirty*, Blackwood tells us that a Hindu student whom he knew while at Edinburgh lent "a fraction of his personality" to both John Silence and Julius LeVallon. Blackwood tells us that this student "made clear a thousand half-conscious dreams and memories in me."

This is what you will discover in *Julius LeVallon*. LeVallon is a being who can remember all of his past lives. It transpires that both he and Mason—and another—had been acquainted in one of those past distant lives and had undertaken forbidden experiments. As a consequence of those LeVallon had set free an elemental. Through successive lives LeVallon had striven to be reunited with the souls of Mason and the other individual in order that they could repeat the experiment and thereby entrap and contain the elemental.

It is through those experiments—and I won't spoil the novel here by revealing their nature or their outcome—that we come to meet the creature who is the eponymous "bright messenger" of the sequel. Though, as I have explained, *The Bright Messenger* is really the book Blackwood had sought to write, only to find he had to write a prequel first in order to set the scene.

This "bright messenger" is a being both human and non-human—indeed, his non-human part is called simply N.H. and efforts to communicate with it are difficult. The one factor that seems to have some affect is love. This raises another interesting point in Blackwood's whole writing career. The best of his work was inspired by his association with Maya Stuart-King. A fey, almost other-worldly character herself, at the time Blackwood first met her she was married to a Russian industrialist, Baron Knoop, but this did not stop Blackwood and Maya finding a powerful spiritual attraction. Exactly when they met is difficult to determine. *Julius LeVallon* is dedicated to her as "To M. S-K. (1906)", but I remain uncertain of the significance of that date. It could be when they first met, though my own researches suggest that they did not meet before the summer of 1910, probably during Blackwood's visit to the Caucasus. There is little doubt that Maya served as a catalyst in Blackwood's work and she appears in most of Blackwood's works of this period. She was the third party in the distant past, the girl Silvatela, who had conducted the forbidden experiments with Mason and LeVallon. She reappears in *The Bright Messenger* as the Russian Nayan Khilkoff whose love strengthens the human side of the *deva*. Both books explore the power of spiritual love as one of the crucial forces in the world.

I have no intention of spoiling the development of *The Bright Messenger* so shall say little about it here. But there is one further point that is crucial to make.

Although Blackwood started *Julius LeVallon* in 1908 he did not finish it until early in 1911, completed in a moment of passion and white heat, inspired by his months of travel the previous summer in the Caucasus. The book was not published until five years later, in 1916. I do not know why he did not seek its publication earlier. It's possible he wanted to complete the sequel first, though it is evident from his correspondence with artist and playwright W. Graham Robertson, that Blackwood did not anticipate writing the sequel straightaway. "And so now I return to our old Centaur till he's finished," he told Robertson in February 1911. "Then, a long way off yet, the second half of Julius."

Blackwood had much else to write and explore. *The Centaur* itself was an intense creative experience, arguably Blackwood's most inspired. But Blackwood was also exploring other threads, most notably his novels of childhood imagination which had started with *The Education of Uncle Paul* and would include *A Prisoner in Fairyland* and *The Extra Day*. All of these books were completed and published before *Julius LeVallon* eventually saw print, and it would be another five years, not until 1921, that *The Bright Messenger* appeared.

It was a different Blackwood who produced that novel, a Blackwood seriously affected by the Great War in which he had served as an intelligence agent and with the Red Cross as a 'searcher'. Before the War Blackwood was an optimist, but after the War he became, at least for a while, a haunted pessimist. His hopes for the spiritual evolution of mankind had been dashed.

Yet he believed the potential remained. This is what he explored in *The Bright Messenger*. It is a book of hope that one day mankind will be able to rise above its base instincts and move on to a new plane of existence. Blackwood is intensely aware, however, that humanity cannot do it alone. It needs the help of the spirit world, of the *Devas*, to achieve this transcendence. And the "bright messenger" itself, that outcome of the experiments of LeVallon and friends, is the intermediary between the two worlds.

The Bright Messenger is dedicated "To the Unstable", meaning to all those suffering the mental and spiritual anguish of the Great War, providing a message of hope and recovery.

The Bright Messenger allows Blackwood to explore the post-War world— perhaps a little too much at times—and you see the contrast between the old world and the new, and the hope for a better world. As such the book is far more a product of its time than *Julius LeVallon*, and has to be read as such. Yet Blackwood does not forsake his original plan, though I am sure he had to adapt it to circumstance. The final chapters of the novel are amongst the most profound that Blackwood wrote, just as the final chapters of *Julius LeVallon* are amongst the most potent.

When Blackwood finished *The Bright Messenger* he believed he had completed his life's work. Thereafter he planned to write his autobiography and then devote his time to journalism. In the end he did write other novels, including another of childhood wonder, *The Fruit Stoners*, and a satire on society, *Dudley & Gilderoy*. And though he wrote more stories, he would never write anything again that had the power or stature of his earlier works. That was because in *The Bright Messenger* he had said it all.

These two novels, therefore, are the culmination of a lifetime's experience, and were themselves thirteen years in the making. You will encounter nothing like them anywhere else in the whole of fantastic literature.

- *Mike Ashley*

Julius Le Vallon: An Episode

TO
M. S·K.
(1906)

BOOK I

SCHOOLDAYS

"Dream faces bloom around your face
Like flowers upon one stem;
The heart of many a vanished race
Sighs as I look on them."
                                                A. E.

CHAPTER I

"Surely death acquires a new and deeper significance when we regard it no longer as a single and unexplained break in an unending life, but as part of the continually recurring rhythm of progress—as inevitable, as natural, and as benevolent as sleep."—"Some Dogma of Religion" (Prof. J. M'Taggart).

It was one autumn in the late 'nineties that I found myself at Bâle, awaiting letters. I was returning leisurely from the Dolomites, where a climbing holiday had combined pleasantly with an examination of the geologically interesting Monzoni Valley. When the claims of the latter were exhausted, however, and I turned my eyes towards the peaks, it happened that bad weather held permanent possession of the great grey cliffs and towering pinnacles, and climbing was out of the question altogether. A world of savage desolation gloomed down upon me through impenetrable mists; the scouts of winter's advance had established themselves upon all possible points of attack; and the whole tossed wilderness of precipice and scree lay safe, from my assaults at least, behind a frontier of furious autumn storms.

Having ample time before my winter's work in London, I turned my back upon the unconquered Marmolata and Cimon della Pala, and made my way slowly, via Bozen and Innsbruck, to Bâle; and it was in the latter place, where my English correspondence was kind enough to overtake me, that I found one letter in particular that interested me more than all the others put together. It bore a Swiss stamp; and the handwriting caused me a thrill of anticipatory excitement even before I had consciously recalled the name of the writer. It was addressed before and behind till there was scarcely room left for a postmark, and it had journeyed from my chambers to my club, from my club to the university, and thence, by way of various poste-restantes, from one hotel to another till, with good luck little short of marvellous, it discovered me in my room of the

Trois Rois Hotel overlooking the Rhine.

The signature, to which I turned at once before reading the body of the message, was Julius LeVallon; and as my eye noted the firm and very individual writing, once of familiar and potent significance in my life, I was conscious that emotions of twenty years ago woke vigorously into being, releasing sensations and memories I had thought buried beyond all effective resurrection. I knew myself swept back to those hopes and fears that, all these years before, had been— me. The letter was brief; it ran as follows:

FRIEND OF A MILLION YEARS, —Should you remember your promise, given to me at Edinburgh twenty years ago, I write to tell you that I am ready. Yours, especially in separation,

Julius LeVallon.

And then followed two lines of instructions how to reach him in the isolated little valley of the Jura Mountains, on the frontier between France and Switzerland, whence he wrote.

The wording startled me; but this surprise, not unmingled with amusement, gave place immediately to emotions of a deeper and much more complex order, as I drew an armchair to the window and resigned myself, half pleasurably, half uneasily, to the flood of memories that rose from the depths and besieged me with their atmosphere of half-forgotten boyhood and of early youth. Pleasurably, because my curiosity was aroused abruptly to a point my dull tutorial existence now rarely, if ever, knew; uneasily, because these early associations grouped themselves about the somewhat unearthly figure of a man with whom once I had been closely intimate, but who had since disappeared behind a veil of mystery to follow pursuits where danger to body, mind and soul—it seemed to me—must be his constant attendant.

For Julius LeVallon, or Julius, as he was known to me in our school and university days, had been once a name to conjure with; a personality who evoked for me a world more vast and splendid, horizons wider, vistas of possibilities more dazzling, than any I have since known—which have contracted, in fact, with my study of an exact science to a dwindled universe of pettier scale and measurement;—and wherein, formerly, with all the terror and delight of vividly imagined adventure, we moved side by side among strange experiences and fascinating speculations.

The name brings back the face and figure of as singular an individual as I have ever known who, but for my saving streak of common sense and inability to imagine beyond a certain point, might well have swept me permanently into his own region of research and curious experiment. As it was, up to the time when I felt obliged to steer my course away from him, he found my nature of great assistance in helping him to reconstruct his detailed mental pictures of the past; we were both "in the same boat together," as he constantly assured me—this boat that travelled down the river of innumerable consecutive lives; and there can be no doubt that my cautious questionings—lack of perspective, he termed it—besides checking certain aspects of his conception, saved us at the same time from results that must have proved damaging to our reputations, if not injurious actually to our persons, physically and mentally. Yet that he captured me so completely at the time was due to an innate sympathy I felt towards his theories, a sympathy that at times amounted to complete acceptance. I freely admit this sympathy. He used another word for it, however: he called it Memory.

As a boy, Julius LeVallon was beyond question one of the strangest beings that ever wore a mortar-board, or lent his soul and body to the conventionalities of an English private school.

I recall, as of yesterday, my first sight of him, and the vivid impression, startling as of shock, he then produced: the sensitive, fine face, pallid as marble, the thatch of tumbling dark hair, and the eyes of changing greeny blue that shone unlike any English eyes I have ever looked upon before or since. "Giglamps" the other boys called them, of course; but when you caught them through the black hair that straggled over the high white forehead, they somehow conveyed the impression of twin lanterns, now veiled, now clear, seen through the tangled shadows of a twilight wood. Unlike the eyes of most dreamers, they looked keenly within, rather than vaguely beyond; and I recall to this day the sharp, half disquieting effect produced upon my mind as a new boy the first instant I saw them—that here was an individual who somehow stood aloof from the mob of noisy, mischief-loving youngsters all about him, and had little in common with the world in which this school was a bustling, practical centre of educational energy.

Nor is it that I recall that first sight with the added judgment of later years. I insist that this moment of his entrance into my life was accompanied by an authentic thrill of wonder that announced his presence to my nerves, or even deeper, to my very soul. My sympathetic nervous system was instinctively aware of him. He came upon me with a kind of rush for which the proper word is startling; there was nothing gradual about it; its nature was electrifying; and in some sense he certainly captivated me, for, immediately upon knowing him, this opening wonder merged in a deep affection of a kind so intimate, so fearless, so familiar, that it seemed to me that I must, somewhere, somehow, have known him always. For years to come it bound me to his side. To the end, moreover, I never quite lost something of that curious first impression, that he moved, namely, in an outer world that did not claim him; that those luminous, inward-peering eyes saw but dimly the objects we call real; that he saw them as counters in some trivial game he deemed it not worth while to play; that, while, perforce, he used them like the rest of us, their face-value was as naught compared to what they symbolised; that, in a word, he stood apart from the vulgar bustle of ordinary ambitious life, and above it, in a region by himself where he was forever questing issues of infinitely greater value.

For a boy of fifteen, as I then was, this seems much to have discerned. At the time I certainly phrased it all less pompously in my own small mind. But that first sense of shock remains: I yearned to know him, to stand where he stood, to be exactly like him. And our speedy acquaintance did not overwhelm me as it ought to have done—for a singular reason; I felt oddly that somehow or other I had the *right* to know him instantly.

Imagination, no doubt, was stronger in me at that time than it is to-day; my mind more speculative, my soul, perhaps, more sensitively receptive. At any rate the insignificant and very ordinary personality I own at present has since largely recovered itself. If Julius LeVallon was one in a million, I know that I can never expect to be more than one *of* a million. And it is something in middle age to discover that one can appreciate the exceptional in others without repining at its absence in oneself.

Julius was two forms above me, and for a day or two after my arrival at mid-term, it appears he was in the sick-room with one of those strange nervous illnesses that came upon him through life at intervals, puzzling the doctors and alarming those responsible for his well-being; accompanied, too, by symptoms that to-day would be recognised, I imagine, as evidence of a secondary personality. But on the third or fourth day, just as afternoon "Preparation" was beginning and we were all shuffling down upon our wooden desks with a clatter of books and pens, the door beside the great blackboard opened, and a figure stole into the room, tall, slender, and unsubstantial as a shadow, yet intensely real.

"Hullo! Giglamps back again!" whispered the boy on my left, and another behind me sniggered audibly "Jujubes"—thus Julius was sometimes paraphrased—"tired of shamming at last!" Then Hurrish, the master in charge, whose head had been hidden a moment behind his desk, closed the lid and turned. He greeted the boy with a few kind words of welcome which, of course, I have forgotten; yet, so strange are the freaks of memory, and so instantaneous and prophetic the first intuitions of sympathy or aversion, that I distinctly recall that I liked Hurrish for his words, and was grateful to him for his kindly attitude towards a boy whose very existence had hitherto been unknown to me. Already, before I knew his name, Julius LeVallon meant, at any rate, this to me.

But from that instant the shadow became most potently real substance. The boy moved forward to his desk, looked about him as though to miss no face, and almost immediately across that big room full of heads and shoulders saw—myself.

That something of psychical import passed swiftly between us is indubitable, for while Julius visibly started, pausing a moment in his walk and staring as though he would swallow me with his eyes, there flashed upon my own mind a thought so vivid, so precise, that it took actual sentence form, and before I could possibly have imagined or invented an idea so uncorrelated with a previous experience of any kind at all, I heard myself murmuring: "He's found me...!"

It seemed audible, at least. I hid my face a second, thinking I had spoken it aloud. No one looked at me, however; Hurrish made no comment. My name did not sound terribly across the class-room. The sentence, after all, had remained a thought. But that it leaped into my mind at all seems to me now, as it did at the time, significant.

His eyes rested for the fraction of a second on my face as he crossed the floor, and I felt—but how describe it intelligibly?—as though a wind had risen and caught me up into another place where there was great light and an impression of vast distances. Hypnotic we should call it to-day; hypnotic let it be. I can only affirm how, with that single glance from a boy but slightly older than myself, seen then for the first time, and with no word yet spoken, there came back to me a larger sense of life, and of the meaning of life. I became aware of an extended world, of wonder, movement, adventure on a scale immensely grander than any-thing I found about me among known external things. But I became aware—"again." In earlier childhood I had known this bigger world. It suddenly flashed over me that time stretched *behind* me as well as before—and that I stretched back with it. Something scared me, I remember, with a faint stirring as of old pains and pleasures suffered long ago. The face and eyes that called into being these fancies, so oddly touched with alarm, were like those seen sometimes in dreams that never venture into daily life—things of composite memory, no doubt, that bring with them an atmosphere, and a range of query, nothing in normal waking life can even suggest.

He passed to his place in front of Hurrish's desk among the upper forms, and a sea of tousled heads intervened to hide him from my sight; but as he went the afternoon sunshine fell through the unfrosted half of the window, and in later years—now, in fact, as I hold his letter in my hand and re-collect these vanished memories—I still see him coming into my life with the golden sunlight about his head and his face wrapped in its halo. I see it reflected in the lamping eyes, glistening on the mop of dark hair, shining on the pallid face with its high ex-pression of other-worldliness and yearning remote from the chaos of modern life.... It was a long time before I managed to bring myself down again to parse the verbs in that passage of *Hecuba*, for, if anything, I have understated rather than exaggerated the effect that this first sight of Julius LeVallon produced upon my feelings and imagination. Some one, lost through ages but ever seeking me, rose suddenly and spoke: "So here you are, at last! I've found you. We've found each other again!"

To say more could only be to elaborate the memory with knowledge that came later, and thus to distort the first simple and profound impression. I merely wish to present, as it occurred, the picture of this wizard face appearing suddenly above the horizon of my small schoolboy world, staring with that deep sug-gestion of having travelled down upon me from immense distances *behind*, bring-ing fugitive and ghostly sensations of things known long ago, and hinting very faintly, as I have tried to describe, of vanished pains and alarms—yet of suf-ferings so ancient that to touch them even with the tenderest of words is to make them crumble into dust and disappear.

CHAPTER II

"'Body,' observes Plotinus, 'is the true river of Lethe.' The memory of definite events in former lives can hardly come easily to a consciousness allied with brain... Bearing in mind also that even our ordinary definite memories slowly become indefinite, and that most drop altogether out of notice, we shall attach no importance to the naive question, 'Why does not Smith remember who he was before?' It would be an exceedingly strange fact if he did, a new Smith being now in evidence along with a new brain and nerves. Still, it is conceivable that such remembrances occasionally arise. Cerebral process, conscious or subconscious, is psychical."—"Individual and Reality" (E. D. Fawcett).

Looking back upon this entrance, not from the present long interval of twenty years, but from a point much nearer to it, and consequently more sympathetically in touch with my own youth, I must confess that his presence—his arrival, as it seemed—threw a momentary clear light of electric sharpness upon certain "inner scenery" that even at this period of my boyhood was already beginning to fade away into dimness and "mere imagining." Which brings me to a reluctant confession I feel bound to make. I say "reluctant," because at the present time I feel intellectually indisposed to regard that scenery as real. Its origin I know not; its reality at the time I alone can vouch for. Many children have similar experiences, I believe; with myself it was exceptionally vivid.

Ever since I could remember, my childhood days were charged with it—haunting and stimulating recollections that were certainly derived from nothing in this life, nor owed their bright reality to anything seen or read or heard. They influenced all my early games, my secret make-believe, my magical free hours after lessons. I dreamed them, played them, lived them, and nothing delighted me so much as to be alone on half-holidays in summer out of doors, or on winter evenings in the empty schoolroom, so that I might reconstruct for myself the gorgeous detail of their remote, elusive splendour. For the presence of others, even of my favourite playmates, ruined their reality with criticising questions, and a doubt as to their genuineness was an intrusion upon their sacredness my youthful heart desired to prevent by—killing it at once. Their nature it would be wearisome to detail, but I may mention that their grandeur was of somewhat mixed authority, and that if sometimes I was a general like Gideon, against whom Amalekites and such like were the merest insects, at others I was a High Priest in some huge, dim-sculptured Temple whose magnificence threw Moses and the Bible tabernacles into insignificance.

Yet it was upon these glories, and upon this sacred inner scenery, that the arrival of Julius LeVallon threw a new daylight of stark intensity. He made them live again. His coming made them awfully real. They had been fading. Going to school was, it seemed, a finishing touch of desolating destruction. I felt obliged to give them up and be a man. Thus ignored, disowned, forgotten of set deliberation, they sank out of sight and were prepared to disappear, when suddenly his arrival drew the entire panorama delightfully into the great light of day again. His presence re-touched, re-coloured the entire series. He made them true.

It would take too long, besides inviting the risk of unconscious invention, were I to attempt in detail the description of our growing intimacy. Moreover, I believe it is true that the intimacy did not grow at all, but suddenly, incomprehensibly was. At any rate, I remember with distinctness our first conversation. The hour's "prep." was over, and I was in the yard, lonely and disconsolate as a new boy, watching the others playing tip-and-run against the high enclosing wall, when Julius LeVallon came up suddenly behind me, and I turned expectantly at the sound of his almost stealthy step. He came softly. He was smiling. In the falling dusk he looked more shadow-like than ever. He wore the school cap at the back of his head, where it clung to his tumbling hair like some absurd disguise circumstances forced him to adopt for the moment.

And my heart gave a bound of excitement at the sound of his voice. In some strange way the whole thing seemed familiar. I had expected this. It had happened before. And, very swiftly, a fragment of that inner scenery, laid like a theatre-inset against the playground of to-day, flashed through the depths of me, then vanished.

"What is your name?" he asked me, very gently.

"Mason," I told him, conscious that I flushed and almost stammered. "John Mason. I'm a new boy." Then, although my brother, formerly Head of the school, had already gone on to Winchester, I added "Mason secundus." My outer self felt shy, but another, deeper self realised a sense of satisfaction that was pleasure. I was aware of a desire to seize his hand and utter something of this bigger, happier sensation. The strength of school convention, however, prevented anything of the sort. I was at first embarrassed by the attention of a bigger boy, and showed it.

He looked closely into my face a moment, as though searching for something, but so penetratingly that I felt his eyes actually inside me. The information I had given did not seem to interest him particularly. At the same time I was conscious that his near presence affected me in a curious way, for I lost the feeling that this attention to a new boy was flattering and unusual, and became aware that there was something of great importance he wished to say to me. It was all right and natural. There was something he desired to find out and know: it was not my name. A vague yet profound emotion troubled me.

He spoke then, slowly, earnestly; the voice gentle and restrained, but the expression in the eyes and face so grave, almost so solemn, that it seemed an old and experienced man who addressed me, instead of a boy barely sixteen years of age.

"Have you then... quite... forgotten... everything?" he asked, making dramatic pauses thus between the words.

And, singular in its abruptness though the question was, there flashed upon me even while he uttered it, a sensation, a mood, a memory—I hardly know what to call it—that made the words intelligible. It dawned upon me that I *had* "forgotten... everything... quite": crowded, glorious, ancient things, that some' how or other I ought to have remembered. A faint sense of guiltiness accom' panied the experience. I felt disconcerted, half ashamed.

"I'm afraid... I have," came my faltering reply. Though bewildered, I raised my eyes to his. I looked straight at him. "I'm—Mason secundus... now...."

His eyes, I saw, came up, as it were, from their deep searching. They rested quietly upon my own, with a reassuring smile that made them kindly and understanding as those of my own father. He put his hand on my shoulder in a protective fashion that gave me an intense desire to remember all the things he wished me to remember, and thus to prove myself worthy of his interest and attention. The desire in me was ardent, serious. Its fervency, moreover, seemed to produce an effect, for immediately there again rose before my inner vision that flashing scenery I had "imagined" as a child.

Possibly something in my face betrayed the change. His expression, at any rate, altered instantly as though he recognised what was happening.

"You're Mason secundus now," he said more quickly. "I know that. But—can you remember nothing of the Other Places? Have you quite forgotten when— we were together ?"

He stopped abruptly, repeating the last three words almost beneath his breath. His eyes rested on mine with such pleasure and expectancy in them that for the moment the world I stood in melted out, the playground faded, the shouts of cricket ceased, and I seemed to forget entirely who or where I was. It was as though other times, other feelings, other scenery battled against the actual present, claiming me, sweeping me away, extending the sense of personal identity towards a previous series. Seductive the sensation was beyond belief, yet at the same time disturbing. I wholly ignored the flattery of this kindness from an older boy. A series of vivid pictures, more familiar than the nursery, more distant than a dream of years ago, swam up from some inner region of my being like memories of places, people, adventures I had actually lived and seen. The near presence of Julius LeVallon drew them upwards in a stream above the horizon of some temporarily veiled oblivion.

"...in the Other Places," his voice continued with a droning sound that was like the sea a long way off, or like wind among the branches of a tree.

And something in me leaped automatically to acknowledge the truth I sud' denly realised.

"Yes, yes!" I cried, no shyness in me any more, and plunged into myself to seize the flying pictures and arrest their sliding, disappearing motion. "I remember, oh, I remember... a whole lot of... dreams... or things like made-up adventures I once had ages and ages ago... with..." I hesitated a second. A rising and inex' plicable excitement stopped my words. I was shaking all over. "...with you!" I added boldly, or rather the words seemed to add themselves inevitably. "It was with you, sir?"

He nodded his head slightly and smiled. I think the "sir," sounding so incon' gruous, caused the smile.

"Yes," he said in his soft, low voice, "it was with me. Only they were not dreams. They were real. There's no good denying what's real; it only prevents your remembering properly."

The way he said it held conviction as of sunrise, but anyhow denial in myself seemed equally to have disappeared. Deep within me a sense of reality answered willingly to his own.

"And myself?" he went on gently yet eagerly at the same time, his eyes searching my own. "Don't you remember—me? Have I, too, gone quite beyond recall?"

But with truth my answer came at once:

"Something... perhaps... comes back to me... a little," I stammered. For while aware of a keen sensation that I talked with someone I knew as well as I knew my own father, nothing at the moment seemed wholly real to me except his sensitive, pale face with the large and beautiful eyes so keenly peering. and the tangled hair escaping under that ridiculous school cap. The pine trees in the cricket-field rose into the fading sky behind him, and I remember being puzzled to determine where his hair stopped and the feathery branches began.

"...carrying the spears up the long stone steps in the sunshine," his voice murmured on with a sound like running water, "and the old man in the robe of yellow standing at the top... and orchards below, all white and pink with blossoms dropping in the wind... and miles of plain in blue distances far away, the river winding... and birds fishing in the shallow places..."

The picture flashed into my mind. I saw it. I remembered it in detail as easily as any childhood scene of a few years ago, but yet through a blur of summery haze and at the end of a stupendous distance that reduced the scale to lilliputian proportions. I looked down the wrong end of a telescope at it all. The appalling distance—and something else as well I was at a loss to define—frightened me a little.

"I... my people, I mean... live in Sussex," I remember saying irrelevantly in my bewilderment, "and my father's a clergyman." It was the upper part of me that said it, no doubt anticipating the usual question "What's your father?" My voice had a lifeless, automatic sound.

"That's now," LeVallon interrupted almost impatiently. "It's thinking of these things that hides the others."

Then he smiled, leaning against the wall beside me while the sunset flamed upon the clouds above us and the tide of noisy boys broke, tumbling about our feet. I see those hurrying clouds, crimson and gold, that scrimmage of boys in the school playground, and Julius LeVallon gazing into my eyes, his expression rapt and eager—I see it now across the years as plainly as I saw that flash of inner scenery far, far away. I even hear his low voice speaking. The whole, strange mood that rendered the conversation not too incredibly fantastic at the time comes over me again as I think of it.

He went on in that murmuring tone, putting true words to the pictures that rolled clearly through me

"...and the burning sunlight on the white walls of the building... the cool deep shadows where we talked and slept... the shouting of the armies in the distance... with the glistening of the spears and shining shields..."

Mixed curiously together, kaleidoscopic, running one into the other without sharp outlines of beginning or end, the scenes fled past me like the pages of a coloured picture-book. I saw figures plainly, more plainly than the scenery beyond. The man in the yellow robe looked close into my eyes, so close, indeed, I could almost hear him speak. He vanished, and a woman took his place. Her back was to me. She stood motionless, her hands upraised, and a gesture of passionate entreaty about her plunged me suddenly into a sea of whirling, poignant drama that had terror in it. The blood rushed to my head. My heart beat violently. I knew a moment of icy horror—that she would turn—and I should recognise her face—worse, that she would recognise my own. I experienced actual fear, a shrinking dread of something that was nameless. Escape was impossible, I could neither move nor speak, nor alter any single detail in this picture which—most terrifying of all—I knew contained somewhere too—myself. But she did not turn; I did not see her face. She vanished like the rest... and I next saw quick, running figures with skins of reddish brown, circlets of iron about their foreheads and red tassels hanging from their loin cloths. The scene had shifted.

"...when we lit the signal fires upon the hills," the voice of LeVallon broke in softly, looking over his shoulder lest we be disturbed, "and lay as sentinels all night beside the ashes... till the plain showed clearly in the sunrise with the encampments marked over it like stones..."

I saw the blue plain fading into distance, and across it a swiftly-moving cloud of dust that was ominous in character, presaging attack. Again the scene shifted noiselessly as a picture on a screen, and a deserted village slid before me, with small houses built of undressed stone, and roomy paddocks, abandoned to the wild deer from the hills. I smelt the keen, fresh air and the scent of wild flowers. A figure, carrying a small blue stick, passed with tearing rapidity up the empty street.

"...when you were a Runner to the tribe," the voice stepped curiously in from a world outside it all, "carrying warnings to the House of Messengers... and I held the long night-watches upon the passes, signalling with the flaming torches to those below..."

"But so far away, so dim, so awfully small, that I can hardly—"

The world of to-day broke in upon my voice, and I stopped, not quite aware of what I had been about to say. Martin, the Fourth Form and Mathematical Master, had come up unobserved by either of us, and was eyeing LeVallon and myself somewhat curiously. It was afterwards, of course, that I discovered who the interrupter was. I only knew at the moment that I disliked the look of him, and also that I felt somehow guilty.

"New boy in tow, LeVallon?" he remarked casually, the tone and manner betraying ill-concealed disapproval. The change of key, both in its character and its abruptness, seemed ugly, almost dreadful. It was so trivial.

"Yes, sir. It's young Mason." LeVallon answered at once, touching his cap respectfully, but by no means cordially.

"Ah," said the master dryly. "He's fortunate to find a friend so soon. Tell him we look to him to follow his brother's example and become Head of the school one day perhaps." I got the impression, how I cannot say, that Martin stood in awe of LeVallon, was even a little afraid of him as well. He would gladly have "scored off" him if it were possible. There was a touch of spite in his voice, perhaps.

"We knew one another before, sir," I heard Julius say quietly, as though his attention to a new boy required explanation—to Martin.

I could hardly believe my ears. This extraordinary boy was indeed in earnest. He had not the smallest intention of saying what was untrue. He said what he actually believed. I saw him touch his cap again in the customary manner, and Martin, the under-master, shrugging his shoulders, passed on without another word. It is difficult to describe the dignity LeVallon put into that trivial gesture of conventional respect, or in what way Martin gained a touch of honour from it that really was no part of his commonplace personality. Yet I can remember perfectly well that this was so, and that I deemed LeVallon more wonderful than ever from that moment for being able to exact deference even from an older man who was a Form Master and a Mathematical Master into the bargain. For LeVallon, it seemed to me, had somehow positively dismissed him.

Yet, to such extent did the pictures in my mind dominate the playground where our bodies stood, that I almost expected to see the master go down the "long stone steps towards the sunny orchard below"—instead of walk up and cuff young Green who was destroying the wall by picking out the mortar from between the bricks. That wall, and the white wall in the dazzling sunshine seemed, as it were, to interpenetrate each other. The break of key caused by the interruption, however, was barely noticeable. The ugliness vanished instantly. Julius was speaking again as though nothing had happened. He had been speaking for some little time before I took in what the words were:

"...with the moonlight gleaming on the bosses of the shields... the sleet of flying arrows... and the hissing of the javelins..."

The battle-scene accompanying the sentence caught me so vividly, so fiercely even, that I turned eagerly to him, all shyness gone, and let my words pour out impetuously as they would, and as they willy-nilly had to. For this scene, more than all the others, touched some intimate desire, some sharp and keen ambition that burned in me to-day. My whole heart was wrapped up in soldiering. I had chosen a soldier's career instinctively, even before I knew quite the meaning of it.

"Yes, rather!" I cried with enthusiasm, staring so close into his face that I could have counted the tiny hairs on the smooth pale skin, "and that narrow ledge high up inside the dome where the prisoners stood until they dropped on to the spearheads in the ground beneath, and how some jumped at once, and others stood all day, and—and how there was only just room to balance by pressing the feet sideways against the curving call... ?"

It all rushed at me as though I had witnessed the awful scene a week ago. Something inside me shook again with horror at the sight of the writhing figures impaled upon the spears below. I almost felt a sharp and actual pain pierce through my flesh. I overbalanced. It was my turn to fall...

A sudden smile broke swiftly over LeVallon's face, as he held my arm a moment with a strength that almost hurt.

"Ah, you remember *that!* And little wonder—" he began, then stopped abruptly and released his grip. The cricket ball came bouncing to our feet across the yard, with insistent cries of "Thank you, ball! Thank you, LeVallon!" impossible to ignore. He did not finish the sentence, and I know not what shrinking impulse of suffering and pain in me it was that felt relieved he had not done so. Instead, he stooped good-naturedly, picked up the ball, and flung it back to the importunate cricketers; and as he did so I noticed that his action was unlike that of any English boy I had ever seen. He did not throw it as men usually throw a ball, but used a violent yet graceful motion that I vaguely remembered to have seen somewhere before. It perplexed me for a moment—then, suddenly, out of that deeper part of me so strangely now astir, the hint of explanation came. It was the action of a man who flings a spear or javelin.

A bell rang over our heads with discordant clangour, and we were swept across the yard with the rush of boys. The transition was abrupt and even painful—as when one comes into the noisy street from a theatre of music, lights and colour. A strong effort was necessary to recover balance and pull myself together. Until we reached the red-brick porch, however, LeVallon kept beside me, and his hurried last phrases, as we parted, were the most significant of all. It seemed as if he kept them for the end, although no such intention was probably in his thought. They left me quivering through and through as I heard them fall from his lips so quietly.

His face was shining. The words came from his inmost heart

"Well, anyhow," he said beneath his breath lest he might be overheard, "I've found you, and we've found each other—at last. That's the great thing, isn't it? No one here understands all that. Now, we can go on together where we left off before; and, having found you, I expect I shall soon find her as well. For we're all three together, and—sooner or later—there's no escaping anything."

I remember that I staggered. The hand I put out to steady myself scraped along the uneven bricks and broke the skin. A boy with red hair struck me viciously in the back because I had stumbled into him; he shouted at me angrily too, though I heard no word he said. And LeVallon, for his part, just had time to bend his head down with "work hard and get up into my form—we shall have more chances then," and was gone into the passage and out of sight—leaving me trembling inwardly as though stricken by some sudden strange attack of nerves.

For his words about the woman turned me inexplicably—into ice. My legs gave way beneath me. A cold perspiration broke out upon my skin. No words of any kind came to me; there was no definite thought; clear recollection, absolutely none. The strange emotion itself I could not put a name to, nor could

I say what part was played in it by any particular ingredient such as horror, terror, or mere ordinary alarm. All these were in it somewhere, linked darkly to a
sense of guilt at length discovered and brought home. I can only say truthfully
that I saw again the picture of that woman with her back towards me; but that,
when he spoke, she turned and looked at me. She showed her face. I knew a sense
of dreadful chill like some murderer who, after years of careful hiding, meets unexpectedly The Law and sees the gallows darkly rise. A hand of justice—of ret-
ribution—seemed stretched upon my shoulder from the empty sky.

I now set down my faithful recollection of what happened; and, incredible as
it doubtless sounds to-day, yet it was most distressingly real. Out of what dim,
forgotten past his words, this woman's face, arose to haunt "me" of To-day, I
had no slightest inkling. What crime of mine, what buried sin, came as with a
blare of trumpets, seeking requital, no slightest hint came whispering. Yet this
was the impression I instantly received. I was a boy. It terrified and amazed me,
but it held no element of make-believe. Julius LeVallon, myself, and an unknown
woman stood waiting on the threshold of the breathless centuries to set some
stone in its appointed place—a stone, moreover, he, I, and she, together breaking mighty laws, had left upon the ground. It seemed no common wrong to her,
to him, to me, and yet we three, working together, alone could find it and replace it.

This, somehow, was the memory his words, that face, struggled to reconstruct.

I saw LeVallon smiling as he left my side. He disappeared in the way already
described. The stream of turbulent boys separated us physically, just as, in his
belief, the centuries had carried us apart spiritually—he—myself—and this
other. I saw a veil drop down upon his face. The lamps in his splendid eyes were
shrouded. At supper we sat far apart, and the bedroom I shared with two other
youngsters of my own age and form, of course, did not include LeVallon.

CHAPTER III

*"Souls without a past behind them, springing suddenly into existence, out of noth-
ing, with marked mental and moral peculiarities, are a conception as monstrous
as would be the corresponding conception of babies suddenly appearing from
nowhere, unrelated to anybody, but showing marked racial and family types."—*
"The Ancient Wisdom" (A. Besant).

As the terms passed and I ceased to be a new boy, it cannot be said that
I got to know Julius LeVallon any better, because our intimacy had
been established, or "resumed" as he called it, from the beginning; but
the chances of being together increased, we became members of the same form,
our desks were side by side, and we shared at length the same bedroom with another Fifth Form boy named Goldingham. And since Goldingham, studious, fat,
good-natured, slept soundly from the moment his head touched the pillow till

the seven o'clock bell rang—and sometimes after it in order to escape his cold bath—we practically had the room to ourselves.

Moreover, from the beginning, it all seemed curiously true. It was not Julius who invented, but I who in my stupidity had forgotten. Long, detailed dreams, too, came to me about this time, which I recognised as a continuation of these of "Other Places" his presence near me in the daytime would revive. They existed, apparently, in some layer deeper than my daily consciousness, recoverable in sleep. In the daytime something sceptical in me that denied, rendered them inaccessible, but once reason slept and the will was in abeyance, they poured through me in a continuous, uninterrupted flow. A word from Julius, a touch, a glance from his eyes perhaps, would evoke them instantly, and I would *see*. Yet he made no potent suggestions that could have caused them; there was no effort; I did not imagine at his bidding; and often, indeed, his descriptions differed materially from my own, which makes me hesitate to ascribe the results to telepathy alone. It was his presence, his atmosphere that revived them. To-day, of course, immediately after our schooldays in fact, they ceased to exist for me—to my regret, I think, on the whole, for they were very entertaining, and sometimes very exquisite. I still retain, however, the vivid recollection of blazing summer landscapes; of people, sometimes barbaric and always picturesque, moving in brilliant colours; of plains, and slopes of wooded mountains that dipped, all blue and thirsty, into quiet seas—scenes and people, too, utterly unlike any I had known during my fifteen years of existence under heavy English skies.

LeVallon knew this inner world far better and more intimately than I did. He lived in it. Motfield Close, the private school among the Kentish hills, was merely for him a place where his present brain and body—instruments of his soul—were acquiring the current knowledge of To-day. It was but temporary. He himself, the eternal self that persisted through all the series of lives, was in quest of other things, "real knowledge," as he called it. For this reason the recollection of his past, these "Other Places," was of paramount importance, since it enabled him to see where he had missed the central trail and turned aside to lesser pursuits that had caused delay. He was forever seeking to recover vanished clues, to pick them up again, and to continue the main journey with myself and, eventually, with—one other.

"I've always been after those things," he used to say, "and I'm searching, searching always—inside myself, for the old forgotten way. We were together, you and I, so your coming back like this will help—"

I interrupted, caught by an inexplicable dread that he would mention another person too. I said the first thing that came into my head. Instinctively the words came, yet right words:

"But my outside is different now. How could you know? My face and body, I mean—?"

"Of course," he smiled; "but I knew you instantly. I shall never forget that day. I felt it at once—all over me. I had often dreamed about you," he added after a moment's pause, "but that was no good, because you didn't dream with me." He looked hard into my eyes. "We've a lot to do together, you know," he said gravely, "a lot of things to put right—one thing, one big thing in particular—when the time comes. Whatever happens, we mustn't drift apart again. We shan't."

Another minute and I knew he would speak of "her." It was strange, this sense of shrinking that particular picture brought. Never, except in sleep occasionally, had it returned to me, and I think it was my dread that kept it out of sight. Yet Julius just then did not touch the topic that caused my heart to sink.

"I must be off," he exclaimed a moment later. "There's 'stinks' to mug up, and I haven't looked at it. I shan't know a blessed word!" For the chemistry, known to the boys by this shorter yet appropriate name, was a constant worry to him. He was learning it for the first time, he found it difficult. But he was a boy, a schoolboy, and he talked like one.

He never doubted for one instant that I was not wholly with him. He assumed that I knew and remembered, though less successfully, and that we merely resumed an interrupted journey. Pre-existence was as natural to him as that a certain man and woman had provided his returning soul with the means of physical expression, termed body. His soul remembered; he, therefore, could not doubt. It was innate conviction, not acquired theory.

"I can't get down properly to the things I want," he said another time, "but they're coming. It's a rotten nuisance—learning dates and all these modern languages keeps them out. The two don't mix. But, now you're here, we can dig up a jolly sight more than I could alone. And you're getting it up by degrees all right enough."

For the principle of any particular knowledge, once acquired, was never lost. It was learning a thing for the first time that was the grind. Instinctive aptitude was subconscious memory of something learned before.

"The pity is we're made to learn a lot of stuff that belongs to one particular section, and doesn't run through them all. It clogs the memory. The great dodge is to recognise the real knowledge and go for it bang. Then you get a bit further every section."

Until my arrival, it seems, he kept these ideas strictly to himself, knowing he would otherwise be punished for lying, or penalised in some other educational manner for being too imaginative. Yet, while he stood aloof somewhat from the common school life, he was popular and of good repute. The boys admired, but stood in awe of him. He pleased the masters almost as much as he puzzled them; for, unlike most dreamy, fanciful youths, he possessed concentration and an imperious will; he worked hard and always knew his lessons. Modern knowledge he found difficult, and only mastered with great labour the details of recent history, elementary science, chemistry, and so forth, whereas in algebra, euclid, mathematics, and the dead languages, especially Greek, he invariably stood at the head of the form. He was merely re-collecting them.

During the whole two years of our schooldays at the Close, I never heard him use such phrases as "former life" or "reincarnation." Life, for him, was eternal simply, and at Motfield he was in eternal life, just as he always had been and al-

ways would be. Only he never said this. He was a boy and talked like a boy. He
just lived it. Death to him was an insignificant detail. His whole mind ran to the
idea that life was continuous, each section casting aside the worn-out instrument
which had been exactly suited to the experience its wearer needed for its development at that time and under those conditions. And, certainly, he never understood that astounding tenet of most religions, that life can be "eternal" by
prolonging itself endlessly in the future, without having equally extended endlessly also in the past!

"But I'm going to be a general," I said, "when I grow up," afraid that the "real
knowledge" might interfere with my main ambition. "I could never think of giving up *that.*"

Julius looked up from tracing figures in the sand with the point of his gymnasium shoe. There was a smile on his lips, a light in his eye that I understood.
I had said something that belonged to To-clay, and not to all To-days.

"You were before," he answered patiently, "a magnificent general, too."

"But I don't remember it," I objected, being in one of my denying moods.

"You want to be it again," he smiled. "It's born in you. That is memory. But,
anyhow," he added, "you call do both—be a general with your mind and the
other thing with your soul. To shirk your job only means to come back to it again
later, don't you see?"

Quite naturally, and with profound conviction, he spoke of life's obligations.
Physical infirmities resulted from gross errors in the past; mental infirmities, from
lost intellectual opportunities; spiritual disabilities, from past moral shirkings and
delinquencies: all were methods, moreover, by which the soul divines her mistakes and grows, through discipline, stronger, wiser. He would point to a
weakness in someone, and suggest what kind of error caused it in a previous section, with the same certainty that a man might show a scar and say "that came
from fooling with a mowing machine when I was ten years old."

The antipathies and sympathies of To-day, the sudden affinities like falling in
love at sight, and the sudden hostilities that apparently had no cause—all were
due to relationships in some buried Yesterday, while those of To-morrow could
be anticipated, and so regulated, by the actions of To-day. Even to the smallest
things. If, for instance, Martin vented his spite and jealousy, working injustice
upon another, he but prepared the way for an exactly adequate reprisal later that
must balance the account to date. For into the most trivial affairs of daily life
dipped the spirit of this remarkable boy's belief, revealing as with a torch's flare
the workings of an implacable justice that never could be mocked. No question
of punishment meted out by another entered into it, but only an impersonal law,
which men call—elsewhere—Cause and Effect.

At the time, of course, I was somewhat carried away by the thoroughness with
which he believed and practised these ideas, though without grasping the
logic and consistency of his intellectual position. I was aware, most certainly,
in his presence of large and vitalising sensations not easily accounted for, of being caught up into some unfamiliar region over vast horizons, where big winds
blew from dim and ancient lands, where a sunlight burned that warmed the in-

most heart in me, and where I seemed to lose myself amid the immensities of an endless, vistaed vision.

This, of course, is the language of maturity. At the time I could not express a tithe of what my feelings were, except that they were vast and wonderful. To think myself back imaginatively, even now, into that period of my youth with Julius LeVallon by my side, is to feel myself eternally young, alive forever beyond all possibility of annihilation or decay: it is, further, to realise an ample measure of lives at my disposal in which to work towards perfection, the mere ageing and casting off of any particular body after using it for sixty years or so—nothing, and less than nothing.

"Don't funk!" I remember his saying once to a boy named Creswick who had "avoided" the charging Hurrish at football. "You can't lose your life. You can only lose your body. And you'll lose that anyhow."

"Crazy lout!" Creswick exclaimed, nursing his ankle, as he confided to another boy of like opinions. "I'm not going to have my bones all smashed to pulp for anybody. Body I'm using at the moment indeed! It'll be life I'm using at the moment next!"

Which, I take it, was precisely what LeVallon meant.

CHAPTER IV

"In the case of personal relations, I do not see that heredity would help us at all. Heredity, however, can produce a more satisfactory explanation of innate aptitudes. On the other hand, the doctrine of pre-existence does not compel us to deny all influence on a man's character of the character of his ancestors. The character which a man has at any time is modified by any circumstances which happen to him at that time, and may well be modified by the fact that his re-birth is in a body descended from ancestors of a particular character."—Prof. J. M'Taggart.

There were numerous peculiarities about this individual with a foreign name that I realise better on looking back than I did at the time.

Of his parentage and childhood I knew nothing, for he mentioned neither, and his holidays were spent at school; but he was always well dressed and provided with plenty of pocket-money, which he generously shared. Later I discovered that he was an orphan, but a certain cruel knowledge of the world whispered that he was something else as well. This mystery of his origin, however, rather added to the wonder of him than otherwise. Compared to the stretch of time behind, it seemed a trifling detail of recent history that had no damaging significance. "Julius LeVallon is my label for this section," he observed, "and John Mason is yours." And family ties for him seemed to have no necessary existence, since neither parents nor relations were of a man's own choosing. It was the ties deliberately formed, and especially the ties renewed, that held real significance.

I thought of him as "foreign," though, in a deeper sense than that he was not quite English. He carried me away from England, but also away from modern times; and something about him belonged to lands where life was sunnier, more passionate, more romantic even, and where the shadows of great Gods haunted blue, wooded mountains, vast plains and deep, sequestered valleys. He claimed kinship somehow with an earlier world, magical, unstained. Even his athletic gifts, admired of all, had this subtle distinction too: the way he ran and jumped and "fielded" was not English. At fives, squash-racquets, or with the cricket-bat he fumbled badly, whereas in any game that demanded speed, adroitness, swift intuitive decision, and physical dexterity of a certain un-English kind—as against mere strength and pluck—he was supreme. He was deer rather than bulldog. The school-games of modern days he was learning, apparently, for the first time.

In a corner of the field, where a copse of larches fringed the horizon against the sloping woods and hoppoles in the distance, we used to lie and talk for hours during playtime. The high-road skirted this field, and a hedge was provided with a gate which, under penalties, was the orthodox means of entrance. Few boys attempted any other, though Peabody was once caught by the Head as he floun-dered through a thorny opening with the jumping pole. But Julius never used the gate—nor was ever caught. He would dart from my side with a few quick steps, leap into the air, and fly soaring over the hedge, his feet tucked neatly un-der him like a bird's.

"Now," he would say, as we flung ourselves down beneath the shade of the larches, "we've got an hour or more. Let's talk, and remember, and get well down into it all."

How it was accomplished I cannot hope to describe. The world about me faded, another took its place. It rose in sheets and layers, shimmering, alive, and amazingly familiar. Space and time seemed to overlap, objects and scenery in-terpenetrated. There was fragrance, light and colour; adventure and alarm; de-light and ceaseless expectation. It was a kind of fairyland where flowers never died, where motion was swift as thought, and life seemed meted out on a more lavish scale than by the meagre measurements of ticking clocks. And, while the memories were often hard to disentangle, the marked idiosyncrasies of our sep-arate natures were never in the least confusion: my passion for adventure, his to find the reality that lay behind all manifested life. For this was the lode-star that guided him over the hills and deserts of all his many "sections"—the un-quenchable fever to learn essential truth, to pierce behind the veil of appearances and discover the secret nature of the soul, its origin, its destiny, the methods of its full realisation.

It was a pastoral people that interested me most, primitive folk with migra-tory habits not yet abandoned. Their herds roamed an enormous territory. There was a Red Tribe and a Blue Tribe. The fighting men used bows, spears and javelins, and carried shields with round, smooth metal bosses to deflect the rain of arrows. And there was cavalry—two thousand men on horseback called a "coorlie." Julius and I both knew it all as if we had lived with them, not merely read an invented tale; and it was pictures of this land and people that had first flared up in me that afternoon in the playground when he asked if I "remembered." Memories of my childhood a few years before had not half the vividness and actuality of these. Nothing could have been more stupid than such undistinguished legends, but for this convincing reality that was their outstanding characteristic.... It all came back to me: the days and nights of hunting, nomad existence, the wild freedom of open plains and trackless forests, of migrations in the spring, wood fires, lawless raids, and also of some kind of mighty worship that stirred me deeply with an old, grand sense of Nature Deities adequately approached.

This latter fact, indeed, rose most possessingly upon me. There came a vague uneasiness and discomfort with it. I was aware of brooding Presences....

"And they are still about us if we care to look for them," interrupted a low voice in my ear, "ready to give us of their strength and happiness, waiting to answer if we call...."

I looked up, disagreeably startled. A breath of wind stirred in the branches overhead. The tufts of ragwort bent their yellow heads. In the sky there was a curious glow and warmth. A sense of hush pervaded all the air, as though someone had crept close to where we lay and overheard our thoughts with sympathy.

And in that very moment, just as I looked up at Julius, the picture of the woman, her face averted and her hands upraised, stole like a ghost before my inner vision. She vanished into mist again; the layer that had so suddenly disclosed itself, sank down; the other shifted up into its former place; and my companion, I saw, with sharp amazement was stretched upon his back, his head turned from me, resting on his folded hands—as though he had not spoken any word at all. For his eyes, as I then leaned over to discover, were gazing into space, and his mind seemed intent upon pictures that he visualised for himself.

"Julius," I said quickly, "you spoke to me just now?"

He turned slowly, as with an effort to tear himself away from what he saw within him; he answered quietly:

"I may have spoken. I can't be sure. Why do you ask? I've been so far away." His face was rapt as with some inner light. It had a radiant look. There was no desire in me to insist.

"Oh, nothing," I answered quickly, and lay down again to follow what memories might come. The slight shiver that undeniably had touched me went its way. There was relief, intense relief—that he had not taken the clue I recklessly had offered. And, almost at once, the world about me faded out once more, the larches dipped away, the field sank out of sight. I plunged down into the sea of older memories....

I saw the sunlight flashing on shield and spear; I saw the hordes all gathered in the plains below, a mass of waving plumes, with red on the head-dress of the chieftains; I saw the river blackened by the thousands crossing it, covering the opposite bank like swarms of climbing ants.... I saw the chieftains lay aside their arms as they entered the sacred precincts of the grove; I smelt the odour of the

sacrificial fires, heard the long-drawn droning of petitions, the cries of the victims.... And then the sentry-fires behind the sleeping camps... the stirring of the
soldiers at dawn... the perfume of leagues of open plain... muffled tramping far
away... wind... fading stars... wild-flowers dripping with the dew....
There was fighting, too, galore; tremendous marches; signalling by night from
the mountain-tops with torches alternately hidden and revealed; and of sacred
rites, primitive and fraught with danger to human life, no end...

In the middle of which up stole again that other layer, breathing terror and
shrinking dread, and with a vividness of actuality that put all the rest into the
shade. It could not, *would* not be dismissed. Its irruption was of but an instant's
duration, but in that instant there flashed upon me a clear intuition of certainty.
I knew that Julius refrained purposely from speaking of this figure, because he
understood my dread might drive me from his side before what we three must
accomplish together was ripe for action, and because he waited—till she should
appear in person. And, before it vanished again, I knew another thing: that what
we three must accomplish together had to do directly with the worship of these
mighty, old-world Nature Deities.

The stirring of these deep, curious emotions in me banished effectually all further scenery. I sat up and began to talk. I laughed a little and raised my voice.
The sky, meanwhile, had clouded over, there was no heat in the occasional
gleams of sunshine.

"I've been hunting and fighting and the Lord knows what else besides," I exclaimed, touching Julius on the shoulder where he lay. "But somehow I didn't
feel that you were with me—always."

"It's too awfully far back, for one thing," he replied dreamily, as if still half withdrawn, "and, for another, we both left that section young. The three of us were
not together then. That was a bit later. All the same," he added, "it was there
you sowed the first seeds of the soldiering instinct which is so strong in you to-
day. I was killed in battle. We were on opposite sides. You fell—"

"On the steps—" I cried, seizing a flashing memory.

"Of the House of Messengers," he caught me up. "You carried the Blue Stick
of warning. You got down the street in safety when the flying javelin caught
you as you reached the very steps—"

There was a sound behind us in the field quite close.

"What in the world do you two boys find to talk about so much?" asked the
voice of Hurrish suddenly. "I'm afraid it's not all elegiacs." And he laughed
good-humouredly.

We turned with a start. Julius looked up, then rose and touched his cap. I followed his example the same moment.

"No, sir," he said, before I could think of anything to answer. "It's the Memory Game."

Hurrish looked at him with a quiet smile upon his face. His expression betrayed
interest. But he said nothing, merely questioning with his eyes.

"The most wonderful game you ever played, sir," continued Julius.

"Indeed! The most wonderful game you ever played?" Hurrish repeated, yet by no means unkindly.

"Getting down among the memories of—of before, sir. Recovering what we did, and what we were—and so understanding what we are to-day."

The master stared without a sign of emotion upon his face. Apparently, in some delightful way, he understood. He was very sympathetic, I remember, to both of us. We thought the world of him, respecting him almost to the point of personal affection; and this in spite of punishments his firm sense of justice often obliged him to impose. I think, at that moment, he divined what Julius meant and even felt more sympathy than he cared to show.

"The Memory Game," he repeated, looking quizzically down at us over the top of his glasses. "Well, well." He hummed and hesitated a moment, choosing his words, it seemed, with care. "There's a good deal of that in the air just now, I know as you'll discover for yourselves when you leave here and get into the world outside. But, remember," he went on with a note of earnestness and warning in his voice, "most of it is little better than a feeble, yet rather dangerous, form of hysteria, with vanity as a basis."

I hardly understood what he meant myself, but I saw the quick flush that coloured the pale cheeks of my companion.

"There are numbers of people about to-day," continued Hurrish, as we walked home slowly across the field, "who pretend to remember all kinds of wonderful things about themselves and about their past, not one of which can be justified. But it only means, as a rule, that they wish to appear peculiar by taking up the fad of the moment. They like to glorify themselves, though few of them understand even the A B C of the serious belief that may lie behind it all."

Julius squeezed my arm; the flush had left his skin; he was listening eagerly.

"You may later come across a good many thinking people, too," said the master, "who play your Memory Game, or think they do, and some among them who claim to have carried it to an extraordinary degree of perfection. There are ways and means, it is said. I do not deny that their systems may be worthy of investigation; I merely say it is a good plan to approach the whole thing with caution and common sense."

He glanced down first at one, then the other of us, with a grave and kindly expression in the eyes his glasses magnified so oddly.

"And most who play it," he added dryly, "remember so much of their wonderful past that they forget to do their ordinary duties in their very commonplace present." He chuckled a little, while Julius again gripped my flesh so hard that I only just prevented crying out.

"I'll remember him in a minute—if only I can get down far enough," he managed to whisper in my ear. "We were together—"

We had reached the gate, and were walking down the road towards the house. It was very evident that Hurrish understood more than he cared to admit about our wonderful game, and was trying to guide us rather than to deride instinctive beliefs.

That night in our bedroom, when Goldingham was asleep and snoring, I felt a touch upon my pillow, and looking up from the edge of unconsciousness, saw the white outline of Julius beside the bed.

"Come over here," he whispered, pointing to a shaded candle on the chest of drawers, "I've got something to show you. Something Hurrish gave me—something out of a book."

We peered together over a page of writing spread before us. Julius was excited and very eager. I do not think he understood it much better than I myself did, but it was the first time he had come across anything approaching his beliefs in writing. The discovery thrilled him. The authority of print was startling.

"He said it was somebody or other of importance, an Authority," Julius whispered as I leaned over to read the fine handwriting. "It's Hurrish's," I announced. "Rather," Julius answered. "But he copied it from a book. *He* knows right enough."

Oddly enough, the paper came eventually into my hands, though how I know not; I found it many years later in an old desk I used in those days. I have it now somewhere. The name of the author, however, I quite forget.

"The moral and educational importance of the belief in metempsychosis," it ran, as our fingers traced the words together in the uncertain candle-light, "lies in the fact that it is a manifestation of the instinct that we are not 'complete,' and that one life is not enough to enable us to reach that perfection whither we are urged by the inmost depths of our being, and also an evidence of the belief that all human action will be inevitably rewarded or punished—"

"Rewards or punishes *itself*," interrupted Julius ; "it's not punishment at all really."

"And this is an importance that must not be underestimated," the interrupted sentence concluded. "In so far," we read on together, somewhat awed, I think, to tell the truth, "as the theory is based upon the supposition that a personal divine power exists and dispenses this retributive justice—"

"Wrong again," broke in Julius, "because it's just the law of natural results—there's nothing personal about it."

"—and that the soul must climb a long steep path to approach this power, does metempsychosis preserve its religious character."

"He means going back into animals as well—which *never* happens," commented the excited boy beside me once again. We read to the end then without further interruption.

"This, however, is not all. The Theory is also the expression of another idea which gives it a philosophical character. It is the earliest intellectual attempt of man, when considering the world and his position in it, to conceive that world, not as alien to him, but as akin to him, and to incorporate himself and his life as an indispensable and eternal element in the past and future of the world with which it forms one comprehensive totality. I say an eternal element, because, regarded philosophically, the belief in metempsychosis seems a kind of unconscious anticipation of the principle now known as 'Conservation of Energy.' Nothing that has ever existed can be lost, either in life or by death. All is but change; and hence souls do not perish, but return again and again in ever-changing forms.

Moreover, later developments of metempsychosis, especially as conceived by Lessing, can without difficulty be harmonised with the modern idea of evolution from lower to higher forms."

"That's all," Julius whispered, looking round at me.

"By George!" I replied, returning his significant stare.

"I promised Hurrish, you know," he added, blowing out the candle. "Promised I'd read it to you."

"All right," I answered in the dark.

And, without further comment or remark, we went back to our respective beds, and quickly so to sleep.

Before taking the final plunge, however, into oblivion, I heard the whisper of Julius, sharply audible in the silence, coming at me across the darkened room "It's all rot," he said. "The chap who wrote that was simply thinking with his brain. But it's not the brain that remembers; it's the other part of you." There was a pause. And then he added, as though after further reflection: "Don't bother about it. There's lots of stuff like that about—all tommy-rot and talk, that's all. Good night! We'll dream together now and p'raps remember."

CHAPTER V

"We have no right whatever to speak of really unconscious Nature, but only of uncommunicative Nature, or of Nature whose mental processes go on at such different time-rates to ours that we cannot easily adjust ourselves to an appreciation of their inward fluency, although our consciousness does make us aware of their presence.... Nature is a vast realm of finite consciousness of which your own is at once a part and an example."—Royce.

There was a great deal more in LeVallon, however, than the Memory Game: he brought a strange cargo with him from these distant shores, where, apparently, I—to say nothing of another—had helped to load it. Bit by bit, as my own machinery of recovery ran more easily, I tapped other layers also in myself. Our freight was slowly discharged. We examined and discussed each bale, as it were, but I soon became aware that there was a great deal he kept back from me. This secrecy first piqued and then distressed me. It brought mystery between us; there stood a shadowy question-mark in our relationship.

I divined the cause, and dreaded it—that is, I dreaded the revelation he would sooner or later make. For I guessed—I *knew*—what it involved and whom. I asked no questions. But I noticed that at a certain point our conversations suddenly stopped, he changed the subject, or withdrew abruptly into silence. And something sinister gripped my heart. Behind it, closely connected in some undiscovered manner, lay two things I have already mentioned: the woman, and the worship.

This reconstruction of our past together, meanwhile, was—for a pair of schoolboys—a thrilling pursuit that never failed to absorb. Stone by stone we built it up. After often missing one another, sometimes by a century, sometimes by a mere decade or so, our return at last had chimed, and we found ourselves on earth again. We had inevitably come together. There was no such thing as missing eventually, it seemed. Debts must be discharged between those who had incurred them. And, chief among these mutual obligations, I gathered, were certain dealings we had together in connection with some form of Nature worship, during a section he referred to as our "Temple Days."

The character of these dealings was one of those secret things that he would not disclose; he knew, but would not speak of it; and alone I could not "dig it up." Moreover, the effect upon me here was decidedly a mixed one, for while there was great beauty in these Temple Days, there lurked behind this portion of them—terror. We had not been alone in this. Involved somehow or other with us was "the woman."

Julius would talk freely of certain aspects of this period, of various practices, physical, mental, spiritual, and of gorgeous ceremonies that were stimulating as well as true, pertaining undoubtedly to some effective worship of the sun, that resulted in the obtaining of enormous energy by the worshippers; but after a certain point he would say no more, and would deliberately try to shift back to some other "layer" altogether. And it was sheer cowardice in me that prevented my forcing a declaration. I burned to know, yet was afraid.

"I do wish I could remember better," I said once.

"It comes gradually of itself," he answered, "and best of all when you're not thinking at all. The top part gets thin, and suddenly you see down into clear deep water. The top part, of course, is recent; it smothers the older things."

"Like thick sand, mine is," I said, "heaps and heaps of it."

He shrugged his shoulders and laughed.

"The pictures of To-day hide those of Yesterday," he explained. "You can't remember two things at once. If your head is stuffed with what's happening at the moment, you can't expect to remember what happened a month ago. Dig back. It's trying that starts it moving."

Ancient as the stars themselves appeared the origins of our friendship and affection of to-day.

"Then I didn't get as far as you—in those Temple Days?" I asked.

He glanced sharply at me beneath his long dark eyelids. He hesitated a moment.

"You began," he answered presently in a low voice, "but got caught later by—something in the world—fighting, or money, or a woman—something sticky like that. And you left me for a time."

Any temptation that enticed the soul from "real knowledge" he described as "sticky."

"For several sections you fooled with things that counted for the moment, but were not carried over through the lot. You came back to the real ones—but too late." His voice sank down into a whisper; his face was grave and troubled. Shrinking stole over me. There was the excitement that he was going to tell me

something, yet the dread, too, that I should hear it. "But now," he went on, half
to himself and half to me, "we can put that right. Our chance—at last—is coming." These last words he uttered beneath his breath.

And then he abruptly shifted the subject, leaving me with a strangely disquieting emotion that I should be drawn against my will into something that I
dreaded yet could not possibly avoid. The expression of his face chilled my heart.
He pulled me down upon the grass beside him. "You've got to burrow down
inside yourself," he went on earnestly, raising his voice again to its normal pitch,
"that's where it all lies buried. Once you get it up by yourself, you'll understand.
Then you can help me."

His own excitement ran across the air to me. I felt grandeur in his wonderful
conception—this immense river of our lives, the justice of inevitable cause and
effect, the ultimate importance of every action, word and thought, and, what
appealed to me most of all, the idea that results depended upon one's own character and will without the hiring of exalted substitutes to make it easy. Even
as a boy this all appealed strongly to me, probably to the soldier fighting-instinct
that was my chief characteristic....

Of these Temple Days with their faint, flying pictures I retain fascinating recollections. In them was nothing to suggest any country I could name, certainly
neither Egypt, Greece nor India. Julius spoke of some great civilisation in which
primitive worship of some true kind combined with accomplishments we might
regard to-day as the result of trained and accurate science. It involved union
somehow with great "natural" forces. There was awe in it, but an atmosphere,
too, of wonder, power and aspiration of a genuinely lofty type.

It left upon me the dim impression that it was not on the earth at all. But, for
me it was too thickly veiled for detailed recovery, though an invincible instinct
whispered that it was here "the woman" first intruded upon our joint relationship. I saw, with considerable sharpness, however, delightful pictures of
what was evidently sun-worship, though of an intelligent rather than a superstitious kind. We seemed nearer to the sun than we are to-day, differently con-
stituted, aware of greater powers; there was vast heat, there were gigantic,
mighty winds. In this heat, through these colossal winds, came deity. The elemental powers were its manifestation. The sun, the planets, the entire universe,
in fact, seemed then alive: we knew it was alive; we were kin with every point
in it; and worship of a sun, a planet, or a tree, as the case might be, somehow
drew their beings into definite relationship with our own, even to the point of
leaving the characteristics of their particular Powers in our systems. A human
being was but *one* living detail of a universe in which all other details were
equally living and equally—possibly more—important. Nature was a power to
be experienced, shared, and natural objects had a meaning in their own right.
We read the phenomena of Nature as signs and symbols, clear as the black signs
of writing on a printed page.

Out of many talks together, Julius and I recovered all this. Alone I could not
understand it. Julius, moreover, believed it still to-day. Though nominally, and
in his life as well, a Christian, he always struck me as being intensely religious,

yet without a definite religion. It was afterwards, of course, I realised this, when my experience of modern life was larger. He was unfettered by any little dogmas of man-made creeds, but obeyed literally the teaching of the Sermon on the Mount, which he knew by heart. It was essential spiritual truth he sought. His tolerance and respect for all the religions of to-day were based upon the belief that each contained a portion of truth at least. His was the attitude of a perfect charity—of an "old soul," as he phrased it later, who "had passed through all the traditions." His belief included certainly God and the gods, Nature and Christ, temples of stone and hills and woods and that temple of the heart which is the Universe itself. True worship, however, was *with* Nature.

A vivid picture belongs to this particular "layer." I saw the light of a distant planet being used, apparently in some curative sense, by human beings. It took place in a large building. Long slits in the roof were so arranged that the planet shone through them exactly upon the meridian. Dropping through the dusky atmosphere, the rays were caught by an immense concave mirror of polished metal that hung suspended above an altar where the smoke of incense rose; and, since a concave mirror forms at its focus in the air before it an image of whatever is reflected in its depths, a radiant image of the planet stood shining there in the heart of the building. It was a picture of arresting beauty and significance. Gleaming overhead, hung a mirror of still mightier proportions that caught the reflected rays and poured them down in a stream of intensified light upon the backs of men and women who lay naked on the ground, waiting to receive them.

"The quality of that particular planet is what they need," whispered Julius, as we watched together; "the light-cures of that age have hardly changed," he laughed; "the principle, at least, remains the same."

There was another scene as well in which I saw motionless, stretched figures. I could never see it clearly, though. Darkness invariably rolled down and hid it; and I had the idea that LeVallon tried to prevent its complete recovery—just then. Nor was I sorry at this, for beyond it lay something that seemed the source of the shrinking dread that haunted me. If I saw all, I should see also—*her*. I should know the secret thing Julius kept back from me, the thing we three had somehow to "set right again." And once, when this particular scene was in my mind and Julius, I felt sure, was seeing it too, as he lay beside me on the grass, there passed into me a sudden sensation of a kind I find it difficult to describe. There was yearning in it, but there was anguish too, and a pain as of deep, unfathomable regret, wholly beyond me to account for. It swept into me, I think, from him.

I turned suddenly. He lay, I saw, with his face hidden in his hands; his shoulders shook as though he sobbed; and it seemed that some memory of great poignancy convulsed him. For several minutes he lay speechless in this way, yet an air of privacy about him, that forbade intrusion. Once or twice I surprised him under these curious attacks; they were invariably connected with this particular "inner scenery"; and sometimes were followed by bouts of that nameless and mysterious illness that kept him in the sick-room for several days. But I asked no questions, and he vouchsafed no explanation.

On this particular point, at least, I asked no questions; but on the general subject of my uneasiness I sometimes probed him.

"This sense of funk when I remember these old forgotten things," I asked, "what is it? Why does it frighten me'"

Gazing at me out of those strange eyes that saw into so huge a universe, he answered softly:

"It's a faint memory, too—of the first pains and trials you suffered when you began to learn. You feel the old wrench and strain."

"It hurt so—?"

He nodded, with that smile of yearning that sometimes shone so beautifully on his face.

"At first," he replied. "It seemed like losing your life—until you got far enough to know the great happiness of the bigger way of living. Coming back to me like this revives it. We began to learn together, you see."

I mentioned the extraordinary feelings of the playground when first I spoke with him, and of the classroom when first we saw each other.

"Ah," he sighed, "there's no mistaking it—the coming together of old friends or enemies. The instant the eyes meet, the flash of memory follows. Only, the tie must have been real, of course, to make it binding."

"How can it ever end?" I asked. "Each time starts it all going again."

"By starting the opposite. Love dissolves the link. Understand why you hate—and at once it lessens. Sympathy follows, feeling-with—that's love; and love sets you both free. It's not thinking, but feeling that make the strongest chains."

And it was speaking of "feeling" that led to his saying things I have never forgotten. For thinking, in those older days, seemed of small account. It was an age of feeling, chiefly. Feeling was the way to knowledge: here was the main difference between To-day and those far-off Yesterdays. The way to know an object was to feel it—feel-with it. The simplicity of the method was as significant as its—impossibility! Yet a fundamental truth was in it.

To know a thing was not to enumerate merely its qualities. To state the weight, colour, texture of stone, for instance, was merely to mention its external characteristics; whereas to think of it till it became part of the mind, seen from its own point of view, was to know it as it actually is. The mind felt-with it. It became a part of yourself. Knowledge, as Julius understood the word, was identifying himself with the object: it became part of the substance of the mind: it was known from within.

Communion with inanimate objects, with Nature itself, was in this way actually possible.

"Dwell upon anything you like," he said, "to the point where you feel it, and you get it all exactly as it *is*, not merely as you see it. Its quality, its power, becomes a part of yourself. Take trees, rivers, mountains, take wind and fire in this way—and you feel their power in you. You can use them. That was the way of worship—then."

"The sun itself, the planets, anything?" I asked eagerly, recognising something that seemed once familiar to me.

"Anything," he replied quietly. "Copy their own movements, too, and you'll get nearer still. Imitate the attitude and gestures of a stranger and you begin to understand what he's up to, his point of view—what he's feeling. You begin to know him. All ceremonies began that way. On that big plain where the worship of the sun was held, the smaller temples represented the planets, the distances all calculated in proper ratio from the heavens. We copied their movements exactly, as we moved, thousands and thousands of us, in circular form about the centre. We felt-with them, got all joined up to the whole system; by imitating their gestures, we understood them and absorbed a portion of their qualities and powers. Our energy became as theirs. Acting the ceremony brought the knowledge, don't you see? Oh, it's scientific, right enough," he added. "It's not going backwards—instinctive knowledge. It's a pity it's forgotten now."

"How do you know all this?" I asked.

"I've done it so often. You've done it with me. Alone, of course, it's difficult to get results: but when a lot together do it—a crowd—a nation—the whole world—you could shift Olympus into the Ægean, or bring Mars near enough to throw a bridge across!"

We burst out laughing together, though his face instantly again grew grave and earnest.

"It will come," he said, "it will come again in time. When the idea of brotherhood has spread, and the separate creeds have merged, and the whole world feels the same thing together—it will come. It's another order of consciousness, that's all."

His passionate conviction certainly stirred joy and wonder in me somewhere. It was stupendous, yet so simple. The universe was knowable: its powers assimilable by human beings. Here was true Nature Magic, the elements co-operating, the stars alive, the sun a deity to be known and felt.

"And that's why concentration gives such power," he added. "By feeling anything till you *feel-with* it and become it, you know every blessed thing about it from inside. You have instinctive knowledge of it. Mistakes become impossible. You live and act with the whole universe."

And, as I listened, it seemed a kind of childish presumption that had shut us off from the sun, the stars, the numerous other systems of space, and that reduced knowledge to the meagre statement of a people dwelling upon one unimportant globe of comparatively recent matter in one of the smaller solar systems.

Our earth, indeed, was not the centre of the universe; it was but a temporary point in the long, long journey of the River of Lives. The soul would eventually traverse a million other points. It was so integral a part of everything, so intimately akin to every corner and aspect of the cosmos, that a "human" being's relative position to the very stars, the angle at which he met their light and responded to the tension of their forces, must necessarily affect his inmost personality. If the moon could raise the tides, she could assuredly cause an ebb and flow in the fluids of the human body, and how could men and women expect to resist the stress and suction of those tremendous streams of power that played upon the earth from the network of great distant suns? Times and seasons, now known as feast-days and the like, were likewise of significance. There were moments, for instance, in the "ceremony" of the heavens when it was possible to see more easily in one direction than in another, when certain powers, therefore, were open and accessible. The bridges then were clear, the channels open. A revelation of intenser life—from the universe, from a star, from mountains, rivers, winds or forests—could then steal down and leave their traces in the heart and passion of a human being. For, just as there is a physical attitude of prayer by which the human body invites communion, so times and seasons were attitudes and gestures of that greater body of Nature when results could be most favourably expected.

It was all very bewildering, very big, very curious; but if I protested that it merely meant a return to the unreasoning superstitious days of Nature Magic, there was something in me at the same time that realised vital, forgotten truth behind it all. Cleansed and scientific, Julius urged, it must return into the world again. What men formerly knew by feeling, an age now coming would justify and demonstrate by brain and reason. Touch with the universe would he restored. We should go back to Nature for peace and power and progress. Scientific worship would be known.

Yet by worship he meant not merely kneeling before an Ideal and praying eagerly to resemble it; but approaching a Power and acquiring it. What heat in itself may be we do not know; only that without it we collapse into inert particles. What lies behind, beyond the physicist's account of air as a gas, remains unknown; deprived of it, however, we cease to breathe and be conscious in matter. Each moment we feel the sun, take in the air, we live; and the more we accomplish this union, the more we are alive. In addition to these physical achievements, however, their essential activities could be known and acquired spiritually. And the means was that worship which is union—feeling-with.

To Julius this achievement was a literal one. The elements were an expression of spiritual powers. To be in touch with them was to be in touch with a Whole in which the Earth or Sirius are, after all, but atoms. Moreover, it was a conscious Whole. In atoms themselves he found life too. Chemical affinity involved intelligence. Certain atoms refuse to combine with certain other atoms, they are hostile to each other; while others rush headlong into each other's arms. How do the atoms know?

Here lay hints of powers he sought to reclaim for human use and human help and human development.

"For they were known once," he would cry. "We knew them, you and I. Their nature is not realized to-day; consciousness has lost touch with them. We recall a broken fragment, but label it superstition, ignorance, and the like. And, being incomplete, these remnants of necessity seem childish. Their meaning cannot come through the brain, and that other mode of consciousness which understood has left us now. The world, pursuing a lesser ideal, denies its forgotten greatness with a sneer!"

A great deal of this he said to me one day while we were walking home from

church, whose "service" has stirred him into vehement. and eager utterance. His
language was very boyish, and yet it seemed to me that I listened to someone
quite as old as Dr. Randall, the Headmaster who had preached. I can see the
hedges, wet and shining after rain; the dull November sky; ploughed fields and
muddy lanes. I can hear again the plover calling above the hill. Nothing could
possibly have been more uninspiring than the dreary hop-poles, the moist, depressing air, the leafless elms, and the "Sunday feeling" amid which the entire
scene was laid.

The boys straggled along the road in twos and threes, hands in pockets, points
of Eton jackets sticking out behind. Hurrish, the nice master, was just in front
of us, walking with Goldingham. I saw the latter turn his face up sideways as
he asked some question, and I suddenly wondered whether he knew how odd
he looked or, indeed, what he looked like at all. I wondered what sort of "sections" and adventures Goldingham, Hurrish, and all these Eton-jacketed boys
had been through before they arrived at *this;* and next it flashed across me what
a grotesque result it was for LeVallon to have reached after so many picturesque
and stimulating lives—an Eton jacket, a mortar-board, and tight Wesleyan
striped trousers.

And now, as I recall these curious recollections of years ago, it occurs to me
as remarkable that, although a sense of humour was not lacking in either of us,
yet neither then nor now could the spirit of the comic, and certainly never of
the ludicrous, rob by one little jot the reality, the deep, convincing actuality of
these strange convictions that LeVallon and I shared together when at Motfield
Close we studied Greek and Latin, while remembering a world before Greeks
or Latins ever existed at all.

CHAPTER VI

*"There seems nothing in pre-existence incompatible with any of the dogmas which
are generally accepted as fundamental to Christianity."*—Prof. M Taggart.

By my last half-year at Motfield Close, when I was Head of the school,
LeVallon had already left, but the summer term preceding his departure
is the one most full of delightful recollections for me. He was Head then-
—which proves that he was sufficiently normal and practical to hold that typ-
ically English position, and to win respect in it—and I was "Follow-on Head,"
as we called it.

I suppose he was verging on eighteen at the time, for neither of us was des-
tined for a Public School later, and we stayed on longer than the general run of
boys. We still shared the room with Goldingham—"Goldie," who went on to
Wellington and Sandhurst, and afterwards lost his life in the Zulu War—and
we enjoyed an unusual amount of liberty. The "triumvirate" the masters called
us, and I remember that we were proud of topping Hurrish by half an inch, each

being over six feet in his socks.

With peculiar pleasure, too, I recall the little class we formed by ourselves in Greek, and the hours spent under Hurrish's sympathetic and enthusiastic guidance, reading Plato for the first time. Hurrish was an admirable scholar, and myself and Goldie, though unable to match LeVallon's singular and intuitive mastery of the language, made up for our deficiency by working like slaves. The group was a group of enthusiasts, not of mere plodding schoolboys. But Julius it undoubtedly was who fed the little class with a special subtle fire of his own, and with a spirit of searching interpretative insight that made the delighted Hurrish forget that he was master and Julius pupil. And in the "Sympathetic Studies" the former published later upon Plotinus and some of the earlier Gnostic writings, I certainly traced more than one illuminating passage to its original inspiration in some remark let fall by LeVallon in those intimate talks round Hurrish's desk at Motfield Close.

But what comes back to me now with a kind of veritable haunting wonder that almost makes me sorry such speculations are no longer possible, were the talks and memories we enjoyed together in our bedroom. For there was a stimulating excitement about these whispered conversations we held by the open window on summer nights—an atmosphere of stars and scented airs and hushed silent spaces beyond the garden—that comes back to me now with an added touch of mystery and beauty both compelling and suggestive. When I think of those bedroom hours I step suddenly out of the London murk and dinginess, out of the tedium of my lecturing and teaching, into a vast picture gallery of vivid loveliness. The scenery of mighty dreams usurps the commonplace realities of the present.

Ten o'clock was the hour for lights out, and by ten-fifteen Goldie, with commendable regularity, was asleep and snoring. We thanked him much for that, as somebody says in "Alice," and Julius, as soon as the signal of Goldie's departure became audible, would creep over to my bed, touch me on the shoulder, and give the signal to drag the bolsters from a couple of unused beds and plant ourselves tailor-wise in our dressing-gowns before the window.

"It's like the old, old days," he would say, pointing to the sky. "The stars don't change much, do they?" He indicated the dim terraces of lawn with the tassel of his dressing-gown. "Can't you imagine it all? I can. There were the long stone steps—don't you see?—below, running off into the plain. Behind us, all the halls and vestibules, cool and silent, veil after veil hiding the cells for meditation, and over there in the corner the little secret passages down to the crypts below ground where the tests took place. Better put a blanket round you if you're cold," he added, noticing that I shivered, though it was excitement and not cold that sent the slight trembling over my body. "And there"—as the church clock sounded the hour across the Kentish woods and fields—"are the very gongs themselves, I swear, the great gongs that swung in the centre of the dome."

Goldie's peaceful snoring, and an occasional closing of a door as one master after another retired to his room in the house below, were the only sounds that reminded me of the present. Julius, sitting beside me in the starlight, his eyes ashine, his pale skin gleaming under the mop of tangled dark hair, whispered words that conjured up not only scenes and memories, but the actual feelings, atmosphere and emotions of days more ancient than any dreams. I smelt the odour of dim, pillared aisles, tasted the freshness of desert air, heard the high rustle of other winds in palm and tamarisk. The Past that never dies swept down upon us from sky and Kentish countryside with the murmur of the night-breeze in the shrubberies below. It enveloped us completely.

"Not the stars we knew together *first*—not the old outlines we once travelled by," he whispered, describing in the air with his finger the constellations presumably of other skies. "That was earlier still. Yet the general look is the same. You can feel the old tinglings coming down from some of them." And he would name the planet that was in ascension at the moment, with invariable correctness I found out afterwards, and describe the particular effect it produced upon his thoughts and imagination, the moods and forces it evoked, the mental qualities it served—in a word, its psychic influence upon the inner personality.

"Look," he whispered, but so suddenly that it made me start. He pointed to the darkened room behind us. "Can't you almost see the narrow slit in the roof where the rays came through and fell upon the metal discs swinging in mid-air? Can't you see the rows of darkskinned bodies on the ground? Can't you feel the minute and crowding vibrations of the light on your flesh, as the disc swung round and the stream fell down in a jolly blaze all over you?"

And, though I saw nothing in the room but faintly luminous patches where the beds stood, and the two tin baths upon the floor, a vivid scene rose before my mind's eye that stirred poignant emotions I was wholly at a loss to explain. The consciousness of some potent magical life stirred in my veins, a vaster horizon, and a larger purpose than anything I had known hitherto in my strict and conventional English life and my quaint worship in a pale-blue tin tabernacle where all was ugly, cramped, and literally idolatrous.

"And the gongs so faintly ringing," I cried.

Julius turned quickly and thrust his face closer into mine. Then he stood up beside the open window and drew in a deep breath of the June night air.

"Ah, you remember that?' he said, with eyes aglow. "The gongs—the big singing gongs! There you had a bit of clean, deep memory right out of the centre. No wonder you feel excited...!"

And he explained to me, though I scarcely recognised the voice or language, so strongly did the savour of shadowy past days inform them, how it was in those old temples when the world was not cut off from the rest of the universe, but claimed some psychical kinship with all the planetary and stellar forces, that each planet was represented by a metal gong so attuned in quality and pitch as to vibrate in sympathy with the message of its particular rays, sound and colour helping and answering one another till the very air trembled and pulsed with the forces the light brought down. No doubt, Julius's words, vibrating with earnestness, completed my confusion while they intensified my enjoyment, for I remember how carried away I was by this picture of the temples acting as sounding-boards to the sky, and by his description of the healing powers of the light and sound thus captured and concentrated.

The spirit of comedy peeped in here and there between the entr'actes, as it were, for even the peaceful and studious Goldie was also included in these adventures of forgotten days, sometimes consciously, sometimes unconsciously.

"By the gods!" Julius exclaimed, springing up, "I've an idea! We'll try it on Goldie, and see what happens!"

"Try what?" I whispered, catching his own excitement.

"Gongs, discs and planet," was the reply.

I stared at him through the gloom. Then I glanced towards the unconscious victim.

"There's no harm. We'll imagine this is one of the old temples, and we'll do an experiment!" He touched me on the back. Excitement ran through me. Something caught me from the past. I watched him with an emotion that was half amazement, half alarm.

In a moment he had the looking-glass balanced upon the window-ledge at a perilous angle, reflecting the faint starlight upon the head of the sleeping Goldingham. Any minute I feared it would fall with a crash upon the lawn below, or break into smithereens upon the floor. Julius fixed it somehow with a hairbrush and a towel against the sash.

"Get the disc," he whispered, and after a moment's reflection I understood what he meant; I emptied one bath as quietly as possible into the other, then dragged it across the carpet to the bedside of the snoring Goldie who was to be "healed." The ridiculous experiment swept me with such a sense of reality, owing to the intense belief LeVallon injected into it, that I never once felt inclined to laugh. I was only vaguely afraid that Goldingham might somehow suffer.

"It's Venus," exclaimed Julius under his breath. "She's in the ascendant too. That's the luck of the gods, isn't it?"

I whispered something in reply, wondering dimly what Goldie might think.

"You bang the bath softly for the sound," said he, "while I hold it up for you. We *may* hit the right note—the vibrations that fit in with the rate of the light, I mean—though it's a bit of a chance, I suppose!"

I obeyed, thinking of masters sleeping down below in the silent building.

"Louder!" exclaimed Julius peremptorily.

I obeyed again, with a dismal result resembling tin cans in orgy. And the same minute the good-natured and studious Goldingham awoke with a start and stretched out a hand for his glasses.

"Feel anything unusual, Goldie?" asked LeVallon at once, tremendously in earnest, as he lowered the tin bath.

"Oh, it's only *you!*" exclaimed the victim, awakened out of his first sleep and blinking in the gloom, "and *you!*" he added, catching sight of me, my fist still upraised to beat; "rotten brutes, both of you! You *might* let a fellow sleep a bit. You know I'm swotting up for an exam!"

"But do you *feel* anything, Goldie?" insisted LeVallon, as though it were a matter of life and death. "It was Venus, you know...."

"Was it?" spluttered the other, catching sight of the big bath between him and the open window. "Well, Venus is beastly cold. Who opened the window?" The sight of the bath apparently unnerved him. He hardly expected it before seven in the morning.

Further explanations were cut short by the sudden collapse of the mirror with a crash of splintering glass upon the floor. The noise of the bath, that pinged and boomed as I balanced it against the bed, completed the uproar. Then the door opened, and there stood—Martin.

It was an awkward moment. Yet it was not half as real, half as vivid, half as alive with the emotion of actual life, as that other memory so recently vanished. Martin, at first, seemed the dream; that other, the reality.

He entered with a lighted candle. The noise of the opening window and the footsteps had, no doubt, disturbed him for some time. Yet, quickly as he came, Goldie and I were "asleep" even before he had time to cross the threshold. Julius stood alone to face him in the middle of the floor. It was characteristic of the boy. He never shirked.

"What's the meaning of all this noise?" asked Martin, obviously pleased to find himself in a position of unexpected advantage. "LeVallon, why are you not in bed? And why is the window open?"

Secretly ashamed of myself, I lay under the sheets, wondering what Julius would answer.

"We always sleep with the window open, sir," he said quietly.

"What was that crash I heard?" asked the master, coming farther into the room, and holding the candle aloft so that it showed every particle of the broken glass. "Who did this?" He glanced suspiciously about him, knowing of course that Julius was not the only culprit.

LeVallon stood there, looking straight at him. Martin—as I think of the incident to-day—had the appearance of a weasel placed by chance in a position of advantage, yet afraid of its adversary. He winced, yet exulted.

"Do you realise that it's long after eleven," he observed frigidly, "and that I shall be obliged to report you to Dr. Randall in the morning...."

"Yes, sir," said Julius.

"It's very serious," continued Martin, more excitedly, and apparently uncertain how to drive home his advantage, "it's very distressing—er—to find you, LeVallon, Head of the School, guilty of mischief like a Fourth-Form boy—at this hour of the night too!"

The reference to the lower form was, of course, intended to be crushing. But Julius in his inimitable way turned the tables astonishingly.

"Very good, sir," he said calmly, "but I was only trying to get the light of Venus, and her sound, into Goldingham's head—into his system, that is—by reflecting it in the looking-glass; and it fell off the ledge. It's an experiment of antiquity, as you know, sir. I'm exceedingly sorry...."

Martin stared. He was a little afraid of LeVallon; the boy's knowledge of mathematics had compelled his admiration as often as his questions, sometimes before the whole class, had floored him.

"It's an old experiment," the boy added, his pale face very grave, "healing, you know, sir, by the rays of the planets—forgotten star-worship—like the light-cures of to-day—"

Martin's somewhat bewildered eye wandered to the flat tin bath still propped against Goldingham's bedside.

"...and using gongs to increase the vibrations," explained Julius further, notic-ing the glance. "We were trying to make it do for a gong—the scientists will dis-cover it again before long, sir."

The master hardly knew whether to laugh or scold. He stood there in his shirt-sleeves looking hard at LeVallon who faced him with tumbled hair and shining eyes in his woolly red dressing-gown. Erect, dignified, for all the absurdity of the situation, the flush of his strange enthusiasm emphasising the delicate beauty of his features, I remember feeling that even the stupid Martin must surely understand that there was something rather wonderful about him, and pass himself beneath the spell.

"I was the priest," he said.

"But I did the gong—I mean, the bath-part, please, sir," I put in, unable any longer to let Julius bear all the blame.

There was a considerable pause, during which grease dripped audibly upon the floor from the master's candle, while Goldingham lay blinking in bed in such a way that I dared not look at him for fear of laughter. I have often wondered since what passed through the mind of Tuke Martin, the senior Master of Math-ematics, during that pregnant interval.

"Get up, all of you," he said at length, "and pick up this mess. Otherwise you'll cut your feet to pieces in the morning. Here, Goldingham, you help too. You're no more asleep than the others." He tried to make his tone severe.

"Goldingham only woke when the glass fell off the ledge, sir," explained LeV-allon. "It was all my doing, really—"

"And mine," I put in belatedly.

Martin watched us gather up the fragments, Goldie, still dazed and troubled, barking his shins against chairs and bedposts, unable to find his blue glasses in the excitement.

"Put the pieces in the bath," continued Martin shortly, "and ring for William in the morning to clear it away. And pay the matron for a new looking-glass," he added, with something of a sneer; "Mason half, and you, LeVallon, the other half."

"Of course, sir," said Julius.

"And don't let me hear any further sounds to-night," said the master finally, closing the window, and going out after another general look of suspicion round the room.

Which was all that we ever heard of the matter! For the Master of Mathe-matics did not particularly care about reporting the Head of the School to Dr. Randall, and incurring the dislike of the three top boys into the bargain. I got the impression, too, that Tuke Martin was as glad to get out of that room with-out loss of dignity as we were to see him go. LeVallon, by his very presence even, had a way of making one feel at a disadvantage.

"Anything particular come to you?" he asked Goldie, as soon as we were alone again, and the victim's temper was restored by finding himself the centre of so much general interest. "I suppose there was hardly time, though—"

"Queer dream's all I can remember," he replied gruffly.

"What sort?"

"Nothing much. I seemed to be hunting through a huge lexicon for verbs, but every time I opened the beastly thing it was like opening the lid of a box instead of the cover of a book; and, in place of pages, I saw rows of people lying face downwards, and streaks of light dodging about all over their skins. Rotten nightmare, that's all!"

Julius and I exchanged glances.

"And then," continued Goldie, "that batty tin bath banged like thunder and I woke up to see you two rotters by my bed."

"If there had been more time—" Julius observed to me in an aside.

"I'm jolly glad it's your last term," Goldingham growled, looking at LeVallon, or LeValion, as he usually called him; "you're as mad as a March hare, anyhow!"—which was the sentence I took into dreamland with me.

CHAPTER VII

"The blue dusk ran between the streets: my love was winged within my mind,
It left to-day and yesterday and thrice a thousand years behind
To-day was past and dead for me, for from to-day my feet had run
Through thrice a thousand years to walk the ways of ancient Babylon."
—A. E

It was another time, very early in the morning, that LeVallon called me from the depths of dreamless sleep with a whisper that seemed to follow me out of some vast place where I had been lying under open skies with the winds of heaven about my face and the stars as close as flowers. It was no dream; I brought back no single detail of incident or person—only this keen, sweet awareness of having been somewhere far away upon an open plain or desert of enormous stretch, waiting for something, watching, preparing—and that I had been awakened. Great hands drew back into the stars; eyes that were mighty closed; heads of majestic aspect turned away; and Presences of some infinite demeanour grandly concealed themselves as when mountains become veiled by the hood of hurrying clouds. I had the feeling that the universe had touched me, then withdrawn.

The room was dark, but shades of tender grey, stealing across the walls and ceiling, told that the dawn was near. Our windows faced the east; a flush of delicate light was in the sky; and, between me and this sky, something moved very softly and came close. It touched me.

Julius, I saw, was bending down above my pillow.

"Are you ready?" he whispered, as I felt his hand upon my hair. "The sun is on the way!"

The words, however, at first, seemed not in English, but in some other half-familiar language that I instantly translated into my own tongue. They drifted away from me like feathers into space. I grew wide awake and rubbed my eyes. It startled me a little to find myself in this modern room and to see his pale visage peering so closely into mine. I surely had dropped from a height, or risen from some hollow of prodigious depth; for it flashed across me that, had I waked a moment sooner, I must have caught a glimpse of other faces, heard other voices in that old familiar language, remembered other well-known things, all of which had fled too suddenly away, plunging with swiftness into the limbo of forgotten times and places.... It was very sweet. There was yearning desire in me to know more.

I sat up in bed.

"What is it?" I asked, my tongue taking the words with a certain curious effort. "What were you saying...? A moment ago... just now?" I tried to arrest the rout of flying sensations. Dim, shadowy remoteness gathered them away like dreams.

"I'm calling you to see the sunrise," he whispered softly, taking my hand to raise me; "the sunrise on the Longest Day upon the plain. Wake up and come!"

Confusion vanished at his touch and voice. Yet a fragment of words just vanished dropped back into my mind. Something sublime and lovely ran between us.

"But you were saying—about the Blue Circle and the robes—that it was time to—" I went on, then, with the effort to remember, lost the clue completely. He had said these other things, but already they had dipped beyond recovery. I scrambled out of bed, almost expecting to find some robe or other in place of my old grey dressing-gown beside the chair. Strong feelings were in me, awe, wonder, high expectancy, as of some grand and reverent worship. No mere bedroom of a modern private school contained me. I was elsewhere, among imperial and august conditions. I was aware of the Universe, and the Universe aware of me.

I spoke his name as I followed him softly over the carpet. but to my amazement, my tongue refused the familiar "Julius" of to-day, and framed instead another sound. Four syllables lay in the name. It was "Concerighé" that slipped from my lips. Then instantly, in the very second of utterance, it was gone beyond recovery. I tried to repeat the name, and could not find it.

Julius laughed softly just below his breath, making no reply. I saw his white teeth shine in the semi-darkness. He moved away on tiptoe towards the window, while I followed....

The lower sash was open wide as usual. I heard Goldingham breathing quietly in his sleep. Still with the mistiness of slumber round me, I felt bewildered, half caught away, as it seemed, into some web of ancient, far-off things that swung earthwards from the stars. In this net of other times and other places, I hung suspended above the world I ordinarily knew. I was not Mason, a Sixth-Form boy at a private school in Kent, yet I was indubitably myself. A flood of memories rose; my soul moved among more spacious conditions; all hauntingly alive and real, yet never recoverable completely....

We stood together by the open window and looked out. The country lay still beneath the fading stars. A faint breath of air stirred in the laurel shrubberies below. The notes of awakening birds, marvellously sweet, came penetratingly from the distant woods. I smelt the night, I smelt the coolness of very early morning, but there was another subtler, wilder perfume, that came to my nostrils with a deep thrill of happiness I could not name. It was the perfume of another day, another time, another land, all three as familiar to me as this Kentish hill where now I lived, yet gone otherwise beyond recall. Deep emotion stirred in me the sense of recognition, as though smell alone had the power to reconstruct the very atmosphere of those dim days by raising the ghosts of feelings that once accompanied them....

To the right I saw the dim cricket-field with hedge of privet and hawthorn that ran away in a dark and undulating line towards the hop-poles standing stiffly in the dusk; and, farther off, to the left, loomed the oast-houses, peaked and hooded, their faces turned the other way like a flock of creatures that belonged to darkness. The past seemed already indistinguishable from the present. I stood upon shifting sands that rustled beneath my feet.... The centuries drove backwards....

And the eastern sky, serene and cloudless, ran suddenly into gold and crimson near to the horizon's rim. It became a river of fire that flashed along the edge of the world with high, familiar speed. It broke the same instant into coloured foam far overhead, with shafts of reddish light that swept the stars and put them out. And then this strange thing happened:

For, as my sight passed from the shadowy woods beyond, the scene before me rose like a lifted map into the air; changed; trembled as though it were a sheet shaken from the four corners, and—disclosed another scene below it, most exquisitely prepared. The world I knew melted and disappeared. I looked a second time. It was gone.

And with it vanished the entire little bundle of thoughts and feelings I was accustomed to regard as John Mason.... I smelt the long and windy odours of the open world. The stars bent down and whispered. Rivers rolled through me. Forests and grass grew thickly in my thoughts. And there was dew upon my face.... It was all so natural and simple. It was divine. The Universe was conscious. I was not separate from it any point.... More, I was conscious with it.

Far off, as an auditorium seen with a bird's-eye view from some gigantic height, yet with the distinctness of a map both scaled and raised, I saw a treeless plain of vast dimensions, grey in the shadows just before the dawn. In the middle distance stood a domed white building upon the summit of a mound, with broad steps of stone in circles all about it, leading to a pillared door that faced the east. On all sides round it, covering the plain like grass, there was a concourse, many thousands strong, of people, upright and motionless, arranged in wide concentric rings, each one a hundred to two hundred deep. Each ring was dressed in coloured robes, from blue to red, from green to a soft pale yellow, purple, brown and orange, and the outermost of all a delicate and tender green that merged into the tint of the plain itself at a distance of a mile beyond the central building.

These concentric rings of colour, this vast living wheel of exquisitely merg-ing tints, standing motionless and silent about the hub of that majestic temple, formed a picture whose splendour has never left my mind; and a sense of in-toxicating joy and awe swept through me as something whispered that long ago, I, too, had once taken my appointed place in those great circles, and had felt the power of the Deity of Living Fire pass into me in the act of worship just about to begin. The courage and sweetness of the sun stole on me; light, heat and glory burned in my heart; I knew myself akin to earth, sea and sky, as also to every human unit in the breathing wheel; and, knowing this, I knew the power of the universe was in me because the universe was my Self.

Imperceptibly at first, but a moment later with measurable speed, a movement ran quivering round the circles. They began to turn. The immense, coloured wheel revolved silently upon the plain. The rings moved alternately, the first to the right, the second to the left, those at the outer rim more swiftly, and those within more slowly, each according to its distance from the centre, so that the entire mass presented the appearance of a single body rotating with a uniform and perfect smoothness. There rose a deep, muffled sound of myriad feet that trampled down the sand. The mighty shuffling of it paced the air. No other sound was audible. The sky grew swiftly brighter. The shafts of light shot out like arms towards the paling zenith. There came a whir of cool, delicious wind that instantly died down again and left the atmosphere more still and empty than before.

And then the sun came up. With the sudden rush of an eastern clime, it rose above the world. One second it was not there, the next it had appeared. The wheel blazed into flame. The circles turned to coloured fire. And a roaring chant burst forth instantaneously—a prodigious sound of countless voices whose vol-ume was as the volume of an ocean. This wind of singing swept like a tempest overhead, each circle emitting the note related to its colour, the total resulting in a chord whose magnificence shook the heart with an ecstasy of joyful wor-ship.... I was aware of the elemental power of fire in myself....

How long this lasted, or how long I listened is impossible to tell... the dazzling glory slowly faded; there came a moment when the brilliance dimmed; a blur of coloured light rose like a sheet from the surface of the wheeling thousands, floating off into the sky as though it were a separate shining emanation the multi-tude gave off. I seemed to lose my feet. I no longer stood on solid earth. There came upon me a curious sense of lightness, as of wings, that yet left my body far below.... I was charged with a deific power, energy.... Long shafts of dark-ness flashed across the sea of light; the pattern of interwoven colour was dis-turbed and broken; and, suddenly, with a shock as though I fell again from some great height, I remembered dimly that I was no longer—that my name was—

I cannot say. I only know confusion and darkness sponged the entire picture from the world; and my sight, I suddenly realised, went groping with difficulty about a little field, a rough, uneven hedge, a strip of ribboned whiteness that was a road, and some ugly, odd-shaped things that I recognised as—yes, as oast-houses just beyond. And a pale, sad-looking sun then crawled above the horizon where the hop-poles stood erect.

"You saw... ?" whispered someone beside me.

It was Julius. His voice startled me. I had forgotten his very presence.

I nodded in reply; no words came to me; there was still a trembling in me, a sense of intolerable yearning, of beauty lost, of power gone beyond recall, of pain and littleness in the place of it.

Julius kept his eyes upon my face, as though waiting for an answer.

"The sun..." I said in a low and shaking voice.

He bent his head a moment, leaning down upon the window-sill with his face in his hands.

"As we knew it then," he said with a deep-drawn sigh, raising himself again. "To-day— !"

He pointed. Across the fields I saw the tin roof of the conventicle where we went to church on Sunday, lifting its modern ugliness beyond the playground walls. The contrast was somehow dreadful. A revulsion of feeling rose within me like a storm. I stared at the meagre building beneath whose roof of corrugated iron, once a week, we knelt and groaned that we were "miserable sinners"—begging another to save us from "punishment" because we were too weak to save ourselves. I saw once more in memory the upright-standing throng, claiming with joy the powers of that other Deity of whom they knew they formed a living portion. And again this intolerable yearning swept me. My soul rose up in a passionate protest that vainly sought to express itself in words. Language deserted me; tears dimmed my eyes and blurred my sight; I stretched my hands out straight towards that misty sunrise of To-day....

And, when at length I turned again to speak to Julius, I saw that he had already left my side and gone back to bed.

CHAPTER VIII

"Not unremembering we pass our exile from the starry ways:
One timeless hour in time we caught from the long night of endless days."
—A. E.

And so, in due course, the period of our schooldays came to its appointed end without one single further reference to the particular thing I dreaded. Julius had offered no further word of explanation, and my instinctive avoidance of the subject had effectively prevented my asking pointed questions. It remained, however; it merely waited the proper moment to reveal itself. It was real. No effort on my part, no evasion, no mere pretence that it was fantasy or imagination altered *that*. The time would come when I should know and understand; evasion would be impossible. It was inevitable as death.

During our last term together it lay in almost complete abeyance, only making an appearance from time to time in those vivid dreams which still presented themselves in sleep. It hid; and I pretended bravely to ignore it altogether.

Meanwhile our days were gloriously happy, packed with interest, and enlivened often with experiences as true and beautiful as the memory of our ancient sun-worship I have attempted to describe. No doubt assailed me; we *had* existed in the past together; those pictures of "inner scenery" were memories. The emotions that particular experience, and many others, stirred in me were as genuine as the emotions I experienced the last term but one, when my mother died; and, whatever my opinion of the entire series may be to-day, on looking back, honesty compels me to admit this positive character of their actuality. There was no make-believe, no mere imagination.

Our intimacy became certainly very dear to me, and I felt myself linked to Julius LeVallon more closely than to a brother. The knowledge that much existed he could not, or would not, share with me was pain, the pain of jealousy and envy, or possibly the deeper pain that a barrier was raised. Sometimes, indeed, he went into his Other Places almost for days together where I could not follow him, and on these occasions the masters found him absent-minded and the boys avoided him; he went about alone; if games or study compelled his attention, he would give it automatically—almost as though his body obeyed orders mechanically while the main portion of his consciousness seemed otherwise engaged. And, while it lasted, he would watch me curiously, as from a distance, expecting apparently that I would suddenly "remember" and come up to join him. His soul beckoned me, I felt, but half in vain. I longed to be with him, to go where he was, to see what he saw, but there was something that effectually prevented.

And these periods of absence I rather dreaded for some reason. It was uncanny, almost creepy. For I would suddenly meet his glowing eyes fixed queerly, searchingly on my own, gazing from behind a veil at me, asking pregnant questions that I could not catch. I would see him lying there beneath the larches of the cricket-field alone, rapt, far away, deep in his ancient recollections, and apart from me; or I would come upon him suddenly in the road, in a sunny corner of the playground, even in the deserted gymnasium on certain afternoons, when he would start to see me, and turn away without a word, but with an expression of unhappy yearning in his eyes as though he shared my pain that he dwelt among these Other Places which, for the moment, I might not know.

Many, many, indeed, are the details of these days that I might mention, but their narration would prove too long. One, however, may be told. He had, for instance, a kind of sign-language that was quite remarkable. On the sandy floor of a disused gravel-pit, where we lay on windy days for shelter while we talked, he would trace with a twig a whole series of these curious signs. They were for him the alphabet of a long-forgotten language—some system of ideograph or pictorial representation that expressed the knowledge of the times when it was used. He never made mistakes; the same sign invariably had the same meaning;

and it all existed so perfectly in his inner vision that he used it even in his work, and kept a book in which the Greek play of the moment was written out entirely in this old hieroglyphic side by side with the original. He read from it in class, even under the eagle eye of the Head, with the same certainty as he read from the Greek itself.

There were characteristic personal habits, too, that struck me later as extraordinary for a boy of eighteen—in England; for he led an inner life of exceeding strictness, not to say severity, and was for ever practising mental concentration with a view to obtaining complete control of his feelings, thoughts and, therefore, actions. Upright as a rod of steel himself, he was tolerant to the failings of others, lenient to their weaknesses, and forgiving to those who wronged him. He bore no malice, cherished no ill-feeling. "It`s as far as they`ve got," he used to say, "and no one can be farther than he is." Indeed, his treatment of others implied a degree of indifference to self that had something really big about it. And, even on the lowest grounds, to bear a grudge meant only casting a net that must later catch the feet.

His wants in the question of food were firmly regulated too; for at an age when most boys consider it almost an aim in life to devour all they can possibly get and to spend half of their pocket-money on tempting eatables, Julius exercised a really Spartan control over these particular appetites. Not only was his fare most frugal in quantity, but he avoided the eating of meat almost entirely, alcohol completely, and sometimes would fast for a period that made me wonder for his health. He never spoke of this. I noticed it. Nor ever once did he use his influence to persuade me to like habits. No boy was ever less a prig than LeVallon. Another practice of his was equally singular. In order to increase control of the body and develop tenacity of will, I have known him, among other similar performances, stand for hours at a time on winter nights, clad only in a nightshirt, fighting sleep, cold, hunger, movement—stand like a statue in the centre of the room, as though the safety of the world depended upon success.

Most curious of all, however, seemed to me his habit of—what I can only call—communing with inanimate things. "You only remember the sections where we were together," he explained, when once I asked the meaning of what he did; "and as you were little with me when this was the way of getting knowledge, it is difficult for you to understand." This fact likewise threw light upon the enormous intervals between remembered sections. We recalled no recent ones at all. We had not come back together in them.

This communing with inanimate things had chiefly to do, of course, with Nature, and I may confess at once that it considerably alarmed me. To read about it comfortably in an armchair over the fire is one thing; to see it done is another. It alarmed me, moreover, for the reason that somewhere, somehow, it linked on to the thing I dreaded above all others—the days when he and I and *she* had made some wrong, some selfish use of it. This, of course, remained an intuition of my own. I never asked; I never spoke of it. Only in my very bones I felt sure that the thing we three must come together to put right again somehow involved, and involved unpleasantly, this singular method of acquiring knowledge and acquiring power. We had abused it together; we had yet to put it right.

To see Julius practising this mysterious process with a stone, a flower, a tree, and to hear him then talk about these three different objects, was like listening to a fairy tale told with the skill of a great imaginative artist. He personified them, gave their life history, rendered their individual experiences, moods, sensations, qualities, adventures—anything and everything that could ever happen to a stone, a flower, a tree. I realised their existence from their own point of view; felt-with them; shared their joys and sufferings, and understood that they were living things, though with a degree of life so far below our own. Communion with Nature was, for him, communion with the very ground of things. All this, though exquisitely wonderful, was within the grasp of sympathetic compre-hension. It was natural.

But when he dealt with things less concrete—and his favourites were ele-mental forces such as air and heat, or as he preferred to call them, wind and fire—the experience, though no whit less convincing owing to the manner of his de-scription, was curiously disturbing, because of the results produced upon himself. I can describe it in two words, though I can give no real idea of it in two thousand. He rushed, he flamed. It was almost as if, in one case, his actual radiation became enormous, and in the other, some power swept, as in the form of torrential enthusiasm, from his very person. I remember my first impression in the class-room—that a great wind blew, and that flaming colours moved upon the air.

When he was "feeling-with" this pair of elemental forces he seemed to draw their powers into his own being so that I, being in close sympathy with him, caught some hint of what was going forward in his heart. Sometimes on drowsy summer afternoons when no air stirred through the open windows of the room, there would come a sudden change in my surroundings, an alteration. I would hear a faint and distant sound of roaring; something invisible drove past me. Julius, at the desk beside me, had finished work, and closed his books. His head in his hands, he sat motionless, an intent expression on both face and body, wrapped deep in concentrated effort of some kind. He was practising.... And once, too, I remember being waked out of sleep in the early morning with an impression of a stimulating heat about me which amounted to an intensification of life almost. There he stood beside the window, arms folded, head bent down upon his breast, and an effect about him that can only be described as glowing. The air immediately round him seemed to shine with a faint, delicate radiance as of tropical starlight, or as though he stood over a dying fire of red-hot coals. It was a half fascinating, half terrifying sight; the light pulsed and trem-bled with distinct vibrations, the air quivered so as to increase his bodily ap-pearance. He looked taller, vaster. And not once I saw this thing, but many times. No single dream could possibly explain it. In both cases, with the wind as with the fire, his life seemed magnified as though he borrowed from these el-emental forces of Nature their own special qualities and powers.

"All the elements," I remember his saying to me once, "are in our bodies. Do you expect Nature to be less intelligent than the life that she produces?" For him, certainly, there was the manifestation of something deeper than physics in the operations of so-called natural laws.

For here, let me say now in conclusion of this broken record of our days at school together, was the rock on which our intercourse eventually suffered interruption, and here was that first sign of the parting of our ways. It frightened me.... Later, in our university days, the cleavage became definite, causing a break in our friendship that seemed at the moment final. For a long time the feeling in me had been growing that his way and mine could not lie much farther together. Julius attributed it to my bringing up, which I was not independent enough to shake off. I can only say that I became conscious uneasily that this curious intercourse with Nature—"communing," as he termed it—led somehow away from the Christianity of my childhood to the gods and deification of the personal self. I did not see at the time, as he insisted, that *both* were true, being different aspects of the central fact that God is the Universe, and that man, being literally part of it, must eventually know Him face to face by actually becoming Him. All this lay far beyond me at the time.

It seemed to me then, and more as I grew older, an illegitimate, dangerous traffic; for paganism, my father taught me sternly, was the Devil, and that the Universe could actually be alive was a doctrine of heathenish days that led straight to hell and everlasting burning. I could not see, as Julius saw, that here was teaching which might unify the creeds, put life into the formal churches, inspire the world with joy and hope, and bring on the spirit of brotherhood by helping the soul to rediscover its kinship with a living cosmos.

One certainty, however, my schooldays with this singular boy bequeathed to me, a certainty I have never lost, and a very gorgeous and inspiring one—that life is continuous.

LeVallon lived in eternal life. He knew that it stretched infinitely behind his present "section," and infinitely ahead into countless other "sections." The results of what lay behind he must inevitably exhaust. Be that harvest painful or pleasant, he must reap what he had sown. But the future lay entirely in his own hands, and in his power of decision: chance or caprice had no word to say at all. And this consciousness of being in eternal life now, at the present moment, master of fate, potentially at least deific—this has remained a part of me, whether I will or no. To Julius LeVallon I owe certainly this unalterable conviction.

Another memory of that early intercourse that has remained with me, though too vaguely for very definite description, is the idea that personal life, even in its smallest details, is part of a cosmic ceremony, that to perform it faithfully deepens the relationship man bears to the Universe as a living whole, and is therefore of ultimate spiritual significance. An inspiring thought, I hold, even in the vagueness of my comprehension of it.

Yet above and beyond such notions, remained the chief memory of all: that in some such ancient cosmic ceremony, Julius, myself and one other had somehow abused our privileges in regard to Nature Powers, and that the act of restoration still awaiting fulfilment at our hands, an act involving justice to the sun and stars as well as to our lesser selves, could not be accomplished until that "other" was found on earth together with himself and me. And that other was a woman.

BOOK II

EDINBURGH

"We do not know where sentient powers, in the widest sense of the term, begin or end. And there may be disturbances and moods of Nature wherein the very elemental forces approach sentient being, so that, perhaps, mythopoeic man has not been altogether a dreamer of dreams. I need not dwell on the striking reflections to which this possibility gives rise; enough that an idealistic dynamism forces the possibility on our view. If the life of Nature is from time to time, and under special conditions, raised to the intense requisite level, we are in the presence of elemental forces whose character primitive man has not entirely misunderstood."—"Individual and Reality" (E. D. Fawcett).

CHAPTER IX

There was an interval of a year and a half before we met again. No letters passed between us, and I had no knowledge of where LeVallon was or what he did. Yet while in one sense we had gone apart, in another sense I knew that our relationship suffered no actual break. It seemed inevitable that we should come together again. Our tie was of such a kind that neither could shake the other off. In the meantime my soldier's career had been abandoned; loss of money in the family decreed a more remunerative destiny; and the interval had been spent learning French and German abroad with a view to a less adventurous profession. At the age of nineteen, or thereabouts, I found myself at Edinburgh University to study for a Bachelor of Science degree, and the first face I saw in Professor Geikie's lecture room for geology was that of my old school-friend of the "Other Places," Julius LeVallon.

I stood still and stared, aware of two opposing sensations. For this unexpected meeting came with a kind of warning upon me. I felt pleasure, I felt dread: I cannot determine which came first, only that, mingled with the genuine gratification, there was also the touch of uneasiness, the sinking of the heart I knew so well.

And I remember saying to myself—so odd are the tricks of memory—"Why, he's as pale as ever! Always that marble skin!" As though during the interval he ought somehow to have acquired more colour. He was tall, over six feet, thin, graceful as an Oriental; an expression of determination in his face had replaced the former dreaminess. The eyes were clear and very strong. There was an expression of great intensity about him.

His greeting was characteristic: he showed eager pleasure, but expressed no surprise.

"Old souls like ours are bound to meet again," he said with a smile, as he shook my hand. "We have so much to do together."

I recalled the last time I had seen him, waiting on the school platform as the train went out, and I realised that there were changes in him that left me standing still, as it were. Perhaps he caught my thought, for his face took on a touch of sadness; he gazed into my eyes, making room for me beside him on the bench. "But you've been dawdling on the way a bit," he added. "You've been after other things, I see."

It was true enough. I had fallen in love, for one thing, besides devoting myself with the ardour of youth to literature, music, sport, and other normal interests of my age. From his point of view, of course, I had not advanced, whereas he obviously had held steadily to the path he had chosen for himself, following always one main thing—this star in the east of his higher knowledge. His attitude to me, I felt moreover, had undergone a change. The old sympathy and affection had not altered, but a strain of pity had crept in, a regret that I suffered the attractions of the world to interfere with my development.

A delay, as he called it, in our relationship there had certainly been, though the instant we met I realised that something bound us together fundamentally with a power that superficial changes or external separation could never wholly dissolve.

Yet, on the whole, I saw little enough of him during these Edinburgh days, far less certainly than at Motfield Close. I was older, for one thing, more of the world for another. As a boy, of course, the idea that we renewed an eternal friendship, faithful to one another through so many centuries, made a romantic appeal that was considerable. But the glamour had evaporated ; I was a man now, I considered, busy with the things of men. At the same time I was aware that these other tendencies were by no means dead in me, and that very little would be required to revive them. Buried by other interests, they were yet ready to assert themselves again.

And LeVallon, for his part, though he saw less of me, and I think cared to see less of me than before, kept deliberately in touch, and of set purpose would not suffer us to go too far apart. We did not live in the same building, but he came often to my rooms, we took great walks together over the Pentland Hills, and once or twice wandered down the coast from Musselburgh to the cliffs of St. Abbs Head above the sea. Why he came to Edinburgh at all, indeed, puzzled me a little; but I am probably not far wrong in saying that two things decided the choice: He wished to keep me in sight, having heard somehow of my destination; and, secondly, certain aspects of Nature that he needed were here easily accessible—the sea, hills, woods, and lonely places that his way of life demanded. Among the lectures he took a curious selection: geology, botany, chemistry, certain from the Medical Course, such as anatomy and materia medica, and, above all, the advanced mental classes. He attended operations, postmortems, and anything in the nature of an experiment, while the grim Dissecting Room knew him as well as if his living depended upon passing the examination in anatomy.

Of his inner life at this period it was not so easy to form an estimate. He worked incessantly, but at something I never could quite determine. At school he was for ever thinking of this "something"; now he was working at it. It seemed remote from the life of the rest of us, students and others, because its aim was different. Pleasure, as such, and the usual forms of indulgence, he left on one side; and women, though his mysterious personality, his physical beauty, and his cold indifference attracted them, he hardly admitted into his personal life at all; to his intimacy, never. His habits were touched with a singular qual-ity of selflessness, very rare, very exquisite, sincere as it was modest, that set him apart in a kind of divine loneliness, giving to all, yet asking of none. My for-mer feeling that his aims were tinged by something dark and anti-spiritual no longer held good; it was due to a partial and limited judgment, to ignorance, even to misunderstanding. His aims were undeniably lofty, his life both good and pure. Respect grew with my closer study of him, for his presence brought an uplifting atmosphere of intenser life whose centre of activity lay so high above the aims of common men as to constitute an "otherworldliness" of a very un-usual kind indeed.

I observed him now as a spectator, more critically. No dreams or imaginative visions—with one or two remarkable exceptions—came to bewilder judgment. I saw him from outside. If not sufficiently unaffected by his ideas to be quite a normal critic, I was certainly more prosaic, and often sceptical. None the less the other deeper tendency in me was still strong; it easily wakened into life. This deep contradiction existed.

The only outward change I noticed, apart from the greater maturity and de-cision in the features, was a look of sadness he habitually wore, that altered when he spoke of the things he cared about, into an expression of radiant joy. The thought of his great purpose then lit flames in his eyes, and brought into the whole countenance a certain touch of grandeur. It was not often, evidently, that he found anyone to talk with; and arguing, as such, he never cared about. He knew. He was one of those fortunate beings who never had felt doubt. Perfect assurance he had.

Julius, at that time, occupied a suite of rooms at the end of Princes Street, where Queensferry Road turns towards the Forth. They were, I think, his only extravagance, for the majority of students were content with a couple of rooms, or a modest flat on the Morningside.

This suite he furnished himself, and there was one room in it that no one but himself might enter. It had, I believe, no stick of furniture in it, and required, therefore, no dusting apparently; in any case, neither landlady, friend nor ser-vant ever passed its door.

My curiosity concerning it was naturally considerable, though never satisfied. He needed a place, it seems, where absolute solitude was possible, an atmosphere uncoloured by others. He made frequent use of it, but whether for that process

of "feeling-with" already mentioned, or for some kind of secret worship, ceremonial, or what not, is more than I can say. Often enough I have sat waiting for
him in the outer room when he was busy within this mysterious sanctum; no
sound audible; no movement; a bright light visible beneath the crack of the door;
a sense of hush, both deep and solemn, about the entire place. Though it may
sound ridiculous to say so, there was a certain air of sanctity that hung like a veil
about that inner chamber, the silence and stillness evoked a hint of reverence.
I waited with something between awe and apprehension for the handle to turn,
aware that behind the apparent stillness something intensely active was going
forward, of which faint messages reached my mind outside. Certainly, while sitting with book or newspaper, waiting for his footstep, my thoughts would glow
and burn within me, rushing with energy along unaccustomed channels, and I
remember the curious feeling that behind those panels of painted deal there lay
a space far larger than the mere proportions of a room.

As in the fairy-tale, that door opened into outer space; and I suspect that Julius
used the solitude for "communing" with those Nature Powers he seemed always
busy with. Once, indeed, when he at length appeared, after keeping me waiting for a longer period than usual, I was aware of two odd things about him: he
brought with him a breath of open air, cool, fresh and scented as by the fragrance
of the forest; about him, too, a faintly luminous atmosphere that lent to his face
a kind of delicate radiance almost shining. My sight for a moment wavered; the
air between us vibrated as he came across the room towards me. There was a
strangeness round about him. There was power. And when he spoke, his
voice, though low as always, had a peculiar resonance that woke echoes, it
seemed, beyond the actual walls.

The impressions vanished as curiously as they came; but their reality was beyond question. And at times like these, I confess, the old haunting splendour
of his dream would come afresh upon me as at Motfield Close. My little world
of ambition and desire seemed transitory and vain. The magic of his personality stole sweetly, powerfully upon me; I was swept by gusts of passionate yearning to follow where he led. For his purpose was not selfish. The knowledge and
powers he sought were for the ultimate service of the world. It was the permanent Self he trained rather than the particular brain and body of one brief and
transient "section," called To-day.

These moods with me passed off quickly, and the practical world in which I
now lived brought inevitable reaction; I mention them to show that in me two
persons existed still: an upper, that took life normally like other people, and a
lower, that hid with Julius LeVallon in strange "Other Places." For in this du-
ality lies the explanation of certain experiences I later shared with him, to be related presently.

Our relations, meanwhile, held intimate and close as of old—up to a certain
point. There was this barrier of my indifference and the pity that it bred in him.
Though never urging it, he was always hoping that I would abandon all and follow him; but, failing this, he held to me because something in the future made
me necessary. Otherwise the gulf between us had certainly not widened.

I see him as he stood before me in those Edinburgh lodgings: young, in the full tide of modern life, with good facilities, health, means, looks, high character, and sane as a policeman! All that men hold dear and the world respects was his. Yet, without a hint of insincerity or charlatanism, he seemed conscious only of what he deemed the long, sweet prizes of the soul, difficult of attainment, and to the majority mere dreams. His was that rare detachment which sees clear to the end, not through avoiding the stress of perilous adventure by the way, but through refusing the conclusion that the adventures were ends in themselves, or could have any other significance than as items in development, justifying all suffering.

Eternal life for him was *now*. He sought the things that once acquired can never be forgotten, since their fruits are garnered by the Self that persists through all the series of consecutive lives. Through all the bewildering rush and clamour of the amazing world he looked ever to the star burning in the depths of his soul. And for a tithe of his certainty, as of the faith and beauty of living that accompanied it, I sometimes felt tempted to give all that I possessed and follow him. The scale at any rate was grand. The fall of empires, the crash of revolutions, the destiny of nations, all to him were as nothing compared with the advance or retreat of a single individual soul in the pursuit of what he deemed "real knowledge."

Yet, while acknowledging the seduction of his dream, and even half yielding to it sometimes, ran ever this hidden thread of lurking dread and darkness that, for the life of me, I could never entirely get rid of. It was lodged too deeply in me for memory to discover, or for argument to eject. Ridicule could not reach it, denial made no difference. To ignore it was equally ineffective. Even during the long interval of our separation it was never quite forgotten. Like something on the conscience it smouldered out of sight, but when the time was ripe it would burst into a blaze.

At school I merely "funked" it; I would not hear about it. Now, however, my attitude had changed a little. The sense of responsibility that comes with growing older was involved—rather to my annoyance and dismay. Here was something I must put right, or miss an important object of my being. It was inevitable; the sooner it was faced and done with, the better.

Yet the time, apparently, was not quite yet.

CHAPTER X

"Instead of conceiving the elements as controlled merely by blindly operative forces, they may be imagined as animated spiritual beings, who strive after certain states, and offer resistance to certain other states. "—Lotze.

In connection with LeVallon's settled conviction that the Universe was everywhere alive and one, and that only the thinnest barriers divided animate from so-called inanimate Nature, I recall one experience in particular. The world men ordinarily know is limited to a few vibrations the organs of sense respond to. Though science, with her delicate new instruments, was beginning to justify the instinctive knowledge of an older time, and wireless marvels and radio-activity were still unknown (at the time of which I write), Julius spoke of them as the groundwork of still greater marvels by which thought would be transmissible. The thought-current was merely a little higher than the accepted wave lengths; moreover, powers and qualities were equally transmissible. Unscientifically, he was aware of all these things, and into this beyond-world he penetrated, apparently, though with the effort of a long-forgotten practice. He linked the human with the non-human. He knew Saturn or the Sun in the same way that he knew a pebble or a wild flower—by feeling-with them.

"It's coming back into the world," he said. "Before we leave this section it will all be known again. The 'best minds,'" he laughed, "will publish it in little primers, and will label it 'extension of consciousness,' or some such laboured thing.. And they will think themselves very wonderful to have discovered what they really only re-collect."

He looked up at me and smiled significantly, as we sat side by side in the Dissecting Room, busily tracing the nerves and muscles in a physical "instrument" some soul had recently cast aside. I use his own curious phraseology, of course. He laid his pointed weapon down a moment upon the tangle of the solar plexus that resembled the central switch-hoard of a great London telegraph office.

"There's the main office," he pointed, "not *that*," indicating the sawn-off skull where the brain was visible. "Feeling is the clue, not thinking."

And, then and there, he described how this greatest nerve-centre of the human system could receive and transmit messages and powers between its owner and the entire universe. His quiet yet impassioned language I cannot pretend at this interval to give; I only remember the conviction that his words conveyed. It was more wonderful than any fairy-tale, for it made the fairy-tale come true. For this "beyond-world" of Julius LeVallon contained whole hierarchies of living beings, whose actuality is veiled to-day in legend, folk-lore, and superstition generally—some small and gentle as the fairies, some swift and radiant as the biblical angels, others, again, dark, powerful and immense as the deities of savage and "primitive" races. But all knowable, all obedient to the laws of their own being, and, furthermore, all accessible to the trained will of the human who understood them. Their great powers could be borrowed, used, adapted. Herein lay for him a means to deeper wisdom, richer life, the recovery of true worship, powers that must eventually help Man to that knowledge of the universe which is, more simply put, the knowledge of one God. At present Man was separate, cut off from all this bigger life, matter "inanimate" and Nature "dead."

And I remember that in this remarkable outburst he touched very nearly upon the origin of my inner dread. Again I felt sure that it was in connection with practices of this nature that he and I and she had involved ourselves in something that, as it were, disturbed the equilibrium of those forces whose balance constitutes the normal world, but something that could only be put right again by the three of us acting in concert and facing an ordeal that was somehow terrible.

One afternoon in October I always associate particularly with this talk about elemental Nature Powers being accessible to human beings, for it was the first occasion that I actually witnessed anything in the nature of definite results. And I recall it in detail; the memory of such an experience could never fade.

We had been walking for a couple of hours, much of the time in silence. My own mind was busy with no train of thought in particular; rather I was in a negative, receptive state, idly reviewing mental pictures, and my companion's presence obtruded so little that I sometimes almost forgot he was beside me. On the Pentlands we followed the sheep tracks carelessly where they led, and presently lay down among the heather of the higher slopes to rest. Julius flung himself down first, and, pleasantly tired, I imitated him at once. In the distance lay the mosaic of Edinburgh town, her spires rising out of haze and mist. Across the uninspiring strip of modern house, called the Morningside, the Castle Rock stood on its blunt pedestal, carved out by the drive of ancient glaciers. At the end of the small green valley where immense ice-chisels once had ploughed their way, we saw the Calton Hill; beyond it, again, the line of Princes Street with its stream of busy humanity; and further still, the lovely dip over the crest of the hill where the Northern ocean lay towards the Bass Rock and the seabirds.

The autumn air drew cool and scented along the heathery ridges, and while Julius lay gazing at the cirrus clouds, I propped myself upon one elbow and enjoyed the scene below. It was my pleasure always to know a thing by name and recognise it—the different churches, the prison, the University buildings, the particular house where my own lodgings were; and I was searching for Frederick Street, trying to pick out the actual corner where George Street cut through it, when I became aware that, across the great dip of intervening valley, something equally saw me. This was my first impression—that something watched me.

I placed it, naturally enough, where my thought was fixed, across the dip; but the same instant I realised my mistake. It was much nearer—close beside me. Something was watching us intently. We were no longer quite alone. And, with the discovery, there grew gradually about me a sense of indescribable loveliness, a soft and tender beauty impossible to define precisely. It came like one of those enveloping moods of childhood, when everything is alive and anything may happen. My heart, it seemed, expanded. It turned wild.

I looked round at Julius. He still lay on his back as before, with the difference that his hands now were folded across his eyes and that his body was motionless and rigid as a log. He hardly breathed. He seemed part and parcel of the earth, merged in the hill-side as naturally as the heather.

Yet something had happened, or was in the act of happening, to him. The forgotten schoolday atmosphere of Other Places stole over me as I gazed.

I made no sound; I did not speak; my eyes passed quickly from the panorama of town and sea to a flock of mountain sheep that nibbled the patches of coarse grass not far away. The feeling that something invisible yet conscious approached us from the empty spaces of the afternoon became a certainty. My spirit lifted. There was a new and vital relationship between my inner nature, so to speak, and my material environment. My nerves were quivering, the sense of beauty remained, but my questioning wonder changed to awe. Somewhere about me on that bare hill-side Nature had become aggressively alive.

Yet no one of my senses in particular conveyed the great impression; it seemed wrought of them all in combination—a large, synthetic, universal report sent forth by the natural things about me. Some flooding energy, like a tide of unknown power, rose through my body. But my brain was clear. One by one I ticked off the different senses; it was neither sight, smell, touch, nor hearing that was individually affected. There was vague uneasiness, it seems, as well, for I sought instinctively what was of commonplace import in the landscape. I stared at the group of nibbling sheep. My sight wandered to the larches on my right, some thirty yards away. Next, seeking things more humanly comforting still, I fixed my gaze upon my nailed and muddy boots.

At the same moment Julius became suddenly alert. He sat erect.

The change in his attitude startled me; he seemed intent upon something in the nearer landscape that escaped me. He, like myself, was aware that other life approached; he shared my strange emotion of delight and power; but in him was no uneasiness, for whereas I questioned nervously, he knew with joy. Yet he was doing nothing definite, so far as I could see. The change of attitude resulted in no act. His face, however, was so intense, so animated, that I understood it was the touch of his mind that had reached my own so stimulatingly, and that what was coming—came through him. His eyes were fixed, I saw, upon the little grove of larches.

I made no movement, but watched the larches and his face alternately. And what I can only call the childhood mood of make-believe enormously increased. It extended, however, far beyond the child's domain; it seemed all-potent, irresistibly imperative. By the mere effort of my will I could—create. Some power in me hidden, lost, unused, seemed trying to assert itself. I merely had to say "Let there be a ball before me in the air," and by the simple fiat of this power it must appear. I had only to will the heather at my feet to move, and it must move—as though, in the act of willing, some intense, intermolecular energy were set free. There was almost the sense that I had this power in me now—that I had certainly once known how to use it.

I can hardly describe intelligently what followed. It is so easy to persuade my-self that I was dreaming or deceived, yet so difficult to prove that I was neither one nor other, but keenly observant and wholly master of my mind. For by this time it was clear to me that the sensation of being watched, of knowing another living presence close, as also of sharing this tender beauty, issued primarily from the grove of larches. My being and their own enjoyed sonic inter-relationship, exquisite yet natural. There was exchange between us. And the wind, blow-ing stiffly up the heather slopes, then lifted the lower branches of the trees, so that I saw deep within the little grove, yet at the same time behind and beyond them. Something that their veil of greenness draped went softly stirring. The same minute it came out towards me with a motion best described as rushing. The heart of the grove became instinct with life, life that I could appreciate and understand, each individual tree contributing its thread to form the composite whole, Julius and myself contributing as well. This Presence swam out through the afternoon atmosphere towards us, whirring, almost dancing, as it came. There was an impression of volume—of gigantic energy. The air in our imme-diate neighbourhood became visible.

Yet to say that I saw something seems as untrue as to say that I saw nothing. Form was indistinguishable from movement. The air, the larches and ourselves were marvellously entangled with the sunshine and the landscape. I was aware of an intelligence different from my own, immensely powerful, but somehow not a human intelligence. Superb, unearthly beauty touched the very air.

"Hush!" I heard LeVallon whisper. "Feel-with it, but do not think."

The advice was unnecessary. I felt; but I had no time to think, no inclination either. A long-forgotten "I" was active. My familiar, daily self shrank out of sight. Vibrant, sensitive, amazingly extended, my being responded in an im-miediate fashion to things about me. Any "thoughts" I had came afterwards.

For the greenness whirled and flashed like sunlight upon water or on flutter-ing silk. With an intricate and complex movement it appeared to spin and revolve within itself; and I cannot dare to say from what detail came the absolute per-suasion that it was alive in the same sense that I myself and Julius were alive, while of another order of intelligence.

Julius rose suddenly to his feet, and a fear came over me that he was going to touch it; for he moved forwards with an inviting gesture that caused me an ex-hilarating distress as when a friend steps too near the edge of a precipice. But the next moment I saw that he was directing it rather, with the immediate re-sult that it swerved sharply to one side, passed with swiftness up the steep hill-side, and—disappeared. It raced by me with a soft and roaring noise, leaving a marked disturbance of the air that was like a wind within a wind. I seemed pushed aside by the fringe of a small but violent whirlwind. The booming al-ready sounded some distance up the slope.

"I've lost it!" I remember shouting with a pang of disappointment. For it seemed that the power and delight in me both ebbed and that energy went with them.

"Because you thought a moment instead of felt!" cried Julius. He turned, holding up one hand by way of warning. His voice was more than ordinarily resonant, his whole body charged with force. "Now—watch the sheep," he added
in a lower tone. And, although the words surprised me in one way, in another
I anticipated them. There passed across his face a momentary expression of intense effort, but even before the sentence was finished I heard the rushing of
the frightened animals, and understood something of what was happening.
There was panic in them. The entire flock ran headlong down the steep slope
of heather. The thunder of their feet is in my ears to-day. I see their heaving backs
of dirty wool climbing in tumbling fashion one upon another as they pressed
tightly in a wedge-shaped outline. They plunged frantically together down the
steep place to some level turf below. But, even then, I think they would not have
stopped, had not a sound, half cry, half word of command, from my companion
brought them to a sudden halt again. They paused in their wild descent. Like
a single animal the entire company of them—twenty or thirty, perhaps, all
told—were arrested. They looked stupidly about them, turned their heads in
the opposite direction, and with one accord began once more peacefully—eating grass.

The incident had occupied, perhaps, three minutes.

"The larches!" I heard, and the same instant that softly-roaring thing, not
wind, yet carried inside the wind, again raced past me, going this time in the
direction of the grove. There was just time to turn, when I heard a clap—not
unlike the sound of an open hand that strikes a pillow, though on a far vaster
scale—and it seemed to me that the bodies of the trees trembled for a moment
where they melted into one another amid the general greenness of stems and
branches.

For the fraction of a second they shone and pulsed and quivered. Something
opened; something closed again. The enthralling sense of beauty left my heart,
the power sank away, the huge energy retired. And, in a flash, all was normal
once again; it was a cool October afternoon upon the Pentland Hills, and a wind
was blowing freshly from the distant sea.

I was lying on the grass again exactly as before; Julius, watching me keenly
beneath the lids of his narrowed eyes, had just flung himself down to keep m
company....

"The barriers, you see, are thin," he said quietly. "There really are no barriers at all."

This was the first sentence I heard, though his voice it seemed, had been speaking for some considerable time. I had closed my eyes—to shut out a rising tide
of wonderful and familiar pictures whose beauty somehow I sought vigorously
to deny. Yet there was this flare of vivid memory: a penetrating odour of acrid
herbs that burned in the clearing of a sombre forest; a low stone altar, the droning of men's voices chanting monotonously as they drew near in robes of
white and yellow... and I seemed aware of some forgotten but exquisite ceremonial by means of which natural forces were drawn upon to benefit the beings

of the worshippers....

"All is transmissible," rose LeVallon's voice out of the picture, "all can be shared. That was the aim and meaning of our worship...."

I opened my eyes and looked at him. The expansion of my consciousness had been a genuine thing; the power and joy both real; the worship authentic. Now they had left me and the shrinkage caused me pain; there was a poignant sense of loss. I felt afraid again.

"But it's all gone," I answered in a hushed tone, "and everything has left me." Reason began to argue and deny. I could scarcely retain the memory of those big sensations which had offered a channel into an extended world.

Julius searched my face with his patient, inward-gazing eyes.

"Your attitude prevented," he replied after a moment's hesitation ; "it became unsafe."

"You brought it?" I faltered.

He nodded. "A human will," he replied, "and a physical body—as channel. Your resistance broke the rhythm and brought danger in." And after a pause he added significantly: "For the return—the animals served well." He smiled. "Ran down a steep place into the sea—almost."

And, abruptly then, the modern world came back, as though what I had just experienced had been but some pictured memory, thrust up, withdrawn. I was aware that my fellow student at Edinburgh University, LeVallon by name, lay beside me in the heather, his face charged with peace and happiness... that the dusk was falling, and that the air was turning chilly.

Without further speech we rose and made our way down from the windy ridge, and the chief change I noticed in myself seemed to be a marked increase of vitality that was singularly exhilarating, yet included the touch of awe already mentioned. The feeling was in me that life of some non-human kind had approached us both. I looked about me, first at Julius, then at the landscape, growing dim. The wind blew strongly from the sea. Far in the distance rose the outline of the Forth Bridge, then a-building, its skeleton, red in the sunset, rearing across the water like a huge sea-serpent with ribs of gleaming steel. I could almost hear the hammering of the iron.... And, at our feet, the first lights of the Old Town presently twinkled through the veil of dusk and smoke that wove itself comfortingly about the habitations of men and women.

My thoughts were busy, but for a long time no speech passed. Occasionally I stole glances at my companion as we plodded downwards through the growing dusk, and there seemed a curious glow about his face that made him more clearly visible than the other objects about us. The way he looked back from time to time across his shoulder increased my impression—by no means a pleasant one just then—that something followed us from those heathery hill-tops, kept close behind us through the muddy lanes, and watched our movements across the fields and hedges.

I have never forgotten that walk home in the autumn twilight, nor the sense of haunting possibilities that hung about it like an atmosphere—the feeling that other life loomed close upon our steps. Before Roslin Chapel was passed, and the welcome lights of the town were near, this Consciousness of a ghostly fol-lowing suite became a certainty, and I felt that every copse and field sent out some messenger to swell the throng. We had established touch with another re-gion of life, of power, and the link was not yet fully broken.

And the sentences Julius let fall from time to time, half to himself and half to me, increased my nervousness instead of soothing it.

"The gods, you see, are not dead," he said, waving his hand towards the hills, "but only distant. They are still accessible to all who can feel-with their pow-ers. In your self-consciousness a door stands open; they can be approached—through Nature. Ages ago, when the sun was younger, and you and I were nearer to the primitive beauty..."

A cat, darting silently across the road like a shadow from a cottage door, gave me such a start that I lost the remainder of the sentence. His arm was linked in mine as he added softly:

"...Only, what is borrowed in this way must always be returned, for otherwise the equilibrium is destroyed, and the borrower suffers until he puts it right again. So utterly exact is the balance of the universe...."

I deliberately turned my head away, aware that something in me *would* not lis-ten. The conviction grew that he had a motive in the entire business. That in-ner secret dread revived. Yet, in spite of it, there was a curiosity that refused to let me escape altogether. It was bound to satisfy itself. The question seemed to force itself out of my lips:

"They are unconscious, though, these Powers?" And, having asked it, I would willingly have blotted out the words. I heard his low voice answer so far away it seemed an echo from the hills behind us.

"Of a different order," he replied, "until they are part of you; and then they share *your* consciousness...."

"Hostile or friendly?" I believed I thought this question only, but apparently I spoke it out aloud. Julius paused a moment. Then he said briefly:

"Neither one nor other, of themselves. Merely that they resent an order be-ing placed upon them. It involves mastery or destruction."

The words sank into me with something like a shudder. It seemed that every-thing I asked and everything he answered were as familiar as though we spoke of some lecture of the day before. What I had witnessed shared this familiarity, too, though more faintly. All belonged to this incalculable past he for ever searched to bring to light. Yet of what dim act of mine, of his, or of another work-ing with us, this mysterious shudder was born, I still remained in ignorance, though an ignorance that seemed now slowly about to lift.

Then, suddenly, the final question was out before I could prevent it. It came irresistibly:

"And if, instead of animals, it had been men... ?"

The effect was instantaneous, and very curious. I could have sworn he had been waiting for that question. For he turned upon me with passion that shone a moment in his pale and eager face, then died away as swiftly as it came. His hand tightened upon my arm; he drew me closer. He bent down. I saw his eyes gleam in the darkness as he whispered:

"Such men would know themselves cut off from their own kind, a gulf between humanity—and themselves. For the elemental powers may be borrowed, but not kept. There would burn in them fires no human hands could quench, because no human hands had lit them. Yet their vast energies might lift our little self-seeking race into that grander universal life where—"

He stopped dead in the darkened road and fixed me with his eyes. He said the next words with a vehement conviction that struck cold into my very entrails:

"He who retains within himself the elemental powers which are the deities in Nature, is both above and below his kind."

A moment he hid his face in his hands; then, opening his arms wide and throwing his head back to the sky, he raised his voice; he almost cried aloud: "A man who has worshipped the Powers of Wind and the Powers of Fire, and has retained them in himself, keeping them out of their appointed places, is born of them. He is become their child. He is a son of Wind and Fire. And though he break and flame with energies that could regenerate the world, he must remain alien and outcast from humanity, untouched by love or sorrow, stranger to joy, aloof, impersonal, until by full and complete restitution, he restore the balance in the surrender of his stolen powers."

It seemed to me he towered; that his stature grew; that the darkness round his very head turned bright; and that a wind from nowhere went driving down the sky behind him with a wailing violence. The amazing outburst took me off my feet by its suddenness. An emotion from the depths rose up and shook me. What happened next I hardly realised, only that he caught my arm and hurried along the road at a reckless, half stumbling speed, and that the lonely hills behind us followed in the darkness....

A few moments afterwards we found ourselves among the busy lights and traffic of the streets. His calm had returned as suddenly as it had deserted him. Such moments with him were so rare, he seemed almost unnatural, superhuman. And presently we separated at the corner of the North Bridge, going home to our respective rooms. He made no single reference to the storm that had come upon him in this extraordinary manner; I likewise spoke no word. We said good night. He turned one way, I another. But, as I went, his burning sentences still haunted me; I saw his face like moonlight through the tangle of a wood; and I knew that all we had seen and heard and spoken that afternoon had reference to a past that we had shared, yet also to a future, which he and I awaited together for the coming of a—third.

CHAPTER XI

"*Strange as it may appear to the modern mind, whose one ambition is to harden and formalise itself... the ancient mind conceived of knowledge in a totally different fashion. It did not crystallise itself into a hardened point, but, remaining fluid, knew that the mode of knowledge suitable to its nature was by intercourse and blending. Its experience was...that it could blend with intelligence greater that itself, that it could have intercourse with the gods.*"—"Some Mystical Adventures" (G. R. S. Mead).

An inevitable result of this experience was that, for me, a reaction followed. I had no stomach for such adventures. Though carried away at the moment by the enthralling character of the feelings roused that afternoon, my normal self, my upper self as I had come to call it, protested—with the result that I avoided Julius. I changed my seat in the classrooms, giving as excuse that I could not hear the lecturer; I gave up attending postmortems and operations where I knew that he would be; and if I saw him in the street I would turn aside or dive into some shop until the danger of our meeting passed. Ashamed of my feebleness, I yet could not bring myself to face him and thrash the matter out.

Other influences also were at work, for my father, it so happened, and the girl I was engaged to marry, her family, too, were all of them in Edinburgh just about that time, and some instinct warned me that they and LeVallon must not meet. In the latter case particularly I obeyed this warning instinct, for in the influence of Julius there hid some strain of opposition towards these natural affections. I was aware of it unconsciously, perhaps. It seemed he made me question the reality of my love; made me doubt and hesitate; sometimes almost made me challenge the value of these ties that meant so much to me. From his point of view, I knew, these emotions belonged to transient relationships of one brief section, and to become centred in them involved the obliteration of the larger view. His attitude was more impersonal: Love everyone, but do not lose perspective by focusing your entire self in one or two. It was *au fond* a selfish pleasure merely; it delayed the development of the permanent personality; it destroyed—more important still—the sense of kinship with the universe which was the basic principle with him. It need not: but it generally did.

For some weeks, therefore, our talks and walks were interrupted; I devoted myself to work, to intercourse with those I loved, and led generally the normal existence of a university student who was reading for examinations that were of importance to his future career in life.

Yet, though we rarely met, and certainly held no converse for some time, interruption actually there was none at all. To pretend it were a farce. The inner relationship continued as before. Physical separation meant absolutely nothing in those ties that so strangely and so intimately knit our deeper lives together. There was no more question of break between us than there is question of a break in time when light is extinguished and the clock becomes invisible. His presence always stood beside me; the beauty of his pale, un-English face kept ever in my thoughts; I heard his whisper in my dreams at night, and the ideas his curious language watered continued growing with a strength I could not question.

There were two selves in me then as in our schooldays: one that resisted, and one that yearned. When together, it was the former that asserted its rights, but when apart, oddly enough, it was the latter. There is little question, however, that the latter was the stronger of the two. Thus, the moment I found myself alone again, my father and my fiancée both gone, we rushed together like two ends of an elastic that had been stretched too long apart.

And almost immediately, as though the opportunity must not be lost, he spoke to me of an experiment he had in view.

By what network of persuasiveness he induced me to witness, if not actually to co-operate in, this experiment, I cannot pretend at this distance to remember. I think it is true that he used no persuasion at all, but that at the first mention of it my deeper being met the proposal with curious sympathy. At the horror and audacity my upper self shrank back aghast; the thing seemed wholly unpermissible and dreadful; something unholy, as of blasphemy, lay in it too. But, as usual, when this mysterious question of "Other Places" was involved, in the end I followed blindly where he led. My older being held the casting vote. And the reason—I admit it frankly—was that somewhere behind the amazing glamour of it all lay—truth. While reason scoffed, my heart remembered and believed.

Moreover, in this particular instance, a biting curiosity had its influence too. I was wholly sceptical of results. The thing was mad, incredible, even wicked. It could never happen. Yet, while I said these words, and more besides, there ran a haunting terror in me underground that, after all... that possibly... I cannot even set down in words the nature of my doubt. I can merely affirm that something in me was not absolutely sure.

"The essential thing," he told me, "is to find an empty 'instrument' that is in perfect order—young, vigorous, the tissues unwasted by decay or illness. There must have been no serious deterioration of the organs, muscles, and so forth."

I knew then that this new experiment was akin to that other I had already witnessed. The experience on the Pentlands had also been deliberately brought about. The only difference was that this second one he announced beforehand. Further, it was of a higher grade. The channel of evocation, instead of being in the vegetable kingdom, was in the human.

I understood his meaning, and suggested that someone in deep trance might meet the conditions, for in trance he held that the occupant, or soul, was gone elsewhere, the tenement of flesh deserted.

But he shook his head. That was not, he said, legitimate. The owner would return. He watched me with a curious smile as he said this. I knew then that he referred to the final emptiness of a vacated body.

"Sudden death," I said, while his eyes flashed back the answer. "And the Elemental Powers?" I asked quickly.

"Wind and fire," he replied. And in order to carry his plan into execution he proposed to avail himself of his free access to the students' Dissecting Room.

During the longish interval between the conception and carrying out of this preposterous experiment I shifted like a weathercock between acceptance and refusal. My doubts were torturing. There were times when I treated it as the proposal of a lunatic that at worst could work no injury to anyone concerned. But there were also times when a certain familiar reality clothed it with a portentous actuality. I was reminded faintly of something similar I had been connected with before. Dim figures of this lost familiarity stalked occasionally across the field of inner sight. Julius and I had done this thing together long, long ago, "when the sun was younger," and when we were "nearer to the primitive beauty," as he phrased it. In reverie, in dreams, in moments when thinking was in abeyance, this odd conviction asserted itself. It had to do with a Memory of some worship that once was mighty and effective; when august Presences walked the earth in stupendous images of power; and traffic with them had been useful, possible. The barrier between the human and the non-human, between Man and Nature, was not built. Wind and fire! It was always wind and fire that he spoke of. And I remember one vivid and terrific dream in particular in which I heard again a voice pronounce that curious name of "Concerighé," and, though the details were blurred on waking, I clearly grasped that certain elemental powers had been evoked by us for purposes of our own and had not been suffered to return to their appointed places; further, that concerned with us in the awful and solemn traffic was—another. We had been three.

This dream, of course, I easily explained as due directly to my talks with Julius, but my dread was not so easily dismissed, and that I overcame it finally and consented to attend was due partly to the extraordinary curiosity I felt, and partly to this inexplicable attraction in my deeper self which urged me to see the matter through. Something inevitable about it forced me. Yet, but for the settled conviction that behind the abhorrent proposal lay some earnest purpose of LeVallon's, not ignoble in itself, I should certainly have refused. For, though saying little, and not taking me fully into his confidence, he did manage to convey the assurance that this thing was not to be carried out as an end, but as a means to an end, in itself both legitimate and necessary. It was, I gathered, a kind of preliminary trial—an attempt that *might* possibly succeed, even without the presence of the third.

"Sooner or later," he said, aware that I hesitated, "it must be faced. Here is an opportunity for us, at least. If we succeed, there is no need to wait for—another. It is a question. We can but try."

And try accordingly we did.

The occasion I shall never forget—a still, cold winter's night towards the middle of December, most of the students already gone down for Christmas, and small chance of the room being occupied. For even in the busiest time before examinations there were few men who cared to avail themselves of the gruesome privilege of nightwork, for which special permission, too, was necessary. Julius,

in any case, made his preparations well, and the janitor of the grey-stone building on the hill, whose top floor was consecrated to this grisly study of life in
death, had surrendered the keys even before we separated earlier in the evening
for supper at the door of the post-mortem theatre.

"Upstairs at eleven o'clock," he whispered, "and if I'm late—the preparations
may detain me—go inside and wait. Your presence is necessary to success." He
laid his hand on my shoulder; he looked at me searchingly a moment, almost be-
seechingly, as though he detected the strain of opposition in me. "And be as sympathetic as you can," he begged. "At least, do not actively oppose." Then, as
he turned away, "I'll try to be punctual," he added, smiling, "but—well, you
know as well as I do—!" He shrugged his shoulders and was gone.

You know! Somehow or other it was true: I did know. The interval of several
hours he would spend in his inner chamber concentrated upon the process of
feeling-with—evoking. He would have no food, no rest, no moment's pause. At
the appointed hour he would arrive, charged with the essential qualities of these
two elemental powers which in dim past ages, summoned by another audacious
"experiment" from their rightful homes, he now sought to "restore." He would
seek to return what had been "borrowed." He would attempt to banish them
again. For they could only be thus banished, as they had been summoned—
through the channel of a human organism. They were of a loftier order, then,
than the Powers for whose return the animal organisms of the sheep had
served.

I went my way down Frederick Street with a heart, I swear, already palpi-
tating.

Of the many thrilling experiences that grew out of my acquaintance with this
extraordinary being, I think that night remains supreme—certainly, until our
paths met again in the Jura Mountains. But, strangest of all, is the fact that
throughout the ghastly horror of what occurred was—beauty! To convey this
beauty is beyond any power that I possess, yet it was there, a superb and awful beauty that informed the meanest detail of what I witnessed. The experiment
failed of course; in the accomplishment of LeVallon's ultimate purpose, that is,
it failed; but the failure was due, apparently, to one cause alone: that the
woman was not present.

It is most difficult to describe, and my pen, indeed, shrinks from setting down
so revolting a performance. Yet this curious high beauty redeems it in my memory as I now recall the adventure through the haze of years, and I believe the
beauty was due to a deeper fact impossible to convey in words. Behind the little "modern" experiment, and parallel to it, ran another, older Memory that was
fraught with some significance of eternity. Till parent memory penetrated and
overshadowed the smaller copy of it; it exalted what was ugly, uplifted what
seemed abominable, sublimated the distressing failure into an image of what
might have been magnificent. I mean, in a word, that this experiment was a poor
attempt to reconstruct an older ritual of spiritual significance whereby those natural forces, once worshipped as the gods, might combine with qualities similar
to their own in human beings. The memory of a more august and effective cer-

emony moved all the time behind the little reconstruction. The beauty was derived from my dim recollection of some transcendent but now forgotten worship.

At the appointed hour I made my way across the Bridge and towards the Old
Town where the University buildings stood. It was, as I said, a bitter night. The
Castle Rock and Cathedral swam in a flood of silvery moonlight; frost sparkled
on the roofs; the spires of Edinburgh shone in the crystal wintry atmosphere.
The air, so keen, was windless. Few people were about at this late hour, and I
had the feeling that the occasional pedestrians, hurrying homewards in tightly-
buttoned overcoats, eyed me askance. No one of them was going in the same direction as myself. They questioned my purpose, looked sharply over their
shoulders, then quickened their pace away from me towards the houses where
the fires burned in cosy human sitting-rooms.

At the door of the great square building itself I hesitated a moment, hiding
in the shadow of the overhanging roof. It was easy to pretend that moral disapproval warned me to turn back, but the simpler truth is that I was afraid. At
the best of times the Dissecting Room, with its silent cargo of dreadful forms
and faces, was a chamber of horrors I could never become hardened to as the
majority of students did; but on this occasion, when a theory concerning life
alien to humanity was to be put to so strange a test, I confess that the prospect
set my nerves a-quivering and made the muscles of my legs turn weak. A cold
sensation ran down my spine, and it was not the wintry night alone that
caused it.

Opening the heavy door with an effort, I went in and waited a moment till
the clanging echo had subsided through the deserted building. My imagination
figured the footsteps of a crowd hurrying away behind the sound down the long
stone corridors. In the silence that followed I slowly began climbing the steps
of granite, hoping devoutly that Julius would be waiting for me at the top. I was
a little late; he might possibly have arrived before me. Up the four flights of stairs
I went stealthily, trying to muffle my footsteps, putting my weight heavily upon
the balustrade, and doing all I could to make no sound at all. For it seemed to
me that my movements were both watched and heard, and that those motionless, silent forms above were listening for my approach, and knew that I was
coming.

On the landings at each turn lay a broad sweet patch of moonlight that fell
through the lofty windows, and but for these the darkness would have been
complete. No light, it seemed to me, had ever looked more clean and pure and
welcome. I thought of the lone Pentland ridges, and of the sea, lying calm and
still outside beneath the same sheet of silver, the air of night all keen and fragrant. The heather slopes came back to me, the larches and the flock of nibbling
sheep. I thought of these in detail, of my fire-lit rooms in Frederick Street, of the
vicarage garden at home in Kent where my boyhood had been spent; I thought
of a good many things, truth to tell, all of them as remote as possible front my
present surroundings; but when I eventually reached the topmost landing and

found LeVallon was not there, I thought of one thing only—that I was alone. Just beyond me, through that door of frosted glass, lay in its most loathsome form the remnant of humanity left behind by death.

In the daytime, when noisy students, callous and unimaginative, thronged the room, the horror of it retreated, modified by the vigorous vitality of these doctors of the future; but now at night, amid the ominous silence, with darkness over the town and the cold of outer space dropping down upon the world, as though linking forces with that other final cold within the solemn chamber, it seemed quite otherwise. I stood shivering and afraid upon the landing, angry that I could have lent myself to so preposterous and abominable a scheme, yet determined, so long as my will held firm, to go through with it to the end.

He had asked me to wait for him—inside.

Knowing that every minute of hesitation must weaken my powers of resolve, I moved at once towards the door, then paused again. The comforting roar of the traffic floated to my ears; I heard the distant tinkle of a tramcar bell, the boom of Edinburgh, a confused noise of feet and wheels and voices, far away, it is true, but distinctly reassuring.

Outside, the life of humanity rolled upon its accustomed way, recking little of the trembling figure that stood on the top floor of this silent building, one hand on the door upon whose further side so many must one day come to final rest. For one hand already touched the freezing knob, and I was in the act of turning it when another sound, that was certainly not the murmur of the town, struck sharply through the stillness and brought all movement in me to a sudden halt.

It came from within, I thought at first; and it was like a wave of sighs that rose and fell, sweeping against the glass door a moment, then passing away as abruptly as it came. Yet it was more like wind than sighs through human lips, and immediately, then, I understood that it was wind. I caught my breath again with keen relief. Wind was rising from the hills, and this was its first messenger running down among the roofs and chimney-pots. I heard its wailing echoes long after it had died away.

But a moment later it returned, louder and stronger than before, and this time, hearing it so close, I know not what secret embassies of wonder touched me from the night outside, deposited their undecipherable messages, and were gone again. I can only say that the key of my emotions changed, changed, moreover, with a swelling rush as when the heavier stops are pulled out upon an organ-board. For, on entering the building, the sky had been serenely calm, and keen frost locked the currents of the air; whereas now that wind went wailing round the walls as though it sought an entrance, almost as though its crying voice veiled purpose. There seemed a note of menace, eager and peremptory, in its sudden rush and drop. It knocked upon the stones and upon the roof above my head with curious and repeated buffets of sound that resembled the "clap" I had heard that October afternoon among the larches, only a hundred times repeated and a hundred-fold increased. The change in myself, moreover, was similar to the change then experienced—the flow and drive of bigger consciousness that helped to banish fear. I seemed to know about that wind, to feel its life and being, indeed, to share it. No longer was I merely John Mason, a student in Edinburgh, separate and distinct from all about me, but was—I realised it amazingly—a bit of life in the universe, not isolated even from the wind.

The beauty of the sensation did not last; it passed through me, linked to that insistent roar; but the fact that I had felt it gave me courage. The stops were instantly pushed in again... and the same minute the swing-door closed behind me with a sullen thud.

I stood within the chamber; Julius, I saw in a moment, was not there. I moved through the long, narrow room, keeping close beside the wall, taking up my position finally about halfway down, where I could command the six tall windows and the door. The moon was already too high to send her rays directly through the panes, but from the extensive sky-lights she shed a diffused, pale glow upon the scene, and my eyes, soon accustomed to the semi-darkness, saw everything quite as clearly as I cared about.

In front of me stretched the silent, crowded room, patchy in the moonshine, but with shadows deeply gathered in the corners; and, row after row upon the white marble slabs, lay the tenantless forms in the grotesque, unnatural positions as the students had left them a few hours before. The picture does not invite detailed description, but I at once experienced the peculiar illusion that attacks new students even in the daytime. It seemed that the sightless eyes turned slowly round to stare at me, that the shrunken lips half opened as in soundless speech, and that the heads with one accord shifted to an angle whence they could observe and watch me better. There went a rustling through that valley of dry bones as though life returned for a moment to drive the broken machinery afresh.

This sensible illusion was, of course, one I could easily dismiss. More difficult, however, was the subtler attack that came upon me from behind the sensory impressions. For, while I stood with my back against the wall, listening intently for LeVallon's step upon the stairs, I could not keep from my mind the terror of those huddled sheep upon the Pentland ridges; the whole weird force of his theories about "life" in Nature came beating against my mind, aided, moreover, by some sympathy in myself that could never wholly ridicule their possible truth.

I gazed round me at the motionless, discarded forms, used for one brief "section," then cast aside, and as I did so my mind naturally focused itself upon a point of dreadful and absorbing interest—which one was to be the subject of the experiment? So short a time ago had each been a nest of keenest activity and emotion, enabling its occupant to reap its harvest of past actions while sowing that which it must reap later again in its new body, already perhaps now a-forming. And of these discarded vehicles, one was to be the channel through which two elemental Powers, evoked in vanished ages, might return to their appointed place. I heard that clamouring wind against the outer walls; I felt within me the warmth of a strange enthusiasm rise and glow; and it seemed to me just then that the whole proposal was as true and simple and in the natural order of things as birth or death, or any normal phenomenon to the terror and glory of which mankind has grown accustomed through prolonged familiarity. To this point, apparently, had the change in my feelings brought me. The dreadful novelty had largely gone. Something would happen, nor would it be entirely unfamiliar.

Then, on a marble slab beside the door, the body of a boy, fresh, white and sweet, and obviously brought in that very day, since it was as yet untouched by knife or scalpel, "drew" my attention of its own accord—and I knew at once that I had found it.

Oddly enough, the discovery brought no increase of fearful thrill; it was as natural as though I had helped to place it there myself. And, again, for some reason, that delightful sense of power swept me; my diminutive modern self slipped off to hide; I remembered that a million suns surrounded me; that the earth was but an insignificant member of one of the lesser systems that man's vaunted Reason was as naught compared to the oceans of what might be known and possible; and that this body I wore and used, like that white, empty one upon the slab, was but a transient vehicle through which I, as a living part of the stupendous cosmos, acted out my little piece of development in the course of an eternal journey. This wind, this fire, that Julius spoke of, were equally the vehicles of other energies, alive as myself, only less tamed and cabined, yet similarly obedient, again, to the laws of their own beings. The extraordinary mood poured through me like a flood—and once more passed away. And the wind fled singing round the building with a shout.

I looked steadily at the beautiful but vacated framework that the soul had used—used well or ill I knew not—lying there so quietly, so calmly, the smooth skin as yet untouched by knife, unmarred by needle, surrounded on all sides by the ugly and misshapen crew of older death; and as I looked, I thought of some fair shell the tide had left among the seaweed wrack, a flower of beauty shining 'mid decay. In the moonlight I could plainly see the thin and wasted ribs, the fixed blue eves still staring as in life, the lank and tangled hair, the listless fingers that a few hours before must have been active in the flush of health, and passionately loved by more than one assuredly. For, though I knew not the manner of the soul's out-passing, this boy must have suddenly met death that very day. And I found it odd that he should now be lying here, since usually the students' work is concerned to study the processes of illness and decay. It confirmed my certainty that here was the channel LeVallon meant to use.

Time for longer reflection, however, there was none, for just then another gust of this newly-risen wind fell against the building with a breaking roar, and at the same moment the swing door opened and Julius LeVallon stood within the room.

Whether windows had burst, or the great skylights overhead been left unfastened, I had no time, nor inclination either, to discover, but I remember that the wind tore past him down the entire length of the high-ceilinged chamber, tossing the hair uncannily upon a dozen heads in front of me and even stirring the dust about my feet. It was almost as though we stood upon an open plain and met the unobstructed tempest in our teeth.

Yet the rush and vehemence with which he entered startled me, for I found myself glad of the support which a high student's stool afforded. I leaned against it heavily, while Julius, after standing by the door a moment, turned immediately then to the left. He knew exactly where to look. Simultaneously, he saw me too.

Our eyes, in that atmosphere of shadow and soft moonlight, met also across centuries. He spoke my name; but it was no name I answered to To-day. "Come, Silvatela," he said, "lend me your will and sympathy. Feel now with Wind and Fire. For both are here, and the time is favourable. At last, I shall perhaps return what has been borrowed." He beckoned me with a gesture of strange dignity. "It is not that time of balanced forces we most desire—the Equinox—but it is the winter solstice," he went on, "when the sun is nearest. That, too, is favourable. We *may* transcend the appointed boundaries. Across the desert comes the leaping wind. Both heat and air are with us. Come!"

And, having vaguely looked for some kind of elaborate preparation or parade, this sudden summons took me by surprise a little, though the language somehow did not startle me. I sprang up; the stool fell sideways, then clattered noisily upon the concrete floor. I made my way quickly between the peering faces. It seemed no longer strange, this abrupt disturbance of two familiar elements, nor did I remark with unusual curiosity that the wind went rushing and crying about the room, while the heat grew steadily within me so that my actual skin was drenched with perspiration. All came about, indeed, quickly, naturally, and without any pomp of dreadful ceremonial as I had expected. Julius had come with power in his hands; and preparation, if any, had already taken place elsewhere. He spoke no further word as I approached, but bent low over the thin, white form, his face pale, stern and beautiful as I had never seen it before. I thought of a star that entered the roof of those Temple Memories, falling beneficently upon the great concave mirrors where the incense rose in a column of blue smoke. His entire personality, when at length I stood beside him, radiated an atmosphere of force as though charged with some kind of elemental activity that was intense and inexhaustible. The wonder and beauty of it swept me from head to foot. The air grew marvellously heated. It rose in beating waves that accompanied the rushing wind, like a furnace driven by some powerful, artificial draught; in his immediate neighbourhood it whirled and roared. It drew me closer. I, too, found myself bending down above the motionless, stretched form, oblivious of the other crowded slabs about us.

So familiar it all seemed suddenly. Some such scene I had witnessed surely many a time elsewhere. I knew it all before. Upon success hung issues of paramount importance to his soul, to mine, to the soul of another who, for some reason unexplained, was not present with us, and, somehow, also, to the entire universe of which we formed, with these two elements, a living, integral portion. A weight of solemn drama lay behind our little show. It seemed to me the universe looked on and waited. The issue was of cosmic meaning.

Then, as I entered the sphere of LeVallon's personality, a touch of dizziness caught me for an instant, as though this running wind, this accumulating heat, emanated directly from his very being; and, before I quite recovered myself, the moonlight was extinguished like a lamp blown out. Across the sky, apparently, rushed clouds that changed the spreading skylights into thick curtains, while into the room of death came a blast of storm that I thought must tear the windows from their very sockets in the stone. And with the wind came also a yet further increase of heat that was like a touch of naked fire on some inner membrane.

I dare not assert that I was wholly master of myself throughout the swift, dramatic scene that followed in darkness and in tumult, nor can I claim that what I witnessed in the gloom, shot with occasional gleams of moonlight here and there, was more than the intense visualisation of an over-wrought imagination. It well may be that what I expected to happen dramatised itself as though it actually did occur. I can merely state that, at the moment, it seemed real and natural, and that what I saw was the opening scene in a ceremony as familiar to me as the Litany in my father's church.

For, with the pouring through the room of these twin energies of wind and fire, I saw, sketched in the dim obscurity, one definite movement—as the body of the boy rose up into a sitting posture close before our faces. It instantly then sank back again, recumbent as before upon the marble slab. The upright movement was repeated the same second, and once more there came the sinking back. There were several successive efforts before the upright position was maintained; and each time it rose slowly, gradually, all of one piece and rigidly, until finally these tentative movements achieved their object—and the boy sat up as though about to stand. Erect before us, the head slightly hanging on one side, the shoulders squared, the chest expanded as with lung-drawn air, he rose steadily above his motionless companions all around.

And Julius drew back a pace. He made certain gestures with his arms and hands that in some incalculable manner laid control upon the movements. I saw his face an instant as the moon fell on it, pale, glorious and stately, wearing a glow that was *not* moonlight, the lips compressed with effort, the eyes ablaze. He looked to me unearthly and magnificent. His stature seemed increased. There was an air of power, of majesty about him that made his presence beautiful beyond words; and yet, most strange of all, it was familiar to me, even this. I had seen it all before. I knew well what was about to happen.

His gesture changed. No word was spoken. It was a Ceremony in which gesture was more significant than speech. There was evidence of intense internal struggle that yet did not include the ugliness of strain. He put forth all his power merely—and the body rose by jerks. Spasmodically, this time, as though pulled by wires, yet with a kind of terrible violence, it floated from that marble slab into the air. With a series of quick, curious movements, half plunge, half jerk, it touched the floor. It stood stiffly upright on its feet. It rose again, it turned, it twisted, moving arms and legs and head, passing me unsupported through the atmosphere some four feet from the ground. The wind rushed round it with a roar; the fire, though invisible, scorched my eyes. This way and that, now up, now down, the body of this boy danced to and fro before me, silent always, the blue eyes fixed, the lips half parted, more with the semblance of some awful marionette than with human movement, yet charged with a colossal potency that drove it hither and thither. Like some fair Ariel, laughing at death, it flitted above the yellow Calibans of horror that lay strewn below.

Yet, from the very nature of these incompleted movements, I was aware that the experiment was unsuccessful, and that the power was insufficient. Instead of spasmodic, the movements should have been rhythmical and easy; there should have been purpose and intention in the performance of that driven body; there should have been commanding gestures, significant direction there should have been spontaneous breathing and—a voice—the voice of Life.

And instead—I witnessed an unmeaning pantomime, and heard the wailing of the dying wind....

A voice, indeed, there was, but it was the voice of Julius LeVallon that eventually came to me across the length of the room. I saw him slowly approaching through the patches of unequal moonlight, carrying over his shoulder the frail, white burden that had collapsed against the further wall. And his words were very few, spoken more to himself apparently than to me. I heard them; they struck chill and ominous upon my heart:

"The conditions were imperfect, the power insufficient. Alone we cannot do it. We must wait for *her*.... And the channel must be another's—as before."

The strain of high excitement passed. I knew once again that small and pitiful sensation of returning to my normal consciousness. The exhilaration all was gone. There came a dwindling of the heart. I was "myself" again, John Mason, student at Edinburgh University. It produced a kind of shock, the abruptness of the alteration took my strength away. I experienced a climax of sensation, disappointment, distress, fear and revolt as well, that proved too much for me. I ran. I reeled. I heard the sound of my own falling.

No recollection of what immediately followed remains with me... for when I opened my eyes much later, I found myself prone upon the landing several floors below, with Julius bending solicitously over me, helping me to rise. The moonlight fell in a flood through a window on the stairs. My recovery was speedy, though not complete. I accompanied him down the remaining flight, leaning upon his arm; and in the street my senses, though still dazed, took in that the night was calm and cloudless, that the moonlight veiled the stars by its serene brightness, and that the clock above the University buildings pointed to the hour of two in the morning.

The cold was bitter. There was no wind!

Julius came with me to my door in Frederick Street, but the entire distance of a mile neither of us spoke a word.

At the door of my lodging-house, however, he turned. I drew back instinctively, hesitating, for my desire was to get upstairs into my own room with the door locked safely behind me. But he caught my hand.

"We failed to-night," he whispered, "but when the real time comes we shall succeed. *You* will not—fail me then?"

In the stillness of very early morning, the moon sinking towards the long dip of the Queensferry Road, and the shadows lying deep upon the deserted streets, I heard his voice once more come travelling down the centuries to where I stood. The atmosphere of those other days and other places came back with incredible appeal upon me.

He drew me within the chilly hall-way, the sound of our feet echoing up the spiral staircase of stone. Night lay silently over everything, sunrise still many hours away.

I turned and looked into his eager, passionate face, into his eyes that still shone with the radiance of the two great powers, at the mouth and lips which now betrayed the exhaustion that had followed the huge effort. And something appealing and personal in his entire expression made it impossible to refuse. I shook my head, I shrank away, but a voice I scarcely recognised as my own gave the required answer. My upper and my under selves conflicted; yet the latter gave the inevitable pledge "Julius... I promise you."

He gazed into my eyes. An inexpressible tenderness stole into his manner. He took my hand and held it. The die was cast.

"She is now upon the earth with us," he said. "I soon shall find her. We three shall inevitably be drawn together, for we are linked by indestructible ties. There is this debt we must repay—we three who first together incurred it."

There was a pause. Far away I heard a cart rumbling over the cobbles of George Street. In another world it seemed, for the gods were still about us where we stood. Julius moved from me. Once more I saw his eyes fixed pleadingly, almost yearningly upon my own. Then the street door closed upon him and he was gone.

CHAPTER XII

> "*Love and pity are pleading with me this hour.*
>   *What is this voice that stays me forbidding to yield,*
> *Offering beauty, love, and immortal power,*
>   *Aeons away in some far-off heavenly field*'" —A. E.

The actual beginnings of a separation are often so slight that they are scarcely noticed. Between two friends, whose acquaintance is of several years' standing, sure that their tie will stand the ordinary tests of life, some unexpected and trivial incident first points to the parting of the ways; each discovers suddenly that, after all, the other is not necessary to him. An emotion unshared is sufficient to reveal some fundamental lack of sympathy hitherto concealed, and they go their different ways, neither claim debited with the least regret. Like the scarce perceptible mist of evening that divides dusk from night, the invisible chill has risen between them; each sees the other through a cloud that first veils, then distorts, and finally obliterates.

For some weeks after the "experiment" I saw LeVallon through some such risen mist, now thin, now thick, but always there and invariably repelling. I remember distinctly, however, that our going apart was to me not without a sense of regret both keen and poignant. I owed him something impossible to describe; a yearning sense of beauty touched common things about me at the sight of him, even at the mention of his name in the University class-rooms, he had given me an awareness of other possibilities, an exhilarating view of life that held immense perspectives ; a feeling that justice determined even the harshest details above all, a sense of kinship with Nature that combined to form a tie of a most un-common order.

Yet I went willingly from his side; for his prospectus of existence led me to-wards heights where I could not comfortably breathe. His entire scheme I never properly grasped, perhaps; the little parts we shared I saw, possibly, in wrong proportion, uncorrelated to the huge map his mind contained so easily. My own personality was insignificant, my powers mediocre; above all I had not always his strange conviction of positive memory to support me. I lagged behind. I left him. The seductive world that touched him not made decided claims upon my heart—love, passion, ambition and adventure called me strongly. I would not give up all and follow where he led. Yet I left him with the haunting con-sciousness that I surrendered a system of belief that was logical, complete and adequate, its scale of possible achievement wonderful, and its unselfish ideal, if immensely difficult, at least noble and inspiring. For all his mysticism, Julius, it seems to me, was practical and scientific.

Yet, the plausibility of his audacious theories would sometimes return ques-tioningly upon me. Man was an integral part of Nature, not alien to it. What was there, after all, so impossible in what he claimed? And what amongst it might not the science of to-morrow, with its X rays, N rays, its wireless messages, its radium, its inter-molecular energy, and its slowly-formulating laws of telepa-thy and the dynamic character of Thought, not come eventually to confirm un-der new-fangled names?

So far as I reflected concerning these things at all, I kept an open mind; my point was simply that I preferred the ordinary pursuits of ordinary men. He was evidently aware of the change in me, while yet he made no effort to prevent my going. Nor did he make, so far as I can recall, any direct reference to the mat-ter. Once only, in a lecture room, with a hand upon my shoulder while we jos-tled out together in the stream of other students, he bent his face towards me and said with the tender, comprehending smile that never failed to touch me deeply: "Our lives are far too deeply knit for any separation. Out of the Past we come, and that Past is not exhausted yet." The crowd had carried us apart be-fore I could reply, but through me like a flash of lightning rose the certainty that this was literally true, and that while my upper, modern Self went off, my older, hidden Self was with him to the end. We merely took two curves that presently must join again.

But, though we saw little of one another all these weeks, I can never forget the scene of our actual leave-taking, nor the extraordinary incidents that led up to it. Now that I set it down on paper such phrases as "imaginative glamour" and the like may tempt me, but at the time it was as real and actual as the weekly battles with my landlady, or the sheaves of laborious notes I made at lecture-time. In some region of my consciousness, abnormal or otherwise, this scene most certainly took place.

It was one late evening towards the close of the session—March or April, therefore—that I had occasion to visit LeVallon's house for some reason in itself of no importance; one of those keen and blustery nights that turn Edinburgh into a scene of unspeakable desolation, Princes Street, a vista of sheeted rain where shop-windows glistened upon black pavements; the Castle smothered in mist; Scott's Monument semi-invisible with a monstrous air about it in the gloom; and the entire deserted town swept by a wind that howled across the Forth with gusts of quite thunderous energy. Even the cable-cars blundered along like weary creatures blindly seeking shelter.

I hurried through the confusion of the tempest, fighting my way at every step, and on turning the corner past the North British Railway Station, the storm carried me with a rush into the porch of the house, whipping the soaked macintosh with a blow across my face. The rain struck the dripping walls down their entire height, then poured splashing along the pavement in a stream. Night seemed to toss me into the building like some piece of wreckage from the crest of a great wave.

Panting and momentarily flustered, I paused in the little hall to recover breath, while the hurricane, having flung me into shelter, went roaring and howling down the sloping street. I wiped the rain from my face and put straight my disordered clothes. My mind just then was occupied with nothing but these very practical considerations. The impression that followed the next instant came entirely unbidden:

For I became aware of a sudden and enveloping sense of peace, beyond all telling calm and beautiful—an interior peace—a calm upon the spirit itself. It was a spiritual emotion. There drifted over me and round me, like the stillness of some perfect dawn, the hush of something serene and quiet as the stars. All stress and turmoil of the outer world passed into an exquisite tranquillity that in some nameless way was solemn as the spaces of the sky. I felt almost as if some temple atmosphere, some inner Sanctuary of olden time, where the tumult of external life dared not intrude, had descended on me. And the change arrested every active impulse in my being; my hurrying thoughts lay down and slept; all that was scattered in me gathered itself softly into an inner fold; unsatisfied desires closed their eyes. It seemed as if all the questing energies of my busy personality found suddenly repose. Life's restlessness was gone. I even forgot momentarily the purpose for which I came.

So abrupt a change of key was difficult to realise; I can only say that the note of spiritual peace seemed far more true and actual than the physical relief due to the escape from wind and rain. Moreover, as I climbed the spiral staircase to the second floor where Julius lived, it deepened perceptibly—as though it emanated from his dwelling quarters, pervading the entire building. It brought back the atmosphere of what at school we called our "Temple Days."

I went on tiptoe, fearful of disturbing what seemed solemn even to the point

of being sacred, for the mood was so strong that I felt no desire to resist or criticise. Whatever its cause, this subjective state of mind was soothing to the point
of actual happiness. A hint of bliss was in it. And it did not lessen either, when
I discovered the landlady, Mrs. Garnier, white of face in the little hall-way,
showing signs of nervousness that she made no attempt whatever to conceal.

She was all eagerness to speak. Before I could ask if Julius was at home, she
relieved her burdened mind

"Oh, it'll be you, Mr. Mason! And I'm that glad ye've come!"

Her round, puffy visage plainly expressed relief, as she came towards me with
a shambling gait, looking over her shoulder across the dim-lit hall. "Mr. LeVallon," she whispered, "has been in there without a sound since mornin', and I'm
thinkin', maybe, something would ha' happened to him." And she stared into
my face as though I could instantly explain what troubled her. Where I felt spiritual peace, she felt, obviously, spiritual alarm.

"He is engaged?" I inquired. Then—though hardly aware why I put the question—I added: "There is someone with him?"

She peered about her.

"He'll be no engaged to you, sir," she replied. Plainly, it was not her lodger's
instructions that prompted the words: by the way she hung back I discerned that
she dreaded to announce me; she hoped I would go in and explore alone.

"I'll wait in the sitting-room till he comes out," I said, after a moment's hesitation. And I moved towards the door.

Mrs. Garnier, however, at once made an involuntary gesture to prevent me.
I can still hear her slippered tread shuffling across the oil-cloth. The gesture became a sort of leap when she saw that I persisted. It reminded me of a frightened
animal.

"There'll be twa gentlemen already waiting," she mumbled thickly, her face
turning a shade paler.

And, hearing this, I paused. The old woman, I saw, was trembling. I was annoyed at the interruption, for it destroyed the sense of delightful peace I had
enjoyed.

"Anyone I know?"

I was close to the door as I asked it, the terrified old woman close beside me.
She thrust her grey face up to mine; her eyes shone in the gleam of the low-
turned gas jet above our heads; and her excitement communicated itself suddenly
to my own blood. A distinct shiver ran down my back.

"I dinna ken them," she whispered behind a hand she held to her mouth, "for,
ye see, I dinna let them in." I stared at her, wondering what was coming next.

The slight trepidation I had felt for a moment vanished, but I kept my voice
at a whisper for fear of disturbing Julius in his inner chamber on the other side
of the wall. "What do you mean? Tell me plainly what's the matter." I said it
with some sharpness.

She replied at once, only too glad to share her anxiety with another.

"They came in by themselves," she whispered with a touch of superstitious
awe; "wonderfu' big men, the twa of them, and dark-skinned as the de'il," and

she drew back a pace to watch the effect of her words upon me.

"How long ago?" I asked impatiently. I remembered suddenly that Julius had friends among the Hindu students. It was more than possible that he had given them his key.

Mrs. Garnier shook her head suggestively. "I went in an hour ago," she told me in a low tone, "thinkin' maybe he would be eatin' something, and, O Lord mercy, I ran straight against the pair of them, settin' there in the darkness wi' oot a word."

"Well?" I said, seeing that she was likely to invent, "and what of it?"

"Neither of them moved a finger at me," she continued breathlessly, "but they looked all over me, and they had eyes like a flame o' fire, and I all but let the lamp fall and came out in a faintin' condeetion, and have been prayin' ever since that someone would come in."

She shuffled into the middle of the hall-way, drawing me after her by my sleeve. She pointed towards a corner of the ceiling. A small square window was let into the wall of the little interior room where Julius sought his solitude, and where at this moment he was busy with his mysterious occupations.

"And what'll be that awfu' licht, then?" she inquired, plucking me by the arm.

A gleam of bright white light, indeed, was visible through the small dusty pane above us, and again a curious memory ran like sheet-lightning across my mind that I had seen this kind of light before and that it was familiar to me. It vanished instantly before I could seize the fleeting picture. The light certainly was of peculiar brightness, coming from neither gas nor candle, nor from any ordinary light that I could have named off-hand.

"It'll be precisely that kind of licht that's in their eyes," I heard her whisper, as she jerked her whole body rather than her head alone towards the sitting-room I was about to enter. She wiped her clammy hands upon the striped apron that hung crooked from her angular hips.

"Mrs. Garnier," I said with authority, "there's nothing to be afraid of. Mr. LeVallon makes experiments sometimes, that's all. He wouldn't hurt a hair of your head—"

"Nae doot," she interrupted me, backing away from the door, "for his bonny face is a face to get well on, but the twa others in there, the darkies—aye, and that'll be another matter, and not one for me to be meddlin' with—"

I cut her short. "If you feel frightened," I said, smiling, "go to your room and pray. You needn't announce me. I'll go in and wait until he's ready to come out and see me."

Her face went white as linen, showing up an old scar on the cheek in an ugly reddish pattern, while I pushed past her and turned the handle of the door. I heard the breath catch in her throat. The next minute, lamp in hand, I was in the room, slamming the door literally in her face lest she might follow and do some foolish thing. I set the lamp down upon the table in the centre. I looked quickly about me. No living person but myself was there—certainly no Hindu gentlemen with eyes of flame. Mrs. Garnier's Celtic imagination had run away with her altogether. I sat down and waited. A line of that same bright, silvery light shone also beneath the crack of the door from the inner chamber. The wind and rain trumpeted angrily at the windows. But the room was undeniably empty.

Yet it is utterly beyond me to describe the sense of exaltation that at once rose over me like some influence of perfect music; "exaltation" is the right word, I think, and "music" conveys best the uplifting and soothing effect that was produced. For here, at closer quarters, the sensation of exquisite peace was doubly renewed. The nervous alarm inspired by the woman fled. This peace flooded me; it stirred the bliss of some happy spiritual life long since enjoyed and long since forgotten. I passed instantly, as it were, under the sway of some august authority that banished the fret and restlessness of the extraneous world; and compared to which the strife and ambition of my modern life seemed, indeed, well lost.

Behind it, however, and behind the solemnity that awed, was at the same time the faint presage of something vaguely disquieting. The memory of some afflicting incompleteness gripped me; the anguish of ideals too lofty for attainment; the sweet pain and passion of some exquisite long suffering; the secret yearning of a soul that had dared sublime accomplishment, then plunged itself and others in the despair of failure—all this lay in the apprehension that stood close behind the bliss.

But, above all else, was the certainty that I remembered definite details of those Temple Days, and that I was upon the verge of still further and more detailed recollection.... That faintness stealing over me was the faintness of immeasurable distance, the ache of dizzy time, the weariness that has no end and no beginning. I felt what Julius LeVallon felt—the deep sickness of eternity that knows no final rest, either of blessed annihilation or of non-existence, until the journey of the soul comes to its climax in the Deity. And, feeling this—realising it—for the first time, I understood, also for the first time, LeVallon's words at Motfield Close two years ago—"If the soul remembered all, it would lose the courage to attempt. Only the vital things are worth recalling, because they guide."

This flashed across me now, as I sat in that Edinburgh lodging-house, waiting for him to come. I knew myself, beyond all doubt or question, caught away in that web of wonderful, far-off things; there revived in me the yearnings of memories exceedingly remote; poignant still with life, because they were unexhausted still, and terrible with that incompleteness which sooner or later *must* find satisfaction. And it was this sense of things left undone that brought the feeling of presentiment. Julius, in that inner chamber, was communing as of old. But also—he was searching. He was hard upon the trail of ancient clues. He was seeking *her*. I knew it in my bones.

For I felt some subtle communication with that other mind beyond the obstructing door—not, however, as it was to-day, but as it was in the recoverable centuries when the three of us had committed the audacious act which still awaited its final readjustment at our hands. Julius, searching by some method of his own among the layers of our ancient lives, reconstructed the particular scenes he needed. Involuntarily, unwittingly, I shared them too. I had stepped into his ancient mood....

My mind grew crowded. The pictures rose and passed, and rose again. ... .

But it was always one in particular that returned, staying longer than the others. He concentrated upon one, then. In his efforts to find *her* soul in its body of to-day, he went back to the source of our original relationship, the immensely remote experience when he and I and she had sown the harvest we had now come back to reap together. Thence, holding the clue, he could trace the thread of her existences down to this very moment. He could find her where she stood upon the earth—to-day.

This seemed very clear to me, though how I realised it is dificult to say. I remember a curious thought—which proves how real the conviction was in me. I asked myself: "Does *she* feel anything now, as she goes about her business on this earth, perhaps in England, perhaps not far removed from us, as distance goes? And is she, too, wherever she stands and waits, aware perhaps of some queer presentiment that haunts her waking or her sleeping mind—the presentiment of something coming, something about to happen—that someone waits for her?"

The one persistent picture rose and captured me again....

In blazing sunlight stood the building of whitened stone against the turquoise sky; and, a little to the left, the yellow cliffs, precipitous and crumbling. At their base were mounds of sand the wind and sun had chiselled and piled up against their feet. The soft air trembled with the heat; fierce light bathed everything—from the small white figures moving up and down the rock-hewn steps, to the Temple hollowed out between the stone paws of an immense outline half animal, half human. To the right, and towards the east, stretched the abundant desert, shimmering grey and blue and green beneath the torrid sun. I smelt the empty leagues of sand, the delicate perfume that gathers among the smooth, baked hollows of a million dunes; I felt the breeze, sharp and exhilarating, that knew no interruption of broken surfaces to break its journey of days and nights; and behind me I heard the faint, sharp rustle of trees whose shadows flickered on the burning ground. This heat and air grew stealthily upon me; fire and wind were here the dominating influences, the natural methods which furnished vehicles for the manifestation of particular Powers. Here was the home of our early worship of the Sun and space, of Fire and Wind. Yet, somehow, it seemed not of this present planet we call Earth, but of some point nearer to the centre.

Beside those enormous paws, where the air danced and shimmered in the brilliant glare, I saw the narrow flight of steps leading to the crypts below—the retreats for solitude. And then, suddenly, with a shock of poignant recognition, I saw a figure that I knew instantly to be myself, the Sower of my harvest of To-day. It slowly moved down the steps behind another figure that I recognised with equal conviction—some inner flash of lightning certainty—as Julius LeVallon, the soul I knew to-day in Edinburgh, the soul that, in another body, now stood near me in a nineteenth century lodging-house. The bodies, too, were lighter, less dense and material than those we used to-day, the spirit occupier less hampered and restricted. That too was clear to me.

I was aware of both times, both places simultaneously. That is, I was not dreaming. The peace, moreover, that stole round me in this modern building was but a faint reflection of the peace once familiar to me in those far-off Temple Days. And somehow it was the older memory that dominated consciousness.

About me the room held still as death, the battle of that earthly storm against the walls and windows half unreal, or so remote as to be not realised. Time paused a moment. I looked back. I lived as I had been then—in another type of consciousness, it seemed. It was marvellous, yet natural as in a dream. Only, as in a dream, subsequent language fails to retain the searching, vivid reality. The living *fact* is not recaptured. I felt. I understood. Certain tendencies and characteristics that were "me" to-day I saw explained—those that derived from this particular period. What must be conquered, and why, flashed sharply; also individuals whom to avoid would be vain shirking, since having sown together we must reap together—or miss the object of our being.

I heard strange names—Concerighé, Silvatela, Ziaz... and a surge of passionate memories caught at my heart. Yet it was not Egypt, it was not India or the East, it was not Assyria or old Chaldea even; this belonged to a civilisation older than them all, some dim ancient kingdom that antedated all records open to possible research to-day....

I was in contact with the searching mind within that inner chamber. His effort included me, making the deeps in me give up their dead. I saw. He sought through many "sections."... I followed.... There was confusion—the pictures of recent days breaking in upon others infinitely remote. I could not disentangle....

Very sharply, then, and with a sensation of uneasiness that was almost pain, another figure rose. I saw a woman. With the same clear certainty of recognition the face presented itself. Hair, lips, and eyes I saw distinctly, yet somehow through a haze that veiled the expression. About the graceful neck hung a soft cloth of gold; dark lashes screened a gaze still starry and undimmed; there was a smile of shining teeth... the eyes met mine....

With a diving rush the entire picture shifted, passing on to another scene, and I saw two figures, her own and his, bending down over something that lay stretched and motionless upon an altar of raised stones. We were in shadow now; the air was cool; the perfume of the open desert had altered to the fragrance that was incense.... The picture faded, flashed quickly back, faded again, and once again was there. I could not hold it for long. Larger, darker figures swam between to confuse and blur its detail, figures of some swarthier race, as though layers of other memories, perhaps more recent, mingled bewilderingly with it. The two passed in and out of one another, sometimes interpenetrating, as when two slides appear upon the magic-lantern sheet together; yet, peering at me through the phantasmal kaleidoscope, shone ever this woman-face, seductively lovely, haunting as a vision of stars, mask of a soul even then already "old," although the picture was of ages before the wisdom of Buddha or the love of Christ had stolen on the world....

Then came a moment of clearer sight suddenly, and I saw that the objects lying stretched and motionless in the obscurity, and over one of which they bent in concentrated effort, were the bodies of men not dead, but temporarily vacated. And I knew that we stood in the Hall of the Vacated Bodies, an atmosphere of awe and solemnity about us. For these were the advanced disciples who in the final initiation lay three days and nights entranced, while their souls acquired "elsewhere and otherwise" the knowledge no brain could attain to in the flesh. During the interval there were those who watched the empty tenements—Guardians of the Vacated Bodies—and two of these I now saw bending low—the woman and a man. The body itself I saw but dimly, but an overmastering curiosity woke in me to see it clearly—to recognise

The intensity of my effort caused a blur, it seemed. Across my inner sight the haze thickened for a moment, and I lost the scene. But this time I understood. The dread of something they were about to consummate blackened the memory with the pain of treachery. Guardians of the Vacated Bodies, they had been faithless to their trust: they had used their position for some personal end. Awe and terror clutched my soul. Who was the leader, who the led, I failed utterly to recover, nor what the motive of the broken trust had been. A sublime audacity lay in it, that I knew. There was the desire for knowledge not yet properly within their reach; there was the ambition to evoke the elemental powers; and there was an "experiment," using the instrument at hand as the channel for an achievement that might have made them—one of them, at any rate—as the gods. But there was about it all an entanglement of personalities and motives I was helpless to unravel. The whole deep significance I could not recover. My own part, the part he played, and the part the woman played, seemed woven in an involved and inextricable knot. It belonged, I felt, to an order of consciousness which is not the order of to-day. I, therefore, failed to understand completely. Only that we three were together, closely linked, emerged absolutely clear.

For one moment the scene returned again. I remember that something drove forcibly against me in that ancient place, that it flung itself roaring like a tempest in my face, that a great burning sensation passed through me, while sheets of what I can only describe as black fire tore through the air about us. There was fire and there was wind... that much I realised.

I rocked—that is my present body rocked. I reeled upon my chair. The entire memory plunged down into darkness with a speed of lightning. I seemed to rise—to emerge from the depths of some sea within me where I had lain sunk for ages. In one sense—I awoke. But, before the glamour passed entirely, and while the reality of the scene hung about me still, I remember that a cry for help escaped my lips, and that it was the name of our leader that I called upon:

"Concerighé...!"

With that cry still sounding in the air, I turned, and saw him whom I had called upon beside me. With a kind of splendid, dazzling light he came. He rested one hand upon my shoulder; he gazed down into my eyes; and I looked into a face that was magnificent with power, radiant, glorious. The atmosphere momentarily seemed turned to flame. I felt a wind of strength strike through me. The

old temptation and the sin—the failure—all were clear at last.
I remembered....

CHAPTER XIII

T he brilliance of the figure dimmed and melted, as though the shadows
ate it from the edges inwards; there came a rattling at the handle of that
inner chamber door; it opened suddenly; and Julius LeVallon, this time
in his body of To-day, stood framed against the square of light that swirled behind him like clouds of dazzlingly white steam. The door swung to and closed.
He moved forward quickly into the room.

By this time I was more in possession of my normal senses again. Here was no
question of memory, vision, or imagination's glamour. Beyond any doubt or am-
biguity, there stood beside me in this sitting-room of the Edinburgh lodging-
house two figures of Julius LeVallon. I saw them simultaneously. There was the
normal Julius walking across the carpet towards me, and there was his double
that stood near me in a body of light—now fading, yet unquestionably wearing the likeness of that Concerighé whom I had seen bending with the woman
above the vacated body.

They moved together swiftly. Almost the same moment they met; they intermingled, much as two outlines of an object slip one into the other when the
finger's pressure on the eyeball is removed. They became one person. Julius was
there before me in the lamp-lit room, just come from his inner chamber that
blazed with brilliance. This light now disappeared. No line showed beneath the
crack of the door. I heard the wild and rain shout drearily past the windows with
the dying storm.

I caught my breath. I stood up to face him, taking a quick step backwards. And
I heard Julius laugh a little. He told me afterwards I had assumed an attitude
of defence.

He was speaking—in his ordinary voice, no sign of excitement in him, nor
about his presence anything unusual.

"You called me," he said quietly; "you called for help. But I could not come
at once; I could not get back; it was such a long way off." He looked at me and
smiled. "I was searching," he added, as though he had been merely turning the
pages of a book.

"Our old Memory Game. I know. I felt it—even out here."

He nodded gravely.

"You could hardly help it," he replied, "being so close," and indicated that inner room with a gesture of his head. "Besides, you were in it all the time. And
she was in it too. Oh," he said with a touch of swift enthusiasm, "I have recovered nearly all. I know exactly now what happened. I was the leader, I the
instigator; you both merely helped me; you with your faithful friendship, even
while you warned; she with her passionate love that asked no questions, but

obeyed."

"She loved you so?" I asked faintly, but with an uncontrollable trembling of the voice. An amazing prescience seized me.

"You," he said calmly. "It was you she loved."

What thrill of romance, deathless and enthralling, stirred in me as I heard these words! What starry glory stepped down upon the world! A memory of bliss poured into me; the knowledge of an undying love constant as the sun itself. Then, hard upon its heels, flashed back the Present with a small and insignificant picture—of my approaching union—with another. An extraordinary revulsion caught me. I remember steadying myself against the chair in front of me.

"For it was your love," Julius went on quietly, "that made you so necessary. You two were a single force together. I had the knowledge, but you together had the greatest power in the world. We were three—a trinity—the strongest union possible. And the temptation was too much for me—"

He turned away a moment so that I could not see his face. He broke off suddenly. There was a new and curious quality in his voice, as though it dwindled in volume and grew smaller, yet was not audibly lowered.

What caused the old sense of dread to quicken in me? What brought this sudden sinking of the heart as he turned again from the cabinet where he stood, and our eyes met steadily through the lamp-lit room?

"I borrowed love, but knew not how to use it," he went on slowly, solemnly. "I had evoked the Powers successfully; through the channel of that vacated body I had drawn them into my own being. Then came the failure—"

"I—we failed you!" I faltered.

"The failure," he replied, still fixing me with his glowing eyes, "was mine, and mine alone. The power lent me I did not understand. It was not my own, and without great love these things cannot be accomplished. I must first know love. What I had summoned I was too weak to banish. The owner of the vacated body returned." Then, after a pause, he added half below his breath: "The Powers, exiled from their appointed place, are about me to this very day. But it is the owner of that body whose forgiveness I need most. And only with your help—with the presence, the sympathetic presence of yourself and her—can this be effected."

Past, present, and future seemed strangely intermingled as I heard, for my thoughts went groping forward, and at the same time diving backwards among desert sands and temples. The passion of an immense love-story caught me; I was aware of intense yearning to resume my place in it all with him, with her, with all the reconstructed conditions of relationships so ancient and so true. It swept over me like a storm unchained. That scene in the cool and sunless crypt flamed forth again, reality in each smallest detail. The meaning of his words I did not wholly grasp, however; there was something lacking in my mind of To-day that withheld the final clue. My present consciousness was not as then. From brain and reason all this seemed so utterly divorced, and I had forgotten how to understand by *feeling* in the way that Julius did. Those last words, however, brought a sudden question to my lips. Almost unconsciously I gave it utterance:

"Through the channel of a body?" I asked, and my voice was lower than his own.

"Through the channel of a human system," was his answer, "an organism that uses consciously both heat and air, and that, therefore, knows the nature of them both. For the Powers can he summoned only by those who understand them; and understanding, being worship, depends ultimately upon *sharing* their natures, though it be in little."

There came a welcome break, then, in the strain of this extraordinary conversation, as Julius, using no bridge to transpose our emotions from one key to the other, walked quietly over to the cupboard. It was characteristically significant of his attitude to life in general, that the solemn things we had been speaking of were yet no more sacred than the prosaic detail of to-day that now concerned him—a student's supper. All was "one" to him in this rare but absolutely genuine way. He was unconscious of any break in the emotional level of what had been—for him there was, indeed, no break—and, watching him, it almost seemed that I still saw that other figure of long ago striding across the granite, sun-drenched slabs.

The voice rose unbidden within me, choked by the stress of some inexplicable emotion:

"Concerighé...!" I cried aloud involuntarily: "Concerighé... Ziaz.... We are all together still... my help is yours... my unfailing help...."

Julius, loaf and marmalade jar in hand, turned from the cupboard as though he had been struck. For a moment he stood and stared. The customary expression melted from his face, and in its place a look of tenderest compassion shone through the strength.

"You do remember, then!" he said very softly; "even the names!"

"And Silvatela," I murmured, moisture rising unaccountably to my eyes. I saw the room in mist.

Julius stood before me like a figure carved in stone. For a long time he spoke no word. Gradually the curious disturbance in my own breast sank and passed. The mist lifted and disappeared. I felt myself slipping back into To-day on the ebb of some shattering experience, already half forgotten.

"You remember," he repeated presently, his voice impassioned but firmly quiet, "the temptation—and—the failure...?"

I nodded, almost involuntarily again.

"And still hold to you—both," I murmured.

He held me with his eyes for quite a minute. Though he used no word or gesture, I felt his deep delight.

"Because we must," he answered presently; "because we must."

He had moved so close to me that I felt his breath upon my face. I could have sworn for a second that I gazed into the shining eyes of that other and audacious figure, for it was the voice of Concerighé, yet the face of Julius. Past and present seemed to join hands, mingling confusedly in my mind. Cause and effect whispered across the centuries, linking us together. And the voice continued deeply, as if echoing down hollow aisles of stone.

I heard the words in the shadowy spaces of that old-world crypt, rather than among the plush furniture of these Edinburgh lodgings.

"We three are at last together again, and must bring the Balance to a final close. As the stars are but dust upon the pathway of the gods, so our mistakes are but dust upon the pathway of our lives. What we let fall together, we must together remove."

Then, with an abruptness that pertained sometimes to these curious irruptions from the past, the values shifted. He became more and more the Julius LeVallon whom I knew to-day. Speech changed to a modern and more usual key. And the effect upon myself was of vague relief, for while the impression of great drama did not wholly pass, the uneasiness lightened in me, and I found my tongue again. I told my own experience—all that I had seen and felt and thought. Brewing the cocoa, and setting out the bread and marmalade upon the table, Julius listened to every word without interruption. Our intimacy was complete again as though no separation, either of lives or days, had been between us.

"Inside me, of course," I concluded the recital; "in some kind of interior sight I saw it all—"

"The only true sight," he declared, "though what you saw was but the reflection at second-hand of memories I evoked in there." He pointed to the inner room. "In there," he went on significantly, "where nothing connected with the Present enters, no thought, no presence, nothing that can disturb or interrupt,— in there you would see and remember as vividly as I myself. The room is prepared.... The channels all are open. As it was, my pictures flashed into you and set the great chain moving. For no life is isolated; all is shared; and every detail, animate or so-called inanimate, belongs inevitably to every other."

"Yet what I saw was so much clearer than our school-day memories," I said. "Those pictures, for instance, of the pastoral people where we came together first."

An expression of yearning passed into his eyes as he answered.

"Because in our Temple Days you led the life of the soul instead of the body merely. The soul alone remembers. There lies the permanent record. Only what has touched the soul, therefore, is recoverable—the great joys, great sorrows, great adventures that have reached it. You *feel* them. The rest are but fugitive pictures of scenery that accompanied the spiritual disturbances. Each body you occupy has a different brain that stores its own particular series. But true memory is in, and of, the Soul. Few have any true soul-life at all; few, therefore, have anything to remember!"

His low voice ran on and on, charged with deep earnestness; his very atmosphere seemed to vibrate with the conviction of his words; about his face occasionally were flashes of that radiance in which his body of light—his inmost being—dwelt for ever. I remember moving the marmalade pot from its precarious position on the table edge, lest his gestures should send it flying! But I remember also that the haunting reality of "other days and other places" lay about us while we talked, so that the howling of the storm outside seemed far away and quite unable to affect us. We knew perfect communion in that dingy room. We *felt* together.

"But it is difficult, often painful, to draw the memories up again," he went on, still speaking of recovery, "for they lie so deeply coiled about the very roots of joy and grief. Things of the moment smother the older pictures. The way of recovery is arduous, and not many would deem the sacrifice involved worth while. It means plunging into yourself as you must plunge below the earth if you would see the starlight while the sun is in the sky. To-day's sunlight hides the stars of yesterday. Yet all is accessible—the entire series of the soul's experiences, and real forgetting is not possible."

A movement as of wind seemed to pass between us over the faded carpet, bearing me upwards while he spoke, sweeping me with his own conviction of our eternal ancestry and of our unending future.

"We have made ourselves exactly what we are. We are making our future at this very minute—now!" I exclaimed. The justice of the dream inspired me. Great courage, a greater hope awoke.

He smiled, opening his arms with a gesture that took in the world.

"Your aspirations, hopes and fears, all that has ever burned vitally at your centre, every spiritual passion that uplifted or enticed, each deep endeavour that seeded your present tendencies and talents—everything, in fact, strong enough to have touched your Soul—sends up its whirling picture of beauty or dismay at the appointed time. The disentangling may be difficult, but all are there, for you yourself are their actual, living Record. Feeling, not thinking, best unravels them—the primitive vision as of children—the awareness of kinship with everything about you. The sense of separateness and isolation vanishes, and the soul recovers the consciousness of sharing all the universe. There is no loneliness; there is no more fear."

Ah, how we talked that night of tempest through! What thoughts and dreams and possibilities Julius sent thundering against my mind as with the power of the loosed wind and rain outside. The scale of life became immense, each tiniest detail of act and thought important with the sacredness of some cosmic ceremonial that it symbolised. Yet to his words alone this power was not due, but rather to some force of driving certitude in himself that brought into me too a similar conviction. The memory of it hardened in the sands of my imagination, as it were, so that the result has remained, although the language by which he made it seem so reasonable has gone.

I smoked my pipe; and, as the smoke curled upwards, I watched his face of pallid marble and the mop of ebony hair that set off so well the brilliance of the eyes. He looked, I thought to myself, like no human being I had ever seen before.

"And sometimes," I remember hearing, "the memories from a later section may suddenly swarm across an earlier one—confusing the sight, perhaps, just when it is getting clear. A few hours ago, for instance, any search was interrupted by an inrush of two more recent layers—Eastern ones—which came to obliterate with their vividness the older, dimmer ones I sought."

I mentioned what the frightened woman imagined she had seen.

"She caught a reflected fragment too," he said. "So strong a picture was bound to spread."

"Then was Mrs. Garnier with us too before?" I asked, as we burst out laughing.

"Not in that sense, no. It was the glamour that touched her only—second-sight, as she might call it. She is sensitive to impressions, nothing more."

He came over and sat closer to me. The web of his language folded closer too. The momentum of his sincerity threw itself against all my prejudices, so that I, too, saw the serpentine vista of these previous lives stretching like a river across the ages. To this day I see his tall, slim figure, his face with the clear pale skin, the burning eyes; now he leaned across the table, now stood up to emphasise some phrase, now paced the floor of that lamp-lit students' lodging-house, while he spoke of the long battling of our souls together, sowing thoughts and actions whose consequences must one day be reaped without evasion. The scale of his Dream was vast indeed, its prospect austere and merciless, yet the fundamental idea of justice made it beautiful, as its inclusion of all Nature made it grand.

To Julius LeVallon the soul was indeed unconquerable, and man master of his fate. Death lost its ugliness and terror; the sense of broken, separated life was replaced by the security of a continuous existence, whole, unhurried, eternal, affording ample time for all development, accepting joy and suffering as the justice of results, but never as of reward or punishment. There was no caprice; there was no such thing as chance.

Then, as the night wore slowly on, and the wind died down, and the wonderful old town lay sleeping peacefully, we talked at last of that one thing towards which all our conversation tended subconsciously: our future together and the experiment that it held in store for us—with her.

I cannot hope to set down here the words by which this singular being led me, half accepting, to the edge of understanding that his conception might be right. To that edge, however, I somehow felt my mind was coaxed. I looked over that edge. I saw for a moment something of his magnificent panorama. I realised a hint of possibility in his shining scheme. But it is beyond me to report the persuasive reasonableness of all I heard, for the truth is that Julius spoke another language—a language incomprehensible to my mind to-day. His words, indeed, were those of modern schools and books, but the spirit that ensouled them belong to a forgotten time. Only by means of some strange inner sympathy did I comprehend him. Another, an older type of consciousness, perhaps, woke in me. As with the pictures, this also seemed curiously familiar as I listened. Something in me old as the stars and wiser than the brain both heard and understood.

For the elemental forces he held to be Intelligences that share the life of the cosmos in a degree enormously more significant than anything human life can claim. Mother Earth, for him, was no mere poetic phrase. There was spiritual life in Nature as there was spiritual life in men and women. The insignificance of the latter was due to their being cut off from the great sources of supply—to their separation from Nature. Under certain conditions, and with certain consequences, it was possible to obtain these powers which, properly directed, might help the entire world. This experiment we had once made—and failed.

The method I already understood in a certain measure; but the rest escaped my comprehension. Memory failed to reconstruct it for me; vision darkened; his words conveyed no meaning. It was beyond me. Somewhere, somehow, personal love had entered to destroy the effective balance that ensured complete success. Yet, equally, the power of love which is quintessential sympathy, was necessary.

What, however, I did easily understand was that the object of that adventure was noble, nothing meanly personal in it anywhere; and, further, that to restore the damaged equilibrium by returning these particular powers to their rightful places, there must be an exact reproduction of the conditions of evocation—that is, the three original participants must be together again—a human system must serve again as channel.

And the essential fact of all that passed between us on this occasion was that I gave again my promise. When the necessary conditions were present—I would not fail him. This is the memory I have carried with me through the twenty years of our subsequent separation. I gave my pledge.

The storm blew itself to rest behind the hills; the rain no longer set the windows rattling; the hush of early morning stole down upon the sleeping city. We had talked the night away. He seemed aware—I know not how—that we stood upon the brink of going apart for years. There was great tenderness in his manner, his voice, his gestures. Turning to me a moment as the grey light crept past the curtains, he peered into my face as though he would revive lost centuries with the passion of his eyes. He took my hand and held it, while a look of peace and trust passed over his features as though the matter of the future were already then accomplished.

He led me silently across the room towards the door. I turned instinctively; words rose up in me, but words that found no utterance. A deep emotion held me dumb. Then as I opened the door, I found the old, familiar name again: "Concerighé... Friend of a million years...!"

But no sentence followed it. He touched my arm. A cold wind seemed to pass between us. I firmly believe that somehow he foresaw the long interval of separation that was coming. Something about him seemed to fade; I saw him less distinctly; my sight, perhaps, was blurred with the strain of these long hours— hours the like of which I was not to know again for many years. That magical name has many a time echoed since in my heart away from him, as it echoed then across the darkened little hall-way of those Edinburgh lodgings: "Concerighé! Friend of a million years!"

Side by side we went down the granite steps of the spiral staircase to the street. Julius opened the big front door. I heard the rattling of the iron chain. A breeze from the sea blew salt against our faces, then ran gustily along the streets. Behind the Calton Hill showed a crimson streak of dawn. A line of clouds, half rosy and half gold, ran down the sky. No living being was astir. I heard only the noisy whirling of the iron chimney-pots against the morning wind.

And then his voice:

"Good-bye— Until we meet again...."

He pressed my hands. I looked into his eyes. He stepped back into the shadow of the porch. The door closed softly.

CHAPTER XIV

> "*Forgive! O yes! How lightly, lightly said!*
> *Forget? No, never, while the ages roll,*
> *Till God slay o`er again the undying dead,*
> *And quite unmake my soul!*"—Mary Coleridge.

I stepped down, it seemed, into a lilliputian world where the grander issues no longer drew the souls of men. The deep and simple things were fled, the old Nature gods withdrawn. The scale of life had oddly shrunk.

I saw the names above the shuttered shops with artificial articles for sale— "11 3/4d. a yard"—on printed paper labels. The cheapness of a lesser day flashed everywhere.

I passed the closed doors of a building where people flocked to mumble that no good was in them, while a man proclaimed in a loud voice things he hardly could believe. A few streets behind me Julius LeVallon stood in the shadows of another porch, solitary and apart, yet communing with stars and hills and seas, survival from a vital, vanished age when life was realised everywhere and the elemental Nature Powers walked hand in hand with men.

Through the deserted streets I made my way across the town to my own little student's flat on the Morningside where I then lived. Gradually the crimson dawn slipped into a stormy sunrise. I watched the Pentlands take the gold, and the Castle rock turn ruddy; a gentle mist lay over Leith below; a pool of deep blue shadow marked the slumbering Old Town.

But about my heart at this magic hour stirred the dawn-winds of a thousand ancient sunrises, and I felt the haunting atmosphere of other days and other places steal up through the mists of immemorial existences. I thought of the whole great series, each life rising and setting like a little day, each with its dawn and noon and sunset, each with its harvest of failure and success, of joy and sorrow, of friendships formed and enemies forgiven, of ideals realised or abandoned—pouring out of the womb of time and slowly bringing the soul through the discipline of all possible experience towards that perfection which proclaims it one with the entire universe—the Deity.

And a profound weariness fell about my spirit as I went. I became aware of my own meagre enthusiasm. I welcomed the conception of some saviour who should do it all for me. I knew myself unequal to the gigantic task. In that moment the heroic figure of Julius seemed remote from reality, a towering outline in the sky, an austere embodiment of legendary myth. The former passionate cer-tainty that he was right dwindled amid wavering doubts. The perplexities of life came back upon me with tormenting power. I lost the coherent vision of con-sistent and logical beauty that he inspired. It was all too vast for me.

This reaction was natural enough, though for a long time mood chased mood across my troubled mind, each battling for supremacy. The materialism of the day, proudly strutting with its boundless assurance and its cock-sure knowledge, regained possession of my thoughts. The emptiness of scholastic theology no longer seemed so hideously apparent. It was pain to let the other go, but go it did—though never, perhaps, so completely as I then believed.

By insignificant details the change revealed itself. I recalled that I was due that very afternoon at a luncheon where "intellectual" folk would explain away the soul with a single scientific formula, and where learned heads would wag con-descendingly as they murmured "But there's no evidence to prove *that*, you know..."... and Julius rose before me in another light at once—Pagan, dreamer, monster of exploded superstitions, those very hills where he evoked the sylvan deities, a momentary hallucination....

Then again, quite suddenly, it was the chatterers at the luncheon party who seemed unreal, and all their clever patter about the "movements" of the day mere shallow verbiage. The hoardings of the town were blue and yellow with gaudy election posters, but the sky was aflame with the grand old message of the Sun God, written in eternal hieroglyphs of gold and red upon the clouds that brushed the hills. The elemental deities stormed thundering by. And, instead of scholars laying down the letter of their little law, I heard the tones of Con-cerighé calling across the centuries the names of great belief, of greater beauty.

And the older pageantry stole back across the world.

Almost it was in me to turn and seek... with him... that soul-knowledge which ran through all the "sections."... Yet the younger fear oppressed me. The endless journey, the renunciation and suffering involved, the incessant, tireless striving, with none to help but one's own unconquerable will—this, and a host of other feelings that lay beyond expression, bore down upon me with their cold, glacier power. I thought of Julius with something of reverence akin to terror.... I despised myself. I also understood why the majority need priests and creeds and formulae to help them.... The will, divorced from Nature, was so small a thing!

When I entered my rooms the sunlight lay upon the carpet, and never before had it seemed so welcome or so comforting. I could then and there have wor-shipped the great body that sent it forth. But, instead, in a state of exhaustion and weariness, I flung myself upon the bed. Yet, while I slept, it seemed I left that little modern room and entered the region of great, golden days "when the sun was younger." In very different attire, I took my place in the blue-robed cir-cle, a portion of some ancient, gorgeous ceremonial that was nearer to the prim-itive beauty, when the "circles swallowed the sun," and the elemental Powers were accessible to every heart.

It was not surprising that I slept till dusk, missing my lectures and the luncheon party as well; but it was distinctly surprising to find myself wakened by a knocking at the door for a telegram that summoned me south forthwith. And only in the train, anxiously counting the minutes in the hope that I might find my father still alive, did the possible significance of LeVallon's final words come back upon my troubled mind: "Until we meet again."

For little did I guess that my father's death was to prevent my returning to the University, that my career would be changed and hastened owing to an unexpected lack of means, that my occasional letters to Julius were to be returned "unknown," or that my next word of him would be received twenty years later in a room overlooking the Rhine at Bâle, where I have attempted to set down these difficult notes of reminiscence....

BOOK III

THE CHÂLET IN THE JURA MOUNTAINS

"He (man) first clothes the gods in the image of his own innermost nature; he per-
sonifies them as modes of his own greater consciousness. All this was native to him
when he still felt himself kin with Nature; when he felt rather than thought, when
he followed instinct rather than ratiocination. But for long centuries this feeling
of kinship with Nature has been gradually weakened by the powerful play of that
form of mind peculiar to man; until he has at last reached a stage when he finds
himself largely divorced from Nature, to such an extent indeed that he treats her
as something foreign and apart from himself....

"He seems at present, at any rate in the persons of most of the accredited thinkers
of the West, to be absolutely convinced that no other mode of mind can exist except his own mode.... To say that Nature thinks, he regards as an entire misuse of
language.... That Nature has feelings even, he will not allow; to speak of love and
hate among the elements is for him a puerile fancy the cultured mind has long out-
grown.

"The sole joy of such a mind would almost seem to be the delight of expelling the
life from all forms and dissecting their dead bodies."—" Some Mystical Adventures" (G. R. S. Mead).

CHAPTER XV

For, a long time that letter lay on my table like a challenge—neither accepted nor refused. Something that had slumbered in me for twenty years
awoke. The enchantment of my youthful days, long since evaporated as
I believed, rose stealthily upon me at the sight of this once familiar handwriting. LeVallon, of course, had found the woman. And my word was pledged.

To say that I hesitated, however, would be no more true than to say that I de-
bated or considered. The first effect upon me was a full-blown amazement that
I could ever have come under the spell of so singular a kind or have promised
co-operation in anything so wildly preposterous as Julius had proposed. The second effect, however—and, as it turned out, the deeper one—was different. I
experienced a longing, a thrill of anticipation. a sense even of joy—I know not
what to call it; while in its train came a hint, though the merest hint, of that
vague uneasiness I had known in my school and university days.

Yet by some obscure mental process difficult to explain, I found myself half
caught already in consent. I answered the letter, asking instructions how to reach
him in his distant valley of the Jura Mountains. Some love of adventure—so I

flattered myself—long denied by my circumscribed conditions of life, prompted the decision in part. For in the heart of me I obviously wished to go; and, briefly, it was the heart of me that finally went.

I passed some days waiting for a reply, LeVallon's abode being apparently inaccessible to the ordinary service of the post—"poste restante" in a village marked only upon the larger maps where, I judged, he had to fetch his letters. And those days worked their due effect upon me; they were filled with questions to which imagination sought the answers. How would the intervening years have dealt with him? What changes would have come upon him with maturity? And this woman—what melancholy splendours brought from "old, forgotten, far-off things" would she bring with her down into the prosaic conditions of this materialistic century? What signs and evidences would there be that she, like himself, was an adept at life, seeking eternal things, discerning what was important, an "old soul" taught of the gods and charged with the ideals of another day? I saw her already in imagination—a woman of striking appearance and unusual qualities. And, how had he found her? A hundred similar questions asked themselves, but, chief among them, two: Would she—should I, *remember*?

The time passed slowly; my excitement grew; sometimes I hesitated, half repented, almost laughed, but never once was tempted really to change my mind. For in the deeper part of me, now so long ignored, something of these ancient passions blew to flame again; symptoms of that original dread increased; there rose once more the whisper "we are eternally together; the thing is true!" And on the seventh day, when the porter handed me the letter, it almost seemed that Julius stood beside me, beckoning. I felt his presence; the old magic of his personality tightened up a thousand loosened threads; belief was unwillingly renewed.

The instructions were very brief, no expression of personal feeling accompanying them. Julius counted on my fidelity. It had never occurred to him that I could fail. I left my heavy luggage in the care of the hotel and packed the few things necessary for the journey. The notes of our school and university days I have just jotted down I sent by post to my London chambers. A spirit of recklessness seemed in me. I was off into fairyland, mystery and wonder about me, possibly romance. Nothing mattered; work could wait; I possessed a small competency of my own; the routine of my life was dull and uninspiring. Also I was alone in the world, for my early attachment had not resulted in marriage, and I knew no other home than that of chambers, restaurants, and the mountain inns where my holidays were usually spent. I welcomed the change with it's promise of adventure—and I went. This feeling of welcome owned perhaps a deeper origin than I realised.

Travelling via Bienne and Neuchâtel to a point beyond the latter town I took thence, according to instructions, a little mountain railway that left the lake behind and plunged straight into the purple valleys of the Jura range. Deep pine woods spread away on all sides as we climbed a winding ravine among the folds of these soft blue mountains that are far older than the Alps. Scarred cliffs and

ridges of limestone gleamed white against the velvet forests, now turning red
and yellow in the sunset, but no peaks were visible and no bare summits
pricked the sky. Thick and soft, the trees clothed all. Their feathery presence
filled the air. The clatter of the train seemed muffled, and the gathering shadows below the eastern escarpments took on that rich black hue that ancient
forests lend to the very atmosphere above them. We passed into a world where
branches, moss and flowers muted every sound with a sense of undisturbable
peace. The softness of great age reigned with delicious silence. The very engine
puffed uphill on wheels of plush.

Occasional hamlets contributed a few wood-cutters by Way of passengers;
strips of half-cleared valley revealed here and there a farm-house with dark
brown walls and spreading roof; little *sentiers* slipped through the pine trees to
yet further recesses of unfrequented woods; but nowhere did I see a modern
building, a country house, nor any dwelling that might be occupied by other
than simple peasant folk. Suggestion of tourists there was absolutely none; no
trees striped blue and yellow by Improvement Committees; no inns with cen-
tral-heating and tin banners stating that touring clubs endorsed them; no ad-
vertisements at all; only this air of remote and kindly peace, the smoke of peat
fires, and the odour of living woods stealing upon the dusk.

The feeling grew that I crossed a threshold into a region that lay outside the
common happenings of the world; life here must be very gentle, wonderful, distinguished, and things might come to pass that would be true yet hard to explain by the standards of the busy cities. Those cities, indeed, seemed very far
away, unreal, and certainly unimportant. For the leisurely train itself was almost
make-believe, and the station officials mere uniformed automata. The normal
world, in a word, began to fade a little. I was aware once more of that bigger
region in which Julius LeVallon lived—the cosmic point of view. The spell of
our early days revived, worked on my nerves and thought, altering my outlook
sensibly even at this early stage of my return.

The autumn afternoon was already on the wane when at length I reached C—
, an untidy little watch-making town, and according to instructions left the train.
I searched the empty platform in vain for any sign of Julius. Instead of the tall,
familiar figure, a little darkfaced man stood abruptly before me, stared into my
face with the questioning eyes of a child or animal, and exclaimed bluntly enough
"*Monsieur le professeur?*" We were alone on the deserted platform, the train already swallowed by the forest, no porter, of course, visible, and signs of civilisation generally somewhat scanty.

This man, sent by Julius, made a curious impression on me as I gave him my
bag and prepared to follow him to the cart I saw standing outside the station.
His mode of addressing me seemed incongruous. Of peasant type, with black
moustaches far too big for his features, and bushy eyebrows reminding me of
tree-lichen, there was something in his simplicity of gesture and address that suggested a faithful animal. His voice was not unlike a growl; he was delighted to
have found me, but did not accept me yet; he showed his pleasure in his honest smile and in certain quick, jerky movements of the body that made me think

how a clever caricaturist could see the dog in him. Yet in his keen and steady eyes there was another look that did not encourage levity; one would not lightly trifle with him. There was something about the alert little fellow that insisted on respect, and a touch of the barbaric counteracted the comedy of the aggressive eyebrows and moustache. In the eyes, unflinching yet respectful, I fancied to detect another thing as well: a nameless expression seen sometimes in the eyes of men who have known uncommon things—habitual amazement grown slowly to unwilling belief. He was a man, certainly, who would serve his master to the death and ask no questions.

But also he would not answer questions; I could get nothing out of him, as the springless cart drove slowly up the steep mountain road behind the pair of sturdy horses. *Oui* and *non* and *peut-être* summed up his conversational powers, till I gave up trying and lapsed into silence. Perhaps he had not "passed" me yet, not quite approved me. He was just the sort of faithful, self-contained servant Julius required, no doubt, and, as a conductor into mysterious adventure, a by no means inadequate figure. Name, apparently, he had also none, for Julius, as I learned later, referred to him as simply "he." But my imagination instantly christened him "The Dog-Man," and as such the inscrutable fellow lives in my memory to this day. He seemed just one degree above the animal stage.

But while thought was busy with a dozen speculations, the dusk had fallen steadily, and the character of the country, I saw, had changed. It was more rugged and inhospitable, the valleys narrower, the forests very deep, with taller and more solemn trees, and no signs anywhere of the axe. An hour ago we had left the main road and turned up a rough, deep-rutted track that only the feet of oxen seemed to have used. We moved in comparative gloom, though far overhead the heights shone still with the gold of sunset. For a long time we had seen no peasant huts, no sign of habitation, nor passed a single human being. Woodcutters and charcoal-burners apparently had not penetrated here, and the track, I gathered, was used in summer only and led to some lonely farm among the upper pastures. It was very silent; no wind stirred the sea of branches; no animal life showed itself; and the only moving things beside ourselves were the jays that now and again flew across the path or announced their invisible presence in the woods by raucous screaming.

Although the ceaseless jolting of the cart was severe, the long journey most fatiguing, I was sensible of the deep calm that brooded everywhere. After the bluster of the aggressive Alps, this peaceful Jura stole on the spirit with a subtle charm. Something whispered that I was not alone, but that a friendly touch of welcome pervaded the cool recesses of these wooded hills. The sense of hostile isolation inspired by the snowy peaks, that faint dismay one knows sometimes at the foot of towering summits, was wholly absent here. I felt myself, not alien to these rolling mountains, but akin. I was known and hospitably admitted, not merely ignored, nor let in at my own grave risk. The spirit of the mountains here was kind.

Yet that I was aware of this at all made me realise the presence of another thing as well: It was in myself, not in these velvet valleys. For, while the charm of the

scenery acted as a sedative, I realised that something alert in me noted the calming influence and welcomed it. *That* did not go to sleep—it resolutely kept
awake. A faint instinct of alarm had been stimulated, if ever so slightly, from the
moment I left the train and touched the atmosphere of my silent guide, the "Dog-
Man." It was, of course, that he brought his master nearer. Julius and I should
presently meet again, shake hands, look into each other's eyes—I should hear
his voice and share again the glamour of his personality. Also there would be—
a third.

It was an element, obviously, in a process of readjustment of my being which
had begun the moment I received his letter; it had increased while I sat in the
Bâle hotel and jotted down those early recollections—an ingredient in the new
grouping of emotions and sensations constituting myself which received the attack, so to speak, of what came later. My consciousness was slowly changing.

Yet this, I think, was all I felt at the moment: a perfectly natural anticipatory
excitement, a stirring wonder, and behind them both a hint of shrinking that
was faint uneasiness. It was the thought of the woman that caused the last, the
old premonition that something grave involving the three of us would happen.
The potent influences of my youth were already at work again.

My entrance into the secluded spot Julius had chosen came unexpectedly; we
were suddenly upon it; the effect was almost dramatic. The last farmhouse had
been left behind an hour or more, and we had been winding painfully up a steep
ascent that led through a tunnel of dark, solemn trees, when the forest abruptly
stopped, and a little, cup-like valley lay before me, bounded on three sides by
jagged limestone ridges. Open to the sky, like some lonely flower, it lay hidden
and remote upon this topmost plateau, difficult of access to the world. I saw
cleared meadows of emerald green beneath the peeping stars; a stream ran gur-
gling past my feet; the surface of a little lake held the shadows of the encircling
cliffs; and at the further end, beneath the broken outline of the ridges, lights
twinkled in a peasant's châlet.

The effect was certainly of Fairyland. The stillness and cool air, after the close-
ness of the heavy forest, seemed to bring the stars much nearer. There was a
clean, fresh perfume; the atmosphere crystal clear, the calm profound. I felt a little private world about me, self-contained, and impressive with a quiet dignity
of its own. Unknown, unspoilt, serene and exquisite, it lay hidden here for some
purpose that vulgar intrusion might not discover. If ever an enchanted valley
existed, it was here before my eyes.

"So this is the chosen place—this isolated spot of beauty!" My heart leaped
to think that Julius stood already within reach of my voice, possibly of my sight
as well. No meeting-place, surely, could have been more suitable.

The cart moved slowly, and the horses, steam rising from their heated bodies against the purple trees, stepped softly upon the meadow-land. The sound
of hoofs and wheels was left behind, we silently moved up the gentle slope towards the lights. Night stepped with us from the hills; the forest paused and
waited at a distance; only the faint creaking of the wheels upon damp grass and
the singing of the little stream were audible. The air grew sharp with upland

perfumes. We passed the diminutive lake that mirrored the first stars. And a curious feeling reached me from the sky and from the lonely ridges; a nameless emotion caught my heart a moment; some thrill of high, unearthly loveliness, familiar as a dream yet gone again before it could be seized, mirrored itself in the depths of me like those buried stars within the water—when, suddenly, a figure detached itself from the background of trees and cliffs, and towards me over the dew-drenched grass moved—Julius LeVallon.

He came like a figure from the sky, the forest, the distant ridges. The spirit of this marvellous spot came with him. He seemed its incarnation. Whether he first drew me from the cart, or whether I sprang down to meet him, is impossible to say, for in that big moment the thousand threads that bound us together with their separate tensions slipped into a single cable of overwhelming strength. We stood upon the wet meadow, close to one another, hands firmly clasped, eyes gazing into eyes.

"Julius—it's really you—at last!" I found to say—then his reply in the old, unchanging voice that made me tremble a little as I heard it: "I knew you would come—friend of a million years!" He laughed a little; I laughed too.

"I promised." It seemed incredible to me that I had ever hesitated.

"Ages ago," I heard his answer. It was like the singing of the stream that murmured past our feet. "Ages ago."

I was aware that he let go my hand. We were moving through the dripping grass, crossing and recrossing the little stream. The mountains rose dark and strong about us. I heard the cart lumbering away with creaking wheels towards the barn. Across the heavens the stars trailed their golden pattern more and more thickly. I saw them gleaming in the unruffled lake. I smelt the odour of wood-smoke that came from the châlet chimney.

We walked in silence. Those stars, those changeless hills, deep woods and singing rivulet—primitive and eternal things—accompanied us. They were the right witnesses of our meeting. And a night-wind, driving the dusk towards the west, woke in the forest and came out to touch our faces. Splendour and loneliness closed about us, heralding Powers of Nature that were here not yet explained away.

CHAPTER XVI

"We cannot limit the types, superhuman or subhuman, that may obtain. We can 'set no bounds to the existence or powers of sentient beings'—a consideration of the highest importance,as well, perhaps, practical as theoretical.... The discovery of Superhumans of an exalted kind may be only a question of time, and the attainment of knowledge on this head one of the most important achievements in the history of races that are to come."—"The Individual and Reality" (Fawcett).

Something certainly tightened in my throat as we went across that soaking grass towards the building that was half châlet, half farm-house, with steep, heavy roof and wide veranda. The lights beckoned to us through the little windows. I saw a shadow slip across the casement window on the tipper floor. And my question was out of its own accord before I could prevent it. My mind held in that moment no other thought at all; my pulses quickened.

"So, Julius, you have—found her?"

And he answered as though no interval of years had been; as though still we stood in the dawn upon the steps of the Edinburgh lodging-house. The tone was matter of fact and without emotion:

"She is with me here—my wife—eager to see you at last."

The words dropped down between us like lightning into the earth, and a sense of chill, so faint I hardly recognised it, passed over me. Emotion followed instantly, yet emotion, again, so vague, so odd, so distant in some curious way, that I found no name for it. A shadow as, perhaps, of disappointment fell on my thoughts. Yet, assuredly, I had expected no different statement. He had said the right and natural thing. He had found the woman of his dream and married her. What lurked, I wondered nervously, behind my lame congratulations? Why was I baffled and ashamed? What made my speech come forth with a slight confusion between the thought and its utterance? For—almost—I had been about to say another thing, and had stopped myself just in time.

"And she—remembers?" I asked quickly—point-blank, and bluntly enough—and felt mortified the same instant by my premature curiosity. Before I could modify my words, or alter them into something less aggressively inquisitive, he turned and faced me, holding my arm to make me look at him. His skin wore the familiar marble pallor as of old; I saw it shine against the dark building where the light from the window caught it.

"'Me?" he asked quietly, "or—you?"

"Anything," I stammered, "anything at all of—of the past, I meant. Forgive me for asking so abruptly; I—"

The words froze on my lips at the expression that came into his face. He merely looked at me and smiled. No more than that, so far as accurate description goes, and yet enough to make my heart stop dead as a stone, then start thumping against my ribs as though a paddlewheel were loose in me. For it was not Julius in that instant who looked at me. His white skin masked another; behind and through his eyes this other stared straight into my own; and this other was familiar to me, yet unknown. The look disappeared again as instantaneously as it came.

"You shall judge for yourself," I heard, as he drew me on towards the house.

His tone made further pointed questioning impossible, rousing my curiosity higher than ever before. Again I saw the woman in my imagination; I pictured her as a figure half remembered. As the shadow had slid past the casement of the upper floor, so her outline slipped now across a rising screen of memory not entirely obliterated.

The presentment was even vivid: she would be superb. I saw her of the Greek goddess type, with calm, inscrutable eyes, majestic mien, the suggestion of strange knowledge in her quiet language and uncommon gestures. She would be genuinely distinguished, remarkable in mind as well as in appearance. Already, as we crossed the veranda, the thrill of anticipation caught me. She would be standing in the hall to greet us, or, seated before an open fire of logs, would rise out of the shadows to meet the friend of whom she had doubtless "heard so much," and with whom such strange things were now to be accomplished. The words Julius next actually uttered, accordingly, reached me with a sense of disappointment that was sharp, and the entire picture collapsed like a house of cards. The reaction touched my sense of comedy almost.

"I think she is still preparing your room," he said. "I had just taken the water up when I heard your cart. We have little help, or need for help. A girl from the farm in the lower valley brings butter sometimes. We do practically everything ourselves." I murmured something, courtesy keeping a smile in check; and then he added, "We chose this solitude on purpose, of course—she chose it, rather—and you are the first visitor since we came here months ago. We were only just ready for you; it was good that you were close—that it was so easy for you to get here."

"I am looking forward immensely to seeing Mrs. LeVallon," I replied, but such a queer confusion of times and places had fallen on my mind that my tongue almost said "to seeing her again."

He smiled. "She will be with us in the morning," he added quietly, "if not tonight."

This simple exchange of commonplaces let down the tension of my emotions pleasantly. He turned towards me as he spoke, and for the first time, beneath the hanging oil lamp, I noted the signature of the intervening years. There was a look of power in eyes and mouth that had not been there previously. I was aware of a new distance between us, and a new respect came with it. Julius had "travelled." He seemed to look down upon me from a height. But, at the same time, the picture his brief words conveyed had the effect of restoring me to my normal world again. For nothing more banal could have been imagined, and side by side with the chagrin to my sense of the theatrical ran also a distinct relief. It came as a corrective to the loneliness and grandeur of the setting, and checked the suggestion lying behind the hint that they were "only just ready" for my coming.

My emotions sank comfortably to a less inflated level. I murmured something politely as we passed into the so-called "sitting-room" together, and for a moment the atmosphere of my own practical world came in strongly with me. The sense of the incongruous inevitably was touched. The immense fabric of my friend's beliefs seemed in that instant to tremble a little. That the woman he—we—had been waiting for through centuries, this "old soul" taught of the ancient wisdom and aware of august, forgotten worship, should be "making a bed upstairs" woke in me a sense of healthy amusement. Julius took up the water! She was engaged in menial acts! A girl brought butter from a distant farm! And I could have laughed—but for one other thing that lay behind and within the comedy. For that other thing was—pathos. There was a kind of yearning pain at the heart of it: a pain whose origins were too remote to be discoverable by the normal part of me.

It touched the poetry in me, too. For after the first disturbing effect—that it was not adequate—I felt slowly another thing: that this commonplace meeting was far more likely to be *true* than the dramatic sort I had anticipated. It was natural, it was simple; all big adventures of the soul begin in a quiet way. Obviously, as yet, the two selves in me were not yet comfortably readjusted.

I became aware, too, that Julius was what I can only call somewhere less human than before—more impersonal. He talked, he acted, he even looked as a figure might outside our world. I had no longer insight into his being as before. His life lay elsewhere, expresses it best perhaps. I can hardly present him as a man of flesh and blood. Emotion broke through so rarely.

And our talk that evening together—for Mrs. LeVallon put in no appearance—was ordinary, too. Julius, of course, as ever, used phrases that belonged to the world peculiarly his own, but he said nothing startling in the sense I had expected. No dramatic announcement came. He took things for granted in the way he always did, assuming my beliefs and theories were his own, and that my scepticism was merely due to the "mind" in me to-day. We had some supper together, a bowl of bread and milk the man brought in, and we talked of the intervening years as naturally as might be—but for this phraseology he favoured. When the man said "good night," Julius smiled kindly at him, and the fellow made a gesture of delight as though the attention meant far more to him than money. He reminded me again irresistibly, yet in no sense comically, of a faithful and devoted animal. Julius had patted him! It was delightful. An inarticulateness, as of the animal world, belonged to him. His rare words came out with effort, almost with difficulty. He looked his master straight in the eye, listened to orders with a personal interest mere servants never have, and, without a trace of servility in face or manner, hurried off gladly to fulfil them. The distress in the eyes alone still puzzled me.

"You have a treasure there," I said. "He seems devoted to you."

"A young soul," he said, "in a human body for the first time, still with the innocence and simplicity of the recent animal stage about his awakening self-consciousness. It is unmistakable..."

"What sleeps in the vegetable, dreams in the animal, wakes in the man," I said, remembering Leibnitz. "I'm glad we've left the earlier stages behind us." His explanation interested me. "But that expression in his eyes," I asked, "that look of searching, almost of anxiety?"

Julius replied thoughtfully. "My atmosphere acts upon him as a kind of forc-ing-house, perhaps. He is dimly aware of knowledge that lies, at present, too far beyond him—and yet he reaches out for it. Instinctive, but not yet intuitional. The privilege brings terror. Opportunities of growth so swift and concentrated involve bewilderment, even pain."

"Pain?" I queried, interested as of old.

"Development is nothing but a series of little deaths. The soul passes so quickly to new stages." He looked up searchingly into my face. "We knew that privi-lege once," he added significantly; "we, too, knew special teaching."

And, though at the moment I purposely ignored this reference to our "Tem-ple Days," I understood that this man's neighbourhood might, indeed, have in unusual and stimulating effect upon a simple, ignorant type of mind. Even in my own case his presence gave me furiously to think. The "Dog-Man," the more I observed him, was little more than a faithful creature standing on his hind legs with considerable surprise and enjoyment that he was able to do so—that "lit-tle more" being quite possibly *self*-consciousness. He showed his teeth when I met him at the station, whereas, now that I was accepted by his master, his ap-proval was unlimited. He gave willing service in the form of love.

While Julius continued speaking, as though nothing else existed at the mo-ment, I observed him carefully. My eyes assessed the changes in the outward "expression" of himself. He was thinner, slighter than before; there was an in-creased balance and assurance in his manner; a poise not present in our earlier days; but to say that he looked older seemed almost a misuse of language. Though the eyes were stronger, steadier, the lines in the skin more deeply cut, the outline of the features chiselled with more decision, these, even in combi-nation, added no signature of age to the general expression of high beauty that was his. The years had not coarsened, but etherealised the face. Two other things, moreover, impressed me: the texture of skin and flesh had refined away, so that the inner light of his enthusiasm shone through; and—there was a marked increase in what I must term the "feel" of his immediate atmosphere or presence. Always electric and alive, it now seemed doubly charged. Against that dark inner screen where the mind visualises pictorially, he rose in terms of ra-diant strength. Immense potency lay suppressed in him; Powers—spiritual or Nature Powers—were in attendance. He had acquired a momentum that was in some sense both natural and super-human. It was not unlike the sense of power that great natural scenes evoke in those who are receptive—mountains, landscapes, forests. It was elemental. I felt him immense, at the head of an in-visible procession, as it were, a procession from the sky, the heights, the woods, the stars.

And a touch of eeriness stole over me. I was aware of strange vitality in this lonely valley; and I was aware of it—through him. I stood, as yet, upon the outer fringe. Its remoteness from the modern world was not a remoteness of space alone, but of—condition.

There was, however, another thing impossible to ignore—that somewhere in this building there moved a figure already for me mysterious and half legendary. Upstairs, not many feet away from us, her step occasionally audible by the creaking of the boards, she moved, breathing, thinking, listening, hearing our voices, almost within touching distance of our hands. There was a hint of the fabulous in it somewhere.

And, realising her near presence, I felt a curious emotion rising through me as from a secret spring. Its character, veiled by interest and natural anticipation, remained without a name. I could not describe it to myself even. Each time the thought of meeting her, that she was close, each time the sound of her soft footfall overhead was audible, this emotion rose in me pleasurably, yet with dread behind it somewhere lurking. I caught it stirring; the stream of it went out to this woman I had never seen with the certain aim of intuitive direction; I surprised it in the act. But always something blocked it, hiding its name away. It escaped analysis. And, never more than instantaneous, passing the very moment it was born, it seemed to me that the opposing force that blocked it thus had to do with the man who was my host and my companion. It emanated from him—this objecting force. Julius checked it; though not with deliberate consciousness—he prevented my discovery of its nature. There was uncommon and mysterious sweetness in it, a sweetness as of long mislaid romance that lifted the heart. Yet it returned each time upon me, blank and unrewarded.

It was noticeable, moreover, that our talk avoided the main object of my presence here. LeVallon talked freely of other things, of the "Dog-Man," of myself—I gave him a quick sketch of my life in the long interval—of anything and everything but the purpose of my coming. There was, doubtless, awkwardness on my side, since my instinct was not to take my visit heavily, but to regard the fulfilment of my old-time pledge as an adventure, even a fantasy, rather than the serious acceptance of a grave "experiment." His reluctance, yet, was noticeable. He told me little or nothing of himself by way of exchange.

"To-morrow, when you are thoroughly rested from your journey," he met my least approach to the matter that occupied our deepest thoughts; or—"later, when you've had a little time to get acclimatised. You must let this place soak into you. Rest and sleep and take things easy; there is no hurry—here." Until I realised that he wished to establish a natural sympathy between my being and the enchanted valley, to avoid anything in the nature of surprise or shock which might disturb a desired harmony, and that, in fact, the absence of his wife and his silence about himself were both probably intentional. Conditions were to flow in upon me of their own accord and naturally, thus reducing possible hostility to a minimum. Before we rose to go to bed an hour later this had become a conviction in me. It was all thought out beforehand.

We stood a moment on the veranda to taste the keen, sweet air and see the dark mountains blocked against the stars. The sound of running water was all we heard. No lights, of course, showed anywhere. The meadows, beneath thin, frosty mist, lay very still. But the valley somehow rushed at me; it seemed so charged to the brim with stimulating activity and life. Something felt on the move in it. I stood in the presence of a crowd, waiting to combine with energies latent in it. I was aware of the idea of co-operation almost.

"One of the rare places," he said significantly when I remarked upon it cautiously, "where all is clean and open still. Humanity has been here, but humanity of the helpful kind. We went to infinite trouble to find it."

It was the first time he had come so near to the actual subject. I was aware he watched me, although his eyes were turned towards the darkness of the encircling forest.

"And—your wife likes it too?" For though I remembered that she had "chosen it," its loneliness must surely have dismayed an ordinary woman.

Still with his eyes turned out across the valley, he replied, "She chose it. Yes"—he hesitated slightly—"she likes it, though not always—" He broke off abruptly, still without looking at me, then added, as he came a little nearer, "But we both agree—we *know* it is the right place for us." That "us," I felt certain, included myself as well.

I did not press for explanation at the moment. I touched upon another thing.

"Humanity, you say, has been here! I should have thought some virgin corner of the earth would have suited your—purpose—better?" Then, as he did not answer for a moment, I added: "This is surely an ordinary peasant's house that you've made comfortable?"

He looked at me. A breath of wind went past us. I had the ghostly feeling someone had been listening; and a faint shiver ran across my nerves.

"A peasant's, yes, but not"—and he smiled—"an ordinary peasant. We found here an old man with his sons: they, or their forbears, had lived in isolation for generations in this valley; they were 'superstitious' in the sense of knowing Nature amid understanding her. They *believed*, though in an imperfect and degraded form, what was once a living truth. They sold out to me quite willingly and are now established in the plains below. In this loneliness, away from modern 'knowledge,' they loved what surrounded them, and in that sense their love was worship. They felt-with the forests, with streams and mountains, with clouds and sky, with dawn and sunset, with the darkness too." He looked about him as he said it, and my eyes followed the direction of his own across the night. Again the valley stirred and moved throughout its whole expanse. "They also," Julius continued in a lower tone, his face closer than before, "felt-with the lightning and the wind."

I could have sworn some subtle change went through the surrounding darkness as he said the words. Fire and wind sprang at me, so vivid was their entrance into my thought. Again that slight shudder ran tingling up my spine.

"The place," he continued, "is therefore already prepared to some extent, for the channels that we need are partly open. The veil is here unthickened. We can work with less resistance."

"There is certainly peace," I agreed, "and an uplifting sense of beauty."

"You feel it?" he asked quickly.

"I feel extraordinarily and delightfully alive," I admitted truthfully.

Whereupon he turned to me with a still more significant rejoinder:

"Because that which worship and consecration-ceremonies ought to accomplish for churches—are meant to accomplish, rather—has never been here *undone*. All places were holy ground until men closed the channels with their unbelief and thus defiled them by cutting them off from the life about them."

I heard a window softly closing above us; we turned and went indoors. Julius put the lamps out one by one, taking a candle to show me up the stairs. We went along the wooden passage. We passed several doors, beneath one of which I saw a line of light. My own room was at the further end, simply, almost barely, furnished, with just the actual necessaries. He paused at the threshold, shook my hand, said a short "good night," and left me, closing the door behind him carefully. I heard his step go softly down the passage. A door in the distance also opened and closed. Then complete silence hushed the entire house about me, yet a silence that was listening and alive. No ancient, turreted castle, with ivied walls and dungeons, with forsaken banqueting-hall or ghostly corridors, could possibly have felt more haunted than this peasant's châlet in the Jura fastnesses.

For a considerable time I sat at my open window, thinking; and yet not thinking so much, perhaps, as—relaxing. I was aware that my mind had been at high tension the entire day, almost on guard—as though seeking unconsciously to protect itself. Ever since the morning I had been on the alert against quasi-attack, and only now did I throw down my arms and abandon myself without reserve. Something I had been afraid of had shown itself friendly after all. A feeling of security stole over me; I was safe; gigantic powers were round me, oddly close, yet friendly, provided I, too, was friendly. It was a singular feeling of being helpless, yet cared for. The valley took hold of me and all my little human forces. To set myself against it would be somehow dangerous, but to go with it, adopting its over-mastering stride, was safety. This became suddenly clear to me—that I must be sympathetic and that hostility on my part might involve disaster.

Here, apparently, was the first symptom of that power which Julius declared was derived from "feeling-with." I began to understand another thing as well; I recalled his choice of words—that the veil hereabouts was "unthickened" and the channels "open." He did not say the veil was thin, the channels cleared. It was in its native, primitive condition.

I sat by the window, letting the valley pour through and over me. It flooded my being with its calm and beauty. The stars were very bright above the ridges; small clouds passed westwards, the water sang and tinkled; the cup-like hollow had its secrets, but it told them. I had never known night so wonderfully articulate. Power brooded here. I felt my blood quicken with the sense of kinship.

And the little room with its unvarnished pine-boards that held a certain forest perfume, was comforting too; the odour of peat fires still clung to the darkened rafters overhead; the candle, in its saucer-like receptacle of wood, gave just the simple, old-fashioned light that was appropriate. Bodily fatigue made bed exceedingly welcome, though it was long before I fell asleep. Figures, at first, stole softly in across the night and peered at me—Julius, pale and rapt, remote from the modern world; the silent "Dog-Man," with those eyes of questioning wonder and half-disguised distress. And another ghostly figure stole in too, though without a face I could decipher; a woman whom the long, faultless balance of the ages delivered, with the rest of us, into the keeping of this lonely spot for some deep purpose of our climbing souls. Their outlines hovered, mingled with the shadows, and withdrew.

And a certain change in myself, though perhaps not definitely noted at the time, was apparent too—I found in my heart a singular readiness to believe. While sleep crept nearer, and reason dropped a lid, there assuredly was in me, as part of something accepted naturally, the likelihood that LeVallon's attitude was an aspect of forgotten truth. Veiled in Nature's operations, perchance directing them, and particularly in spots of loneliness such as this, dwelt those mighty elemental Potencies he held were accessible to humanity. A phrase from some earlier reading floated back to me, as though deliberately supplied—not that Nature "works towards what are called 'ends,' but that it was possible or rather probable, that 'ends' which implied conscious superhuman activities, are being realised." The sentence, for some reason, had remained in my memory. When life was simpler, closer to Nature, some such doctrine may have been objectively verifiable, and worship, in the sense that Julius used the word, might well promise to restore the grandeur of forgotten beliefs which should make men as the gods....

With the delightful feeling that in this untainted valley, the woods, the mountains, the very winds and stormy lightnings, were yet but the physical vehicle of powers that expressed intelligence and true *being*, I passed from dozing into sleep, the cool outside air touching my eyelids with the beauty of the starry Jura night. An older, earlier type of consciousness—though I did not phrase it to myself thus—was asserting itself and taking charge of me. The spell was on my heart.

Yet the human touch came last of all, following me into the complicated paths of slumber, and haunting me as with half-recovered memories of far-off, enchanted days. Uncommon visions met my descending or ascending consciousness, so that while brain and body slept, some deeper part of me went travelling swiftly backwards. I knew the old familiar feeling that the whole of me did not sleep... and, though remembering nothing definite, my first thought on awakening was the same as my final thought on falling into slumber: What manner of marvellous woman would *she* prove to be?

CHAPTER XVII

"Thy voice is like to music heard ere birth,
Some spirit lute touched ors a spirit sea;
Thy face remembered is from other worlds.
It has been died for, though I know not when,
It has been sung of, though I know not where.
It has the strangeness of the luring West,
And of sad sea-horizons; beside thee
I am aware of other times and lands,
Of birth far back, of lives in many stars."
                 —"Marpessa" (Stephen Phillips).

During sleep, however, the heavier emotions had sunk to the bottom, the lighter had risen to the top. I woke with a feeling of vigour, and with the sense called "common" distinctly in the ascendant. Through the open window came sunshine in a flood, the crisp air sparkled. I could taste it from my bed. Youth ran in my veins and ten years seemed to drop from my back as I sprang up and thrust my face into the radiant morning. Drawing a deep draught into my lungs, I must at the same time have unconsciously exclaimed, for the peasant girl gathering vegetables below—the garden, such as it was, merged into the pastures—looked up startled. She had been singing to herself. I withdrew my pyjamaed figure hurriedly, while she, as hurriedly, let drop the skirts the dew had made her lift so high; and when I peeped a moment later, she had gone. I, too, felt inclined to sing with happiness, so invigorating was the clear brilliance of the opening day. A joyful irresponsibility, as of boyhood, coursed in my tingling blood. Everything in this enchanted valley seemed young and vigorous; the stream ran gaily past the shining trees; the meadows glistened; the very mountains wore a lustre as of life that ran within their solid frames.

It was impossible to harbour the slightest thought of dread before such peace and beauty; all ominous forebodings fled away; this joy and strength of Nature brought in life. Even the "Dog-Man" smiled with eyes unclouded when, a little later, he brought a small pail of boiling water, and informed me that there was a pool in the forest close at hand where I could bathe. He nosed about the room—only thus can I describe his friendly curiosity for my welfare—fussed awkwardly with my boots and clothes, looked frankly into my eyes with an expression that said plainly "How are you this morning? I'm splendid!" grunted, sniffed, almost wagged his tail for pleasure—and trotted out. And he went, I declare, as though he had heard a rabbit and must be after it. The laughter in me was only just suppressed, for I could have sworn that he expected me to pat him, with the remark "Good fellow! Sick 'em, then!" or words to that effect.

The secluded valley, walled-in from the blustering world like some wild, prim-

itive garden, was drenched in sunshine by the time I went downstairs; the limestone cliffs a mile away of quite dazzling brilliance; and the pine woods across
the meadow-land scented the whole interior of the little châlet. But for stray
wisps of autumn mist that still clung along the borders of the stream, it might
have been a day in June the mountains still held prisoner. My heart leaped with
the beauty. This lonely region of woods and mountain tops suggested the presence of some Nature Deity that presided over it, and as I stood a moment on the
veranda, I turned at a sound of footsteps to see the figure of my imagination face
to face. "If *she* is of equal splendour!" flashed instantly through my mind. For
Julius wore the glory of the morning in his eyes, the neck was bare and the shirt
a little open; standing there erect in his mountain clothes, he was as like the
proverbial Greek god as any painter could have possibly desired.

"Whether I slept well?" I answered his inquiry. "Why, Julius, I feel positively
like a boy again. This place has worked magic on me while I slept. There's the
idea in me that one must live for ever."

And, even while I said it, my eyes glanced over his shoulder into the hall for
a sight of someone who any moment might appear. Excitement was high in me.

Julius quietly held my hand in his own firm grasp a second.

"Life came to you in sleep," he said. "I told you—I warned you, the channels
here were open and easily accessible. All power—all powers—everywhere are
natural. Our object is to hold them, isn't it?"

"You mean control them?" I said, still watching the door behind him.

"They visit the least among us; they touch us, and are gone. The essential is
to harness them—in this case before they harness us—again.

I made no reply. The other excitement was too urgent in me.

Linking his arm in mine, he led me towards a corner of the main room, half
hall, half kitchen, where a white tablecloth promised breakfast. The "man" was
already busying himself to and fro with plates and a gleaming metal pot that
steamed. I smelt coffee and the fragrance of baked bread. But I listened half-heart-
edly to my host's curious words because every minute I expected the door to
open. There was a nervousness in me what I should find to say to such a woman
when she came.

Was there, as well, among my bolder feelings, a faint suspicion of something
else—something so slight and vague it hardly left a trace, while yet I was aware
that it had been there? I could not honestly say. I only knew that, again, there
stirred about my heart unconsciously a delicate spider-web of resentment,
envy, disapproval—call it what one may, since it was too slight to own a definite name—that seemed to wake some ghost of injustice, of a grievance almost,
in the hidden depths of me. It passed, unexplained, untraceable. Perhaps I smothered it, perhaps I left it unacknowledged. I know not. So elusive an emotion I
could not retain a second, far less label. "Julius has found her; she is his," was
the clear thought that followed it. No more than that. And yet—like the
shadow of a leaf, it floated down upon me, darkening, though almost imperceptibly, some unknown corner of my heart.

And, remembering my manners, I asked after her indisposition, while he laughed and insisted upon our beginning breakfast; she would presently join us; I should see her for myself. He looked so happy that I yielded to the momentary temptation.

"Julius," I said, by way of compliment and somewhat late congratulation, "she must be wonderful. I'm so—so very pleased—for you."

"Yes," he said, as he poured coffee and boiling milk into my wooden bowl, "and we have waited long. But the opportunity has come at last, and this time we shall not let it slip."

The simple words were not at all the answer I expected. There was a mingling of relief and anxiety in his voice; I remembered that she "did not always like it here," and I wondered again what my "understanding" was to be that he had promised would "come later." What determined her change of mood? Why did she sometimes like it, and sometimes not like it? Was it loneliness, or was it due to things that—happened? Any moment now she would be in the room, holding my hand, looking into my eyes, expecting from me words of greeting, speaking to me. I should hear her voice. Twice I turned quickly at the sound of an opening door, only to find myself face to face with the "man"; but at length came a sound that was indisputably the rustle of skirts, and, with a quickening of the heart, I pushed my plate away, and rose from my chair, turning half way to greet her.

Disappointment met me again, however, for this time it was merely the peasant girl I had seen from my window; and once more I sat down abruptly, covering my confusion with a laugh and feeling like a schoolboy surprised in a foolish mistake. And then a movement from Julius opposite startled me. He had risen from his seat. There was a new expression on his face, an extraordinary expression—observation the most alert imaginable, anxiety, question, the tension of various deep emotions oddly mingled. He watched me keenly. He watched us both.

"My wife," he said quietly, as the figure advanced towards us. Then, turning to her: "And this is my friend, Professor Mason." He indicated myself.

I rose abruptly, startled and dismayed, nearly upsetting the chair behind me in my clumsiness. The "Professor Mason" sounded ludicrous, almost as ludicrous as the "Mrs. LeVallon" he had not uttered. I stared. She stared. There was a moment of blank silence. Disappointment petrified me. There was no distinction, there was no beauty. She was tall and slim, and the face, of a commonplace order, was slightly pock-marked. I forgot all manners.

She was the first to recover. We both laughed. But if there was nervousness of confused emotion in my laugh, there was in hers a happy pleasure, frankly and naturally expressed.

"How do you do, sir—Professor?" she instantly corrected herself, shaking true vigorously, yet almost timidly, by the hand. It was a provincial and untutored voice.

"I'm—delighted to see you," my lips stammered, stopping dead before the modern title. The control of my breath was not quite easy for a moment.

We sat down. In her words—or was it in her manner, rather?—there was a

hint of undue familiarity that tinged my disappointment with a flash of disapproval too, yet caught up immediately by a kind of natural dignity that denied
offence, or at any rate, corrected it. Another impression then stole over me. I
was aware of charm. The voice, however, unquestionably betrayed accent. Of
the "lady," in the restricted, ordinary meaning of the word, there was no pretence. A singular revulsion made me tremble. For a moment she had held my
hand with deliberate pressure, while her eye remained fixed upon my face with
a direct, a searching intentness. She too, like her husband, watched me. If she
formed a swift, intuitive judgment regarding myself, nothing at first betrayed
it. I was aware, however, at once, that, behind the decision of her natural frankness, something elusive hovered. The effect was highly contradictory, even captivating, certainly provocative of curiosity. Accompanying her laughter was a
delicate, swift flush, and the laugh, though loud in some other sense than of
sound alone, was not unmusical. A breath of glamour, seductive as it was fleeting, caught me as I heard.

For a moment or two my senses certainly reeled. It seemed that swift shut-
ters rose and fell before my eyes. One screen rolled up, another dropped, vistas
opened, vanishing before their depths showed anything. The châlet, with our
immediate surroundings, faded; I was aware of ourselves only, chiefly, however,
of her. This first sight of her had the effect that years before Julius had produced:
the peculiar sense of "other places." And this in spite of myself, without any decided belief of my own as yet to help it....

The confusion of my senses passed then, and consciousness focused clearly
once more on my surroundings. The disturbed emotions, however, refused
wholly to quiet down. Her face, I noted, beneath the disfiguring marks, was
rosy, and the grey-green eyes were very bright. They were luminous, changing
eyes, their hue altering of its own accord apart from mere play or angle of the
light. Sometimes their grey merged wholly into green, but a very wonderful
deep green that made them like the sea; later, again, they were distinctly blue.
They lit the entire face, its expression changing when they changed. The frank
and open innocence of the child in them was countered, though not injuriously,
by an unfathomed depth that had its effect upon the whole physiognomy. An
arresting power shone in them as if imperiously. There were two faces there.

And the singular and fascinating effect of these dominating eyes left further
judgment at first disabled. I noticed, however, that her mouth had that generous width that makes for strength rather than for beauty: that the teeth were
fine and regular; and that the brown hair, tinged with bronze, was untidy about
the neck and ears. A narrow band of black velvet encircled the throat; she wore
a blouse, short skirt, and high brown boots with nails that clattered on the stone
flooring when she moved. Since gathering vegetables in the dawn she had
changed her costume, evidently. A certain lightness, I saw now, had nothing
of irresponsibility in it, but was merely youth, vitality, and physical vigor. She
was fifteen years younger than Julius, if a day, and I judged her age no more than
twenty-five perhaps.

"It's a pore house to have your friends to," she said in her breezy, uncultivated voice, "but I hope you managed all right with your room—Professor:" It was the foundation of the voice that had the uncultivated sound; on the top of it, like a layer of something imitated or acquired, there was refinement. I got the impression that, unconsciously, she aped the better manner of speech, yet was not aware she did so.

Burning questions rose within me as I listened to this opening conversation: How much she knew, and believed, of her husband's vast conceptions; what explanation of my visit he had offered her, what explanation of myself; chief of all, how much—if anything—she remembered? For our coming together in this hidden Jura valley under conditions that seemed one minute ludicrous, and the next sublime, was the alleged meeting of three Souls who had not recognised each other through bodily, human eyes for countless centuries. And our pur' pose, if not madness, held a solemnity that might well belong to a forgotten method of approaching deity.

"He's told me such a lot about you, Julius has," she continued half shyly, jerk' ing her thumb in the direction of her husband, "that I wanted to see what you were like." It was said naturally, as by a child; yet the freedom might equally have been assumed to conceal an admitted ignorance of manners. "You're such—very old friends, aren't you?" She seemed to look me up and down. I thought I detected disappointment in her too.

"We were together at school and university, you see," I made reply, shirking the title again. "but it's a good many years now since we met. We've been out of touch for a long time. I hadn't even heard of his marriage. My congratulations are late, but most sincere."

I bowed. Strange! Both in word and gesture some faintest hint of sarcasm or resentment forced itself against my conscious will. The blood rose—I hoped un' noticed—to my cheeks. My eyes dropped quickly from her face.

"That's reely nice of you," she said simply, and without a touch of embar' rassment anywhere. She cut a lump of bread from the enormous loaf in front of us and broke it in little pieces into her bowl of milk. Her spoon remained stand' ing in her coffee cup. It seemed impossible for me to be unaware of any detail that concerned her, either of gesture or prononciation. I noticed every tiniest de' tail whether I would or no. Her charm, I decided, increased. It was wholly in' dependent of her looks. It took me now and again by surprise, as it were.

"'Maybe—I suppose he didn't know where you were," she added, as Julius volunteered no word. "But he was shore you'd come if you got the letter."

"It was a promise," her husband put in quietly. Evidently he wished us to make acquaintance in our own way. He left us alone with purpose, content to watch and show his satisfaction. The relationship between them seemed natu' ral and happy, utterly devoid of the least sign of friction. She certainly—had I perhaps, anticipated otherwise?—showed no fear of him.

The "man" came in with a plate of butter, clattering out noisily again in his heavy boots. He gave us each a look in turn, of anxiety first, and then of pleas' ure. All was well with us, he felt. His eyes, however, lingered longest on his mis' tress, as though she needed his protective care more than we did. It was the at' titude and expression of a faithful dog who knows he has the responsibility of a child upon his shoulders, and is both proud and puzzled by the weight of honour.

A pause followed, during which I made more successful efforts to subdue the agitation that was in me. I broke the silence by a commonplace, expressing a hope that my late arrival the night before had not disturbed her.

"Lord, no!" she exclaimed, laughing gaily, while she glanced from me to Julius. "Only I thought you and he'd like to be alone for a bit after such a long time apart.... Besides, I didn't fancy my food somehow—I get that way up here sometimes," she added, "don't I, Julius?"

"You've been here some time already?" I asked sympathetically, before he could reply.

"Ever since the wedding," she answered frankly. "Seven—getting on for eight—months ago, it is now—we came up straight from the Registry Office. At times its a bit funny, an' no mistake—lonely, I mean," she quickly corrected herself. And she looked at her husband again with a kind of childish mischief in her expression that I thought most becoming.

"It's not for ever, is it?" he laughed with her.

"And I understand you chose it, didn't you?" I fell in with her mood. "It must be lonely, of course, sometimes," I added.

"Yes, we chose it," she replied. "We choose everything together." And they looked proudly at each other like two children. For a moment it flashed across me to challenge him playfully, yet not altogether playfully, for burying a young wife in such a deserted place. I did not yield to the temptation, however, and Mrs. LeVallon continued breezily in her off-hand manner:

"Julius wanted you badly, I know. You must stay here now we've got you. There's reelly lots to do, once you get used to it; only it seems strange at first after city life—like what I've had, and sometimes"—she hesitated a second—" well, of an evening, or when it gets stormy—the thunder-storms are something awful—you feel wild and want to do things, to rush about and take your clothes off." She stopped; and the deep green of the sea came up into her eyes. Again, for an instant, I caught two faces in her. "It turns you wild here when the wind gets to blowing," she added, laughing, "and the lightning's like loose, flying fire." The way she said it made me forget the physical disabilities. There was even a hint of fascination somewhere in the voice.

"It takes you back to the natural, primitive state," I said. "I can well believe it." And no amount of restraint could keep the admiration out of my eyes. "Civilisation is easily forgotten in a place like this."

"Oh, is that it?" she said shortly, while we laughed, all three together. "Civilisation—eh?"

I got the impression that she felt left out of something, something she knew was going on, but that didn't include her quite. Her intuition, I judged, was very keen. Beneath this ordinary conversation she was aware of many things. She was fully conscious of a certain subdued excitement in the three of us, and that between her husband and her guest there was a constant interplay of half-dis-

covered meaning, half-revealed emotion. She was reading me too. Yet all without deliberation; it was intuitive, the mind took no conscious part in it. And,
when she spoke of the effect of the valley upon her, I saw her suddenly a little
different, too—wild and free, untamed in a sense, and close to the elemental side
of life. Her enthusiasm for big weather betrayed it. During the whole of breakfast, indeed, we all were "finding" one another, Julius in particular making notes.
For him, of course, there was absorbing interest in this meeting of three souls
whom late had kept so long apart—the signs of recognition he detected or imagined, the sympathy, the intimacy betrayed by the way things were *taken for
granted* between us. He said no word, however. He was very quiet.

My own feelings, meanwhile, seemed tossed together in too great and violent
confusion for immediate disentanglement. My sense of the dramatic fitness of
things was worse than unsatisfied—it was shattered. Julius unquestionably had
married a superior domestic servant.

"Is the bread to your liking, Professor?"

"I think it's quite delicious, Mrs. LeVallon. It tempts me even to excess," I
added, facetious in my nervousness. I had used her name at last, but with an effort.

"I made it," she said proudly. "Mother taught me that before I was fifteen."

"And the butter, too?" I asked.

"No," she laughed, with a touch of playful disappointment. "We get that from
a farm five miles down the valley. It's in special honour of your arrival, this."

"Our nearest contact with the outside world," added Julius, "and over a thousand feet below us. We're on a little plateau here all by ourselves—"

"Put away like," she interrupted gaily, "as though we'd been naughty," and
then she added, "or for something special and very mysterious." She looked into
his face half archly, half inquisitively, as if aware of something she divined yet
could not understand. Her honesty and sincerity made every little thing she said
seem dignified. I was again aware of pathos.

"The peace and quiet," I put in quickly, conscious of something within me
that watched and listened intently, "must be delightful—after the cities—and
with the great storms you mention to break the possible monotony."

She looked at me a full moment steadily, and in her eyes, no longer green but
sky-blue, I read the approach of that strange expression I called another "face,"
that in the end, however, did not fully come. But the characteristic struck me,
for Julius had it too.

"O, you find out all about yourself in a place like this," she said slowly, "a
whole lot of things you didn't know before. You'll like it; but it's not for everybody. It's very elite." She turned to Julius. "The Professor'll love it, won't he?
And we must keep him," she repeated, "now we've got him."

Something moved between the three of us as she said it. There was no inclination in me to smile, even at the absurd choice of a word. An upheaving sense
of challenge came across the air at me, including not only ourselves at the breakfast table, but the entire valley as well. Against some subterranean door in me
rose sudden pressure, and the woman's commonplace words had in them some-

thing incalculable that caused the door to yield. Out rushed a pouring, bursting flood. A wild delight of beauty ran suddenly in my civilised veins; I felt uplifted, stimulated, carried off my feet.

It was but the flash and touch of a passing mood, of course, yet it marked a change in me, another change. *She* was aware of elemental powers even as her husband was. First through him, but now through her, I, too, was becoming similarly—aware.

I glanced at Julius, calmly devouring bread and milk beyond all reach of comedy—Julius who recognised an "old soul" in a servant girl with the same conviction that he invoked the deific Powers of a conscious Nature; to whom nothing was trivial, nothing final, the future magnificent as the past, and behind whose chair stood the Immensities whispering messages of his tireless evolutionary scheme. And I saw him "unclassable"—merely an eternal, travelling soul, working out with myself and with this other "soul" some detail long neglected by the three of us. Marriage, class, social status, education, culture—what were they but temporary external details, whose sole value lay in their providing conditions for acquiring certain definite experiences? Life's outer incidents were but episodic, after all.

And this flash of insight into his point of view came upon me thus suddenly through *her*. The mutual sympathy and understanding between the three of us that he so keenly watched for had advanced rapidly. Another stage was reached. The foundations seemed already established here among us.

Thus, while surprise, resentment and distress fought their battle within me against something that lay midway between disbelief and acceptance, my mind was aware of a disharmony that made judgment extremely difficult. Almost I knew the curious feeling that one of us had been fooled. It was all so incongruous and disproportioned, on the edge of the inconceivable. And yet, at the same time, some sense of keen delight awoke in me that satisfied. Joy glowed in some depth I could not reach or modify.

Had the "woman" proved wonderful in some ordinary earthly way, I could have continued to share in a kind of dramatic make-believe LeVallon's imagination of an "old soul" returned. The sense of fitness would have felt requited. Yet what so disconcerted me was that this commonplace disclosure of the actual facts did not destroy belief, but even increased it! This unexpected and banal *dénouement*, denying, apparently, all the requirements of his creed, fell upon me with a crash of reality that was arresting in an entirely unexpected way. It made the conception so much more likely—possible—true!

Out of some depth in me I could not summon to the bar of judgment or analysis rose the whisper that in reality the union of these two was not so incongruous and outrageous as it seemed. To a penetrating vision such as his, what difference could that varnish of the mind called "education" pretend to make? Or how could he be deceived by the surface tricks of "refinement," in accent, speech, and manner, that so often cloak essential crudeness and vulgarity? These were to him but the external equipment of a passing To-day, whereas he looked for the innate acquirements due to real experience—age in the soul itself. Her social status, education and so forth lead nothing to do with—her actual Self. In some ultimate region that superficial human judgment barely acknowledges the union of these two seemed right, appropriate and inevitably true.

This breakfast scene remains graven in my mind. LeVallon talked little, even as he ate little, while his wife and I satisfied our voracious appetites with the simple food provided. She chattered *sans gêne*, eating not ungracefully so much as in a manner untaught. Her smallest habits drew my notice and attention of their own accord. I watched the velvet band rising and falling as she swallowed—noisily, talking and drinking with her mouth full, and holding her knife after the manner of the servants' hall. Her pronunciation at times was more than marked. For instance, though she did not say "gime," she most assuredly did not say "game," and her voice, what men call "common," was undeniably of the upper servant class. While guilty now and again of absurd solecisms, she chose words sometimes that had an air of refinement above the ordinary colloquial usage—the kind affected by a lady's-maid who has known service in the "upper suckles" of the world—"close" the door in place of simply "shut" it, "commence" in preference to the ordinary "begin," "costume" rather than merely "clothes," and a hundred others of similar kind. Sofa, again, was "couch." She missed a sentence, and asked for it with "What say?" while her "if you please" and "pardon" held a suspicion of that unction which, it seemed, only just remembered in time not to add "sir," or even "my lady." She halted instinctively before a door, as though to let her husband or myself pass out in front, and even showed surprise at being helped at the table before ourselves. These and a thousand other revealing touches I noticed acutely, because I had expected something so absolutely different. I was profoundly puzzled.

Yet, while I noted closely these social and mental disabilities, I was aware also of their flat and striking contradiction; and her beautifully-shaped hands, her small, exquisite feet and ankles, her natural dignity of carriage, gesture, hearing, were the least of these. Setting her beside maid or servitor, my imagination recoiled as from something utterly ill-placed. I could have sworn she owned some secret pedigree that no merely menial position could affect, most certainly not degrade. In spite of less favourable indications, so thick about her, I caught unmistakable tokens of a superiority she herself ignored, which yet proclaimed that her soul stood erect and four-square to the winds of life, independent wholly of the "social position" her body with its untutored brain now chanced to occupy.

Exactly the nature of these elusive signs of innate nobility I find it more than difficult to describe. They rose subtly out of her, yet evaded separate subtraction from either the gestures or conversation that revealed them. They explained the subtle and increasing charm. They were of the soul.

For, even thus early in our acquaintance, there began to emerge these other qualities in this simple girl that at first the shock of disappointment and surprise had hidden from me. The apparent emptiness of her face was but a mask that cloaked an essential, native dignity. From time to time, out of those strange, arresting eyes that at first had seemed all youth and surface, peered forth that other look, standing a moment to query and to judge, then, like moods of sky which reveal and hide a depth of sea, plunged out of sight again. It betrayed an inner, piercing sight of a far deeper kind. Out of this deeper part of her I felt she watched me steadily—to wonder, ask, and weigh. It was hence, no doubt, I had the curious impression of two faces, two beings, in her, and the moments when I surprised her peering thus were, in a manner, electrifying beyond words. For then, into tone and gesture, conquering even accent and expression, crept flash-like this "something" that would not be denied, hinting at the distinction of true spiritual independence superior to all local, temporary, or worldly divisions implied in mere "class" or "station."

This girl, behind her ignorance of life's snobbish values, possessed that indefinable spiritual judgment best called "taste." And taste, I remember Julius held, was the infallible evidence of a soul's maturity—of age. The phrase "old soul" acquired more meaning for me as I watched her. I recalled that strange hint of his long years before, that greatness and position, as the world accepts them, are actually but the kindergarten stages for the youngest, crudest souls of all. The older souls are not "distinguished" in the "world." They are beyond it.

Moreover, during the course of this singular first meal together, while she used the phraseology of the servant class and betrayed the manners of what men call "common folk," it was borne in upon me that she, too, unknowingly, touched the same vast sources of extended life that her husband claimed to realise, and that her being unknowingly swept that region of elemental Powers with which he now sought conscious union. In her infectious vitality beat the pulse of vaster tides than she yet knew.

Already, in our conversation, this had come to me; it increased from minute to minute as our atmospheres combined and mingled. The suggestion of what I must call great exterior Activities that always accompanied the presence of Julius made themselves felt also through the being of this simple and uneducated girl. Winds, cool and refreshing, from some elemental region blew soundlessly about her. I was aware of their invigorating currents. And this came to me with my first emotions, and was not due to subsequent reflection. For, in my own case, too, while resenting the admission, I felt something more generously scaled than my normal self, scientifically moulded, trying to urge up as with great arms and hands that thrust into my mind. What hitherto had seemed my complete Self opened, as though it were but a surface tract, revealing depths of consciousness unguessed before.

And this, I think, was the disquieting sensation that perplexed me chiefly with a sense of unstable equilibrium. The idea of pre-existence, with its huge weight of memory lost and actions undischarged, pressed upon a portion of my soul that was trying to awake. The foundations of my known personality appeared suddenly insecure, and what the brain denied, this other part accepted, even half remembered. The change of consciousness in me was growing. While observing Mrs. LeVallon, listening to the spontaneous laughter that ran between her sentences, meeting her quick eyes that took in everything about them, these varied and contradictory judgments of my own worked their inevitable effect upon me. The quasi-memory, with its elusive fragrance of far-off, forgotten things; the promised reconstruction of passionate emotions that had burned the tissues of our earlier bodies before even the foundations of these "eternal" hills were laid; the sense of being again among ancient friends, netted by deathless forces of spiritual adventure and desire—Julius, his wife, myself, mutually involved in the intricate pattern of our souls' development:—all this, while I strove to regard it as mere telepathic reflection from his own beliefs, yet made something in me, deeper than any ratiocination, stand up and laugh in my face with the authoritative command that it was absolutely—true.

Our very intimacy, so readily established as of its own accord—established, moreover, among such unlikely and half antagonistic elements—seemed to hint at a relationship resumed, instead of now first beginning. The fact that the three of us took so much for granted almost suggested memory. For the near presence of this woman—I call her woman, though she was but girl—disturbed me more than uncommonly; and this curious, soft delight I felt raging in the depths of me—whence did it come? Whence, too, the depth and power of other feelings that she roused in me, their reckless quality, their certainty, the haunting pang and charm that her face, not even pretty apart from its disfigurement, stirred in my inmost being? There was mischief and disaster in her sea-green eyes, though neither mischief nor disaster quite of this material world.

I confessed—the first time for many years—to something moving beyond ordinary. More and more I longed to learn of her first meeting with the man she had married, and by what method he claimed to have recognised in this servant girl the particular ancient soul he waited for, and by what unerring instinct he had picked her out and set her upon so curious a throne.

I watched the velvet band about the well-shaped neck....

> "I have been here before,
>   But when or how I cannot tell:
> I know the grass beyond the door,
>   The sweet keen smell,
> The sighing sound, the lights around the shore.
>
> "You have been mine before,
>   How long ago I may not know:
> But just when at that swallow's soar
>   Your neck turned so...
> Some veil did fall—I knew it all of yore."

"And now," she exclaimed, springing up and turning to her husband, "I'm going to leave you and the Professor together to talk out all your old things without me intervening! Besides I've got the bread to make," she added with a swift, gay smile in my direction, "that bread you called delicious. I generally do it of a morning."

With a swinging motion of her lithe young body she was gone; the room seemed strangely empty; the disfiguring marks upon her girlish face were already forgotten; and a sense of companionship within me turned somehow lonely and bereft.

CHAPTER XVIII

To MEMORY

"Yet, when I would command thee hence,
Thou mockest at the vain pretence,
Murmuring in mine ear a song
Once loved, alas! forgotten long;
And on my brow I feel a kiss
That I would rather die than miss."
—Mary Coleridge.

"Well?" Julius asked me, as we strolled across the pastures that skirted the main forest, "and does it seem anywhere familiar to you—the three of us together again? You recall—how much?" A rather wistful smile passed over his face, but the eyes were grave. He was in earnest if ever man was. "She doesn't seem wholly a stranger to you?"

My mind searched carefully for words. To refer to any of my recent impressions was difficult, even painful, and frank discussion of my friend's wife impossible—though, probably, there was nothing Julius would not have understood and even welcomed.

"I—cannot deny," I began, "that somewhere—in my imagination, perhaps, there seems—"

He interrupted me at once. "Don't suppress the imaginative pictures—they're memory. To deny them is only to forget again. Let them come freely in you."

"Julius!" I exclaimed, conscious that I flushed a little, "but she is wonderful; superior, too, in some magnificent way to—any—"

"Lady," he came abruptly to my assistance, no vestige of annoyance visible.

"To anyone of our own class," I completed the sentence more to my liking. "I admit I feel drawn to her—in a kind of understanding sympathy—though how can I pretend that I—that this sense of familiarity is really memory?" It was impossible to treat him lightly; his belief was his life, commanding a respect due to all great convictions of the soul. "You have found someone you can love," I went on, aware that it gave me no pleasure to say it, "and someone who loves you. I—am delighted."

He turned to me, standing hatless, the sunlight in his face, his eyes fixed steadily upon my own.

"We had to meet—all three," he said slowly; "sooner or later. It's an old, old debt we've got to settle up together, and the opportunity has come at last. I only ask your sympathy—and hers." He shrugged his shoulders slightly. "To you it may seem a small thing, and, if you have no memory, a wild, impossible thing as well, even with delusion in it. But nothing is really small." He paused. "I only ask that you shall not resist." And then he added gravely: "The risk is mine."

I felt uneasiness; the old schooldays' basis of complete sincerity was not in me quite. I had lived too long in the world of ordinary men and women. His marriage seemed prompted by an impersonal sense of justice to the universe rather than by any desire for the companionship and sweetness that a woman's love could give him. For a moment I knew not what to say. Could such a view be hers as well? Had she yielded herself to him upon a similar understanding? And if not—the thought afflicted me—might not this debt he spoke of have been discharged without claiming the whole life of another in a union that involved also physical ties?

Yet, while I could not find it in me to utter all I thought, there was a burning desire to hear details of the singular courtship. Almost I felt the right to know, yet shrank from asking it.

"Then nothing more definite stirs in you?" he asked quietly, his eyes still holding mine, "no memory you can recognise? No wave of feeling; no picture, even of that time when we—we three—"

"Julius, old friend," I exclaimed with sudden impulsiveness, and hardly knowing why I said it, "it only seems to me that these pine woods behind you are out of the picture rather. They should be palms, with spaces of sand shimmering in a hot sun. And the châlet"—pointing over his shoulder—"seems still less to belong to you when I recall the temples we talked about before the plain where the worship of the rising sun took place—"

I broke off abruptly with a little shamefaced laughter: my invention, or imagination, seemed so thin. But Julius turned eagerly, his face alight.

"Laugh as you please," he said, "but what makes you feel me out of the picture, as you call it, *is* memory—memory of where we three were last together. That sense of incongruity is memory. Don't resist. Let the pictures rise and grow as they will. And don't deny any instinctive feelings that come to you—they're memory too. "

A moment of revolt swept over me, yet with it an emotion both sweet and painful. Dread and delight both troubled me. Unless I resisted, his great conviction would carry me away again as of old. And what if she should come to aid him? What if she should bring the persuasion of her personality to the attack, and with those eyes of mischief and disaster ask me questions out of a similar conviction and belief? If she should hold me face to face: "Do you remember me—*as I remember you?*"

"Julius," I cried, "let me speak plainly at once and so prevent your disappointment later." I forced the words out against my will, it seemed. "For the truth, my dear fellow, is simply—that I remember—nothing! Definitely—I remember nothing."

Yet there was pain and sadness in me suddenly. I had prevaricated. Almost I had told a lie. Some vague fear of involving myself in undesirable consequences had forced me against my innate knowledge. Almost I had denied—her.

From the forest stole forth a breath too soft and perfumed for an autumn wind. It stirred the hair upon his forehead, left its touch of dream upon my cheeks, then passed on to lift a wreath of mist in the fields below. And, as though a spirit older than the wind moved among my thoughts, this modern world seemed less real when it had gone. I heard the voice of Julius answering me. His words came very slowly, fastening upon my own. The resentment, the disappointment I had looked for were not there, nor the comparison of myself—in her favour—I had half anticipated.

The answer utterly nonplussed me:

"Neither does she remember—anything."

I started. A curious pang shot through me—something of regret, even of melancholy in it. That she had forgotten "everything" was pain. She had forgotten me.

"But we you, I mean—can make her?"

The words were out impulsively before I could prevent them. He did not look at me. I did not look at him.

"I should have put it differently, perhaps," he answered. "She is not *aware* that she remembers."

He drew me further along the dewy meadow towards the upper valley, and drew me deeper, as it seemed, into his own strange region whence came these perplexing statements.

"But, Julius," I stammered, seeing that he kept silence, "if she remembers nothing—how could you know—how could you feel sure, when you met her—?"

My sentences stopped dead. Even in these unusual circumstances it was not possible to question a friend about the woman he had married. Had she proved some marvel of physical beauty or of intellectual attainment, curiosity might have been taken as a compliment. But as it was—!

Yet all the time I *knew* that her insignificant worldly value was a clean stroke of proof that he had not suffered himself to be deceived in this recovery and recognition of the spiritual maturity he meant by the term "old soul." His voice reached me, calm and normal as though he talked about the weather. "I'll tell you," he said, "for it's interesting, and, besides, you have the right to know."

And the words fell among my tangled thoughts like deft fingers that put confusion straight. The incredible story he told me as a child might relate a fairy-tale it knows is true, yet thinks may not be quite believed. Without the slightest emphasis, and certainly without the least embarrassment or sense that it was unusual. Even of comedy I was not properly once aware. All through the strange recital rang in my mind, "She is not aware that she remembers."

" 'The Dardanelles,' " he began, smiling a little as though at the recollection, "was where I met her, thus recovered. Not on the way from Smyrna to Constantinople; oh, no! It was not romantic in that little sense. 'The Dardanelles' was a small and ugly red-brick villa in Upper Norwood, with a drive ten yards long, ragged laurel bushes, and a green five-barred gate, gold-lettered. Maennlich lives there—the Semitic language man and Egyptologist; you know. She was his parlour-maid at the time, and before that had been lady's-maid to the daughter of some undistinguished duchess. In this way," he laughed softly, "may old souls wait upon the young ones sometimes! Her father," he continued, "was a market-gardener and fruiterer in a largish way at East Croydon, and she herself had been brought up upon the farm whence his supplies came. 'Chance,' as they call it, led her into these positions I have mentioned, and so, inevitably—to me."

He looked up at me a moment. "And so to you as well."

His manner was composed and serious. He spoke with the simple conviction of some Christian who traces the Hand of God in the smallest details of his daily life, and seeks His guidance in his very train journeys. There was something rather superb about it all.

"A fruiterer in East Croydon! A maid in service! And—you knew—you recognised her?"

"At once. The very first day she let me in at the front door and asked if I wished to see her master, what name she might announce, and so forth."

"It was all—er—unexpected and sudden like that?" came the question from a hundred others that crowded together in me. "To find a lost friend of years only—in such a way—the shock, I mean, to you—!" I simply could not find my words. He told it all so calmly, naturally. "You were wholly unprepared, weren't you? Nothing had led you to expect?" I ended with a dash.

"Not wholly unprepared," was his rejoinder; "nor was the meeting altogether unexpected—on my side, that is. Intimations, as I told you at Motfield Close twenty years ago—when she was born—had come to me. No soul draws breath for the first time, without a quiver of response running through all that lives. Souls intimately connected with each other may feel the summons. There are ways! I knew that she was once more in the world, that, like ourselves, her soul had reincarnated and ever since I have been searching—"

"Searching—!"

"There are clues that offer themselves—that come, perhaps in sleep, perhaps by direct experiment, and, regardless of space, give hints—"

"Psychometry?" I asked, remembering a word just coined.

He shrugged his shoulders. "All objects radiate," he said, "no matter how old they are. Their radiation never ceases till they are disintegrated; and if you are sensitive you can receive their messages. If you have certain powers, due to relation and affinity, you may interpret them. There is an instantaneous linking-up—in picture-form—impossible to mistake."

"You knew, then, she was somewhere on the earth—waiting for you?" I repeated, wondering what was coming next. That night in the Edinburgh lodgings, when he had been "searching," came back to me.

"For *us*," he corrected me. "It was something from a Private Collection that gave me the clue by which I finally traced her—something from the older sands."

"The sands! Egyptian?"

Julius nodded. "Egypt, for all of us, was a comparatively recent section—nearer to To-day, I mean. Many a time has each of us been back there—Thebes,

Memphis, even as lately ago as Alexandria at its zenith, learning, developing, reaping what ages before we sowed—for in Egypt the knowledge that was *our* knowledge survived longer than anywhere else. Yet never, unfortunately, re-turning together, and thus never finding the opportunity to achieve the great purpose of our meeting."

"Put the clue?" I asked breathlessly.

He smiled again at the eagerness that again betrayed me.

"This old world," he resumed quietly, "is strewn, of course, with the remnants of what once has been our bodies—'suits of clothes' we have inhabited, used, and cast aside. Here and there, from one chance or another, some of these may have been actually preserved. The Egyptians, for instance, went to considerable trouble to ensure that they should survive as long as possible, thus assisting mem-ory later."

"Embalming, you mean?"

"As you wander through the corridors of a modern museum," he continued imperturbably, "you may even look through a glass covering at the very tene-ment your soul has occupied at an earlier stage! Probably, of course, without the faintest whisper of recognition, yet, possibly, with just that acute and fascinated interest which *is* the result of stirring memory. For the 'old clothes' still radi-ate vibrations that belong to *you; the* dried blood and nerves once thrilled with emotions, spiritual or otherwise, that were you—the link may be recoverable. You think it is wild nonsense! I tell you it is in the best sense scientific. And, similarly," he added, "you may chance upon some such remnant of another— the body of ancient friend or enemy." He paused abruptly in his extraordinary recital. "I had that good fortune," he added, "if you like to call it so."

"You found *hers?*" I asked in a low voice. "Her, I mean?"

"Maennlich," he replied with a smile, "has the best preserved mummies in the world. He never allowed them even to he unwrapped. The object I speak of— a body she had occupied in a recent Egyptian section—though not when *we* were there, unfortunately—lay in one of his glass cases, while the soul who once had used it answered his bell and walked across his carpets—two of her bod-ies in the house at once. Curious, wasn't it? A discarded instrument and the one in present use! The rest was comparatively easy. I traced her whereabouts at once, for the clue furnished the plainest possible directions. I went straight to her."

"And you knew instantly—when you saw her? You had no doubt?"

"Instantly—when the door swung open and our eyes met on the threshold."

"Love at first sight, Julius, you mean? It was love you felt?" I asked it beneath my breath, for my heart was beating strangely.

He raised his eyebrows. "Love?" he repeated, questioningly. "Deep joy, in-tuitive sympathy, content and satisfaction, rather. I knew her. I knew who she was. In a few minutes we were more intimate in mind and feeling than souls who meet for the first time can become after years of living together. You under-stand?"

I lowered my eyes, not knowing what to say. The standards of modern conduct, so strong about me, prevented the comments or questions that I longed to utter.

There flashed upon me in that instant's pause a singular conviction—that these two had mated for a reason of their own. They had not known the clutch of elemental power by which Nature ensures the continuance of the race. They had not shuddered, wept, and known the awful ecstasy, but had slipped between her fingers and escaped. They had not loved. While he knew this consciously, she was aware of it unconsciously. They mated for another reason, yet one as holy, as noble, as pure—if not more so, indeed—as those that consecrate marriage in the accepted sense. And the thought, strange as it was, brought a sweet pleasure to me, though shot with a pain that was equally undeniable and equally perplexing. While my thoughts floundered between curiosity, dismay and something elusive that yet was more clamorous than either, Julius continued without a vestige of embarrassment, though obviously omitting much detail that I burned to hear.

"And that very week—the next day, I think, it was—I asked Maennlich to allow me an hour's talk with her alone—"

"She—er—?"

"She liked me—from the very first, yes. She felt me."

"And showed it?" I asked bluntly.

"And showed it," he repeated, "although she said it puzzled her and she couldn't understand."

"On her side, then, it was love—love at first sight?"

"Strong attraction," he put it, "but an attraction she thought it her duty to resist at first. Her present conditions made any relationship between us seem incongruous, and when I offered marriage—as I did at once—it overwhelmed her. She made sensible objections, but it was her brain of To-day that made them. You can imagine how it went. She urged that to marry a man in another class of life, a 'gentleman,' a 'wealthy' gentleman and an educated, 'scholar gentleman,' as she called me, could only end in unhappiness—because I should tire of her. Yet, all the time—she told me this afterwards—she had the feeling that we were meant for one another, and that it must surely be. She was shy about it as a child."

"And you convinced her in the end!" I said to myself rather than aloud to him. There were feelings in me I could not disentangle.

"Convinced her that we needed one another and could never go apart," he said. "We had something to fulfil together. The forces that drove us together, though unintelligible to her, were yet acknowledged by her too, you see."

"I see," my voice murmured faintly, as he seemed to expect some word in reply. "I see." Then, after a longer pause than usual, I asked: "And you told her of your—your theories and beliefs—the purpose you had to do together?"

"No single word. She could not possibly have understood. It would have frightened her." I heard it with relief, yet with resentment too.

"Was that quite fair, do you think?"

His answer I could not gainsay. "Cause and effect," he said, "work out,

whether memory is there or not. To attempt to block fulfilment by fear or shrinking is but to delay the very thing you need. I told her we were necessary to each
other, but that she must come willingly, or not at all. I used no undue persuasion, and I used no force. I realised plainly that her upper, modern, uncultured
and uneducated self was merely what she had acquired in the few years of her
present life. It was this upper self that hesitated and felt shy. The older self below was not awake, yet urged her to acceptance blindly—as by irresistible instinctive choice. She knew subconsciously; but, once I could succeed in arous-
ing her knowledge consciously, I knew her doubts would vanish. I suggested
living away from city life, away from any conditions that might cause her annoyance or discomfort due to what she called our respective 'stations' in life; I
suggested the mountains, some beautiful valley perhaps, where in solitude for
a time we could get to know each other better, untroubled by the outer
world—until she became accustomed—"

"And she approved?" I interrupted with impatience.

"Her words were 'That's the very thing; I've always had a dream like that.'
She agreed with enthusiasm, and the opposition melted away. She knew the kind
of place we needed," he added significantly.

We had reached the head of the valley by this time, and I sat down upon a
boulder with the sweep of Jura forests below us like a purple carpet. The sun
and shadow splashed it everywhere with softest colouring. The morning wind
was fresh; birds were singing; this green vale among the mountains seemed some
undiscovered paradise.

"And you have never since felt a moment's doubt—uncertainty—that she really is this 'soul' you knew before?"

He lay back, his head upon his folded hands, and his eyes fixed upon the blue
dome of sky.

"A hundred proofs come to me all the time," he said, stretching himself at full
length upon the grass. "And in her atmosphere, in her presence, the memories
still revive in detail from day to day—just as at school they revived in you—
those pictures you sought to stifle and deny. From the first she never doubted
me. She was aware of a great tie and bond between us. 'You're the only man,'
she said to me afterwards, 'that could have done it like that. I belonged to you—
oh! I can't make it out—but just as if there wasn't any getting out of it possible. I felt stunned when I saw you. I had always felt something like this coming, but thought it was a dream.' Only she often said there was something else
to come as well, and that we were not quite complete. She knew, you see; she
knew." He broke off suddenly and turned to look at me. He added in a lower
tone, as he watched my face: "And you see how pleased and happy she is to have
you here!"

I made no reply. I reached out for a stone and flung it headlong down the steep
slope towards the stream five hundred feet below.

"And so it was settled then and there?" I asked, after a pause that Julius
seemed inclined to prolong.

"Then and there," he said, watching the rolling stone with dreamy eyes. "In the hall-way of that Norwood villa, under the very eyes of Maennlich who paid her wages and probably often scolded her, she came up into my arms at the end of our final talk, and kissed me like a happy child. She cried a good deal at the time, but I have never once seen her cry since!"

"And it's all gone well—these months?" I murmured.

"There was a temporary reaction at first—at the very first, that is," he said, "and I had to call in Maennlich to convince her that I was in earnest. At her bidding I did that. Some instinct told her that Maennlich ought to see it—perhaps, because it would save her awkward and difficult explanations afterwards. There's the woman in her, you see, the normal, wholesome woman, sweet and timid."

"A fascinating personality," I murmured quickly, lest I might say other things—before their time.

"No looks, no worldly beauty," he nodded, "but the unconscious charm of the old soul. It's unmistakable."

Worlds and worlds I would have given to have been present at that interview; Julius LeVallon, so unusual and distinguished; the shy and puzzled serving-maid, happy and incredulous; the grey-bearded archæologist and scholar; the strange embarrassment of this amazing proposal of marriage!

"And Maennlich?" I asked, anxious for more detail.

Julius burst out laughing. "Maennlich lives in his own world with his specimens and theories and memories of travel—more recent memories of travel than our own! It hardly interested him for more than a passing moment. He regarded it, I think, as an unnecessary interruption—and a bothering one—some joke he couldn't quite appreciate or understand. He pulled his dirty beard, patted me on the back as though I were a boy running after some theatre girl, and remarked with a bored facetiousness that he could give her a year's character with a clear conscience and great pleasure. Something like that it was; I forget exactly. Then he went back to his library, shouting through the door some appointment about a Geographical Society meeting for the following week. For how could he know"—his voice grew softer as he said it and his laughter ceased—"how could he divine, that old literal-minded savant, that he stood before a sign-post along the route to the eternal things we seek, or that my marrying his servant was a step towards something we three owe together to the universe itself?"

It was some time before either of us spoke, and when at length I broke the silence it was to express surprise that a woman, so long ripened by the pursuit of spiritual, or at least exalted aims, should have returned to earth among the lowly. By rights, it seemed, she should have reincarnated among the great ones of the world. I knew I could say this now without offence.

"The humble," Julius answered simply, "*are* the great ones."

His fingers played with the fronds of a piece of staghorn moss as he said it, and to this day I cannot see this kind of moss without remembering his strange words.

"It's among what men call the lower ranks that the old souls return," he went on; "among peasants and simple folk, unambitious and heedless of material power, you always find the highest ones. They are there to learn the final lessons of service or denial, neglected in their busier and earlier—kindergarten sections. The last stages are invariably in humble service—they are by far the most difficult; no young, 'ambitious' soul could manage it. But the old souls, having already mastered all the more obvious lessons, are content."

"Then the oldest souls are not the great minds and great characters of history?" I exclaimed.

"Not necessarily," he answered; "probably never. The most advanced are unadvertised, in the least assuming positions. The Kingdom of Heaven belongs to them, hard of attainment by those the world applauds. The successful, so called, are the younger, cruder souls, passionately acquiring still the external prizes men hold so dear. Maturer souls have long since discarded these as worthless. The qualities the world crowns are great, perhaps, at that particular stage, but they never are the highest. Intellect, remember, is not of the soul, and all that reason teaches must he unlearned again. Theories change, knowledge shifts, facts are forgotten or proved false; only what the soul itself acquires remains eternally the same. The old are the intuitional; and the oldest of all—ah! how wonderful!—He who came back from loftier heights than most of us can yet even conceive of, was the—son of a carpenter."

I left my seat upon the boulder and lay beside him, listening for a long time while he talked, and if there was much that seemed visionary, there was also much that thrilled me with emotions beyond ordinary. Nothing, certainly, was foolish—because of the man who said it. And, while he took it for granted that all Nature was alive and a manifestation of spiritual powers, the elements themselves but forces to be mastered and acquired, it grew upon me that I had indeed entered an enchanted valley where, with my strange companions, I might witness new, incredible things. Finding little to reply, I was content to listen, wondering what was coming next. And in due course the talk came round again to ourselves, and so to the woman who was now his wife.

"Then she has no idea," I said at length, "that we three—you and I and she—have been together before, or that there is any particular purpose in my being here at this moment?"

"In her normal condition—none," he answered. "For she has no memory."

"There is a state, however, when she does remember?" I asked. "You have helped her to remember? Is that it, Julius?"

"Yes," he replied; "I have reached down and touched her soul, so that she remembers for herself."

"The deep trance state?"

"Where all the memories of the past lie accumulated," he answered, "the subconscious state. Her Self of Today—with new body and recent brain—she has forgotten; in trance—the subconscious Self where the soul dwells with all its past—she remembers."

CHAPTER XIX

*"Proof of the reality of a personal sovereign of the universe will not be obtained.
But proof of the reality of a power or powers, not unworthy of the title of gods, in*
respect of our corner of the cosmos, *may be feasible."*—"The Individual and Reality" (E. D. Fawcett).

I shrank. Certain memories of our Edinburgh days revived unpleasantly.
They seemed to have happened yesterday instead of years ago. A shadowy
hand from those distant skies he spoke of, from those dim avenues of
thickly written Time, reached down and touched my heart, leaving the chill of
an indescribable uneasiness. The change in me since my arrival only a few hours
before was too rapid not to bring reaction. Yet on the whole the older, deeper
consciousness gained power.

Possibilities my imagination had unwisely played with now seemed stealing
slowly toward probabilities. I felt as a man might feel who, having never
known fire, and disbelieved in its existence, becomes aware of the warmth of
its approach—a strange and revolutionary discomfort. For Julius was winning
me back into his world again, and not with mere imaginative, half-playful acceptance, but with practical action and belief. Yet the change in me was somehow welcome. No feeling of resentment kept it in check, and certainly neither
scorn nor ridicule. Incredulity glanced invitingly at faith. They would presently
shake hands.

I made, perhaps, an effort to hold back, to define the position, my position,
at any rate.

"Julius," I said gravely, yet with a sympathy I could not quite conceal, "as boys
together, and even later at the University, we talked of various curious things,
remarkable, even amazing things. You even showed me certain extraordinary
things which, at the time, convinced me possibly. I ought to tell you now—and
before we go any further, since you take it for granted that my feelings and—
er—beliefs are still the same as yours—that I can no longer subscribe to all the
articles of your wild conviction. I have been living in the world, you see, these
many years, and—well, my imagination has collapsed or dried up or whatever
you like to call it. I don't really see, or remember—anything—quite in the way
you mean—"

"The 'world' has smothered it—temporarily," he put in gently.

"And what is more," I continued, ignoring his interruption, "I must confess
that I have no stomach now for any 'great experiment' such as you think our
coming together in this valley must involve. Your idea of reincarnation may be
true—why not? It's a most logical conception. And we three may have been
together before—granted I admit I rather like the notion. It may even be conceivable that the elemental powers of Nature are intelligent, that men and

women could use them to their advantage, and that worship and feeling-with is the means to acquire them—it's just as likely as that some day we shall send telegrams without wires, thoughts and pictures too!"

I drew breath a moment, while he waited patiently, linking his arm in mine and listening silently.

"It may even be possible, too," I went on, finding some boyish relief in all these words, "that we three together in earlier days did—in some kind of primitive Nature Worship—make wrong use of an unconscious human body to evoke those particular Powers you say exist behind Wind and Fire, and that, having thus upset the balance of material forces, we must readjust that balance or suffer accordingly—you in particular, since you were the prime mover—"

"How well you state it," he murmured. "How excellent your memory is after all."

"But even so," I continued, nettled by his calm interpretation of my long and plodding objection, "and even if all you claim is true—I—I mean bluntly—that the transitory acceptance you woke in me years ago no longer holds. I am with you now merely to keep a promise, a boy's promise, but my heart is no longer in the matter—except out of curiosity—curiosity pure and simple."

I stopped, or rather it was his face and the expression in his eyes that stopped me. I felt convicted of somewhat pompous foolishness, my sense of humour and proportion gone awry. Fear, with its ludicrous inhibitions, made me strut in this portentous fashion. His face, wearing the child's expression of belief and confidence, arrested me by its sheer simplicity. But the directness of his rejoinder, however—of his words, at least, for it was not a reply—struck me dumb.

"You are afraid for her," he said without a trace of embarrassment or emotion, "because you love her still, even as she loves you—beneath."

If unconsciously or consciously I avoided his eye, he made no attempt to avoid my own. He looked calmly at me like some uncannily clairvoyant lawyer who has pierced the elaborate evasions of his cross-examined witness—yet a witness who believed in his own excuses, quite honestly self-deceived.

At first the shock of his words deprived me of any power to think. I was not offended, I was simply speechless. He forgot who I was and what my life had been, forgot my relation with himself, forgot also the brevity of my acquaintance with his wife. He forgot, too, that I had accepted her, an inferior woman, accepted her without a hint of regret—nay, let me use the word I mean—of contempt that he, my friend, had linked his life with such a being—married her. And, further, he forgot all that was due to himself, to me, to her! It was too distressing. What could he possibly think of me, himself, of her, that so outrageous a statement, and without a shred of evidence, could pass his lips? I, a middle-aged professor of geology, with an established position in the world! And she, a parlour-maid he had been wild enough to marry for the sake of some imagined dream, a woman, moreover, I had seen for the first time a short hour before, and with whom I had exchanged a few sentences in bare politeness, remembering that this uneducated creature was the wife of my old friend, and—!

Thought galloped on in indignant disorder and agitation. The pretence was

so apparent even to myself. But I remained speechless. For while he spoke, looking me calmly in the eye, without a sign of *arrière pensée*, I realised in a flash—
that it all was true. Like the witness who still believes in his indignant answers
until the lawyer puts questions that confound him by unexpected self-revelation—I suddenly saw—myself. My own heart opened in a blaze of fire. It was
the truth.

And all this came upon me, not in a flash, but in a series of flashes. I had not
known it. I now discovered myself, but for the first time. Layer after layer
dropped away. The naked fact shone clearly.

"It is exactly what I hoped," he went on quietly. "It proves memory beyond
all further doubt. A love like yours and hers can never die. Even another thirty
thousand years could make no difference—the instant you met you would be
bound to take it up again—exactly where you left it off—no matter how long
the interval of separation. The first sign would be this divine and natural intimacy."

"Of course."

How I said it passes my understanding. I swear my lips moved without my
mind's consent. The words slipped out. I couldn't help myself. The same instant
some words he had used in our Edinburgh days came back to me: that human
love was somehow necessary to him, since love was the greatest power in the
world, the supreme example of "feeling-with." Without its aid—that majestic
confidence it brings—his great experiment must be impossible and fail. That
union which is love was necessary.

I felt an extraordinary exultation, an extraordinary tumult of delight, and—
a degrading flush of shame. I felt myself blushing under his quiet gaze while the
blood rushed over neck and cheeks and forehead. Both guilty and innocent I felt.
The very sun and trees, it seemed, witnessed my nakedness. I stumbled as I
moved beside my friend, and it was my friend who caught my arm and steadied me.

"Good God, Julius," I remember stammering, "but what in the name of
heaven are you saying?"

"The truth," he answered, smiling. "And do not for a moment think of me
as unnatural or a monster. For this is all inevitable and right and good. It means
our opportunity has come at last. It also means that you have not failed me."

I was glad he went on talking. I am a fool, I know it. I am weak, susceptible
and easily influenced. I have no claim to any strength of character, nor ever had.
But, without priggishness or self-righteousness, I can affirm that hitherto I have
never done another man deliberate, conscious injury, or wronged a personal
friend—never in all my days. I can say that, and for the satisfaction of my conscience I did say it, and kept on saying it in my thought while listening to the
next words that Julius uttered there beside me.

"And so, quite naturally, from your point of view," he pursued, "you are
afraid for *her*. I am delighted; for it proves again the strength of the ineradicable, ancient tie. My union, remember, is not, properly speaking, love it is the
call of sympathy, of friendship, of something that we have to do together, of a

claim that has the drive of all the universe behind it. And if I have felt it wise and right and necessary to"—he must have felt the shudder down the arm he held, for he said it softly, even tenderly—"give to her a child, it is because her entire nature needs it, and maternity is the woman's first and ultimate demand of her present stage in life. Without it she is never quite complete..."

"A child!"

"A child," he repeated firmly but with a kind of reverent gravity, "for otherwise her deepest functions are not exercised and—"

"And?" I asked, noticing the slight pause he made.

"The soul—her complete and highest self—never takes full possession of her body. It hovers outside. She misses the full, entire object of her reincarnation. The child, you see, was necessary—for her sake as well as for my own—for ours."

Thought, speech and action—all three stood still in me. I stopped in my walk, half paralysed. I remember we sat down.

"And she," I said at length, "knows nothing—of all this?"

"She," he replied, "knows everything, and is content. Her mind and brain of To-day may remain aware; but she—the soul now fully in her—knows and is content, as you shall see. She has her debt to as well as myself—and you."

For a long time we sat there silent in that sweet September sunshine. The birds sang round us, the rivulet went murmuring, the branches sighed and rustled just behind us, as though no problems vexed their safe, unconscious lives. Yet to me just then they all seemed somehow to participate in this complex plot of human emotion. Nature herself in some deep fashion was involved.

No man, I realised, knows himself, nor understands the acts of which he is potentially capable, until certain conditions bring them out. We imagine we know exactly how we should act in given circumstances—until those circumstances actually arrive and dislocate all our preconceived decisions. For the "given circumstances" produce emotions before whose stress—not realised when the decisions were so lightly made—we act quite otherwise. I could have sworn, for instance, that in a case like this—incredible though its ever happening must have seemed—I should then and there have taken my departure. I should have left. I would have gone without a moment's hesitation, and let him follow his own devices without my further assistance at any rate. I would have been furious with anyone who dared to state the contrary.

Yet it was exactly the opposite I did. The first instinct to clear out of this outrageous situation—proved impossible. It was not for her I remained; it was equally not for him; and it was assuredly not for myself in any meaning of the words. But yet I stayed. I could no more have gone away than I could have—made love to her before his eyes, or even not before his eyes. I argued, reasoned, moralized—but I stayed. It was over very soon—what there was of doubt and hesitation. While we sat there side by side upon that sunny mountain slope, I came to the clear decision that I could not go. But why, or how, I stayed is something beyond my powers to explain. Perhaps, *au fond*, it was because I believed in Julius LeVallon—believed, that is, in his innate uprightness and rectitude and

nobility of soul. It was all beyond me. I could not understand. But—I had this
strange belief in him. My relationship with her was, and would remain on both
sides, a subconscious one—a memory. There would be no betrayal anywhere.
I resolved to see it through.

"I ask nothing but your presence," I heard him saying presently; "if not actively sympathetic, at least not actively hostile. It is the sum of forces you bring
with you that I need. They are in your atmosphere, whether expressed or merely
latent. You are *you*." He watched me as he said this. "I failed once before, you
remember," he added, "because *she* was absent. Your desertion now would render success again impossible."

He took my hand in his. A tender, even beseeching note crept into his deep
voice. "Help me," he concluded, "if you will. You bring your entire past with
you, though you know it not. It is that Past that our reconstruction needs."

A wind from the south, I remember, blew the firs behind us into low, faint
sighing, and with the exquisite sound there stole a mingled joy and yearning on
my soul. Perhaps some flower of memory in that moment yielded up its once familiar perfume, dim, ancient, yet not entirely forgotten. The sighing of the forest wafted it from other times and other places. Wonder and beauty touched me;
I knew longing, but a longing so acutely poignant that it seemed not of this little earth at all. A fragrance and power of other stars, I could have sworn, lay in
it. The pang of some long, long sweetness made me tremble. An immense ideal
rose and beckoned with that whispering wind among the Jura pine woods, and
a grandeur, remote but of ineffable sweetness, stirred through the under-
growths of a half-claimed, half-recognised consciousness within me.

I was aware of this incalculable emotion. Ancient yearnings seemed on the
verge of coaxing loved memories into the light of day. I burned, I trembled, I
suffered atrociously, yet with a rush of blind delight never before realised by
me on earth. Then, suddenly, and wholly without warning, the desire for tears
came over me in a flood.... Control was possible, but left no margin over. Somehow I managed it, so that no visible sign of this acute and extraordinary collapse
should appear. It seemed, for a moment, that the frame of my modern personality was breaking down under the stress of new powers unleashed by my meeting with these two in this enchanted valley. Almost, another order of consciousness supervened... then passed without being quite accomplished.... I heard the
singing of the trees in the low south wind again. I saw the clouds sailing across
the blue foreign sky. I saw *his* eyes upon me like twin flames. With the greatest
difficulty I found speech possible in that moment.

"I can promise, at least, that I will not be hostile. I can promise that," I said
in a low and faltering tone.

He made no direct reply; least of all did it occur to him to thank me. The storm
that had shaken me had apparently not touched him. His tone was quiet and normal as he continued speaking, though its depth and power, with that steady
drive of absolute conviction behind, could never leave it quite an ordinary voice.

"She, as I told you, knows nothing in her surface-mind," I heard. "Beyond occasional uprushes of memory that have come to her lately in dreams—she tells

them naively, confusedly in the morning sometimes—she is aware of no more than a feeling of deep content, and that our union is right in the sense of being inevitable. Her pleasure that you have come is obvious. And more," he added, "I do not wish the older memories to break through yet, for that might wake pain or terror in her and, therefore, unconscious opposition."

He touched my arm a moment, looking at me with a significant expression. It was a suggestive thing he said: "For human consciousness is different at differ-ent periods, remember, and ages remotely separated cannot understand each other. Their points of view, their modes of consciousness, are too different. In *her* deeper state—separated by so huge an interval from the nineteenth cen-tury—with its origin long before we came to live upon this little earth—she would not, could not understand. There would be no sympathy; there might be terror; there must certainly be failure."

I murmured something or other, heaven alone knows what it was.

"What we think fine and wonderful may then have seemed the crudest folly, superstition, wickedness—and vice versa. Look at the few thousand years of his-tory we have—and you'll see the truth of this. We cannot grasp how certain periods could possibly have done the things they did." He paused, then added in a lower tone, more to himself than to me: "So with what we have to do now—though exceptional, utterly exceptional—it is a remnant that we owe to Na-ture—to the universe—and we must see it through..." His voice died away.

"I understand," my voice dropped into the open pause he left.

"Though you neither believe nor welcome," he replied.

"My promise," I said quietly, "holds good. Also"—I blushed and half-stam-mered over the conventional words—"I will do nothing that can cause possible offence—to anyone."

The hand that rested on my arm tightened its grasp a little. He made no other sign. It was remarkable how the topic that must have separated two other men—any two other men in the world, I suppose—had been subtracted from our re-lationship, laid aside as dealt with and admitted, calling for no further mention even. It all seemed, in some strange way, impersonal almost—another attitude to life—a faint sign, it may well have been, of that older mode of consciousness he spoke about.

I hardly recognised myself, so complete was the change in me, and so swiftly going forward. This dragnet from the Past drew ever closer. If the mind in me resisted still, it seemed rather from some natural momentum acquired by habit, than from any spontaneous activity due to the present. The modern, upper self surrendered.

"How soon?" was the question that seemed to come of its own accord; it was certainly not my confused and shaken mind that asked it. "When do you pro-pose to—"

He answered without a sign of hesitation. "The Autumnal Equinox. You've forgotten *that*," he added as though he justified my lack of memory here, "for all the world has forgotten it too—the science of Times and Seasons—the old-est known to man. It was true cosmic knowledge, but so long ago that it has left our modern consciousness as though it never had existed even."

He stopped abruptly. I think he desired me to discover for myself, unguided, unhampered by explanation. And, at the words, something remote and beautiful did stir, indeed, within me. A curtain drew aside....

CHAPTER XX

S ome remnant of ghostly knowledge quickened. Behind the mind and brain, in that region, perhaps, where thought ceases and intuition offers her amazing pageant, there stirred—reality. Times and seasons, I seemed to realise, have spiritual importance; there is a meaning in months and hours; if noon is different from six o'clock, what happens at noon varies in import from what happens at six o'clock, although the happening itself at both moments be identical. An event holds its minimum or its maximum of meaning according to the moment when it happens. Its effectiveness varies with the context.

Power is poured out, or power is kept back. To ask a man for energetic action when he is falling asleep is to court refusal; to expect life of him when he is overflowing with vitality and joy is probably to obtain it. The hand is stretched out to give, or the hand is withheld.

With the natural forces of the earth—it now dawned upon me—the method was precisely similar. Nature and human-nature reacted differently at different moments. At the moment of equilibrium called "equinox," there was a state of balance so perfect that this balance could be most easily, most naturally—transcended.

And objects in the outer world around me changed. Their meaning, ordinarily superficial, appeared of incalculable significance. The innate activities of Nature, the elements, I realised indeed as modes of life; the communication Julius foreshadowed, a possible and *natural* thing.

Someone, I believe, was speaking of these and similar things—words came floating on the wind, it seemed—yet with meanings so remote from all that my mind of To-day deemed possible, that I scarcely knew whether it was the voice of my companion speaking, or a voice of another kind, whispering in my very blood.

In Bâle a week ago, or in London six weeks ago, such theories would have left me cold. Now, at this particular juncture, they came with a solemn beauty I can only account for by the fact that I had changed into almost another being. My mind seemed ready for anything and everything. No modern creeds and dogmas could confine my imagination....

I had entered a different cycle of operation. I felt these ideas all-over-me. The brain might repeat insistently "this is false, this is superstition"; but something bigger than reason steadily overrode the criticism. My point of view had changed. In some new way, strangely exciting, I saw everything at once. My entire Self became the percipient, rather than my five separate senses. In Nature all around me another language uttered. It was the cosmic sense that stirred and woke. It was another mode of consciousness.

We three, it came upon me, were acting out some omitted detail of a great world-purpose. The fact that *she* forgot, that I was ignorant, that Julius LeVallon seemed guilty of unmoral things—these were but ripples upon the deep tide that bore us forward. We were uttering a great sentence we had left unfinished. I knew not exactly what was coming, only that we had begun its utterance ages before the present, and probably upon a planet nearer to the sun than our younger earth. The verb had not yet made its appearance in this sentence, but it would presently appear and explain the series of acts, and, meanwhile, I must go on acting and wondering what it all could mean. I thought of a language that first utters the nouns and adjectives, then adds the verb at the end, explaining the whole series of unmeaning sounds. Our "experiment" was the verb.

Then came the voice of Julius suddenly:

"Fate is the true complement of yourself; it completes your nature. By doing it, you become one with your surroundings. Note attitude and gesture—of yourself and of everything. They are signs. Our attitudes must coincide with that of the earth to the heavens—possible only at the Equinox. We must feel-with her. We then act with her. Do not resist. Let this valley say to you what it will. Regard it, and regard our life here at the moment, as a symbol, clothed in a whole story of information, the story varying with every hour of the day and with the slightest change of the earth in relation to the universe."

It seemed I watched the track of some unknown animal upon the ground, and tried to reconstruct the entire creature. Such imprint is but a trace of the invisible being that has made it. All about this valley there were tracks offering a hint of Beings that had left them—that any moment might reveal themselves. Julius talked on in his calm and unimpassioned way. I both understood and could not understand. I realised that there is a language for the mind, but no language for the spirit. There are no words in which to express big cosmic meanings. Action—a three-dimensional language—alone could be their vehicle. The knowledge must be performed—acted out in ceremony. Comprehension filtered into me, though how I cannot say.

"Symbols are merely the clues," he went on. "It is a question of stimulating your own imagination. Into the images created by your own activities the meaning flows. You must play with them and let them play with you. They depend for their meaning on history and happenings, and vary according to their setting—the time of day or night, the season of the year, the year itself, the exact relation of your Self to every other Self, human *or otherwise*, in the universe. Let your life and activities now arrange themselves in such a way that they shall demonstrate the workings of the elemental powers you feel about you. Every automatic activity of your body, every physiological process in you, links you on to this great elemental side of things. Be open now to the language of action. Think of the motion of all objects here as connected with the language of symbols, a living, ever-moving language, and do not allow your mind to mutilate the moods that come upon you. Let your nerves, if they will, come into contact with the Nature Powers, and so realise that the three kingdoms are alive. Watch your own automatic activities—I mean what you do unconsciously without deliberate thinking. For what you do consciously you are learning, but what you do unconsciously you have learned before. We have to *become* the performance by acting it—instantaneous understanding. All such attitudes are language, and the power to read it comes from a synthetical, intuitive feeling of the entire being. The heart may get one letter only, but that letter is a clue, an omen. A moth flies into the room and everything immediately looks different; it remains the same, yet means something different. It's like the vowel in the ancient languages—put in later, according to the meaning. You have, I know, forgotten"— he paused a moment and put his hand on my shoulder—"but every wind that blows across our valley here, and every change in temperature that lowers or raises the heat and fire of your own particular system"—he looked at me with a power in bearing and gesture impossible to describe—"is a sign and hint of whether—"

He stopped, glancing suddenly down the steep grass slopes. A breeze stirred the hair upon his forehead. It brushed my eyes and cheeks as well. I felt as though a hand had touched me as it passed invisibly. A momentary sensation of energy, of greater life swept over me, then disappeared as though the wind had borne it off.

"Of whether your experiment will be successful?" I broke in.

Turning his eyes from the sunny valley to my face again, he said slowly:

"These Powers can only respond to the language they understand. My deliverance must be experienced, acted out."

"A ceremony?" I asked, wondering uneasily what "acts of language" he might demand of me and of another.

"To restore them finally—where they rightfully belong." he answered, "I must become them. There is no other way."

How little intelligible result issued from this conversation must be apparent from the confused report here given, yet that something deep and true was in his mind lay beyond all question. At the back of my own, whence no satisfactory sentences could draw it out into clean description, floated this idea that the three of us were already acting out some vast, strange ceremonial in which Nature, indeed the very earth and heavens themselves, were acting with us. There was this co-operation, this deep alliance. The "experiment" we approached would reveal itself in natural happenings and circumstances. Action was to take the place of words, conveying meaning as speech or handwriting conveys a message. The attitude of ourselves, the very grouping of inanimate objects, of trees and hills, the effects of light and shade, the moods of day and night, above all, the time and season of the year which is nothing but the attitude of the earth towards the rest of the universe—all these, as modes of intelligent expression, would belong to the strange performance. They were the conscious gestures of the universe. If I could *feel-with* them, interpretation would be mine.

And, that I understood even this proved memory. "You will gradually become conscious," he said, "of various signs about you. Analyse these signs. But analyse them with a view to creating language. For language does not create ideas; Ideas become language. Put the vowels in. When communication begins to be established, the inanimate world here will talk to you as in the fairy tales— seem alive. Play with it, as you play with symbols in algebra before you rise to the higher mathematics. So, notice and think about anything that"—he emphasised the verb significantly—" draws your attention. Do not point out at the moment; that's compulsion and rouses opposition; just be aware and accept by noticing. And do not concentrate too much; what flows in must also be able to flow out; otherwise there comes congestion, and so—fear. In this valley the channels all are open, and wonder everywhere. The more you wonder, the more your memory will come back and consciousness extend. Great language has no words. The only way to grow in consciousness is to be for ever changing your ideas and point of view. Accept Nature here. Feel like a tree and then like a star. Be violent with wind, and burn with fire. These things are forgotten To-day because Wonder has left the world—and with it worship. So do not be ashamed to wonder at anything you notice. It all lies in you—I know that—and here it will rise to the surface." He laughed. "If a woman," he went on, "wears embroidered lilies on her dress, all London seems full of flower-sellers. They were there before, but she had nothing in herself to make her conscious of them. Notice all the little things, for you are a portion of the universe as much as Sirius or Vega, and in living relation with every other atom. You can share Nature, and here in our secret valley you may welcome her without alarm. The cosmic organism, denied by civilisation, survives in you as it survives also in myself and in—my wife. Through that, and through that alone, is the experiment possible to us."

And it flashed into me that my visit to this enchanted valley would witness no concentrated, miniature "ceremonial," reduced in form for worship as in a church or temple, but that all we did and experienced in the course of normal, every-day life would mark the outlines of this vast performance. Understanding would come that way.

And then the mention of his "wife" brought me sharply back to emotions of— another kind. My thought leaped back again—by what steps I cannot say, it seemed so disconnected with what had just occupied my mind—to his statement of ten minutes before.

"By becoming them," I asked, "you mean that you must feel-with wind and fire to the point of being them?"

"You think this might be done alone, without your help or hers?" he asked, picking the thought straight out of my mind. "But only a group could have done what we did—a group, moreover, in perfect sympathy. For as love between the three of us was essential to success then, so is love between us essential now. A group, combined by love into a unit, exerts a power impossible to an individual. The secret of our power lies in that—ideal love and perfect sympathy."

I listened, sure of one thing only—that I would keep an open mind. To deny, object, criticise, above all to ridicule would rob me of an experience. I believe honestly this was my attitude: to miss no value that might be in it by assuming it was nonsense merely because it was so strange. Apart from the curious fact that something in me was sympathetic to a whole world of deep ideas behind his language, I felt the determined desire to see the matter through. There was no creed or religious dogma in me to offend. I made myself receptive. For, out of this singular exposition the conviction grew that I was entering almost a new order of existence, and that an earlier mode of consciousness revived.

In this lonely valley, untouched by the currents of modern thought and feeling, companioned by Julius LeVallon and that old, recovered soul, his wife, the conditions of our previous existence together perhaps reformed themselves. Behind his talk came ideas that wore an aspect of familiarity, although my present brain, try as it might, failed to mould them into any acceptable form. The increasing change in myself was certainly significant. The crumbling of old shibboleths continued. A relationship between my inner nature and the valley seemed established in some way that was new, yet not entirely forgotten. The very sunlight and the wind assisted. Closer to the natural things I felt, the earth not alien to me....

We had neared the châlet again. I saw the peat smoke rising against the background of the ridges. The "man" was whistling at his work in the yard behind the building. The column of smoke, I remember, was agitated by the wind towards the top; it turned, blew downwards. No other sign of movement was anywhere visible, for in the bottom of the hollow where we now stood, the wind did not even stir the isolated larches or tall yellow gentians. Sunshine flooded everything. Out of this peace and stillness then came a sudden cry and the sight of something moving rapidly—both from the châlet.

"Julius!" called a shrill voice, as the figure of Mrs. LeVallon, with flying hair and skirts, came running over the meadow towards us. "Julius!—Professor! Quick!"

The voice and figure startled me; both came, it seemed, out of some other place; a picture from my youth rose up—a larch grove in October upon the Pentland Hills. I experienced a sense of deep and thrilling beauty similar to what I had felt then. But as I watched the slim, hurrying figure I was aware of another thing that left me breathless: For with her, as she passed through chequered sun and shadow along the fringe of forest, there moved something else enormously larger than herself. It was in the air about her. Like that strange Pentland memory, it whirled. It was formless, and owing to its huge proportions gave the impression of moving slowly, yet its very formlessness was singularly impressive and alive, so that the word "body" sprang instantly into my mind. Actually it moved at a tremendous speed.

In my first confusion and bewilderment I remember saying aloud in sheer amazement: "a fragment of the day has broken off; it's clothed in wind and sunlight!"

A phrase quite meaningless, of course, yet somehow accurately descriptive, for it appealed to me as a fragment of conditionless, universal activity that had seized upon available common elements to furnish itself a visible appearance. I

got the astounding suggestion that it was heat and air moving under intelligent
and conscious direction. Combined with its airy lightness there was power, for
in its brief, indeed its instantaneous, appearance I felt persuaded of an irresistible
strength that no barrier of solid matter could possibly withstand. At the same
time it was transparent, for I saw the trees upon its further side. It passed ahead
of the human figure, so close it seemed to touch her dress, rose with a kind of
swift, driving plunge into the air, slipped meltingly into the clean blue colour
of the atmosphere—and disappeared.

And so swift was the entire presentment of the thing, that even while I tried
to focus my sight upon it to make sure I was not deceived, it had both come and
gone. The same second Julius caught my arm. I heard him utter a quick, low cry,
stifled instantly. He gasped. He quivered. I heard him whispering:

"Already! Your presence here—the additional forces that you bring—are
known and recognised! See, how complete we are—a unit—you, she and I—
a trinity!"

A coldness not of this world touched me as I heard. But that first sense of joy
and beauty followed. I felt it true—the three of us were somehow one.

"You saw it too?" I asked, exhilaration still about me.

"They are everywhere and close," he whispered quickly, as the running figure came on toward us, "breaking out into visible manifestation even. Hold yourself strong and steady. Remember, your attitude of mind and feeling are important. Each detail of behaviour is significant."

His anxiety, I realised, was for us, not for himself. Already, it seemed, our souls
were playing vital roles in some great dramatic ceremonial just beginning. What
we did and felt and thought was but a partial expression of something going forward with pregnant completeness behind the visible appearances all round. Mrs.
LeVallon stood breathless in front of us. She was hatless, her hair becomingly
dishevelled; her arms bare to the elbow and white with flour. She stopped,
placed her hands upon her hips, and panted for a full minute before she could
get breath enough to speak. Her eyes, a deep, luminous sea-green, looked into
ours. Her face was pale, yet the emotion was excitement rather than alarm. I was
aware of a superb, nymph-like grace and charm about her. I caught my breath.
Julius made no movement, spoke no word. I wondered. I made a step forward
to catch her. But she did not fall; she merely sank down upon the ground at our
feet.

"Julius," she panted, "that thing I've dreamed about so often—"

She stopped short, glancing up at me, the eyes, charged with a sweet agitation, full upon my own. I turned to Julius with a gesture of uncontrollable impatience.

He spoke calmly, sitting down on the slope beside her. "You felt it again—
the effect of your vivid dreaming? Or did you this time—see anything?"

The swiftness and surprise of the little scene had been bewildering, but the
moment he spoke confusion and suspense both vanished. The sound of his quiet
voice restored the threatened balance. Peace came back into the sunlight and the
air. There was composure again.

"You certainly were not frightened!" he added, as she made no reply. "You look too happy and exhilarated for that." He put his hand on hers.

I sat down then beside her, and she turned and looked at me with a pathetic mingling of laughter and agitation still in her wide-opened eyes. The three of us were close together. He kept his hand on hers. Her shoulder touched me. I was aware of something very wonderful there between us. We comforted her, but it was more, far more, than that. There was sheer, overflowing happiness in it.

"It came into the house," she said, her breath recovered now, and her voice gentle. "It follered me—out here. I ran." She looked swiftly round at me. The radiance in her face was quite astonishing, turning her almost beautiful. Her eye-lids quivered a moment and the corners of her lips seemed trying to smile—or not to smile. She was happy there, sitting between us two. Yet there was noth-ing light or foolish in her. Something of worship rose in me as I watched her.

"Well," urged Julius, "and then—what?" I saw him watching me as well as her. "You remembered your dream, you felt something, and—you ran out here to us. What else?"

She hesitated deliciously. But it was not that she wanted coaxing. She evi-dently knew not how to tell the thing she had to say. She looked hard into my face, her eyes keenly searching.

"It has something to do with *him*, you mean?" asked Julius, noting the di-rection of her questioning gaze.

"Oh, I'm glad he's here," she answered quickly. "It's the best thing that could happen." And she looked round again at Julius, moving her hand upon his own.

"We need him," said Julius simply with a smile. Then, suddenly, she took my hand too, and held it tightly. "He's a protection, I think, as well," she added quite gravely; "that's how I feel him." Her hand lay warm and fast on mine.

There was a pause. I felt her fingers strongly clasp my own. The three of us were curiously linked together somehow by those two hands of hers. A great harmony united us. The day was glorious, the power of the sun divine, there was power in the wind that touched our faces.

"Yes," she continued slowly, "I think it had to do with him—with *you*, Pro-fessor," she repeated emphatically, fixing her bright gaze upon me. "I think you brought it—brought my dream back—brought that thing I dreamed about into—the house itself." And in her excitement she said distinctly " 'ouse."

I found no word to say at the moment. She kept her hand firmly upon mine.

"I was making bread there, by the back winder as usual," she went on, "when suddenly I started thinking of that splendid dream I've had so often—of you," looking at her husband, "and me and another man—that's *you* I'm sure," she gazed at me "all three of us doing some awful thing together in a place underground somewhere, but dressed quite different to what we are now, and standing round a lot of people sleeping in a row—when something we expected, yet were frightened at, used to come in—and give me such a start that I always woke up before knowing what was really going to happen."

She paused a second. She was confused. Her sentences ran into each other. "Well, I was making the bread there when the wind came in with a bang and sent the flour in a cloud all over everything—look! You can see it over my dress still—and with it, sort of behind it, so to speak, something followed with a rush—oh, an enormous rush and scurry it was—and I thought I was rising in the air, or going to burn to pieces by the heat that came in with it. I felt big like— as the sea when you get out of your depth and feel yourself being carried away. I screamed—and the three of us were all together in a moment, just as in the dream, you know—and we were glad, tremendously glad, because we'd got something we wanted that made us feel as if we could do anything, oh, anything in the world—a sort of 'eavenly power I think it was—and then, just as we were going to use our power and do all kinds of things with it, someone—I don't know who it was, for I never can see the face—a man, though—one of those sleeping figures—rose up and came at us all in a fury, and—well, I don't know exactly, but it all turned out a failure somehow—It got terrible then—" She looked like a flash of lightning into my face, then dropped her eyes again.

"You acted out your dream, as it were?" interrupted Julius a moment.

She looked at him with a touch of wonder. "I suppose so," she said, and let go both our hands. "Only this time someone really did come in and caught me just as I seemed going out of myself—it may have been fainting, but I don't think so, for I'm never one to faint—more like being carried off in a storm, a storm with wind and fire in it—"

"It was the 'man' caught you?" I asked quickly.

"The man, yes," she continued. "I didn't fall. He caught me just in time; but my wind was gone—gone clean out of me as though someone had knocked me down."

"He said nothing?" Julius asked.

She looked sharply at him. "Nothing," she answered, "not a single word. I ran away. He frightened me. For a moment—I was that confused with remembering my dream, I suppose; so I just pushed him off and ran out here to find you both. I'd been watching you for a long time while I was mixing the dough."

"I'm glad he was close enough to help you," put in Julius.

"Well," she explained, "I've a sort of idea he was watching me and saw the thing coming, for he'd been in and out of the kitchen for half an hour before, asking me silly questions about whether I wanted this or that, and fussing about"—she laughed at her own description —"just like an old faithful dog or something."

We all laughed together then.

"I'm glad I found you so quickly," she concluded, "because while I was running up here I felt that something was running with me—something that was burning and rushing—like a bit of what was in the house."

She stopped, and a shadow passed across her eyes, changing their colour to that nondescript grey tint they sometimes wore. The wonderful deep green went out of them. And for a moment there was silence that seemed to fill the entire valley. Julius watched her steadily, strong and comforting in his calmness. The valley, I felt, watched us too, something protective in its perfect stillness. All signs of agitation were gone; the wind sank down; the trees stood by in

solemn rows; the very clouds moved more slowly down the calm blue sky. I
watched the bosom of Mrs. LeVallon rise and fall as she recovered breath again.
She put her hands up to gather in the hair at the back of her head, deftly tidy-
ing its disordered masses, and as she did so I felt her gaze draw my own with a
force I could not resist. We looked into each other's eyes for a full two minutes,
no one speaking, no signs anywhere exchanged, Julius watchfully observant
close beside us; and though I know not how to tell it quite, it is a fact that something passed from those clear, discerning eyes into my heart, convincing me more
than any words of Julius ever could, that all he claimed about her and myself
was true. She was imperial somewhere.... She had once been mine....

The cloud passed slowly from her face. To my intense relief—for I had the
dread that the silent gaze would any moment express itself in fateful words as
well—the muscles of her firm, wide mouth relaxed. She broke into happy
laughter suddenly.

"It's very silly of me to think and feel such things, or be troubled by a dream,"
she exclaimed, still holding my eyes, and her laughter running over me like some
message of forgiveness. "We shall frighten him away," she went on, turning now
to Julius, "before he's had time to taste the new bread I'm making—for him."
Her manner was quiet and composed again, natural, prettily gracious. I searched
in vain for something to say; the turmoil of emotion within offered too many possible rejoinders; I could not choose. Julius, however, relieved me of the necessity by taking her soothingly in both his arms and kissing her. The next second,
before I could move or speak, she leaned over against my shoulder and kissed
me on the cheek as well.

Yet nothing happened; there was no sign anywhere that an unusual thing had
occurred; I felt that the sun and wind had touched me. It was as natural as shaking hands. Ah! but the sun and wind were magical with life!

"There!" she laughed happily, "we're all three together and understanding,
and nothing can go wrong. Isn't it so, Julius?" And, if there was archness in her
voice and manner, there was certainly no trace of that mischief which can give
offence. "And you understand, Professor, don't you?"

I saw him take her hand and stroke it. He showed no more resentment than
if she had handed me a flower. And I tried to understand. I struggled. I at least
succeeded in keeping my attitude of thought and feeling above destructive lev-
els. We three were one; love made us so. A devouring joy was in me, but with
it the strange power of a new point of view.

"We couldn't be together like this," she laughed naïvely, "in a city. It's only
here. It's this valley and the sun and wind what does it." She looked round her.
"All this sun and air, and the flowers, and the forest and the clear cold little
stream. Why, I believe, if we stay here we shall never die at all. We'd turn into
gods or something."

She murmured on half to herself, the voice sinking towards a whisper—leaning
over upon her husband's breast, she stretched out her hand and quietly took
my own again. "It's got much stronger," I heard, "since he's come, it makes me
feel closer to you too, Julius. Only—he's with us as well, just like—just as if

we were all meant for each other somehow."

There was pressure, yet no suggestive pressure, in the hand that held my own. It just took me firmly, with a slight gesture of drawing me closer to herself and to Julius too. It united us all three. And, strange as it all was, I, for my part, was aware of no uneasiness, no discomfort, no awkwardness certainly. I only felt that what she said was true: we were linked together by some deep sympathy of feeling-with; we were at one; we were marvellously fused by some tie of universal life that this enchanted valley made apparent. Nature fused with human nature, raising us all to a diviner level.

There was a period of silence in which no one moved or spoke; and then, to my relief, words came from Julius—natural and unforced, yet with a meaning that I saw was meant for me:

"The presence of so distinguished a man," he said lightly, looking down into her face with almost a boyish smile, "is bound to make itself felt anywhere." He glanced across at me significantly. "Even the forces of Nature in this peaceful valley, you see, are aware of his arrival and have sent out messengers to greet him. Only," he added, "they need not be in such a hurry about it, need they— or so violent?"

We all laughed together. It was the only reference he made in her presence to what had happened. Nor did she ask a single question. We lay a little longer, basking in the sunlight and breathing the fragrant mountain air, and then Mrs. LeVallon sprang to her feet alertly, saying that she must go and finish her bread. Julius went with her. I was left alone—with the eerie feeling that more than these two had just been with me....

Less than an hour later the horizon darkened suddenly. Out of a harmless sky appeared masses of ominous cloud. Wild gusts of hot, terrific wind rushed sideways over the swaying forest. The trees shook to their roots, groaning; they shouted; loosened stones fell rattling down the nearer gullies; and, following a minute of deep silence, there blazed forth then a wild glory of lightning such as I have never witnessed. It was a dancing sea of white and violet. It came from every quarter of the sky at once with a dazzling fury as though the entire atmosphere were set on fire. The wind and thunder shook the mountains. From a cupful of still, sweet sunshine, our little valley changed into a scene of violent pandemonium. The precipices tossed the echoing thunder back and forth, the clear stream beside the châlet became a torrent of foaming, muddy water, and the wind was of such convulsive turbulence that it seemed to break with explosive detonations that menaced the upheaval of all solid things. There was a magnificence in it all as though the universe, and not a small section of the sky, produced it.

It passed away again as swiftly as it came. At lunch time the sun blazed down upon a drenched and laughing scene, washed as by magic, brilliant and calm as though made over all afresh. The air was limpid; the forest poured out perfume; the meadows shone and twinkled.

During the assault I saw neither Julius nor the Man, but in the occasional deep pauses I heard the voice of Mrs. LeVallon singing gaily while she kneaded bread at the kitchen "winder" just beneath my own. She, at any rate, was not afraid. But, while it was in progress, I went alone to my room and watched it, caught by a strange sensation of power and delight its grandeur woke in me, and also by a sense of wonder that was on the increase.

CHAPTER XXI

"Why is she set so far, so far above me,
    And yet not altogether raised above?
I would give all the world that she should love me,
    My soul that she should never learn to love."
                    —Mary Coleridge.

"The channels here are open."
As the days went by the words remained with me. I recognised their truth. Nature was pouring through me in a way I had never known before. I had gone for a walk that afternoon after the sudden storm, and tried to think things out. It was all useless. I could only feel. The stream of this strange new point of view had swept me from known moorings; I was in deep water now; there was ex-hilaration in the rush of an unaccustomed tide. One part of me, hourly fading, weighed, criticised and judged; another part accepted and was glad. It was like the behaviour of a divided personality.

"Your brain of To-day asks questions, while your soul of long ago remembers and is sure."

I was constantly in the presence of Mrs. LeVallon. My "brain" was active with a thousand questions. The answers pointed all one way. This woman, so humbly placed in life to-day, rose clearer and clearer before me as the soul that Julius claimed to be of ancient lineage. Respect increased in me with every word, with every act, with every gesture. Her mental training, obviously, was small, and of facts that men call knowledge she had but few; but in place of these re-cent and artificial acquirements she possessed a natural and spontaneous intel-ligence that was swiftly understanding. She seized ideas though ignorant of the words that phrased them; she grasped conceptions that have to be hammered into minds the world regards as well equipped—seized them naively, yet with exquisite comprehension. Something in her discriminated easily between what was transitory and what was real, and the glory of this world made evidently small appeal to her. No ordinary ambition of vulgar aims was hers. Fame and position were no bait at all; she cared nothing about being "somebody." There was a touch of unrest and impatience about her when she spoke of material things that most folk value more than honour, some even more than character. Something higher, yet apparently forgotten, drew her after it. The pursuit of pleasure and sensation scarcely whispered to her at all, and though her self-es-

teem was strong, personal vanity in the little sense was quite a negligible quantity.

This young wife had greatness in her. Domestic servant though she certainly
had been, she was distinguished in her very bones. A clear ray of mental guidance and intuition ran like a gleam behind all her little blunders of speech and
action. To her, it was right and natural, for instance, that her husband's money
should mostly be sent away to help those who were without it. "We're much better this way," she remarked lightly, remembering, perhaps, the life of detailed
and elaborate selfishness she once had served, "and anyhow I can't wear two
dresses at the same time, can I? Or live in two houses—what's the good of all
that? But for those who like it," she added, "I expect it's right enough. They need
it—to learn, or something. I've been in families of the best that didn't want for
anything—but really they had nothing at all." It was in the little things I
caught the attitude. Although conditions here made it impossible to test it, I had
more and more the impression, too, that she possessed insight into the causes of
human frailty, and understood temptations she could not possibly have experienced personally in this present life.

An infallible sign of younger souls was their pursuit hot-foot of pleasure and
sensation, of power, fame, ambition. The old souls leave all that aside; they have
known its emptiness too often. Their hall-mark lies in spiritual discernment, the
power to choose between the permanent and the transitory. Brains and intellect were no criterion of development at all. And I reflected with a smile how
the "educated" and "social" world would close its doors to such a woman—the
common world of younger, cruder souls, insipid and undistinguished, many of
them but just beyond the animal stage—the "upper classes"! The Kingdom of
Heaven lies within, I remembered, and the meek and lowly shall inherit the
"earth."

And the "Dog-Man" also rose before me in another light—this slow-minded,
instinctive being whom elsewhere I should doubtless have dismissed as "stupid."
His approximation to the instinctive animal life became so clear. In his character and essential personality lay the curious suggestion. Out of his frank gaze
peered the mute and searching appeal of the soul awakening into self-consciousness—a look of direct and simple sincerity, often questioning, often
poignant. The interval between Mrs. LeVallon and himself was an interval of
countless lives. How welcome to him would be the support of a thought-out religious creed, to her how useless! The different stages individuals occupy, how
far apart, how near, how various! I felt it all as true, and the effect of this calm
valley upon me was not sympathy with Nature only, but a certain new sympathy with all the world. It was very wonderful.

I watched the "man" with a new interest and insight—the proud and self-con-
scious expression on his face as he moved constantly about us, his menial services earnest and important. The safety of the entire establishment lay upon his
shoulders. He made the beds as he served the coffee, cleaned the boots or lit the
lamps at dusk, with a fine dignity that betrayed his sense of our dependence on
him—he would never fail. He was ever on the watch. I could believe that he

slept at night with one eye open, muscles ready for a spring in case of danger. In myself, at any rate, his signal devotion to our interest woke a kind of affec' tionate wonder that touched respect. He was so eager and ready to learn, more' over. The pathos in his face when found fault with was quite appealing—the curious dumb attitude, the air of mortification that he wore: "I'm rather puz' zled, but I shall know another time. I shall do better. Only—I haven't got as far as you have!"

In myself, meanwhile, the change worked forward steadily. I was much alone, for Julius, preoccupied and intense, was now more and more engaged upon purposes that kept him out of sight. Much of the time he kept to his room upstairs, but he spent hours, too, in the open, among the woods and on the fur' ther ridges, especially at night. Not always did he appear at meals even, and what intercourse I had was with Mrs. LeVallon, so that our intimacy grew quickly, ripening with this sense of sudden and delightful familiarity as though we had been long acquainted. There was at once a happy absence of formality between us, although a dignity and sweet reserve tempered our strange relationship in a manner the ordinary world—I feel certain—could hardly credit. Out of all common zones of danger our intercourse was marvellously lifted, yet in a way it is difficult to describe without leaving the impression that we were hardly hu' man in the accepted vulgar meaning of the words.

But the truth was simple enough, the explanation big with glory. It was that Nature included us, mothering all we said or did or thought, above all, *felt*. Our intercourse was not a separate thing, apart, shut off, two little humans merely aware of the sympathetic draw of temperament and flesh. It was part of Nature, natural in the biggest sense, a small, true incident in the processes of the entire cosmos whose life we shared. The physical thing called passion, of course, was present, yet a passion that the sun and wind took care of, spreading it every' where about us through the hourly happenings of "common" things—in the wind that embraced the trees and then passed on, in the rushing stream that caught the flowers on its bank, then let them go again, in the fiery sunshine that kissed the earth while leaving the cooling shadows beside every object that it glorified.

All this seemed in some new fashion clear to me—that passion degrades be' cause it is set exclusive and apart, magnified, idolatrised into a false importance due to Nature's being neglected and left outside. For not alone the wind and sun and water shared our intercourse, knowing it was well, but in some further sacramental way the whole big Earth, the movements of the Sun, the Seasons, aye, and the armies of the other stars in all their millions, took part in it, justi' fying its necessity and truth. Without a trace of false exaltation in me I saw far, far beyond even the poet's horizon of love's philosophy:

> "Nothing in the world is single;
>   All things by a law divine
> In one another's being mingle—
>   Why not I with thine?"

and so came again with a crash of fuller comprehension upon the words of Julius that here we lived and acted out a Ceremony that conveyed great teach-ing from a cosmic point of view. My relations with Mrs. LeVallon, as our rela-tions all three together, seen from this grander angle, were not only possible and true: they were necessary. We were a unit formed of three, a group-soul affirming truths beyond the brain's acceptance, proving universal, cosmic teaching in the only feasible way—by acting it out.

The scale of experience grew vast about me. This error of the past we would set right was but an episode along the stupendous journey of our climbing souls. The entire Present, the stage at which humanity found itself to-day, was but a moment, and values worshipped now, and by the majority rightly worshipped, would pass away, and be replaced by something that would seem entirely new, yet would be in reality not discovery but recovery.

CHAPTER XXII

> "This mighty sea of Love, with wondrous tides,
>   Is sternly just to suit and grain;
> 'Tis laving at this moment Saturn's sides,
>   'Tis in my blood and brain."
>   —Alexander Smith.

One evening, as the shadows began to lengthen across the valley, I came in from my walk, and saw Mrs. LeVallon on the veranda, looking out towards the ridges now tipped with the sunset gold. Her back was to me. One hand shaded her eyes; her tall figure was like a girl's; her attitude con-veyed expectancy. I got the impression she had been watching for me.

She turned at the sound of my footstep on the boards. "Ah, I hoped you'd get back before the dark," she said, with a smile of welcome that betrayed a touch of relief. "It's so easy to get lost in those big woods." She led the way indoors, where a shaded lamp stood on the table laid for tea. She talked on easily and sim-ply. She had been washing "hankercheefs," and as the dusk came on had felt she "oughter" be seeing where I'd got to. I thanked her laughingly, saying that she must never regard me as a guest who had to he looked after, and she replied, her big eyes penetratingly on my own—"Oh, I didn't mean *that*, Professor. I knew by instinct you were not one to need entertaining. I saw it reely the mo-ment you arrived. I was just wondering where you'd got to and—whether you'd find your way back all right." And then, as I made no reply, she went on to talk about the housework, what fun it was, how it amused her, and how different it was from working for other people. "I could work all day and night, you see, when the results are there, in sight. It's working for others when you never see the result, or what it leads to, and jest get paid so much a week or month, that makes you tired. Seeing the result seems to take away fatigue. The other's simply toil. Now, come to tea. I do relish my cup of tea."

It was very still and peaceful in the house; the logs burned brightly on the open hearth; Julius was upstairs in his room. The winds had gone to sleep, and the hush of dusk crept slowly on the outside world.

I followed my hostess into the corner by the fire where two deep arm-chairs beside the table beckoned us. Rather severe she looked now in a dark stuff dress, dignified, something half stately, half remote about her attitude. The poise in her physical expression came directly from the mind. She moved with grace, sure of herself, seductive too, yet with a seduction that led the thoughts far beyond mere physical attraction. It was the charm of a natural simplicity I felt.

"I've taken up Julius his," I heard her saying in her uncultivated voice, as she began to pour out tea. "And I've made these—these sort of flat unleavened cakes for us." The adjective startled me. She pointed to thin, round scone-like things that lay steaming in a plate. But her eyes were fixed on mine as though they questioned.

"You used to like 'em...."

Or, whether she said "I hope you'll like 'em," I am not certain—for a sudden sense of intimacy flashed between us and disconcerted me. Perhaps it was tone and gesture rather than the actual words. A sweetness as of some deep, remembered joy rose in me.

I started. There had been disclosure, a kind of revelation. A door had opened. They were familiar to me—those small "unleavened cakes." Something of happiness that had seemed lost slipped back of its own accord into my heart. My head swam a second. Some part of me was drawn backwards. For, as I took the offered cake, there stole to my nostrils a faint perfume that made me tremble. Elusive, ghostly sensations dropped their hair-like tracery on the brain, then vanished utterly. It was all dim, yet haunting as a dream. The perfume faded instantly.

"Thank you," I murmured. "You make them deliciously..." aware at the same moment I had been about to say another thing in place of the empty words, but had deliberately kept it back.

The bewilderment came and went. Mrs. LeVallon dropped her eyes from mine, although the question in their penetrating gaze still lingered. I realised this new sense of intimacy that seemed uncannily perfect, it was so natural. No suggestion lay in it of anything that should not be, but rather the close-knit comfortable atmosphere of two minds that were familiar and at home in silence. It deepened with every minute. It seemed the deep companionship that many, many years had forged.

Yet the moment of wonder had mysteriously come and gone. Even the aroma of the little steaming cake was lost as well—I could not recapture the faint odour. And it was my surface consciousness, surely, that asked then about the recipe, and joined in the soft, familiar laughter with which she answered that she "reely couldn't say quite," because "it seemed to have come of its own accord while I was doing nothing in particular with odds and ends about the cooking-stove."

"A very simple way," I suggested, trying to keep my thoughts upon the present, "a very easy way of finding new recipes," whereupon, her manner graver somewhat, she replied: "But, of course, I could make them better if I stopped to think a bit first... and had the proper things. It's jest my laziness. I know how—only"—she looked peeringly at me again as with an air of searching for something I might supply—"I've sort of mislaid something—forgot it, rather... and I can't, for the life of me, remember where I learned it first."

There stirred between us into that corner of the lamp-lit room an emotion that made me feel we used light words together as men use masks upon their faces for disguise, fully aware that while the skin is hidden the eyes are clear. My happiness seemed long-established. There was a little pause in which the key sank deeper. Before I could find anything to say, Mrs. LeVallon went on again:

"There's several things come to me like that the last few days—"

"Since I came?" I could not prevent the question; nor could I hide the pleasure in my voice.

"That's it," she agreed instantly; "it's as though you brought them—back—simply by being here. It's got to do with you." Her elbows were on the table, the chin resting on her folded hands as she stared at me, both concentration and absent-mindedness in her expression at the same time. Her thoughts were travelling, searching, beating backwards into time. She leaned a little nearer to me suddenly, so that I could almost feel her breath upon my face.

"Like memories of childhood revived," I said. My heart beat quickly. There was great sweetness in me.

"That's it," she repeated, but in a lowered tone. "That's it, I think; as if we'd been children together, only so far back I can't hardly remember."

She gazed again into my eyes, searching for words her untutored brain could not supply. There was a moment of extraordinary tenseness. I felt unsure of myself; uneasiness was in it, but a strange, lifting joy as well. I knew an instant's terror that either she or I might say an undesirable thing.

And to my relief just then the Man came clattering in with a cup containing—cream! Her eyes left mine as with an effort. Drawing herself free, yet not easily, from some inner entanglement that had captured both of us, she turned and took the little cup. "There is no proper cream jug," she observed with a smile, dropping back into the undisguised accent of the East Croydon fruiterer's daughter, "but the cream's thick and good jest the same, and we'll take it like this, won't we?" She stirred it with a spoon into my teacup.

The "Man" stood watching us a moment with a questioning, puzzled look, and then went out again. At the door he turned once more to assure himself that all was as it should be, decided that it was so, and vanished with a little run. Slowly, then, upon her face stole back that graver aspect of the eyes and mouth; and into my own mind stole equally a sense of deep confusion as I watched her—very delightful, strangely sweet, but my first uneasiness oddly underlying it. Instinctively I caught myself shrinking as from vague pain or danger. I made a struggle to get free, but it was a feeble and half-hearted effort. Mrs. LeVallon was saying exactly what I had known she was going to say.

"I'm all upset to-day," she said with blunt simplicity,   "and you must excuse my manners. I feel sort of lost and queer. I can't make it out, but I keep forgettin' who I am, and sometimes even where I am. You"—raising her eyes from the plate to mine—"oughter be able to help me. D'you know what I mean? Professor, sometimes, especially nights," her voice sinking as she said it, "I feel afraid of something—" She paused, correcting herself suddenly. "Oh, no, it isn't fear exactly, you see, but a great happiness that seems too big to get hold of quite. It's jest out of reach always, and something'll go wrong before it reely comes." She looked very hard at me. The strange sea-green eyes became luminous. I felt power in her, a power she was not aware of herself. "As if," she continued earnestly, "there was some price to pay for it—first. And somehow it's for *you*— it's what you've come for—" She broke off suddenly.

A touch of rapture caught me. It was only with strong effort that I made a commonplace reply:

"This valley, Mrs. LeVallon"—I purposely used the name and title—"is exceedingly lonely; you are shut off from the world you are accustomed to." I tried to put firmness and authority into my words and manner. "You have no companionship—of your own sex—"

She brushed my explanation aside impatiently. "Oh, but it ain't nothing of that sort," she exclaimed, seeing through my conventional words, and knowing I realised that she did so; "it's not loneliness, nor anything ordin'ry like that. Julius is everything to me in *that* way. It's something bigger and quite different— that's got worse, got stronger I mean, since you came. But I like your being here," she added quickly, "because I feel it's jest the thing for Julius and for— for all of us. Only, since you've been here it seems—well, it's sort of coming to a head."

I remained speechless. A kind of helplessness came over me. I could not prevent it.

"And mixed up with it," she continued, not waveringly, but wholly mistress of herself, "is the feeling that you've been here before too—been with me. We've been together, and you know we have." Her cheek turned a shade paler; she was very earnest; there was deep emotion in her. "That's what I keep feelin' for one thing. Everything is that familiar—as if all three of us had been together before and had come back again." Her breath came faster.

"You understand me, don't you? When Julius told me you were coming, it seemed quite natural, and I didn't feel nothing of any kind except that it was so natural; but the day you arrived I felt—afraid, though always with this tremendous happiness behind it. And *that's* why I didn't come down to meet you!" The words came pouring out, yet without a sign of talking wildly. Her eyes shone; the velvet band on her throat rose and fell; I was aware of happiness and amazement, but never once of true surprise. I had expected this, and more besides. "The moment I saw you—up there at the winder in the early mornin'—it came bursting over me, Professor, as sure as anything in this world, that we've come together again like old, old friends."

And it was still my conventional sense of decent conduct that held me to make a commonplace rejoinder. Yet how the phrases came, and why the thin barrier between us did not fall with a crash is more than I can tell.

"Julius had spoken about me, and no doubt your imagination—here in this deserted place—"

She shook her head almost contemptuously. "Julius said nothing," she put in quickly, "nothing in particular, I mean; only that you were old friends and he was positive sure you'd come because you'd promised. It's since you've come here that I've felt all this so strong. You come as familiar and natural to me as my own mother," she continued, a faint flush rising on the former pallor; "and what's more, your coming has brought a whole lot of other things nearer, too," adding in a whisper suddenly, "things that make me afraid and happy at the same time."

She paused a moment, peering round the room and out of the blindless windows into the darkening valley. "Now, *he*"—pointing with her thumb in the direction of the kitchen—"is all new to me, and I have no feeling about him at all. But you! Why, I always know where you are, and what you'll be doing next, and saying, and even what you're thinking and feeling half the time—jest as I do with Julius—almost."

The next minute came the direct question that I dreaded. It was like a pistol shot:

"And you feel the same, Professor? You feel it, too? You know all about me—and this great wonderful thing that's creepin' up nearer all the time Don't you, now?"

I looked straight at her over the big lamp-shade, feeling that some part of me went lost in the depths of those strange, peering eyes. There was a touch of authority in her face—about lips and mouth—that I had seen once before. For an instant it hovered there while she waited for my reply. It lifted the surface plainness of her expression into a kind of solemn beauty. Her charm poured over me envelopingly.

"There is," I stammered, "a curious sense of intimacy between us—all, and it is very delightful. It comes to me rather like childhood memories revived. The loneliness of this valley," I added, sinking my voice lest its trembling should be noticeable, "may account for a good many strange feelings, but it's the peace and loveliness that should make the chief appeal."

The searching swiftness of the look she flashed upon me, faintly touched with scorn, I have seen sometimes in the eyes of a child who knows an elder says vain things for its protection in the dark. Such weak attempts but bring the reality nearer.

"Oh, I feel that too—the loveliness—right enough." she said at once, her eyes still fixed on mine, "but I mean these other things as well." Her tone, her phrase, assumed that I also was aware of them. "Where do they come from? What are they exactly? I often fancy there's lots of other people up here besides ourselves, only they're hidden away always—watchin', waitin' for something to happen—something that's being got ready like. Oh, but it's a splendid feeling, too, and makes me feel alive all over." She sat up and clapped her hands softly like a child, but there was awe as well as joy in her. "And it comes from the woods and sky somehow—like wind and lightning. God showed Himself once, didn't He, in a burnin' bush and in a mighty rushin' wind?"

"Nature seems very real in a place like this," I said hurriedly. "We see no other human beings. Imagination grows active and constructs—"

The instant way she swept aside the evasive reply I was so proud of made me feel foolish.

"Imagination," she said firmly, yet with a bewitching smile, "is not making up. It's finding out. You know that!"

We stared at one another for a moment without speech. It seemed as if the forest, the meadows, the little rivulet of cool, clear water, the entire valley itself became articulate—through her. Her personality rushed over me like a gush of wind. In her enthusiasm and belief rose the glow of fire.

"You feel the same," she went on, with conviction in her voice, "or you wouldn't try to pretend you don't. You wouldn't try to hide it." And the authority grew visibly upon her face. There was a touch of something imperious as well. "You see, I can't speak to *him* about it, I can't ask him"—jerking her head towards the room upstairs—"because"—she faltered oddly for a second"—because it's about himself. I mean he knows it *all*. And if I asked him—my God, he'd tell me!"

"You prefer not to know?"

She smiled and shrugged her shoulders with a curious gesture impossible to interpret. "I long to know," she replied, "but I'm half afraid"—she shivered slightly"—to hear everything. I feel as if it would change me—into—someone else." The last words were spoken almost below her breath.

But the joy broke loose in me as I heard. It was another state of consciousness she dreaded yet desired. This new consciousness was creeping over her as well. She shared it with me; our innate sympathy was so deep and perfect. More, it was a type of consciousness we had shared together before. An older day rose hauntingly about us both. We felt with one another.

"For yourself?" I asked, dropping pretence as useless any longer. "You feel afraid for yourself?"

She moved the lamp aside with a gesture so abrupt it seemed almost violent; no object intervened between our gaze; and she leaned forward, folding her hands upon the white tablecloth. I sat rigidly still and watched her. Her face was very near to mine. I could see myself reflected in her glowing eyes.

"Not for myself, Professor, nor for you," she said in a low voice. Then, dropping the tone to a whisper, "but for him. I've felt it on and off ever since we came up here last spring. But since you've come, I've known it positive—that something'll happen to Julius—before we leave—and before you leave...."

"But, Mrs. LeVallon—"

"And it's something we can't prevent," she went on whispering, "neither of us—nor oughter prevent either—because it's something we've got to do all three together."

The intense conviction in her manner blocked utterance in me.

"Something I want to do, what's more," she continued, "because it's sort of magnificent—if it comes off proper and as it should—magnificent for all of us, and like a great vision or something. You know what I mean. We are together in it, but this old valley and the whole world is somehow in it, too. I can't quite understand. It's very wonderful. Julius will suffer, too, only he'll call it jest development." Her voice sank lower still, "D'you know, Professor, I sometimes feel there's something in Julius that seems to me like—God."

She stood up as she said it, tall, erect, her figure towering above me; and as she rose her face passed out of the zone of yellow lamplight into comparative shadow, the eyes fixed always penetratingly upon my own. And I could have sworn that not alone their expression altered, growing as with fiery power, but that the very outline of her head and shoulders shifted into something else, something dark, remote and solemn as a tree at midnight, drawn almost visibly into larger scale.

She bent lower again a little over the table, leaning her hands upon the back of the chair she had just occupied. I knew exactly what she was going to say. The sentences dropped one by one from her lips just as I expected.

"I've always had a dread in me, ever since I can remember," I heard this familiar thing close in my ear, "a sinking like—of some man that I was bound to meet—that there was an injury I'd got to put right, and that I'd have to suffer a lot in doing it. When I met Julius first I thought it might be him. Then I knew it wasn't him, but that I'd meet the other—the right man—through him sooner or later." She stopped and watched me for a second. Her eyes looked through and through me. "It's you, Professor," she concluded; "it's you."

She straightened up again and passed behind my chair. I heard her retreating steps. A thousand words rose up in me, but I kept silence. What should I say? How should I confess that I, too, had known a similar dread of meeting—her? A net encompassed me, a web was flung that tightened as it fell—a web of justice, marvellously woven, old as the stars and certain as the pull of distant planets, closing us all together into a pattern of actions necessary and inexorable.

I turned. I saw her against the window where she stood looking out into the valley, now thick with darkness about the little house. And for one passing instant it seemed to me that the entire trough of that dark valley brimmed with the forces of wind and fire that were waiting to come in upon us.

And Mrs. LeVallon turned and looked at me across the room. There was a smile upon her lips.

"But we'll play it out," her whisper reached me, "and face it all without fear or shirking... when it... comes...." And as she whispered it I hid my face in my hands so as not to meet her gaze. For my own dread of years ago returned in force upon me, and I knew beyond all doubt or question, though without a shred of evidence, that what she said was true.

And when I lifted my eyes a moment later Mrs. LeVallon had gone from the room, and the Man, I saw, was clearing away the tea things, glancing at me from time to time for a word or smile, as though to show that whatever happened he was always faithful, ready to fight for all of us to the death if necessary, and to be depended upon absolutely.

CHAPTER XXIII

"*A thousand ages onward led*
Their joys and sorrows to that hour;
No wisdom weighed, no word was said,
For only what we were had power."—A. E.

Meanwhile my intercourse with Nature now began to betray itself in curious little ways, and none more revealing of this mingled joy and nervousness than my growing excitement on being abroad after dark alone.

In the far more desolate Monzoni Valley a few weeks before I had passed whole nights in the open without the least suspicion of uneasiness, yet here, amid these friendly woods, covered by this homely, peaceful valley, it was suddenly made clear to me that I had nerves. And the reason, briefly put, was that there I knew myself alone, whereas here I knew myself never alone.

This sense of a populated Nature grew. After dusk it fairly mastered me, but even in broad daylight, when the September sunshine flooded the whole trough of valley with warmth and brightness, there clung to me the certainty that my moods and feelings, as my very footsteps, too, were noted—and understood. This sense of moving Presences, as in childhood, was stirred by every wind that blew. The feeling of co-operation increased. It was conscious, intelligent co-operation.

"Over that limestone ridge against the sky," I caught myself feeling, rather than definitely thinking; "from just beyond the crests of those tall pines, will presently come—" What? I knew not, even as the child knows not. Only, it would come—appearing suddenly from the woods, or clouds, or from behind the big boulders that strewed the open spaces.

In the fields about the châlet this was manifest too, but especially on the naked ridges above the forests and in the troughs that held the sunlight. Where the wind had unobstructed motion, and where the heat of the sun accumulated in the hollows, this sense of preparation, of co-operation, chiefly touched me. There was behind it pressure—as of purpose and direction, the idea that intelligence stirred within these natural phenomena. Some type of elemental life, enormous yet generally diffused through formlessness, moved and had its being behind natural appearances.

More and more, too, I realised that "inanimate" Nature was a script that it was possible to read; that certain objects, certain appearances drew my attention because they had a definite meaning to convey, whereas others remained unnoticed, as though not necessary to the sentence of some message or communication. The Language of Happenings that Julius talked about—the occurrences of daily life as words in some deep cosmical teaching—connected itself somewhere with this meaning that hid in common objects.

That my awareness of these things was known to others of the household besides myself was equally clear, for I never left the immediate neighbourhood of the châlet after dark without the Man following my movements with a kind of anxiety, sometimes coming on my very tracks for a considerable distance, or hanging about until I returned to light and safety. In sleep, too, as I passed slowly into unconsciousness, it seemed that the certainty of these Presences grew startlingly distinct, and more than once I woke in the night without apparent cause, yet with the conviction that they brooded close upon the châlet and its inmates, pressing like a rising flood against the very walls and windows. And on these occasions I usually heard Julius moving in his room just across the narrow passage, or the Man astir in the lower regions of the house. Outside, the moonlight, cold and gleaming, silvered the quiet woods and limestone heights. Yet not all the peace and beauty of the scene, nor the assurance of the steady stars themselves, could quite dispel this conviction that something was in active progress all about me, and that the elements themselves urged forward towards the deliverance of some purpose that had relation to ourselves.

Julius, I knew, was at the root of it.

One night—a week or so after my arrival—I woke from a dreamless sleep with the impression that a voice had called me. I paused and listened, but the sound was not repeated. I lay quietly for some minutes, trying to discover whose voice it was, for I seemed bereft of some tender companionship quite recently enjoyed. Someone who had been near me had gone again. I was aware of loneliness.

It was between one and two in the morning and I had slept for several hours, yet this mood was not the one in which I had gone to bed. Sleep, even ten minutes' sleep, brings changes on the heart; I woke to this sense of something desirable just abandoned. Someone, it seemed, had called my name. There was a tingling of the nerves, a poignant anticipation that included high delight. I craved to hear that voice again. Then, suddenly, I knew.

I rose and crossed the room. The warmth of the house oppressed me, although the wood-fire in the hearth downstairs was long since out, and by the open window I drank in the refreshing air. The valley lay in a lake of silver. There was mist upon the meadows, transparent, motionless, the tinkling of the rivulet just audible beneath its gauzy covering. The cliffs rose in the distance, gaunt and watchful; the forest was a pool of black. I saw the lake, a round blot upon the fields. Over the shingled roof occasional puffs of wind made a faint rushing sound under the heavy eaves. The moonlight was too bright for stars, and the ridges seemed to top the building with the illusion of nearness that such atmosphere engenders. The hush of a perfect autumn night lay over all.

I stood by that open window spellbound. For the clear loveliness seemed to take my hand and lead me forth into a vale of beauty that, behind the stillness, was brimming with activity. Vast energy paused beneath the immobility. The moonlight, so soft and innocent, yet gleamed with a steely brightness as of hid den fire; the puffs of wind were but the trickling draughts escaping from reservoirs that stored incalculable reserves. A terrific quality belied the appearance of this false repose. I was aware of elemental powers, pressed down and eager to run over. It came to me they also had been—called. Their activity, moreover, was in some very definite relation to myself. The voice that summoned me had warned as well.

I stood listening, trembling with an anticipation of things called unearthly. Nature, dressed in the Night, stepped in and took my hand. There seemed an enormous gesture; and it was a gesture, I felt, of adoration. Somewhere behind the calm picture there lay worship.

And I realised, then, that I stood before a page of writing. Out of this inanimate map that was composed of earth, air, fire and water, a deep sentence of elemental significance thrust up into my consciousness. Objects, forced into syllables of this new language, spoke to me. The cosmic language which is the language of the gods stood written on the moonlit world. "We lie here ready for your use," I read. "Worship is the link. We may be known on human terms. You can use us. We can work with you."

The message was so big, it seemed to thunder. Close to this window-sill on which I leaned the rising energy swayed like a sea. It was obedient to human will, and human will could harness it for practical purposes. I was *feeling-with* it. Immense, far-spreading, pouring down in viewless flood from the encircling heights, the surge of it came round the lonely châlet. The valley brimmed. The blindly-heaving lift of it—thus it presented itself to my imagination—could alter the solid rocks until they flowed like water, could float the trees as though they were but straws. For this also came to me with a conviction no less significant than the rest—that the particular elemental powers at hand were the familiar ones of heat and air. With those twin powers, which in their ultimate physical manifestation men know as wind and fire, my mind had established contact. But it was with the spiritual prototypes of these two elements my own small personal breath and heat linked on. There was co-operation. I had been called by name; yet my summoning was but a detail in some vaster evocation. There was no barrier between the not-me, as I must call it, and the me. Others had been called as well.

So strong was the sense that some unusual manifestation of these two "elements" approached, that I instinctively drew back; and in that same instant there flashed into me a vision, as it were, of sheeted flame and of gigantic wind. In my heart the picture rushed, for outwardly still reigned the calm and silence of the autumn night. Yet any moment, it seemed, the barrier into visible, sensible appearance would be leaped. And it was then, while I stood hesitating half-way between the window and the bed, that the sound rose again with sharp distinctness, and my name was called a second time.

I heard the voice; I recognised it; but the name was not the one I answer to to-day. It was another—first uttered at Edinburgh many years ago—Silvatela. And strong emotion laid a spell upon my senses, masking the present with a veil of other times and other places. I stood entranced.... I heard Julius moving softly on the bare boards of the passage as he came towards my room; the door opened quietly; he held a lighted candle; I saw him framed against the darkness on the threshold.

For a fraction of a second then, before either of us spoke, it was as though he stood before me in another setting. For the meagre wood on either side of him gave place somehow to pylons of grey stone, hewn massively; the ceiling lifted into vaulted space where stars hung brightly; cool air breathed against my skin; and through an immense crepuscular distance I was aware of moving figures, clothed like his own in flowing white with napkined heads, their visages swarthier than those I knew to-day. He took a step forward into the room, and the shifting shadows from the moving candle dispelled the entire scene as though the light and darkness had constructed it. He spoke at once:

"She calls you," he said quietly.

He set the candle down upon the table by my bed and gently closed the door. The draught, as he did so, shook the flame, sending a flutter of shadows dancing through the air. Yet it was no play of light and shadow that this time laid the strange construction on his face and gestures. So stately were his movements, so radiant his pale, passionless features, so touched with high, unearthly glory his whole appearance, that I watched him for a minute in silence, conscious of respect that bordered upon awe. He had been, I knew, in direct communication with the very sources of his strange faith, and a remnant of the power still clung to the outer body of his flesh. Into that small, cramped chamber Julius brought the touch of other life, of other consciousness that yet was not wholly unfamiliar to me. I remained close beside him. I drank in power from him. And, again, across my thoughts swept that sheet of fire and that lift of violent wind.

"*She* calls you," he repeated calmly; and by the emphasis on the pronoun I knew he meant her Self of older times.

"She—" I whispered. "Your wife!"

He bowed his head. "She knows, now for the first time, that *you* are here."

She remembers?" I asked falteringly, knowing the "you" he meant was also of an older day.

"She lies in trance," he answered, "and the buried Self is in command. She felt your presence, and she called for you—by name."

"In trance?" I had the feeling of distress that he had forced her. But he caught my thought and set it instantly at rest.

"From deep sleep she passed of her own accord," he said, "into the lucid state. Her older Self, which retains the memories of all the sections, is now consciously awake."

"And she knows you too? Knows you as you were—remembers?" I asked breathlessly, thinking of my first sight of him in the doorway.

"She is aware at this very moment of both you and me," he answered, "but as she knew us in that particular past. For the old conditions are gathering to-night about the house, and the Equinox is nearer."

"Gathered, then, by you," I challenged, conscious that an emotion of protection rose strong in me—protection of the woman.

"Gathered, rather," he at once rejoined, "by our collective presence, by our collective feeling, thought and worship, but also by necessity and justice which bring the opportunity."

He spoke with solemnity. I stared for several minutes in silence, facing him and holding his brilliant eyes with an answering passion in my own. Through the open window came a sighing draught of wind; a sense of increasing warmth came with it; it seemed to me that the pictured fire and wind were close upon me, as though the essential life of these two common elements were rising upon me from within; and I turned, trembling slightly, aware of the valley behind me in the moonlight. The châlet, it seemed, already was surrounded. The Presences stood close.

"They also know," he whispered; "they wait for the moment when we shall require them—the three of us together. She, too, desires them. The necessity is upon us all."

With the words there rose a certainty in me that knew no vain denial. The sense of reality and truth came over me again. He was in conscious league with powers of Nature that held their share of universal intelligence; we three had returned at last together. The approach of semi-spiritual intelligences that operate through phenomenal effects—in this case wind and fire—was no imaginative illusion. The channels here were open.

"No sparrow falls, no feather is misplaced," he whispered, "but it is known and the furthest star responds. From our life in another star we brought our knowledge first. But we used it here—on the earth. It was you—your body— that we used as channel. It was your return that prevented our completion. Your dread of to-day is memory—"

There broke in upon his unfinished sentence an interrupting voice that turned me into stone. Ringing with marvellous authority, half sweet, half terrible, it came along the wooden walls of that narrow corridor, entered the very room about our ears, then died away in the open valley at our backs. The awakened Self of "Mrs. LeVallon" called us:

"Concerighé... Silvatela... !" sounded through the quiet night.

The voice, with its clear accents, plunged into me with an incredible appeal of some forgotten woe and joy combined. It was a voice I recognised, yet one unheard by me for ages. Power and deep delight rose in me, but with them a flash of stupid, earthly terror. It sounded again, breaking the silence of the early morning, but this time nearer than before. It was close outside the door. I felt Julius catch me quickly by the arm. My terror vanished at his touch.

The tread of bare feet upon the boards was audible; the same second the door pushed open and *she* stood upon the threshold, a tall, white figure with fixed and luminous eyes, and hair that fell in a dark cloud to the waist. Into the zone of pallid candle-light that the moon made paler still, she passed against the darkness of the outer passage, white and splendid, like some fair cloud that swims into the open sky. And as wind stirs the fringes of a cloud, the breeze from the window stirred the edges of her drapery where the falling hair seemed to gather it in below the waist.

It was the wife of Julius, but the wife of Julius changed. Like some vision of ethereal beauty she stood before us, yet a vision that was alive. For she moved, she breathed, she spoke. It was both the woman as I knew her actually To-day, and the woman as I had known her—Yesterday. The partial aspect that used this modern body was somehow supplemented—fulfilled by the presentment of her entire Self. The whole series of past sections came up to reinforce the little present, and I gazed upon the complete soul of her, rather than upon the fragment that made bread now in the kitchen and had known domestic service. The bearing was otherwise, the attitude another, the very fashion of her features changed. Her walk, her gestures, her mien had undergone enthralling alteration.

The stream of time went backwards as I gazed, or, rather, it stopped flowing altogether and held steady in a sea that had no motion. I sought the familiar points in her, plunging below the surface with each separate one to find what I—remembered. The eyes, wide open in the somnambulistic lucidity, were no longer of a nondescript mild grey, but shone with the splendour I had already half surprised in them before; the poise of the neck, the set of the shoulders beneath the white linen of her simple night-dress, had subtly, marvellously changed. She stood in challenge to a different world. It seemed to me that I saw the Soul of her, attended by the retinue of memories, experience, knowledge of all its past, summed up sublimely in a single moment. She was superb.

The outward physical change was, possibly, of the slightest, yet wore just that touch of significant alteration which conveyed authority. The tall, lithe figure moved with an imperial air; she raised her arm towards the open window; she spoke. The voice was very quiet, but it held new depth, sonority and accent. She had not seen me yet where I stood in the shadows by the wall, for Julius screened me somewhat, but I experienced that familiar clutch of dread upon the heart that once before—ages and ages ago—had overwhelmed me. Memory poured back upon my own soul too.

"Concerighé," she uttered, looking full at Julius while her hand pointed towards the moonlit valley. "They stand ready. The air is breaking and the fire burns. Then where is _he?_ I called him."

And Julius, looking from her face to mine, answered softly: "He is beside you—close. He is ready with us too. But the appointed time—the Equinox— is not quite yet."

The pointing hand sank slowly to her side. She turned her face towards me and she—saw. The gaze fell full upon my own, the stately head inclined a little. We both advanced; she took my outstretched hand, and at the touch a shock as of wind and fire seemed to drive against me with almost physical violence. I heard her voice.

"Silvatela—we meet—again!" Her eyes ran over in a smile of recognition as the old familiar name came floating to me through the little room. But for the firm clasp of her hand I should have dropped, for there was a sudden weakness in my knees, and my senses reeled a moment. "We meet again," she repeated, while her splendid gaze held mine, "yet to you it is a dream. Memory in you lies unawakened still. And the fault is ours."

She turned to Julius; she took his hand too; we stood linked together thus; and she smiled into her husband's eyes. "His memory," she said, "is dim. He has forgotten that we wronged him. Yet forgiveness is in his soul that only half remembers." And the man who was her husband of To-day said low in answer: "He forgives and he will help us now. His love forgives. The delay we caused his soul he may forget, but to the Law there is no forgetting possible. We must— we shall—repay."

The clasp of our hands strengthened; we stood there linked together by the chain of love both past and present that knows neither injustice nor forgetting.

Then, with the words, as also with the clasping hands that joined us into one, some pent up barrier broke down within my soul, and a flood of light burst over me within that made all things for a moment clear. There came a singular commotion of the moonlit air outside the window, as if the tide that brimmed the valley overflowed and poured about us in the room. I stood transfixed and speechless before the certainty that Nature, in the guise of two great elements, flooded in and shared our passionate moment of recognition. A blinding confusion of times and places struggled for possession of me. For a tempest of memories surged past, driven tumultuously by sheeted flame and rushing wind. The inner hurricane lasted but a second. It rose, it fell, it passed away.

I was aware that I saw down into deep, prodigious depths as into a pool of water, crystal clear; veil lifted after veil; memory revived.

I shuddered; for it seemed my present self slipped out of sight while this more ancient consciousness usurped its place. My little modern confidence collapsed; the mind that doubts and criticises, but never knows, fell back into its smaller role. The sum-total that was Me remembered and took command. And realising myself part of a living universe, I answered her:

"With love and sympathy," I uttered in no uncertain tones, "and with complete forgiveness too."

In that little bedroom of a mountain châlet, lit by the moon and candle-light, we stood together, our bodies joined by the clasp of hands, and our ancient souls united in a single purpose.

I looked into the eyes of this great woman, imperially altered in her outward aspect, magnificent in the towering soul of her; I looked at Julius, stately as some hierophantic figure who mastered Nature by comprehending her; I felt their hands, his own firm and steady, hers clasping softly, tenderly, yet with an equal strength; and I realised that I stood thus between them, not merely in this isolated mountain valley, but in the full tide of life whose source rose in the fountains of an immemorial past, Nature and human-nature linked together in a relationship that was a practical reality. Our three comrade-souls were re-united in an act of restitution; sharing, or about to share, a ceremony that had cosmic meaning.

And the beauty of the woman stole upon my heart, bringing the loveliness of the universe, while Julius brought its strength.

"This time," I said aloud, "you shall not fail. I am with you both in sympathy, forgiveness,—love."

Their hands increased the pressure on my own.

Her eyes held mine as she replied: "This duty that we owe to Nature and to you—so long—so long ago."

"To me—?" I faltered.

With shining eyes, and a smile divinely tender, she answered: "Love shall repay. We have delayed you by our deep mistake."

"We shall undo the wrong we worked upon you," I heard Julius say. "We stole the channel of your body. And we failed."

"My love and sympathy are yours," I repeated, as we drew closer still together. "I bear you no ill-will...."

And then she continued gravely, but ever with that solemn beauty lighting up her face:

"Oh, Silvatela, it seems so small a thing in the long, long journey of our souls. We were too ambitious only. The elemental Powers we tried to summon through your vacated body are still unhoused. The fault was not yours; it was our ambition and our faithlessness. I loved you to your undoing—you sacrificed yourself so willingly, loving me, alas, too well. The failure came. Instead of becoming as the gods, we bear this burden of a mighty debt. We owe it both to you and to the universe. Fear took us at the final moment—and you returned too soon—robbed of the high teaching that was yours by right, your progress delayed thereby, your memory clouded *now*...."

"My development took another turning," I said, hardly knowing whence the knowledge came to me, "no more than that. It was for love of you that I returned too soon—the fault was mine. It was for the best—there has been no real delay." But there mingled in me a memory both clouded and unclouded. There was a confusion beyond me to unravel. I only knew our love was marvellous, although the fuller motives remained entangled. "It is all forgiven," I murmured.

"Your forgiveness," she answered softly, "is of perfect love. We loved each other then—nor have we quite forgotten now. This time, at least, we shall ensure success. The Powers stand ready, waiting; we are united; we shall act as one. At the Equinox we shall restore the balance; and memory and knowledge shall be yours a hundredfold at last."

The voice of Julius interrupted, though so low it was scarcely audible: "I offer myself. It is just and right, not otherwise. The risk must be all mine. Once accomplished"—he turned to me with power in his face—"we shall provide you with the privilege you lost through us. Our error will then be fully expiated and the equilibrium restored. It is an expiation and a sacrifice. Nature in this valley works with us now, and behind it is the universe—all, all aware..."

It seemed to me she leaped at him across the space between us. Our hands released. Perhaps, with the breaking of our physical contact, some measure of receptiveness went out of me, or it may have been the suddenness of the unexpected action that confused me. I no longer fully understood. Some bright clear flame of comprehension wavered, dimmed, went out in me. Even the words that passed between them then I did not properly catch. I saw that she clasped him round the neck while she uttered vehement words that he resisted, turning aside as with passionate refusal. It was—this, at least, I grasped before the return of reason in me broke our amazing union and left confusion in the place of harmony—that each one sought to take the risk upon himself, herself. The channel of evocation—a human system—I dimly saw, was the offering each one burned to make. The risk, in some uncomprehended way, was grave. And I stepped forward, though but half understanding what it was I did. I offered, to the best of my memory and belief—offered myself as a channel, even as I had offered or permitted long ago in love for her.

For I had discerned the truth, and knew deep suffering, nor cared what happened to me. It was the older Self in her that gave me love, while her self of Today—the upper self—loved Julius. Mine was the old subconscious love unrecognised by her normal self; the love of the daily, normal self was his.

The look upon their faces stopped me. They moved up closer, taking my hands again. The moonlight fell in a silver pool upon the wooden flooring just between us; it clothed her white-clad figure with its radiance; it shone reflected in the eyes of Julius. I heard the tinkling of the little stream outside, beginning its long journey to an earthly sea. The nearer pine trees rustled. And *her* voice came with this moonlight, wind and water, as though the quiet night became articulate.

"So great is your forgiveness, so deep our ancient love," she murmured. And while she said it, both he and she together made the mightiest gesture I have ever seen upon small human outlines—a gesture of resignation and refusal that yet conveyed power as though a forest swayed or some great sea rolled back its flood. There was this sublime suggestion in the wordless utterance by which they made me know my offering was impossible. For Nature behind both of them said also No....

Then, with a quiet motion that seemed gliding rather than the taking of actual steps, her figure withdrew slowly towards the door. Her face turned from me as when the moon slips down behind a cloud. Erect and stately, as though a marble statue passed from my sight by some interior motion of its own, her figure entered the zone of shadow just beyond the door. The sound of her feet upon the boards was scarcely audible. The narrow passage took her. She was gone.

CHAPTER XXIV

I stood alone with Julius, Nature alive and stirring strangely, as with aggressive power, just beyond the narrow window-sill on which he leaned. "You understand," he murmured, "and you remember too—at last."

I made no reply. There are moments when extraordinary emotions, beyond expression either of tears or laughter, move the heart as with the glory of another world. And one of these was certainly upon me now. I knew things that

I did not understand. A pageant of incomparable knowledge went past me, yet, as it were, just out of reach. The memories that offered themselves were too enormous—and too different—to be grasped intelligently by the mind.

And yet one thing I realised clearly: that the elemental powers of Nature already existing in every man and woman in small degree, could know an increase, an intensification, which, directed rightly, might exalt humanity. The consciousness of those olden days knew direct access to Nature. And the method, for which no terms exist To-day in any spoken language, was that *feeling-with* which is adoration, and that desiring sympathy which is worship. The script of Nature wrote it clear. To read it was to act it out. The audacity of their fire-stealing ambition in the past I understood, and so forgave. My memory, further than this, refused to clear....

I remember that we talked together for a space; and it was longer than I realised at the time, for before we separated the moon was down behind the ridges and the valley lay in a single blue-black shadow. There was confusion on my heart and mind. The self in me that asked and answered seemed half of To-day and half of Yesterday.

"She remembered," Julius said below his breath yet with deep delight; "she recognised us both. In the morning she will have again forgotten, for she knows not how to bring the experiences of deep sleep over into her upper consciousness."

"She said 'they waited.' There are—others—in this valley?" It was more a statement to myself than a question, but he answered it:

"Everywhere and always there are others. But just now in this valley they are near to us and active. I have sent out the call."

"You have sent out the call," I repeated without surprise and yet with darkened meaning. "Yes, I knew—I was aware of it." My older consciousness was sinking down again.

"By worship," he interrupted, "the worship of many weeks. We have worshipped and felt-with, intensifying the link already established by those who lived before us here. Your attitude is also worship. Together we shall command an effective summons that cannot fail. Already they are aware of us, and at the Equinox their powers will come close—closer than love or hunger."

"In ourselves," I muttered. "Aware of their activities in ourselves!"

And my mouth went suddenly dry as I heard his quiet answer:

"We shall feel their immense activities in ourselves as they return to their appointed places whence we first evoked them. Through one of our three bodies they must pass—the bodiless ones." A silence fell between us. The blood beat audibly in my ears like drums.

They need a body—again?" I whispered.

He bowed his head. "The channel, as before " he whispered with deep intensity, "of a human organism—a brain, a mind, a body." And, seeing perhaps that I stared with a bewilderment half fear and half refusal, he added quietly, "In the raw, they are too vast for human use, their naked, glassy essence impossible to hold. They must mingle first with our own smaller powers that are akin to them, and thus take on that restraint which enables the human will to harness their colossal strength. Alone I could not accomplish this, but with the three of us, merged by our love into a single unit

"But the risk—you both spoke of—?" I asked it impatiently, yet it was only a thick whisper that I heard.

There was a little pause before he answered me.

"There are two risks," he said with utmost gravity in his voice and face. "The descent of such powers *may* cause a shattering of the one on whom they first arrive—he is the sacrifice. My death—any consequent delay—might thus be the expiation I offer in the act of their release. That is the first, the lesser risk."

He paused, then added: "But I shall not fail."

"And—should you—!" My voice had dwindled horribly.

"The Powers, once summoned, would—automatically—seek another channel: the channel for their return—in case I failed. That is the second and the greater risk."

"Your wife?" The words came out with such difficulty that they were scarcely audible. But Julius heard them.

He shook his head. "For herself there is no danger, he answered. "My love of to-day, and yours of Yesterday protect her. Nor has it anything to do with you," he added, seeing the touch of fear that flashed from my eyes beyond my power to conceal it. The Powers, deprived of my control in the case of my collapse beneath the strain, would follow the law of their own beings automatically. They would seek the easiest channel they could find. They would follow the line of least resistance."

And, realising that it was the other human occupant of the house he meant, I experienced a curious sensation of pity and relief; and with a hint of grandeur in my thought, I knew with what fine pathetic willingness, with what whole-hearted simplicity of devotion, this faithful "younger soul" would offer himself to help in so big a purpose—if he understood.

It was with an appalling shock that I realised my mistake. Julius, watching me closely, divined my instant thought. He made a gesture of dissent. To my complete amazement, I saw him shake his head.

"An empty and deserted organism, as yours was at the time we used it for our evocation," he said slowly; "an organism unable to offer resistance owing to its being unoccupied—that is the channel, if it were available, which they would take. When the soul is out—or *not yet—in.*"

We gazed fixedly at one another for a time I could not measure. I knew his awful meaning. For to me, in that first moment of comprehension, it seemed too terrible, too incredible for belief. I staggered over to the open window. Julius came after me and laid his hand upon my shoulder.

"The body is but the instrument," I heard him murmur: "the vehicle of the soul that uses it. Only at the moment of birth does a soul move in to take possession. The parents provide it, helpless and ignorant as to who eventually shall take command. And if this thing happened—though the risk is small—"

I turned and faced him as he stopped.

"A monster!"

"An elemental being, a child of the elements—"

"Non-human?" I gasped.

"Nature and human-nature linked," he replied with curious reverence. "A cosmic being born in a human body. Only—I shall not fail."

And before I could find another word to utter, or even acknowledge the quick pressure of his hand upon my own, I heard his step upon the passage boards, and found myself alone again. I stood by the open window, gazing into the deep, star-lit sky above this mountain valley on our little, friendly Earth, prey to emotions that derived from another, but forgotten planet—emotions, therefore, that no "earthly" words can attempt to fathom or describe....

BOOK IV

THE ATTEMPTED RESTITUTION

CHAPTER XXV

"*Let us consider* wisdom *first.*

"*Can we be wiser by reason of something which we have forgotten? Unquestionably we can.... A man who dies after acquiring knowledge—and all men acquire
some—might enter his new life, deprived indeed of his knowledge, but not deprived
of the increased strength and delicacy of mind which he had gained in acquiring the
knowledge. And if so, he will be wiser in the second life because of what has happened in the first.*

"*Of course he loses something in losing the actual knowledge... But... is not even
this loss really a gain.? For the mere accumulation of knowledge, if memory never
ceased, would soon become overwhelming, and worse than useless. What better fate
would we wish for than to leave such accumulations behind us, preserving their
greatest value in the mental faculties which have been strengthened by their acquisition.*" —J. M'Taggart.

As I sit here in the little library of my Streatham house, trying to record
faithfully events of so many years ago, I find myself at a point now
where the difficulty well-nigh overwhelms me. For what happened in
that valley rises before me now as though it had been some strange and prolonged enchantment; it comes back to me almost in the terms of dream or vision.

If it be possible for a man to enjoy two states of consciousness simultaneously,
then that possibility was mine. I know not. I can merely state that at the time
my normal consciousness seemed replaced by another mode, another order, that
usurped it, and that this usurping consciousness was incalculably older than anything known to men to-day; further, also, that the three of us had revived it from
some immemorial pre-existence. It was memory.

Thus it seemed to me at the time; thus, therefore, I must record it. And so completely was the change effected in me that belief came with it. In no one of us,
indeed, lay the slightest hint of doubt. What happened must otherwise have been
the tawdriest superstition, whereas actually there was solemnity in it, even grandeur. The performance our sacramental attitude of mind made holy, was true
with the reality of an older time when Nature-Worship was effective in some
spiritual sense far beyond what we term animism in our retrospective summary
of the past. We did, each one of us, and in more or less degree, share the life of
Nature by the inner process of feeling-with that life. Her natural forces augmented us indubitably—there was intelligent co-operation.

To-day, of course, the forces in humanity drive in quite another direction; Nature is inanimate and Pan is dead; another attitude obtains—thinking, not feeling, is our ideal; men's souls are scattered beyond the hope of unity and the sword of formal creeds sharply separates them everywhere. We regard ourselves proudly as separate from Nature. Yet, even now, as I struggle to complete this record in the suburban refuge my old age has provided for me, I seem aware of changes stealing over the face of the world once more. Like another vast dream beginning, I feel, perhaps, that man's consciousness is slowly spreading outwards once again; it is re-entering Nature, too, in various movements; the wireless note is marvellously sounding; on all sides singular phenomena that *seem* new suggest that there is no limit—to extension of consciousness—to interior human activity. Some voice from the long ago is divinely trumpeting across our little globe.

This, possibly, is an old man's dream. Yet it helps me vaguely to understand how, in that enchanted valley, the three of us may actually have realised another, older point of view which amounted even to a different type of consciousness. The slight analogy presents itself; I venture to record it. Only on some such supposition could I, a normal, commonplace product of the day, have consented to remain in the valley without repugnance and distress, much less to have participated willingly as I did in all that happened. For I was almost whole-heartedly in and of it. My moments of criticism emerged, but passed. I saw existence from some cosmic point of view that presented a human life as an insignificant moment in an eternal journey that was related both to the armies of the stars and to the blades of grass along the small, cool rivulet. At the same time this vast perspective lifted each tiny detail into a whole that inspired these details with sacramental value whose meaning affected everything. To live with the universe made life the performance of a majestic ceremony; to live against it was to creep aside into a *cul de sac*. And so this small item of balance we three, as a group, desired to restore was both an insignificant and a mighty act of worship.

Yet, whereas to myself the happenings were so intense as to seem terrific even, to one who had not *felt* them—as I did—they must seem hardly events or happenings at all. I say "felt," because my perception of what occurred was "feeling" more than anything else. I enjoyed this other mode of existence known to the human spirit in an earlier day, and brought, apparently, to earth from our experience upon another planet.

The happenings, to me, seemed momentous—yet they consisted largely of interior changes. They were inner facts. And such inner facts "To-day" regards as less real than outer events, dismissing them as subjective. The collapse of a roof is real, the perception of an eternal verity is a mood! And if my attempt to describe halts between what is alternately bald and overstrained, it is because modern words can only stammer in dealing with experiences that have so entirely left the racial memory.

For myself the test of their actuality lies in the death that resulted—an indubitable fact at any rate!—and in the birth that followed it a little later—another unquestionable "fact."

I may advantageously summarise the essential gist of the entire matter. I would do so for this reason: that physical memory grows dim on looking back so many years and that the events in the châlet grow more and more elusive, so that I find a sharp general outline helpful to guide me in this subsequent record. Further, the portion I am now about to describe depends wholly upon a yet older memory, the memory as it seemed to me of thousands of years ago. This more ancient memory came partially to me only. I saw much I could not understand or realise, and so can merely report baldly. There was fluctuation. Perhaps, after all, my earlier consciousness was never restored with sufficient completeness to reconstitute the entire comprehension that had belonged to it when it was my *natural* means of perceiving, knowing, being. Words, therefore, obviously fail.

Let me say then, as Julius himself might have said, that in some far-off earlier existence the three of us had offended a cosmic law, and that for the inevitable readjustment of this error, its expiation, the three of us must first of all find ourselves reincarnated once again together. This, after numerous intervening centuries, had come to pass.

The nature of the offence seemed crudely this: that, in the days when elemental Nature-Powers were accessible to men, we used two of these—those operating behind wind and fire—for selfish instead of for racial purposes. Apparently they had been evoked by means of a human body which furnished their channel of approach. It was available because untenanted, as already described. I state merely the belief and practice of an earlier day. Special guardians protected the vacated bodies from undesirable invasion, and while Julius and the woman performed this duty, they had been tempted to unlawful use for purposes of their own. The particular body was my own: I was the channel of evocation. That I had, however, been persuaded to permit such usage was as certain as that it was the love between the woman and myself that was the reason of such permission. How and why I cannot state, because, simply, I could not—remember. But that the failure of their experiment resulted in my sudden recall into the body, and the loss, therefore, of teaching and knowledge I should have otherwise enjoyed—this had delayed my soul's advance and explained also why, To-day, memory failed in me and my soul had lagged behind in its advance. Somewhat in this way LeVallon stated it.

Where this ancient experiment took place, in what country and age, I cannot pretend to affirm. The knowledge made use of, however, seems to have been, in its turn, a yet earlier memory still, and of an existence upon a planet nearer to the sun, since Fire and Wind were there recognised as a means by which deific Powers became accessible—through worship. That the human spirit was then clothed in bodies of lighter mould, and that Wind and Fire were viewed as manifestations of deity, turns my imagination, if not my definite memory, to a planet like Mercury, where gigantic Heat and therefore mighty Winds would be imposing vehicles of conveying energy from their source—the Sun.

For the expiation of the error, a re-enactment of the actual scene of its committal was necessary. It must be acted out to be effective—a ceremony. The channel, again, of a human system was essential as before. The struggles that eventually ensued, complicated by the stress of personal emotion—the individual attempts each participator made to become the channel and so the possible sacrifice—this caused, apparently, the awful failure. Emotion destroyed the unity of the group. For Julius was unable to direct the Powers evoked. They were compelled to seek a channel elsewhere, and they automatically availed themselves of that which offered the least resistance. The birth that subsequently followed, accordingly, was a human body informed literally by these two elemental Powers; and it is in the hope that of those who chance to read these notes, someone may perhaps be aware of the existence in the world of this unique being—it is in this hope primarily, I say, that the record I have attempted is made, that it may survive my death which cannot now be very long delayed.

One word more, however, I am compelled to add:

I am aware that my so easy surrender to the spell of LeVallon's personality and ideas must seem difficult to justify. Even those of my intimates, who may read this record after I am gone, may feel that my capitulation was due to what men now term hypnotic influence; whereas, that some part of me accepted with joy and welcome is the actual truth—it was some lesser part that objected and disapproved.

To myself, as to those few who may find these notes, I owe this somewhat tardy confession of personal bias. That I have concealed it in this Record hitherto seems because my "educated" self must ever struggle to deny it.

For there have always been two men in me—more than in the usual sense of good and evil. One, up to date and commonplace, enjoys the game of nineteenth century life, interests itself in motors, telephones, and mechanical progress generally, finds Socialism intriguing and even politics absorbing; while the other, holding all that activity of which such things are symbols, in curious contempt, belongs to the gods alone know what. It remains essentially inscrutable, incalculable, its face masked by an indecipherable smile. It worships the sun, believes in Magic, accepts the influences of the stars, and acknowledges with sweet reverence extended hierarchies of Beings, both lower and higher than the stage at which humanity now finds itself.

In youth, of course, this other self was stronger than in later years; yet, though submerged, it has never been destroyed. It seemed an older aspect of my divided being that declined to die. For periods of varying duration, the modern part would deny it as the superstition of primitive animistic ignorance; but, biding its time, it would rise to the surface and take the reins again. The modern supremacy passed, the older attitude held authoritative sway. The Universe then belonged to it, alive in every detail; there was communion with trees and winds and streams; the thrill of night became articulate; it was concerned with distant stars; the sun changed the earth once more into a vast temple-floor. I was not apart from any item, large or small, on earth or in the heavens, while myth and legend, poetry and folk-lore were but the broken remnants of a once extended faith, a mighty worship that was both of God and knew the gods.

At such times the drift of modern life seemed in another—a minor—direction altogether. The two selves in me could not mingle, could not even compromise. The recent one seemed trivial, but the older one pure gold. It dwelt, this latter, in loneliness, sweetly-prized, perhaps, but isolated from all minds of to-day worth knowing, because its mode of being was not theirs. A loneliness, however, not intolerable, since it was aware of lifting joy, of power no mere contrivance could conceive, and of a majestic beauty nothing of to-day could even simulate.... Societies, moreover, called secret, fraternities labelled magical and hierophantic, were all too trumpery to feed its ancient longings, too charlatan to offer it companionship, too compromising to obtain result. Among modern conditions I found no mode of life that answered to its imperious call in me. It seemed an echo and a memory.

As I grew older, both science and religion told me it must be denied. Respectful of the former, I sought some reasonable basis for these strange burning beliefs that flamed up with this older self—in vain. Unjustifiable, according to all knowledge at my disposal, they remained. History went back step by step to that darkness whence ignorance emerged; evolution traced a gradual rise from animal conditions; to no dim, former state of exalted civilisation, either remembered or imagined, could this deeper part of me track its home and origin. Yet that home, that origin, I felt, existed, and were accessible. I could no more resign their actuality than I could cease to love, to hate, to live. The mere thought of them woke emotions independent of my will, contemptuous of my intellect— emotions that were of indubitable reality. They remained convictions.

Had I, then, known some state antedating history altogether, some unfabled land of which storied Atlantis, itself a fragment, lingered as a remnant of some immenser life? Had I experienced a mode of being less cabined than the one I now experienced in a body of blood and flesh—another order of consciousness, yet identity retained—upon another star?... The centuries geology counts backwards were but moments, the life of a planet only a little instant in the universal calendar. Was there, a million years ago, a civilisation of another kind, too ethereal to leave its signatures in sand and rocks, yet in its *natural* simplicity nearer, perhaps, to deity? Was here the origin of my unrewarded yearnings? Could reincarnation, casting back across the æons to lovelier or braver planets, give the clue? And did this older self trail literally clouds of glory from a golden age of light and heat and splendour that lay nearer to the shining centre of our corner of the heavens...?

At intervals I flung my queries like leaves upon the wind; and the leaves came back to me upon the wind. I found no answer. Speculation became gradually less insistent, though the yearnings never died. Deeper than doubt or question, they seemed ingrained—that my preexistence has been endless, that I continue always.... And it was this strange, buried self in me, already beginning to fade a little when I went to Motfield Close to train my modern mind in modern knowledge—it was this curious older self that Julius LeVallon vitalised anew. Back came the flood of mighty questions: Whence have we come? From what dim corner of the unmeasured cosmos are we derived, descended, making our little way on to the earth? Where have these hints of an immenser life their sweet, terrific origin, and—why this unbridged hiatus in our memory...?

The subsequent events lie somewhat confused in me until the night that her-
alded the Equinox. Whether two days or three intervened between the night-
scene of LeVallon's Older Self already described, and the actual climax, I cannot remember clearly. The sequence of hours went so queerly sliding; incidents
of external kind were so few that the interval remained unmarked; little happened in the sense of outward happenings on which the mind can fasten by way
of measurement. We lived, it seems, so close to Nature that those time-divisions
we call hours and days flowed with us in a smooth undifferentiated stream. I
think we were too much in Nature to observe the size or length of any particular parcels. We just flowed forward with the tide itself. Yet to explain this, now
that for years I am grown normal and ordinary again, is hardly possible. I only
remember that larger scale; I can no longer realise it.

I recall, however, the night of that conversation when Julius left me to my hurricane of thoughts and feelings, and think I am right in saying it immediately pre-
ceded the September day that ushered in the particular "attitude" of our earth
towards the rest of the Universe we call the Autumnal Equinox.

Sleep and resistance were equally impossible; I swam with an enormous current upon a rising tide. And this tide bore stars and worlds within its irresistible
momentum. It bore also little flowers; moisture felt, before it is seen, as dew or
rain; heat that is latent before the actual flame is visible; and air that lies everywhere until the rush of wind insists on recognition. I was aware of a prophecy
that included almost menace. An uneasy sense that preparations of immense, portentous character were incessantly in progress, not in the house and in ourselves
alone, but in the entire sweep of forest, vale and mountain, pressed upon me
from all sides. Nature conspired, I felt, through her most usual channels to drive
into a corner where she would drip over, so to speak, into amazing manifestation. And that corner, waiting and inviting, was ourselves....

Towards morning I fell asleep, and when I woke a cloudless day lay clear and
fresh upon the world, the meadows shone with dew, cobwebs shimmered past
my open window, and a keen breeze from the heights stung my nostrils with
the scent from miles of forest. A sparkling vitality poured almost visibly with
the air and sunshine into my human blood. I bathed and dressed. Frost had laid
silvery fingers upon the valley during the night, and the shadows beneath the
woods still shone in white irregular patches of a pristine loveliness. The feeling
that Nature brimmed over was even stronger than before, and I went downstairs half conscious that the "corner" we prepared would show itself somehow
fuller, *different*. The little arena waiting for it—that arena occupied by our human selves—would proclaim the risen tide. I almost expected to find Julius and
his wife expressing in their physical persons the advent of this power, their very
bodies, gestures, voices increased and grown upon a larger scale. And when I
met them at the breakfast table, two normal, ordinary persons, merely full of the
exhilarating autumn morning, I knew a moment of surprise that at the same time
included relief, though possibly, too, a touch of disappointment. They were both

so simple and so natural.

It brought me up short, as though before a promised hope not justified, a balked anticipation. But the next moment my mistake was clear. The sense of something dwindled gave place to its very opposite—a fuller realisation. The three of us were so intimate—I might say so divinely intimate—that my failure to see them "grander" arose from my attempt to see them "separate"—from my-self. For actually we floated, all three, upon the risen tide together. It was the "mind" in me that sounded the old false note. Having increased like themselves, I was of equal stature with them; to see them "different" was impossible.

And this amazing quality was characteristic of all that followed. Ever since my arrival I had been slowly rising with the tide that brimmed the valley now to the very lips of the surrounding mountains. It brimmed our hearts as well. My companions were quiet because they, like myself, were part of it. There was no sense of disproportion or exaggeration, much less of dislocation; we shared Nature's powers without effort, without struggle, as naturally as sunshine, wind or rain. We stood within; the day contained all three. The Ceremony, which was living-with Nature, tuned to the universal life, had been in progress from the instant Julius had welcomed me a week ago. Our attitude and the earth's were one. The Equinox was in us too.

In that moment when we met at breakfast, the flash of clearer sight left all this beyond dispute. Memory shot back in a lightning glance over recent sensations and events. I realised my gradual growth into the larger scale, I grasped the sig-nificance of the various moods and tenses my changing consciousness had known as in a kind of initiation. Premonitions of another mode of mind had stolen upon me out of ordinary things. The habitual had revealed its marvellous hid-den beauty. There had been transmutation. The ensouling life behind broke loose everywhere, even through the elements themselves: but particularly through the two of them that are so closely levelled to the little division we call human life: air-things and fire-things had become alert and eager. There was commotion in the palaces of Wind and Fire.

And so the bigger truth explained itself to me. What happened later seems only incredible on looking back at it from my present dwindled consciousness. At the time it was natural and quiet. A tourist, passing through our lonely val-ley, need not have been aware either of tumult or of wonder. He would have been too remote from us, too centred in the consciousness of To-day that accepts only what is expected, or explicable—too different, in a word, to have noticed anything beyond the presence of three strangely quiet people in a lonely châlet of the mountains.

But for us, the gamut of experience had stretched; there was in our altered state both a microscope and telescope; but a casual intruder, unprovided with either, must have gone his way, I think, unaware, unstimulated, and uninformed.

CHAPTER XXVI

"*With virtue the point is perhaps clearer.... I have forgotten the greater number of the good and evil acts which I have done in my present life. And yet each must have left a trace on my character. And so a man may carry over into his next life the dispositions and tendencies which he has gained by the moral contests of this life, and the value of those experiences will not have been destroyed by the death which has destroyed the memory of them.*"—Ibid.

T he day that followed lives with me still as an experience of paradise beyond intelligible belief. Yet I unquestionably experienced it. The touch of dread was but the warning of the little mind, which shrank from a joy too vast for it to comprehend. Of Mrs. LeVallon this was similarly true. Julius alone, sure and steadfast in the state from which since early boyhood he had never lapsed, combined Reason and Intuition in that perfect achievement towards which humanity perhaps slowly seems moving now. He remained an image of strength and power; he lived in full consciousness what she and I lived half unconsciously. Yet to record the acts and words which proved it I find now stammeringly difficult; they were so ordinary. The point of view which revealed their "otherness" I have so wholly lost.

"The Equinox comes to-night—the pause in Nature," he said at breakfast, joy in his voice and eyes. "We shall have greater life. The moment is ours, because we know how to use it." Yet what pregnant truth came with the quiet words, what realisation of simple, overflowing beauty, what incalculable power, no language known to me can possibly express.

And his wife, equally, was aglow with happiness and splendour as of a forgotten age. In myself, too, remained no vestige of denial or alarm. The day seemed a long, sweet period without divisions, a big, simple sacrament of unconditioned bliss. Memory came back upon me in a flood, yet a memory of states, and never once of scenes or places. I re-lived a time, a state, when men knew greater purposes than they realised, dimly and instinctively perhaps, not blindly altogether, yet taught of Nature and the Nature Powers close upon their daily lives. They knew these Powers direct, experiencing them, existing side by side with them in definite mutual relationship. They neither reasoned nor, possibly, even thought. They knew.

For my nature was no longer in opposition to the rest of things, nor set over against the universe, as apart from it. I felt my acts related in a vital manner to the planet, as to the entire cosmos, and the elemental side of Nature moved alongside of my most trivial motions. The drift of happenings, in things "external" to me, were related to that drift of inner sensation that I called myself. Thoughts, desires, emotions found themselves completed in trees and grass, in rocks and flowers, in the flowing rivulet, in the whir of wind, the drip of water, the fire of the sunshine. They told me things about myself; they revealed a pregnant story of information by their attitudes and aspects; they were related to my very fate and character. The sublime simplicity of it lies beyond description. For this sacramental tone changed ordinary daily life into something splendid as eternity. I shared the elemental power of "inanimate" things. They affected me and I affected them. The Universe itself, but especially the known and friendly Earth, was hand in hand and arm in arm with me. It was feeling-with; it was the cosmic point of view.

And thus, I suppose, it was that I realised humanity as but a little portion of the whole—important, of course, as the animalculæ in a drop of water are important, yet living towards extinction only if they live apart from the surrounding ocean which divinely mothers them. To this divinity seemed due the presumption with which man To-day imagines himself the centre of this colossal ocean, and lays down the law so insolently for the entire Universe. The birth of a soul—its few years of gaining experience in a material form called body—was vital certainly for itself, yet whether that body should be informed by a "human" soul, or by another type of life of elemental kind—this, seen in proportion to the gigantic scale of universal life, left me unshocked and undismayed. To provide a body for any life was a joy, a proud delight, a duty to the whole, but whether Mrs. LeVallon bore a girl or a boy, or furnished a vehicle for some swift marvellous progeny of another kind, seemed in no sense to offer an afflicting alternative. My *present* point of view may be imagined—the ghastliness and terror, even the horror of it—but at the time I faced it otherwise, regarding the possibility with a kind of reverent wonder only. It was not terrible, but grand.

The certainty of all this I realised at the time. I see it now less vividly. The intensity has left me. So overwhelming was its perfection, however, that, as I have said, the contingency to which Mrs. LeVallon, as mother was exposed, held no dire or unmoral suggestion for me, as it now must hold. Nor did the correlative conditions appear otherwise than true and possible. And that these two, Julius and his wife, staked an entire lifetime to correct an error of the past, meant no more—viewed in this vaster proportion—than if I ran upstairs to close a door I had foolishly left open. An open door is a little thing, yet may cause currents of air that can disarrange the harmony of the objects in its path, upsetting the purpose and balance of the entire household. It must be closed before the occupants of the house can do their work effectively. They owe it to the house as well as to themselves. There was this door left open. It must be closed.

But it could not be closed by one. We three, a group, alone could compass this small act. We who had opened it alone could close it. The potential strength of three in one was the oldest formula of effective power known to life. Such a group was capable of a claim on Nature impossible to an individual—the method of evocation we had used together in the long ago.

CHAPTER XXVII

"There remains love. The gain which the memory of the past gives us here is that the memory of past love for any person can strengthen our present love of him. And this is what must be preserved if the value of past love is not to be lost. But love has no end but itself. If it has gone, it helps us little that we keep anything it has brought us...

"What more do we want? The past is not preserved separately in memory, but it exists, concentrated and united in the present.... If we still think that the past is lost, let us ask ourselves whether we regard, as lost all those incidents in a friend-ship which, even before death, are forgotten."—Ibid.

Here, then, as well as the mind in me can set it down, was the background against which the various incidents of this final day occurred. This was my "attitude" towards them; these thoughts and feelings, though unexpressed in words, were the "mood" which accepted and understood each slightest incident of those extraordinary hours.

The length of the day amazed me; it seemed endless. Time went another gait. The sequence of little happenings that marked its passage remains blurred in the memory, and I look back to these with the curious feeling that they happened all at once. Yet the strongest impression, perhaps, is that time, the sense of du-ration, was arrested or at least moved otherwise. There was a pause in Nature, the pause before the approaching Equinox. A river halted a moment at the bend. And hence came, of course, the sensation of pressure accumulating everywhere in the valley. Acceleration would come afterwards, but first this wondrous pause.

And this pressure that brimmed the valley forced common details into an un-common view. The rising tide drove objects on the banks above high-water mark. There was exhilaration without alarm, as when an exceptional tide throws a full ocean into unaccustomed inlets. The thrill was marvellous. The forest made response, offering its secret things without a touch of fear... as when the deer came out and grazed upon the meadow before the châlet windows, not singly but in groups, and invariably, I noticed, groups of three and three. We passed close in and out among them; I stroked the thick rough hair upon their flanks; I remember Mrs. LeVallon's arm about their necks, and once in partic-ular, when she was lying down, that a fawn, no hint of fear in its beautiful, gra-cious eyes, pushed her hair aside with its shining muzzle to nibble the grass against her neck. The mood of an ancient and divining prophecy lay in the sight, linking Nature with human-nature in natural harmony when the lion and the lamb might play together, and a little child might lead them. For—significant, arresting item—the very air came sweetly down among us too, and the friendly intimacy of the birds brought this exquisite touch of love into the entire day. There was communion everywhere between our Selves and Nature. The birds were in my room when I went upstairs, one hopping across the pillow on my bed, its bright eyes shining as it perched an instant on my shoulder, two others twittering and dancing along the narrow window-sill. There was no fear in them; they fluttered here and there at will, and my quickest movements caused them no alarm. From the table they peeped up into my face; they were downstairs flitting in and out among the chairs and sofas; they did not fly away when we came in. And in threes I saw them, always in threes together. It was like reading natural omens; I understood the significance that lay in omens; and in this delightful sense, but in no other, these natural signs were—ominous.

Over the face of Nature, and in our hearts as well, lay everywhere this attitude of divine carelessness. Everything felt-with everything else, and all were neighbours. The ascension of the soul through all the natural kingdoms seemed written clear upon the trees and rocks and flowers, upon birds and animals, upon the huge, quiet elements themselves.

For the pause and stillness, these were ominous, too. This hush of Nature upon the banks of Time, this beautiful though solemn pause upon the heart of things, was but the presage of an accelerated rushing forward that would follow it. The world halted and took breath. It was the moment just before the leap.

With midnight the climax would be reached—the timeless instant of definite arrest, too brief, too swift for mechanism to record, the instant when Julius would enforce his ancient claim. Then the impetuous advance would be resumed, but resumed with the increased momentum, moreover, of natural forces whose outward manifestation men call the equinoctial gales. Those elemental disturbances, that din and riot in the palaces of heat and air, of wind and fire— how little the sailors, the men upon the heights, the dwellers in the streets of crowded cities might guess the free divinity loose upon the earth behind the hurricanes! The forgotten majesty of it broke in upon me as I realised it. For realise it I most assuredly did. The channels here, indeed, were open.

There seemed a halo laid upon the day; sanctity and peace in all its corners; the valley was a temple, the splendour of true old-world worship ushering in the Equinox: Earth's act of adoration to the sun, the breathless moment when she sank upon her knees before her source of life, her progeny aware, participating.

For the joy and power that vibrated with every message of light and sound about us came to me in the terms of love, as though a love which broke all barriers down flowed in from Nature. It woke in me an unmanageable, an infinite yearning; I burned to sweep all modern life into this lonely mountain valley, to share its happiness with the entire world; the tired ones, the sick and weary, the poor, those who deem themselves outcast and useless in the scheme of things, the lonely, the destitute in spirit, the failures, the wicked, and, above all, the damned. For here all broken and shattered lives, it seemed to me, must find that sense of wholeness which is confidence and that peace due to the certainty of being cared for by the universe—divinely mothered. The natural sacrament of elemental powers, in its simplicity, could heal the nations. I yearned to bring humanity into the power of Nature and the joy of Nature-Worship.

So complete, moreover, was my inclusion in this sacramental attitude towards Nature, that I saw the particular purpose for which we three were here—as Julius saw it. I experienced a growing joy, an ever lessening alarm. Three human souls met here upon this island of a moment's restitution, important certainly, yet after all an episode merely, set between a series of lives long past and of countless lives to follow after. The elements, and the Earth to which they were consciously related, the Universe of which, with ourselves, she formed an integral constituent—all were relatively and in their just proportions involved in this act of restitution. Hence, in a dim way, it was out of time and space. Our very acts and feelings were those of Nature and of that vaster Whole, wherein Nature, herself but a little item, lies secure. The Universe felt and acted with us. The gentian in the field would he aware, but Sirius, too.

Three human specks would act out certain things, but the wind in the forest would co-operate and feel glad, and the fire in Orion's nebula would be aware.

An older form of consciousness was operative. We were not separate. Instead of *thinking* as separate items apart from the rest of the cosmos, we *felt* as integral bits of it—and here, perhaps, lay the essence of what I call another kind of consciousness than the one known to-day.

CHAPTER XXVII

My mind retains with photographic accuracy the detail of that sinister yet gorgeous night. One thing alone vitiates the value of my report—while I remember what happened, I cannot remember *why* it happened.

At the actual time, I understood the meaning of every word and action because the power to do so was in me. I was in another state of consciousness. That state has passed, and with it the ability to interpret. I am in the position of a man who remembers clearly the detail of some dream to which, on waking, he has lost the key. While dreaming it, the meaning was daylight clear. The return to normal consciousness has left him with a photograph he no longer can explain.

The first tentative approach, however, of those Intelligences men call Fire and Wind—their first contact with this other awakened Self in me, I remember perfectly. Wind came first, then Fire; yet at first it was merely that they made their presence known. I became aware of them. And the natural, simple way in which this came about I may describe to some extent perhaps.

The ruins of a flaming sunset lay above the distant ridges when Julius left my room, and, after locking away the private papers entrusted to my charge, I stood for some time watching the coloured storm-clouds hurrying across the sky. For, though the trees about the châlet were motionless, a violent wind ran high overhead, and on the sunmits it would have been impossible to stand. Round the building, however, sunken in its protected valley, and within the walls especially, reigned a still, delightful peace. The wind kept to the summits. But of some Spirit of Wind I was aware long before the faintest movement touched a single branch.

Upon me then, gathering with steady power, stole the advance-guard of these two invasions—air and warmth, yet an inner air, an inner warmth. For, while I watched, the silence of those encircling forests conveyed the sound and move-ment of approaching life. There grew upon me, first as by dim and curious sug-gestion, a sense of ordered preparation slowly accumulating behind the mass of shadowy trees. The picture then sharpened into more definite outline. The for-est was busy with the stirrings of a million thread-like airs that built up together the body of a rising wind, yet not of wind as commonly experienced, but rather of some subtler, more acute activity of which wind is but the outer vehicle. The inner activity, of which it is the sensible manifestation—the body—was be-ginning to move. The soul of air itself was stirring. These million ghost-like airs were lifting wings from their invisible, secret lairs, all running as by a word of command towards a determined centre whence, obeying a spiritual summons, they would presently fall upon the valley in that sensible manifestation called the equinoctial gales. Behind the material effect, the spiritual Cause was active.

This imaginative picture grew upon me, as though in some way I was let into the inner being of that life which prompts all natural movements and hides, se-curely veiled, in every stock and stone. A new interpretative centre was awake in me. In the movement of wind I was aware of—life. Then, while this subtle perception that an intelligent, directing power lay behind the very air I breathed, a similar report reached me from another, equally elemental, quarter, though it is less easy to describe.

From the sun? Originally, yes—since primarily from the sun emerges all the heat the earth contains. It first stirred definite sensation in me when my eye caught the final gleam upon the turreted walls of vapour where still the sunset stood emblazoned. From that coloured sea of light, and therefore of heat, some-thing flashed in power through me; a vision of running fire broke floodingly above the threshold of my mind, ran into every corner of my being, left its in-spiring trail, became part of my very nerves and blood. Consciousness was deep-ened and intensified.

Yet it was neither common heat I felt nor common flame I pictured, but rather a touch of that primordial and ethereal fire which dwells at the heart of all mani-fested life—latent heat. For it was neither yellow, red, nor white with any as-pect of common flame, but what I can only dare to describe as a fierce, dark splen-dour, black and shining, yet of intense, incandescent brilliance. The contradictory adjectives catch a ghost of it. Moreover, I was aware of no dis-comfort, for while it threatened to overwhelm me, the chief effect was to leave a glow, a radiance, an enthusiasm of strengthened will and confidence, combined with a sense of lightning's power. It was spiritual heat, of which fire is but a physical vehicle. The central fire of the universe burned in my heart.

I realised, in a word, that both elements were vehicles of intelligent and liv-ing Agencies. Of their own accord they became active, and natural laws were but their method of activity. They were alert; the valley was alive, combining, co-operating with myself—and taking action.

This was their first exquisite approach. But presently, when I moved away from the window, the sunset clouds grown dark and colourless again, I realised lesser manifestations of this new emotion which may seem more intelligible when I set them down in words. The candle flame, for instance, and the flaring match with which I lit my cigarette seemed not so much to produce fire by a chemi- cal device, as to puncture holes through a curtain into that sea of latent fire that lies in all material things. The breath of air, moreover, that extinguished the flame did not annihilate it, but merged it into the essential being of its own self. The two acted in sympathy together. Both Wind and Fire drew attention to them- selves of set intention, insisting upon notice, as if inviting co-operation.

And something leviathan leaped up in me to welcome them. The standing mir- acle of fire lit up the darkened valley. Pure flame revealed itself suddenly as the soul in me, the eternal part that remembered and grew wise, the deathless part that survived all successive bodies.

And I realised with a shock of comprehension the danger that Julius ran in the evocation that his "experiment" involved: Fire, once kindled, and aided nat- urally by air, must seek to destroy the prison that confines it....

I remained for some time in my room. My will, my power of choice, seemed taken from me. My life moped with these vaster influences. I argued vehemently with some part of me that still offered a vague resistance. It was the merest child's play. I figured myself in my London lecture room, explaining to my stu- dents the course and growth of the delusion that had captured me. The result was futile; I convinced neither my students nor myself. It was the thinking mind in me that opposed, but it was another thing in me that *knew*, and this other thing was enormously stronger than the reasoning mind, and overwhelmed it. No amount of arguing could stand against the power of knowledge that had be- come established in me by feeling-with. I felt-with Nature, especially with her twin elemental powers of wind and fire. And this wisdom of feeling-with domi- nated my entire being. Denial and argument were merely false.

All that evening this sense of the companionship of Wind and Fire remained vividly assertive. Everywhere they moved about me. They acted in concert, each assisting the other. I was for ever aware of them; their physical manifestations were as great dumb gestures of two living and intelligent Immensities in Nature. Yet it was only in part, perhaps, I knew them. Their full amazing power never came to me completely. The absolute realisation that came to Julius in full con- sciousness was not mine. I shared at most, it seems, a reflected knowledge, see- ing what happened as through some lens of half-recovered memory.

Moreover, supper, when I came downstairs to find Julius and his wife already waiting for me, was the most ordinary and commonplace meal imaginable. We talked of the weather! Mrs. LeVallon was light-hearted, almost gay, though I felt it was repressed excitement that drove outwards this trivial aspect of her. But for the fact that all she did now seemed individual and distinguished, her talk and gestures might have scraped acquaintance with mere foolishness. Indeed,

our light talk and her irresponsibility added to the sense of reality I have mentioned. It was a mask, and the mask dropped occasionally with incongruous
abruptness that was startling.

Such insignificant details revealed the immediate range of the Powers that
watched and waited close beside our chairs. That sudden, fixed expression in
her eyes, for instance, when the Man brought in certain private papers, handed
them to Julius who, after reading them, endorsed them with a modern fountain
pen, then passed them on to me! That fountain pen and her accompanying remark—how incongruous and insignificant they were! Both seemed symbolical
items in some dwindled, trivial scale of being!

"It isn't everybody that's got a professor for a secretary, Julius, is it?"

She said it with her mouth full, her elbows on the able, and only that other
look in the watchful eyes seemed to contradict the awkward, untaught body.
There was a flash of tenderness and passion in them, a pathetic questioning and
wonder, as though she saw in her husband's act an acknowledgment of dim forebodings in her own deep heart. She appealed, it seemed, to me. Was it that she
divined he was already slipping from her, farewells all unsaid, yet that she was—
inarticulate?... The entire little scene, the words, the laughter and the look, were
but evidence of an attempt to lift the mask. Her choice of words, their accent
and pronunciation, that fountain pen, the endorsement, the stupid remark
about myself—were all these lifted by those yearning eyes into the tragedy of
a fateful good-bye message?...

More significant still, though even less direct, was another moment—when
the Man stretched his arm across the table to turn the lamp up. For in this unnecessary act she saw—the intuition came sharply to me—an effect of the approaching Powers upon his untutored soul. The wick was already high enough
when, with an abrupt, impulsive movement, he stooped to turn it higher; and
instantly Mrs. LeVallon was on her feet, her face first pale, then hotly flushed.
She rose as though to strike him, then changed the gesture as if to ward a blow—
almost to protect. It was an impetuous, revealing act.

Out of some similar impulse, too, only half understood, I sprang to her assistance.

"There's light enough," I exclaimed.

"And heat," she added quickly. "Good Lord! The room's that hot, it's like a
furnace!"

She flashed a look of gratitude at me. What exactly was in her mind I cannot
know, but in my own was the strange feeling that the less *visible* fire in the air
the better. An expression of perplexed alarm showed itself in the face of the
faithful but inarticulate serving man. Unwittingly he had blundered. His distress was acute. I almost thought he would drop to his knees and lick his mistress's hand for forgiveness.

Whether Julius perceived all this is hard to say. He looked up calmly, watching us; but the glance he gave, and the fact that he spoke no word, made me think
he realised what the energy of her tone and gesture veiled. The desire to assist
the increase of heat, of fire—co-operation—had acted upon the physical medium

least able to resist—the most primitive system present. The approach of the two Activities affected us, one and all.

There were other incidents of a similar kind before the meal was over, quite ordinary in themselves, yet equally revealing; my interpretation of them due to this enhanced condition of acute perception that pertained to awakening memory. Air and fire accumulated, flake by flake. A kind of radiant heat informed all common objects. It was in our hearts as well. And wind was waiting to blow it into flame.

CHAPTER XXIX

"Not yet are fixed the prison bars;
The hidden light the spirit owns
If blown to flame would dim the stars
And they who rule them from their thrones:
And the proud sceptred spirits thence
Would bow to pay us reverence."
—A. E.

It was out of this accumulation of unusual emotion that a slight but significant act of Julius recalled me to the outer world. I was lighting my pipe—from the chimney of the lamp rather than by striking a match—when I overheard him telling the Man that, instead of sitting up as usual, he might go to bed at once. He went off obediently, but with some latent objection, half resentment, half opposition, in his manner. There was a sulkiness as of disappointment in his face. He knew that something unusual was on foot, and he felt that he should by rights be in it—he might be of use, he might be needed. There was this dumb emotion in him, as in a faithful dog who, scenting danger, is not called upon to fight, and so retires growling to his kennel.

He went slowly, casting backward glances, and at the door he turned and caught my eye. I had only to beckon, to raise my hand a moment, to say a word—he would have come running back with a bound into the room. But the gaze of his master was upon him, and he went; and though he may have lain down in his room beyond the kitchen, I felt perfectly sure he did not sleep. His body lay down, but not his excited instincts.

For this dismissal of the Man was, of course, a signal. The three of us were then in that dim-lit peasant's room—alone; and for a long time in a silence broken only by the sparks escaping from the burning logs upon the hearth, and by the low wind that now went occasionally sighing past the open window. We sat there waiting, not looking at each other, yet each aware of the slightest physical or mental movement. It was an intense and active silence in which deep things were being accomplished; for, if Mrs. LeVallon and myself were negative, I was alert to immense and very positive actions that were going forward in the being of our companion. Julius, sitting quietly with folded hands, his face just beyond the lamp's first circle of light, was preparing, and with a stress of extreme internal effort that made the silence seem a field of crashing battle. The entire strength of this strange being's soul, co-operating with Nature, and by methods of very ancient acquirement known fully to himself alone, sought an achievement that should make us act as one. Through two natural elemental powers, fire and wind—both vitally part of us since the body's birth—we could claim the incalculable support of the entire universe. It was a cosmic act. Ourselves were but the channel. Later this channel would define itself still more.

Beneath those smoke-stained rafters, as surely as beneath the vaulted roof of some great temple, stepped worship and solemnity. The change came gradually. From the sky above the star-lit valley this grave, tremendous attitude swung down into our hearts. Not alone the isolated châlet, but the world itself contained us, a temple wherein we, insignificant worshippers, knelt before the Universe. For the powers we invoked were not merely earthly powers, but those cosmic energies that drove and regulated even the flocks of stars.

Mrs. LeVallon and I both knew it dimly, as we waited with beating hearts in that great silence. She scarcely moved. Somehow divining the part she had to play, she sat there motionless as a figure in stone, offering no resistance. Her reawakened memory must presently guide us; she knew the importance of her role, and the composure with which she accepted it touched grandeur. Yet each one of us was necessary. If Julius took the leader's part, her contribution, as my own, were equally essential to success. If the greater risk was his, our own risk was yet not negligible. The elemental Powers would take what channel seemed best available. It was not a personal consideration for us. We were most strangely one.

My own measure of interpretation I have already attempted to describe. Hers I guess intuitively. For we shared each other's feelings as only love and sympathy know how to share. These feelings now grew steadily in power; and, obeying them, our bodies moved to new positions. We changed our *attitudes*.

For I remember that while Julius rose and stood beside the table, his wife went quietly from my side and seated herself before the open window, her face turned towards the valley and the night. Instinctively we formed a living triangle, Mrs. LeVallon at the apex. And, though at the time I understood the precise significance of these changes, reading clearly the language they acted out in motion, that discernment is now no longer in me, so that I cannot give the perfect expression of meaning they revealed. Upon Julius, however, some appearance, definite as a robe upon the head and shoulders, proclaimed him a figure of command and somehow, too, of tragedy. It set him in the centre. Close beside me, within the circle of the lamplight, I watched him—so still, so grave, the face of marble pallor, the dark hair tumbling as of old about the temples whereon the effort of intensest concentration made the pulsing veins stand out as thick as cords. Calm as an image he stood there for a period of time I cannot state. Beyond him, in the shadows by the window, his wife's figure was just visible as she leaned, half reclining, across the wooden sill into the night. There was no sound from the outer valley, there was no sound in the room. Then, suddenly of itself, a change approached. The silence broke.

"Julius... !" came faintly from the window, as Mrs. LeVallon with a sudden gesture drew the curtain to shut out the darkness. She turned towards us. "Julius!" And her voice, using the tone I had heard before when she fled past me up that meadow slope, sounded as from some space beyond the walls. I looked up, my nerves on the alert, for it came to me that she was at the limit of endurance and that something now must break in her.

Julius moved over to her side, while she put her hands out first to welcome him, then half to keep him off. He spoke no word. He took her outstretched hands in both of his, leading her back a little nearer towards the centre of the room.

"Julius," she whispered, "what frightens me to-night? I'm all a-shiver. There's something coming?—but what is it? And why do I seem to know, yet not to know?"

He answered her quietly, the voice deep with tenderness:

"We three are here together"—I saw the shining smile I knew of old—"and there is no cause to feel afraid. You are tired with your long, long waiting." And he meant, I knew, the long fatigue of ages that she apprehended, but did not grasp fully yet. She was Mrs. LeVallon still.

"I'm both hot and cold together, and all oppressed," she went on; "like a fever it is—icy and yet on fire. I can't get at myself, to keep it still. Julius... what is it?" The whisper held somehow for me the potentiality of scream. Then, tak-ing his two hands closer, she raised her voice with startling suddenness. "Julius," she cried, "I know what frightens me—it's *you!* What are you to-night?" She looked searchingly a moment into his face. "And what is this thing that's going to happen to you? I hear it coming nearer—outside"—she moved further from the curtained window with small, rushing steps, looking back across her shoulder—"all down the valley from the mountains, those awful mountains. Oh, Julius, it's coming—for you—my husband—! And for him," she added, laying her eyes upon me like a flame.

I thought the tears must come, but she held them back, looking appealingly at me, and clutching Julius as though he would slip from her. Then, with a quick movement and a little gust of curious laughter, she clapped her hand upon her mouth to stop the words. Something she meant to say to me was left unspoken, she was ashamed of the momentary weakness. "Mrs. LeVallon" was still up-permost.

"Julius," she added more softly, "there's something about to-night I haven't known since childhood. There's such heat and—oh, hark!"—she stopped a mo-ment, holding up her finger—"there's a sound—like riggin' in the wind. But it ain't wind. What is it, Julius? And why is that wonderful?"

Yet no sound issued from the quiet valley; it was as still as death. Even the sighing of the breeze had ceased about the walls.

"If only I understood," she went on, looking from his face to mine, "if only I knew exactly. It was something," she added almost to herself, "that used to come

to me when I was little—on the farm—and I put it away because it made me"—
she whispered the last two words below her breath—"feel crazy—"

"Crazy?" repeated Julius, smiling down at her.

"Like a queen," she finished proudly, yet still timid. "I couldn't feel that way
and do my work." And her long lashes lifted, so that the eyes flashed at me across
the table. "It made everything seem too easy."

I cannot say what quality was in his voice, when, leading her gently towards
a wicker chair beside the fire, he spoke those strange words of comfort. There
seemed a resonant power in it that brought strength and comfort in. She smiled
as she listened, though it was not her brain his language soothed. That other look
began to steal upon her face as he proceeded.

"*You!*" he said gently, "so wonderful a woman, and so poised with the discipline these little nerves forget—you cannot yield to the fear that loneliness and
darkness bring to children." She settled down into the chair, gazing into his face
as he settled the cushions for her back. Her hands lay in her lap. She listened to
every syllable, while the expression of perplexity grew less marked. And the
change upon her features deepened as he continued: "There are moments when
the soul sees her own shadow, and is afraid. The Past comes up so close. But the
shadow and the fear will pass. We three are here. Beyond all chance disaster, we
stand together... and to our real inner selves nothing that is sad or terrible can
ever happen."

Again her eyes flashed their curious lightning at me as I watched; but the sudden vague alarm was passing as mysteriously as it came. She said no more about
the wind and fire. The magic of his personality, rather than the words which
to her could only have seemed singular and obscure, had touched the sources
of her strength. Her face was pale, her eyes still bright with an unwonted brilliance, but she was herself again—I think she was no longer the "upper" self I
knew as "Mrs. LeVallon." The marvellous change was slowly stealing over her.

" You're cold and tired," he said, bending above her "Come closer to the fire—
with us all."

I saw her shrink, for all the brave control she exercised. The word "fire" came
on her like a blow. "It's not my body," she answered; "that's neither cold nor
tired. It's another thing—behind it." She turned toward the window, where
the curtain at that moment rose and fell before a draught of air. "I keep getting
the feeling that something's coming to-night for—one of us." She said it half to
herself, and Julius made no answer. I saw her look back then at the glowing fire
of wood and peat. At the same moment she threw out both hands first as if to
keep the heat away, then as though to hold her husband closer.

"Julius! If you went from me! If I lost you—!"

I heard his low reply:

"Never, through all eternity, can *we* go—away from one another—except for
moments."

She partly understood, I think, for a great sigh, but half suppressed, escaped
her.

"Moments," she murmured, "that are very long... and lonely."

It was then, as she said the words, that I noticed the change which so long had been rising, establish itself definitely in the luminous eyes. That other colour fastened on them—the deep sea-green. "Mrs. LeVallon" before my sight sank slowly down, and a completer, far more ancient self usurped her. Small wonder that my description halts in confusion before so beautiful a change, for it was the beginning of an actual transfiguration of her present person. It was bewildering to watch the gradual, enveloping approach of that underlying Self, shrine of a million memories, deathless, and ripe with long-forgotten knowledge. The air of majesty that she wore in the sleep-walking incident gathered by imperceptible degrees about the uninspired modern presentment that I knew. Slowly her face turned calm with beauty. The features composed themselves in some new mould of grandeur. The perplexity, at first so painfully apparent, but marked the singular passage of the less into the greater. I saw it slowly disappear. As she lay back in that rough chair of a peasant's châlet, there was some calm about her as of the steadfast hills, some radiance as of stars, a suggestion of power that told me—as though some voice whispered it in my soul—she knew the link with Nature reestablished finally within her being. Her head turned slightly towards me. I stood up.

Instinctively I moved across the room and drew the curtain back. I saw the stars; I saw the dark line of mountains; the odours of forest and meadow came in with sweetness; I heard the tinkling of the little stream—yet all contained somehow in the message of her turning head and shoulders.

There was no sound, there was no spoken word, but the language was one and unmistakable. And as I came slowly again towards the fire Julius stood over her, uttering in silence the same stupendous thing. The sense of my own inclusion in it was amazing. He smiled down into her lifted face. These two, myself a vital link between them, smiled across the centuries at one another. We formed—I noticed then—with the fire and the open window into space—a circle.

To say that I grasped some spiritual import in these movements of our bodies, realising that they acted out an inevitable meaning, is as true as my convinced belief can make it. It is also true that in this, my later report of the event, that meaning is no longer clear to me. I cannot recover the point of view that discerned in our very positions a message of some older day. The significance of attitude and gesture then were clear to me; the translation of this three-dimensional language I have lost again. A man upon his knees, two arms outstretched to clasp, a head bowed down, a pointing finger—these are interpretable gestures and attitudes that need no spoken words. Similarly, following some forgotten wisdom, our related movements held a ceremonial import that, by way of acceptance or refusal, helped or hindered the advance of the elemental powers then invoked. In some marvellous fashion one consciousness was shared amongst us all. We worked with a living Nature, and a living Nature worked actively with us, and it was attitude, movement, gestures, rather than words, that assisted the alliance.

Then Julius took the hand that lay nearest to him, while the other she lifted to place within my own. And a light breeze came through the open window at that moment, touched the embers of the glowing logs, and blew them into flame. I felt our hands tighten as that slight increase of heat and air passed into us. For in that passing breeze was the eternal wind which is the breath of God, and in that flame upon the hearth was the fire which burns in suns and lights the heart in men and women....

There came with unexpected suddenness, then, a moment of very poignant human significance—because of the great perspective against which it rose. She sat erect; she gazed into his face and mine; in her eyes burned an expression of beseeching love and sacrifice, but a love and sacrifice far older than this present world on which her body lay. Her arms stretched out and opened, she raised her lips, and, while I looked aside, she kissed him softly. I turned away from that embrace, aware in my heart that it was a half-divined farewell... and when I looked back again the little scene was over.

He bent slightly down, releasing the hand he held, and signifying by a gesture that I should do the same. Her body relaxed a little; she sank deeper into the chair; she sighed. I realised that he was assisting her into that artificial slumber which would lead to the full release of the subconscious self whose slow approach she already half divined. Stooping above her, he gently touched the hypnogenic points above the eyes and behind the ears. It was the oldest memories he sought. She offered them quite willingly.

"Sleep!" he said soothingly, command and tenderness mingled in the voice. "Sleep... and remember!" With the right hand he made slow, longitudinal passes before her face. "Sleep, and recover what you... knew! We need your guidance."

Her body swayed a little before it settled; her feet stretched nearer to the fire; her respiration rapidly diminished, becoming deep and regular; with the movement of her bosom the band of black velvet rose and fell about the neck, her hands lay folded in her lap. And, as I watched, my own personal sensations of quite nameless joy and anguish passed into a curious abandonment of self that merged me too completely in the solemnity of worship to leave room for pain. Hand in hand with the earthly darkness came in to us that Night of Time which neither sleeps nor dies, and like a remembered dream up stole our inextinguishable Past.

"Sleep!" he repeated, lower than before.

Cold, indeed, touched my heart, but with it came a promise of some deep spiritual sweetness, rich with the comfort of that life which is both abundant and universal. The valley and the sky, stars, mountains, forests, running water, all that lay outside of ourselves in Nature everywhere, came with incredible appeal into my soul. Confining barriers crumbled, melted into air; the imprisoned human forces leaped forth to meet the powers that "inanimate" Nature holds. I knew the drive of tireless wind, the rush of irresistible fire. It seemed a state in which we all joined hands, a state of glory that justified the bravest hopes, annihilating doubt and disbelief.

She slept. And in myself something supremely sure, supremely calm, looked on and watched.

"It helps," Julius murmured in my ear, referring to the sleep; "it makes it eas' ier for her. She will remember now... and guide."

He moved to her right side, I to her left. Between the fire and the open win' dow we formed then—a line.

Along a line there is neither tension nor resistance. It was the primitive, ul' timate figure.

CHAPTER XXX

A rush of air ran softly round the walls and roof, then dropped away into silence. There was this increased activity outside. A roar next sounded in the chimney, high up rather; a block of peat fell with a sudden crash into the grate, sending a shower of sparks to find the outer air. Behind us the pine boards cracked with miniature, sharp reports.

Julius continued the longitudinal passes, and "Mrs. LeVallon" passed with every minute into deeper and more complete somnambulism. It was a natural, willing process. He merely made it easier for her. She sank slowly into the deep subconscious region where all the memories of the soul lie stored for use.

It seemed that everything was in abeyance in myself, except the central fact that this experience was true. The rest of existence fell away, clipped off as by a pair of mighty shears. Both fire and wind seemed actively about me; yet not unnaturally. There was this heat and lift, but there was nothing frantic. The native forces in me were raised to their ultimate capacity, though never for a mo' ment beyond the limit that high emotion might achieve. Nature accomplished the abnormal, possibly, but still according to law and what was—or had been once—comprehensible.

The passes grew slower, with longer intervals between; Mrs. LeVallon lay mo' tionless, the lips slightly parted, the skin preternaturally pale, the eyelids tightly closed.

"Hush!" whispered Julius, as I made an involuntary movement, "it is still the normal sleep, and she may easily awake. Let no sound disturb her. It must go gradually." He spoke without once removing his gaze from her face. "Be ready to write what you hear," he added, "and help by 'thinking' fire and wind—in my direction."

A long'drawn sigh was audible, accompanied by the slightest possible con' vulsive movement of the reclining body.

"She sinks deeper," he whispered, ceasing the passes for a moment. "The con' sciousness is already below the deep'dream stage. Soon she will wake into the interior lucidity when her Self of To'day will touch the parent source behind. They are already with her: they light—and lift—her soul. She will remember all her past, and will direct us."

I made no answer; I asked no questions; I stood and watched, willingly sym' pathetic, yet incapable of action. The curious scene held something of tragedy and grandeur. There was triumph in it. The sense of Nature working with us increased, yet we ourselves comparatively unimportant. The earth, the sky, the universe took part and were involved in our act of restitution. It was beyond all experience. It was also—at times—intolerable.

The body settled deeper into the chair; the crackling of the wicker making sharp reports in the stillness. The pallor of the face increased; the cheeks sank in, the framework of the eyes stood out; imperceptibly the features began to re-arrange themselves upon another, greater scale, most visible, perhaps, in the strong, delicate contours of the mouth and jaw. Upon Julius, too, as he stood beside her, came down some indefinable change that set him elsewhere and oth-erwise. His dignity, his deep solicitous tenderness, and at the same time a hint of power that emanated more and more from his whole person, rendered him in some intangible fashion remote and inaccessible. I watched him with growing wonder.

For over the room as well a change came stealing. In the shadows beyond the fringe of lamplight, perspective altered. The room ran off in distances that yet just escaped the eye: I *felt* the change, though it was so real that the breath caught in me each time I sought to focus it. Space spread and opened on all sides, above, below, while so naturally that it was never actually unaccountable. Wood seemed replaced by stone, as though the solidity of our material surroundings deepened. I was aware of granite columns, corridors of massive build, gigantic pylons towering to the sky. The atmosphere of an ancient temple grew about my heart, and long-forgotten things came with a crowding of half-familiar de-tail that insisted upon recognition. It was an early memory, I knew, yet not the earliest....

"Be ready." I heard the low voice of Julius. "She is about to wake—within," and he moved a little closer to her, while I took up my position by the table by the lamp. The paper lay before me. With fingers that trembled I lifted the pen-cil, waiting. The hands of the sleeping woman raised themselves feebly, then fell back upon the arms of the chair. It seemed she tried to make signs but could not quite complete them. The expression on the face betrayed great internal ef-fort.

"Where are you?" Julius asked in a steady but very gentle tone.

The answer came at once, with slight intervals between the words:

"In a building... among mountains...."

"Are you alone?"

"No... not alone," spoken with a faint smile, the eyes still tightly closed.

"Who, then, is with you?"

"You... and he," after a momentary hesitation.

"And who am I?"

The face showed slight confusion; there was a gesture as though she felt about her in the air to find him.

"I do not know... quite," came the halting answer. "But you—both—are mine... and very near to me. Or else you own me. All three are so close I cannot see ourselves apart... quite."

"She is confused between two memories," Julius whispered to me. "The true regression of memory has not yet begun. The present still obscures her consciousness."

"It is coming," she said instantly, aware of his lightest whisper.

"All in due time," he soothed her in a tender tone; "there is no hurry. Nor is there anything to fear—"

"I am not afraid. I am... happy. I feel safe." She paused a moment, then added: "But I must go deeper... further down. I am too near the surface still."

He made a few slow passes at some distance from her face, and I saw the eyelids flutter as though about to lift. She sighed deeply. She composed herself as into yet deeper sleep.

"Ah! I see better now," she murmured. "I am sinking... sinking..."

He waited for several minutes and then resumed the questioning.

"Now tell me who *you* are," he enjoined.

She faintly shook her head. Her lips trembled, as though she tried to utter several names and then abandoned all. The effort seemed beyond her. The perplexed expression on the face with the shut eyes was movingly pathetic, so that I longed to help her, though I knew not how.

"Thank you," she murmured instantly, with a gentle smile in my direction. Our thoughts, then, already found each other!

"Tell me who you are," Julius repeated firmly. "It is not the name I ask."

She answered distinctly, with a smile:

"A mother. I am soon to be a mother and give birth."

He glanced at me significantly. There was both joy and sadness in his eyes. But it was not this disclosure that he sought. She was still entangled in the personality of To-day. It was far older layers of memory and experience that he wished to read. "Once she gets free from this," he whispered, "it will go with leaps and bounds, whole centuries at a time." And again I knew by the smile hovering round the lips that she had heard and understood.

"Pass deeper; pass beyond," he continued, with more authority in the tone. "Drive through—sink down into what lies so far behind."

A considerable interval passed before she spoke again, ten minutes at the lowest reckoning, and possibly much longer. I watched her intently, but with an afflicting anxiety at my heart. The body lay so still and calm, it was like the immobility of death, except that once or twice the forehead puckered in a little frown and the compression of the lips told of the prolonged internal effort. The grander aspect of her features came for moments flittingly, but did not as yet establish itself to stay. She was still confused with the mind and knowledge of To-day. At length a little movement showed itself; she changed the angle of her head in an effort to look up and speak; a scarcely perceptible shudder ran down the length of her stretched limbs. "I cannot," she murmured, as though glancing at her husband with closed eyelids. "Something blocks the way. I cannot see. It's too thickly crowded... crowded."

"Describe it, and pass on," urged Julius patiently. There was unalterable decision in his quiet voice. And in her tone a change was also noticeable. I was profoundly moved; only with a great effort I controlled myself.

"They crowd so eagerly about me,"—the choice of words seemed no longer quite "Mrs. LeVallon's"—with little arms outstretched and pleading eyes. They seek to enter, they implore..."

"Who are they?"

"The Returning Souls." The love and passion in her voice brought near, as in a picture, the host of reincarnating souls eager to find a body for their development in the world. They besieged her, clamouring for birth—for a body.

"Your thoughts invite them," replied Julius, "but you have the power to decide." And then he asked more sternly: "Has any entered yet?"

It was unspeakably moving—this mother willing to serve with anguish the purpose of advancing souls. Yet this was all of To-day. It was not the thing he sought. The general purpose must stand aside for the particular. There was an error to be set right first. She had to seek its origin among the ages infinitely far away. The guidance Julius sought lay in the long ago. But the safety of the little unborn body troubled him, it seemed.

"As yet," she murmured, "none. The little body of the boy is empty... though besieged."

"By whom besieged?" he asked more loudly. "Who hinders?"

The little body of the boy! And it was then a further change came suddenly, both in her face and voice, and in the voice of Julius too.

That larger expression of some forgotten grandeur passed into her features, and she half sat up in the chair; there was a stiffening of the frame; resistance, power, an attitude of authority, replaced the former limpness. The moment was, for me, electrifying. Ice and fire moved upon my skin.

She opened her lips to speak, but no words were audible.

"Look close—and tell me," came from Julius gravely.

She made an effort, then shrank back a little, this time raising one arm as though to protect herself from something coming, then sharply dropping it again over the heart and body.

"I cannot see," she murmured, slightly frowning; "they stand so close and... are... so splendid. They are too great... to see."

"Who—what—are they?" he insisted. He took her hand in his. I saw her smile.

The simple words were marvellously impressive. Depths of untold memory stirred within me as I heard.

"Powers... we knew... so long ago."

Some ancient thing in me opened an eye and saw. The Powers we evoked came seeking an entrance, brought nearer by our invitation. They came from the silent valley; they were close about the building. But only through a human channel could they emerge from the spheres where they belonged.

"Describe them, and pass on," I heard Julius say, and there came a pause then that I thought would never end. The look of power rolled back upon her face. She spoke with joy, with a kind of happiness as though she welcomed them.

"They rush and shine.... They flood the distance like a sea, and yet stand close against my heart and blood. They are clothed in wind and fire. I see the diadems of flame ascending and descending. Their breath is all the winds. There is such roaring. I see mountains of wind and fire... advancing... nearer... nearer.... We used them—we invited... long, long ago.... And so they... come again about us....

His following command appalled me:

"Keep them back. You must protect the vacant body from invasion."

And then he added in tones that seemed to make the very air vibrate, although the voice but whispered, "You must direct them—towards me."

He moved to a new position, so that we formed a triangle again. Dimly at the time I understood. The circle signified the union which, having received, enclosed the mighty forces. Only it enclosed too much; the danger of misdirection had appeared. The triangle, her body forming the apex towards the open night, aimed at controlling the immense arrival by lessening the entry. Another thing stood out, too, with crystal clearness—at the time: the elemental Powers sought the easiest channel, the channel of least resistance, the body still unoccupied: whereas Julius offered—himself. The risk must be his and his alone. There was—in those few steps he took across the dim-lit room—a sense of tremendous, if sinister, drama that swept my heart with both tenderness and terror. The significance of his changed position was staggering.

I watched the sleeper closely. The lips grew more compressed, and the fingers of both hands clenched themselves upon the dark dress on her lap. I saw the muscles of the altering face contract with effort; the whole framework of the body became more rigid. Then, after several minutes, followed a gradual relaxation, as she sank back again into her original position.

"They retire..." she murmured with a sigh. "They retire... into darkness a little. But they still... wait and hover. I hear the rush of their great passing.... I see the distant shine of fire... still."

"And the souls?" he asked gently, "do they now return?"

She lowered her head as with a gesture of relief. "They are crowding, crowding. I see them as an endless flight of birds...." She held out her arms, then shrank back sharply. An expression I could not interpret flashed across the face. Behind a veil, it seemed. And the stern voice of Julius broke in upon the arrested action:

"Invite them by your will. Draw to you by desire and love one eager soul. The little vacant body must be occupied, so that the Mighty Ones, returning, shall find it thus impossible of entry."

It was a command; it was also a precaution; for if the body of the child were left open it would inevitably attract the invading rowers from—himself. I watched her very closely then. I saw her again stretch out her arms and hands, then once again—draw sharply back. But this time I understood the expression on the quivering face. The veil had lifted.

By what means this was clear to me, yet hidden from Julius, I cannot say. Perhaps the ineradicable love that she and I bore for one another in that long-forgotten time supplied the clue. But of this I am certain—that she disobeyed him. She left the little waiting body as it was, empty, untenanted. Life—a soul returning to re-birth—was not conceived and did not enter in. The reason, more-over, was also clear to me in that amazing moment of her choice: she divined his risk of failure, she wished to save him, she left open the channel of least resist-ance of set purpose—the unborn body. For a love known here and now, she sac-rificed a love as yet unborn. If Julius failed, at least he would not now be de-stroyed; there would be another channel ready.

That thus she thought, intended, I felt convinced. If her mistake was fraught with more danger than she knew, my lips were yet somehow sealed. Our deeper, ancient bond gave me the clue that to Julius was not offered, but no words came from me to enlighten him. It seemed beyond my power; I should have broken faith with her, a faith unbelievably precious to me.

For a long time, then, there was silence in the little room, while LeVallon con-tinued to make slow passes before. The anguish left her face, drowned wholly in the grander expression that she wore. She breathed deeply, regularly, with-out effort, the head sunk forward a little on the breast. The rustle of his coat as his arm went to and fro, and the creaking of the wicker chair were all I heard. Then, presently, Julius turned to me—with a low whisper I can hear to this very day. "I, and I alone," he said, "am the rightful channel. I have waited long." He added more that I have forgotten; I caught something about "all the aspects being favourable," and that he felt confidence, sure that he would not fail.

"You will not," I interrupted passionately, "you dare not fail...." And then speech suddenly broke down in me, and some dark shadow seemed to fall upon my senses so that I neither heard nor saw nor felt anything for a period I can-not state.

An interval there certainly was, and of some considerable length probably, for when I came to myself again there was change accomplished, though a change I could not properly estimate. His voice filled the room, addressing the sleeper as before, yet in a way that told me there had been progress accomplished while I had been unconscious.

"Deeper yet," I heard, "pass down deeper yet, pass back across a hundred in-tervening lives to that far-off time and place when first—*first*—we called Them forth. Sink down into your inmost being and remember!"

And in her immediate answer there was a curious faintness as of distance: "It is... so... far away... so far beyond..."

"Beyond what?" he asked, the expression "Other Places" deepening upon his face.

Her forehead wrinkled in a passing frown. "Beyond this earth," she murmured, as though her closed eyes saw within. "Oh, oh, it hurts. The heat is awful... the light... the tremendous winds... they blind, they tear me... !" And she stopped abruptly.

"Forget the pain," he said; "it is already gone." And instantly the tension of her face relaxed. She drew a sigh of deep relief. Before I could prevent it, my own voice sounded: "When we were nearer to the sun!"

She made no reply. He took my hand across the table and laid it on her own. "She cannot hear your voice," he said, "unless you touch us. She is too far away.

She does not even know that you are here beside me. You of To-day she has forgotten, and the you of that long ago she has not yet found."

"You speak with someone—but with whom?" she asked at once, turning her head a little in my direction. Not waiting for his reply she at once went on: "Upon another planet, yes... but oh, so long ago...." And again she paused.

"The one immediately before this present one?" asked Julius.

She shook her head gently. "Still further back than that... the one before the last, when first we knew delight of life... without these heavy, closing bodies. When the sun was nearer... and we knew deity in the fiery heat and mighty winds... and Nature was... ourselves...." The voice wavered oddly, broke, and ceased upon a sigh. A thousand questions burned in me to ask. An amazing certainty of recognition and remembrance burst through my heart. But Julius spoke before my tongue found words.

"Search more closely," he said with intense gravity. "The time and place we summoned Them is what we need—not where we first learned it, but where we practised it and failed. Confine your will to that. Forget the earlier planet. To help you, I set a barrier you cannot pass...."

"The scene of our actual evocation is what we must discover," he whispered to me. "When that is found we shall be in touch with the actual Powers our worship used."

"It was not there, in that other planet," she murmured. "It was only there we first gained the Nature-wisdom. Thence—we brought it with us... to another time and place... later... much nearer to To-day—to Earth."

"Remember, then, and see—" he began, when suddenly her unutterably wonderful expression proclaimed that she at last had found it.

It was curiously abrupt. He moved aside. We waited. I took up my pencil between fingers that were icy cold. My gaze remained fixed upon the motionless body. Those fast-closed eyes seemed cut in stone, as if they never in this world could open. The forehead gleamed pale as ivory in the lamplight. The soft gulping of the lamp oil beside me, the crumbling of the firewood in the grate deepened the silence that I feared to break. The pallid oval of the sleeper's countenance shone at me out of a room turned wholly dark. I forgot the place wherein we sat, our names, our meanings in the present. For there grew vividly upon that disc-like countenance the face of another person—and of one I knew.

And with this shock of recognition—there came over me both horror and undying sweetness—a horror that the face would smile into my own with a similar recognition, that from those lips a voice must come I should remember; that those arms would lift, those hands stretch out; an ecstasy that I should be remembered.

"Open!" I heard, as from far away, the voice of Julius.

And then I realised that the eyes *were* open. The lids were raised, the eyeballs faced the lamp. Some tension drew the skin sideways. They were other eyes. The eternal Self looked out of them bringing the message of a vast antiquity. They gazed steadily and clearly into mine.

CHAPTER XXXI

To-day retired. I remembered Yesterday, but a Yesterday more remote, perhaps, than the fire-mist out of which our little earth was born....

I half rose in my chair. The first instinct—strong in me still as I write this here in modern Streatham—was to fall upon my knees as in the stress of some immense, remembered love. That glory caught me, that power of an everlasting passion that was holy. Bathed in a sea of perfect recollection, my eyes met hers, lost themselves, lived back into a Past that had been joy. A flood of shame broke fiercely over me that such a union could ever have seemed "forgotten." That To-day could smother Yesterday so easily seemed sacrilege. For this memory, uprising from the mists of hoary pre-existence, brought in its train other great emotions of recovered grandeur, all stirred into life by this ancient ceremony we three acted out. Our purpose then had been, I knew, no ordinary, selfish love, no lust of possession or ownership behind it. Its aim and end were not mere personal contentment, mere selfish happiness that excluded others, but, rather, a part of some vast, co-ordinated process that involved all Nature with her powers and workings, and fulfilled with beauty a purpose of the entire Universe. It was holy in the biggest sense; it was divine. The significance of our attitudes To-day was all explained—Julius, herself and I, exquisitely linked to Nature, a group-soul formed by the loves of Yesterday and Now.

We gazed at one another in silence, smiling at our recovered wonder. We spoke no word, we made no gesture; there was perfect comprehension; we were, all three, as we had been—long ago. An earlier state of consciousness took this supreme command.... And presently—how long the interval I cannot say—her eyelids dropped, she drew a deep sigh of happiness, and lay quiescent as before.

It was then, I think, that the sense of worship in me became so imperative that denial seemed impossible. Some inner act of adoration certainly accomplished itself although no physical act resulted, for I remember dropping back again into my chair, not knowing what exactly I meant to do. The old desire for the long, sweet things of the soul burst suddenly into flame, the inner yearning to know the deathless Nature Powers which were the gods, and to taste divinity by feeling-with their mighty beings. That early state of simpler consciousness, it seems, lay too remote from modern things to be translatable in clear language. Yet at the time I knew it, felt it, realised it, because I lived it once again. The flood of aspiration that bore me on its crest left thinking and reason utterly out of account. No link survives To-day with the state we then recovered....

And both she and Julius changed before my eyes. The châlet changed as well, slipping into the shadowy spaces of some vast, pillared temple. The soul in me realised its power and *knew* its origin divine. Bathed in a sea of long-forgotten glory, it rose into a condition of sublimest bliss and confidence. It recognised its destiny and claimed all Heaven. And this raging fire of early spiritual ambition passed over me as upon a mighty wind; desire and will became augmented as though wind blew them into flame.

"Watch... and listen," I heard, "and feel no fear!"

The change visibly increased; it seemed that curtains lifted in succession.... The sunken head was raised; the lips quivered with approaching speech; the pale cheeks deepened with a sudden flush that set the cheekbones in a quick, high light; the neck bent slightly forward, foreshortening, as it were, the presentment of the head and shoulders; while some indescribable touch of power painted the marble brows cold and almost stern. The entire countenance breathed the august passion of a remoter age dropped close.... And to see the little face I knew as Mrs. LeVallon, domestic servant in the world To-day, unscreen itself thus before me, while its actual structure yet remained unchanged, broke down the last resistance in me, and rendered my subjugation absolute. Transfiguration was visibly accomplished....

Once more she turned her head and looked at me. I met the eyes that saw me and remembered. And, though I would have screened myself from their tremendous gaze, there was no remnant of power in me that could do so.... She smiled, then slowly withdrew her eyes.... I passed, with these two beside me, back into the womb of pre-existence. We were upon the Earth—at the very time and place where we had used the knowledge brought from a still earlier globe.

"What do you see?" came in those quiet tones that rolled up time and distance like a scroll. "Tell me now!" It was the scene of the lost experiment he sought. We were close upon it.

She spread her arms; her hands waved slowly through the air to indicate these immense enclosing walls of stone about us. The voice reverberated as in great hollow space.

"Darkness... and the Vacated Bodies," was the reply. I knew that we stood in the Hall of Silence where the bodies lay entranced while their spirits went forth upon the three days' quest. And one of these, I knew, was mine.

"What besides?"

"The Guardians—who protect."

"Who are they? Who are these Guardians?"

An expression of shrinking passed across her face, and disappeared again. The eyes stared fixedly before her into space.

"Myself," she answered slowly, "you—Concerighé...and..."

"There was another?" he asked. "Another who was with us?"

She hesitated. At first no answer came. She seemed to search the darkness to discover it.

"He is not near enough to see," she murmured presently. "Somewhere beyond... he stands... he lies... I cannot see him clearly."

Julius touched my hand, and with the contact the expression on her face grew clear. She smiled.

"You see him now," he said with decision.

She turned her face towards me with a tender, stately movement. The sterner aspect deepened into softness on the features. Great joy for an instant passed into the strange sea-green eyes.

"Silvatela," she whispered, slightly lowering the head. "He offered himself— for me. He lies now—empty at our feet." And the utterance of the name passed through me with a thrill of nameless sweetness. An infinite desire woke, yet desire not for myself alone.

"The time... ?" asked Julius in that calm, reverent tone.

She rose with a suddenness that made me start, though, somehow, I had expected it. At her full height she stood between us. Then, spreading her hands from both the temples outwards, she bowed her head to the level of the breast. Julius, I saw, did likewise, and before I realised it, the same deep, instinctive awe had brought me to my feet in a similar obeisance. A breath of air from the night outside passed sensibly between us, enough to stir the hair upon my head and increase the fire on the hearth behind. It ceased, and a wave of comforting heat moved in, paused a moment, settled like a great invisible presence, and held the atmosphere.

"It is the Pause in Nature," I heard the answer, and saw that she was seated in the chair once more. "The Third Day nears its end.... The Questing Souls... draw near again to enter. We have kept their vacated bodies safe for them. Our task is almost over...."

She drew a deep, convulsive sigh. Then Julius, taking her right hand, guided my left to hold the other one. I touched her fingers and felt them instantly clasp about my own; she sighed again, the frown went from her forehead, and turning her gaze upon us both she murmured:

"I see clearly, I see everything."

The past surged over me in a drowning flood.

"This is the moment, this the very place," came the voice of Julius. "It was at this moment we were faithless to our trust. We used your body as the channel...." He turned slightly in my direction.

"The moment and the place," she interrupted. "There is just time. Before the Souls return.... You have called upon the Powers.... Yet both cannot enter!... he... and they...."

There was a mighty, echoing cry.

She stopped abruptly. Her face darkened as with some great internal effort. I darkened too. My vision broke.... There was a sense of interval....

"And the channel—?" he asked below his breath.

She shook her head slowly to and fro. "It lies waiting still in the Iron Slumber.... You used it... it is shattered.... The soul returning finds it not.... His soul... whom I loved..."

The voices ceased. A sudden darkness dropped. I had the sensation that I was rushing, flying, whirling. The hand I clasped seemed melted into air. I lost the final remnant of present things about me. The circle of my own sensations, my identity, the identity of my two companions vanished. A remarkable feeling of triumph came upon me, of joyful power that lifted me high above all injury and death, while something utterly gigantic asserted itself in the place of what had just been "me"—something that could never be maimed, subdued, held prisoner. The darkness then lilted, giving way before a hurricane of light that swept me, as it were, upon a pinnacle. Secure and strong I felt beyond all possible disaster, yet breathless amid things too long unfamiliar... And then, abruptly, I knew searing pain, the pain of something broken in me, of spiritual incompleteness, disappointment.... I was called back to lesser life—before my time—before some high fulfilment due to me... .

Julius and Mrs. LeVallon were no longer there beside me, but in their place I saw two solemn figures standing motionless and grave above a prostrate body. It lay upon a marble slab, and sunlight fell over the face and folded hands. The two moved forward. They knelt... there was a sound of voices as in prayer, a powerful, drawn-out sound that produced intense vibrations, vibrations so immense that the motion in the air was felt as wind. I saw gestures... the body half rose up upon its marble slab... and then the blaze of some incredible efflugence descended before my eyes, so fiercely brilliant, and accompanied by such an intolerable, radiant heat... that the entire scene went lost behind great shafts of light that splintered and destroyed it... and an awful darkness followed, a darkness that again had pain and imcompleteness at the heart of it....

One thing alone I understood—that body on the shining slab was mine. My absent soul, deprived of high glory elsewhere that was mine by right, returned into it unexpectedly, aware of danger. It had been used for the purposes of evocation. I had met the two Powers evoked by means of it midway: Fire and Wind....

The vision vanished. I was standing in the chalet room again, he and the woman by my side. There was a sense of enormous interval.

We were back among the present things again. I had merely re-lived in a moment's space a vision of that Past where these two had sinned against me. The memory was gone again. We now resumed our present reconstruction, by means of which the balance should be finally restored. The same two elemental Powers were with us still. Summoned once again—but this time that they might be dismissed.

"The Messengers of Wind and Fire approach," Julius was saying softly. "Be ready for the Powers that follow after."

"But—there poured through me but a moment ago—" I began, when his face stopped my speech sharply.

"That 'moment' was sixty centuries ago! Keep hold now upon your will," he interrupted, yet without a trace of the vast excitement that I felt, "lest they invade your heart instead of mine. The glory that you knew was but the shadow of their coming—as long ago you returned *and met them*—when we failed. Keep close watch upon your will. It is the Equinox.... The pause now comes with midnight."

Even before he had done speaking the majesties of Wind and Fire were upon us. And Nature came in with them. A dislocating change, swift as the shaking of some immense thick shutter that hides life behind material things, passed in a flash about us. We stood in a circle, hands firmly clasped. There was a first effect as if those very hands were fused and ran into a single molten chain. There was no outer sound. The silence in the air was deathlike. But the sensation in my soul was—life. The momentary confusion was stupendous, then passed away. I stood in that room, but I stood in the valley too. I was in Nature everywhere. I heard the deer go past me, I heard them on the soft, sweet grass, I heard their breathing and the beating of their hearts. Birds fluttered round my face and shoulders, I heard their singing in my blood and ears, I knew their wild desires and freedom, their darting to and fro, their swaying on the boughs. My feet were running water, while yet the solid mass of earth and cliff stood up in me. I also knew the growing of the flowers by the forests, tasted their fragrance in my breath, their tender, delicate essence all unwasted. It passed understanding, yet was natural as sight, for my hands went far away, while still quite close, dipping among the stars that grew and piled like heaps of gathered sand. It all was simple, easy, mine by right. Nature gave me her myriad sensations without stint. I had forgotten. I remembered. The universe stood open. "I" had entered with these other two beside me.

She raised her arms aloft, taking our hands up with her own, and cried with a voice like wind against great branches:

"They come! The Doors of Fire are wide, and the Gates of Wind stand open! They enter the channel that is offered."

And his voice, like a roar of flame, came answering hers:

"The salutations of the Fire and Wind are made! The channel is prepared! There is no resistance!"

They stood erect and rigid, their outlines merged with some strange extension into space. They were superb, tremendous. There was no shrinking there. The deities of wind and fire came up, seeking their channel of return.

And so "They" came. Yet not outwardly; nor was the terrific impact of their advent known completely to any but himself alone who sought to harbour them now within his little human organism. Into my heart and soul poured but a fragment of their radiant, rushing presences. About us all some intelligent power as of a living wind brought in its mighty arms that ethereal fire which is not merely living, but is life itself. Material objects wavered, then disappeared, thin as transparent glass that increases light and heat. Walls, ceiling, floor were burned away, yet not consumed; the atoms composing all physical things glowed with a radiant energy they no longer could conceal. The latent heat of inanimate Nature emerged, not rebellious but triumphant. It was a deific manifestation of those natural powers which are the first essentials of human existence—heat and air. We were not alien to Nature, nor was Nature set apart from us; we shared her inexhaustible life, and the glory of the Universe in which she is a fragment.

"The Doors of the Creative Fire stand wide," rang out her triumphant voice again. "The golden splendour of the invisible Fire loosens and flows free. The Breath of Life is everywhere... our own.... But what, oh what of—*him!*" The scene of their past audacious error swept again before me. And, partially, I caught it.

Into a gulf of silence her words fell, recaptured from a mode of invocation effective in forgotten ages. Quivering lightnings, like a host of running stars, flashed marvellously about us, with bars of fire that seemed to map all space, while there was a sense of prodigious lifting in the heart as though some power like rushing wind drove will and yearning to the summit of all possible achievement. I realised simply this—that Nature's powers and purposes became mine too.

How long this lasted is impossible to state; duration disappeared. The Universe, it seemed, had caught me up, joyful and unafraid, into her bosom. It was too immense for little terrors.... And it was only after what seemed an interminable interval that I became aware of something that marred; of effort somewhere to confine and limit; of conflict, in a word, as though some smaller force strove to impose an order upon Powers that resented it. And I understood the meaning of this too. Julius battled in his soul. He wrestled with the Energies he had invoked, exerting to the utmost a trained, spiritual will to influence their direction into himself, as expiatory channel. Julius, after the lapse of centuries, fought to restore the balance he had long ago disturbed.

Her voice, too, occasionally reached me with a sound as of wind that rushed, but very far away. The words went past me with a heat like flame. I caught fragments only... "The King of Breath.... The Master of the Diadems of Fire... they seek to enter... the channel of safe return.... Oh, beware... beware..."

And it was then I saw this wonderful thing happen, poignant with common human drama, intensifying the reality of the whole amazing experience. For she turned suddenly to him, her face alight and radiant. She would not let him accept the awful risk. Her arms went out to hold him to her. He drove her back.

"I open wide the channel of my life and soul!" he cried, with a gesture of the entire body that made it relaxed and unresisting. He stepped backwards a little from her touch. "It must be through me!"

And there was anguish in her tone that seemed to press all possible human passion into the single sentence:

"I, too, throw myself open! I cannot let you go from me!"

He moved still further from her. It seemed to me he went at prodigious speed, yet grew no smaller to the eye. The withdrawal belonged to some part of his being that I was aware of inwardly. Streams of fire and wind went with him. They followed. And I heard her voice in agonised pursuit. She raised her hands as in supplication, but to whom or what I knew not. She fought to prevent. She fought to offer herself instead.

But also she offered the body as yet unclaimed—untenanted.

"He who is in the Fire and in the Sun... I call upon His power. I offer myself!" I heard her cry. His answering voice seemed terrible:

"The Law forbids. You hold Them back from me." And then as from a greater distance, the voice continued more faintly: "You prevent. It has to be! Help me before it is too late; help me... or... I... fail!"

Fail! I heard the awful word like thunder in the heavens.

The conflict of their wills, the distress of it was terrible. At this last moment she realised that the strain was more than he could withstand—he would go from her in that separation which is the body's death. She saw it all; there was division in her will and energies. Opposing herself to the justice he had invoked, she influenced the invasion of the elemental Powers, offering herself as channel in the hope of saving him. Her human desire weighed the balance—turning it just against him. Her insight clouded with emotion. She increased the risk for him, and at the same time left open to the great invading Powers another chan-nel—the line of least resistance, the empty vehicle all prepared within herself.

To me it was mercilessly clear. I tried to speak, but found no words to utter; my tongue refused to frame a single sound; nor could I move my limbs. I heard Julius only, his voice calling like a distant storm.

"I call upon the Fire and Wind to enter me, and pass to their eternal home... whence you and I... and he..."

His voice fell curiously away into a gulf; there was weakness in it. I saw her frail body shake from head to foot. She swayed as though about to fall. And then her voice, strong as a bugle-call, rang out:

"I claim it by—my *love....!*"

There was a burst of wind, a rush of sheeted fire. Then darkness fell. But in that instant before the fire passed, I saw his form stand close before my eyes. The face, alight with compassion and resignation, was turned towards her own. I saw the eyes; I saw the hands outstretched to take her; the lips were parted in a fi-nal attempt at utterance which never knew completion. And I knew—the cer-tainty stopped the beating of my heart—that he had failed. There was no ac-tual sound. Like a gleaming sword drawn swiftly from its scabbard, he rose past me through the air, borne from his body, as it were, on wings of ascending flame. There was a second of intolerable radiance, a rush of driving wind—and he was gone.

And far away, at the end of some stone corridor in the sunshine, yet at the same time close beside me upon the floor of the little mountain châlet, I heard the falling body as it dropped with a thud before my feet—untenanted....

CHAPTER XXXII

I remember what followed very much as one remembers the confusion after an anæsthetic—fragments of extraordinary dream and of sensational expe-rience jostling one another on the threshold of awakening. Then, very swiftly, like a train of gorgeous colour disappearing into a tunnel of darkness, the memory slipped down within me and was gone. The Past with a rush of lightning swept back into its sheath.

The glory and sense of exaltation, that is, were gone, but not the memory that they had been. I knew what had happened, what I had felt, seen, yearned for;

but it was the cold facts alone remained, the feelings that had accompanied them vanished. Into a dull, chilled world I dropped back, wondering and terrified. A long interval had passed.

And the first thing I realised was that Mrs. LeVallon still lay sleeping in that chair of wicker—profoundly sleeping—that the lamp had burned low, and that the châlet felt like ice. Her face, even in the twilight, I saw was normal, the older expression gone. I turned the wick up higher, noting as I did so that the paper strewn about me was thick with writing, and it was then my half-dazed senses took in first that Julius was not standing near us, and that a shadow, oddly shaped and huddled, lay on the floor where the lamplight met the darkness.

The moving portion seemed at once to disentangle itself from the rest, and a face turned up to stare at me. It was the serving-man upon his knees. The expression in his eyes did more to bring me to my normal senses than anything else. That scared and anguished look made me understand the truth—that, and the moaning that from time to time escaped his lips.

Of speech from him I hardly got a word; he was inarticulate to the last as ever, and all that I could learn was that he had felt his master's danger and had come....

We carried the body upstairs and laid it on the bed. I strove to regard it merely as the "instrument" *he* had used awhile, strove to find still his real undying Presence close to me—but that comfort failed me too. The face was very white. Upon the pale marble features lay still that signature of "Other Places" which haunted his life and soul. We closed the staring eyes and covered him with a sheet. And there the servant crouched upon the floor for the remaining five hours until the dawn, when I came up from watching that other figure of sleep in the room below, and found him in the same position. All that day as well he watched indeed, until at last I made him realise that the sooner he got the farmer's horse below and summoned a doctor, the better for all concerned.

But that was many hours later in the day, and meanwhile he just crouched there, difficult of approach, eyeing me savagely almost when I came, his eyes aflame with a kind of ugly, sullen resentment, but faithful to the last. What the silent, devoted being had heard or seen during our long hours of sinister struggle and experiment, I never knew, nor ever shall know.

My memory hardly lingers upon that; nor upon the unprofitable detail of the doctor's tardy arrival in the evening, his ill-concealed suspicion and eventual granting of a death certificate according to Swiss law; nor, again, upon his obvious verdict of a violent heart-stroke, or the course of procedure that he bade us follow.

Even the distressing details of the burial have somewhat faded, and I recall chiefly the fact that the Man established himself in the village where the churchyard was and began his watch that kept him near the grave, I believe, till death relieved him. My memory lingers rather upon the hours that I watched beside the sleeping woman, and upon the dreadful scene of her awakening and discovery of the truth.

For hours we had the darkness and the silence to ourselves, a silence broken only by the steady breathing of her slumber. I dared not wake her; knowing that the trance condition in time exhausts itself and the subject returns to normal waking consciousness without effort or distress, I let her slumber on, dreading the moment when the eyes would open and she must question me. The cold increased with the early hours of the morning, and I spread a rug about her stretched-out form. Slowly with the failing of the oil, the little lamp flame flickered and died, then finally went out, leaving us in the chill gloom together. All heat had long since left the fire of peat.

It was a vigil never to be forgotten. My thoughts revolved the whole time in one and the same circle, seeking in vain support from common things. Slowly and by degrees my mind found steadiness, though with returning balance my pain grew keener and more searching. The poignant minutes stretched to days and years. For ever I fell to reconstructing those vanished scenes of memory, while striving to believe that the whole thing had been but a detailed vivid dream, and that presently I, too, should awake to find our life in the châlet as before, Julius still alive and close....

The moaning from the room overhead, where the Man watched over that other, final sleep, then brought bitterly again the sad reality, and set my thoughts whirling afresh with anguish. I was distraught and trembling.... London and my lectures, the recent climbing in the Dolomites, cities and trains and the business of daily modern life, these were the dreams.... The reality, truth, lay in that world of vision just departed.... Concerighé, Silvatela, the woman of that ancient, splendid past, the re-capture of the Temple Days when we three trod together that strange path of questing; the broken fragment of it all; the Chamber of the Vacated Bodies, and the sin of long ago; then, chief of all, the attempt to banish the Powers, evoked in those distant ages, back to their eternal home—his effort to offer himself as channel—her fear to lose him and her offering of herself—the failure... and that appalling result upstairs.

For, ever and again, my thoughts returned to that: the spirit of the chief transgressor hovering now without a body, waiting for the River of the Lives to bring in some dim future another opportunity for atonement.

The failure...! In the glimmer of that pale, cold dawn I watched the outline of her slumbering form. I remembered her cry of sacrificing love that drew the great rushing Powers down into herself, and thus into the unresisting little body gathered now in growth against her heart. That human love the world deems great, seeking to save him to her own distress, had only blocked the progress of his soul she yearned to protect, so little understanding.... I heard her deep-drawn breathing in the darkness and wondered... for the child that she would bear... come to our modern strife and worldly things with this freight of elemental forces linked about his human heart and mind—fierce child of Wind and Fire...! A "natural," perhaps a "super-natural" being....

This sense of woe and passion, haunting my long, silent vigil from night to dawn, and after it when the sunshine of the September morning lit the room and turned her face to silver—this it is that, after so many years, clings to the memory as though of yesterday.

And then, without a sign or movement to prepare me, I saw that the eyes had opened and were fixed upon my face.

The whispered words came instantly:

"Where is he? Has he gone away?"

Stupid with distress and pain, my heart was choked. I stared blankly in return, the channels of speech too blocked to find a single syllable.

I raised my hands, though hardly knowing what I meant to do. She sat up in the chair and looked a moment swiftly about the room. Her lips parted for another question, but it did not come. I think in my face, or in my gesture perhaps, she read the message of despair. She hid her face behind her hands, leaned back with a dreadful drooping of the entire frame, and let a sigh escape her that held the substance of all unutterable words of grief.

I yearned to help, but it was my silence, of course, that brought the truth so swiftly home to her returning consciousness. The awakening was complete and rapid, not as out of common sleep. I longed to touch and comfort her, yet my muscles refused to yield in any action I could manage, and my tongue clung dry against the roof of my mouth.

Then, presently, between her fingers came the words below a whisper:

"I knew that this would happen... I knew that once I slept, he'd go from me... and I should lose him. I tried... that hard... to keep awake.... But sleep *would* take me. An' now... it's took him... too. He's gone for—for very long again!" She did not say "for ever."

It was the voice, the accent and the words again of Mrs. LeVallon.

"Not for ever," I whispered, "but for a little time."

She rose up like a figure of white death, taking my hand. She did not tremble, and her step was firm. And more than this I never heard her say, for the entire contents of the interval since she first fell asleep beneath her husband's passes had gone beyond recall.

"Take me to him," she said gently. "I want to say good-bye."

I led her up those creaking wooden stairs and left her with her dead.

Her strength was wonderful. I can never forget the quiet self-control she showed through all the wretched details that the situation then entailed. She asked no questions, shed no tears, moving brave and calm through all the ghastly duties. Something in her that lay deeper than death understood, and with the resignation of a truly great heart, accepted. Far stronger than myself she was; and, indeed, it seemed that my pain for her—at the time anyhow—absorbed the suffering that made my own heart ache with a sense of loss that has ever since left me empty and bereaved. Only in her eyes was there betrayal of sorrow that was itself, perhaps, another half revival of yet dimmer memories... "eyes in which desire of some strange thing unutterably burned, unquenchable...." For the first time I understood the truth of another's words—so like a statue was her appearance, so set in stone, her words so sparing and her voice so dead:

"I tell you, hopeless grief is passionless;
That only men incredulous of despair,
Half taught in anguish, through the midnight air

Beat upward to God's throne in loud access
Of shrieking and reproach. Full desertness
Its souls as countries lieth silent-bare..."

Her soul lay silent-bare; her grief was hopeless.... To my shame it must be confessed that I longed to escape from all the strain and nightmare of what had
passed. The few days had been charged with material for a lifetime. I knew the
sharp desire to find myself in touch once more with common, wholesome
things—with London noise and bustle, trains, telephones and daily newspapers,
with stupid students who could not even remember what they had learned the
previous week, and with all the great majority who never even dreamed of a consciousness less restricted than their own. I saw the matter through, however,
to the bitter end, and did not lose sight of Mrs. LeVallon until I left her safely
in Lausanne, and helped her find a woman who should be both maid and companion, at least for the immediate future. It cannot be of interest or value to relate here. She did not cross my path again; while, on the other hand, it has never
been possible for me to forget her. To this day I hear her voice and accent, I feel
the touch of that hand that drew me softly into such depths of inexplicable vision; above all, I see her luminous, strange eyes and her movements of strange
grace across the châlet floor.... And sometimes, even now, I half... remember.

Yet never, till after this long interval of years, could I bring myself to set down
any record of what had happened. Perhaps—most probably, I think—I feared
that dwelling upon the haunting details that writing would involve might revive too obsessingly the memory of an experience so curiously overwhelming.

Now time has brought the necessity, as it were, of this confession; and I have
done my best with material that really resists the mould of language, at least as
I can use it. Later reading—for I devoured the best authorities and ransacked
even the most extravagant records in my quest—has come to throw a little curious light upon some parts of it; and the results of this subsequent study no
doubt appear in this report. At the time, however, I was ignorant of all such
things, and the effect upon me of what I witnessed thus for the first time may
be judged accordingly. It was dislocating.

Two facts alone remain to mention. And the first seems to me perhaps the
most singular of the entire experience. For the pages I had covered with writing showed suddenly an abrupt and extraordinary change of script. Although
the earlier sheets were in my own handwriting, roughly jotting down question
and reply as they fell from the lips of Julius or his wife, there came midway in
them this inexplicable change that altered them into the illegible scribble of a
language that I could not read, yet recognised. It changed into that curious kind
of ideograph that Julius used at school, that he showed me many a time in the
sand at the end of the football field where we used to lie and talk, and that he
claimed then was the ancient sacerdotal cipher we had used together in our remotest "Temple Days." I cannot read a word of it, nor can any to whom I have
shown it decipher a single outline. The change began, it seems, at the point
where "Mrs. LeVallon" went "deeper" at his word of command, and entered

the layer of memories that dealt with that most ancient "section." This accounts, too, for the confusion and incompleteness of my record as written. A page of this script is framed upon my walls to-day; my eye rests on it as I write these words upon a modern typewriter—in Streatham.

The other fact I have to mention might well be the starting point for study and observation of an interesting kind. Yet, though it sorely tempted me, I resisted the temptation, and now, after twenty years, it is too late, and I, too old. This record, if published, may fall beneath the eye of someone to whom the chance and the desire may possibly combine to bring the opportunity.

For some weeks after the events that have been here described, Mrs. LeVallon gave birth to a boy, surviving him, alas! by but a single day.

This I heard long afterwards by the merest chance. But my strenuous efforts to trace the child proved unavailing, and I only learned that he was adopted by a French family whose name even was not given to me. If alive he would be now about twenty years of age.

THE END

The Bright
Messenger

TO THE UNSTABLE

CHAPTER I

Edward Fillery, so far as may be possible to a man of normal passions and emotions, took a detached view of life and human nature. At the age of thirty-eight he still remained a spectator, a searching, critical, analytical, yet chiefly, perhaps, a sympathetic spectator, before the great performance whose stage is the planet and whose performers and auditorium are humanity.

Knowing himself outcast, an unwelcome deadhead at the play, he had yet felt no bitterness against the parents whose fierce illicit passion had deprived him of an honourable seat. The first shock of resentment over, he had faced the situation with a tolerance which showed an unusual charity, an exceptional understanding, in one so young.

He was twenty when he learned the truth about himself. And it was his wondering analysis as to why two loving humans could be so careless of their offspring's welfare, when the rest of Nature took such pains in the matter, that first betrayed, perhaps, his natural aptitude. He had the innate gift of seeing things as they were, undisturbed by personal emotion, while yet asking himself with scientific accuracy why and how they came to be so. These were invaluable qualities in the line of knowledge and research he chose for himself as psychologist and doctor. The terms are somewhat loose. His longing was to probe the motives of conduct in the first place, and, in the second, to correct the results of wrong conduct by removing faulty motives. Psychiatrist and healer, therefore, were his more accurate titles; psychiatrist and healer, in due course, he became.

His father, an engineer of ability and enterprise, prospecting in the remoter parts of the Caucasus for copper, and making a comfortable fortune in so doing, was carried off his feet suddenly by the beauty of a Khaketian peasant girl, daughter of a shepherd in these lonely and majestic mountains, whose intolerable grandeur may well intoxicate a man to madness. A dangerous and disgraceful episode it seems to have been between John Fillery, hitherto of steady moral fibre, and this strange, lovely, pagan girl, whose savage father hunted the pair of them high and low for weeks before they finally eluded him in the azalea valleys beyond Artvine.

Great passion, possibly great love, born of this enchanted land whose peaks touch heaven, while their lower turfy slopes are carpeted with lilies, azaleas, rhododendrons, contributed to the birth of Edward, who first saw the light in a secret chamber of a dirty Tiflis house, above the Koura torrent. That same night, when the sun dipped beneath the Black Sea waters two hundred miles to the westward, his mother had looked for the last time upon her northern lover and her wild Caucasian mountains.

Edward, however, persisted, visible emblem of a few weeks' primal passion in a primal land. Intense desire, born in this remote wilderness of amazing loveliness, lent him, perhaps, a strain of illicit, almost unearthly yearning, a secret nostalgia for some lost vale of beauty that held fiercer sunshine, mightier winds and fairer flowers than those he knew in this world.

At the age of four he was brought to England; his Russian memories faded, though not the birthright of his primitive blood. Settling in London, his father increased his fortune as consulting engineer, but did not marry. To the short vehement episode he had given of his very best; he remained true to his gorgeous memory and his sin; the cream of his life, its essence and its perfume, had been spent in those wild wind-swept azalea valleys beyond Artvine. The azalea honey was in his blood, the scent of the lilies in his brain; he still heard the Koura and Rion foaming down towards ancient Colchis. Edward embodied for him the spirit of these sweet, passionate memories. He loved the boy, he cherished and he spoilt him.

But Edward had stuff in him that rendered spoiling harmless. A vigorous, independent youngster, he showed firmness and character as a lad. To the delight of his father he knew his own mind early, reading and studying on his own account, possessed at the same time by a vehement love of nature and outdoor life that was far more than the average English boy's inclination to open air and sport. There lay some primal quality in his blood that was of ancient origin and leaned towards wildness. There seemed almost, at the same time, a faunish strain that turned away from life.

As a tiny little fellow he had that strange touch of creative imagination other children have also known—an invisible playmate. It had no name, as it, apparently, had no sex. The boy's father could trace it directly to no fairy tale read or heard; its origin in the child's mind remained a mystery. But its characteristics were unusual, even for such fanciful imaginings: too full-fledged to have been created gradually by the boy's loneliness, it seemed half goblin and half Nature-spirit; it replaced, at any rate, the little brothers and sisters who were not there, and the father, led by his conscience, possibly, to divine or half divine its origin, met the pretence with sympathetic encouragement.

It came usually with the wind, moreover, and went with the wind, and wind accordingly excited the child. "Listen! Father!" he would exclaim when no air was moving anywhere and the day was still as death. Then: "Plop! So there you are! " as though it had dropped through empty space and landed at his feet. "It came from a tremenjus height," the child explained. "The wind's up *there*, you see, to-day." Which struck the parent's mind as odd, because it proved later true. An upper wind, far in the higher strata of air, came down an hour or so afterwards and blew into a storm.

Fire and flowers, too, were connected with this invisible playmate. "*He*'ll make it burn, father," the child said convincingly, when the chimney smoked and the coals refused to catch, and then became very busy with his friend in the grate and about the hearth, just as though he helped and superintended what was being invisibly accomplished. "It's burning better, anyhow," agreed the father, astonished in spite of himself as the coals began to glow and spurt their gassy flames. "Well done; I am very much obliged to you and your little friend."

"But it's the only thing he can do. He likes it. It's his work really, don't you see—keeping up the heat in things."

"Oh, it's his natural job, is it? I see, yes. But my thanks to him, all the same."

"Thank you very much," said grave Edward, aged five, addressing his tiny friend among the fire-irons. "I'm much mobliged to you."

Edward was a bit older when the flower incident took place—with the geranium that no amount of care and coaxing seemed able to keep alive. It had been dying slowly for some days, when Edward announced that he saw its "inside" flitting about the plant, but unable to get back into it. "It's got out, you see, and can't get back into its body again, so it's dying."

"Well, what in the world are we to do about it?" asked his father.

"I'll ask," was the solemn reply. "Now I know!" he cried, delighted, after asking his question of the empty air and listening for the answer. "Of course. Now I see. Look, father, there it is—its spirit! " He stood beside the flower and pointed to the earth in the pot.

"Dear me, yes! Where d'you see it? I—don't see it quite."

"He says I can pick it up and put it back and then the flower will live." The child put out a hand as though picking up something that moved quickly about the stem.

"What's it look like?" asked his father quickly.

"Oh, sort of trinangles and things with lines and corners," was the reply, making a gesture as though he caught it and popped it back into the red drooping blossoms. "There you are! Now you're alive again. Thank you very much, please"—this last remark to the invisible playmate who was superintending.

"A sort of geometrical figure, was it?" inquired the father next day when, to his surprise, he found the geranium blooming in full health and beauty once again. "That's what you saw, eh?"

"It was its spirit, and it was shiny red, like fire," the child replied. "It's heat. Without these things there'd be no flowers at all."

"Who makes everything grow?" he asked suddenly, a moment later.

"You mean *what* makes them grow."

"Who," he repeated with emphasis. "Who builds the bodies up and looks after them?"

"Ah! the structure, you mean, the form?"

Edward nodded. His father had the feeling he was not being asked for information, but was being cross-examined. A faint pressure, as of uneasiness, touched him.

"They develop automatically—that means naturally, under the laws of nature," he replied.

"And the laws—who keeps them working properly?"

The father, with a mental gulp, replied that God did.

"A beetle's body, for instance, or a daisy's or an elephant's?" persisted the child, undeceived by the theological evasion. "Or mine, or a mountain's—? "

John Fillery racked his brain for an answer, while Edward continued his list to include sea-anemones, frost-patterns, fire, wind, moon, sun and stars. All these forms to him were bodies apparently.

"I know!" he exclaimed suddenly with intense conviction, clapping his hands together and standing on his toes.

"Do you, indeed! Then you know more than the rest of us."

"*They* do, of course," came the positive announcement. "The other kind! It's their work. Yours, for instance"—he turned to his playmate, but so naturally and convincingly that a chill ran down his father's spine as he watched—"is fire, isn't it? You showed me once. And water stops you, but wind helps you..." and he continued long after his father had left the room.

With advancing years, however, Edward either forgot his playmate or kept its activities to himself. He no longer referred to it, at any rate. His energies demanded a bigger field; he roamed the fields and woods, climbed the hills, stayed out all night to see the sunrise, made fires even when fires were not exactly needed, and hunted with Red Indians and with what he called "Windy-Fire people" everywhere. He was never in the house. He ran wild. Great open spaces, trees and flowers were what he liked. The sea, on the other hand, alarmed him. Only wind and fire comforted him and made him happy and full of life. He was a playmate of wind and fire. Water, in large quantities at any rate, was inimical.

With concealed approval, masking a deep love fulfilled yet incomplete, his father watched the growth of this fiercer strain that mere covert shooting could not satisfy, nor ordinary sporting holidays appease.

"England's too small for you, Edward, isn't it?" he asked once tentatively, when the boy was about fifteen.

"The English people, you mean, father?"

"You find them dull, don't you? And the island a bit cramped—eh?"

Edward waited without replying. He did not quite understand what his indulgent father intended, or was leading up to.

"You'd like to travel and see things and people for yourself, I mean?"

He watched the boy without, as he thought, the latter noticing. The answer pleased but puzzled him.

"We're all much the same, aren't we?" said Edward.

"Well—with differences—yes, we are. But still—"

"It's only the same over and over again, isn't it?" Then, while his father was thinking of this reply, and of what he should say to it, the boy asked suddenly with arresting intensity:

"Are we the only people—the only sort of beings, I mean? Just men and women like us all over the world? No others of any sort—bigger, for instance, or—more wild and wonderful?" Then he added, a thrust of strange yearning in his face and eyes: "More beautiful?" He almost whispered the last words.

His father winced. He divined the origin of that strange inquiry. Upon those immense and lonely mountains, distant in space and time for him, imagination, rich and pagan, ran, he well knew, to vast and mighty beings, superior to human, benignant and maleficent, akin to the stimulating and exhilarating conception of the gods, and certainly non-human.

"Nothing, Edward, that we know of. Why should there be?"

"Oh, I don't know, dad. I just wondered—sometimes. But, as you say, we've not a scrap of evidence, of course."

"Not a scrap," agreed his father. "Poetic legends ain't evidence."

The mind ruled the heart in Edward; he had his father's brains, at any rate; and all his powers and longings focused in a single line that indicated plainly what his career should be. The Public Schools could help him little; he went to Edinburgh to study medicine; he passed eventually with all possible honours; and the day he brought home the news his father, dying, told him the secret of his illegitimate birth.

CHAPTER II

The subsequent twenty years or so may be summarized.

Alone in the world, of a loving, passionate nature, he deliberately set all thought of marriage on one side as an impossibility, and directed his entire energy into the acquirement of knowledge; reading, studying, experimenting far outside the circle of the ordinary medical man. The attitude of detachment he had adopted became a habit. He believed it was now his nature.

The more he learned of human frailty and human faculties, the greater became the charity he felt towards his fellow-kind. In his own being, it seemed, lay something big, sweet, simple, a generosity that longed to share with others, a tolerance more ready to acquit than to condemn, above all, a great gift of understanding sympathy that, doubtless, was the explanation of his singular insight. Rarely he found it in him to blame; forgiveness, based upon the increasing extent of his experience, seemed his natural view of human mistakes and human infirmities. His one desire, his one hope, was to serve the Race.

Yet he himself remained aloof. He watched the Play but took no part in it. This forgiveness, too, began at home. His grievance had not soured or dejected him, his father's error presenting itself as a problem to be pondered over, rather than a sin to blame. Some day, he promised himself, he would go and see with his own eyes the Khaketian tribe whence his blood was partially derived, whence his un-English yearnings for a wilder scale of personal freedom amid an unstained, majestic Nature were first stolen. The inherited picture of a Caucasian vale of loveliness and liberty lay, indeed, very deep in his nature, emerging always like a symbol when he was profoundly moved. At any crisis in his life it rose beckoning, seductive, haunting beyond words... Curious, ill-defined emotions with it, that drove him towards another standard, another state, to something, at any rate, he could neither name nor visualize, yet that seemed to dwarf the only life he knew. About it was a touch of strange unearthly radiance that dimmed existence as he knew it. The shine went out of it. There was involved in this symbolic "Valley" something wholly new both in colour, sound and outline, yet that remained obstinately outside definition.

First, however, he must work, develop himself, and broaden, deepen, extend in every possible way the knowledge of his kind that seemed his only love.

He began in a very practical way, setting up his plate in a mean quarter of the great metropolis, healing, helping, learning with his heart as well as with his brain, observing life at closest quarters from its beginning to its close, his sympathies becoming enriched the more he saw, and his mind groping its way towards clearer insight the more he read, thought, studied. His wealth made him independent; his tastes were simple; his wants few. He observed the great Play from the Pit and Gallery, from the Wings, from Behind the Scenes as well.

Moving then, into the Stalls, into a wealthier neighbourhood, that is, he repeated the experience among another class, finding, however, little difference except in the greater artificiality of his types, the larger proportion of mental and nervous ailments, of hysteria, delusion, imaginary troubles, and the like. The infirmities due to idleness, enflamed vanity and luxury offered a new field, though to him a less attractive one. The farther from simplicity, from the raw facts of living, the more complicated, yet the more trivial, the resulting disabilities. These, however, were quite as real as those, and harder, indeed, to cure. Idle imagination, fostered by opportunity and means, yet forced by conventionality to wear infinite disguises, brought a strange, if far from a noble, crop of disorders into his ken. Yet he accepted them for serious treatment, whatever his private opinion may have been, while his patience, tact and sympathy, backed by his insight and great knowledge, brought him quick success. He was soon in a fair way to become a fashionable doctor.

But the field, he found, was restricted somewhat. His quest was knowledge, not fame or money. He chose his cases where he could, though actually refusing nothing. He specialized more and more with afflictions of a mental kind. He was immensely successful in restoring proportion out of disorder. He revealed people to themselves. He taught them to recover lost hope and confidence. He used little medicine, but stimulated the will towards a revival of fading vitality. Auto-suggestion, rather than suggestion or hypnotism, was his method. He healed. He began to be talked about.

Then, suddenly, his house was sold, his plate was taken down, he vanished.

Human beings object to sudden changes whose secret they have not been told and cannot easily guess; his abrupt disappearance caused talk and rumours, led, of course, by those, chiefly disappointed women, who had most reason to be grateful for past services. But, if the words charlatan and quack were whispered, he did not hear them; he had taken the post of assistant in a lunatic asylum in a northern town, because the work promised him increase of knowledge and experience in his own particular field. The talk he left behind him mattered as little as the small pay attached to the humble duties he had accepted.

London forgot him, but he did not forget what London had taught him.

A new field opened, and in less than two years, opportunity, combined with his undoubted qualifications, saw him Head of an establishment where he could observe at first hand the facts and phenomena that interested him most. Humane treatment, backed by profound insight into the derangements of the

poor human creatures under his charge, brought the place into a fame it had
never known before. He spent five years there in profound study and experiment; he achieved new results and published them. His *Experimental Psychology* caused a sensation. His name was known. He was an Authority.

At this time he was well past thirty, a tall, dark, distinguished-looking man,
of appearance grave and even sombre; imposing, too, with his quiet, piercing
eyes, but sombre only until the smile lit up his somewhat rugged face. It was a
face that nobody could lie to, but to that smile the suffering heart might tell its
inmost secrets with confidence, hope, trust, and without reserve.

There followed several years abroad, in Paris, Rome, St. Petersburg, Moscow;
Vienna and Zurich he also visited to test there certain lines of research and to
meet personally their originators.

This period was partly a holiday, partly an opportunity to know at first hand
the leaders in mental therapeutics, psychology and the rest, and also that he
might find time to digest and arrange his own accumulation of knowledge with
a view, later, to undertaking the life-work to which his previous experience was
but preliminary. Fame had come to him unsought; his published works alone ensured his going down to posterity as a careful but daring and original judge of
the human species and its possibilities. It was the supernormal rather than the
merely abnormal powers that attracted him. In the subconscious, as, equally, in
the superconscious, his deep experience taught him, lay amazing powers of both
moral and physical healing, powers as yet but little understood, powers as limitless as they seemed incredible, as mysterious in their operation as they were simple in their accessibility. And auto-suggestion was the means of using them. The
great men whom he visited welcomed him with open arms, added to his data,
widened yet further his mental outlook. Sought by high and low in many countries and in strangest cases, his experience grew and multiplied, his assortment
of unusual knowledge was far-reaching; till he stood finally in wonder and amazement before the human being and its unrealized powers, and his optimism concerning the future progress of the race became more justified with every added
fact.

Yet, perhaps, his greatest achievement was the study of himself; it was probably to this deep, intimate and honest research into his own being that his success in helping others was primarily due. For in himself, though mastered and
co-ordinated by his steady will, rendered harmless by his saving sense of humour
and (as he believed) by the absence of any harboured grievance against others—
in his very own being lay all those potential elements of disorder, those loose un-
ravelled threads of alien impulse and suppressed desire, which can make for dangerous disintegration, and thus produce the disturbing results classed generally
under alienation and neurosis.

The incongruous elements in him were the gift of nature; γνῶθι σεαυτόν
was the saving attitude he brought to that gift, redeeming it. This phrase, borrowed, he remembered with a smile, for the portal of the ancient Mysteries, remained his watchword. He was able to thank the fierce illicit love that furnished
his body and his mental make-up for a richer field of first-hand study than years

of practice among others could have supplied. He belonged by temperament to the unstable. But—he was aware of it. He realized the two beings in him: the reasoning, scientific man, and the speculative dreamer, visionary, poet. The latter wondered, dreamed among a totally different set of values far below and out of sight. This deeper portion of himself was forever beating up for recognition, clamouring to be used, yet with the strange shyness that reminded him of a loving woman who cannot be certain her passion is returned. It hinted, threatened, wept and even sulked. It rose like a flame, bringing its own light and wind, blessed his whole being with some divine assurance, and then, because not instantly accepted, it retired, leaving him empty, his mind coloured with unearthly yearnings, with poignant regrets, yet perfumed as though the fairness of Spring herself had lit upon his heart and kissed it into blossom on her passage north. It presented its amazing pictures, and withdrew. Elusive, as the half memory of some radiant dream, whose wonder and sweetness have been intense to the point of almost pain, it hovered, floating just out of reach. It lay waiting for that sincere belief which would convince that its passion was returned. And a fleeting picture of a wild Caucasian valley, steeped in sunshine and flowers, was always the first sign of its awakening.

Though not afraid of reason, it seemed somehow independent of the latter's processes. It was his reason, however, he well knew that dimmed the light in its grand, terrible eyes, causing it to withdraw the instant he began to question. Precise, formal thinking shut the engines off and damped the furnaces. His love, his passion, none the less, were there, hiding with belief, until some bright messenger, bringing glad tidings, should reveal the method of harmonious union between reason and vision, between man's trivial normal faculties and his astounding supernormal possibilities.

"This element of feeling in our outlook on Nature is a satisfaction in itself, but our plea for allowing it to operate in our interpretation of Nature is that we get closer to some things through feeling than we do through science. The tendency of feeling is always to see things whole. We cannot, for our life's sake, and for the sake of our philosophical reconstruction, afford to lose in scientific analysis what the poets and artists and the lovers of Nature all see. It is intuitively felt, rather than intellectually perceived, the vision of things as totalities, root and all, all in all; neither fancifully, nor mystically, but sympathetically in their wholeness."

To these words of Professor T. Arthur Thomson's, he heartily subscribed. applying their principle to his own particular field.

CHAPTER III

The net result of his inquiries and research, when, at the age of nearly forty, he established his own Private Home for unusual, so-called hope-less cases in North-West London—it was free to all, and as Spiritual Clinique he thought of it sometimes with a smile—may be summed up in the single sentence that man is greater than he knows, and that completer realiza-tion of his full possibilities lies accessible to his subconscious and superconscious powers. Herein he saw, indeed, the chief hope of progress for humanity.

And it was to the failures, the diseased, the evil and the broken that he owed chiefly his inspiring optimism, since it was largely in collapse that occurred the sporadic upheaval of those super-normal forces which, controlled, co-ordinated, led, must eventually bring about the realization he foresaw.

The purpose, however, of these notes is not to furnish a sensational story of various patients whom he studied, healed, or failed to heal. Its object is to give some details of one case in particular whose outstanding peculiarities affected his theories and convictions, leaving him open-minded still, but with a breath of awe in his heart perhaps, before a possibility his previous knowledge had ruled entirely out of court, even if—which is doubtful—he had ever considered it as a possibility at all.

He had realized early that the individual manifests but an insignificant por-tion of his being in his ordinary existence, the normal self being the tip of his consciousness only, yet whose fuller expression rises readily to adequate evo-cation; and it was the study of genius, of prodigies, so-called, and of certain fac-ulties shown sometimes in hysteria, that led him to believe these were small jets from a sea of power that might, indeed ought, to be realizable at will. The phe-nomena all pointed, he believed, to powers that seemed as superior to cerebral functions as they were independent of these.

Man's possible field of being, in other words, seemed capable of indefinite ex-tension. His heart glowed within him as he established, step by step, these greater powers. He dared to foresee a time when the limitations of separate per-sonality would have been destroyed, and the vast brotherhood of the race be-come literally realized, its practical unity accomplished.

The difficulties were endless and discouraging. The inventive powers of the bigger self, its astonishing faculty for dramatizing its content in every conceiv-able form, blocked everywhere the search for truth.

It could, he found, also, detach a portion of its content into a series of sepa-rate personalities, each with its individual morals, talents, tendencies, each with its distinct and separate memory. These fragments it could project, so to speak, masquerading convincingly as separate entities, using strange languages, offer-ing detailed knowledge of other conditions, distant in time and space, suggest-ing, indeed, to the unwary that they were due to obsessing spirits, and leaving

the observer in wonder before the potential capacity of the central self dis-
gorging them.

The human depths included, beyond mere telepathy and extended telepathy,
an expansion of consciousness so vast as to be, apparently, limitless. The past,
on rare occasions even the future, lay open; the entire planetary memory,
stored with rich and pregnant accumulated experience, was accessible and
shareable. New aspects of space and time were equally involved. A vision of incredible grandeur opened gradually before his eyes.

The surface consciousness of to-day was really rather a trumpery affair; the
gross lethargy of the vast majority viz à vis the greater possibilities afflicted him.
To this surface consciousness alone was so-called evil possible—as ignorance. As
"ugly is only half-way to a thing," so evil is half-way to good. With the greater
powers must come greater knowledge, shared as by instantaneous wireless
over the entire planet, and misunderstanding, chief obstacle to progress always,
would be impossible.

A huge unity, sense of oneness must follow. Moral growth would accompany
the increase of faculty. And here and there, it seemed to him, the surface ice had
thawed already a little; the pressure of the great deeps below caused cracks and
fissures. Auto-suggestion, prototype of all suggestion, offered mysterious hints
of the way to reach the stupendous underworld, as the Christian Scientists, the
miraculous healers, the New Thought movement, saints, prophets, poets,
artists, were finding out.

The subliminal, to state it shortly, might be the divine. This was the hope,
though not yet the actual belief, that haunted and inspired him. Behind his personality lurked this strange gigantic dream, ever beating to get through...

In his Private Home, helping, healing, using his great gifts of sympathy and
insight, he at the same time found the material for intimate study and legitimate
experiment he sought. The building had been altered to suit his exact requirements; there were private suites, each with its door and staircase to the street;
one part of it provided his own living quarters, shut off entirely from the patients' side; in another, equally cut off and self-contained, yet within easy communication of his own rooms, lived Paul Devonham, his valued young assistant.
There was a third private suite as well. The entire expenses he defrayed himself.

Here, then, for a year or two he worked indefatigably, with the measure of
success and failure he anticipated; here he dreamed his great dream of the future
of the race, in whose progress and infinite capacities he hopefully believed. Work
was his love, the advancement of humanity his god. The war availed itself of
his great powers, as also of his ready-made establishment, both of which he gave
without a thought of self. New material came as well from the battlefields into
his ken.

The effect of the terrible five years upon him was in direct proportion to his
sincerity. His mind was not the type that shirks conclusions, nor fears to look
facts in the face. For really new knowledge he was ever ready to yield all previous theories, to scrap all he had held hitherto for probable. His mind was open,

he sought only Truth.

The war, above all the Peace, shook his optimism. If it did not wholly shatter his belief in human progress, it proved such progress to be so slow that his Utopia faded into remotest distance, and his dream of perfectibility became the faintest possible star in his hitherto bright sky of hope.

He felt shocked and stupefied. The reaction was greater than at first he realized. He had often pitied the mind that, aware only of its surface consciousness, uninformed by thrill or shift of the great powers below and above, lived unwarned of its own immenser possibilities. To such, the evidence for extended human faculties must seem explicable by fraud, illusion, derangement, to be classed as abnormal rubbish worthy only of the alienist's attention as disease. To him such minds, though able, with big intellects among them, had ever seemed a prejudiced, fossilized, prehistoric type. Restricted by their very nature, violently resisting new ideas, they might be intense within their actual scope, but, with vision denied them, they never could be really great.

One effect of the shock he had undergone will be evident by merely stating that he now understood this type of mind a good deal better than before.

CHAPTER IV

The war was over, though the benefits of the long anticipated peace still kept provocatively, exasperatingly, out of reach, when, about the middle of September, Dr. Fillery received a letter that interested him deeply.

The shattered world was still distraught, uneasy. Nervously eager to resume its former activities, it was yet waiting for the word that should give it the necessary confidence to begin. Doubt, insecurity, uncertainty everywhere dominated human minds. Those who hoped for a renewal of the easy, careless mood of pre-war days were dismayed to find this was impossible; others who had allowed an optimistic idealism to prophesy a New Age, looked about them bewilderingly and in vain for signs of its fair birth. The latter, to whom, perhaps, Dr. Fillery belonged, were more bitterly disappointed, more cruelly shocked, than the former. The race, it seemed to many unshirking eyes, had leaped back centuries at a single spring; the gulf of primal savagery which had gaped wide open for five years, proving the Stone Age close beneath the surface of so-called civilization, had not yet fully closed. Its jaws still dripped blood, hatred, selfishness; the Race was still dislocated by the convincing disproof of progress, horrified at the fierce reality which had displaced the two-pence coloured dream it had been complacently worshipping hitherto. Men in the mass undoubtedly were savages still.

To Dr. Fillery, an honest, though not a necessarily fundamental pessimism, seemed justified. He believed in progress still, but as his habit was, he faced the facts. His attitude lost something of its original enthusiasm. Looking about him, he saw no big constructive movement; the figure who more than any other was altering the face of the world with his ideas as well as his armies, was avowedly de-structive only. He found himself a sobered and a saddened man.

His Private Home, having accomplished splendid work, had just discharged its last shell-shocked patient; it was now empty again, the staff, carefully chosen and proved by long service, dismissed on holidays, the building itself renovated and repaired against the arrival later of new patients that were expected.

Devonham, his assistant, away for a period of rest in Switzerland, would be back in a week or two, and Dr. Fillery, before resuming his normal work, found himself with little to do but watch the progress of the cleaners, painters and carpenters at work.

Into this brief time of leisure dropped the strange, perplexing letter with an effect distinctly stimulating. It promised an unusual case, a patient, if patient the case referred to could properly be called, a young man "who if you decide after careful reflection to reject, can be looked after only by the State, which means, of course, an Asylum for the Insane. I know you are no longer head of the Establishment in Liverpool, but that you confine yourself to private work along similar lines, though upon a smaller scale, and that you welcome only cases that have been given up as hopeless. I honour your courage and your sympathy, I know your skill. So far as a cure is conceivable, this one is hopeless certainly, but its unusual, indeed, its unique character, entitles it, I believe, to be placed among your chosen few. Love, sympathy, patience, combined with the closest observation, it urgently demands, and these qualities, associated with unrivalled skill, you must allow me, again, to think you alone possess, among healers and helpers of strange minds.

"For over twenty years, in the solitudes of these Jura forests and mountains, I have cared for him as best I could, and with a devotion a child of my own might have expected. But now, my end not far away, I cannot leave him behind me here uncared for, yet the alternative, the impersonal and formal care of an Institute, must break my heart and his. I turn to you.

"My advanced age and growing infirmities, in these days of unkind travel, prohibit my bringing him over. Can your great heart suggest a means, since I feel sure you will not refuse the care of this strange being whose nature and peculiarities indicate your especial care, and yours alone? Is it too much to wonder if you yourself could come and see him—here in the remote mountain châlet where I have tended and cared for him ever since his mother died in bearing him over twenty years ago?

"I have taught him what seemed wise and best; I have guarded and observed him; he knows little or nothing of an outside world of men and women, and is ignorant of life in the ordinary meaning of the word. What precisely he may be, to what stratum of consciousness he belongs, what kind of being he is, I mean...." The last two lines were then scored through, though left legible. "I feel with Arago, that he is a rash man who pronounces the word 'impossible' anywhere outside the sphere of pure mathematics." More sentences were here scored through.

"Dare I say—to you, as master, teacher, great open-minded soul—that to human life, as we know it, he does not, perhaps, belong?

"In writing—in this letter—I find it impossible to give you full details. I had intended to set them down; my pen refuses; in the plain English at my disposal—well, simply, it is not credible. But I have kept full notes all these years, and the notes belong to you. I enclose an imperfect painting I made of him some four years ago. I am no artist; for background you must imagine what lay beyond my little skill—the blazing glory of the immense wood-fires that he loves to make upon the open mountain side, usually at dawn after a night of prayer and singing, while waiting for the strange power he derives (as we all do, indeed, at second or third hand), from the worship of what is to him his mighty father, the life-giving sun. Wind, as the 'messengers' of the sun, he worships too.... Both sun and wind, that is, produce an unusual state approaching ecstasy.

"Counting upon you, I have hypnotized him, suggesting that he forget all the immediate past (in fact to date), and telling him he will like you in place of me—though with him it is an uncertain method.

I am now old in years. I have lived and loved, suffered and dreamed like most of us; my hands have been warmed at the fires of life, of which, let me add, I am not ignorant. You have known, I believe, my serious, as also my lighter imaginative books; my occasional correspondence with your colleague Paul Devonham has been of help and guidance to me. We are not, therefore, wholly strangers.

"The twenty years spent in these solitudes among simple peasant folk, with a single object of devotion to fill my days, have been, I would tell you, among the best of my long existence. My renouncement of the world was no renouncement. I am enriched with wonder and experience that amaze me, for the world holds possibilities few have ever dreamed of, and that I myself, filled as I am with the memory of their contemplation, can hardly credit even now. Perhaps in an earlier stage of evolution, as Delboeuf believes, man was fully aware of *all* that went on within himself—a region since closed to us, owing to attention being increasingly directed outwards. Into some such region I have had a glimpse, it seems. I feel sometimes there was as much fact as fancy, perhaps, in the wise old Hebrew who stated poetically—recently, too, compared with the stretch of time my science deals with—'The Sons of God took to themselves daughters of the children of men. . '"

The letter here broke off, as though interrupted by something unexpected and unusual; it was signed, indeed, "John Mason," but signed in pencil and at the bottom of an unwritten blank sheet. It had not all been written, either, at one time, or on the same day; there were intervals, evidently, perhaps of hours, perhaps of days, between the paragraphs. Dr. Fillery read, re-read, then read again the strange epistle, coming each time to the same conclusion—the writer was dying in the very act of forming the last sentences. Their incoherence, the alteration in the style, were thus explained. He had felt the end of life so close that he had written his signature, probably addressed the envelope as well, knowing the page might never be filled up. It had not been filled up.

Something behind the phrases, behind the intensity of the actual words, beyond the queer touches that revealed a mind betrayed by solitude, the hints possibly of a deluded intelligence—there was something that rang true and stimulated him more than ordinarily. The reference to Devonham, too, was definite enough. Dr. Fillery remembered vaguely a correspondence during recent crowded years with a man named Mason, living away in Switzerland somewhere, and that Devonham had asked him questions from time to time about what he called, with his rough-and-ready and half-humorous classification, "pagan obsession," "worshipper of fire and wind," referring it to the writer of the letters, named John Mason. "Non-human delusion," he had also called it sometimes. They had come to refer to it, he remembered, as "N.H." in fact.

He now looked up those Notes, for the mention of the books caused him an uncomfortable feeling of neglected opportunity, and John Mason was an honoured name.

"You know, I believe... my books," the writer said. Could this be, he asked himself anxiously, John Mason, the eminent geologist? Had Devonham not realized who he was? Must he blame his assistant, whose jealous care and judgment saved him so many foolish, futile, un-real cases, reserving what was significant and important only?

The Notes established his mistake and his assistant's—perhaps intentional?—ignorance. The writer of this curious letter was unquestionably the author of those fairy books for children, old and young, whose daring speculations had suggested that other types and races, ages even before the Neanderthal man, had dwelt side by side with what is known as modern man upon this time-worn planet. Behind the literary form of legend and fairy tale, however, lay a curious conviction. Atlantis was of yesterday compared with earlier civilizations, now extinct by fire and flood and general upheaval, which once may have inhabited the globe. The present evolutionary system, buttressed by Darwin and the rest, was but a little recent insignificant series, trivial both in time and space, when set beside the mightier systems that had come and gone. Their evidence he found, not in clumsy fossils and footprints on cooled rocks, but in the *minds* of those who had followed and eventually survived them: memories of Titan Wars and mighty beings, and gods and goddesses of nonhuman kind, to whose different existence the physical conditions of an over-heated planet presented no impossibility. The human species, this trumpery, limited, self-satisfied super-animal man, was not the only type of being.

Yet John Mason, in his day, had held the chair at Edinburgh University, his lectures embodied commonsense and knowledge, with acutest imaginative insight. His earliest writings were the text-books of the time. His name, when Edward Fillery was medical student there, still hovered like well-loved incense above the old-town towers.

The Notes now intrigued him. No blame attached to Devonham for having missed the cue, Devonham could not know everything; geology was not in his line of work and knowledge; and Mason was a common name. Rather he blamed himself for not having been struck by the oddness of the case—the Mason letters, the pagan obsession, worshipper of wind and fire, the strange " N. H."

"A competent indexer, at any rate," he said to himself with a smile, as he turned up the details easily.

These were very scanty. Devonham evidently had deemed the case of questionable value. The letters from Mason, with the answers to them, he could not find.

The slight record was headed "*Mason*, John," followed by an address "Chez Henri Petavel, peasant, Jura Mountains, Vaud, French Switzerland," and details how to reach this apparently remote valley by mule and carriage and footpath. Name of Mason's protégé not given.

"*Sex*, male; age—born 1895; parentage, couple of mystical temperament, sincere, but suffering from marked delusions, believers in Magic (various, but chiefly concerned with Nature and natural forces, once known, forgotten to-day, of immense potency, accessible to certain practices of logical but undetailed kind, able apparently to intensify human consciousness).

"*Subject*, of extremely quick intelligence, yet betrays ignorance of human conditions; intelligence superior to human, though sometimes inferior; long periods of quiescence, followed by immense, almost super-human, activity and energy; worships fire and air, chiefly the former, calling the sun his father and deity.

"Abhors confined space; this shown by intense desire for heat, which, together with free space (air), seem conditions of well-being.

"Fears (as in claustrophobia) both water and solidity (anything massive).

"Has great physical power, yet indifferent to its use; women irresistibly attracted to him, but his attitude towards other sex seems one of gentleness and pity; love means nothing. Has, on the other hand, extraordinarily high ideal of service. Is puzzled by quarrels and differences of personal kind. Half-memories of vast system of myriad workers, ruled by this ideal of harmonious service. Faithful, true, honest; falseness or lies impossible... lovable, pathetic, helpless type—"

The Notes broke off abruptly.

Dr. Fillery, wondering a little that his subordinate's brief but suggestive summary had never been brought to his notice before, turned a moment to glance at the rough water-colour drawing he held in his hand. He looked at it for some moments with absorption. The expression of his face was enigmatical. He was more than surprised that Devonham had not drawn his attention to the case in detail. Placing his hand so as to hide the lower portion of the face, he examined the eyes, then turned the portrait upside down, gazing at the eyes afresh. He seemed lost in thought for a considerable time. A faint flush stole into his cheek, and a careful observer might have noticed an increase of light about the skin. He sighed once or twice, and presently, laying the portrait down again, he turned back to the *dossier* upon the table in front of him.

"Very accurate and careful," he said to himself with satisfaction as he noticed the date Devonham had set against the entries—"June 20th, 1914."

The war, therefore, had interrupted the correspondence.

Devonham had made further notes of his own in the margin here and there:

"Does this originate primarily from Mason's mind, communicated thence to his protégé?" He agreed with his assistant's query.

"If so, was it transferred to Mason's mind before that? By the father or mother? The mother was, obviously, his—Mason's—great love. Yet the father was his life friend. Mason's great passion was suppressed. He never told it. It found no outlet."

"Admirable," was the comment spoken below his breath.

"Boy born as result of some 'magical' experiment intensely believed (not stated in detail), during course of which father died suddenly.

"Mason tended mother, then lived on alone in remote place where all had occurred.

"Did Mason inherit entire content of parents' beliefs, dramatizing this by force of unexpressed but passionate love?

"Did not Mason's mind, thus charged, communicate whole business to the young mind he has since formed, a plastic mind uninfluenced by normal human surroundings and conditions of ordinary life?

"Transfer of a sex-inspired mania?"

Then followed another note, summarizing evidently Devonham's judgment:

"Not worth F.'s investigation until examined further. N.B.—Look up Mason first opportunity and judge at first hand."

Dr. Fillery, glancing from the papers to the portrait, smiled a little again as he signified approval.

But the last entry interested him still more. It was dated July 13, 1914.

"Mason reports boy's prophecy of great upheaval coming. Entire race slips back into chaos of primitive life again. Entire Western Civilization crumbles. Modern inventions and knowledge vanish. Nature spirits reappear.... Desires return of all previous letters. These sent by registered post."

A few scattered notes on separate sheets of paper lay at the end of the carefully typed *dossier*, but these were very incomplete, and Devonham's handwriting, especially when in pencil, was not of the clearest.

"Non-human claim, though absurd, not traceable to any antecedent causes given by letters. What is Mason's past mental and temperamental history? Is he not, through the parents, the cause? Mania seems harmless, both to subject and others. No suffering or unhappiness. Therefore not a case for F., until further examined by self. Better see Mason and his subject first. Wrote July 24th proposing visit."

Dr. Fillery's eyes twinkled. His forehead relaxed. He looked back. He remembered details. Devonham's holiday that year, he recalled, was due on August 1st; he had intended going out mountain climbing in Switzerland.

The final note of all, also in half-legible writing, seemed to refer to the treatment Mason had asked advice about, and the line Devonham had suggested

"Natural life close to Nature cannot hurt him. But I advise watch him with fire and with heights—heat, air! That is, he may decide his physical body is irksome and seek to escape it. Teach him natural history—botany, geology, insects, animals, even astronomy, but always giving him reasons and explanations. *Above all*—let him meet girls of his own age and fall in love. Fullest natural expression, but guarded without his knowing it..."

For a long time Dr. Fillery sat with the notes and papers before him, thinking over what he had read. Devonham's advice was clever enough, but without insight, sound and astute, yet lacking divination.

The twinkle in his eyes, caused by the final entry, died away. His face was grave, his manner preoccupied, intense. He gazed long at the portrait in his hand.... It was dusk when he finally rose, replaced the *dossier*, locked the cabinet, and went out into another room, and thence into the hall. Taking his hat and stick, he left the house, already composing in his mind the telegram instructing Devonham, while apologizing for the interrupted holiday, to bring the subject of the Notes to England with him. A telegraph girl met him on the very steps of the house. He took the envelope from her, and opened it. He read the message. It was dated Bâle, the day before:

"Arriving end week with interesting patient. Details index under Mason. Prepare private suite.

"DEVONHAM."

CHAPTER V

It was, however, some two weeks later before Dr. Fillery was on his way to the station to meet Devonham and his companion. A slight delay, caused apparently by the necessity of buying an outfit, had intervened and given time for an exchange of letters, but Devonham had contented himself chiefly with telegrams. He did not wish his chief to know too much about the case in advance. "Probably he regrets the Notes already," thought the doctor, as the car made its way slowly across crowded London. "He wants my first unbiased judgment; he's right, of course, but it's too late for that now."

The delay, however, had been of value. The Home was in working order again, the staff returned, the private suite all ready for its interesting occupant, whom in thought he had already named "N. H."; for in the first place he did not know his name as yet, and in the second he felt towards him a certain attitude of tolerant, half-humorous scepticism.

Cut off from his own kind for so many years, educated, perhaps half-educated only, by too speculative and imaginative a mind, equally warped by this long solitude, a mind unduly stretched by the contemplation of immense geological perspectives, filled, too, with heaven knows what strange stories of pantheistic Nature-feeling—"N. H." might be distinctly interesting, but hardly all that Mason had thought him. "Unique" was a word rarely justified; the peculiarities would prove to be mere extravagances that had, of necessity, remained uncorrected by the friction of intercourse with his own kind. The rest was inheritance, equally unpruned; a mind living in a side-eddy, a backwater with

Nature...

At the same time Dr. Fillery admitted a certain anticipatory excitement he could not wholly account for, an undercurrent of wonder he ascribed to his Khaketian blood.

He had written once only to his assistant, sending briefest instructions to say the rooms would be ready, and that the young man must believe he was an invited guest coming on a visit. "Let him expect complete freedom of movement and occupation without the smallest idea of restraint in any way. He is merely coming to stay for as long as he pleases with a friend of Mason. Impress him with a sense of hearty welcome." And Devonham, replying, had evidently understood the wisdom of this method. "He is also greatly pleased with your name—the sound of it," was stated in the one letter that he wrote, "and as names mean a lot to him, so much the better. The sound of it gives him pleasure; he keeps repeating it over to himself; he already likes you. My name he does not care about, saying it quickly, sharply. But he trusts me. His trust in anyone who shows him kindness is instantaneous and complete. He invariably expects kindness, however, from everyone—gives it himself equally—and is baffled and puzzled by any other treatment."

So Devonham, with "N. H.," who attached importance to names and expected kindness from people as a natural thing, would be in London town within the hour. Straight from his forests and mountains for the first time in his life, he would find himself in the heart of the greatest accumulation of human beings on the planet, the first city of the world, the final expression of civilization as known to the human race.

"'N. H.' in London town," thought Dr. Fillery, his mouth twitching with the smile that began in his quiet eyes. "Bless the lad! We must make him feel at home and happy. He shall indeed have kindness. He'll need a woman's touch as well." He reflected a moment. "Women are a great help in doubtful cases—the way a man reacts to them," he mused. "Only they must be distinct in type to be of value." And his mind ran quickly, comprehensively over the women of his acquaintance, pausing, as it did so, upon two in particular—a certain Lady Gleeson, and Iraida—sometimes called Nayan—Khilkoff, the daughter of his Russian friend, the sculptor.

His mind pondered for some moments the two he had selected. It was not the first time he had made use of them. Their effect respectively upon a man was invariably instinctive and illuminating.

The two were radically different feminine types, as far removed from one another as pole from pole, yet each essentially of her sex. Their effect, respectively, upon such a youth must be of value, and might be even illuminating to the point of revelation. Both, he felt sure, would not be indifferent to the new personality.

It was, however, of Nayan Khilkoff that he thought chiefly. Of that rare, selfless, maternal type which men in all ages have called saint or angel, she possessed that power which evoked in them all they could feel of respect, of purity, of chivalry, that love, in a word, which holds as a chief ingredient, worship. Her beauty, beyond their reach, was of the stars; it was the unattainable in her they loved; her beauty was of the soul. Nayan was spiritual, not as a result of painful effort and laborious development, but born so. Her life, moreover, was one of natural service. Personal love, exclusive devotion to an individual, concentration of her being upon another single being—this seemed impossible to her. She was at the same time an enigma, an elusive flavour about her that made people a little in awe of her, a flavour not of this earth, quite. She carried an impersonal attitude almost to the point of seeming irresponsive to common human things and interests.

The other woman, Lady Gleeson, Angela her Christian name, was equally a simple type, though her simplicity was that of the primitive female who is still close to the Stone Age—a savage. She adorned herself to capture men. She was the female spider that devours its mates. She wanted slaves. To describe her as selfish were inadequate, for she was unaware that any other ideal existed in life but that of obtaining her own pleasure. There was instinct and emotion, but, of course, no heart. Without morals, conscience or consideration, she was the animal of prey that obeys the call of hunger in the most direct way possible, regardless of consequences to herself or others. Her brain was quick, her personality shallow. When talking she "rattled on." Devonham had well said once: "You can hear her two thoughts clicking, both of them in trousers! " Sir George, recently knighted, successful with large concessions in China, was indulgent. The male splendour of the youth was bound to stimulate her hunger, as his simplicity, his loneliness, and in a sense his pathetic helplessness, would certainly evoke the tenderness in Nayan. "He'll probably like her dear, ridiculous name, too," Dr. Fillery felt, "the nickname they gave her because she's the same to everybody, whichever way you take her—Nayan Khilkoff." Yet her real name was more beautiful—Iraida. And, as he repeated it half aloud, a soft light stole upon his face, shone in the deep clear eyes, and touched even the corners of the rather grim mouth with another, a tenderer expression, before the sternness quickly returned to it.

"N. H." would meet, thus, two main types of female life. He, apparently an exceedingly male being, would face the onslaught of passion and heart, of lust and love, respectively; and it was his reactions to these onslaughts that Fillery wished to observe. They would help his diagnosis, they might guide his treatment.

It was a warm and muggy afternoon, the twilight passing rapidly into darkness now; one of those late autumn days when summer heat flits back, but light is weak. The covered sky increased the clammy warmth, which was damp, unhealthy, devitalizing. No wind stirred. The great city was sticky and depressing. Yet people approved the heat, although it tired them. "It shortens the winter, anyhow," was the general verdict, when expressed at all. They referred unconsciously to the general dread of strikes.

London was hurried and confused. An air of feverish overcrowding reigned in the great station, when he left the car and went in on foot. No sign of order, system, direction, was visible. The scene might have been a first rehearsal of some entirely new experiment. Grumbling and complaint rose from all sides in an exasperated chorus. He tried to ascertain how late the train was and on which platform it might be expected, but no one knew for certain, and the grudging replies to questions seemed to say, "You've no right to ask anything, and if you keep on asking there will be a strike. So that's that!"

He listened to the talk and watched the facial expressions and the movements of the half-resigned and half-excited concourse of London citizens. The clock was accurate, and everyone was kind to ladies; stewed tea, stale cake with little stones in it, vile whisky and very weak beer were obtainable at high prices. There were no matches. The machine for supplying platform-tickets was broken. He saw men paying more thought and attention to the comfort of their dogs than to their own. The great, marvellous, stupid, splendid race was puzzled and exasperated. Then, suddenly, the train pulled in, full of returned exiles longing to be back again in "dear old England."

"Thank God, it's come," sighed the crowd. "Good! We're English. Forgive and forget!" and prepared to tip the porters handsomely and carry their own baggage.

The confusion that followed was equally characteristic, and equally remarkable, displaying greatness side by side with its defects. There was no system; all was muddled, yet all was safe. Anyone could claim what luggage they liked, though no one did so, nor dreamed, it seemed, of doing so. There was an air of decent honesty and trust. There were ladies who discovered that all men are savages; there were men—and women—who were savages. People shook hands warmly, smiled with honest affection, said light, careless good-byes that hid genuine emotion; helped one another with parcels, offered one another lifts. There were few taxicabs, one perhaps to every thirty people. And in this general scrimmage, Dr. Fillery, at first, could see no sign of his expected arrivals; he walked from end to end of the platform littered with luggage and thronged with bustling people, but nowhere could he discover the familiar outline of Devonham, nor anyone who answered to the strange picture that already stood forth sharply in his mind.

"There's been a mistake somewhere," he said to himself; "I shall find a telegram when I get back to the house explaining it"—when, suddenly and without apparent cause, there stole upon him a curious lift of freedom—a sharp sense of open spaces he was at a loss to understand. It was accompanied by an increase of light. For a second it occurred to him that the great enclosing roof had rolled back and blown away, letting in air and some lost ray of sunshine. A lovely valley flitted across his thought. Almost he was aware of flowers, of music, of rhythmic movement.

"Edward! there you are. I thought you hadn't come," he heard close behind him, and, turning, saw the figure of Devonham, calm and alert as usual. At his side stood a lean, virile outline of a young man, topping Devonham by several inches, with broad but thin shoulders, figure erect yet flexible, whose shining and inquiring eyes of blue were the most striking feature in a boyish face, where strength, intensity and radiant health combined in an unusual degree.

"Here is our friend, LeVallon," added Devonham, but not before the figure had stepped lightly and quickly forward, already staring at him and shaking his outstretched hand.

So this was "N. H.," and LeVallon was his name. The calm, searching eyes held a touch of bewilderment in them, the eyes of an honest, intelligent animal, thought Fillery quickly, adding in spite of himself and almost simultaneously, "but of a divine animal." It was a look he had never in his life before encountered in any human eyes. Mason's water-colour sketch had caught something, at least, of their innocence and question, of their odd directness and intensity, something, too, of the golden fire in the hair. He wore a broad-brimmed felt hat of Swiss pattern, a Bernese overcoat, a low, soft-collared shirt, with blue tie to match.

Buffeted and pushed by the frenzied travellers, they stood and faced each other, shaking hands, eyes looking into eyes, two strangers, doctor and patient possibly, but friends most certainly, both felt instantly. They liked one another. Once again the scent of flowers danced with light above the piled-up heaps of trunks, rugs, packages. A cool wind from mountains seemed to blow across the dreadful station.

"You've arrived safely," began Dr. Fillery, a little taken aback perhaps. "Welcome! And not too tired, I hope—" when the other interrupted him in a man's deep voice, full of pleasant timbre:

"Fill-er-y," he said, making the "F" sound rather long, "I need you. To see you makes me happy."

"'Tired," put in Devonham breathlessly, "good heavens, not he! But I am. Now for a porter and the big luggage. Have you got a taxi?"

"The car is here," said Fillery, letting go with a certain reluctance the hand he held, and paying little attention to anything but the figure before him who used such unexpected language. What was it? What did it mean? Whence came this sudden sense of intensity, light, of order, system, intelligence into the racial scene of muddled turmoil all about him? There seemed an air of speeding up in thought and action near him, compared to which the slow stupidity, unco-ordinated and confused on all sides, became painful, gross, and even ludicrous.

Someone bumped against him with violence, but quite needlessly, since the simplest judgment of weight and distance could have avoided the collision. In such ordinary small details he was aware of another, a higher, standard close. A man on his left, trying to manage several bundles, appeared vividly as of amazing incompetence, with his miscalculation, his clumsy movement, his hopeless inability to judge cause and effect. Yet he had two arms, ten fingers, two legs, broad shoulders and deep chest. Misdirection of his great strength made it impossible for him to manage the assortment of light parcels. Next to him, however, stood a woman carrying a baby—there was no error there. The panting engine just beyond them, again, set a standard of contemptuous, impersonal intelligence that, obeying Nature's laws, dwarfed the humans generally. But it was another, a quasi-spiritual standard, that had flashed to him above all. In some curious way the competent "dead" machinery that obeyed the Law with faultless efficiency, and the woman obeying instinct with equally unconscious skill—these two energies were akin to the new standard he was now startlingly aware of.

He looked up, as though to trace this sudden new consciousness of bright, quick, rapid competence—almost as of some immense power building with consistent scheme and system—that had occurred to him; and he met again the direct, yet slightly bewildered eyes that watched him, watched him with confidence, sweetness, and with a questioning intensity he found intriguing, captivating, and oddly stimulating. He felt happiness.

"By yer leave!" roared a porter, as they stepped aside just in time to save being pushed by the laden truck—just in time to save himself, that is, for the other, Fillery noticed, moved like a chamois on its native rocks, so surely, lightly, swiftly was he poised.

"This! Ah, you must excuse it," the doctor exclaimed with a smile of apology almost, "we've not yet had time to settle down after the war, you see." He pointed with a sweep of his hand to the roaring, dim-lit cavern where confusion reigned supreme, the G.H.Q. of travel in the biggest city of the Empire.

"I've got a porter," cried Devonham, beckoning vigorously a little further down the platform. "You wait there. I'll be along in a minute with the stuff." He was hot, flustered, exhausted.

"You struggle. It was like this all the way. Is there no knowledge?" LeVallon asked in his deep, quiet tones.

"We do," said Fillery. "With us life is always struggle. But there is more system than appears. The confusion is chiefly on the surface."

"It is dark and there is so little air," observed the other. "And they all work against each other."

Fillery laughed into the other's eyes; they laughed together; and it seemed suddenly to the doctor that their beings somehow merged, so that, for a second, he knew the entire content of his companion's mind—as if there was nothing in LeVallon he did not understand.

"You—are a builder," LeVallon said abruptly. But as he said it his companion caught, on the wing as it were, another meaning. He became curiously aware of the smallness, of the remote insignificance of the little planet whereon this dialogue took place, yet at the same time of its superb seductive loveliness. In him rose a feeling, as on wings, that he was not chained in his familiar, daily personality, but that an immense, delicious freedom lay within reach. He could be everywhere at once. He could do everything.

"Wait here while I help Devonham. Then we'll get into the car and be off." He moved away, threading a path with difficulty.

"I wait in peace. I am happy," was the reply.

And with those few phrases, uttered in the quiet, deep voice, sounding in his ears and in his very blood, the older man went towards the spot where Devonham struggled with a porter, a pile of nondescript luggage and a truck: "I wait in peace.... You struggle, you work against each other.... It is dark, there is little air.... You are a builder...."

But not these singular words alone remained alive in his mind; there re-mained in his heart the sense of that vitality of open spaces, keen air and brighter light he had experienced—and, with it, the security of some higher, faultless standard. His brain, indeed, had recognized a consciousness of swifter reactions, of surer movements, of more intelligent co-ordination, compared to which the people about him behaved like stupid, almost like half-witted beings, the one exception being the instinctive action of the mother in carrying her baby, and the other, the impersonal, accurate, competence of the dead machinery.

But, more than this reasoned change, there burned suddenly in his heart an in-explicable exhilaration and brightness, a wonder that he could attribute only to another mode of life. His Khaketian blood, he knew, might be responsible for part of it, but not for all. The invigorating mountain wind, the sunlight, the rhythmic sound, the scent of wild flowers, these were his own personal interpretations of a quickened sense he could not analyse as yet. As he held the young man's hand, as he gazed into his direct blue eyes, this sense had increased in intensity. LeV-allon had some marvellous quality or power that was new to him, while yet not entirely unfamiliar. What was it? And how did the youth perceive this sense in him so surely that he took its presence for granted, accepted, even played upon it? He experienced, as it were, a brilliant intensification of spirit. Some portion of him already knew exactly what LeVallon was.

Across the ugly turmoil and confusion of the huge dingy railway terminus had moved wondrously some simple power that brought in—Beauty. Some very deep and ancient conception had touched him and gone its way again. The stu-pendous beauty of a simple, common day appeared to him. His subconscious be-ing, of course, was deeply stirred. That was the truth, phrase it as he might. His heart was lifted as by a primal wind at dawn upon some mountain top. The heav-iness of the day was gone. Fatigue, too, vanished. The "civilized" folk appeared contemptible and stupid. Something direct from Nature herself poured through him. And it was from the atmosphere of LeVallon this new vitality issued ra-diating.

He found a moment or two, while alone with Devonham, to exchange a few hurried sentences. As they bent over bags and bundles he asked quick questions. These questions and answers between the two experienced men were brief but significant:

"Yes, quiet as a lamb. Just be kind and sympathetic. You looked up the Notes? Well, that can't be helped now, though I had rather you knew nothing. My mistake, of course."

"The content of his mind is accessible to me—telepathically—in any case."

"But at one remove more distant, because unexpressed."

Fillery laughed. "Quite right. I admit it's a pity. But tell me more about him—anything I ought to know—at once."

"Quiet as a lamb, I told you," repeated the other, "and most of the way over too. But puzzled—my god, Edward, his criticisms would make a book."

"Normal? Intelligent criticisms?"

"Intelligent above ordinary. Normal—no."

"Hysteria? "

"Not a sign."

"Health?"

"Perfect, magnificent, as you see. He's less tired now than when we started three days ago, whereas I'm fagged out, though in climbing condition."

"Origin of delusions—any indication?"

Devonham looked up quickly. His eyes flashed a peculiarly searching glance—something watchful in it perhaps. "No delusion at all of any sort. As for origin of his ideas—the parents probably, but stimulated and allowed unchecked growth by Mason. Affected by Nature beyond anything *we* know."

"By Nature. Ah!" He checked himself. "And what peculiarities?" he asked.

"His terror of water, for instance. Crossing the Channel he was like a frightened child. He hid from it, kept his hands over his eyes even, so as not to see it."

"Give any reason?"

"All he said was 'It is unknown, an enemy, and can destroy me. I cannot understand its secret ways. Fire and wind are not in it. I cannot work with it.' No, it was not fear of drowning that he meant. He found comfort, too, in the repetition of your name."

"Appetite, pulse, temperature?" asked Fillery, after a brief pause.

"First two very strong; temperature always slightly above normal."

"Other peculiarities?"

"He became rather excited before a lighted match once—tried to kneel, almost, but I stopped it."

"Fire?"

"That's it. Instinct of worship presumably."

The barrow was laden, the porter was asking where the car was. They prepared to move back to the companion, whom Fillery had never failed to observe carefully over his shoulder during this rapid conversation. "N. H." had not moved the whole time: he stood quietly, looking about him, a curious figure, aloof somehow from his surroundings, so tall and straight and unconcerned he seemed, yet so poised, alert, virile, vigorous. It was not his clothes that made him appear unusual, nor was it his eyes and hair alone, though all three contributed their share. Yet he seemed dressed up, his clothes irksome to him. He was uncommon, an attractive figure, and many a pair of eyes, female eyes especially, Fillery noticed, turned to examine him with undeniable curiosity.

"And women?" the doctor asked quickly in a lowered voice, as they followed the porter's barrow towards LeVallon, who already smiled at their approach—the most engaging, trustful, welcoming smile that Fillery had ever seen upon a human countenance.

He lowered his head to catch the reply. But Devonham only laughed and shrugged his shoulders. "All attracted," he mumbled in a half whisper, "and eager to help him."

"And he—?"

"Gentle, astonished, but indifferent, oh, supremely indifferent."

LeVallon came forward to meet them, and Fillery took his hand and led him to the car. The luggage was bundled in, some behind and some on the roof. Fillery and LeVallon sat side by side. The car started.

"We shall get home in half an hour," the doctor mentioned, turning to his companion. "We'll have a good dinner and then get to bed. You are hungry, I know."

"Thank you," was the reply, "thank you, dear Fillery. I want sleep most. Will there be trees and air near me? And stars to see?"

"Your windows open on to a garden with big trees, there will be plenty of fresh air, and you will hear the sparrows chattering at dawn. But London, of course, is not the country. Oh, we'll make you comfortable, never fear."

"Dear Fillery, I thank you," said LeVallon quietly, and without more ado lay back among the soft cushions and closed his eyes. Hardly a word was said the whole way out to the north-west suburb, and when they arrived the "patient" was too overcome with sleep to wish to eat. He went straight to his room, found a hot bath into which he tumbled first, and then leaped into his bed and was sound asleep almost before the door was closed. Upon a table beside the bed Dr. Fillery, with his own hands, arranged bread, butter, eggs and a jug of milk in case of need. Nurse Robbins, an experienced, tactful young woman, he put in special charge. He thought of everything, divining his friend's possible needs instinctively, noticing with his keen practised eye several details for himself at the same time. The splendid physical condition, frame-work, muscular development he noted—no freakish bulky masses produced by gymnastic exercises, but the muscles laid on flowingly, smooth and firm and ample, without a trace of fat, and the whole in the most admirable proportion possible. The leanness was deceptive; the body was of immense power. The quick, certain, unerring movements he noticed too; perfect, swift co-ordination between brain and physical response, no misdirection, no miscalculation, the reactions extremely rapid. He thought with a smile of something between deer and tiger. The poise and balance and accuracy conveyed intense joy of living. Yet above and beyond these was something else he could not name, something that stirred in him wonder, love, a touch of awe, and a haunting suggestion of familiarity.

He saw him into bed, he saw him actually asleep. The strong blue eyes looked up into his own with their intense and innocent gaze for a moment; he held the firm, dry muscular hand; ten seconds later the eyes were closed in sleep, the grip of the powerful but slender fingers relaxed.

"Good night, my friend, and sleep deeply. To-morrow we'll see to everything you need. Be happy here and comfortable with us, for you are welcome and we love you." His voice trembled slightly.

"Good night, dear Fill-er-y," the musical tones replied, and he was off.

The windows were wide open. "N. H." had thrown aside the pyjamas and blankets. On this cool, damp night of late autumn he covered his big, warm, lithe body with a single sheet only.

Fillery went out quietly, an expression of keen approval and enjoyment on his face—not a smile exactly, but that look of deep content, betraying a fine inner excitement of happiness, which is the mother of all smiles. As he softly opened the door the draught blew through from the open windows, stirring the white curtains by the bed. It came from the big damp garden where the trees stood, already nearly leafless, and where no flowers were. And yet a scent of flowers came faintly with it. He caught an echo of faint sound like music. There was the invigorating hint of forests too. It seemed a living wind that blew into the house.

Dr. Fillery paused a moment, sniffed with surprise and sharp enjoyment, listened intently, then switched the light off and went out, closing the door behind him. There was a flash of wonder in his eyes, and a thrill of some remote, inexplicable happiness ran through his nerves. An instant of complete comprehension had been his, as if another consciousness had, for that swift instant, identified itself with his own.

CHAPTER VI

E dward Fillery was glad that Paul Devonham, good friend and skilful colleague, was his assistant; for Devonham, competent as himself in knowledge and experience, found explanations for all things, and had in his natural temperament a quality of sane judgment which corrected extravagances. Devonham was agnostic, because reason ruled his life. Devoid of imagination, he had no temptations. Speculative, within limits, he might be, but he belonged not to the unstable. Not that he thought he knew everything, but that he refused to base action on what he regarded as unknown. A clue into the unknown he would follow up as keenly, carefully, as Fillery himself, but he went step by step, with caution, declining to move further until the last step was of hardened concrete. To the powers of the subconscious self he set drastic limits, admitting their existence of course, but attaching small value to their use or development. His own deeper being had never stirred or wakened. Of this under-sea, this vast background in himself, he remained placidly uninformed. A comprehensive view of a problem—the flash of vision he never knew—thus was perhaps denied him, but so far as he went he was very safe and sure. And his chief was the first to appreciate his value. He appreciated it particularly now, as the two men sat smoking after their late dinner, discussing details of the new inmate of the Home.

Fillery, aware of the strong pull upon his own mixed blood, aware of a half-wild instinctive sympathy towards "N. H.," almost of a natural desire now, having seen him, to believe him "unique" in several ways, and, therefore, conscious of a readiness to accept more than any evidence yet justified—feeling these symptoms clearly, and remembering vividly his experiences in the railway station, he was glad, for truth's sake, that Devonham was there to clip extravagance before it injured judgment. A weak man, aware of his own frailties, excels a stronger one who thinks he has none at all. The two colleagues were a powerful combination.

"In your view, it's merely a case of a secondary—anyhow of a divided—personality?" he asked, as soon as the other had recovered a little from his journey, and was digesting his meal comfortably over a pipe. "You have seen more of him than I have. Of insanity, at any rate, there is no sign at all, I take it? His relations with his environment are sound?"

"None whatever." Devonham answered both questions at once. "Exactly."

He took off his pince-nez, cleaned them with his handkerchief, and then replaced them carefully. This gave him time to reflect, as though he was not quite sure where to begin his story.

"There are certainly indications," he went on slowly, "of a divided personality, though of an unusual kind. The margin between the two—between the normal and the secondary self—is so very slight. It is not clearly defined, I mean. They sometimes merge and interpenetrate. The frontier is almost indistinguishable."

Fillery raised his eyebrows.

"You feel uncertain which is the main self, and which the split-off secondary personality?" he inquired, with surprise.

Devonham nodded. "I'm extremely puzzled," he admitted. "LeVallon's most marked self, the best defined, the richest, the most fully developed, seems to me what *we* should call his Secondary Self—this 'Nature-being' that worships wind and fire, is terrified by a large body of water, is ignorant of human ways, probably also quite *un*-moral, yet alive with a kind of instinctive wisdom we credit usually to the animal kingdom—though far beyond anything animals can claim—"

"Briefly, what we mean by the term 'N. H.,'" suggested Fillery, not anxious for too many details at the moment.

"Exactly. And I propose we always refer to that aspect of him as 'N. H.,' the other, the normal ordinary man, being LeVallon, his right name." He smiled faintly.

"Agreed," replied his chief. "We shall always know then exactly which one we're talking of at a given moment. Now," he went on, "to come to the chief point, and before you give me details of what happened abroad, let me hear your own main conclusion. What is LeVallon? What is 'N. H.'?"

Devonham hesitated for some time. It was evident his respect for his chief made him cautious. There was an eternal battle between these two, keen though always good-natured, even humorous, the victory not invariably perhaps with the assistant. Later evidence had often proved Fillery's swifter imagination correct after all, or, alternately, shown him to be wrong. They kept an accurate score of the points won and lost by either.

"You can always revise your conclusions later," Fillery reminded him slyly. "Call it a preliminary conclusion for the moment. You've not had time yet for a careful study, I know."

But Devonham this time did not smile at the rally, and his chief noticed it with secret approval. Here was something new, big, serious, it seemed. Devonham, apparently, was already too interested to care who scored or did not score. His Notes of 1914 indeed betrayed his genuine zeal sufficiently.

"LeVallon," he said at length—"to begin with him! I think LeVallon—without any flavour of 'N. H.'—is a fine specimen of a normal human being. His physique is magnificent, as you have seen, his health and strength exceptional. The brain, so far as I have been able to judge, functions quite normally. The intelligence, also normal, is much above the average in quickness, receptivity of ideas, and judgment based on these. The emotional development, however, puzzles me; the emotions are not—entirely normal. But"—he paused again, a grave expression on his face—"to answer your question as well as my limited observation of him, of LeVallon, allows—I repeat that I consider him a normal young man, though with peculiarities and idiosyncrasies of his own, as with most other normal young fellows who are individuals, that is," he added quickly, "and not turned out in bundles cut to measure."

"So much for LeVallon. Now what about 'N. H.'?"

He repeated the question, fixing the assistant with his steady gaze. He had noticed the confusion in the reply.

"My dear Edward—" began Devonham, after a considerable pause. Then he stuck fast, sighed, settled his glasses carefully upon his aquiline, sharp nose, and relapsed into silence. His forehead became wrinkled, his mouth much pursed.

"Out with it, Paul! This isn't a Court of Law. I shan't behead you if you're wrong." Yet Fillery, too, spoke gravely.

The other kept his eyes down; his face still wore a puzzled look. Fillery detected a new expression on the keen, thoughtful features, and he was pleased to see it.

"To give you the truth," resumed his assistant, "and all question of who is right or who is wrong aside, I tell you frankly—I am not sure. I confess myself up against it. It—er—gives me the creeps a little—" He laughed awkwardly. That swift watchful look, as of a man who plays a part, flashed and vanished.

"Your feeling, anyhow?" insisted his friend. "Your general feeling?"

"A general judgment based on general feeling," said the other in a quiet tone, "has little value. It is based, necessarily, as you know, upon intuition, which I temperamentally dislike. It has no facts to go upon. I distrust generalizations." He took a deep breath, inhaled a lot of smoke, exhaled it with relief, and made an effort. It went against the grain in him to be caught without an explanation.

"'N. H.' in my opinion, and so far as my limited observation of him—"

Fillery allowed himself a laugh of amused impatience. "Leave out the personal extras for once, and burn your bridges. Tell me finally what you think about 'N. H.' We're not scoring points now."

Thus faced with an alternative, Devonham found his sense of humour again and forgot himself. It cost him an effort, but he obeyed the bigger and less personal mind.

"I really don't know exactly *what* he is," he confessed again. "He puzzles me completely. It may be"—he shrugged his shoulders, compelled by his temperament to hedge—"that he represents, as I first thought, the content of his parents' minds, the subsequent addition of Mason's mind included."

"That's possible, usual and comprehensible enough," put in the doctor, watching him with, amused concentration, but with an inner excitement scarcely concealed.

"Or" resumed Devonham, "it may be that through these—"

"Through his mental inheritance from his parents and from Mason, yes—"

"—he taps the most primitive stores and layers of racial memory we know. The world-memory, if I dare put it so, full proof being lacking, is open to him—"

"Through his subconscious powers, of course?"

"That is your usual theory, isn't it? We have there, at any rate, a working hypothesis, with a great mass of evidence—generally speaking—behind it."

"Don't be cynical, Paul. Is this 'N. H.' merely a Secondary Personality, or is it the real central self? That's the whole point."

"You jump ahead, as usual," replied Devonham, really smiling for the first time, though his face instantly grew serious again. "Edward," he went on, "I do not know, I cannot say, I dare not—dare not guess. 'N. H.' is something entirely new to me, and I admit it." He seemed to find his stride, to forget himself. "I feel far from cynical. 'N. H.,' in my opinion, is exceptional. My Notes suggested it long ago. He has, for instance—at least, so it seems to me—peculiar powers."

"Ah!"

"Of suggestion, let us put it."

"Of suggestion, yes. Get on with it, there's a good fellow. I felt myself an extraordinary vitality about him. I noticed it at once at Charing Cross."

"I saw you did." Devonham looked hard at him. "You were humming to yourself, you know."

"I didn't know," was the surprised reply, "but I can well believe it. I felt a curious pleasure and exhilaration."

Devonham, shrugging his shoulders slightly, resumed: "During the 'LeVallon' periods he is ordinary, though unusually observant, critical and intelligent; during the 'N. H.' periods he becomes—er—super-normal. If you felt this—felt anything in the station, it was because something in you—called up the 'N. H.' aspect."

"It's quick of you to guess that," said Fillery, with quick appreciation. "You noticed a change in me, well—but the other—? He divined my 'foreign' blood, you think?"

"It is enough that you responded and felt kinship. Put it that way. 'N H.' seems to me"—he took a deeper breath and gave a sort of gasp—"in some ways—a unique—being—as I said before."

"Tell me, if you can," said Fillery, lighting his own pipe and settling back into his chair, "tell me a little about your first meeting with him in the Jura Mountains, what happened and so forth. I remember, of course, your Notes. After your telegram, I read 'em carefully." He glanced round at his companion. "They were very honest, Paul, I thought. Eh?" He was unable to refuse himself the pleasure of the little dig. "Honest you always are," he added. "We couldn't work together otherwise, could we?"

Devonham, deep in his own thoughts, did not accept the challenge. He turned in his chair, puffing at his pipe.

"I can give you briefly what happened and how things went," he said. "The place, then, first: an ordinary peasant châlet in a remote Jura valley, difficult of access, situated among what they call the upper pastures. I reached it by *diligence* and mule late in the afternoon. A peasant in a lower valley directed me, adding that 'le monsieur anglais' was dead and buried two days before—"

"Mason, that is?"

The other nodded. "And adding that 'le fou' —"

"LeVallon, of course?"

"—would eat me alive at sight. He spoke with respect, however, even awe. He hoped I had come to take him away. The countryside was afraid of him.

"The valley struck me as intolerably lonely, but of unusual beauty. Big forests, great rocks, and tumbling streams among cliffs and pastures made it exceptional. The châlet was simple, clean and comfortable. It was really an ideal spot for a thinker or a student. The first thing I noticed was a fire burning on a pile of rock in front of the building. The sun was setting, and its last rays lit the entire little glen—a mere gully between precipices and forest slopes—but especially lit up the pile of rocks where the fire burned, so that I saw the smoke, blue, red and yellow, and the figure kneeling before it. This figure was a man, half naked, and of magnificent proportions. When I shouted—"

"You *would* shout, of course." Yet he did not say it critically.

"—the figure rose and turned and came to meet me. It was LeVallon."

Devonham paused a moment. Fillery's eyes were fixed upon him.

"I admit," Devonham went on, conscious of the other's inquiring and intent expression, "I was surprised a bit." He smiled his faint, unwilling smile. "The figure made me start. I was aware of an emotion I am not subject to—what I called just now the creeps. I thought, at last, I had really seen a—a vision. He looked so huge, so wonderful, so radiant. It was, of course, the effect of coloured smoke and magnifying sunset, added to his semi-nakedness. To the waist he was stripped. But, at first, his size, his splendour, a kind of radiance borrowed from the sunlight and the fire, seemed to enlarge him beyond human. He seemed to dominate, even to fill the little valley.

"I stood still, uncertain of my feelings. There was, I think, a trace of fear in me. I waited for him to come up to me. He did so. He stretched out a hand. I took it. And what do you think he said?"

Fillery, the inner excitement and delight increasing in him as he listened, stared in silence. There was no lightness in him now.

"'Are you Fillery?' That's what he said, and the first words he uttered. 'Are you Fillery?' But spoken in a way I find difficult to reproduce. He made the name sound like a rush of wind. 'F,' of course, involves a draught of breath between the teeth, I know. But *he* made the name sound exactly like a gush of wind through branches—that's the nearest I can get to it."

"Well—and then ?"

"Don't be impatient, Edward. I try to be accurate. But really—what happened next is a bit beyond any experience that we—I—have yet come across. And, as to what I felt—well, I was tired, hungry, thirsty. I wanted, normally, rest and food and drink. Yet all these were utterly forgotten. For a moment or two—

I admit it—I felt as if I had come face to face with something not of this earth quite." He grinned. "A touch of gooseflesh came to me for the first time in my life. The fellow's size and radiance in the sunlight, the fact that he stood there worshipping fire—always, to me, the most wonderful of natural phenomena— his grandeur and nakedness—the way he pronounced your name even—all this—er—upset my judgment for the moment." He paused again. He hesitated. "A visual hallucination, due to fatigue, can be, of course, very detailed some-times," he added, a note of challenge in his tone.

Fillery watched his friend narrowly, as he stumbled among the details of what he evidently found a difficult, almost an impossible description.

"Natural enough," he put in. "You'd hardly be human yourself if you felt noth-ing at such a sight."

"The loneliness, too, increased the effect," went on the other, "for there was no one nearer than the peasants who had directed me a thousand feet below, nor was there another building of any sort in sight. Anyhow, it seemed, I man-aged my strange emotions all right, for the young man took to me at once. He left the fire, if reluctantly, singing to himself a sort of low chanting melody, with perhaps five or six notes at most in it, and far from unmusical—"

"He explained the fire? Was he actually worshipping, I mean?"

"It was certainly worship, judging by the expression of his face and his ges-tures of reverence and happiness. But I asked no questions. I thought it best just to accept, or appear to accept, the whole thing as natural. He said something about the Equinox, but I did not catch it properly and did not ask. This had ev-idently been taught him. It was, however, the 22nd of September, oddly enough, though the gales had not yet come."

"So you got into the châlet next?" asked the other, noticing the gaps, the in-coherence.

"He put his coat on, sat down with me to a meal of bread and milk and cheese—meat there seemed none in the building anywhere. This meal was, if you understand me, obeying a mere habit automatically. He did just what it had been his habit to do with Mason all these years. He got the stuff himself— quickly, effectively, no fumbling anywhere—and, from that moment, hardly spoke again until we left two days later. I mean that literally. All he said, when I tried to make him talk, was, 'You are not Fillery,' or 'Take me to Fillery. I need him.'

"I almost felt that I was living with some marvellously trained animal, of ex-traordinary intelligence, gentle, docile, friendly, but unhappy because it had lost its accustomed master. But on the other hand—I admit it—I was conscious of a certain power in his personality beyond me to explain. That, really, is the best description I can give you."

"You mentioned the name of Mason?" asked Fillery, avoiding a dozen more obvious and natural questions.

"Several times. But his only reply was a smile, while he repeated the name him-self, adding your own after it: 'Mason Fillery, Mason Fillery,' he would say, smil-ing with quiet happiness. 'I like Fillery!' "

"The nights?"

"Briefly—I was glad to see the dawn. We had separate rooms, my own being the one probably where Mason had died a few days before. But it was not that I minded in the least. It was the feeling—the knowledge in fact—that my companion was up and about all night in the building or out of doors. I heard him moving, singing quietly to himself, the wooden veranda creaked beneath his tread. He was active all through the darkness and cannot have slept at all. When I came down soon after dawn he was running over the slopes a mile away, running towards the châlet, too, with the speed and lightness of a deer. He had been to some height, I think, to see the sun rise and probably to worship it—"

"And your journey? You got him away easily?"

"He was only too ready to leave, for it meant coming to you. I arranged with the peasants below to have the châlet closed up, took my charge to Neuchâtel, and thence to Berne, where I bought him an outfit, and arrived in due course, as you know, at Charing Cross."

"His first sight of cities, people, trains, steamers and the rest, I take it. Any reactions?"

"The troubles I anticipated did not materialize. He came like a lamb, the most helpless and pathetic lamb I ever saw. He stared but asked no questions. I think he was half dazed, even stupefied with it all."

"Stupefied?"

"An odd word to use, I know. I should have said perhaps 'automatic' rather. He was so open to my suggestions, doing what my mind expected him to do, but nothing more—ah! with one exception."

Fillery meant to hear an account of that exception, though the other would willingly have foregone its telling evidently. It was related, Fillery felt sure, to the unusual powers Devonham had mentioned.

"Oh, you shall hear it," said the latter quickly, "for what it's worth. There's no need to exaggerate, of course." He told it rapidly, accurately, no doubt, because his mind was honest, yet without comment or expression in his voice and face. He supplied no atmosphere.

"I had got him like a lamb, as I told you, to Paris, and it was during the Customs examination the—er—little thing occurred. The man, searching through his trunk, pulled out a packet of flat papers and opened it. He looked them over with puzzled interest, turning them upside down to examine them from every possible angle. Then he asked a trifle unpleasantly what they were. I hadn't the smallest idea myself, I had never seen them before; they were very carefully wrapped up. LeVallon, whose sudden excitement increased the official's interest, told him that they were star-and-weather maps. It doubtless was the truth; he had made them with Mason; but they were queer-looking papers to have at such a time, hidden away, too, at the bottom of the trunk; and LeVallon's manner and expression did not help to disarm the man's evident suspicion. He asked a number of pointed questions in a very disagreeable way—who made them, for what purpose, how they were used, and whether they were connected with aviation. I translated, of course. I explained their innocence—"

"LeVallon's excitement?" asked Fillery. "What form did it take? Rudeness, anger, violence of any sort? "He was aware his friend would have liked to shirk these details.

"Nothing of the kind." He hesitated briefly, then went on. "He behaved, rather, as though—well, as a devout Catholic might have behaved if his crucifix or some holy relic were being mauled. The maps were sacred. Symbols possibly. Heaven knows what! He tried to take them back. The official, as a natural result, became still more suspicious and, of course, offensive too. My explanations and expostulations were quite useless, for he didn't even listen to them."

Devonham was now approaching the part of the story he least wished to describe. He played for time. He gave details of the ensuing altercation.

"What happened in the end?" Fillery at length interrupted. "What did LeVallon do? There were no arrests, I take it?" he added with a smile.

Paul coughed and fidgeted. He told the literal truth, however.

"LeVallon, after listening for a long time to the conversation he could not understand, suddenly took his fingers off the papers. The man's dirty hand still held them tightly on the grimy counter. LeVallon began—er—he suddenly began to breathe—well—heavily rather."

"Rhythmically?"

"Heavily," insisted the other. "In a curious way, anyhow," he added, determined to keep strictly to the truth, "not unlike Heathcote when he put himself automatically into trance and then told us what was going on at the other end of England. You remember the case." He paused a moment again, as if to recall exactly what had occurred. "It's not easy to describe, Edward," he continued, looking up. "You remember that huge draughty hall where they examine luggage at the Lyons Station. I can't explain it. But that breathing somehow caught the draughts, used them possibly, in any case increased them. A wind came through the great hall. I can't explain it," he repeated, "I can only tell you what happened. That wind most certainly came pouring steadily through, for I felt it myself, and saw it blow upon the fluttering papers. The heat in the *salle* at the same moment seemed to grow intense. Not an oppressive heat, though. Radiant heat, rather. It felt, I mean, like a fierce sunlight. I looked up, almost expecting to see a great light from which it came. It was then—at this very moment—the Frenchman turned as if someone touched him."

"*You* felt anything, Paul?"

"Yes," admitted the other slowly. Fillery waited.

"A—what I must call—a thrill." His voice was lower now.

"Of—?" his Chief persisted.

Devonham waited a full ten seconds before reply. He again shrugged his shoulders a little. Apparently he sought his words with honest care that included also intense reluctance and disapproval:

"Loveliness, romance, enchantment; but, above all, I think—power." He ground out the confession slowly. "By power I mean a sort of confidence and happiness."

"Increase of vitality, call it. Intensification of your consciousness."

"Possibly. A bigger perspective suddenly, a bigger scale of life; something—er—a bit wild, but certainly—er—uncommonly stimulating. The best word, I think, is liberty, perhaps. An immense and careless sense of liberty." And Fillery, knowing the value of superlatives in Devonham's cautious mind, felt satisfied. He asked quietly what the official did next.

"Stood stock still at first. Then his face changed; he smiled; he looked up understandingly, sympathetically, at LeVallon. He spoke: 'My father, too,' he said with admiration, 'had a big telescope. Monsieur is an astronomer.'

"'One of the greatest,' I added quickly; 'these charts are of infinite value to France.' No sense of comedy touched me anywhere, the ludicrous was absent. The man bowed, as carefully, respect in every gesture, he replaced the maps, marked the trunk with his piece of chalk, and let us go, helping in every way he could."

Devonham drew a long breath, glad that he had relieved himself of his unwelcome duty. He had told the literal truth.

"Of course, of course," Fillery said, half to himself perhaps. "A breath of bigger consciousness, his imagination touched, the subconscious wakened, and intelligence the natural result." He turned to his colleague. "Interesting, Paul, very," he added in a louder tone, "and not easy to explain, I grant. The official we do not know, but you, at any rate, are not a good subject for hypnotic suggestion!"

For some time Devonham said nothing. Presently he spoke:

"Fillery, I tell you—really I love the fellow. He's the most lovable thing in human shape I ever saw. He gets into your heart so strangely. We must heal him."

The other sighed, quickly smothering it, yet not before Devonham had noticed it. They did not look at one another for some seconds, and there was a certain tenseness, a sense of deep emotion in the air that each, possibly, sought to hide from the other.

Devonham was the first to break the silence that had fallen between them.

"To be quite frank—it's LeVallon that appeals most to me," he said, as if to himself, "whereas you, Edward, I believe, are more—more interested in the other aspect of him. It's 'N. H.' that interests you."

No challenge was intended, yet the glove was flung. Fillery said nothing for a minute or two. Then he looked up, and their eyes met across the smoke-laden atmosphere. It was close on midnight. The world lay very still and hushed about the house.

"It is," he said quietly, "a pathetic and inspiring case. He is deserving of"—he chose his words slowly and with care—"our very best," he concluded shortly.

"And now," he added quickly, "you're tired out, and I ought to have let you have a night's sleep before taxing you like this." He poured out two glasses of whisky. "Let us drink anyhow to success and healing of body, mind—and soul."

"Body, mind and—nerves," said Devonham slowly, as he drank the toast.

"The reason I had none of the trouble I anticipated," remarked Devonham, as he sipped the reviving liquor, "is simple enough."

"There are two periods, of course. I guessed that."

"Exactly. There is the LeVallon period, when he is quiescent, normal, very charming into the bargain, more like a good child or trained animal or happy peas-ant, if you like it better, than a grown man. And there is the 'N. H.' period, when he is—otherwise."

"Ah!"

"I arrived just at the transition moment, so to speak. It was during the change I reached the châlet."

"Precisely." Fillery looked up, smiled and nodded.

"That's about the truth," repeated Devonham, putting his glass down. He thought for a moment, then added slowly, "I think that fire of his, the worship, singing—at the autumnal equinox—marked the change. 'N. H.,' at once after that, slipped back into the unconscious state. LeVallon emerged. It was with LeVallon only, or chiefly, I had to deal. He became so very quiet, dazed a lit-tle, half there, as we call it, and almost entirely silent. He retained little, if any, memory of the 'N. H.' period, although it lies, I think, just beneath the surface only. The LeVallon personality, you see, is not very positive, is it? It seems a quiet, negative state, a condition almost of rest, in fact."

Fillery listening attentively, made no rejoinder.

"We may expect," continued Devonham, "these alternating states, I think. The frontier between them is, as I said, a narrow one. Indeed, often they merge or interpenetrate. In my judgment, the main, important part of his consciousness, that parent Self, is LeVallon—not 'N. H.'" The voice was slightly strident.

"Ah!"

It so happened that, in the act of exchanging these last words, they both looked up toward the ceiling, where a moth buzzed round and round, banging itself occasionally against the electric light. Whether it was this that drew their sight upwards simultaneously, or whether it was that some other sound in the still-ness of the night had caught their strained attention, is uncertain. The same thought, at any rate, was in both minds at that instant, the same freight of mean-ing trailing behind it invisibly across the air. Their hearts burned within them; the two faces upward turned, the lips a little parted as when listening is intense, the heads thrown back. For in the room above that ceiling, asleep at this moment, lay the subject of their long discussion; only a few inches of lath and plaster sep-arated them from the strange being who, dropping out of space, as it were, had come to make his home with them. A being, lonely utterly in the world, unique in kind perhaps, his nature as yet undecipherable, lay trustingly uncon-scious in that upper chamber. The two men felt the gravity, the responsibility of their charge. The same thought had vividly touched them both at the same instant.

A few minutes later they were still standing, facing one another. They were of a height, but compared to Fillery's big frame and rugged head, his friend's appearance was almost slight. Devonham, for all his qualifications, looked painfully like a shopwalker. They exchanged this steady gaze for a few seconds without speaking. Then the older man said quietly:

"Paul, I understand, and I respect your reticence. I think I can agree with it."

He placed a hand upon the other's shoulder, smiling gently, even tenderly.

"You have told me much, but you have not told me *all!* The chief part—you have intentionally omitted."

"For the present, at any rate," was the reply, given without flinching.

"Your reasons are sound, your judgment perhaps right. I ask no questions. What happened, what you saw, at the châlet; the 'peculiar powers' you mentioned; all, in fact, that you think it wise to keep to yourself for the moment, I leave there willingly."

He spoke gravely, sincere emotion in the eyes and tone. It was in a lower voice he added:

"The responsibility, of course, is yours."

Devonham returned the steady gaze, pondering his reply a moment.

"I can—and do accept it," he answered. "You have read my thoughts correctly as usual, Edward. I think you know quite enough already—what with my Notes and Mason's letter—even too much. Besides, why complicate it with an account of what were doubtless mere mental pictures—hallucinations—on my part? This is a matter," he went on slowly, "a case, we dare not trifle with; there may be strange and terrible afflictions in it later; we must remain unbiased." The anxiety deepened on his face.

"True, true," murmured the other. "God bless the boy! May his own gods bless him!"

"In other words, it will need your clearest, soundest judgment, your finest skill, your very best, as you said yourself just now." He used a firmer, yet also a softer tone suddenly: "Edward, you know your own mind, its contents, its suppressions, its origin; your refusal of the love of women, your deep powerful dreams that you have suppressed and put away. Promise me"—the voice and manner were very earnest—"that you will not communicate these to him in any way, and that you will keep your judgment absolutely unbiased and untainted." He looked at his old friend and paused. "Only your purest judgment of what is to come can help. You promise."

Fillery sighed a scarcely noticeable sigh. "I promise you, Paul. You are wise— and you are right," he said. "On the other hand, let me say one thing to you in my turn. This theory of heredity and of mental telepathic transference—the idea that all his mind's content is derived from his parents and from Mason—we cannot, remember, force this transference and interchange *too* far. I ask only this: be fair and open yourself with all that follows."

Devonham raised his voice: "Nor can we, apparently, set limits to it, Edward. But—to be fair and open-minded—I give my promise too."

Thus, in the little downstairs room of a Private Home for Incurable Mental Cases, *not* a Lunatic Asylum, though sometimes perhaps next door to it, these two men, deeply intrigued by a new "Case" that passed their understanding, as it exceeded their knowledge, practice and experience, swore to each other to observe carefully, to report faithfully, and to experiment, if experiment proved necessary, with honest and affectionate uprightness.

Their views were, obviously, not the same. Devonham, temperamentally opposed to radical innovations, believed it was a case of divided personality—hundreds of such cases had passed through their hands. Forced to accept extended telepathy—that all minds can on occasion share one another's content, and that even a racial and a world-memory can be tapped—he feared that his Chief might influence LeVallon, and twist, thus, the phenomena to a special end. He knew Edward Fillery's story. He feared, for the sake of truth, the mental transference. He had, perhaps, other fears as well.

Fillery, on the other hand, believing as much, and knowing more than his colleague, saw in "N. H." a unique possibility. He was thrilled and startled with a half-impossible hope. He felt as if someone ran beside his life, bearing impossible glad tidings, an unexpected, half-incredible figure, the tidings marvellously bright. He hoped, he already wished to think, that "N. H." might shadow forth a promise of some magical advance for the ultimate benefit of the Race....

The thinkers were crying on the housetops that progress was a myth, that each wave of civilization at its height reached the same average level without ever passing further. The menace to the present civilization, already crumbling, was in full swing everywhere; knowledge, culture, learning threatened in due course with the chaos of destruction that has so far been the invariable rule. The one hope of saving the world, cried religion, lay in substituting spiritual for material values—a Utopian dream at best. The one chance, said science, on the other hand, was that civilization to-day is continuous and not isolated.

The best hope, believed Fillery, the only hope, lay in raising the individual by the drawing up into full consciousness of the limitless powers now hidden and inactive in his deeper self—the so-called subliminal faculties. With these greater powers must come also greater moral development.

Already, with his uncanny insight, derived from knowledge of himself, he had piercingly divined in "N. H." a being, whatever he might be, whose nature acted automatically and directly upon the subconscious self in everybody.

That bright messenger, running past his life, had looked, as with fire and tempest, straight into his eyes.

It was long after one o'clock when the two men said good-night, and went to their rooms. Devonham was soon in bed, though not soon asleep. Exhausted physically though he was, his mind burned actively. His recent memories were vivid. All he had purposely held back from Fillery returned with power....

The uncertainty whether he had experienced hallucination, or had actually, as by telepathic transfer from LeVallon, touched another state of consciousness, kept sleep far away....

His brain was far too charged for easy slumber. He feared for his dear, faithful friend, his colleague, the skilful, experienced, yet sorely tempted mind—tempted by Nature and by natural weaknesses of birth and origin—who now shared with him the care and healing of a Case that troubled his being too deeply for slumber to come quickly.

Yet he had done well to keep these memories from Edward Fillery. If Fillery once knew what he knew, his judgment and his scientific diagnosis must be drawn hopelessly away from what he considered the best treatment: the suppression of "N. H." and the making permanent of "LeVallon."...

He fell asleep eventually, towards dawn, dreaming impossible, radiant dreams of a world he might have hoped for, yet could not, within the limits of his little cautious, accurate mind, believe in. Dreams that inspire, yet sadden, haunted his release from normal consciousness. Someone had walked upon his life, leaving a growth of everlasting flowers in their magical tread, though his mind—his stolid, cautious mind—had no courage for the plucking...

And while he slept, as the hours slipped from west to east, his chief and colleague, lying also sleepless, rose suddenly before the late autumn dawn, and walked quietly along the corridor towards the Private Suite where the new patient rested. His mind was quiet, yet his inner mind alert. His thoughts, his hopes, his dreams, these lay, perhaps, beyond human computation. He was calmer far than his assistant, though more strangely tempted.

It was just growing light, the corridor was cold. A cool, damp air came through the open windows and the linoleum felt like ice against the feet. The house lay dead and silent. Pausing a moment by a window, he listened to the chattering of early sparrows. He felt chill and hungry, unrested too, though far from sleepy. He was aware of London—bleak, heavy, stolid London town. The troubles of modern life, of Labour, Politics, Taxes, cost of living, all the common, daily things came in with the cheerless morning air.

He reached the door he sought, and very softly opened it.

The radiance met him in the face, so that he almost gasped. The scent of flowers, the sting of sharp, keen forest winds, the exhilaration of some distant mountaintop. There was, actually, a tang of dawn, known only to those who have tasted the heights at sunrise with the heart. And into his heart, singing with happy confidence, rose a sense of supreme joy and confidence that mastered all little earthly woes and pains, and walked among the stars.

The occupant of the bed lay very still. His shining hair was spread upon the pillow. The splendid limbs were motionless. The chest and arms were bare, the single covering sheet tossed off. The strange, wild face wore happiness and peace upon its skin, the features very calm, the mouth relaxed. It almost seemed a god lay sleeping there upon a little human bed.

How long he stood and stared he did not know, but suddenly, the light increased. The curtains stirred about the bed.

With a marvellous touch—the separate details merged and quickened into life. The room was changed. The occupant of the bed moved very swiftly, as through the open window came the first touch of exhilarating light. Gold stole across the lintel, breaking over the roofs of slates beyond. The leafless elm trees shimmered faintly. The telegraph wires shone. There was a running sparkle. It was dawn.

The figure leaped, danced—no other word describes it—to the open window where the light and air gushed in, spread wide its arms, lowered its radiant head, began to sing in low, melodious rhythmic chant—and Fillery, as silently as he had come, withdrew and closed the door unseen. His heart moved strangely, but—his promise held him....

CHAPTER VII

The following days it seemed to both Fillery and Devonham that their discussion of the first night had been pitched in too intense, too serious a key. Their patient was so commonplace again, so ordinary. He made himself quite at home, seemed contented and uncurious, taking it for granted he had come to stay for ever, apparently.

Apart from his strange beauty, his size, virility and a general impression he conveyed of immense energies he was too easy-going to make use of, he might have passed for a peasant, a countryman to whom city life was new; but an educated, or at least half-educated, countryman. He was so big, yet never gauche. He was neither stupid nor ill-informed; the garden interested him, he knew much about the trees and flowers, birds and insects too. He discussed the weather, prevailing wind, moisture, prospects of change and so forth with a judgment based on what seemed a natural, instinctive knowledge. The gardener looked on him with obvious respect.

"Such nice manners and such a steady eye," Mrs. Soames, the matron, mentioned, too, approvingly to Devonham. "But a lot in him he doesn't understand himself, unless I'm wrong. Not much the matter with his nerves, anyhow. Once he's married—unless I'm much mistaken—eh, sir?"

He was quiet, talking little, and spent the morning over the books Fillery had placed purposely in his sitting-room, books on simple physics, natural history and astronomy. It was the latter that absorbed him most; he pored over them by the hour.

Fillery explained the situation so far as he thought wise. The young man was honesty and simple innocence, but only vaguely interested in the life of the great city he now experienced for the first time. He had in his luggage a copy of the Will by which Mason had left him everything, and he was pleased to know himself well provided for. Of Mason, however, he had only a dim, uncertain, almost an impersonal memory, as of someone encountered in a dream.

"I suppose something's happened to me," he said to Fillery, his language normal and quite ordinary again. He spoke with a slight foreign accent. "There was somebody, of course, who looked after me and lived with me, but I can't remember who or where it was. I was very happy," he added, "and yet... I miss something."

Dr. Fillery, remembering his promise, did not press him.

"It will all come back by degrees," he remarked in a sympathetic tone. "In the meantime, you must make yourself at home here with us, for as long as you like.

You are quite free in every way. I want you to be happy here."

"I live with you always," was the reply. "There are things I want to tell you, ask you too." He paused, looking thoughtful. "There was someone I told all to once."

"Come to me with everything. I'll help you always, so far as I can." He placed a hand upon his knee.

"There are feelings, big feelings I cannot reach quite, but that make me feel different"—he smiled beautifully—"from—others." Quick as lightning he had changed the sentence at the last word, substituting "others" for "you." Had he been aware of a slight uneasy emotion in his listener's heart? It had hardly betrayed itself by any visible sign, yet he had instantly divined its presence. Such evidences of a subtle, intimate understanding were not lacking. Yet Fillery admirably restrained himself.

"There are bright places I have lost," he went on frankly, no sign of shy reserve in him. "I feel confused, lost somewhere, as if I didn't belong here. I feel"—he used an odd word—"doubled." His face shaded a little.

"Big overpowering London is bound to affect you," put in Fillery, who had noticed the rapid discernment, "after living among woods and mountains, as you have lived, for years. All will come right in a little time; we must settle down a bit first—"

"Woods and mountains," repeated the other, in a half-dreamy voice, his eyes betraying an effort to follow thought elsewhere. "Of course, yes—woods and mountains and hot living sunlight—and the winds—"

His companion shifted the conversation a little. He suggested a line of reading and study.... They talked also of such ordinary but necessary things as providing a wardrobe, of food, exercise, companionship of his own age, and so forth—all the commonplace details of ordinary daily life, in fact. The exchange betrayed nothing of interest, nothing unusual. They mentioned theatres, music, painting, and, beyond the natural curiosity of youth that was ignorant of these, no detail was revealed that need have attracted the attention of anybody, neither of doctor, psychologist, nor student of human nature. With the single exception that the past years had been obliterated from memory, though much that had been acquired in them remained, there was no noticeable peculiarity of any sort. Both language and point of view were normal.

This was obviously LeVallon. The "N. H." personality scarcely cast a shadow even. Yet "N. H.," the doctor was quick to see, lay ready and waiting just below the surface. There was no doubt in his mind which was the central self and which its transient projection, the secondary personality. Again, as he sat and talked, he had the odd impression that someone with bright tidings ran swiftly past his life, perhaps towards it.

The swift messenger was certainly not LeVallon. LeVallon, indeed, was but a shadow cast before this glad, bright visitant. Thus he felt, at any rate. LeVallon was an empty simulacrum left behind while "N. H." rested, or was active upon other things, things natural to him, elsewhere. LeVallon was an arm, a limb, a feeler that "N. H." thrust out. At Charing Cross, for instance, for a brief moment only, "N. H." had peered across his shoulder, then withdrawn again. In the car had sat by his side LeVallon. The being he now chatted with was also LeVallon only.

But in his own heart, deep down, hidden yet eager to break loose, lay his own deeper self that burned within him. This, the important part of him, yearned towards "N. H." And up rose the strange symbol that always appeared when his deepest, perhaps his subliminal self was stirred. That lost radiant valley in the haunted Caucasus shone close and brimming over... with light, with flowers, with splendid winds and fire, symbols of a vaster, grander, happier life, though perhaps a life not yet within the range of normal human consciousness.... The fiery symbol flashed and passed.

Curious thoughts and pictures rose flaming in his mind, persistent ideas that bore no possible relation to his intellectual, reasoning life. Passing across the background of his brain, as with waves of heat and colour, they were correlated somewhere with harmonious sound. Music, that is, came with them, as though inspiration brought its own sound with it that made singing natural. They haunted him, these vague, pleasurable phantasmagoria that were connected, he felt sure, with music, as with childhood's lost imaginings. For a long time he searched in vain for their source and origin. Then, suddenly, he remembered. He heard his father's gruff, humorous voice: "There's not a scrap of evidence, of course...." And, sharply, vividly, the buried memory gave up its dead. His childish question went crashing through the air: "Are we the only beings in the world?"

"Nothing is ever lost," he reminded himself with a smile that Devonham assuredly never saw. "Every seed must bear its fruit in time."

And emotion surged through him from the remorseless records of his underself. The childhood's love, with its correlative of deep, absolute belief, returned upon him, linked on somehow to that old familiar symbol he knew to mean his awakening subconscious being—a flowering Caucasian vale of sun and wind. A belief, he realized, especially a belief of childhood, remains for ever inexpungable, eternal, prolific seed of future harvests.

The unstable in him betrayed its ineradicable, dangerous streak. There rose upon him in a cloud strange notions that inflamed imagination sweetly. Later reading, indeed, had laid flesh upon the skeleton of the boyish notion, though derived in the first instance he certainly knew not whence. The literature and tradition of the East, he recalled, peopled the elements with conscious life, to which the world's fairy-tales—remnant of lost knowledge possibly—added nerves and heart and blood. In all human bodies, at any rate, dwelt not necessarily always human spirits, human souls....

He checked himself with a smile he would have liked to call a chuckle, but that yet held some inexplicable happiness at its heart. His rugged, eager face, its expression bitten deeply by experience, turned curiously young. There rushed through him the Eastern conception of another system of life, another evolution, deathless, divine, important, the Order of the *Devas*, a series of Nature Beings entirely apart from human categories. They included many degrees, from fairies to planetary spirits, the gods, so called; and their duties, work and purposes were concerned, he remembered, with carrying out the Laws of Nature, the busy tending of all forms and structures, from the elaborately marvellous infusoria in a drop of stagnant water, the growth of crystals, the upbuilding of flowers and trees, of insects, animals, humans, to the guidance and guardianship of those vaster forms of heavenly bodies, the stars, the planets and the mighty suns, whose gigantic "bodies," inhabited by immenser consciousness, people empty space.... A noble, useful, selfless work, God's messengers....

He checked himself again, as the rich, ancient notion flitted across his stirring memory.

"Delightful, picturesque conceptions of the planet's young, fair ignorance!" he reminded himself, smiling as before.

Whereupon rose, bursting through his momentary dream, with full-fledged power, the great hope of his own reasoned, scientific Dream—that man is greater than he knows, and that the progress of the Race was demonstrable.

For, to the subliminal powers of an awakened Race these Nature Beings with their special faculties, must lie open and accessible. The human and the non-human could unite! Nature must come back into the hearts of men and win them again to simple, natural life with love, with joy, with naked beauty. Death and disease must vanish, hope and purity return. The Race must develop, grow, become in the true sense *universal.* It could know God!

The vision flashed upon him with extraordinary conviction, so that he forgot for the moment how securely he belonged to the unstable. The smile of happiness spread, as it were, over his entire being. He glowed and pulsed with its delicious inward fire. Light filled his being for an instant—an instant of intoxicating belief and certainty and vision. The instant inspiration of a dream went lost and vanished. He had drawn upon childhood and legendary reading for the substance of a moment's happiness. He shook himself, so to speak. He remembered his patients and his duties, his colleague too....

Nothing, meanwhile, occurred to arouse interest or attention. Le Vallon was quite docile, ordinary; he needed no watching; he slept well, ate well, spent his leisure with his books and in the garden. He complained often of the lack of sunlight, and sometimes he might be seen taking some deep breaths of air into his lungs by the open window or on the balcony. The phases of the moon, too, interested him, and he asked once when the full moon would come, and then, when Devonham told him, he corrected the date the latter gave, proving him two hours wrong. But, on the whole, there seemed little to differentiate him from the usual voting man whose physique had developed in advance of his mental faculties; his knowledge in some respects certainly was backward, as in the case of arrested development. He seemed an intelligent countryman, but an unusually intelligent countryman, though all the time another under-intelligence shone brightly, betraying itself in remarks and judgments oddly phrased.

Dr. Fillery took him, during the following day or two, to concerts, theatres, cinemas. He enjoyed them all. Yet in the theatres he was inclined to let his attention wander. The degree of alertness varied oddly. His critical standard, moreover, was curiously exacting; he demanded the real creative interpretation of a part, and was quick to detect a lack of inspiration, of fine technique, of true conception in a player. Reasons he failed to give, and argument seemed impossible to him, but if voice or gesture or imaginative touch failed anywhere, he lost interest in the performer from that moment.

"He has poor breath," he remarked. "He only imitates. He is outside." Or, "She pretends. She does not feel and know. Feeling—the feeling that comes of fire— she has not felt."

"She does not understand her part, you mean?" suggested Fillery.

"She does not burn with it," was the reply.

At concerts he behaved individually too. They bored as well as puzzled him; the music hardly stirred him. He showed signs of distress at anything classical, though Wagner, Debussy, the Russians, moved him and produced excitement.

"He," was his remark, with emphasis, "has *heard*. He gives me freedom. I could fly and go away. He sets me free..." and then he would say no more, not even in reply to questions. He could not define the freedom he referred to, nor could he say where he could go away to. But his face lit up, he smiled his delightful smile, he looked happy. "Stars," he added once in a tone of interest, in reply to repeated questions, "stars, wind, fire, away from *this!*"—he tapped his head and breast—"I feel more alive and real."

"It's real and true, that music? That's what you feel?"

"It's beyond this," he replied, again tapping his body. "*They* have *heard*."

The cinema interested him more. Yet its limits seemed to perplex him more than its wonder thrilled him. He accepted it as a simple, natural, universal thing.

"They stay always on the sheet," he observed with evident surprise. "And I hear nothing. They do not even sing. Sound and movement go together!"

"The speaking will come," explained Fillery. "Those are pictures merely."

"I understand. Yet sound is natural, isn't it? They ought to be heard."

"Speech," agreed his companion, "is natural, but singing isn't."

"Are they not alive enough to sing?" was the reply, spoken to himself rather than to his neighbour, who was so attentive to his least response. "Do they only sing when"—Fillery heard it and felt something leap within him—"when they are paid or have an audience?" he finished the sentence quickly.

"No one sings naturally of their own accord—not in cities, at any rate," was the reply.

LeVallon laughed, as though he understood at once. "There is no sun and wind," he murmured. "Of course. They cannot."

It was the cinemas that provided most material for observation, Fillery found. There was in a cinema performance something that excited his companion, but excited him more than the doctor felt he was justified in encouraging. Obviously the other side of him, the "N. H." aspect, came up to breathe under the stimulus of the rapid, world-embracing, space-and-time destroying pictures on the screen. Concerts did not stimulate him, it seemed, but rather puzzled him. He remained wholly the commonplace LeVallon—with one exception he drew involved patterns on the edge of his programmes, patterns of a very complicated yet accurate kind, as though he almost saw the sounds that poured into his ears. And these ornamented programmes Dr. Fillery preserved. Sound—music—seemed to belong to his interpretation of movement. About the cinema, however, there seemed something almost familiar, something he already knew and understood, the sound belonging to movement only lacking.

Apart from these small incidents, LeVallon showed nothing unusual, nothing that a yokel untaught yet of natural intelligence might not have shown. His language, perhaps, was singular, but, having been educated by one mind only, and in a region of lonely forests and mountains, remote from civilized life, there was nothing inexplicable in the odd words he chose, nor in the peculiar—if subtle and penetrating—phrases that he used. Invariably he recognized the spontaneous, creative power as distinguished from the derivative that merely imitated.

He found ways of expressing himself almost immediately, both in speech and writing, however, and with a perfection far beyond the reach of a half-educated country lad; and this swift aptitude was puzzling until its explanation suddenly was laid bare. He absorbed, his companion realized at last, as by telepathy, the content of his own, of Fillery's mind, acquiring the latter's mood, language, ideas, as though the two formed one being.

The discovery startled the doctor. Yet what startled him still more was the further discovery, made a little later, that he himself could, on occasions, become so identified with his patient that the slightest shade of thought or feeling rose spontaneously in his own mind too.

He remained, otherwise, almost entirely "LeVallon"; and, after a full report made to Devonham, and the detailed discussion thereon that followed, Dr. Fillery had no evidence to contradict the latter's opinion: "LeVallon is the real true self. The other personality—'N. H.' as we call it—is a mere digest and accumulation of material supplied by his parents and by Mason."

"Let us wait and see what happens when 'N. H.' appears and *does* something," Fillery was content to reply.

"If," answered Devonham, with sceptical emphasis, " it ever does appear."

"You think it won't?" asked Fillery.

"With proper treatment," said Devonham decisively, "I see no reason why 'N. H.' should not become happily merged in the parent self—in LeVallon, and a permanent cure result."

He put his glasses straight and stared at his chief, as much as to say "You promised."

"Perhaps," said Fillery. "But, in my judgment, 'LeVallon' is too slight to count at all. I believe the whole, real, parent Self is 'N. H.,' and the only life LeVallon has at all is that which peeps up through him—from 'N. H.'"

Fillery returned his serious look.

"If 'N. H.' is the real self, and I am right," he added slowly, "you, Paul, will have to revise your whole position."

"I shall," returned Devonham. "But—you will allow this—it is a lot to expect. I see no reason to believe in anything more than a subconscious mind of unusual content, and possibly of unusual powers and extent," he added with reluctance. "It is," said Fillery significantly, "a lot to expect—as you said just now. I grant you that. Yet I feel it possible that—" he hesitated.

Devonham looked uncomfortable. He fidgeted. He did not like the pause. A sense of exasperation rose in him, as though he knew something of what was coming.

"Paul," went on his chief abruptly in a tone that dropped instinctively to a lower key—almost a touch of awe lay behind it—"you admit no deity, I know, but you admit purpose, design, intelligence."

"Well," replied the other patiently, long experience having taught him iron restraint, "it's a blundering, imperfect system, inadequately organized—if you care to call that intelligence. It's of an extremely intricate complexity. I admit that. Deity I consider an unnecessary assumption."

"The love and hate of atoms alone bowls you over," was the unexpected comment. "The word 'Laws' explains nothing. A machine obeys the laws, but intelligence conceived that machine—and a man repairs and keeps it going. Who—what—keeps the daisy going, the crystal, the creative thought in the imagination? An egg becomes a leaf-eating caterpillar, which in turn becomes a honey-eating butterfly with wings. A yolk turns into feathers. Is that accomplished without intelligence?"

"Ask our new patient," interrupted Devonham, wiping his glasses with unnecessary thoroughness.

"Which?"

Devonham startled, looked up without his glasses. It seemed the question made him uneasy. Putting the glasses on suddenly, he stared at his chief. "I see what you mean, Edward," he said earnestly, his interest deeply captured. "Be careful. We know nothing, remember, nothing of life. Don't jump ahead like this or take your dreams for reality. We have our duty—in a case like this."

Fillery smiled, as though to convey that he remembered his promise.

"Humanity," he replied, "is a very small section of the universe. Compared to the minuter forms of life, which *may* be quite as important, if not more so, the human section is even negligible; while, compared to the possibility of greater forms—" He broke off abruptly. "As you say, Paul, we know nothing of life after all, do we? Nothing, less than nothing! We observe and classify a few results, that's all. We must beware of narrow prejudice, at any rate—you and I."

His eyes lost their light, his speech dried up, his ideas, dreams, speculations returned to him unrewarded, unexpressed. With natures in whom the subconscious never stirred, natures through whom its magical fires cast no faintest upward gleam, intercourse was ever sterile, unproductive. Such natures had no background. Even a fact, with them, was detached from its true big life, its full significance, its divine potentialities!....

"We must beware of prejudice," he repeated quietly. "We seek truth only."

"We must beware," replied Devonham, as he shrugged his shoulders, "of suggestion—of auto-suggestion above all. We must remember how repressed desires dramatize themselves—especially," he added significantly, "when aided by imagination. We seek only facts." On his face appeared swiftly, before it vanished again, an expression of keen anxiety, almost of affliction, yet tempered, as it were, by surprise and wonder, by pity possibly, and certainly by affection.

CHAPTER VIII

To Devonham, meanwhile, LeVallon's behaviour was polite and kind and distant; he did not show distrust of any sort, but he betrayed a certain diffidence, reserve and caution. Trust he felt; sympathy he did not feel. To the amusement of Fillery, he suggested almost a kind of mild contempt when dealing with him, and this amusement was increased by the fact that it obviously annoyed Devonham, while it gratified his chief. For towards Fillery, LeVallon behaved with an intimate and understanding sympathy that proved his instantaneous affection based upon mutual comprehension. It seemed that LeVallon and Fillery had known one another always.

It was, doubtless, due to this innate sympathy between them that Edward Fillery's rare gift of absorbing the content of another's mind, even to the point of taking on that other's conditions, physical and emotional at the same time, was so successful. By means of a highly developed power of auto-suggestion, he had learned so to identify his own mind, thought, feeling with those of a patient, that there resulted a kind of merging by which he literally became that patient. He felt with him. As a subject sees the pictures in the hypnotiser's mind, perceives his thoughts, divines his slightest will, so Fillery, reversing the process, could realize for the moment exactly what his patient was thinking, feeling, desiring. It was of great use to him in his strange practice.

This gift, naturally, varied in degree, and was not invariably successful. In some cases he only felt, the emotion alone being thus transferred; in others he only saw what the patient saw, or thought he saw, the accompanying emotion being omitted; in others again, as in cases of vision at a distance, either of time or space, he had been able to follow the "travelling sight " of his patient, whose consciousness in trance was operating far away, and thus to check for subsequent verification exactly what that patient saw. He had shared strange experiences with others—with a man, for instance, in whom sight was transferred to the tip of his index finger, so that he could read a book by passing that finger along the printed line; with a woman, again, in whom "exteriorized consciousness" manifested itself, so that, if the air several inches from her face was pinched or struck, the impact was received and an actual bruise produced upon her skin.

This extension of consciousness, its seeds already in his nature, he had trained and developed to a point where he could almost rely upon auto-suggestion bringing about quickly the desired conditions. Its success, however, as mentioned, was variable. With "N. H.," especially now, this variableness was marked; sometimes it was so easily accomplished as to seem natural and without a conscious effort, while at other times it failed completely. Since it was in no sense an attempt to transfer anything from his own mind to that of the patient, Fillery felt that his promise to his colleague was not involved.

The following scene describes the first time in which the process took place with his new patient. Fillery himself wrote down the words, supplied the detailed description, filled in the emotion and psychology, but exactly as these occurred and as he felt them, both when these took place, respectively, in his own consciousness and in that of his patient. Part of the time he was present, part of it he was not visibly so, being screened from observation, yet so placed that he could note everything that happened. It is clear, however, that his mind was so intimately *en rapport* with the thoughts and feelings of "N. H.," that he experienced in his own being all that 'N. H." experienced. The description was written immediately after the occurrence, though some of it, the spoken language in particular, was jotted down in his hiding place at the actual moment.

The interlacing of the two minds, their interpenetration, as it were, one occasionally dominating the other, is curious to trace and far from difficult to disentangle. Similarly, the interweaving of LeVallon and "N.H." is noticeable. The description given by Devonham of the portion of the occurrence he witnessed personally, or heard about from Nurse Robbins and the attendants—this description reduces the whole thing to the commonplace level of "a slight seizure accompanied by signs of violence and moments of delirium due to excitement and fatigue, and soon cured by sleep."

The occurrence took place precisely at the period when the moon was at the full.

CHAPTER IX

The body I'm in and using is 22, as they call it, and from a man named Mason, a geologist, I receive sums of money, regularly paid, with which I live. They call it "live." A roof and walls protect me, who do not need protection; my body, which it irks, is covered with wool and cloth and stuff, fitting me as bark fits a tree and yet not part of me; my feet, which love the touch of earth and yearn for it, are cased in dead dried skin called leather; even my head and hair, which crave the sun and wind, are covered with another piece of dead dried skin, shaped like a shell, but an ugly shell, in which, were it shaped otherwise, the wind and rustling leaves might sing with flowers.

Before 22 I remember nothing—nothing definite, that is. I opened my eyes in a soft, but not refreshing case standing on four iron legs, and well off the ground, and covered with coarse white coverings piled thickly on my body. It was a bed. Slabs of transparent stuff kept out the living sunshine for which I hungered; thick solid walls shut off the wind; no stars or moon showed overhead, because an enormous lid hid every bit of sky. No dew, therefore, lay upon the sheets. I smelt no earth, no leaves, no flowers. No single natural sound entered except the chattering of dirty sparrows which had lost its freshness. I was in a hospital.

One comely figure alone gave me a little joy. It was soft and slim and grace- ful, with a smell of fern and morning in its hair, though that hair was lustreless and balled up in ugly lumps, with strips of thin metal in it. They called it nurse and sister. It was the first moving thing I saw when my eyes opened on my lim- ited and enclosed surroundings. My heart beat quicker, a flash of thin joy came up in me. I had seen something similar before somewhere; it reminded me, I mean, of something I had known elsewhere; though but a shabby, lifeless, clumsy copy of this other glorious thing. Though not real, it stirred this faint memory of reality, so that I caught at the skirts of moonlight, stars and flowers reflected in a forest pool where my companion played for long periods of hap- piness between our work. The perfume and the eyes did that. I watched it for a bit, as it moved away, came close and looked at me. When the eyes met mine, a wave of life, but of little life, surged faintly through me.

They were dim and pitiful, these eyes; mournful, unlit, unseeing. The stars had set in them; dull shadows crowded. They were so small. They were hun- gry too. They were unsatisfied. For some minutes it puzzled me then I under- stood. That was the word—unsatisfied. Ah, but I could alter that! I could com- fort, help, at any rate. My strength, though horribly clipped and blocked, could manage a little thing like that! My smaller rhythms I could put into it.

The eyes, the smile, the whole soft comely bundle, so pitifully hungry and un- satisfied, I rose and seized, pressing it close inside my own great arms, and bury- ing it all against my breast. I crushed it, but very gently, as I might crush a sapling. My lips were amid the ferny hair. I breathed upon it willingly, glad to help.

It was a poor unfinished thing, I felt at once, soft and yielding where it should have been resilient and elastic as fresh turf; the perfume had no body, it faded instantly; there was so little life in it.

But, as I held it in my big embrace, smothering its hunger as best I could within my wave of being, this bundle, this poor pitiful bundle, screamed and struggled to get free. It bit and scratched and uttered sounds like those squeaks the less swift creatures make when the swifter overtake them.

I was too surprised to keep it to me; I relaxed my hold. The instant I did so the figure, thus released, stood upright like a young birch the wind sets free. The figure looked alive. The hair fell loose, untidily, the puny face wore colour, the eyes had fire in them. I saw that fire. It was a message. Memory stirred faintly in me.

"Ah!" I cried. "I've helped you anyhow a little!"

The scene that followed filled me with such trouble and bewilderment that I cannot recall exactly what occurred. The figure seemed to spit at me, yet not with grace and invitation. There was no sign of gratitude. I was entirely mis- understood, it seemed. Bells rang, as the figure rushed to the door and flung it open. It called aloud; similar, though quite lifeless figures came in answer and filled the room. A doctor—Devonham, they called him—followed them. I was most carefully examined in a dozen curious ways that tickled my skin a little so that I smiled. But I lay quite still and silent, watching the whole performance with a confusion in my being that baffled my comprehending what was going on. Most of the figures were frightened.

Then the doctor gave place to Fillery, whose name has rhythm.

To him I spoke at once:

"I wished to comfort and revive her," I told him. " She is so starved. I was most gentle. She brings a message only."

He made no reply, but gazed at me with the corners of his mouth both twitch-ing, and in his eyes—ah, his eyes had more of the sun in them—a flash of some-thing that had known fire, at least, if it had not kept it.

"My God! I worship thee," I murmured at the glimpse of the Power I must own as Master and creator of my being. Even when thou art playful, I adore thee and obey."

Then four other figures, shaped like the doctor but wholly mechanical, a mere blind weight operating through them, held my arms and legs. Not the least de-sire to move was in me luckily. I say "luckily," because, had I wished it, I could have flung them through the roof, blown down the little walls, caught up a dozen figures in my arms, and rushed forth with them towards the Powers of Fire and Wind to which I belonged.

Could I? I felt that I could. The sight of the true fire, small though it was, in the comely figure's and the doctor's eyes, had set me in touch again with my home and origin. This touch I had somehow lost; I had been "ill," with what they called nervous disorder and injured reason. The lost touch was now re-stored. But, luckily, as I said, there was no desire in me to set free these other figures, to help them in any way, after the reception my first kindly effort had experienced. I lay quite still, held by these four grotesque and puny mechanisms. The comely one, with the others similar to her, had withdrawn. I felt very kindly towards them all, but especially towards the doctor, Fillery, who had shown that he knew my deity and origin. None of them were worth much trou-ble, anyhow. I felt that too. A mild, sweet-toned contempt was in me.

"Dangerous," was a word I caught them whispering as they went. I laughed a little. The four faces over me made odd grimaces, tightening their lips, and grip-ping my legs and arms with greater effort. The doctor—Fillery—noticed it.

"Easy, remember," he addressed the four. "There's really no need to hold. It won't recur." I nodded. We understood one another. And, with a smile at me, he left the room, saying he would come back after a short interval. A link with my source, a brother as it were, went with him, I was lonely....

I began to hum songs to myself, little fragments of a great natural music I had once known but lost, and I noticed that the four figures, as I sang, relaxed their grip of my limbs considerably. To tell the truth, I forgot that they were hold-ing me; their grip, anyhow, was but a thread I could snap without the smallest effort. The songs were happiness in me. Upon free leaping rhythms I careered with an exhilarating rush of liberty; all about space I soared and sank; I was picked up, flung far, riding the crest of immense waves of orderly vibration that delighted me. I let myself go a bit, let my voice out, I mean. No effort accompanied my singing. It was automatic, like breathing almost. It was natural to me. These rhythmical sounds and the patterns that they wove in space were the outlines of forms it was my work to build. This expressed my nature. Only my power was blocked and stifled in this confining body. The fire and air which were my tools I could not control. I have forgotten—forgotten—!

"Got a voice, ain't he?" observed one of the figures admiringly.

"Lunies can do 'most anything they have a mind to."

"Grand Opera isn't in it."

"Yes," mentioned the fourth, "but he'll lift the roof off presently. We'd better stop him before there's any trouble."

I stopped of myself, however: their remarks interested me. Also while I had been singing, although I called it humming only, they had gradually let go of me, and were now sitting down on my bed and staring with quite pleasant faces. All their dim eight eyes were fixed on me. Their forms were not built well.

"Where did you get that from, Guv'nor?" asked the one who had spoken first. "Can you give me the name of it?"

The sound of his own voice was like the scratching of a pin after the enormous rhythm that now ceased.

"Ain't printed, is it?" he went on, as I stared, not understanding what he meant. "I've got a sister at the Halls," he explained. "She'd make a hit with that kind of thing. Gave me quite a twist inside to hear it," he added, turning to the others.

The others agreed solemnly with dull stupid faces. I lay and listened to their talk. I longed to help them. I had forgotten how.

"A bit churchy, I thought it," said one. "But, I confess, it stirred me up."

"Churchy or not, it's the stuff," insisted the first.

"Oh, it's the stuff to give 'em, right enough." And they looked at me admiringly again. "Where did you get it, if I may ask?" repeated Number One in a more respectful tone. His face looked quite polite. The lips stretched, showing yellow teeth. It was his smile. But his eyes were a little more real. Oh, where was my fire? I could have built the outline better so that he was real and might express far more. I have forgotten—!

"I hear it," I told him, "because I'm in it. It's all about me. It never stops. It's what we build with—"

Number One seemed greatly interested.

"Hear it, do you? Why, that's odd now. You see"—he looked at his companions apologetically, as though he knew they would not believe him—"my father was like that. He heard his music, he always used to say, but we laughed at him. He was a composer by trade. Oh, his stuff was printed too. Of course," he added, "there's musical talent in the family," as though that explained everything. He turned to me again. "Give us a little more, Mister—if you don't object, that is," he added. And his face was soft as he said it. "Only gentle like—if you don't mind."

"Yes, keep it down a bit," another put in, looking anxiously in the direction of the closed door. He patted the air with his open palm, slowly, carefully, as though he patted an animal that might rise and fly at him.

I hummed again for them, but this time with my lips closed. The waves of rhythm caught me up and away. I soared and flew and dropped and rose again upon their huge coloured crests. Curtains and sheets of quiet flame in palest gold flared shimmering through the sound, while winds that were full of hurricanes and cyclones swept down to lift the fire and dance with it in spirals. The perfume of great flowers rose. There were flowers everywhere, and stars shone through it all like showers of gold. Ah! I began to remember something. It was flowers and stars as well as human forms we worked to build....

But I kept the fire from leaping into actual flame; the mighty winds I held back. Even thus pent and checked, their powerful volume made the atmosphere shake and pulse about us. Only I could not control them now.... With an effort I came back, came down, as it were, and saw the funny little faces staring at me with opened eyes and mouths, and yellow teeth, pale gums, their skins gone whitish, their figures rigid with their tense emotion. They were so poorly made, the patterns so imperfect. The new respect in their manner was marked plainly. Suddenly all four turned together towards the door. I stopped. The doctor had returned. But it was Fillery again. I liked the feel of him.

"He wanted to sing, sir, so we let him. It seemed to relieve him a bit," they explained quickly and with an air of helpless apology.

"Good, good," said the doctor. "Quite good. Any normal expression that brings relief is good." He dismissed them. They went out, casting back at me expressions of puzzled thanks and interest. The door closed behind them. The doctor seated himself beside me and took my hand. I liked his touch. His hand was alive, at any rate, although within my own it felt rather like a dying branch or bunch of leaves I grasped. The life, if thin, was real.

"Where's the rest of it?" I asked him, meaning the music. "I used to have it all. It's left me, gone away. What's cut it off?"

"You're not cut off really," he said gently. "You can always get into it again when you really need it." He gazed at me steadily for a minute, then said in his quiet voice—a full, nice tone with wind through a forest running in it: "Mason.... Dr. Mason...."

He said no more, but watched me. The name stirred something in me I could not get at quite. I could not reach down to it. I was troubled by a memory I could not seize.

"Mason," I repeated, returning his strong gaze. "What—who—was Mason? And where?" I connected the name with a sense of liberty, also with great winds and pools of fire, with great figures of golden skin and radiant faces, with music, too, the music that had left me.

"You've forgotten for the moment," came the deep running voice I liked. "He looked after you for twenty years. He gave his life for you. He loved you. He loved your mother. Your father was his friend."

"Has he gone—gone back?"

"He's dead."

"I can get after him though," I said, for the name touched me with a sense of lost companionship I wanted, though the reference to my father and mother left me cold. "I can easily catch him up. When I move with my wind and fire, the fastest things stand still." My own speed, once I was free again, I knew outpaced easily the swiftest bird, outpaced light itself.

"Yes," agreed the doctor; "only he doesn't want that now. You can always catch him up when the time comes. Besides, he's waiting for you anyhow."

I knew that was true, I sank back comforted upon the stuffy pillows and lay silent. This tinkling chatter wearied me. It was like trickling wind. I wanted the flood of hurricanes, the pulse of storms. My building, shaping powers, my great companions—oh! where were they?

"He taught you himself, taught you all you know," I heard the tinkling go on again, "but he kept you away from life, thinking it was best. He was afraid for you, afraid for others too. He kept you in the woods and mountains where, as he believed, you could alone express yourself and so be happy. A hundred times, in babyhood and early childhood, you nearly died. He nursed you back to life. His own life he renounced. Now he is dead. He has left you all his money."

He paused. I said no word. Faint memories passed through my mind, but nothing I could hold and seize. The money I did not understand at all, except that it was necessary.

"He thought at first that you could not possibly live to manhood. To his surprise you survived everything—illness, accident, disaster of every sort and kind. Then, as you grew up, he realized his mistake. Instead of keeping you away from life, he ought to have introduced you to it and explained it—as I and Devonham are now trying to do. You could not live for ever alone in woods and mountains; when he was gone there would be no one to look after you and guide you."

The trickling of wind went on and on. I hardly listened to it. He did it for his own pleasure, I suppose. It pleased and soothed him possibly. Yet I remembered every syllable. It was a small detail to keep fresh when my real memory covered the whole planet.

"Before he died, he recognized his mistake and faced the position boldly. It was some years before the end; he was hale and hearty still, yet the end, he knew, was in sight. While the power was still strong in him, therefore, he did the only thing left to him to do. He used his great powers. He used suggestion. He hypnotized you, telling you to forget—from the moment of his death, but not before—forget everything— It was only partially successful."

The door opened, the comely figure glanced in, then vanished.

"She wants more help from me," I interrupted the monotonous tinkling instantly, for pity stirred in me again as I saw her eager, hungry and unsatisfied little eyes. "Call her back. I feel quite willing. It is one of the lower forms we made. I can improve it."

Dr. Fillery, as he was called, looked at me steadily, his mouth twitching at the corners as before, a flash of fire flitting through his eyes. The fire made me like and trust him; the twitching, too, I liked, for it meant he knew how absurd he was. Yet he was bigger than the other figures.

"You can't do that," he said, "you mustn't," and then laughed outright. "It isn't done, you know—here."

"Why not, sir?" I asked, using the terms the figures used. "I feel like that."

"Of course, you do. But all you feel can't be expressed except at the proper times and places. The consent of the other party always is involved," he went on slowly, "when it's a question of expressing—anything you feel."

This puzzled me, because in this particular instance the other party had asked me with her eyes to comfort her. I told him this. He laughed still more. Caught by the sound—it was just like wind passing among tall grasses on a mountain ridge—I forgot what he was talking about for the moment. The sound carried me away towards my own rhythms.

"You've got such amazing insight," he went on tinkling to himself, for I heard, although I did not listen. "You read the heart too easily, too quickly. You must learn to hide your knowledge." The laughter which ran with the words then ended, and I came back to the last thing I had definitely listened to—"express, expressing," was the phrase he used.

"You told me that self-expression is the purpose for which I'm here—?"

"I believe it is," he agreed, more solemnly.

"Only sometimes, then?"

"Exactly. If that expression involves another in pain or trouble or discomfort—"

"Ah! I have to choose, you mean. I have to know first what the other feels about it."

I began to understand better. It was a game. And all games delighted me.

"You may put it roughly so, yes," he explained, "you're very quick. I'll give you a rule to guide you," he went on. I listened with an effort; this tinkling soon wearied me; I could not think long or much; my way, it seemed, was feeling. "Ask yourself always how what you do will affect another," Dr. Fillery concluded. "That's a safe rule for you."

"That is of children," I observed. We stared at each other a moment. "Both sides keep it?" I asked.

"Childish," be agreed, "it certainly is. Both sides, yes, keep it."

I sighed, and the sigh seemed to rise from my very feet, passing through my whole being. He looked at me most kindly then, asking why I sighed.

"I used to be free," I told him. "This is not liberty. And why are we not all free together?"

"It is liberty for two instead of only for one," he said, "and so, in the long run, liberty for all."

"So that's where they are," I remarked, but to myself and not to him. "Not further than that." For what I had once known, but now, it seemed, forgotten, was far beyond such a foolish little game. We had lived without such tiny tricks. We lived openly and unafraid. We worked in harmony. We lived. Yes—but who was "we"? That was the part I had forgotten.

"It's the growth and development of civilization," I heard the little drift of wind go whistling thinly, "and it won't take you long to become quite civilized at this rate, more civilized, indeed, than most—with your swift intelligence and lightning insight."

"Civilization," I repeated to myself. Then I looked at his eyes which hid carefully in their depths somewhere that tiny cherished flame I loved. "Your ways are really very simple," I said. "It's all easy enough to learn. It is so small."

"A man studying ants," he tinkled, "finds them small, but far from simple. You may find complications later. If so, come to me."

I promised him, and the fire gleamed faintly in his eyes a moment. "'He entrusted you to me. Your mother," he added softly, "was the woman he loved."

"Civilization," I repeated, for the word set going an odd new rhythm in me that I rather liked, and that tired me less than the other things he said. "What is it then? You are a Race, you told me."

"A Race of human beings, of men and women developing—"

"The comely ones?"

"Are the women. Together we make up the Race."

"And civilization?"

"Is realizing that we are a community, learning, growing, all its members living for the others as well as for themselves."

Dr. Fillery told me then about men and women and sex, how children are made, and what enormous and endless work was necessary merely to keep them all alive and clothed and sheltered before they could accomplish anything else of any sort at all. Half the labour of the majority was simply to keep alive at all. It was an ugly little system he described. Much I did not hear, because my thinking powers gave out. Some of it gave me an awful feeling he called pain. The confusion and imperfection seemed beyond repair, even beyond the worth of being part of it, of belonging to it at all. Moreover, the making of children, without which the whole thing must end gave me spasms of irritation he called laughter. Only the Comely Ones, and what he told me of them, made me want to sing.

"The men," I said, "but do they see that it is ugly and ludicrous and—"

"Comic," he helped me.

"Do they know," I asked, taking his unknown words, "that it's comic?"

"The glamour," he said, "conceals it from them. To the best among them it is sacred even."

"And the Comely Ones?"

"It is their chief mission," he replied. "Always remember that. It's Sacred." He fixed his kind eyes gravely on my face.

"Ah, worship, you mean," I said. "I understand." Again we stared for some minutes. "Yet all are not comely, are they?" I asked presently.

The fire again shone faintly in his eyes as he watched me a moment without answering. It caught me away. I am not sure I heard his words, but I think they ran like this:

"That's just the point where civilization—so far—has always stopped."

I remember he ceased tinkling then; our talk ceased too. I was exhausted. He told me to remember what he had said, and to lie down and rest. He rang the bell, and a man, one of the four who had held me, came in.

"Ask Nurse Robbins to come here a moment, please," he said. And a moment later the Comely One entered softly and stood beside my bed. She did not look at me. Dr. Fillery began again his little tinkling. "...wishes to apologize to you most sincerely, nurse, for his mistake. He meant no harm, believe me. There is no danger in him, nor will he ever repeat it. His ignorance of our ways, I must ask you to believe—"

"Oh, it's nothing, sir," she interrupted. "I've quite forgotten it already. And usually he's as good as gold and perfectly quiet." She blushed, glancing shyly at me with clear invitation.

"It will not recur," repeated the Doctor positively. "He has promised me. He is very, very sorry and ashamed."

The nurse looked more boldly a moment. I saw her silver teeth. I saw the hint of soft fire in her poor pitiful eyes, but far, far away and, as she thought, safely hidden.

"Pitiful one, I will not touch you," I said instantly. "I know that you are sacred."

I noticed at once that her sweet natural perfume increased about her as I said the words, but her eyes were lowered, though she smiled a little, and her little cheeks grew coloured. I saw her small teeth of silvery marble again. Our work was visible. I liked it.

"You have promised me," said Dr. Fillery, rising to go out.

"I promise," I said, while the Comely One was arranging my pillows and sheets with quick, clever hands, sometimes touching my cheek on purpose as she did so. "I will not worship, unless it is commanded of me first. The increased sweetness of her smell will tell me."

But indeed already I had forgotten her, and I no longer realized who it was that tripped about my bed, doing numerous little things to make me comfortable. My friend, the understanding one, companion of my big friend, Mason, who was dead, also had left the room. His twitching mouth, his laughter, and his shining eyes were gone. I was aware that the Comely One remained, doing all manner of little things about me and my bed, unnecessary things, but my pity and my worship were not asked, so I forgot her. My thinking had wearied me, and my feeling was not touched. I began to hum softly to myself; my giant rhythms rose; I went forth towards my Powers of Wind and Fire, full of my own natural joy. I forgot the Race with its men, its women, its rules and games, its tiny tricks, its civilization. I was free for a little with my own.

One detail interfered a little with the rhythms, but only for a second and very faintly even then. The Comely One's face grew dark.

"He's gone off asleep—actually," I heard her mutter, as she left the room with a fling of her little skirts, shutting the door behind her with a bang.

That bang was far away. I was already rising and falling in that natural happy state which to me meant freedom. It is hard to tell about, but that dear Fillery knows, I am sure, exactly what I know, though he has forgotten it. He has known us somewhere, I feel. He understands our service. But, like me, he has forgotten too.

What really happened to me? Where did I go, what did I see and feel when my rhythms took me off?

Thinking is nowhere in it—I can tell him that. I am conscious of the Sun.

One difficulty is that my being here confuses me. Here I am already caught, confined and straitened. I am within certain limits. I can only move in three ways, three measurements, three dimensions. The space I am in here allows only little rhythms; they are coarse and slow and heavy, and beat against confining walls as it were, are thrown back, cross and recross each other, so that while they themselves grow less, their confusion grows greater. The forms and outlines I can build with them are poor and clumsy and insignificant. Spirals I cannot make. Then I forget.

Into these small rhythms I cannot compress myself; the squeezing hurts. Yet neither can I make them bigger to suit myself. I would break forth towards the Sun.

Thus I feel cramped, confused and crippled. It is almost impossible to tell of my big rhythms, for it is an attempt to tell of one thing in terms of another. How can I fix fire and wind upon the point of a pin, for instance, and examine them through a magnifying-glass? The Sun remains. What I experience, really, when I go off into my own freedom is release. My rhythms are of the Sun. They are his messengers, they are my law, they are my life and happiness. By means of them I fulfil the purpose of my being. I work, so Fillery calls it. I build.

That, at any rate, is literally true. My thinking stops at that point, perhaps; but "I think" I mean by "release" that I escape back from being trapped by all these separate little individualities, human beings each working on his own, for his own, and against all the others—escape from this stifling tangle into the sweep of my big rhythms which work together and in unison. I search for lost companions, but do not find them—the golden skins and radiant faces, the mighty figures and the splendid shapes.

They work without effort, however. That is another difference.

I, too, work, only I work with them, and never against them. I can draw upon them as they can draw upon me. We do draw on one another. We know harmony. Service is our method and system.

My dear Fillery also wants to know who "we" are. How can I tell him? The moment I try to "think," I seem to forget. This forgetting, indeed, is one of the limits against which I bang myself, so that I am flung back upon the tangle of criss-cross, tiny rhythms which confuse and obliterate the very thing he wants to know. Yet the Sun I never forget—father of fire and wind. My companions are lost temporarily. I am shut off from them. It seems I cannot have them and the Race at the same time. I yearn and suffer to rejoin them. The service we all know together is great joy. Of love, this love between two isolated individuals the Race counts the best thing they have—we know nothing.

Now, here is one thing I can understand quite clearly

I have watched and helped the Race, as he calls it, for countless ages. Yet from outside it. Never till now have I been inside its limits with it. And a dim sense of having watched it through a veil or curtain comes to me. I can faintly recall that I tried to urge my big rhythms in among its members, as great waves of heat or sound might be launched upon an ant-heap. I used to try to force and project my vast rhythms into their tiny ones, hoping to make these latter swell and rise and grow—but never with success. Though a few members, here and there, felt them and struggled to obey and use their splendid swing, the rest did not seem to notice them at all... Indeed, they objected to the struggling efforts of the few who did feel them, for their own small accustomed rhythms were interfered with. The few were generally broken into little pieces and pushed violently out of the way.

And this made me feel pitiful, I remember dimly; because these smaller rhythms, though insignificant, were exquisite. They were of extraordinary beauty. Could they only have been increased, the Race that knew and used them must have changed my own which, though huge and splendid of their kind, lacked the intense, perfect loveliness of the smaller kind.

The Race, had it accepted mine and mastered them, must have carried themselves and me towards still mightier rhythms which I alone could never reach.

This, then, is clear to me, though very faint now. Fillery, who can think for a long time, instead of like me for seconds only, will understand what I mean. For if I tell him what "we" did, he may be able to think out what "we" were.

"Your work?" he asked me too.

I'm not sure I know what he means by "work." We were incessantly active, but not for ourselves. There was no effort. There was easy and sure accomplishment—in the sense that nothing could stop or hinder our fulfilling our own natures. Obstacles, indeed helped our power and made it greater, for everything feeds fire and opposition adds to the Pressure of wind. Our main activity was to make perfect forms. We were form-builders. Apart from this, our "work" was to maintain and keep active all rhythms less than our own, yet of our kind. I speak of my own kind alone. We had no desire to be known outside our kind. We worked and moved and built up swiftly, but out of sight—an endless service.

"You are the Powers behind what we call Nature, then?" the dear Fillery asked me. "You operate behind growing things, even behind inanimate things like trees and stones and flowers. Your big rhythms, as you call them, are our Laws of Nature. Your own particular department, your own elements evidently, were heat and air."

I could not answer that. But, as he said it, I saw in his grey eyes the flash of fire which so few of his Race possessed; and I felt vaguely that he was one of the struggling members who was aware of the big rhythms and who would be put away in little pieces later by the rest. It made me pitiful. "Forget your own tiny rhythms," I said, "and come over to us. But bring your tiny rhythms with you because they are so exquisitely lovely. We shall increase them."

He did not answer me. His mouth twitched at the corners, and he had an attack of that irritation which, he says, is relieved and expressed by laughter. Yet the face shone.

The laughter, however, was a very quick, full, natural answer, all the same.

It was happy and enthusiastic. I saw that laughter made his rhythms bigger at once. Then laughter was probably the means to use. It was a sort of bridge.

"Your instantaneous comprehension of our things puzzles me," he said. "You grasp our affairs in all their relations so swiftly. Yet it is all new to you." His voice and face made me wish to stroke and help him, he was so dear and eager. "How do you manage it?" he asked point blank. "Our things are surely foreign to your nature."

"But they are of children," I told him. "They are small and so very simple. There are no difficulties. Your language is block letters because your self-expression, as you call it, is so limited. It all comes to me at a glance. I and my kind can remember a million tiniest details without effort."

He did not laugh, but his face looked full of questions. I could not help him further. "A scrap, probably, of what you've taught us," I heard him mumble, though no further questions came. "Well," he went on presently, while I lay and watched the pale fire slip in tiny waves about his eyes, "remember this: since our alphabet is so easy to you, follow it, stick to it, do not go outside it. There's a good rule that will save trouble for others as well as for yourself."

"I remember and I try. But it is not always easy. I get so cramped and stiff and lifeless with it."

"This sunless, chilly England, of course, cannot feed you," he said. "The sense of beauty in our Race, too, is very poor."

Once he suddenly looked up and fixed his eyes on my face. His manner became very earnest.

"Now, listen to me," he said. "I'm going to read you something; I want you to tell me what you make of it. It's private; that is, I have no right to show it to others, but as no one would understand it—with the exception possibly of yourself—secrecy is not of importance." And his mouth twitched a little.

He drew a sheaf of papers from an inner pocket, and I saw they were covered with fine writing. I laughed; this writing always made me laugh—it was so laborious and slow. The writing I knew best, of course, lay all over and inside the earth and skies. The privacy also made me laugh, so strange seemed the idea to me, and so impossible—this idea of secrecy. It was such an admission of ignorance.

"I will understand it quickest by reading it," I said. "I take in a page at once—in your block letters."

But he preferred to read it out himself, so that he could note the effect upon me, he explained, of definite passages. He saw that I guessed his purpose, and we laughed together a moment. "When you tire listening," he said, "just tell me and I'll pause." I gave him my hand to hold. "It helps me to stay here," I explained, and he nodded as he grasped me in his warm firm clasp.

"It's written by one who *may* have known you and your big rhythms, though I can't be sure," he added. "One of—er—my patients wrote it, someone who believed she was in communication with a kind of immense Nature-spirit."

Then he began to read in his clear, windy voice:

"'I sit and I weave. I feel strange; as if I had so much consciousness that words cannot explain it. The failure of others makes my work more hard, but my own purposes never fail. I am associated with those who need me. The universal doors are open to me. I compass Creation.'"

But already I began to hum my songs, though to please him I kept the music low, and he, dear Fillery, did not bid me stop, but only tightened his grasp upon my hand. I listened with pleasure and satisfaction. Therefore I hummed.

"'I am silent seeking no expression, needing no communication, satisfied with the life that is in me. I do not even wish to be known about—'"

"That's where your Race," I put in, "is to me as children. All they do must be shouted about so loud or they think it has not happened."

"'I do not wish to be forced to obtrude myself,'" he went on. "'There are hosts like me. We do not want that which does not belong to us. We do not want that hindrance, that opposition which rouses an undesirable consciousness; for without that opposition we could never have known of disobedience. We are formless. The formless is the real. That cannot die. It is eternal.'"

Again he tightened his grasp, and this time also laid his eyes a moment on my own, over the top of his paper, so that I kept my music back with a great effort. For it was hard not to express myself when my own came calling in this fashion.

He continued reading aloud. He selected passages now, instead of going straight through the pages. The words helped memory in me; flashes of what I had forgotten came back in sheets of colour and waves of music; the phrases built little spirals, as it were, between two states. Of these two states, I now divined, he understood one perfectly—his own, and the other—mine—partially. Yet he had a little of both, I knew, in himself. With me it was similar, only the understood state was not the same with us. To the Race, of course, what he read would have no meaning.

"The Comely One and the four figures," I said, "how they would turn white and run if they could hear you, showing their yellow teeth and dim eyes!"

His face remained grave and eager, though I could see the laughter running about beneath the tight brown skin as he went on reading his little bits.

"'We heard nothing of man, and were rarely even conscious of him, although he benefited by our work in all that sustained and conditioned him. The wise are silent, the foolish speak, and the children are thus led astray, for wisdom is not knowledge, it is a realization of the scheme and of one's own part in it.'"

He took a firmer, broader grip of my hand as he read the next bit. I felt the tremble of his excitement run into my wrist and arm. His voice deepened and shook. It was like a little storm:

"'Then, suddenly, we heard man's triumphant voice. We became conscious of him as an evolving entity. Our Work had told. We had built his form and processes so faithfully. We knew that when he reached his height we must be submissive to his will.'"

A gust of memory flashed by me as I heard. Those small but perfect, exquisite, lovely rhythms!

"Who called me here? Whose voice reached after me, bringing me into this undesirable consciousness?" I cried aloud, as the memory went tearing by, then vanished before I could recover it. At the same time Fillery let go my hand, and the little bridge was snapped. I felt what he called pain. It passed at once. I found his hand again, but the bridge was not rebuilt. How white his skin had grown, I noticed, as I looked up at his face. But the eyes shone grandly. "I shall find the way," I said. "We shall go back together to our eternal home."

He went on reading as though I had not interrupted, but I found it less easy to listen now.

I realized then that he was gone. He had left the room, though I had not seen him go. I had been away.

It was some days ago that this occurred. It was to-day, a few hours ago, that I seized the Comely One and tried to comfort her, poor hungry member of this little Race.

But both occurrences help us—help dear Fillery and myself—to understand how difficult it is to answer his questions and tell him exactly what he wants to know.

"How long, O Lord, how long.'" I hear his yearning cry. "Yet other beings cannot help us; they can only tell us what their own part is."

After the door had clicked I knew release for a bit—release from a state I partially understood and so found irksome, into another where I felt at home and so found pleasurable. In the big rhythms my nature expressed itself apparently. I rose, seeking my lost companions. They—the Devonham and his busy little figures—called it sleep. It may be "sleep." But I find there what I seek yet have forgotten, and that with me were dear Fillery and another—a Comely One whom he brings—as though we belong together and have a common origin. But this other Comely One—who is it?

CHAPTER X

About a week after the arrival of LeVallon in London, Dr. Fillery came out of the Home one morning early, upon some uninteresting private business. He had left "LeVallon " happy with his books and garden, Devonham was with him to answer questions or direct his energies; the other "cases" in the establishment were moving nicely towards a cure.

The November air was clear and almost bright; no personal worries troubled him. His mind felt free and light.

It was one of those mornings when Nature slips, very close and sweet, into the heart, so close and sweet that the mind wonders why people quarrel and disagree, when it is so easy to forgive, and the planet seems but a big, lovely, happy garden, evil an impossible nightmare, and personal needs few and simple.

He walked by cross roads towards Primrose Hill, entering Regent's Park near the Zoo. An early white frost was rapidly melting in the sun. The sky showed a faint tinge of blue. He saw floating sea-gulls. These, and a faint breeze that stirred the yellowing last leaves of autumn, gave his heart a sudden lift.

And this lift was in the direction of a forbidden corner. He was aware of some exquisite dawn-wind far away stirring a million flowers, dew sparkled, streams splashed and murmured. A valley gleamed and vanished, yet left across his mind its shining trail.... For this lift of his heart made him soar into a region where it was only too easy to override temptation. Fillery, however, though his invisible being soared, kept both visible feet firmly on the ground. The surface was slippery, being melted by the sun, but frost kept the earth hard and frozen underneath. His balance never was in danger. He remained detached and a spectator.

She walked beside him nevertheless, a figure of purity and radiance, perfumed, soft, delicious. She was so ignorant of life. That was her wonder partly; for beauty was her accident and, while admirable, was not a determining factor. Life, in its cruder sense, she did not know, though moving through the thick of it. It neither touched nor soiled her; she brushed its dirt and dust aside as though a non-conducting atmosphere surrounded her. Her emotions, deep and searching, had remained untorn. A quality of pristine innocence belonged to her, as though, in the noisy clamour of ambitious civilized life, she remained still aware of Eden. Her grace, her loveliness, her simplicity moved by his side as naturally, it seemed to him, as air or perfume.

"Iraida," he murmured to himself, with a smile of joy. "Nayan Khilkoff. All the men worship and adore you, yet respect you too. They cannot touch you. You remain aloof, unstained." And, remembering LeVallon's remarks in cinema and theatre, he could have sung at this mere thought of her.

"Untouched by coarseness, something unearthly about your loveliness of soul, a baby, a saint, and to all the men in Khilkoff's Studio, a mother. Where do you really come from? Whence do you derive? Your lovely soul can have no dealings with our common flesh. How many young fellows have you saved already, how many floundering characters redeemed! They crave your earthly, physical love. Instead you surprise and disappoint and shock them into safety again—by giving to them Love....!"

And, as he half repeated his vivid thoughts aloud, he suddenly saw her coming towards him from the ornamental water, and instantly, wondering what he should say to her, his mind contracted. The thing in him that sang went backward into silence. He put a break upon himself. But he watched her coming nearer, wondering what brought her so luckily into Regent's Park, and all the way from Chelsea, at such an hour. She moved so lightly, sweetly; she was so intangible and lovely. He feared her eyes, her voice.

They drew nearer. From looking to right and left, he raised his head. She was close, quite close, a hundred yards away. That walk, that swing, that poise of head and neck he could not mistake anywhere. His whole being glowed, thrilled, and yet contracted as in pain.

A sentence about the weather, about her own, her father's health, about his calling to see them shortly, rose to his lips. He turned his eyes away, then again looked up. They were now not twenty yards apart; in another moment he would have raised his hat, when, with a sensation of cold disappointment in him, she went past in totally irresponsive silence. It was a stranger—a shop girl, a charwoman, a bus-conductor's wife—anybody but she whom he had thought.

How could he have been so utterly mistaken? It amazed him. It was, indeed, months since they had met, yet his knowledge of her appearance was so accurate and detailed that such an error seemed incredible. He had experienced, besides, the actual thrill.

The phenomenon, however, was not new to him. Often had he experienced it, much as others have. He knew, from this, that she was somewhere near, coming deliciously, deliberately towards him, moving every minute firmly nearer, from a point in great London town which she had left just at the precise moment which would time her crossing his own path later. They would meet presently, if not now. Fate had arranged all details, and something in him was aware of it before it happened.

The phenomenon, as a matter of fact, was repeated twice again in the next half-hour: he saw her—on both occasions beyond the possibility of question—coming towards him, yet each time it was a complete stranger masquerading in her guise.

It meant, he knew, that their two minds—hearts, too, he wondered, with a sense of secret happiness, enjoyed intensely then instantly suppressed—were wirelessing to one another across the vast city, and that both transmitter and receiver, their physical bodies, would meet shortly round the corner, or along the crowded street. Strong currents of desiring thought, he knew, he hoped, he wondered, were trying to shape the crude world nearer to the heart's desire, causing the various intervening passers-by to assume the desirable form and outline in advance.

He reflected, following the habit of his eager mind; this wireless discovery, after all, was the discovery of a universal principle in Nature. It was common to all forms of life, a faint beginning of that advance towards marvellous inter-communicating, semi-telepathic brotherhood he had always hoped for, believed in.... Even plants, he remembered, according to Bosé....

Then, suddenly, half-way down Baker Street he found her close beside him.

She was dressed so becomingly, so naturally, that no particular detail caught his eye, although she wore more colour than was usual in the dull climate known to English people. There was a touch of fur and there were flowers, but these were part of her appearance as a whole, and the hat was so exactly right, though it was here that Englishwomen generally went wrong, that he could not remember afterwards what it was like. It was as suitable as natural hair. It looked as if she had grown it. The shining eyes were what he chiefly noticed. They seemed to increase the pale sunlight in the dingy street.

She was so close that he caught her perfume almost before he recognized her, and a sense of happiness invaded his whole being instantly, as he took the slender hand emerging from a muff and held it for a moment. The casual sentences he had half prepared fled like a flock of birds surprised. Their eyes met.... And instantly the sun rose over a far Khaketian valley; he was aware of joy, of peace, of deep contentment, London obliterated, the entire world elsewhere. He knew the thrill, the ecstasy of some long-forgotten dawn....

But in that brief second while he held her hand and gazed into her eyes, there flashed before him a sudden apparition. With lightning rapidity this picture darted past between them, paused for the tiniest fraction of a second, and was gone again. So swiftly the figure shot across that the very glance he gave her was intercepted, its angle changed, its meaning altered. He started involuntarily, for he knew that vision, the bright rushing messenger, someone who brought glad tidings. And this time he recognized it—it was the figure of "N. H."

The outward start, the slight wavering of the eyelids, both were noticed, though not understood, much less interpreted by the young woman facing him.

"You are as much surprised as I am," he heard the pleasant, low-pitched voice before his face. "I thought you were abroad. Father and I came back from Sark only yesterday."

"I haven't left town," he replied. "It was Devonham went to Switzerland."

He was thinking of her pleasant voice, and wondering how a mere voice could soothe and bless and comfort in this way. The picture of the flashing figure, too, preoccupied him. His various mind was ever busy with several trains of thought at once, though all correlated. Why, he was wondering, should that picture of "N. H." leave a sense of chill upon his heart? Why had the first radiance of this meeting thus already dimmed a little? Her nearness, too, confused him as of old, making his manner a trifle brusque and not quite natural, until he found his cen-tre of control again. He looked quickly up and down the street, moved aside to let some people pass, then turned to the girl again. "Your holiday has done you good, Iraida," he said quietly; "I hope your father enjoyed it too."

"We both enjoyed ourselves," she answered, watching him, something of a pro-tective air about her. "I wish you had been with us, for that would have made it perfect. I was thinking that only this morning—as I walked across Hyde Park."

"How nice of you! I believe I, too, was thinking of you both, as I walked through Regent's Park." He smiled for the first time.

"It's very odd," she went on, "though you can explain it probably," she added, with a smile that met his own, increasing it, "or, at any rate, Dr. Devonham could—but I've seen you several times this morning already—in the last half-hour. I've seen you in other people in the street, I mean. Yet I wasn't thinking of you at the actual moment, it's two months since we've met, and I imagined you were abroad."

"Odd, yes," he said, half shyly, half curtly. "It's an experience many have, I believe."

She gazed up at him. "It's very natural, I think, when people like each other, Edward, and are in sympathy."

"Yet it happens with people who don't like each other too," he objected, and at the same moment was vexed that he had used the words.

Iraida Khilkoff laughed. He had the feeling that she read his thoughts as easily as if they were printed in red letters on his grey felt hat.

"There must be some bond between them, though," she remarked, "an emotion, I mean, whatever it may be—even hatred."

"Probably, Nayan," he agreed. "It's you now, not Devonham, that wants to explain things. I think I must take you into the Firm, you could take charge of the female patients with great success."

Whereupon she looked up at him with such a grave mothering expression that he was aware of her secret power, her central source of strength in dealing with men. Her innocence and truth were an atmosphere about her, protecting her as naturally and neatly as the clothes upon her body. She believed in men. He felt like a child beside her.

"I'm in the Firm already," she said, "for you made me a partner years ago when I was so high," and her small gloved hand indicated the stature of a little girl. "You taught me first."

He remembered the bleak northern town where fifteen years ago he had known her father as a patient for some minor ailment, and the friendship that grew out of the relationship. He remembered the child of nine or ten who sat on his knee and repeated to him the Russian fairy tales her mother told her; he recalled the charm, the wonder, the extraordinary power of belief. Her words brought back again that flowered Caucasian valley in the sunlight and this, again, flashed upon the screen the strange bright figure that had already once intercepted their glance, as though it somehow came between them.

"You have one advantage over me," he rejoined presently, "for in my Clinique the people know that they need treatment, whereas in the Studio you catch your patients unawares. They do not know they're ill. You heal them without their being aware that they need healing."

"Yet some of our *habitués* have found their way later to your consultingroom," she reminded him.

"Merely to finish what you had first begun—a sort of convalescence. You work in the big, raw world, I in a mere specialized corner of it."

He turned away, lest the power in her eyes overcome him. The traffic thundered past, the people crowded, jostling them. He could have stood there talking to her all day long, the London street forgotten or full of flowers and Eden's trees and rippling summer streams. The pale sunlight caught her face beside him and made it shine....

He longed to take her in his arms and fly through the dawn for ever, for his clean mind saw her without clothing, her hair loose in the wind, her white shape fleeing from him, yet beckoning across a gleaming shoulder that he most overtake and capture her....

"I'm on my way to St. Dunstan's," he heard the musical voice. "A friend of father's.... Come with me, will you?" And with her muff she touched his arm, trying to make him turn her way. But just as he felt the touch he saw the bright figure again. Swifter than himself and far more powerful, it leaped dancing past and carried her away before his very eyes. She waved her hand, her eyes faded like stars into the distance of some unearthly spring—and she was gone. A pang of peculiar anguish seized him, as the mental picture flashed with the speed of light and vanished. For the figure seemed of elemental power, taking its own with perfect ease....

He shook his head. "I'll come to see you to-morrow instead," he told her. "I'll come to the Studio in the afternoon, if you'll both be in. I'd like to bring a friend with me, if I may."

"Good-bye then." She took his hand and kept it. "I shall expect you to tell me all about this—friend. I knew you had something on your mind, for your thoughts have been elsewhere all the time."

"Julian LeVallon," he replied quickly. "He's staying with me indefinitely." His face grew stern a moment about the mouth. "I think he may need you," he added with abrupt significance.

"Julian LeVallon," she repeated, the name sounding very musical the way her slightly foreign accent touched it. "And what nationality may that be?"

Dr. Fillery hesitated. "His parents, Nayan, I believe, were English," he said. "He has lived all his life in the Jura Mountains, alone with an old scholar, poet and geologist, who brought him up. Of our modern life he knows little. I think you may—" He broke off. "His mother died when he was born," he concluded.

"And of women he knows nothing," she replied, understandingly, "so that he will probably fall in love with the first he sees—with Nayan."

"I hope so, Nayan, and he will be safe with you."

She watched her companion's face for a minute or two with her clear searching eyes. She smiled. But his own face wore a mask now; no figure this time flashed between their deep understanding gaze.

"A woman, you think, can teach and help him more than a man," she said, without lowering her eyes.

"Probably—perhaps, at any rate. The material, I must warn you at once, is new and strange. I want him to meet you."

"Then I am in the Firm," was all she answered, "and you can't do without me." She let go the hand she had held all this time, and turned from him, looking once across her shoulder as he, too, went upon his way.

"About three o'clock we shall expect you—and Mr. Julian LeVallon," she added. "The Prometheans are coming too, as of course you know, but that won't matter. Father has let the Studio to them."

"The more the merrier," he answered, raised his hat, and went on at a rapid pace up Baker Street.

But with him up the London street went a flock of thoughts, hopes, fears and memories that were hard to disentangle. Lost, forgotten dreams went with him too. He had known that one day he must be "executed," yet with his own hands he had just slipped the noose about his neck. Detachment from life, he realized, keeping aloof from the emotions that touch one's fellow beings, can only be, after all, a pose. In his case it was evidently a pose assumed for safety and self-protection, an artificial attitude he wore to keep his heart from error. His love, born of some far unearthly valley, undoubtedly consumed him, while yet he said it nay....

He had himself suggested bringing together the girl and "N. H." There had been no need to do this. Yet he had deliberately offered it, and she had instantly accepted. Even while he said the words there was a volcano of emotion in him, several motives fighting to combine. The fear for himself, being selfish, he had set aside at once; there was also the fear for her—the odd certainty in him that at last her woman's nature would be waked; lastly, the fear for "N. H." himself. And here he clashed with his promise to Devonham. Behind the simple proposal lay these various threads of motive, emotion and qualification.

Now, as he hurried along the street, they rushed to and fro about his mind, each at its own speed and with its own impetuous strength. It was the last one, however, the certainty that her mere presence must evoke the "N. H." personality, banishing the commonplace LeVallon; it was this that, in the end, perhaps troubled him most. An intuitive conviction assured him that this was bound to be the result of their meeting. LeVallon would sink down out of sight; "N. H." would emerge triumphant and vital, bringing his elemental power with him. The girl would summon him....

"I must tell Paul first," he decided. "I must consult his judgment. Otherwise I'm breaking my promise. If Paul is against it, I will send an excuse...."

With this proviso, he dismissed the matter from his mind, noting only how clearly it revealed his own keen desire to let LeVallon disappear and "N. H. " become active. He himself yearned for the interest, stimulus and companionship of the strange new being that was "N. H."

The other aspect of the problem he dismissed quickly too: he would lose Nayan. Yes, but he had never possessed the right to hold her. He was strong, indifferent, detached.... His life in any case was a sacrifice upon the altar of a mistake with regard to which he had not been consulted. His whole existence must he passed in worship before this altar, unless he was to admit himself a failure. His ideal possession of the girl, he consoled himself, need know no change. To watch her womanhood, hitherto untouched by any man, to watch this bloom and ripen at the bidding of another must mean pain. But he faced the loss. And a curious sense of compensation lay in it somewhere—the strange notion that she and he would share "N. H." in a sense between them. He was already aware of a deep subtle kinship between the three of them, a kinship hardly of this physical world. And, after all, the interests of "N. H." must come first. He had chosen his life, accepted it, at any rate; he must remain true to his high ideal. This strange being, blown by the winds of chance into his keeping, must be his first consideration.

"LeVallon" needed no special help, neither from himself, nor from her, nor from others. "LeVallon" was ordinary enough, if not commonplace, his only interest being at those thin places in his being where the submerged personality of "N. H." peeped through. Paul Devonham, he felt convinced, was wrong in thinking "N. F." to be the transient manifestation.

It was the reverse that Dr. Fillery believed to be the truth. He saw in "N. H." almost a new type of being altogether. In that physical body warred two personalities certainly, but "N. H." was the important one, and LeVallon merely the transient outer one, masquerading on the surface merely, a kind of automatic and mechanical personality, gleaned, picked up, trained and educated, as it were, by the few years spent among the human herd.

And this "N. H. " needed help, the best, the wisest possible. Both male and female help "N. H." demanded. He, Edward Fillery, could supply the former, but the latter could be furnished only by some woman in whom innocence, truth and a natural mother-love—the three deepest feminine qualities—were happily combined. Nayan possessed them all. "N. H.," the strange bright messenger, bringing perhaps glad tidings into life, had need of her.

And Fillery, as his thoughts ran down these sad and happy paths of that lost valley in his blood, realized the meaning of the flashing intuition that had pained yet gladdened him half an hour before with its convincing symbolic picture.

This private Eden secreted in his depths he revealed to no one, though Paul, his intimate friend and keen assistant, divined its general neighbourhood and geography to some extent. It was the girl who invariably opened its ivory gates for him. They had but to meet and talk a moment, when, with a sudden drift of wonder, beauty, wildness, this Khaketian inheritance rose before him. Its sunny brilliance, its flowers, its perfumes seduced and caught him away. The unearthly mood stole over him. Thought took wings of imagination and soared beyond the planet. He foresaw, easily, the effect she would produce upon "LeVallon."...

He came back to earth again at the door of the Home, smiling, as so often before, at these brief wanderings in his secret Eden, yet perfectly able to pigeonhole the experience, each detail explained, labelled, docketed, and therefore harmless....

He found Devonham in the study and at once told him of his suggestion and its possible results, and his assistant, resting before lunch after a long morning's work, looked up at him with his quick, observant air. Noticing the light in the eyes, the softer expression about the mouth, the general appearance of a strong and recent stimulus, he easily divined their origin, and showed his pleasure in his face. He longed for his old friend to be humanized and steadied by some deep romance. There was a curious new watchful attitude also about him, though cleverly concealed.

"I'm glad the Khilkoffs are back in town," he said easily. "As for LeVallon— he's been quiet and uninteresting all the morning. He needs the human touch, as I already said, and the Studio atmosphere, especially if the Prometheans are to be there, seems the very thing."

"And Nayan—?"

"Her influence is good for any man, young or old, and if LeVallon worships at her shrine like the rest of 'em, so much the better. You remember my Notes. Nothing will help towards his finding his real self quicker than an abandoned passion—unreturned."

"Unreturned? "

" You can't think she will give to LeVallon what so many—?"

"But may she not," the other interrupted, "stimulate 'N. H.' rather than LeVallon?"

Devonham was surprised—he had quickly divined the subconscious fear and jealousy. For this detached, impersonal attitude he was not prepared. Only the keenest observer could have noticed the sharp, anxious watchfulness he hid so well.

"Edward, there's only one thing I feel we—you rather—have to be careful about. And the girl has nothing to do with *that*. In your blood, remember, lies an unearthly spiritual vagrancy which you must not, dare not, communicate to him, if you ever hope to see him cured."

Devonham regarded him keenly as he said it. He was as earnest as his chief, but the difference between the two men was fundamental, probably un-bridgeable as well. The affection, trust, respect each felt for the other was sin-cere. Devonham, however, having never known a thought, a feeling, much less an actual experience outside the normal gamut of humanity, regarded all such as pathogenic. Fillery, who had tasted the amazing, dangerous sweetness of such experiences, in his own being, had another standard.

"You must not exaggerate," observed Fillery slowly. "Your phrase, though, is good. 'Spiritual vagrancy' is an apt description, I admit. Yet to the 'spiritual,' if it exists, the whole universe lies open, remember, too."

They laughed together. Then, suddenly, Devonham rose, and a new inex-pressible uneasiness was in his face. He thrust his hands deep into his trouser pockets, turned his eyes hard upon the floor, stood with his legs apart. Abruptly turning, he came a full step closer. "Edward," he said, furious with himself, and yet fiercely determined to be honest, "I may as well tell you frankly—though explanation lies beyond me—there's something in this—this case I don't quite like." Behind his lowered eyelids his observation never failed.

Quick as a flash, his companion took him up. "For yourself, for others, or for himself?" he asked, while a secret touch of joy ran through him.

"For myself perhaps," was the immediate rejoinder. "It's intolerable. It's the panic sense he touches in me. I admit it frankly. I've had—once or twice—the desire to turn and run. But what I mean is—we've got to be uncommonly care-ful with him," he ended lamely.

"LeVallon you refer to? Or 'N. H.'?"

"'N. H.'"

"The panic sense," repeated Fillery to himself more than to his friend. "The old, old thing. I understand."

"Also," Devonham went on presently, "I must tell you that since he came here there's been a change in every patient in the building—without exception." He looked over his shoulder as though he heard a sound. He listened certainly, but his mind was sharply centred on his friend.

"For the better, yes," said Fillery at once. "Increased vitality, I've noticed too."

"Precisely," whispered the other, still listening.

There came a pause between them.

"And when we have found the real, the central self," pursued Fillery presently. "When we have found the essential being—what is it?"

"Exactly," replied Devonham with extraordinary emphasis. "*What is it?*" But even then he did not look up to meet the other's glance.

CHAPTER XI

The meeting with Dr. Fillery and his friends, the Khilkoffs, father and daughter, had, for one reason or another, to be postponed for a week, during which brief time even, no single day wasted, LeVallon's education proceeded rapidly. He was exceedingly quick to learn the usages of civilized society in a big city, adapting himself with an ease born surely of quick intelligence to the requirements and conventions of ordinary life.

In his perception of the rights of others, particularly, he showed a natural aptitude; he had good manners, that is, instinctively; in certain houses where Fillery took him purposely, he behaved with a courtesy and tact that belong usually to what England calls a gentleman. Except to Fillery and Devonham, he talked little, but was an excellent and sympathetic listener, a quality that helped him to make his way. With Mrs. Soames, the stern and even forbidding matron, he made such headway, that it was noticed with a surprise, including laughter. He might have been her adopted son.

"She's got a new pet," said Devonham, with a laugh. "Mason taught him well. His aptitude for natural history is obvious; after a few years' study he'll make a name for himself. The 'N. H.' side will disappear now more and more, unless *you* stimulate it for your own ends—" He broke off, speaking lightly still, but with a carelessness some might have guessed assumed.

"You forget," put in his Chief, "I promised."

Devonham looked at him shrewdly. "I doubt," he said, "whether you can help yourself, Edward," the expression in his eyes for a moment almost severe.

Fillery remained thoughtful, making no immediate reply.

"We must remember," he said presently, "that he's now in the quiescent state. Nothing has again occurred to bring 'N. H.' uppermost again."

Devonham turned upon his friend. "I see no reason why 'N. H.'—he spoke with emphasis—"should ever get uppermost again. In my opinion we can make this quiescent state—LeVallon—the permanent one."

"We can't keep him in a cage like Mrs. Soames's mice and parrot. Are you, for instance, against my taking him to the Studio? Do you think it's a mistake to let him meet the Prometheans?"

"That's just where Mason went wrong," returned Devonham. "He kept him in a cage. The boy met only a few peasants, trees, plants, animals and birds. The sun, making him feel happy, became his deity. The rain he hated. The wind inspired and invigorated him. If we now introduce the human element wisely, I see no danger. If he can stand the Khi—the Studio and the Prometheans, he can stand anything. He may be considered cured."

The door opened and a tall, radiant figure with bright eyes and untidy shining hair came into the room, carrying an open book.

"Mrs. Soames says I've nothing to do with stars," said a deep musical voice, "and that I had better stick to animals and plants. She says that star-gazing never was good for anyone except astronomers who warn us about tides, eclipses and dangerous comets."

He held out the big book, open at an enlarged stellar photograph. "What, please, is a galaxy, a star that is suddenly brilliant, then disappears in a few weeks, and a nebula?"

Before either of the astonished men could answer, LeVallon turned to Devonham, his face wearing the gravity and intense curiosity of a child. "And, please, are *you* the only sort of being in the universe? Mrs. Soames says that the earth is the only inhabited place. Aren't there other beings besides you anywhere? The Earth is such a little planet, and the solar system, according to this book, is one of the smallest too."

"My dear fellow," Devonham said gently, "do not bother your head with useless speculations. Our only valuable field of study is this planet, for it is all we know or ever can know. Whether the universe holds other beings or not, can be of no importance to us at present."

LeVallon stared fixedly at him, saying nothing. Something of his natural radiance dimmed a little. "Then what are all these things that I remember I've forgotten?" he asked, his blue eyes troubled.

"It will take you all your lifetime to understand beings like me, and like yourself and like Dr. Fillery. Don't waste time speculating about possible inhabitants in other stars."

He spoke good-humouredly, but firmly, as one who laid down certain definite lines to be followed, while Dr. Fillery, watching, made no audible comment. Once long ago he had asked his own father a somewhat similar question.

"But I shall so soon get to the end of you," replied LeVallon, a disappointed expression on his face. "I may speculate *then?*" he asked.

"When you get to the end of me and of yourself and of Dr. Fillery—yes, then you may speculate to your heart's content," said Devonham in a kindly tone. "But it will take you longer than you think perhaps. Besides, there are women, too, remember. You will find them more complicated still."

A curious look stole into the other's eager eyes. He turned suddenly towards the older man who had his confidence so completely. There was in the movement, in the incipient gesture that he made with his arms, his hands, almost with his head and face as well, something of appeal that set the doctor's nerves alert. And the change of voice—it was lower now and more musical than before—increased the nameless message that flashed to his brain and heart. There was a hint of song, of chanting almost, in the tone. There was music in him. For the voice, Fillery realized suddenly, brought in the over-tones, somewhat in the way good teachers of singing and voice production know. There was the depth, sonority, singing quality which means that the "harmonics" are made audible, as with a violin played in perfect tune. The sound seemed produced not by the vocal cords alone, but by the entire being, so to speak. Yet, "LeVallon's " voice had not this rich power, he noticed. Its appearance was a sign that "N. H." was stirring into activity and utterance.

"Women, yes," the young man repeated to himself. "Women—bring back something. Their eyes make me remember—" he turned abruptly to the open book upon the doctor's knee. "It's something to do with stars, these memories," he went on eagerly, the voice resonant. "Stars, women, memories... where are they all gone to...? Why have I lost...? What is it that...?"

It seemed as if a veil passed from his face, a thin transparency that dimmed the shining effect his hair and eyes and radiant health produced. A far-away expression followed it.

"'N. H.'!" Devonham quickly flashed the whispered warning. And in the same instant, Fillery rose, holding out the open book.

"Come, LeVallon," he said, putting a hand upon his shoulder, "we'll go into my room for an hour, and I'll tell you all about the galaxies and nebulæ. You shall ask as many questions as you like. Devonham is a very busy man and has duties to attend to just now."

He moved across to open the door, and LeVallon, his face changing more and more, went with him; the light in his eyes increased; he smiled, the far-away expression passed a little.

"Dr. Devonham is quite right in what he says about useless speculations," continued Fillery, as they went out arm in arm together, "but we can play a bit with thought and imagination, for all that—you and I. 'Let your thought wander like an insect which is allowed to fly in the air, but is at the same time confined by a thread.' Come along, we'll have an hour's play. We'll travel together among the golden stars, eh?"

"Play!" exclaimed the youth, looking up with flashing eyes. "Ah! in the Spring we play! Our work with sap, roots, crystals, fire, all finished out of sight, so that their results followed of their own accord." He was talking at great speed in a low voice, a deep, rolling voice, and half to himself. "Spring is our holiday, the forms made perfect and ready for the power to rush through, and we rush with it, playing everywhere—"

"Spring is the wine of life, yes," put in Fillery, caught away momentarily by something behind the words he listened to, as though a rhythm swept him. "Creative life racing up and flooding into every form and body everywhere. It brings wonder, joy—play, as you call it."

"We—we build the way—" The youth broke off abruptly as they reached the study door. Something flowed down and back in him, emptying face and manner of a mood which had striven for utterance, then passed. He returned to the previous talk about the stars again

"Who attends to them? Who looks after them? " he inquired, a deep, peculiar interest in his manner, his eyes turning a little darker.

"What we call the laws of Nature," was the reply, "which are, after all, merely our 'descriptive formulæ summing up certain regularities of recurrence,' the laws under which they were first set alight and then sent whirling into space. Under these same laws they will all eventually burn out and come to rest. They will be dead."

"Dead," repeated the other, as though he did not understand. "They are the children of the laws," he stated, rather than asked. "Are the laws kind and faithful? They never tire?"

Fillery explained with one-half of his nature, and still as to a child. The other half of him lay under firm restraint according to his promise. He outlined in general terms man's knowledge of the stars. "The laws never tire," he said.

"But the stars end! They burn out, stop, and die! You said so."

The other replied with something judicious and cautious about time and its immense duration. But he was startled.

"And those who attend to the laws," came then the words that startled him, "who keeps them working so that they do not tire?"

It was something in the tone of voice perhaps that, once again, produced in his listener the extraordinary sudden feeling that Humanity was, after all, but an insignificant, a microscopic detail in the Universe; that it was, say, a mere ant-heap in the colossal jungle crowded with other minuter as well as immenser life of every sort and kind, and, moreover, that "N. H." was aware of this "other life," or at least of some vast section of it, and had been, if he were not still, associated with it. The two letters by which he was designated acquired a deeper meaning than before.

A rich glow came into the young face, and into the eyes, growing ever darker, a look of burning; the skin had the effect of radiating; the breathing became of a sudden deep and rhythmical. The whole figure seemed to grow larger, expanding as though it extended already and half filled the room. Into the atmosphere about it poured, as though heat and light rushed through it, a strange effect of power.

"You'd like to visit them, perhaps—wouldn't you?" asked Fillery gently.

"I feel—" began the other, then stopped short.

"You feel it would interest you," the doctor helped—then saw his mistake.

"I feel," repeated the youth. The sentence was complete. " I am there."

"Ah! when you feel you're there, you *are* there?"

The other nodded.

He leaned forward. "*I* know," he whispered as with sudden joy. "*You* help me to remember, Fillery." The voice, though whispering, was strong; it vibrated full of over-tones and under-tones. The sound of the "F" was like a wind in branches. "You wonderful, *you* know too! It is the same with flowers, with everything. We build with wind and fire." He stopped, rubbing a hand across his forehead a moment. "Wind and fire," he went on, but this time to himself, "my splendid mighty ones...." Dropping his hand, he flashed an amazing look of enthusiasm and power into his companion's face. The look held in concentrated form something of the power that seemed pulsing and throbbing in his atmosphere. "Help me to remember, dear Fillery," his voice rang out aloud like singing. " Remember with me why we both are here. When we remember we can go back where we belong."

The glow went from his face and eyes as though an inner lamp had been suddenly extinguished. The power left both voice and atmosphere. He sank back
in his chair, his great sensitive hands spread over the table where the star charts
lay, as through the open window came the crash and clatter of an aeroplane tearing, like some violent, monstrous insect, through the sunlight.

A look of pain came into the eyes. "It goes again. I've lost it."

"We were talking about the stars and the laws of Nature," said Fillery
quickly, though his voice was shaking, "when that noisy flying-machine disturbed us." He leaned over, taking his companion's hand. His heart was beating. He smelt the open spaces. The blood ran wildly in his veins. It was with
the utmost difficulty he found simple, common words to use. "You must not ask
too much at once. We will learn slowly—there is so much we have to learn together."

LeVallon's smile was beautiful, but it was the smile of "LeVallon" again only.

"Thank you, dear Fillery," he replied, and the talk continued as between a tutor and his backward pupil.... But for some time afterwards the "tutor's" mind
and heart, while attending to LeVallon now, went travelling, it seemed, with
"N. H." There was this strange division in his being . . for "N. H." appealed with
power to a part of him, perhaps the greatest, that had never yet found expression, much less satisfaction.

Many a talk together of this kind, with occasional semi-irruptions of "N. H.,"
he had already enjoyed with his new patient, and LeVallon was by now fairly
well instructed in the general history of our little world, briefly but pic-
turesquely given. Evolution had been outlined and explained, the rise of man
sketched vividly, the great war, and the planet's present state of chaos described
in a way that furnished a clear enough synopsis of where humanity now stood.
LeVallon was able to hold his own in conversation with others; he might pass
for a simpleminded but not ill-informed young man, and both Paul Devonham
and Edward Fillery, though each for different reasons, were, therefore, well satisfied with the young human being entrusted to their care, a human being to
be eventually discharged from the Home, healed and cured of extravagances,
made harmonious with himself, able to make his own way in the world alone.
To Devonham it appeared already certain that, within a reasonable time, LeV-
allon would find himself happily at home among his fellow kind, a normal, even
a gifted young man with a future before him. "N. H." would disappear and be
forgotten, absorbed back into the parent Self. To his colleague, on the other
hand, another vision of his future opened. Sooner or later it was LeVallon that
would disappear and "N. H." remain in full control, a strange, possibly a new
type of being, not alone marvellously gifted, but who might even throw light
upon a vista of research and knowledge hitherto unknown to humanity, and
with benefits for the Race as yet beyond the reach of any wildest prophecy.

Both men, therefore, went gladly with him to the Khilkoff Studio that early
November afternoon, anxious to observe him, his conduct, attitude, among the
curious set of people to be found there on the Prometheans' Society day, and
to note any reactions he might show in such a milieu. Each felt fully justified

in doing so, though they would have kept an ordinary "hysterical" patient safely from the place. LeVallon, however, betrayed no trace of hysteria in any meaning of the word, big or little; he was stable as a navvy, betraying no undesirable reaction to the various well-known danger points. The visit might be something of an experiment perhaps, but an experiment, a test, they were justified in taking. Yet Devonham on no account would have allowed his chief to go alone. He had insisted on accompanying them.

And to both men, as they went towards Chelsea, their quiet companion with them, came the feeling that the visit might possibly prove one of them right, the other wrong. Fillery expected that Nayan Khilkoff alone, to say nothing of the effect of the other queer folk who might he present, must surely evoke the "N. H." personality now lying quiescent and inactive below the threshold of LeVallon. The charm and beauty of the girl he had never known to fail with any male, for she had that in her which was bound to stimulate the highest in the opposite sex. The excitement of the wild, questing, picturesque, if unbalanced, minds who would fill the place, must also, though in quite another way, affect the *real* self of anyone who came in contact with their fantastic and imaginative atmosphere. Attraction or repulsion must certainly be felt. He expected at any rate a vital clue.

"Ivan Khilkoff," he told LeVallon, as they went along in the car, "is a Russian, a painter and sculptor of talent, a good-hearted and silent sort of old fellow, who has remained very poor because he refuses to advertise himself or commercialize his art, and because his work is not the kind of thing the English buy. His daughter, Nayan, teaches the piano and Russian. She is beautiful and sweet and pure, but of an independent and rather impersonal character. She has never fallen in love, for instance, though most men fall in love with her. I hope you may like and understand each other."

"Thank you," said LeVallon, listening attentively, but with no great interest apparently. "I will try very much to like her and her father too."

"The Studio is a very big one, it is really two studios knocked into one, their living rooms opening out of it. One half of the place, being so large, they sometimes let out for meetings, dances and that sort of thing, earning a little money in that way. It is rented this evening by a Society called the Prometheans—a group of people whose inquisitive temperaments lead them to believe, or half believe—"

"To imagine, if not deliberately to manufacture," put in Devonham.

"—to imagine, let us call it," continued the other with a twinkle, "that there are other worlds, other powers, other states of consciousness and knowledge open to them outside and beyond the present ones we are familiar with."

"They *know* these?" asked LeVallon, looking up with signs of interest. "They have experienced them?"

"They know and experience," replied Fillery, "according to their imaginations and desires, those with a touch of creative imagination claiming the most definite results, those without it being merely imitative. They report their experiences, that is, but cannot—or rarely—show the results to others. You will hear their talk and judge accordingly. They are interesting enough in their way. They have, at any rate, one thing of value—that they are open to new ideas. Such people have existed in every age of the world's history, but after an upheaval, such as the great war has been, they become more active and more numerous, because the nervous system, reacting from a tremendous strain, produces exaggeration. Any world is better than an uncomfortable one in revolution, they think. They are, as a rule, sincere and honest folk. They add a touch of colour to the commonplace—"

"Tuppence coloured," murmured Devonham below his breath.

"And they believe so much in other worlds to conquer, other regions, bigger states of consciousness, other powers," concluded Fillery, ignoring the interruption, "that they are half in this world, half in the next. Hence Dr. Devonham's name, the name by which he sometimes laughs at them—of Half Breeds."

LeVallon's eyes, he saw, were very big; his interest and attention were excited.

"They will probably welcome you with open arms," he added, "if you care to join them. They consider themselves pioneers of a larger life. They are not mere spiritualists—oh no! They are familiar with all the newest theories, and realize that an alternative hypothesis can explain all so-called psychic phenomena without dragging spirits in. It is in exaggerating result, they go mostly wrong."

"Eccentrics," Devonham remarked, "out of the circle, and hysterical to a man. They accomplish nothing. They are invariably dreamers, usually of doubtful morals and honesty, and always unworthy of serious attention. But they may amuse you for an hour."

"We all find it difficult to believe what we have never experienced," mentioned Fillery, turning to his colleague with a hearty laugh, in which the latter readily joined, for their skirmishes usually brought in laughter at the end. Just now, moreover, they were talking with a purpose, and it was wise and good that LeVallon should listen and take in what he could—hearing both sides. He watched and listened certainly with open eyes and ears, as he sat between them on the wide front seat, but saying, as usual, very little.

The car turned down a narrow lane with slackening speed, and slowed up before a dingy building with faded Virginia creepers sprawling about stained dirty walls. The neighbourhood was depressing, patched and dishevelled, and almost bordering on a slum. The November light was passing into early twilight.

"You," said LeVallon abruptly, turning round and staring at Devonham, "make everything seem unreal to me. I do not understand you. You know so much. Why is so little real to you?"

But Devonham, in the act of getting out of the car, made no reply, and probably had not heard the words, or, if he had heard, thought them more suitable for Fillery.

CHAPTER XII

The Prometheans were evidently in full attendance; possibly the rumour had reached them that Dr. Fillery was coming. No one announced the latter's arrival, there was no servant visible; the party hung up their hats and coats in a passage, then walked into the lofty, dim-lit studio which was already filled with people and the hum of many voices.

At once, standing in a hesitating group beside the door, they were observed by everyone in the room. All asked, it seemed, "Who is this stranger they have brought?" Fillery caught the curious atmosphere in that first moment, an instant whiff, as it were, of excitement, interest, something picturesque, if possibly foolish, fantastic, too, yet faintly stimulating, breathing along his extremely sensitive nerves.

He glanced at his companions. Devonham, it struck him, looked more than ever like a floor-walker come to supervise, say, a Department where the sales and assistants were not satisfactory or—he laughed inwardly as the simile occurred to him—a free-thinker entering a church whose teaching he disapproved, even despised, and whose congregation touched his contemptuous pity. "Who would ever guess," thought his friend and colleague, "the sincerity and depth of knowledge in that insignificant appearance? Paul hides his value well!" He noticed, in his quick fashion, touched by humour, the hard challenging eyes, the aquiline nose on which a pair of pince-nez balanced uneasily, the narrow shoulders, the poorly fitting clothes. The heart, of course, remained invisible. Yet suddenly he felt glad that Devonham was with him. "Nothing unstable there," he reflected, "and stability combined with competence is rare." This rapid judgment, it occurred to him, was possibly a warning from his own subconscious being.... A red flag signalled, flickered, vanished.

He glanced next at LeVallon, towering above the other. LeVallon was now well dressed in London clothes that suited him, though, for that matter, any clothes must have looked well upon a male figure so virile and upstanding. His great shoulders, his leanness, covered so beautifully with muscle, his height, his colouring, his radiant air; above all, his strange, big penetrating eyes, marked him as a figure one would notice anywhere. He stood, somehow, alone, apart, though the ingredients that contributed to this strange air of aloofness would be hard to define.

It was chiefly, perhaps, the poise of the great powerful frame that helped towards this odd setting in isolation and independence. Motionless, he gazed about him quietly, but it was the way he stood that singled him out from other men. Even in his stillness there was grace; neither hands nor feet, though it was difficult to describe exactly how he placed them or used them, were separate from this poise of perfect balance. To put it colloquially, he knew what to do with his extremities. Self-consciousness, in sight of this ardent throng, the first he had encountered at close, intimate quarters, was entirely absent.

This Fillery noticed instantly, but other impressions followed during the few brief seconds while they waited by the door; and first, the odd effect of tremendous power he managed to convey. Nothing could have been less aggressive than the tentative, questioning, half inquiring, half wondering attitude in which he stood, waiting to be introduced to the buzzing throng of humans; yet there hung about him like an atmosphere this potential strength, of confidence, of superiority, even of beauty too, that not only contributed much to the aloofness already mentioned, but also contrived to make the others, men and women, in the crowded room—insignificant. Somehow they seemed pale and ineffective against a larger grandeur, a scale entirely beyond their reach.

"Gigantic" was the word that leaped into the mind, but another perhaps leaped with it—"elemental."

Fillery was aware of envy, oddly enough, of pride as well. His heart warmed more than ever to him. Almost, he could have then and there recalled his promise given to Devonham, cancelling it contemptuously with a word of self-apology for his smallness and his lack of faith....

LeVallon, aware of a sympathetic mind occupied closely with himself, turned in that moment, and their eyes met squarely; a smile of deep, inner understanding passed swiftly between them over Devonham's head and shoulders. In which moment, exactly, a short, bearded man, detaching himself from the crowd, came forward and greeted them with sincere pleasure in his voice and manner. He was broad-shouldered, lean, his clothes hung loosely; his glance was keen but kindly. Introductions followed, and Khilkoff's sharp eye rested for some seconds with unconcealed admiration upon LeVallon, as he held his hand. His discerning sculptor's glance seemed to appraise his stature and proportions, while he bade him welcome to the Studio. His big head and short neck, his mane of hair, the width of his face, with its squat nose and high cheek-bones, the half ferocious eyes, the heavy jaw and something sprawling about the mouth, gave him a leonine expression. And his voice was not unlike a deep-toned growl, for all its cordiality.

A stir, meanwhile, ran through the room, more heads turned in their direction; they had long ago been observed; they were being now examined.

"Nayan," Khilkoff was saying, while he still held LeVallon's hand as though its size and grip contented him, "had a late Russian lesson. She will be here shortly, and very glad to make your acquaintance," looking up at LeVallon, as the new-comer. His gruffness and brevity had something pleasing in them. "To-day the Studio is not entirely mine," he explained. "I want you to come when I'm alone. Some studies I made in Sark this summer may interest you." He turned to Fillery. "That lonely place was good for both of us," he said; "it gave me new life and inspiration, and Nayan benefited immensely too. She looks more like a nymph than ever."

He shook hands with Devonham, smiling more grimly. "I'm surprised you, too, have honoured us," he exclaimed with genuine surprise. "Come to damn them all as usual, probably! Good! Your common-sense and healthy criticism are needed in these days—cool, cleaning winds in an over-heated conservatory." He broke off abruptly and looked down at LeVallon's hand he was still holding. He examined it for a second with care and admiration, then turned his eye upon the young man's figure. He grunted.

"When I know you better," he said, with a growl of earnest meaning, "I shall ask a favour, a great favour, of you. So, beware!"

"Thank you," replied LeVallon, and at the sound of his voice the sculptor's interest deepened. A gleam shone in his eye.

"You've begun some work," said Fillery, "and models are hard to come by, I imagine." His eye never left LeVallon.

Khilkoff chuckled. "Thought-reader!" he exclaimed. "If Povey heard that, he'd make you join the Society at once—as honorary member or vice-president. Anything to get you in. Dr. Fillery understands us all *too* well," he went on to LeVallon. "In Sark, that lonely island in the sea, I began four figures—four elemental figures—of earth, air, fire and water—a group, of course. The air figure, I've done—"

"With Nayan as model," suggested Fillery, smiling.

"One morning, yes, I caught her bathing from a rock, hair streaming in the wind, no clothes on, white foam from the big breakers fluttering about her, slim, shining, unconscious and half dancing, fierce sunlight all over her. Ah"—he broke off—"here's Povey coming. I mustn't monopolize you all. Devonham, you know most of 'em. Make yourselves at home." He turned to LeVallon again, with a touch of something gentler, almost of respect, thought Fillery, as he noticed the delicate change of voice and manner quickly. "Come, Mr. LeVallon," he said courteously, "I should like to show you the figure as I've done it. We'll go for a moment into my own private rooms. But it's a model for fire I'm looking for, as Fillery guessed. You may be interested." He led him off. LeVallon went with evident content, and the advance of skirmishers that were already approaching for introductions was temporarily defeated.

For the three men standing by the door had formed a noticeable group, and Khilkoff's presence added to their value. Dr. Fillery, known and much respected, regarded with a touch of awe by many, had not come for nothing, it was doubtless argued; his colleague, moreover, accompanied him, and he, too, was known to the Society, though not much cultivated by its members owing to his downright, critical way of talking. They deemed him prejudiced, unsympathetic. It was the third member of the group, LeVallon, who had quickly caught all eyes, and the attention immediately paid to him by their host set the value of a special and important guest upon him instantly. All watched him led away by Khilkoff to the private quarters of the Studio, where none at first presumed to follow them; but it was the eyes of the women that remained glued to the open door where they had disappeared, waiting with careful interest for their reappearance. In particular Lady Gleeson, the "pretty Lady Gleeson," watched from the corner where she sat alone, sipping some refreshment.

Fillery and Devonham, having observed the signs about them, exchanged a glance; their charge was safe for the moment, at any rate; they felt relieved; yet it was for the entry of Nayan, the daughter, that both waited with interest and impatience, as, meanwhile, the bolder ones among the crowd came up one by one and captured them.

"Oh, Dr. Fillery, I *am* glad to see you here. I thought you were always too busy for unscientific people like us. Yet, in a way, we're all seekers, are we not? I've been reading your Physiology book, and I did so want to ask you about something in it. I wonder if you'd mind."

He shook hands with a young-old woman, wearing bobbed hair and glasses, and speaking with an intense, respectful, yet self-apologetic manner.

"You've forgotten me, but I *quite* understand. You see so many people. I'm Miss Lance. I sent you my little magazine, 'Simplicity,' once, and you acknowledged it *so* sweetly, though, of course, I understood you had not the time to write for it." She continued for several minutes, smiling up at him, her hands clasping and unclasping themselves behind a back clothed with some glittering coloured material that rather fascinated him by its sheen. She kept raising herself on her toes and sinking back again in a series of jerky rhythms.

He gave her his delightful smile.

"Oh, Dr. Fillery!" she exclaimed, with pleasure, leading him to a divan, upon which he let himself down in such a position that he could observe the door from the street as well as the door where LeVallon had disappeared. "This is really too good-natured of you. Your book set me on fire simply"—her eyes wandering to the other door—"and what a wonderful looking person you've brought with you—"

"I fear it's not very easy reading," he interposed patiently.

"To me it was too delightful for words," she rattled on, pleased by the compliment implied. "I devour *all* your books and always review them myself in the magazine. I wouldn't trust them to anyone else. I simply can't tell you how physiology stimulates me. Humanity needs imaginary books, especially just now." She broke off with a deprecatory smile. "I do what I can," she added, as he made no remark, "to make them known, though in such a very small way, I fear." Her interest, however, was divided, the two powerful attractions making her quite incoherent. "Your friend," she ventured again, "he must be Eastern perhaps? Or is that merely sunburn? He looks *most* unusual."

"Sunburn merely, Miss Lance. You must have a chat with him later."

"Oh, thank you, *thank* you, Dr. Fillery. I do so love unusual people...."

He listened gravely. He was gentle, while she confided to him her little inner hopes and dreams about the "simple life." She introduced adjectives she believed would sound correct, if spoken very quickly, until, between the torrent of "psychical," "physiological" and once or twice, "psychological," she became positively incoherent in a final entanglement from which there was no issue but a convulsive gesture. None the less, she was bathed in bliss. She monopolized the great man for a whole ten minutes on a divan where everybody could see that they talked earnestly, intimately, perhaps even intellectually, together side by side.

He observed the room, meanwhile, without her noticing it, scanning the buzzing throng with interest. There was confusion somewhere, something was lacking, no system prevailed; he was aware of a general sense of waiting for a leader. All looked, he knew, for Nayan to appear. Without her presence, there was no centre, for, though not a member of the Society herself, she was the heart always of their gatherings, without which they straggled somewhat aimlessly. And "heart," he remembered, with a smile that Miss Lance took proudly for herself, was the appropriate word. Nayan mothered them. They were but children, after all....

"When you talk of a 'New Age,' what *exactly* do you mean? I wish you'd define the term for me?" Devonham meanwhile was saying to an interlocutor, not far away, while with a corner of his eye he watched both Fillery and the private door. He still stood near the entrance, looking more than ever like a disapproving floor-walker in a big department store, and it was with H. Millington Povey that he talked, the Honorary Secretary of the Society. The Secretary had aimed at Fillery, but Miss Lance had been too quick for him. He was obliged to put up with Devonham as second best, and his temper suffered accordingly. He was in aggressive mood.

Povey, facing him, was talking with almost violent zeal. A small, thin, nervous man, on the verge of middle age, his head prematurely bald, with wildish tufts of patchy hair, a thin, scraggy neck that he lengthened and shortened between high hunched shoulders, Povey resembled an eager vulture. His keen bright eyes, hooked nose, and a habit of twisting head and neck apart from his body, which held motionless, increased this likeness to a bird of prey. Possessed of considerable powers of organization, he kept the Society together. It was he who insisted upon some special "psychic gift" as a qualification of membership; an applicant must prove this gift to a committee of Povey's choosing, though these proofs were never circulated for general reading in the Society's Reports. Talkers, dreamers, faddists were not desired; a member must possess some definite abnormal power before he could be elected. He must be clairvoyant or clairaudient, an automatic writer, trance-painter, medium, ghost-seer, prophet, priest or king.

Members, therefore, stated their special qualification to each other without false modesty: "I'm a trance medium," for instance; "Oh, really! *I* see auras, of course"; while others had written automatic poetry, spoken in trance—"inspirational speakers," that is—photographed a spirit, appeared to someone at a distance, or dreamed a prophetic dream that later had come true. Mediums, spirit-photographers, and prophetic dreamers were, perhaps, the most popular qualifications to offer, but there were many who remembered past lives and not a few could leave their bodies consciously at will.

Membership cost two guineas, the hat was occasionally passed round for special purposes, there was a monthly dinner in Soho, when members stood up, like saved sinners at a revivalist meeting, and gave personal testimony of conversion or related some new strange incident. The Prometheans were full of stolen fire and life.

Among them were ambitious souls who desired to start a new religion, deeming the Church past hope. Others, like the water-dowsers and telepathists, were humbler. There was an Inner Circle which sought to revive the Mysteries, and gave very private performances of dramatic and symbolic kind, based upon recovered secret knowledge, at the solstices and equinoxes. New Thought members despised these, believing nothing connected with the past had value; they looked ahead; "live in the present," "do it now" was their watchword. Astrologers were numerous too. These cast horoscopes, or, for a small fee, revealed one's secret name, true colour, lucky number, day of the week and month, and so forth. One lady had a tame "Elemental." Students of Magic and Casters of Spells, wearers of talismans and intricate designs in precious or inferior metal, according to taste and means, were well represented, and one and all believed, of course, in spirits.

None, however, belonged to any Sect of the day, whatever it might be; they wore no labels; they were seekers, questers, inquirers whom no set of rules or dogmas dared confine within fixed limits. An entirely open mind and no prejudices, they prided themselves, distinguished them.

"Define it in scientific terms, this New Age—I cannot," replied Povey in his shrill voice, "for science deals only with the examination of the known. Yet you only have to look round you at the world to-day to see its obvious signs. Humanity is changing, new powers everywhere—"

Devonham interrupted unkindly, before the other could assume he had proved something by merely stating it:

"What *are* these signs, if I may ask?" he questioned sharply. "For if you can name them, we can examine them—er—scientifically." He used the word with malice, knowing it was ever on the Promethean lips.

"There you are, at cross-purposes at once," declared Povey. "I refer to hints, half-lights, intuitions, signs that only the most sensitive among us, those with psychic divination, with spiritual discernment—that only the privileged and those developed in advance of the Race—can know. And, instantly you produce our microscope, as though I offered you the muscles of a tadpole to dissect."

They glared at one another. "We shall never get progress your way," Povey fumed, withdrawing his head and neck between his shoulders.

"Returning to the Middle Ages, on the other hand," mentioned Devonham, "seems like advancing in a circle, doesn't it?"

"Dr. Devonham," interrupted a pretty, fair-haired girl with an intense manner, "forgive me for breaking up your interesting talk, but you come so seldom, you know, and there's a lady here who is dying to be introduced. She has just seen crimson flashing in your aura, and she wants to ask—do you mind *very* much?" She smiled so sweetly at him, and at Mr. Povey, too, who was said to be engaged to her, though none believed it, that annoyance was not possible. "She says she simply must ask you if you were feeling anger. Anger, you know, produces red or crimson in one's visible atmosphere," she explained charmingly. She led him off, forgetting, however, her purpose *en route*, since they presently sat down side by side in a quiet corner and began to enjoy what seemed an interesting tête-à-tête, while the aura-seeing lady waited impatiently and observed them, without the aid of clairvoyance, from a distance.

"And *your* qualifications for membership?" asked Devonham. "I wonder if I may ask—?"

"But you'd laugh at me, if I told you," she answered simply, fingering a silver talisman that hung from her neck, a six-pointed star with zodiacal signs traced round a rose, *rosa mystica*, evidently. "I'm so afraid of doctors."

Devonham shook his head decidedly, asserting vehemently his interest, whereupon she told him her little private dream delightfully, without pose or affectation, yet shyly and so sincerely that he proved his assertion by a genuine interest.

"And does that protect you among your daily troubles?" he asked, pointing to her little silver talisman. He had already commented sympathetically upon her account of saving her new puppies from drowning, having dreamed the night before that she saw them gasping in a pail of water, the cruel under-gardener looking on. "Do you wear it always, or only on special occasions like this?"

"Oh, Miss Milligan made that," she told him, blushing a little. "She's rather poor. She earns her living by designing—"

"Oh!"

"But I don't mean *that*. She tells you your Sign and works it in metal for you. I bought one. Mine is Pisces." She became earnest. "I was born in Pisces, you see."

"And what does Pisces do for you? " he inquired, remembering the heightened colour. The sincerity of this Rose Mystica delighted him, and he already anticipated her reply with interest. Here, he felt, was the credulous, religious type in its naked purity, forced to believe in something marvellous.

"Well, if you wear your Sign next your skin it brings good luck—it makes the things you want happen." The blush reappeared becomingly. She did not lower her eyes.

"Have your things happened then?"

She hesitated. "Well, I've had an awfully good time ever since I wore it—"

"Proposals?" he asked gently.

"Dr. Devonham!" she exclaimed. "How ever did you guess?" She looked very charming in her innocent confusion.

He laughed. "If you don't take it off at once," he told her solemnly, "you may get another."

"It was two in a single week," she confided a little tremulously. "Fancy!"

"The important thing, then," he suggested, "is to wear your talisman at the right moment, and with the right person."

But she corrected him promptly.

"Oh, no. It brings the right moment and the right person together, don't you see, and if the other person is a Pisces person, you understand each other, of course, at once."

"Would that I too were Pisces!" he exclaimed, seeing that she was flattered by his interest. "I'm probably—"taking a sign at random—"Scorpio."

"No," she said with, grave disappointment, "I'm afraid you're Capricornus,

you know. I can tell by your nose and eyes—and cleverness. But—I wanted really to ask you," she went on half shyly, "if I might—" She stuck fast.

"You want to know," he said, lancing at her with quick understanding,
"who *he* is." He pointed to the door. "Isn't that it?"

She nodded her head, while a divine little blush spread over her face. Devonham became more interested. "Why?" he asked. "Did he impress you so?"

"*Rather*," she replied with emphasis, and there was something in her earnestness curiously convincing. A sincere impression had been registered.

"His appearance, you mean?"

She nodded again; the blush deepened; but it was not, he saw, an ordinary
blush. The sensitive young girl had awe in her. "He's a friend of Dr. Fillery's,"
he told her; "a young man who's lived in the wilds all his life. But, tell me—
why are you so interested? Did he make any particular impression on you?"

He watched her. His own thoughts dropped back suddenly to a strange memory of woods and mountains... a sunset, a blazing fire... a hint of panic.

"Yes," she said, her tone lower, "he did."

"Something *very* definite?"

She made no answer.

"What did you see?" he persisted gently. From woods and mountains, memory stepped back to a railway station and a customs official....

Her manner, obviously truthful, had deep wonder, mystery, even worship in
it. He was aware of a nervous reaction he disliked, almost a chill. He listened for
her next words with an interest he could hardly account for.

"'Wings," she replied, an odd hush in her voice. "I thought of wings. He
seemed to carry me off the earth with great rushing wings, as the wind blows
a leaf. It was too lovely: I felt like a dancing flame. I thought he was—"

"What?" Something in his mind held its breath a moment.

"You *won't* laugh, Dr. Devonham, will you? I thought—for a second—of—
an angel." Her voice died away.

For a second the part of his mood that held its breath struggled between anger
and laughter. A moment's confusion in him there certainly was.

"That makes two in the room," he said gently, recovering himself. He smiled.
But she did not hear the playful compliment; she did not see the smile. "You've
a delightful, poetic little soul," he added under his breath, watching the big
earnest eyes whose rapt expression met his own so honestly. Having made her
confession she was still engrossed, absorbed, he saw, in her own emotion.... So
this was the picture that LeVallon, by his mere appearance alone, left upon an
impressionable young girl, an impression, he realized, that was profound and true
and absolute, whatever value her own individual interpretation of it might have.
Her mention of space, wind, fire, speed, he noticed in particular—"off the
earth... rushing wind... dancing flame... an angel!"

It was easy, of course, to jeer. Yet, somehow, he did not jeer at all.

She relapsed into silence, which proved how great had been the emotional discharge accompanying the confession, temporarily exhausting her. Dr. Devonham
keenly registered the small, important details.

"Entertaining an angel unawares in a Chelsea studio," he said, laughingly; then reminding her presently that there was a lady who was "dying to be introduced" to him, made his escape, and for the next ten minutes found himself listening to a disquisition on auras which described "visible atmospheres whose colour changes with emotion... radio-activity... the halo worn by saints"... the effect of light noticed about very good people and of blackness that the wicked emanated, and ending up with the "radiant atmosphere that shone round the figure of Christ and was believed to show the most lovely and complicated geometrical designs."

"God geometrizes—you, doubtless, know the ancient saying?" Mrs. Towzer said it like a challenge.

"I have heard it," admitted her listener shortly, his first opportunity of making himself audible. "Plato said some other fine things too —"

"I felt sure you were feeling cross just now," the lady went on, "because I saw lines and arrows of crimson darting and flashing through your aura while you were talking to Mr. Povey. He is very annoying sometimes, isn't he? I often wonder where all our subscriptions go to. I never could understand a balance-sheet. Can you?"

But Devonham, having noticed Dr. Fillery moving across the room, did not answer, even if he heard the question. Fillery, he saw, was now standing near the door where Khilkoff and LeVallon had disappeared to see the sculpture, an oddly rapt expression on his face. He was talking with a member called Father Collins. The buzz of voices, the incessant kaleidoscope of colour and moving figures, made the atmosphere a little electric. Extricating himself with a neat excuse, he crossed towards his colleague, but the latter was already surrounded before he reached him. A forest of coloured scarves, odd coiffures, gleaming talismans, intervened; he saw men's faces of intense, eager, preoccupied expression, old and young, long hair and bald; there was a new perfume in the air, incense evidently; tea, coffee, lemonade were being served, with stronger drink for the few who liked it, and cigarettes were everywhere. The note everywhere was *exalté* rather.

Out of the excited throng his eyes then by chance, apparently, picked up the figure of Lady Gleeson, smoking her cigarette alone in a big armchair, a half-empty glass of wine-cup beside her. She caught his attention instantly, this "pretty Lady Gleeson," although personally he found neither title nor adjective justified. The dark hair framed a very white skin. The face was shallow, trivial, yet with a direct intensity in the shining eyes that won for her the reputation of being attractive to certain men. Her smile added to the notoriety she loved, a curious smile that lifted the lip oddly, showing the little pointed teeth. To him, it seemed somehow a face that had been over-kissed; everything had been kissed out of it; the mouth, the lips, were worn and barren in an appearance otherwise still young. She was very expensively dressed, and deemed her legs of such symmetry that it were a shame to hide them; clad in tight silk stockings, and looking like strips of polished steel, they were now visible almost to the knee, where the edge of the skirt, neatly trimmed in fur, cut them off sharply.

Some wag in the Society, paraphrasing the syllables of her name, wittily if un-kindly, had christened her *fille de joie*. When she heard it she was rather pleased than otherwise.

Lady Gleeson, too, he saw now, was watching the private door. The same mo-ment, as so often occurred between himself and his colleague at some significant point in time and space, he was aware of Fillery's eye upon his own across the intervening heads and shoulders. Fillery, also, had noticed that Lady Gleeson watched that door. His changed position in the room was partly explained.

A slightly cynical smile touched Dr. Devonham's lips, but vanished again quickly, as he approached the lady, bowed politely, and asked if he might bring her some refreshment. He was too discerning to say "more" refreshment. But she dotted every i, she had no half tones.

"Thanks, kind Dr. Devonham," she said in a decided tone, her voice thin, a trifle husky, yet not entirely unmusical. It held a strange throaty quality. "It's so absurdly light," she added, holding out the glass she first emptied. "The mys-tics don't hold with anything strong apparently. But I'm tired, and you dis-covered it. That's clever of you. It'll do me good."

He, malevolently, assured her that it would.

"Who's your friend?" she asked point blank, with an air that meant to have a proper answer, as he brought the glass and took a chair near her. "He looks un-usual. More like a hurdle-race champion than a visionary." A sneer lurked in the voice. She fixed her determined clear grey eyes upon him, eyes sparkling with interest, curiosity in life, desire, the last-named quality of unmistakable kind. "I think I should like to know him perhaps." It was mentioned as a favour to the other.

Devonham, who disliked and disapproved of all these people collectively, felt angry suddenly with Fillery for having brought LeVallon among them. It was after all a foolish experiment; the atmosphere was dangerous for anyone of un-stable, possibly of hysterical temperament. He had vengeance to discharge. He answered with deliberate malice, leading her on that he might watch her reac-tions. She was so transparently sincere.

"I hardly think Mr. LeVallon would interest you," he said lightly. "He is nei-ther modern nor educated. He has spent his life in the backwoods, and knows nothing but plants and stars and weather and—animals. You would find him dull."

"No man with a face and figure like that can be dull," she said quickly, her eyes alight.

He glanced at her rings, the jewelry round her neck, her expensive gown that would keep a patient for a year or two. He remembered her millionaire South African husband who was her foolish slave. She lived, he knew entirely for her own small, selfish pleasure. Although he meant to use her, his gorge rose. He produced his happiest smile.

"You are a keen observer, Lady Gleeson," he remarked. "He doesn't look quite ordinary, I admit." After a pause he added, "It's a curious thing, but Mr. LeV-allon doesn't care for the charms that we other men succumb to so easily. He seems indifferent. What he wants is knowledge only.... Apparently he's more interested in stars than in girls."

"Rubbish," she rejoined. "He hasn't met any in his woods, that's all."

Her directness rather disconcerted him. At the same time, it charmed him a little, though he did not know it. His dislike of the woman, however, remained. The idle, self-centred rich annoyed him. They were so useless. The fabulous jewelry hanging upon such trash now stirred his bile. He was conscious of the lust for pleasure in her.

"Yet, after all, he's rather an interesting fellow perhaps," he told her, as with an air of sudden enthusiasm. "Do you know, he talks of rather wonderful things, too. Mere dreams, of course, yet, for all that, out of the ordinary. He has vague memories, it seems, of another state of existence altogether. He speaks sometimes of—of marvellous women, compared to whom our women here, our little dressed-up dolls, seem commonplace and insignificant." And, to his keen enjoyment, Lady Gleeson took the bait with open mouth. She recrossed her shapely legs. She wriggled a little in her chair. Her be-ringed fingers began fidgeting along the priceless necklace.

"Just what I should expect," she replied in her throaty voice, "from a young man who looks as he does."

She began to play her own cards then, mentioning that her husband was interested in Dr. Fillery's Clinique. Devonham, however, at once headed her off. He described the work of the Home with enthusiasm. "It's fortunate that Dr. Fillery is rich," he observed carelessly, "and can follow out his own ideas exactly as he likes. I, personally, should never have joined him had he been dependent upon the mere philanthropist."

"How wise of you," she returned. "And I should never have joined this mad Society but for the chance of coming across unusual people. Now, your Mr. LeVallon is one. You may introduce him to me," she repeated as an ultimatum.

Her directness was the one thing he admired in her. At her own level, she was real. He was aware of the semi-erotic atmosphere about these Meetings and realized that Lady Gleeson came in search of excitement, also that she was too sincere to hide it. She wore her insignia unconcealed. Her talisman was of base metal, the one cheap thing she wore, yet real. This foolish woman, after all, might be of use unwittingly. She might capture LeVallon, if only for a moment, before Nayan Khilkoff enchanted him with that wondrous sweetness to which no man could remain indifferent. For he had long ago divined the natural, unspoken passion between his Chief and the daughter of his host, and with his whole heart he desired to advance it.

"My husband, too, would like to meet him, I'm sure," he heard her saying, while he smiled at the reappearance of the gilded bait. "My husband, you know, is interested in spirit photography and Dr. Frood's unconscious theories."

He rose, without even a smile. "I'll try and find him at once," he said, "and bring him to you. I only hope," he added as an afterthought, "that Miss Khilkoff hasn't monopolized him already—"

"She hasn't come," Lady Gleeson betrayed herself. Instinctively she knew her rival, he saw, with an inward chuckle, as he rose to fetch the desired male.

He found him the centre of a little group just inside the door leading into the sculptor's private studio, where Khilkoff had evidently been showing his new group of elemental figures. Fillery, a few feet away, observing everything at close range, was still talking eagerly with Father Collins. LeVallon and Kempster, the pacifist, were in the middle of an earnest talk, of which Devonham caught an interesting fragment. Kempster's qualification for membership was an occasional display of telepathy. He was a neat little man exceedingly well dressed, over-dressed in fact, for his tailor's dummy appearance betrayed that he thought too much about his personal appearance. LeVallon, towering over him like some flaming giant, spoke quietly, but with rare good sense, it seemed. Fillery's con-densed education had worked wonders on his mind. Devonham was astonished. About the pair others had collected, listening, sometimes interjecting opinions of their own, many women among them, leaning against the furniture or sitting on cushions and movable, dump-like divans on the floor. It was a picturesque little scene. But LeVallon somehow dwarfed the others.

"I really think," Kempster was saying, "we might now become a comfortable little third-rate Power—like Spain, for instance—enjoy ourselves a bit, live on our splendid past, and take the sun in ease." He looked about him with a self-satisfied smirk, as though he had himself played a fine rôle in the splendid past.

LeVallon's reply surprised him perhaps, but it surprised Devonham still more. The real, the central self, LeVallon, he thought with satisfaction, was wak-ing and developing. His choice of words was odd too.

"No, no! You—the English—are the leaders of the world; the best quality is in you. If you give up, the world goes down and backwards." The deep, musi-cal tones vibrated through the little room. The speaker, though so quiet, had the air of a powerful athlete, ready to strike. His poise was admirable. Faces turned up and stared. There was a murmur of approval.

"We're so tired of that talk," replied Kempster, no whit disconcerted by the evident signs of his unpopularity. "Each race should take its turn. We've borne the white man's burden long enough. Why not drop it, and let another nation do its bit? We've earned a rest, I think." His precise, high voice was persuasive. He was a good public speaker, wholly impervious to another point of view. But the resonant tones of LeVallon's rejoinder seemed to bury him, voice, exquisite clothes and all.

"There is no other—unless you hand it back to weaker shoulders. No other race has the qualities of generosity, of big careless courage of the unselfish kind required. Above all, you alone have the chivalry."

Two things Devonham noted as he heard: behind the natural resonance in the big voice lay a curious deepness that made him think of thunder, a volume of sound suppressed, potential, roaring, which, if let loose, might overwhelm, sub-merge. It belonged to an earnestness as yet unsuspected in him, a strength of conviction based on a great purpose that was evidently subconscious in him, as though he served it, belonged to it, without realizing that he did so. He stood there like some new young prophet, proclaiming a message not entirely his own.

Also he said "you" in place of the natural "we."

Devonham listened attentively. Here, too, at any rate, was an exchange of ideas above the "psychic" level he so disliked.

LeVallon, he noticed at once, showed no evidence of emotion, though his eyes shone brightly and his voice was earnest.

"America—" began Kempster, but was knocked down by a fact before he could continue.

"Has deliberately made itself a Province again. America saw the ideal, then drew back, afraid. It is once more provincial, cut off from the planet, a big island again, concerned with local affairs of its own. Your Democracy has failed."

"As it always must," put in Kempster, glad perhaps to shift the point, when he found no ready answer. "The wider the circle from which statesmen are drawn, the lower the level of ability. We should be patriotic for ideas, not for places. The success of one country means the downfall of another. That's not spiritual...." He continued at high speed, but Devonham missed the words. He was too preoccupied with the other's language, penetration, point of view. LeVallon had, indeed, progressed. There was nothing of the alternative personality in this, nothing of the wild, strange, nature-being whom he called "N. H."

"Patriotism, of course, is vulgar rubbish," he heard Kempster finishing his tirade. "It is local, provincial. The world is a whole."

But LeVallon did not let him escape so easily. It was admirable really. This half-educated countryman from the woods and mountains had a clear, concentrated mind. He had risen too. Whence came his comprehensive outlook?

"Chivalry—you call it sporting instinct—is the first essential of a race that is to lead the world. It is a topmost quality. Your race has it. It has come down even into your play. It is instinctive in you more than any other. And chivalry is unselfish. It is divine. You have conquered the sun. The hot races all obey you."

The thunder broke through the strange but simple words which, in that voice, and with that quiet earnestness, carried some weight of meaning in them that print cannot convey. The women gazed at him with unconcealed, if not with understanding admiration. "Lead us, inspire us, at any rate!" their eyes said plainly; "but love us, O love us, passionately, above all!"

Devonham, hardly able to believe his ears and eyes, turned to see if Fillery had heard the scrap of talk. Judging by the expression on his face, he had not heard it. Father Collins seemed saying things that held his attention too closely. Yet Fillery, for all his apparent absorption, had heard it, though he read it otherwise than his somewhat literal colleague. It was, nevertheless, an interesting revelation to him, since it proved to him again how unreal "LeVallon" was; how easily, quickly this educated simulacrum caught up, assimilated and reproduced as his own, yet honestly, whatever was in the air at the moment. For the words he had spoken were not his own, but Fillery's. They lay, or something like them lay, unuttered in Fillery's mind just at that very moment. Yet, even while listening attentively to Father Collins, his close interest in LeVallon was so keen, so watchful, that another portion of his mind was listening to this second conversation, even taking part in it inaudibly. LeVallon caught his language from the air....

Devonham made his opportunity, leading LeVallon off to be introduced to Lady Gleeson, who still sat waiting for them on the divan in the outer studio.

As they made their way through the buzzing throng into the larger room, Devonham guessed suddenly that Lady Gleeson must somehow have heard in advance that LeVallon would be present; her flair for new men was singular; the sexual instinct, unduly developed, seemed aware of its prey anywhere within a big radius. He owed his friend a hint of guidance possibly. "A little woman," he explained as they crossed over, "who has a weakness for big men and will probably pay you compliments. She comes here to amuse herself with what she calls 'the freaks.' Sometimes she lends her great house for the meetings. Her husband's a millionaire." To which the other, in his deep, quiet voice, replied: "Thank you, Dr. Devonham."

"She's known as 'the pretty Lady Gleeson.' "

"That?" exclaimed the other, looking towards her.

"Hush!" his companion warned him.

As they approached, Lady Gleeson, waiting with keen impatience, saw them coming and made her preparations. The frown of annoyance at the long delay was replaced by a smile of welcome that lifted the upper lip on one side only, showing the white even teeth with odd effect. She stared at LeVallon, thought Devonham, as a wolf eyes its prey. Deftly lowering her dress—betraying thereby that she knew it was too high, and a detail now best omitted from the picture—she half rose from her seat as they came up. The instinctive act of deference, though instantly corrected, did not escape Paul Devonham's too observant eye.

"You were kind enough to say I might introduce my friend," murmured he. "Mr. LeVallon is new to our big London, and a stranger among all these people."

LeVallon bowed in his calm, dignified fashion, saying no word, but Lady Gleeson put her hand out, and, finding his own, shook it with her air of brilliant welcome. Determination lay in her smile and in her gesture, in her voice as well, as she said familiarly at once: "But, Mr. LeVallon, how tall *are* you, really? You seem to me a perfect giant." She made room for him beside her on the divan. "Everybody here looks undersized beside you!" She became intense.

"I am six feet and three inches," he replied literally, but without expression in his face. There was no smile. He was examining her as frankly as she examined him. Devonham was examining the pair of them. The lack of interest, the cold indifference in LeVallon, he reflected, must put the young woman on her mettle, accustomed as she was to quick submission in her victims.

LeVallon, however, did not accept the offered seat; perhaps he had not noticed the invitation. He showed no interest, though polite and gentle.

"He towers over all of us," Devonham put in, to help an awkward pause. Yet he meant it more than literally; the empty prettiness of the   shallow little face before him, the triviality of Miss Rosa Mystica, the cheapness of Povey, Kempster, Mrs. Towzer, the foolish air of otherworldly expectancy in the whole room, of deliberate exaggeration, of eyes big with wonder for sensation as story followed story—all this came upon him with its note of poverty and tawdriness as he used the words.

Something in the atmosphere of LeVallon had this effect—whence did it come? he questioned, puzzled—of dwarfing all about him.

"All London, remember, isn't like this," he heard Lady Gleeson saying, a dangerous purr audible in the throaty voice. "Do sit down here and tell me what you think about it. I feel you don't belong here quite, do you now? London cramps you, doesn't it? And you find the women dull and insipid?" She deliberately made more room, patting the cushions invitingly with a flashing hand, that alone, thought Devonham contemptuously, could have endowed at least two big Cliniques. "Tell me about yourself, Mr. LeVallon. I'm dying to hear about your life in the woods and mountains. Do talk to me. I *am* so bored!"

What followed surprised Devonham more than any of the three perhaps. He ascribed it to what Fillery had called the "natural gentleman," while Lady Gleeson, doubtless, ascribed it to her own personal witchery.

With that easy grace of his he sat down instantly beside her on the low divan, his height and big frame contriving the awkward movement without a sign of clumsiness. His indifference was obvious—to Devonham, but the vain eyes of the woman did not notice it.

"That's better," she again welcomed him with a happy laugh. She edged closer a little. "Now, do make yourself comfortable"—she arranged the cushions again—"and please tell me about your wild life in the forest, or wherever it was. You know a lot about the stars, I hear." She devoured his face and figure with her shining eyes.

The upper lip was lifted for a second above a gleaming tooth. Devonham had the feeling she was about to eat him, licking her lips already in anticipation. He himself would be dismissed, he well knew, in another moment, for Lady Gleeson would not tolerate a third person at the meal. Before he was sent about his business, however, he had the good fortune to hear LeVallon's opening answer to the foolish invitation. Amazement filled him. He wished Fillery could have heard it with him, seen the play of expression on the faces too—the bewilderment of sensational hunger for something new in Lady Gleeson's staring eyes, arrested instantaneously; the calm cold look of power, yet power tempered by a touch of pity, in LeVallon's glance, a glance that was only barely aware of her proximity. He smiled as he spoke, and the smile increased his natural radiance. He looked extraordinarily handsome, yet with a new touch of strangeness that held even the cautious doctor momentarily almost spellbound.

"Stars—yes, but I rarely see them here in London, and they seem so far away. They comfort me. They bring me—they and women bring me—nearest to a condition that is gone from me. I have lost it." He looked straight into her face, so that she blinked and screwed up her eyes, while her breathing came more rapidly. "But stars and women," he went on, his voice vibrating with music in spite of its quietness, "remind me that it is recoverable. Both give me this sweet message. I read it in stars and in the eyes of women. And it is true because no words convey it. For women cannot express themselves, I see; and stars, too, are silent—here."

The same soft thunder as before sounded below the gently spoken words; Lady Gleeson was trembling a little; she made a movement by means of which she shifted herself yet nearer to her companion in what seemed a natural and unconscious way. It was doubtless his proximity rather than his words that stirred her. Her face was set, though the lips quivered a trifle and the voice was less shrill than usual as she spoke, holding out her empty glass.

"Thank you, Dr. Devonham," she said icily.

The determined gesture, a toss of the head, with the glare of sharp impatience in the eyes, he could not ignore; yet he accepted his curt dismissal slowly enough to catch her murmured words to LeVallon:

"How wonderful! How wonderful you are! And what sort of women...?" followed him as he moved away. In his heart rose again an uncomfortable memory of a Jura valley blazing in the sunset, and of a half-naked figure worshipping before a great wood fire on the rocks.

He fancied he caught, too, in the voice, a suggestion of a lilt, a chanting resonance, that increased his uneasiness further. One thing was certain: it was not quite the ordinary "LeVallon" that answered the silly woman. The reaction was of a different kind. Was, then, the other self awake and stirring? Was it "N. H." after all, as his colleague claimed?

Allowing a considerable interval to pass, he returned with a glass—of lemonade—reaching the divan in its dimlit corner just in time to see a flashing hand withdrawn quickly from LeVallon's arm, and to intercept a glance that told him the intrigue evidently had not developed altogether according to Lady Gleeson's plan, although her air was one of confidence and keenest self-satisfaction. LeVallon sat like a marble figure, cold, indifferent, looking straight before him, listening, if only with half an ear, to a stream of words whose import it was not difficult to guess.

This Devonham's practised eye read in the flashing look she shot at him, and in the quick way she thanked him.

"Coffee, dear Dr. Devonham, I asked for."

Her move was so quick, his desire to watch them a moment longer together so keen, that for an instant he appeared to hesitate. It was more than appearance; he did hesitate—an instant merely, yet long enough for Lady Gleeson to shoot at him a second swift glance of concentrated virulence, and also long enough for LeVallon to spring lightly to his feet, take the glass from his hand, and vanish in the direction of the refreshment table before anything could prevent. "I will get your coffee for you," still sounded in the air, so quickly was the adroit manoeuvre executed. LeVallon had cleverly escaped.

"How stupid of me," said Devonham quickly, referring to the pretended mistake. Lady Gleeson made no reply. Her inward fury betrayed itself, however, in the tight-set lips and the hard glitter of her brilliant little eyes. "He won't be a moment," the other added. "Do you find him interesting? He's not very talkative as a rule, but perhaps with you—" He hardly knew what words he used.

The look she gave him stopped him, so intense was the bitterness in the eyes. His interruption, then, must indeed have been worse—or better?—timed than he had imagined. She made no pretence of speaking. Turning her glance in the direction whence the coffee must presently appear, she waited, and Devonham might have been a dummy for all the sign she gave of his being there. He had made an enemy for life, he felt, a feeling confirmed by what almost immediately then followed. Neither the coffee nor its hearer came that evening to pretty Lady Gleeson in the way she had desired. She laid the blame at Devonham's door.

For at that moment, as he stood before her, secretly enjoying her anger a lit-tle, yet feeling foolish, perhaps, as well, a chord sounded on the piano, and a hush passed instantly over the entire room. Someone was about to sing. Nayan Khilkoff had come in, unnoticed, by the door of the private room. Her singing invariably formed a part of these entertainments. The song, too, was the one in-variably asked for, its music written by herself.

All talk and movement stopped at the sound of the little prelude, as though a tap had been turned off. Even Devonham, most unmusical of men, prepared to listen with enjoyment. He tried to see Nayan at the piano, but too many peo-ple came between. He saw, instead, LeVallon standing close at his side, the cup of coffee in his hand. He had that instant returned.

"For Lady Gleeson. Will you pass it to her? Who's going to sing?" he whis-pered all in the same breath. And Devonham told him, as he bent down to give the cup. "Nayan Khilkoff. Hush! It's a lovely song. I know it—'The Vagrant's Epitaph.'"

They stood motionless to listen, as the pure voice of the girl, singing very sim-ply but with the sweetness and truth of sincere feeling, filled the room. Every word, too, was clearly audible:

"Change was his mistress; Chance his counsellor.
  Love could not hold him; Duty forged no chain.
The wide seas and the mountains called him,
  And grey dawns saw his camp-fires in the rain.

"Sweet hands might tremble!—aye, but he must go.
  Revel might hold him for a little space;
But, turning past the laughter and the lamps,
  His eyes must ever catch the luring Face.

"Dear eyes might question! Yea, and melt again;
  Rare lips a-quiver, silently implore;
But he must ever turn his furtive head,
  And hear that other summons at the door.

"Change was his mistress; Chance his counsellor.
  The dark firs knew his whistle up the trail.

Why tarries he to-day?... And yesternight
Adventure lit her stars without avail."

CHAPTER XIII

L ady Gleeson, owing to an outraged vanity and jealousy she was unable
to control, missed the final scene, for before the song was actually finished
she was gone. Being near a passage that was draped only by a curtain, she
slipped out easily, flung herself into a luxurious motor, and vanished into the
bleak autumn night.

She had seen enough. Her little heart raged with selfish fury. What followed
was told her later by word of mouth.

Never could she forgive herself that she had left the studio before the thing
had happened. She blamed Devonham for that too.

For LeVallon, it appears, having passed the cup of coffee to her through a third
person—in itself an insult of indifference and neglect—stood absorbed in the
words and music of the song. Being head and shoulders above the throng, he easily saw the girl at the piano. No one, unless it was Fillery, a few yards away,
watched him as closely as did Devonham and Lady Gleeson, though all three for
different reasons. It was Devonham, however, who made the most accurate note
of what he saw, though Fillery's memory was possibly the truer, since his own
inner being supplied the fuller and more sympathetic interpretation.

LeVallon, tall and poised, stood there like a great figure shaped in bronze. He
was very calm. His bright hair seemed to rise a little; his eyes, steady and
wondering, gazed fixedly; his features, though set, were mobile in the sense that
any instant they might leap into the alive and fluid expression of some strong
emotion. His whole being, in a word, stood at attention, alert for instant action
of some uncontrollable, perhaps terrific kind. "He seemed like a glowing pillar
of metal that must burst into flame the very next instant," as a Member told
Lady Gleeson later.

Devonham watched him. LeVallon seemed transfixed. He stared above the intervening tousled heads. He drew a series of deep breaths that squared his shoulders and made his chest expand. His very muscles ached apparently for instant
action. An intensity of wondering joy and admiration that lit his face made the
eyes shine like stars. He watched the singing girl as a tiger watches the keeper
who brings its long-expected food. The instant the bar is tip, it springs, it leaps,
it carries off, devours. Only, in this case, there were no bars. Nor was the wild
desire for nourishment of a carnal kind. It was companionship, it was intercourse
with his own that he desired so intensely.

"He divines the motherhood in her," thought Fillery, watching closely, pain
and happiness mingled in his heart. "The protective, selfless, upbuilding power
lies close to Nature." And as this flashed across him he caught a glimpse by
chance of its exact opposite—in Lady Gleeson's peering, glittering eyes—the

destructive lust, the selfish passion, the bird of prey.

"*The dark firs knew his whistle up the trail*," the song in that soft true voice drew to its close. LeVallon was trembling.

"Good Heavens!" thought Devonham. "Is it 'N. H.? Is it 'N. H.,' after all, waking—rising to take possession? " He, too, trembled.

It was here that Lady Gleeson, close, intuitive observer of her escaping prey, rose up and slipped away, her going hardly noticed by the half-entranced, half-dreaming hearts about her, each intent upon its own small heaven of neat desire. She went as unobtrusively as an animal that is aware of untoward conditions and surroundings, showing her teeth, feeling her claws, yet knowing herself helpless. Not even Devonham, his mind ever keenly alert, observed her going. Fillery, alone, conscious of LeVallon's eyes across the room, took note of it. She left, her violent little will intent upon vengeance of a later victory that she still promised herself with concentrated passion.

Yet Devonham, though he failed to notice the slim animal of prey in exit, noticed this—that the face he watched so closely changed quickly even as he watched, and that the new expression, growing upon it as heat grows upon metal set in a flame, was an expression he had seen before. He had seen it in that lonely mountain valley where a setting sun poured gold upon a burning pyre, upon a dancing, chanting figure, upon a human face he now watched in this ridiculous little Chelsea studio. The sharpness of the air, the very perfume, stole over him as he stared, perplexed, excited and uneasy. That strange, wild, innocent and tender face, that power, that infinite yearning! LeVallon had disappeared. It was "N. H." that stood and watched the singer at the little modern piano.

Then with the end of the song came the rush, the bustle of applause, the confusion of many people rising, trotting forward, all talking at once, all moving towards the singer—when LeVallon, hitherto motionless as a statue, suddenly leaped past and through them like a vehement wind through a whirl of crackling dead leaves. Only his deft, skillful movement, of poise and perfect balance combined with accurate swiftness, could have managed it without bruised bodies and angry cries. There was no clumsiness, no visible effort, no appearance of undue speed. He seemed to move quietly, though he moved like fire. In a moment he was by the piano, and Nayan, in the act of rising from her stool, gazed straight up into his great lighted eyes.

It was singular how all made way for him, drew back, looked on. Confusion threatened. Emotion surged like a rising sea. Without a leader there might easily have been tumult; even a scene. But Fillery was there. His figure intervened at once.

"Nayan," he said in a steady voice, "this is my friend, Mr. LeVallon. He wants to thank you."

But, before she could answer, LeVallon, his hand upon her arm, said quickly, yet so quietly that few heard the actual words, perhaps—his voice resonant, his eyes alight with joy: "You are here too—with me, with Fillery. We are all exiles together. But you know the way out—the way back! You remember!..."

She stared with delicious wonder into his eyes as he went on:

"O star and woman! Your voice is wind and fire. Come!" And he tried to seize
her. "We will go back together. We work here in vain!..." His arms were round
her; almost their faces touched.

The girl rose instantly, took a step towards him, then hung back; the stool fell
over with a crash; a hubbub of voices rose in the room behind; Povey, Kempster, a dozen Members with them, pressed up; the women, with half-shocked,
half-frightened eyes, gaped and gasped over the forest of intervening male
shoulders. A universal shuffle followed. The confusion was absurd and futile.
Both male and female stood aghast and stupid before what they saw, for behind
the mere words and gestures there was something that filled the little scene with
a strange shaking power, touching the panic sense.

LeVallon lifted her across his shoulders.

The beautiful girl was radiant, the man wore the sudden semblance of a god.
Their very stature increased. They stood alone. Yet Fillery, close by, stood with
them. There seemed a magic circle none dared cross about the three. Something
immense, unearthly, had come in the room, bursting its little space. Even Devonham, breaking with vehemence through the human ring, came to a sudden
halt.

In a voice of thunder—though it was not actually loud—LeVallon cried:

"Their little personal loves! They cannot understand!" He bore Nayan in his
arms as wind might lift a loose flower and whirl it aloft. "Come back with me,
come home! The Sun forgets us here, the Wind is silent. There is no Fire. Our
work, our service calls us." He turned to Fillery. "You too. Come!"

His voice boomed like a thundering wind against the astonished frightened
faces staring at him. It rose to a cry of intense emotion: "We are in little exile
here! In our wrong place, cut off from the service of our gods! We will go back!"
He started, with the girl flung across his frame. He took one stride. The others
shuffled back with one accord.

"*The other summons at the door.* But, Edward!—you—you too!"

It was Nayan's voice, as the girl clung willingly to the great neck and arms,
the voice of the girl all loved and worshipped and thought wonderful beyond
temptation; it was this familiar sound that ran through the bewildered, startled
throng like an electric shock. They could not believe their eyes, their ears. They
stood transfixed.

Within their circle stood LeVallon, holding the girl, almost embracing her,
while she lay helpless with happiness upon his huge enfolding arms. He paused,
looked round at Fillery a moment. None dared approach. The men gazed, wondering, and with faculties arrested; the women stared, stock still, with beating
hearts. All felt a lifting, splendid wonder they could not understand. Devonham, mute and motionless before an inexplicable thing, found himself bereft of
judgment. Analysis and precedent, for once, both failed. He looked round in vain
for Khilkoff.

Fillery alone seemed master of himself, a look of suffering and joy shone in his
face; one hand lay steady upon LeVallon's arm.

Within the little circle these three figures formed a definite group, filling the beholders, for the first time in their so-called "psychic" experience, with the thrill of something utterly beyond their ken—something genuine at last. For there seemed about the group, though emanating, as with shining power, from the figure of LeVallon chiefly, some radiating force, some elemental vigour they could not comprehend. Its presence made the scene possible, even right.

"Edward—you too! What is it, O, what is it? There are flowers—great winds! I see the fire—!"

A searching tenderness in her tone broke almost beyond the limits of the known human voice.

There swept over the onlookers a wave of incredible emotion then, as they saw LeVallon move towards them, as though he would pass through them and escape. He seemed in that moment stupendous, irresistible. He looked divine. The girl lay in his arms like some young radiant child. He did not kiss her, no sign of a caress was seen; he did no ordinary, human thing. His towering figure, carrying his burden almost negligently, came out of the circle "like a tide" towards them, as one described it later—or as a poem that appeared later in "Simplicity" began:

> "With his hair of wind
> And his eyes of fire
> And his face of infinite desire..."

He swept nearer. They stirred again in a confused and troubled shuffle, opening a way. They shrank back farther. They shivered, like crying shingle a vast wave draws back. Only Fillery stood still, making no sign or movement; upon his face that look of joy and pain—wild joy and searching pain—no one, perhaps, but Devonham understood.

"Wind and fire!" boomed LeVallon's tremendous voice. "We return to our divine, eternal service. O Wind and Fire! We come back at last!" An immense rhythm swept across the room.

Then it was, without announcement of word or action, that Nayan, suddenly leaping from the great enfolding arms, stood upright between the two figures, one hand outstretched towards—Fillery.

At which moment, emerging apparently from nowhere, Khilkoff appeared upon the scene. During the music he had left the studio to find certain sketches he wished to show to LeVallon; he had witnessed nothing, therefore, of what had just occurred. He now stood still, staring in sheer surprise. The people in a ring, gazing with excited, rapt expression into the circle they thus formed, looked like an audience watching some performance that dazed and stupefied them, in which Fillery, LeVallon and Nayan—his own daughter—were the players. He took it for an impromptu charade, perhaps, something spontaneously arranged during his absence. Yet he was obviously staggered.

As he entered, the girl had just leaped from the arms that held her, and run towards Fillery, who stood erect and motionless in the centre of the circle; and LeVallon's wild splendid cry in that instant shook its grand music across the vaulted room. So well acted, so dramatic, so real was the scene thus interrupted that Khilkoff stood staring in silence, thinking chiefly, as he said afterwards, that the young man's pose and attitude were exactly—magnificently—what he wanted for the figure of Fire and Wind in his elemental group.

This enthusiastic thought, with the attempt to engrave it permanently in his memory, filled his mind completely for an instant, when there broke in upon it again that resonant voice, half cry, half chant, vibrating with depth and music, yet quiet too:

"Wind and Fire! My Wind and Fire! O Sun—your messengers are come for us! . . . Oh, come with power and take us with you!..." Its rhythm was gigantic.

So extraordinary was the volume, yet the sweetness, too, in the voice, though its actual loudness was not great—so arresting was its quality, that Khilkoff, as he put it afterwards, thought he heard an entirely new sound, a sound his ears had never known before. He, like the rest of the astonished audience, was caught spellbound. But for an instant only. For at once there followed another voice, releasing the momentary spell, and, with the accompanying action, warned him that what he saw was no mere game of acting. This was real.

"*I hear that other summons at the door!...*"

Her hands were outstretched, her eyes alight with yearning, she was oblivious of everyone but Fillery, LeVallon and herself.

And her father, then, breaking through the crowding figures, packed shoulder to shoulder nearest to him, entered the circle. His mind was confused, perhaps, for vague ideas of some undesirable hypnotic influence, of some foolish experiment that had become too real, passed through it. He knew one thing only—this scene, whether real or acted, pretence or sincere, must be stopped. The look on his daughter's face—entirely new and strange to him—was all the evidence he needed. He shouldered his way through like an angry bear, making inarticulate noises, growling.

But, before he reached the actors, before Nayan reached Fillery's side, and while the voice of the girl and of LeVallon still seemed to echo simultaneously in the air, a new thing happened that changed the scene completely. In these few brief seconds, indeed, so much was concentrated, and with such rapidity, that it was small wonder the reports of individual witnesses differed afterwards, almost as if each one had seen a separate detail of the crowded picture. Its incredibility, too, bewildered minds accustomed to imagined dreams rather than to real action.

LeVallon, at any rate, all agreed, turned with that ease and swiftness peculiarly his own, caught Nayan again into the air, and with one arm swung her back across his shoulder. He moved, then, so irresistibly, with a great striding rush in the direction of the door into the street, and so rapidly, that the onlookers once more drew back instinctively pell mell, tumbling over each other in their frightened haste.

This, all agreed, had happened. One second they saw LeVallon carrying the girl off, the next—a flash of intense and vivid brilliance entered the big studio, flooding all detail with a blaze of violet light. There was a loud report, there was a violent shock.

"The Messengers! Our Messengers!..." The thunder of LeVallon's cry was audible.

The same instant this dazzling splendour, so sparkling it was almost painful, became eclipsed again. There was complete obliteration. Darkness descended like a blow. An inky blackness reigned. No single thing was visible. There came a terrific splitting sound.

The effect of overwhelming sudden blackness was natural enough. In every mind danced still the vivid memory of that last amazing picture they had seen: Khilkoff, with alarmed face, breaking violently into the circle where his daughter, Nayan, swinging from those giant shoulders, looked back imploringly at Dr. Fillery, who stood motionless as though carved in stone, a smile of curious happiness yet pain upon his features. Yet the figure of LeVallon dominated. His radiant beauty, his air of superb strength, his ease, his power, his wild swiftness. Something unearthly glowed about him. He looked a god. The extraordinary idea flashed into Fillery's mind that some big energy as of inter-stellar spaces lay about him, as though great Sirius called down along his light-years of distance into the little tumbled Chelsea room.

This was the picture, set one instant in dazzling violet brilliance, then drowned in blackness, that still hung shining with intense reality before every mind.

The following confusion had a moment of real and troubling panic; women screamed, some fell upon their knees; men called for light; various cries were heard; there was a general roar:

"To the door, all men to the door! He's controlled! There's an Elemental in him!" It was Povey's shrill tones that pierced.

"Strike a match!" shouted Kempster. "The electric light has fused. Stay where you are. Don't move—everybody!"

"Lightning," the clear voice of Devonham was heard. "Keep your heads. It's only a thunderstorm!"

Matches were struck, extinguished, lit again; a patch of dim light shone here and there upon a throng of huddled people; someone found a candle that shed a flickering glare upon the walls and ceiling, but only made the shadows chiefly visible. It was an unreal, fantastic scene.

A moment later there descended a hurricane gust of wind against the building, with splintering glass as though from a hail of bullets, that extinguished candle and matches, and plunged the scene again into total darkness. A terrific clap of thunder, followed immediately by a rushing sound of rain that poured in a flood upon the floor, completed the scene of terror and confusion. The huge north window had blown in.

The consternation was, for some moments, dangerous, for true panic may become an unmanageable thing, and this panic was unquestionably real. The superstitious thread that lies in every human being, stretched and shivered, beginning to weave its swift, ominous pattern. The elements dominated the human too completely just then even for the sense of wonder that was usually so active in the Society's mental make-up to assert itself intelligently. Most of them lost their heads. All associated that picture of LeVallon and the girl with this terrific demonstration of overpowering elemental violence. Povey's startled cry had given them the lead. The human touch thus added the flavour of something both personal and supernatural.

Some stood screaming, whimpering, unable to move; some were numb; others cried for help; not a few remained on their knees; the name of God was audible here and there; many collapsed and several women fainted. To one and all came the realization of that panic fear which dislocates and paralyses. This was a manifestation of elemental power that had intelligence somewhere driving too suggestively behind it....

It was Devonham and Khilkoff who kept their heads and saved the situation. The sudden storm was, indeed, of extreme violence and ferocity; the force of the wind, with the nearness of the terrible lightning and the consequent volume of the overwhelming thunder, were certainly bewildering. But a thunderstorm, they began to realize, was a thunderstorm.

"Everyone stay exactly where he is," suddenly shouted Khilkoff through the darkness. His voice brought comfort. "I'll light candles in the inner studio." He did so a moment later; the faint light was reassuring; a pause in the storm came to his assistance, the wind had passed, the rain had ceased, there was no more lightning. With a whispered word to Devonham, he disappeared through the door into the passage; "You look after 'em; I must find my girl."

"One by one, now," called Devonham. "Take careful steps! Avoid the broken glass!"

Voices answered from dark corners, as the inner room began to fill; all saw the candle light and came to it by degrees. "Povey, Kempster, Imson, Father Collins! Each man bring a lady with him. It's only a thunderstorm. Keep your heads!"

The smaller room filled gradually, people with white faces and staring eyes coming, singly or in couples, within the pale radiance of the flickering candle light. Feet splashed through pools of water; the furniture, the clothing, were soaked; the heat in the air, despite the great broken window, was stifling. One or two women were helped, some were carried; there were cries and exclamations, a noise of splintered glass being trodden on or kicked aside; drinks were brought for those who had fainted; order was restored bit by bit. The collective consciousness resumed gradually its comforting sway. The herd found strength in contact. A single cry—in a woman's voice—"Pan was among us!..." was instantly smothered, drowned in a chorus of "Hush! Hush!" as though a mere name might bring a repetition of a terror none could bear again.

The entire scene had lasted perhaps five minutes, possibly less. The violent storm that had hung low over London, accumulating probably for hours, had dissipated itself in a single prodigious explosion, and was gone. Through the gaping north window, torn and shattered, shone the stars. More candles were brought and lighted, food and drink followed, a few cuts from broken glass were attended to, and calm in a measure came back to the battered and shaken yet thrilled and delighted Prometheans.

But all eyes looked for a couple who were not there; a hundred heads turned searching, for in every heart lay one chief question. Yet, oddly enough, none asked aloud; the names of Nayan and LeVallon were not spoken audibly; some touch of awe, it seemed, clung to a memory still burning in each individual mind; it was an awe that none would willingly revive just then. The whole occurrence had been too devastating, too sudden; it all had been too real.

There was little talk, nor was there the whispered discussion even that might have been expected; individual recovery was slow and hesitating. What had happened lay still too close for the comfort of detailed comparison or analysis by word of mouth. With common accord the matter was avoided. Discussion must wait. It would fill many days with wonder afterwards....

It was with a sense of general relief, therefore, that the throng of guests, bedraggled somewhat in appearance, eyes still bright with traces of uncommon excitement, their breath uneven and their attitude still nervous, saw the door into the passage open and frame the figure of their returning host. He held a lighted candle. His bearded face looked grim, but his slow deep voice was quiet and reassuring—he smiled, his words were commonplace.

"You must excuse my daughter," he said firmly, "but she sends her excuses, and begs to he forgiven for not coming to bid you all good-night. The lightning—the electricity—has upset her. I have advised her to go to bed."

A sigh of relief from everybody came in answer. They were only too glad to take the hint and go.

"The little impromptu act we had prepared for you we cannot give now," he added, anticipating questions. "The storm prevented the second part. We must give it another time instead."

CHAPTER XIV

Khilkoff, Edward Fillery and Paul Devonham, between them, it seems, were wise in their generation. The story spread that the scene in the Studio had been nothing but a bit of inspired impromptu acting, to which the coincidence of the storm had lent a touch of unexpected conviction where, otherwise, all would have ended in a laugh and a round or two of amused applause.

The spreading of an undesirable story, thus, was to a great extent prevented, its discussion remaining confined, chiefly, among the few startled witnesses. Yet the Prometheans, of course, knew a supernatural occurrence when they saw one. They were not to be so easily deprived of their treasured privilege. Thrilled to their marrows, individually and collectively, they committed their versions to writing, drew up reports, compared notes and, generally, made the feast last as long as possible. It was, rnoreover, a semi-sacred feast for them. Its value increased portentously. It bound the Society together with fresh life. It attracted many new members. Povey and his committee increased the subscription and announced an entrance fee in addition.

The various accounts offered by the Members, curious as these were, may be left aside for the moment, since the version of the occurrence as given by Edward Fillery comes first in interest. His report, however, was made only to himself; he mentioned it in full to no one, not even to Paul Devonham. He felt unable to share it with any living being. Only one result of his conclusions he shared openly enough with his assistant: he withdrew his promise.

Upon certain details, the two men agreed with interest—that everybody in the room, men and women, were on the *qui vive* the moment LeVallon made his entrance. His appearance struck a note. All were aware of an unusual presence. Interest and curiosity rose like a vapour, heads all turned one way as though the same wind blew them, there was a buzz and murmur of whispered voices, as though the figure of LeVallon woke into response the same taut wire in every heart. "Who on earth is that? What is he?" was legible in a hundred questioning eyes. All, in a word, were aware of something unaccustomed.

Upon this detail—and in support of the Society's claim to special "psychic" perception, it must be mentioned—Fillery and Devonham were at one. But another detail, too, found them in agreement. It was not the tempest that caused the panic; it was LeVallon himself. Something about LeVallon had produced the abrupt and singular sense of panic terror.

Fillery was glad; he was satisfied, at any rate. The transient, unreal personality called "LeVallon" had disappeared and, as he believed, for ever; a surface apparition after all, it had been educated, superimposed, the result of imitation and quick learning, a phantom masquerading as an intelligent human being. It was merely an acquired surface-self, a physical, almost an automatic intelligence. The deep nature underneath had now broken out. It was the sudden irruption of "N. H." that touched the subconscious self of everyone in the room with its strange authentic shock. "N. H." was in full possession.

Towards this real Self he felt attraction, yearning, even love. He had felt this from the very beginning. Why, or what it was, he did not pretend to know as yet. Towards "N. H." he reacted as towards his own son, as to a comrade, ancient friend, proved intimate and natural playmate even. The strange tie was difficult to describe. In himself, though faint by comparison, lay something akin in sympathy and understanding.... They belonged together in the same unknown region. The girl, of course, belonged there too, but more completely, more absolutely, even than himself. He foresaw the risks, the dangers. His heart, with a leap of joy, accepted the responsibilities.

Unlike Devonham, he had not come that afternoon to scoff; his smile at the vagaries of what his assistant called "hysterical psychics" had no bitterness, no contempt. If their excesses were pathogenic often, he believed with Lombroso that genius and hysteria draw upon a common origin sometimes, also that, from among this unstable material, there emerged on occasions hints of undeniable value. To the want of balance was chiefly due the ineffectiveness of these hints. This class, dissatisfied with present things, kicking over the traces which herd together the dull normal crowd into the safe but uninteresting commonplace, but kicking, of course, too wildly, alone offered hints of powers that might one day, obedient to laws at present unknown, become of value to the race. They were temperamentally open to occasional, if misguided, inspiration, and all inspiration, the evidence overwhelmingly showed, is due to an intense, but hidden mental activity. The hidden nine-tenths of the self peeped out here and there periodically. These people were, at heart, alert to new ideas. The herd instinct was weak in them. They were individuals.

Fillery had not come to scoff. His chief purpose on this particular occasion had been to observe any reactions produced in LeVallon by the atmosphere of these unbalanced yet questing minds, and by the introduction to a girl, whose beauty, physical and moral, he considered far far above the standard of other women. Iraida Khilkoff, as he saw her, rose head and shoulders, like some magical flower in a fairy-tale, beyond her feminine kind.

His hopes had in both respects proved justified. LeVallon was gone. "N. H." had swept up commandingly into full possession.

If it is the attitude of mind that interprets details in a given scene, it is the heart that determines their selection. Devonham saw collective hallucination, delusion, humbug—useless and undesirable weeds, where his chief saw strange imperfect growths that might one day become flowers in a marvellous garden. That this garden blossomed upon the sunny slopes of a lost Caucasian valley had a significance he did not shirk. Always he was honest with himself. It was this symbolic valley he longed to people. Its radiant loveliness stirred a forgotten music in his heart, he watched golden bees sipping that wild azalea honey, of which even the natives may not rob them without the dangerous delight of exaltation; his nostrils caught the delicious perfumes, his cheek felt the touch of happy winds... as he stood by the door with Devonham and LeVallon, looking round the crowded Chelsea studio.

Aware of this association stirring in his blood, he believed he had himself well in hand; he knew already in advance that a spirit moved upon the face of those waters that were his inmost self; he had that intuitive divination which anticipates a change of spiritual weather. The wind was rising, the atmosphere lay prepared, already the flowers bent their heads one way. All his powers of self-control might well be called upon before the entertainment ended. Glancing a moment at LeVallon, tall, erect and poised beside him, he was conscious— it was an instant of vivid self-revelation—that he steadied himself in doing so. He borrowed, as it were, something of that poise, that calm simplicity, that potential energy, that modest confidence. Some latent power breathed through the great stalwart figure by his side; the strength was not his own; LeVallon emanated this power unconsciously,

Khilkoff, as described, had then led the youth away to see the sculpture, Devonham was captured by a Member, and Fillery found himself alone. He looked about him, noticing here and there individuals whom he knew. Lady Gleeson he saw at once on her divan in the corner, with her cigarette, her jewels, her glass, her background of millions through which an indulgent husband floated like a shadow. His eye rested on her a second only, then passed in search of something less insignificant. Miss Lance, who had heard of his books and dared to pretend knowledge of them monopolised him for ten minutes. A little tactful kindness managed her easily, while he watched the door where LeVallon had disappeared with Khilkoff, and through which Nayan might any moment now enter. Already his thoughts framed these two together in a picture; his heart saw them playing hand in hand among the flowers of the Hidden Valley, one flying, the other following, a radiance of sunny fire and a speed of lifting winds about them both, yet he himself, oddly enough, not far away. He, too, was somehow with them. While listening with his mind to what Miss Lance was saying, his heart went out playing with this splendid pair.... He would not lose her finally, it seemed; some subtle kinship held them together in this trinity. The heart in him played wild against the mind.

He caught Devonham's eye upon him, and a sudden smile that Miss Lance fortunately appropriated to herself, ran over his too thoughtful face. For Devonham's attitude towards the case, his original Notes, his obvious concealment of experiences in the Jura Mountains, flashed across him with a flavour of something half comic, half pathetic. "With all that knowledge, with all the accumulation of data, Paul stops short of Wonder!" he thought to himself, his eyes fixed solemnly upon Miss Lance's face. He remembered Coleridge: "All knowledge begins and ends with wonder, but the first wonder is the child of ignorance, while the second wonder is the parent of adoration." A thousand years, and the dear fellow will still regard adoration as hysteria! He chuckled audibly, to his companion's surprise, since the moment was not appropriate for chuckling.

Making his peace with his neighbour, he presently left her for a position nearer to the door, Father Collins providing the opportunity.

Father Collins, as he was called, half affectionately, half in awe, as of a parent with a cane, was an individual. He had been evangelical, high church, Anglican, Roman Catholic, in turn, and finally Buddhist. Believing in reincarnation, he did not look for progress in humanity; the planet resembled a form at school—individuals passed into it and out of it, but the average of the form remained the same. The fifth form was always the fifth form. Earth's history showed no advance as a whole, though individuals did. He looked forward, therefore, to no Utopia, nor shared the pessimism of the thinkers who despaired of progress.

A man of intense convictions, yet open mind, he was not ashamed to move. Before the Buddhist phase, he had been icily agnostic. He thought, but also he felt. He had vision and intuition; he had investigated for himself. His mind was of the imaginative-scientific order. Buddhism, his latest phase, attracted him because it was "a scientific, logical system rather than a religion based on revelation." He belonged eminently to the unstable. He found no resting place. He came to the meetings of the Society to listen rather than to talk. His net was far flung, catching anything and everything in the way of new ideas, experiments, theories, beliefs, especially powers. He tested for himself, then accepted or discarded. The more extravagant the theory, the greater its appeal to him. Behind a grim, even a repulsive ugliness, he hid a heart of milk and honey. In his face was nobility, yet something slovenly ran through it like a streak.

He loved his kind and longed to help them to the light. Although a rolling stone, spiritually, his naked sincerity won respect. He was composed, however, of several personalities, and hence, since these often clashed, he was accused of insincerity too. The essay that lost him his pulpit and parish, "The Ever-moving Truth, or Proof Impossible," was the poignant confession of an honest intellect where faith and unbelief came face to face with facts. The Bishop, naturally, preferred the room of "Father" Collins to his company.

"I should like you to meet my friend," Fillery mentioned, after some preliminary talk. "He would interest you. You might help him possibly." He mentioned a few essential details. "Perhaps you will call one day—you know my address—and make his acquaintance. His mind, owing to his lonely and isolated youth, is *tabula rasa*. For the same reason, a primitive Nature is his Deity."

Father Collins raised his bushy dlark eyebrows.

"I took note of him the moment he came in," he replied. "I was wondering who he was—and what! I'll come one day with pleasure. The innocence on his face surprised me. Is he— may I ask it—friend or patient?"

"Both."

"I see," said the other, without hesitation. He added: "You are experimenting?"

"Studying. I should value the help—the view of a religious temperament."

Father Collins looked grim to ugliness. The touch of nobility appeared.

"I know your ideals, Dr. Fillery; I know your work," he said gruffly. "In you lies more true religion than in a thousand bishops. I should trust your treatment of an unusual case. If," he added slowly, "I can help him, so much the better." He then looked up suddenly, his manner as if galvanized: "Unless *he* can perhaps help us."

The words struck Fillery on the raw, as it were. They startled him. He stared into the other's eyes. "What makes you think that? What do you mean exactly?"

Father Collins returned his gaze unflinchingly. He made an odd reply. "Your friend," he said, "looks to me—like a man who—might start a new religion— Nature for instance—back to Nature being, in my opinion, always a possible solution of over-civilization and its degeneracy." The streak of something slovenly crept into the nobility, smudging it, so to speak, with a blur.

Dr. Fillery, for a moment, waited, listening with his heart.

"And find a million followers at once," continued the other, as though he had not noticed. "His voice, his manner, his stature, his face, but above all—something he brings with him. Whatever his nature, he's a natural leader. And a sincere, unselfish leader is what people are asking for nowadays."

His black bushy eyebrows dropped, darkening the grim, clean-shaven face. "You noticed, of course—you—the women's eyes?" he mentioned. "It isn't, you know, so much what a man says, nor entirely his looks, that excite favour or disfavour with women. It's something he emanates—unconsciously. They can't analyze it, but they never fail to recognize it."

Fillery moved sideways a little, so that he could watch the inner studio bet-

ter. The discernment of his companion was somewhat unexpected. It disconcerted him. All his knowledge, all his experience clustered about his mind as
thick as bees, yet he felt unable to select the item he needed. The sunshine upon
his Inner Valley burned a brighter fire. He saw the flowers glow. The wind ran
sweet and magical. He began to watch himself more closely.

"LeVallon is an interesting being," he admitted finally, "but you make big deductions surely. A mind like yours," he added, "must have its reasons?"

"Power," replied the other promptly; "power. 'The earlier generations,' said
Emerson, 'saw God face to face; we through their eyes. Why should not we also
enjoy an original relation to Nature?' Your friend has this original relation, I feel;
he stands close—terribly close—to Nature. He brings open spaces even into this
bargain sale—" He drew a deep breath. "There is a power about him—"

"Perhaps," interrupted the other.

"Not of this earth."

"You mean that literally?"

"Not of this earth quite—not of humanity, so to speak," repeated Father
Collins half irritably, as though his intelligence had been insulted. "That's the
best way I can describe how it strikes me. Ask one of the women. Ask Nayan,
for instance. Whatever he is, your friend is elemental."

Like a shock of fire the unusual words ran deep into Fillery's heart, but, at
that same instant a stirring of the figures beyond the door caught his attention.
His main interest revived. The inner door of the private studio, he thought, had
opened.

"Elemental!" he repeated, his interest torn in two directions simultaneously.
He looked at his companion keenly, searchingly. "You—a man like you—does
not use such words—" He kept an eye upon the inner studio.

"Without meaning," the other caught him up at once. "No. I mean it. Nor do
I use such words idly to a man—Fillery—like you." He stopped. "He has what
you have," came the quick blunt statement; "only in your case it's indirect, while
in his it's direct—essential."

They looked at each other. Two minds, packed with knowledge and softened
with experience of their kind, though from different points of view, met each
other fairly. A bridge existed. It was crossed. Few words were necessary, it
seemed. Each understood the other.

"Elemental," repeated Fillery, his pulse quickening half painfully.

At which instant he knew the inner door had opened. Nayan had come in. The
same instant almost she had gone out again. So quick, indeed, was the interval
between her appearance and disappearance, that Fillery's version of what he
then witnessed in those few seconds might have been ascribed by a third person who saw it with him to his imagination largely. Imaginative, at any rate, the
version was; whether it was on that account unreal is another matter. The swift,
tiny scene, however, no one witnessed but himself. Even Devonham, unusually
alert with professional anxiety, missed it; as did also the watchful Lady Gleeson, whom jealousy made clairvoyante almost. Khilkoff and LeVallon, standing
sideways to the door, were equally unaware that it had opened, then quickly

closed again. None saw, apparently, the radiant, lovely outline.

It was a curtained door leading out of the far end of the inner studio into a passage which had an exit to the street; Fillery was so placed that he could see it over his companion's shoulder; Khilkoff, LeVallon and the little group about them stood in his direct line of sight against the dark background of the curtain. The light in this far corner was so dim that Fillery was not aware the curtained door had swung open until he actually saw the figure of Nayan Khilkoff framed suddenly in the clear space, the white passage wall behind her. She wore gloves, hat and furs, having come, evidently, straight from the street. Ten seconds, perhaps twenty, she stood there, gazing with a sudden fixed intensity at LeVallon, whose figure, almost close enough for touch, was sideways to her, the face in profile.

She stopped abruptly as though a shock ran through her. She remained motionless. She stared, an expression in her eyes as of life momentarily arrested by wild, glorious, intense surprise. The lips were parted; one gloved hand still held the swinging curtained door. To Fillery it seemed as if a flame leaped into her eyes. The entire face lit up. She seemed spellbound with delight.

This leap of light was the first sign he witnessed. The same second her eyes lifted a fraction of an inch, changed their focus, and, gazing past LeVallon, looked straight across the room into his own.

In his mind at that instant still rang the singular words of Father Collins; in his heart still hung the picture of the flowered valley: it was across this atmosphere the eyes of the girl flashed their message like a stroke of lightning. It came as a cry, almost a call for help, an audible message whose syllables fled down the valley, yearning sweet, yet a tone of poignant farewell within the following wind. It was a moment of delicious joy, of exquisite pain, of a blissful, searching dream beyond this world....

He stood spellbound himself a moment. The look in the girl's big eloquent eyes threatened a cherished dream that lay too close to his own life. He was aware of collapse, of ruin; that old peculiar anguish seized him. He remembered her words in Baker Street a few days before: "Please bring your friend"—the accompanying pain they caused. And now he caught the echo on that following wind along the distant valley. The cry in her eyes came to him:

"Why—O why—do you bring this to me? It must take your place. It must put out—You!"

The reasoning and the inspirational self in him knew this momentary confusion, as the cry fled down the wind.

> "O follow, follow
> Through the caverns hollow
> As the song floats, thou pursue
> Where the wild bee never flew..."

The curtained door swung to again; the face and figure were no longer there; Nayan had withdrawn quickly, noticed by none but himself. She had gone up to make herself ready for her father's guests; in a few minutes she would come down again to play hostess as her custom was.... It was so ordinary. It was so dislocating.... For at that moment it seemed as if all the feminine forces of the universe, whatever these may be, focused in her, and poured against him their concentrated stream to allure, enchant, subdue. He trembled. He remembered Devonham's admission of the panic sense.

"It's the air," said a voice beside him, "all this tobacco smoke and scent, and no ventilation."

Father Collins was speaking, only he had completely forgotten that Father Collins was in the world. The steadying hand upon his arm made him realize that he had swayed a moment.

"The perfume chiefly," the voice continued. "All this cheap nasty stuff these women use. It's enough to sicken any healthy man. Nobody knows his own smell, they say." He laughed a little.

Collins was tactful. He talked on easily of nothing in particular, so that his companion might let the occasion slip, or comment on it, as he wished.

"Worse than incense." Fillery gave him the clue perhaps intentionally, certainly with gratitude. He made an effort. He found control. "It intoxicates the imagination, doesn't it?" That note of sweet farewell still hung with enchanting sadness in his brain. He still saw those yearning eyes. He heard that cry. And yet the conflict in his nature bewildered him—as though he found two persons in him, one weeping while the other sang.

Father Collins smiled, and Fillery then knew that he, too, had seen the girl framed in the doorway, intercepted the glance as well. No shadow of resentment crossed his heart as he heard him add: "She, too, perhaps belongs elsewhere." The phrase, however, brought to his own personal dream the conviction of another understanding mind. "As you yourself do, too," was added in a thrilling whisper suddenly.

Fillery turned with a start to meet his eye. "But *where?*"

"That is *your* problem," said Father Collins promptly. "You are the expert— even though you think—mistakenly—that your heart is robbed." His voice held the sympathy and tenderness of a woman taught by suffering. The nobility was in his face again, untarnished now. His words, his tone, his manner caught Fillery in amazement. It did not surprise him that Father Collins had been quick enough to understand, but it did surprise him that a man so entangled in one formal creed after another, so netted by the conventional thought of various religious Systems, and therefore stuffed with old, rigid, commonplace ideas—it did, indeed surprise him to feel this sudden atmosphere of vision and prophecy that abruptly shone about him. The extravagant, fantastic side of the man he had forgotten.

"Where?" he repeated, gazing at him. "Where, indeed?"

"Where the wild bee never flew... perhaps!"

Father Collins's eyebrows shot up as though worked by artificial springs. His eyes, changing extraordinarily, turned very keen. He seemed several persons at once. He looked like—contradictory description—a spiritual Jesuit. The ugly mouth—thank Heaven, thought Fillery—showed lines of hidden humour. His sanity, at any rate, was unquestioned. Father Collins watched the planet with his soul, not with his brain alone. But which of his many personalities was now in the ascendancy, no man, least of all himself, could tell. His companion, the expert in him automatically aware of the simultaneous irruption and disruption, waited almost professionally for any outburst that might follow. "Arcades ambo," he reflected, making a stern attempt to keep his balance.

"The subconscious, remember, doesn't explain everything," came the words. "Not everything," he added with emphasis. "As with heredity"—he looked keenly half humorously, half sympathetically at the doctor—"there are gaps and lapses. The recent upheaval has been more than an inter-tribal war. It was a planetary event. It has shaken our nature fundamentally, radically. The human mind has been shocked, broken, dislocated. The prevalent hysteria is not an ordinary hysteria, nor are the new powers—perhaps—quite ordinary either."

"Mental history repeats itself," Fillery put in, now more master of himself again. "Unbalance has always followed upheaval. The removal of known, familiar foundations always lets in extravagance of wildest dissatisfaction, search and question."

"Upheaval of this kind," rejoined the other gravely, "there has never been since human beings walked the earth. Our fabulous old world trembles in the balance." And, as he said it, the dreamer shone in the light below the big, black eyebrows, noticed quickly by his companion. "Old ideals have been smashed beyond recovery. The gods men knew have been killed, like Tommy, in the trenches. The past is likewise dead, its dreams of progress buried with it by a Black Maria. The human mind and heart stand everywhere empty and bereft, while their hungry and unanswered questions search the stars for something new."

"Well, well," said Fillery gently, half stirred, half amused by the odd language. "You may be right. But mental history has always shown a desire for something new after each separate collapse. Signs and wonders are a recurrent hunger, remember. In the days of Abraham, of Paul, of Moses it was the same."

"Questions to-day," replied the other, "are based on an immense accumulated knowledge unknown to Moses or to Abraham's time. The phenomenon, I grant you, is the same, but—the shock, the dislocation, the shattering upheaval comes in the twentieth century upon minds grounded in deep scientific wisdom. It was formerly a shock to the superstitious ignorance of intuitive feeling merely. To-day it is organized scientific knowledge that meets the earthquake."

"You mentioned gaps and lapses," said Fillery, deeply interested, but still half professionally, perhaps, in spite of his preoccupations. "You think, perhaps, those gaps—?" One eye watched the inner studio. The unstable in him gained more and more the upper hand.

"I mean," replied Father Collins, now fairly launched upon his secret hobby, evidently his qualification for membership in the Society, "I mean, Edward Fillery, that the time is ripe, if ever, for a new revelation. If Man is the only type of being in the universe, well and good. We see his finish plainly, for the war has shown that progress is a myth. Man remains, in spite of all conceivable scientific knowledge, a savage, of low degree, irredeemable, and intellect, as a reconstructive force, but of small account."

"It seems so, I admit."

"But if"—Father Collins said it as calmly as though he spoke of some new food or hygienic treatment merely—"if mankind is not the only life in the universe, if, for instance, there exist—and why not?—other evolutionary systems besides our own somewhat trumpery type—other schemes and other beings—perhaps parallel, perhaps quite different—perhaps in more direct contact with the sources of life—a purer emanation, so to say—"

He hesitated, realizing perhaps that in speaking to a man of Edward Fillery's standing he must choose his words, or at least present his case convincingly, while aware that his inability to do so made him only more extravagant and incoherent.

"Yes, quite so," Fillery helped him, noting all the time the suppressed intensity, the half-concealed conviction of an *idée fixe* behind the calmness, while the balance of his own attention remained concentrated on the group about LeVallon. "If, as you suggest, there are other types of life—" He spoke encouragingly. He had noticed the slovenly streak spread and widen, breaking down, as it were, the structure of the face. He was aware also of the increasing insecurity in himself.

"Now is the moment," cried the other; "now is the time for their appearance." He turned as though he had hit a target unexpectedly.

"Now," he repeated, "is the opportunity for their manifestation. The human mind lies open everywhere. It is blank, receptive, ready. On all   sides it waits ready and inviting. The gaps are provided. If there is any other life, it should break through and come among us *now!*"

Fillery, startled, withdrew for the first time his attention from that inner room. With keen eyes he gazed at his companion. With an abrupt, unpleasant shock it occurred to him that all he heard was borrowed, filched, stolen out of his own mind. Before words came to him, the other spoke:

"Your friend," he mentioned quietly, but with intentional significance, "and patient."

"LeVallon!"

But it was at this moment that Nayan Khilkoff, entering again without her hat and furs, had moved straight to the piano, seated herself, and begun to sing.

CHAPTER XV

To retail the following scene as Dr. Fillery saw it in detail is not necessary, the sequence of acts, of physical events being already known. The reactions of his heart and mind, however, have importance. What be felt, thought, hoped and feared, what he believed as well, his point of view in a word, remain essential.

Edward Fillery, being what he was, witnessed it from his own individual angle; his mind, with its heredity, his soul, with its mysterious background, these held the glasses to his eyes, adjusting, as with a Zeiss instrument, each eye separately. In his case the analyst and thinker checked the unstable dreamer with acute exactitude. This was his special gift. He studied himself best while studying others. His sight, moreover, was exceptionally keen, his glasses of consummate workmanship. He saw, it seems, considerably beyond the normal range. He believed, at least, that he did so.

He saw, for instance, that the girl, while her fingers ran over the keys before she sang, searched the room and found LeVallon in a second. Following her rapid glance, he took in the picture that she also saw—LeVallon, coffee cup in hand, before Lady Gleeson languishing on the divan, and Devonham just beside them. LeVallon was obviously unaware of Lady Gleeson's presence; he had forgotten her existence. Devonham, a floor walker with nothing particular to do at the moment, looked uncomfortable and ill at ease, scared a little, fearing a scene, a possible outbreak even. The meaning of the group was easily read. The girl herself, undoubtedly, read it clearly too.

This flashed upon the cinema screen, and Fillery divined it without the help of tedious letterpress.

The same instant he was aware that the girl and LeVallon looked for the first time straight into each other's faces, and that both seemed simultaneously caught into the air as though a star had lifted them. Not even a question lay in their clear eyes. It was an instantaneous understanding, so complete and perfect that the expression of happy surprise was too convincing to be missed even by the slow-witted Lady Gleeson. Vanity usually delays intelligence, and her vanity was abnormal. But she saw the expression on the two faces, and interpreted it aright. Fillery noticed that she squirmed; she would presently, he felt positive, disappear. Before the singing ended he had seen her slink away.

The song began. He had heard it before, "The Vagrant's Epitaph," sung by the same clear, sweet voice, had felt his heart stirred by the true simple feeling she put into it. He knew every word and every bar; the music was her own. He loved it. Both words and music awoke in him invariably a picture of his own lost valley, a physical desire to be over the hills and far away with the homeless liberty of winds and stars and waters, and at the same time, its spiritual equivalent—a yearning that the Race should discover the immense fair region of its greater hidden self and enjoy its new powers without restraint. All this was familiar to him. But now, as she sang, there came another, deeper meaning that sublimated the essential spirit of it, lifting it out of the known ditch of space and time. Never yet had he heard such yearning passion, such untold desire in her voice. The physical vagrancy changed subtly, exquisitely, to a symbol of a vaster meaning—a spiritual vagrancy that suddenly captured him in bitter pain. "Love could not hold him, Duty forged no chain"—as he listened to the sweetness, struck him between the joints of armour he had not realized before was so insecurely bound about him. The anguish of lonely souls, alien among their kind, hungry for companionship they might not find, unclothed, uncared for, desired of none and understanding none—this rose tumultuously in his blood. "The wide seas and the mountains called him..." the words and music pierced him like a flame. "Revel might hold him for a little space..."—her voice made it sound like a description of man's brief moment on the whirling planet, tasting adventure with men and women, playing a moment with love and hope and fear, till, "turning past the laughter and the lamps," he heard that "other summons at the door."

This bigger version, this deeper meaning, caught at him with power as he heard the song in the sweet, familiar voice, and realized in a flash that what he felt faintly LeVallon felt terrifically. His own detachment was a pose, a shadow, at best a bodiless yearning; in LeVallon it was a reality of consuming fire. Also it was an explanation of the girl's own singular aloofness from the world of admiring men. Both belonged, as Father Collins put it, "elsewhere."

He watched them. LeVallon's eyes, he saw, remained fixed and motionless on the singer; her own did not leave the notes for a single moment; the words and music poured into the room like a shower of dancing silver. The personality of the girl flowed out with them to meet the newly-found companion they addressed. An extraordinary thing then happened: to Fillery it almost seemed that there formed then and there between them a new vehicle—as it were, a body—that gave expression to their own great secret. Something in each of them, unable to manifest through their minds, their brains, their earthly bodies, formed for itself an elastic subtle vehicle, using the sound, the words, the feeling for this purpose—and as literally as a human spirit uses the familiar physical body for its manifestation.

The experience was amazing, but it was real. He watched it carefully. In the room about him, formed on the waves of this sweet singing, shaped by feeling that found normally no other expression, inspired by emotions, yearnings, desires alien to their normal kind, these two created between them a new vehicle or body that could and did express all this.

They heard that "other summons at the door...." And they were off.

Yet he, too, heard the summons, and in the depths of his being he answered to it. His essential weakness, wearing the guise of strength, rose naked....

These thoughts and feelings lay unexpressed, perhaps—too deep actually, too remote from any experience he had yet known, to find actual words, even in his mind. What did find expression, in thought at any rate, was that, before his very eyes, he witnessed the transfiguring change come over Nayan. Like some flower that has been growing in the shade, then meets the flood of sunshine for the first time, she knew a fresh tide of life sweep over her entire being. She seemed to blossom, breaking almost into flower and fruit before his very eyes, as though sun and wind brought her into a sudden bloom of exquisite maturity. He was aware of rich, deep purple, the faint gold of fruits and flowers, the creamy softness of a rose, the amber of wild grapes bathed in sparkling dew. The luscious promise of the Spring matured about her whole presentment into full summer glory. And it was the sun and wind of LeVallon's enigmatic, stimulating presence close to her that caused the miracle. The essential flower of her life poured forth to meet his own, as he had always felt it must. LeVallon`s was the mighty wind that lifted her, was the sun in whose heat she basked, expanded, soared. She experienced a strange increase of her natural vitality and being. Her consciousness knew an abrupt intensification.

The signs, in that brief moment, were as clear to Fillery`s divining heart as though he read them in black printed letters on a page of whitest paper. He knew the cipher and the code. He watched the signals flash. They had not even spoken, yet the relationship was established beyond doubt. He witnessed the first exchange; the wireless message of joy and sympathy that flashed he intercepted.

Through his extremely rapid mind, as he watched, poured memories, reflections, judgments in concentrated form, yet calmly, steadily, though against a background of deep and troubled emotion. There seemed actually a disruption of his personality. Father Collins, standing beside him, divined nothing, he believed, of his agitation, standing, mere figure of a man, listening to the music with attentive pleasure; at least, he gave no outward sign....

The song drew to its close. Once Nayan raised her eyes, instantly finding those of LeVallon across the room, then shifting again for a fleeting second with a rapidly changing focus to his own. He met them without a quiver; he caught again her tender, searching question; he sent no answer back.

In his own heart burned, however, a score of questions that beat against his soul for answers. What was it that each had found thus intuitively within the other? Was it her maternal instinct only that was reached as with all other men hitherto, was it at last the woman in her that leaped towards its own divine, creative sun, or was it that hidden, nameless aspect of her which had never yet found a vehicle for manifestation among her own kind and had therefore remained hitherto unexpressed—bodiless?

The answer to this he found easily enough. No jealousy stirred; pain for himself had been long ago uprooted. Yet pain of a kind he felt. Would LeVallon injure, drag her down, bring suffering, perhaps of an atrocious sort, into her hitherto so innocent life? Was she yet qualified to withstand the fierce fire, the rushing wind, that the full force of his strange nature must bring to hear upon her?

His questions went prophesying, flying like swift birds to such great distances that no audible answers could return. His pain, at any rate, chiefly was for her. He divined that she was frightened, yet exhilarated, before the unexpected apparition of an unusual presence. Accustomed to smaller jets of admiration from smaller men, this deep flood overwhelmed her. This motionless figure watching her among the shadows, listening to her singing, devouring her beauty with an innocence, power, worship she had never yet encountered—could she, Fillery asked himself, withstand its elemental flood and not be broken by its waves?

For at the back of all his questions, haunting his prophecies, filling his hopes and fears with substance, stood one outstanding certainty:

The motionless figure in the shadows was not LeVallon. It was "N. H."

The thing he had expected had now happened. Instinctively he turned to find his colleague.

For what followed, Fillery, of course, was as unprepared as anyone. In some way, difficult to describe, the whole thing had a strangely natural, almost an inevitable touch. The exaggeration that others felt he was not conscious of. He never, for a single moment, lost his head. The wonder of the elemental violence appealed and stimulated without once touching the sense of fear, much less of panic, in him.

Searching for Devonham's familiar figure, he found it in the seat that Lady Gleeson had vacated shortly before, but the face turned away towards the inner room, so that it was not possible to catch his eye. It was an attentive, critical, almost anxious expression his chief surprised, and while a faint smile perhaps flitted across his own mouth, he became aware that Father Collins—he had again completely forgotten his proximity—was staring with a curious intentness at him. The same instant the song came to an end. Into the brief pause of a second before the applause burst forth, Father Collins's voice was suddenly audible in his ear:

"LeVallon's gone," Fillery was saying to himself, "'N. H.' is in control," when his neighbour's words broke in. The two sentences were simultaneously in his mind:

"A man in *his own place* is the Ruler of his Fate!"

And Fillery's astonishment was only equalled by the fact that the grim face was soft with sympathy, and that in the eyes shone moisture that was close to tears. Before he could reply, however, the applause burst forth, making an uproar against which no voice could possibly contend. The subsequent events, following so swiftly, made rejoinder equally out of the question, nor did he see Father Collins again that evening.

These Fillery witnessed much as already described through Devonham's eyes. The storm, the panic took place as told. Yet a detail here and there belong to Fillery's version, for they were a part of his own being. He had, for instance, a warning that something was about to happen, although warning seems not quite the faithful word. He saw the Valley for one fleeting second, the three familiar figures, Nayan, "N. H.," himself, flying through the bright sunshine before a wind that stirred a million flowers. In the farthest possible background of his mind it shone an instant. The shutter dropped again, it vanished.

Yet enough to set him on the alert. Into the air about him, into his heart as well, fell an exhilarating and immense refreshment. It rose, as it were, from the most deeply submerged portion of his own hidden being, now stirred, even actually summoned, into activity.

The shutter meanwhile rose and fell and rose again; the Valley reappeared and vanished, then reappeared again.

For the truth came smashing against him—smashing his being open, and bursting the doors of his carefully instructed, carefully guarded nature. The doors flung from their hinges and a blinding light poured in and flooded the strangest possible hidden corners.

He saw what followed with an accuracy of observation impossible to anyone else, with an intimate sympathy the others could not feel—because he himself took part in the entire scene. But the scene, for him, was not the Chelsea studio with its tobacco smoke and perfume, it was the Caucasian valley whence his own blood derived. Clean, fragrant winds swept past him across mighty space. The walls melted into distances of forest and mountain peaks, the ceiling was a dome of stainless blue, the floor ran deep in flowers. A drenching sunshine of crystal purity bathed the world. It was across bright emerald turf that he saw "N. H." dance forward like a wind of power, cry with a joyful resonant voice to the radiant girl who stood laughing, half hiding, yet at the same time beckoning, that she should fly with him. He caught and lifted her, her hair, the whiteness of her skin flashing in the sun like some marvellous bird in the act of taking wing, for before he had touched her she leapt through the air to meet his outstretched arms. Yet one hand, one silvery arm, waved towards himself, towards Fillery; their fingers met and clasped; the three of them, three dancing, free and joyful figures, fled like the wind across the enormous mountains, but fled, he knew beyond all question—home.

He saw this in the space of those few seconds in which Nayan was swung over the youth's shoulders beside the piano. The two scenes ran parallel, as it were, before his eyes, outer and inner sight keeping equal pace together. His balance and judgment here were never once disturbed. In the studio: he had just introduced LeVallon to the girl and the latter had caught her up. In the valley: she had leapt into his arms and the three of them were off.

It was this inner interpretation, keeping always level pace with what was happening outwardly, that furnished Fillery with the hint of an astounding explanation. The figure in the valley, it flashed to him, was, of course, "N. H." in all his natural splendour, but a figure unknown surely to all records of humanity as such. Here danced and sang a happy radiant being, by whom the limitations of the human species were not experienced, even if the species were familiar to him at all. A being from another system, another evolution, an elemental being, whose ideal, development, mode of existence, were not those of men and women. "N. H." was not a human being, a human soul, a human spirit. He belonged elsewhere and otherwise. Under the guise of LeVallon he had drifted in. He inhabited LeVallon's frame.

In the Studio, at this instant, Fillery heard him using the singular words already noted, and in the Studio they sounded, indeed, senseless, foolish, even mad. It was, he realized, an attempt to stammer in human language some meaning that lay beyond, outside it. In the Valley, however, and at the same moment, they sounded natural and true. The evolutionary system to which "N. H." belonged, from which he had in some as yet unknown manner passed into humanity, but to which, though almost entirely forgotten, he yearned with his whole being to return—this other system had, it seemed, its own conditions, its own methods of advance, its ideals and its duties. Were, then, its inhabitants—this flashed upon him in the delicious wind and sunshine—the workers in what men call the natural kingdoms, the builders of form and structure, the directing powers that expressed themselves through the elemental energies everywhere behind the laws of Nature? Was this their tireless and wondrous service in the planet, in the universe itself?

"N. H." called the girl to service, not to personal love. Alone, cut off from his own kind, alien and derelict amid the conditions of a humanity strange, perhaps unknown to him, he sought companionship where he could. Drawn instinctively to the more impersonal types, such as Fillery and the girl, he felt there the nearest approach to what he recognized as his own kind; their ideal of selfless service was a beacon that he understood; he would return to his own kingdom, carrying them both with him. From somewhere, at any rate, this all flashed into his too willing mind....

At which second precisely in Fillery's valley-vision, Khilkoff entered, and— yet before he could take action—the lightning struck and the sudden explosion of the ferocious storm blackened out both the outer and the inner scene.

The shock of elemental violence, the astounding revelation as well that an entirely new type had possibly come within his ken, this, combined with the emotional disturbance caused by the change produced in Nayan, seemed enough to upset the equilibrium of even the most balanced mind. The darkness added its touch of helplessness besides. Yet Fillery never for a moment lost his head. Two natures in him, cause of his radical instability, merged for a moment in amazing harmony. The panic now dominating all about him seemed so small a thing compared to the shattering discovery life had just offered to him. Across it, finding his way past kneeling women and shrieking girls, drenched to the skin by the flood of entering rain, moving over splintered glass, he found the figure he sought, as though by some instinctive sympathy. They came together in the darkness. Their hands met easily. A moment later they were in the street, and "N. H.'s" instinctive terror amid the sheets of falling water, an element hostile to his own natural fire, made it a simple matter to get him home—in Lady Gleeson's motor car.

CHAPTER XVI

When relative order had been restored, Devonham realized, of course, that his colleague had cleverly spirited away their "patient"; also that the sculptor had carried off his daughter. Relieved to escape from the atmosphere of what he considered collective hysteria, he had borrowed mackintosh and umbrella, and declining several offers of a lift, had walked the four miles to his house in the rain and wind. The exercise helped to work off the emotion in him; his mind cleared healthily; personal bias gave way to honest and unprejudiced reflection; there was much that interested him deeply, at the same time puzzled and bewildered him beyond anything he had yet experienced. He reached the house with a mind steady if unsatisfied; but the emotions caused by prejudice had gone. His main anxiety centred about his chief.

He was glad to notice a light in an upper window, for it meant, he hoped, that LeVallon was now safely home. While his latchkey sought its hole, however, this light was extinguished, and when the door opened, it was Fillery himself who greeted him, a finger on his lips.

"Quietly!" he whispered. "I've just got him to bed and put his light out. He's asleep already." Paul noticed his manner instantly—its happiness. There was a glow of mysterious joy and wonder in his atmosphere that made the other hostile at once.

They went together towards that inner room where so often together they had already talked both moon and sun to bed. Cold food lay on the table, and while they satisfied their hunger, the rain outside poured down with a steady drenching sound. The wind had dropped. The suburb lay silent and deserted. It was long past midnight. The house was very still, only the occasional step of a night-nurse audible in the passages and rooms upstairs. They would not be disturbed.

"You got him home all right, then?" Paul asked presently, keeping his voice low.

He had been observing his friend closely; the evident pleasure and satisfaction in the face annoyed him; the light in the eyes at the same time profoundly troubled him. Not only did he love his chief for himself, he set high value on his work as well. It would be deplorable, a tragedy, if judgment were destroyed by personal bias and desire. He felt uneasy and distressed.

Fillery nodded, then gave an account of what had happened, but obviously an account of outward events merely; he did not wish, evidently, to argue or explain. The strong, rugged face was lit up, the eyes were shining, some inner enthusiasm pervaded his whole being. Evidently he felt very sure of something—something that both pleased and stimulated him.

His account of what had happened was brief enough, little more than a statement of the facts.

Finding himself close to LeVallon when the darkness came, he had kept hold of him and hurried him out of the house at once. The sudden blackness, it seemed, had made LeVallon quiet again, though he kept asking excitedly for the girl. When assured that he would soon see her, he became obedient as a lamb. The absence of light apparently had a calming influence. They found, of course, no taxis, but commandeered the first available private car, Fillery using the authoritative influence of his name. And it was Lady Gleeson's car, Lady Gleeson herself inside it. She had thought things over, put two and two together, and had come back. Her car might be of use. It was. For the rain was falling in sheets and bucketfuls, the road had become a river of water, and Fillery's automobile, ordered for an hour later, had not put in an appearance. It was the rain that saved the situation....

An exasperated expression crossed Devonham's face as he heard this detail emphasized. He had meant to listen without interruption. The enigmatical reference to the rain proved too much for him.

"Why 'the rain'? What d'you mean exactly, Edward?"

"Water," was the reply, made in a significant tone that further annoyed his listener's sense of judgment. "You remember the Channel, surely! Water and fire mutually destroy each other. They are hostile elements."

There was a look almost of amusement on his face as he said it. Devonham kept a tight hold upon his tongue. It was not impatience or surprise he felt, though both were strong; it was perhaps sorrow.

"And so Lady Gleeson drove you home?"

He waited with devouring interest for further details. The throng of questions, criticisms and emotions surging in him he repressed with admirable restraint.

Lady Gleeson, yes, had driven the party home. Fillery made her sit on the back seat alone, while he occupied the front one, LeVallon beside him, but as far back among the deep cushions as possible. The doctor held his hand. At any other time, Devonham could have laughed; but he saw no comedy now. Lady Gleeson, it seemed, was awed by the seriousness of the "Chief," whom, even at the best of times, she feared a little. Her vanity, however, persuaded her evidently that she was somehow the centre of interest.

Yet Devonham, as he listened, had difficulty in persuading himself that he was in the twentieth century, and that the man who spoke was his colleague and a man of the day as well.

"LeVallon talked little, and that little to himself or to me. He seemed unaware that a third person was present at all. Though quiet enough, there was suppressed vehemence still about him. He said various things: that '*she* belonged to us,' for instance; that he 'knew his own'; that *she* was 'filled with fire in exile'; and that he would 'take her back.' Also that I, too, must go with them both. He often mentioned the sun, saying more than once that the sun had 'sent its messengers.' Obviously, it was not the ordinary sun he referred to, but some source of central heat and fire he seems aware of—"

"You, I suppose, Edward," put in his listener quickly, "said nothing to encourage all this? Nothing that could suggest or stimulate?"

Fillery ignored, even if he noticed, the tone of the question. "I kept silence rather. I said very little. I let him talk. I had to keep an eye on the woman, too."

"You certainly had your hands full—a dual personality and a nymphomaniac."

"She helped me, without knowing it. All he said about the girl, she evidently took to herself. When he begged me to keep the water out, she drew the window up the last half-inch.... The water frightened him; she was sympathetic, and her sympathy seemed to reach him, though I doubt if he was aware of her presence at all until the last minute almost—"

"And 'at the last minute'?"

"She leaned forward suddenly and took both his hands. I had let go of the one I held and was just about to open the door, when I heard her say excitedly that I must let her come and see him, or that he must call on her; she was sure she could help him; he must tell her everything.... I turned to look.... LeVallon, startled into what I believe was his first consciousness of her presence, stared into her eyes, and leaned forward among his cushions a little, so that their faces were close together. Before I could interfere, she had flung her bare arms about his neck and kissed him. She then sat back again, turning to me, and repeating again and again that he needed a woman's care and that she must help and mother him. She was excited, but she knew what she was saying. She showed neither shame nor the least confusion. She tasted—of course with her it cannot last—a bigger world. She was most determined."

"His reaction?" inquired Devonham, amused in spite of his graver emotions of uneasiness and exasperation.

"None whatever. I scarcely think he realized he had been kissed. His interest was so entirely elsewhere. I saw his face a moment among the white ermine, the bare arms and jewels that enveloped him." Fillery frowned faintly. "The car had almost stopped. Lady Gleeson was leaning back again. He looked at me, and his voice was intense and eager: 'Dear Fillery,' he said, 'we have found each other, I have found her. She knows, she remembers the way back. Here we can do so little.'

"Lady Gleeson, however, had interpreted the words in another way.

"'I'll come to-morrow to see you,' she said at once intensely. 'You *must* let me come,' —the last words addressed to me, of course."

The two men looked at one another a moment in silence, and for the first time during the conversation they exchanged a smile....

"I got him to bed," Fillery concluded. "In ten minutes he was sound asleep." And his eyes indicated the room overhead.

He leaned hack, and quietly began to fill his pipe. The account was over.

As though a great spring suddenly released him, Paul Devonham stood up. His untidy hair hung wild, his glasses were crooked on his big nose, his tie askew. His whole manner bristled with accumulated challenge and disagreement.

"*Who?*" he cried. "*Who?* Edward, I ask you?"

His colleague, yet knowing exactly what he meant, looked up questioningly. He looked him full in the face.

"Hush! " he said quietly. "You'll wake him."

He gazed with happy penetrating eyes at his companion. "Paul," he added gently, "do you really mean it? Have you still the faintest doubt?"

The moment had drama in it of unusual kind. The conflict between these two honest and unselfish minds was vital. The moment, too, was chosen, the place as well—this small, quiet room in a commonplace suburb of the greatest city on the planet, drenched by earthly rain and battered by earthly wind from the heart of an equinoctial storm; the mighty universe outside, breaking with wondrous, incredible impossibilities upon a mind that listened and a mind that could not hear; and upstairs, separated from them by a few carpenter's boards, an assortment of "souls," either derelict and ruined, or gifted supernormally, masters of space and time perhaps, yet all waiting to be healed by the best knowledge known to the race—and one among them, about whom the conflict raged... sound asleep... while wind and water stormed, while lightning fires lit the distant horizons, while the great sun lay hidden, and darkness crept soundlessly to and fro....

"Have you still the slightest doubt, Paul? " repeated Fillery. "You know the evidence. You have an open mind."

Then Devonham, still standing over his Chief, let out the storm that had accumulated in him over-long. He talked like a book. He talked like several books. It seemed almost that he distrusted his own personal judgment.

"Edward," he began solemnly—not knowing that he quoted—"you, above all men, understand the lower recesses of the human heart, that gloomy, gigantic oubliette in which our million ancestors writhe together inextricably, and each man's planetary past is buried alive—"

Fillery nodded quietly his acquiescence.

"You, of all men, know our packed, limitless subterranean life," Devonham went on, "and its impenetrable depths. You understand telepathy, 'extended telepathy ' as well, and how a given mind may tap not only forgotten individual memories, but memories of his family, his race, even planetary memories into the bargain, the memory, in fact, of every being that ever lived, right down to Adam, if you will—"

"Agreed," murmured the other, listening patiently, while he puffed his pipe and heard the rain and wind. "I know all that. I know it, at any rate, as a possible theory."

"You also know," continued Devonham in a slightly less strident tone, "your own—forgive me, Edward—your own idiosyncrasies, your weaknesses, your dynamic accumulated repressions, your strange physical heritage and spiritual—I repeat the phrase—your spiritual vagrancies towards—towards—" He broke off suddenly, unable to find the words he wanted.

"I'm illegitimate, born of a pagan passion," mentioned the other calmly. "In that sense, if you like, I have in me a 'complex' against the race, against humanity—as such."

He smiled patiently, and it was the patience, the evident conviction of superiority that exasperated his cautious, accurate colleague.

"If I love humanity, I also tolerate it perhaps, for I try to heal it," added Fillery. "But, believe me, Paul, I do not lose my scientific judgment."

"Edward," burst out the other, "how can you think it possible, then—that *he* is other than the result of tendencies transmitted by his mad parents, or acquired from Mason, who taught him all he knows, or—if you will—that he has these hysterical faculties—supernormal as we may call them—which tap some racial, even, if you will, some planetary past—"

He again broke off, unable to express his whole thought, his entire emotion, in a few words.

"I accept all that," said Fillery, still calmly, quietly, "but perhaps now—in the interest of truth"—his tone was grave, his words obviously chosen carefully—"if now I feel it necessary to go beyond it! My strange heritage," he added, "is even possibly a help and guide. How," he asked, a trace of passion for the first time visible in his manner, "shall we venture—how decide—for we are not wholly ignorant, you and I—between what is possible and impossible? Is this trivial planet, then," he asked, his voice rising suddenly, ominously perhaps, "our sole criterion? Dare we not venture—beyond—a little? The scientific mind should be the last to dogmatize as to the possibilities of this life of ours...."

The authority of chief, the old tie of respectful and affectionate friendship, the admiring wonder that pertained to a daring speculator who had often proved himself right in face of violent opposition—all these affected Devonham. He did not weaken, but for an instant he knew, perhaps, the existence of a vast, incredible horizon in his friend's mind, though one he dared not contemplate. Possibly, he understood in this passing moment a huger world, a new outlook that scorned limit, though yet an outlook that his accurate, smaller spirit shrank from.

He found, at any rate, his own words futile. "You remember," he offered— "'We need only suppose the continuity of our own consciousness with a mother sea, to allow for exceptional waves occasionally pouring over the dam.'"

"Good, yes," said Fillery. "But that 'mother sea,' what may it not include? Dare we set limits to it?"

And, as he said it, Fillery, emotion visible in him, rose suddenly from his chair. He stood up and faced his colleague.

"Let us come to the point," he said in a clear, steady voice. "It all lies—doesn't it?—in that question you asked—"

"Who?" came at once from Devonham's lips, as he stood, looking oddly stiff and rigid opposite his Chief. There was a touch of defiance in his tone. "Who?" He repeated his original question.

No pause intervened. Fillery's reply came sharp and firm:

"'N. H.,'" he said.

An interval of silence followed, then, between the two men, as they looked into each other's eyes. Fillery waited for his assistant to speak, but no word came.

"LeVallon," the older man continued, "is the transient, acquired personality. It does not interest us. There is no real LeVallon. The sole reality is 'N. H.'"

He spoke with the earnestness of deep conviction. There was still no reply or comment from the other.

"Paul," he continued, steadying his voice and placing a hand upon his colleague's shoulder, "I am going to ask you to—consider our arrangement—cancelled. I must—"

Then, before he could finish what he had to say, the other had said it for him: "Edward, I give you back your promise."

He shrugged his shoulders ever so slightly, but there was no unpleasant, no antagonistic touch now either in voice or manner. There was, rather, a graver earnestness than there had been hitherto, a hint of reluctant acquiescence, but also there was an emotion that included certainly affection. No such fundamental disagreement had ever come between them during all their years of work together. "You understand," he added slowly, "what you are doing—what is involved." His tone almost suggested that he spoke to a patient, a loved patient, but one over whom he had no control. He sighed.

"I belong, Paul, myself to the unstable—if that is what you mean," said his old friend gently, "and with all of danger, or of wonder, it involves."

The faint movement of the shoulders again was noticeable. "We need not put it that way, Edward," was the quiet rejoinder; "for that, if true, can only help your insight, your understanding, and your judgment." He hesitated a moment or two, searching his mind carefully for words. Fillery waited. "But it involves—I think"—he went on presently in a firmer voice—"his fate as well. He must become permanently—one or other."

No pause followed. There was a smile of curious happiness on Fillery's face as he instantly answered in a tone of absolute conviction

"There lies the root of our disagreement, Paul. There is no 'other.' I am positive for once. There is only one, and that one is—'N. H.'"

"Umph!" his friend grunted. Behind the exclamation hid an attitude confirmed, as though he had come suddenly to a big decision.

"You see, Paul—I *know*."

CHAPTER XVII

It was not long after the scene in the Studio that the Prometheans forgathered at dinner in the back room of the small French restaurant in Soho and discussed the event. The prices were moderate, conditions free and easy. It was a favourite haunt of Members.

To-night, moreover, there was likely to be a good attendance. The word had gone out.

The Studio scene had, of course, been the subject of much discussion already. The night of its occurrence it had been talked over till dawn in more than one flat, and during the following days the Society, as a whole, thought of little else. Those who had not been present had to be informed, and those who had witnessed it found it an absorbing topic of speculation. The first words that passed when one member met another in the street was: "What *did* you make of that storm? Wasn't it amazing? Did your solar plexus vibrate? Mine did! And the light, the colour, the vibrations—weren't they terrific? What do you think *he* is?" It was rumoured that the Secretary was asking for individual reports. Excitement and interest were general, though the accounts of individual witnesses differed extraordinarily. It seemed impossible that all had seen and heard the same thing.

The back room was pleasantly filled to-night, for it was somehow known that Millington Povey and possibly Father Collins, too, were coming. Miss Milligan, the astrologist, was there early, arriving with Mrs. Towzer, who saw auras and had already, it was rumoured, painted automatically a strange rendering of "forces" that were visible to her clairvoyantly during the occurrence. Miss Lance, in shining beads and a glittering scarf, arrived on their heels, an account of the scene in her pocket—to be published in her magazine "Simplicity" after she had modified it according to what she picked up from hearing other, and better, descriptions.

Kempster, immaculate as ever, ordering his food as he ordered his clothes, like a connoisseur, was one of the first to establish himself in a comfortable seat. He knew how to look after himself, and was already eating in his neat dainty way while the others still stood about, studying the big white *menu* with its illegible hieroglyphics in smudged violet ink. He supplemented his meals with special patent foods of vegetarian kind he brought with him. He had dried bananas in one pocket and spirit photographs in another, and he was invariably pulling out the wrong thing. Meat he avoided. "A man is what he eats," he held, and animal blood was fatal to psychic development. To eat pig or cow was to absorb undesirable characteristics.

Next to him sat Lattimer, a lanky man of thirty, with loose clothes, long hair, and eyes of strange intensity. Known as "occultist and alchemist," he was also a chemist of some repute. His life was ruled by a master-desire and a master-fear: the former, that he might one day project his double consciously; the latter, that in his next earthly incarnation he might be—the prospect made him shudder—a woman. He sought to keep his thought as concrete as possible, the male quality.

He believed that the nervous centre of the physical body which controlled all such unearthly, if not definitely "spiritual," impulses, was the solar plexus. For him it was *the* important portion of his anatomy, the seat of intuition. Brain came second.

"The fellow," he declared emphatically, "stirred my solar plexus, my *kundalini*—that's all I know." He referred, as all understood, to the latent power the *yogis* claim lies coiled, but only rarely manifested, in that great nervous centre.

His statement, he knew, would meet with general approval and understanding. It was the literal Kempster who spoiled his opening:

"Paul Devonham," said the latter, "thinks it's merely a secondary personality that emerged. I had a long argument with him about it—"

"Never argue with the once-born," declared Povey flatly, producing his pet sentence. "It's waste of time. Only older souls, with the experience of many earthly lives stored in their beings, are knowledgeable." He filled his glass and poured out for others, Lattimer and Mrs. Towzer alone declining, though for different reasons.

"It destroys the 'sight,'" explained the former. "Alcohol sets up coarse vibrations that ruin clairvoyance."

"I decided to deny myself till the war is over," was Mrs. Towzer's reason, and when Povey reminded her of the armistice, she mentioned that Turkey hadn't "signed yet."

"I think his soul—" began Miss Lance.

"If he has a soul," put in Povey, electrically.

"—is hardly in his body at all," concluded Miss Lance, less convincingly than originally intended.

"It was love at first sight. His sign is Fire and hers is Air," Miss Milligan said.

"That's certain. *Of course* they came together."

"A clear case of memory, at any rate," insisted Kempster. "Two old souls meet-ing again for the first time for thousands of years, probably. Love at first sight, or hate, for that matter, is always memory, isn't it?" He disliked the astrology explanation; it was not mysterious enough, too mathematical and exact to please him.

"Secondary personalities *are* invariably memories of former selves, of course," agreed young Dickson, the theosophist, who was on the verge now of becom-ing a psycho-analyst and had already discarded Freud for Jung. "If not memo-ries of past lives, then they're desires suppressed in this one."

"The less you think, the more you know," suggested Miss Lance. She dis-trusted intellect and believed that another faculty, called instinct or intuition, according to which word first occurred to her, was the way to knowledge. She was about to quote Bergson upside down, when Povey, foreseeing an interval of boredom, took command:

"One thing we know, at any rate," he began judiciously; "we aren't the only beings in the universe. There are non-human intelligences, both vast and small. The old world-wide legends can't be built on nothing. In every age of history—the reports are universal—we have pretty good evidence for other forms of life than humans—"

"Though never yet in human *form*," put in Lattimer, yet sympathetically. "Their bodies, I mean, aren't human," he added.

"Exactly. That's true. But the gods, the fauns, the satyrs, the elemental be-ings, as we call 'em—sylphs, undines, gnomes and salamanders—to say noth-ing of fairies et hoc genus omne—there must be *some* reasonable foundation for their persistence through all the ages."

"They all belong to the *Deva* Evolution," Dickson mentioned with conviction. "In the East it's been known and recognized for centuries, hasn't it? Another evolutionary system that runs parallel to ours. From planetary spirits down to elementals, they're concerned with the building up of form in the various king-doms—"

"Yes, yes," Povey interrupted impatiently. Dickson was stealing what he had meant to say himself and to say, he flattered himself, far better. "We know all that, of course. They stand behind what we call the laws of nature, non-human activities and intelligences of every grade and kind. They work for humanity in a way, are in other space and time, deathless, of course, yet—in some strange way, always eager to cross the gulf fixed between the two and so find a soul. They are impersonal in a sense, as impersonal as, say, wind and fire through which some of them operate as bodies."

He paused and looked about him, noting the interested attention he awaked.

"There may be times," he went on, "there probably *are* certain occasions, when the gulf is more crossable than others." He laid down his knife and fork as a sympathetic murmur proved that the point he was leading up to was favourably understood already. "We have had this war, for instance," he stated, his voice taking on a more significant and mysterious tone. "Dislodged by the huge upheaval, man's soul is on the march again." He paused once more. "*They,*" he concluded, lowering his voice still more, and emphasizing the pronoun, "are possibly already among us! Who knows?"

He glanced round. "We do; we know," was the expression on most faces. All knew precisely what he meant and to whom he referred, at any rate.

"You might get him to come and lecture to us," said Dickson, the first to break the pause. "You might ask Dr. Fillery. *You* know him."

"That's an idea—" began the Secretary, when there was a commotion near the door. His face showed annoyance.

It was the arrival of Toogood that at this moment disturbed the atmosphere and robbed Povey of the effect he aimed at. It provided Kempster, however, with an idea at the same time. "Here's a psychometrist!" he exclaimed, making room for him. "He might get a bit of his hair or clothing and psychometrize it. He might tell us about his past, if not exactly what he is."

The suggestion, however, found no seconder, for it seemed that the new arrival was not particularly welcomed. Judging by the glances, the varying shades of greeting, too, he was not fully trusted, perhaps, this broad, fleshy man of thirty-five, with complexion blotchy, an over-sensual mouth and eyes a trifle shifty. His claim to membership was two-fold: he remembered past lives, and had the strange power of psychometry. An archæologist by trade, his gift of psychometry—by which he claimed to hold an object and tell its past, its pedigree, its history—was of great use to him in his calling. Without further trouble he could tell whether such an object was genuine or sham. Dealers in antiquities offered him big fees—but "No, no; I cannot prostitute my powers, you see"—and he remained poor accordingly.

In his past lives he had been either a famous Pharaoh, or Cleopatra—according to his audience of the moment and its male or female character—but usually Cleopatra, because, on the whole, there was more money and less risk in her. He lectured—for a fee. Lately, however, he had been Pharaoh, having got into grave trouble over the Cleopatra claim, even to the point of being threatened with expulsion from the Society. His attitude during the war, besides, had been unsatisfactory—it was felt he had selfishly protected himself on the grounds of being physically unfit. Apart from archæology, too, his chief preoccupation, derived from past lives of course, was sex, in the form of other men's wives, his own wife and children being, naturally, very recent and somewhat negligible ties.

His gift of psychometry, none the less, was considered proved—in spite of the backward and indifferent dealers. His mind was quick and not unsubtle. He became now au fait with the trend of the conversation in a very few seconds, but he had not been present at the Studio when the occurrence all discussed had taken place.

"Hair would be best," he advised tentatively, sipping his whisky-and-soda. He had already dined. "It's a part of himself, you see. Better than mere clothing, I mean. It's extremely vital, hair. It grows after death."

"If I can get it for you, I will," said Povey. "He may be lecturing for us before long. I'll try."

"With psychometry and a good photograph," Kempster suggested, "a time exposure, if possible, we ought to get *some* evidence, at any rate. It's first-hand
evidence we want, of course, isn't it? What do you think of this, for instance,
I wonder?" He turned to Lattimer, drawing something from his pocket and
showing it. "It's a time exposure at night of a haunted tree. You'll notice a queer
sort of elemental form *inside* the trunk and branches. Oh!" He replaced the shriv-
elled banana in his pocket, and drew out the photograph without a smile.
"This," he explained, waving it, "is what I meant." They fell to discussing it.

Meanwhile, Povey, anxious to resume his lecture, made an effort to recover
his command of the group-atmosphere which Toogood had disturbed. The latter had a "personal magnetism" which made the women like him in spite of their
distrust.

"I was just saying," he resumed, patting the elbow of the psychometrist, "that
this strange event we've been discussing—you weren't present, I believe, at
the time, but, of course, you've heard about it?—has features which seem to
point to something radically new, or at least of very rare occurrence. As Lattimer
mentioned, a human body has never yet, so far as we know, been occupied, ob-
sessed, by a non-human entity, but that, after all, is no reason why it should not
ever happen. What is a body, anyhow? What is an entity, too?" Povey's
thought was wandering, evidently; the thread of his first discourse was broken;
he floundered. "Man, anyway, is more than a mere chemical machine," he went
on, "a crystallization of the primitive nebulæ, though the instrument he uses,
the body he works through, is undoubtedly thus describable. Now, we know
there are all kinds of non-human intelligences busy on our planet, in the Universe itself as well. Why, then, I ask, should not one of these—?"

He paused, unable to find himself, his confusion obvious. He was as glad of
the interruption that was then provided by the arrival of Imson as his audience
was. Toogood certainly was not sorry; he need find no immediate answer. He
sipped his drink and made mental notes.

Imson arrived in a rough brown ulster with the collar turned up about his ears,
a low flannel shirt, not strictly clean, lying loosely round his neck. His colourless face was of somewhat flabby texture, due probably to his diet, but its simple, honest expression was attractive, the smile engaging. The touch of foolishness might have been childlike innocence, even saintliness some thought, and
though he was well over forty, the unlined skin made him look more like
thirty. He enjoyed a physiognomy not unlike that of a horse or sheep. His big,
brown eyes stared wide open at the world, expecting wonder and finding it. His
hobby was inspirational poems. One lay in his breast pocket now. He burned
to read it aloud.

Pat Imson's ideal was an odd one—detachment; the desire to avoid all ties that
must bring him back to future incarnations on the earth, to eschew making fresh
karma, in a word. He considered himself an "old soul," and was rather weary
of it all—of existence and development, that is. To take no part in life meant to
escape from those tangles for whose unravelling the law of rebirth dragged the

soul back again and again. To sow no Causes was to have no harvest of Effects to reap with toil and perspiration. Action, of course, there must be, but "indifference to results of action" was the secret. Imson, none the less, was always entangled with wives and children. Having divorced one wife, and been divorced by another, he had recently married a third; a flock of children streamed behind him; he was a good father, if a strange husband.

"It's old Karma I have to work off," he would explain, referring to the wives. "If I avoid the experience I shall only have to come back again. There's no good shirking old Karma." He gave this explanation to the wives themselves, not only to his friends. "Face it and it's done with, worked off, you see." That is, it had to be done nicely, kindly, generously.

An entire absence of the sense of humour was, of course, his natural gift, yet a certain quaint wisdom helped to fill the dangerous vacuum. He was known usually as "Pat."

"Come on, Pat," said Povey, making room for him at his side. "How's Karma? We're just talking about LeVallon and the Studio business. What do you make of it? You were there, weren't you?" The others listened, attentively, for Imson had a reputation for "seeing true."

"I saw it, yes," replied Imson, ordering his dinner with indifference—soup, fried potatoes, salad, cheese and coffee—but declining the offered wine. The group waited for his next remark, but none was forthcoming. He sat crumbling his bread into the soup and stirring the mixture with his spoon.

"Did you see the light about him, Mr. Imson?" asked Miss Lance. "The brilliant aura of golden yellow that he wore? I thought—it sounds exaggerated, I know—but to me it seemed even brighter than the lightning. Did you notice it?"

"Well," said Imson slowly, putting his spoon down. "I'm not often clairvoyant, you know. I did notice, however, a sort of radiance about him. But with hair like that, it's difficult to be certain—"

"Full of lovely patterns," said Mrs. Towzer. "Geometrical patterns."

"Like astrological designs," mentioned Miss Milligan. "He's Leo, of course—fire."

"Almost as though he brought or caused the lightning—as if it actually emanated out of his atmosphere somehow," claimed Miss Lance, for it was *her* conversation after all.

"I saw nothing of that," replied Imson quietly. "No, I can't say I saw anything *exactly* like that." He added honestly, with his engaging smile that had earned for him in some quarters the nickname of "The Sheep": "I was looking at Nayan, you see, most of the time."

A smile flickered round the table, for rumour had it that the girl had once seemed to him as possible "Karma."

"So was I," put in Kempster with kindly intention, though his sympathy was evidently not needed. Imson was too simple even to feel embarrassment. "She came to life suddenly for the first time since I've known her. It was amazing." To which Imson, busy over his salad-dressing, made no reply.

Povey, lighting his pipe and puffing out thick clouds of smoke, was cleverer. "LeVallon's effect upon her, whatever it was, seemed instantaneous," he informed the table. "I never saw a clearer case of two souls coming together in a flash."

"As I said just now," Kempster quickly mentioned.

"They are similar," said. Imson, looking up, while the group waited expectantly.

"Similar," repeated Kempster. "Ah!"

"It was the surprise in her face that struck me most," observed Povey quickly, making an internal note of Imson's adjective, but knowing that indirect methods would draw him out better than point-blank questions. "LeVallon showed it too. It was an unexpected recognition on both sides. They are 'similar,' as you say; both at the same stage of development, whatever that stage may be. The expression on both faces—"

"Escape," exclaimed Imson, giving at last the kernel of what he had to say. And the effect upon the group was electrical. A visible thrill ran round the Soho table.

"The very word," exclaimed Povey and Miss Lance together. "Escape!" But neither of them knew exactly what they meant, nor what Imson himself meant.

"LeVallon has, of course, already escaped," the latter went on quietly. "He is no longer caught by causes and effects as we are here. He's got out of it all long ago—if he was ever in it at all."

"If he ever was in it at all," said Povey quickly. "You noticed that too. You're very discerning, Pat."

"Clairvoyant," mentioned Miss Lance.

"I've seen them in dreams like that," returned Imson calmly. "I often see them, of course." He referred to his qualification for membership. "The great figures I see in dream have just that unearthly expression."

"Unearthly," said Mrs. Towzer with excitement.

"Non-human," mentioned Kempster suggestively.

"Not of this world, anyhow," suggested Miss Lance mysteriously.

"Divine?" inquired Miss Milligan below her breath.

"Really," murmured Toogood, "I must get a bit of his hair and psychometrize it at once." He was sipping a second glass of whisky.

Imson looked round at each face in turn, apparently seeing nothing that need increase his attachment to the planet by way of fresh Karma.

"The *Deva* world," he said briefly, after a pause. "Probably he's come to take Nayan off with him. She—I always said so—has a strong strain of the elemental kingdom in her. She may be his *Devi*. LeVallon, I'm sure, is here for the first time. He's one of the nonhuman evolution. He's slipped in. A *Deva* himself probably." It was as though he said that the waiter was Swiss or French, or that the proprietor's daughter had Italian blood in her.

Povey looked round him with an air of triumph.

"Ah!" he announced, as who should say, "You all thought my version a bit wild, but here's confirmation from an unbiased witness."

"Oh, well, I can't be certain," Imson reminded the group. If he deceived them enough to change their lives in any respect, it involved fresh Karma for himself. Care was indicated. "I can't be positive, can I?" he hedged. "Only—I must say—the great deva-figures I've seen in dream have exactly that look and expression."

"That's interesting, Pat," Povey put in, "because, before you came, I was suggesting a similar explanation for his air of immense potential power. The elemental atmosphere he brought—we all noticed it, of course."

"Elemental *is* the only word," Miss Lance inserted. "A great Nature Being." She was thinking of her magazine. "He struck me as being so close to Nature that he seemed literally part of it."

"That would explain the lightning and the strange cry he gave about 'messengers,'" replied Imson, wiping the oil from his chin and sprinkling his *petit suisse* with powdered sugar. "It's quite likely enough."

"I wish you'd jot down what you think—a little report of what you saw and felt," the Secretary mentioned. "It would be of great value. I thought of making a collection of the different versions and accounts."

"They might be published some day," thought Miss Lance. "Let's all," she added aloud with emphasis.

Imson nodded agreement, making no audible reply, while the conversation ran on, gathering impetus as it went, growing wilder possibly, but also more picturesque. A man in the street, listening behind a curtain, must have deemed the talkers suffering from delusion, mad; a good psychologist, on the other hand, similarly screened, and knowing the antecedent facts, the Studio scene, at any rate, must have been struck by one outstanding detail—the effect, namely, upon one and all of the person they discussed. They had seen him for an hour or so among a crowd, a young man whose name they hardly knew; only a few had spoken to him; there had been, it seemed, neither time nor opportunity for him to produce upon one and all the impression he undoubtedly had produced. For in every mind, upon every heart, LeVallon's mere presence had evidently graven an unforgettable image, scored an undecipherable hieroglyph. Each felt, it seemed, the hint of a personality their knowledge could not explain, nor any earthly explanation satisfy. The consciousness in each one, perhaps, had been quickened. Hence, possibly, the extravagance of their conversation. Yet, since all reported differently, collective hysteria seemed discounted.

Meanwhile, as the talk continued, and the wings of imaginative speculation fanned the thick tobacco smoke, others had dropped in, both male and female members, and the group now filled the little room to the walls. The same magnet drew them all, in each heart burned the same huge question mark: Who—what—is this LeVallon? What was the meaning of the scene in Khilkoff's Studio?

Here, too, was a curious and significant fact about the gathering—the amount of knowledge, true or otherwise, they had managed to collect about LeVallon. One way or another, no one could say exactly how, the Society had picked up an astonishing array of detail they now shared together. It was known where he had spent his youth, also how, and with whom, as well as something of the different views about him held by Dr. Devonham and Edward Fillery. To such temperaments as theirs the strange, the unusual, came automatically perhaps, percolating into their minds as though a collective power of thought-reading operated. Garbled, fanciful, askew, their information may have been, but a great deal of it was not far wrong.

Imson, for instance, provided an account of LeVallon's birth, to which all listened spellbound. He evaded all questions as to how he knew of it. "His parents," he assured the room, "practised the old forgotten magic; his father, at any rate, was an expert, if not an initiate, with all the rites and formulæ of ancient times in his memory. LeVallon was born as the result of an experiment, its origins dating back so far that they concerned life upon another planet, I believe, a planet nearer to the sun. The tremendous winds and heat were vehicles of deity, you see—*there*."

"The parents, you mean, had former lives upon another planet?" asked someone in a hushed tone. "Or he himself?"

"The parents—and Mason. Mason was involved in the experiment that resulted in the birth of LeVallon here to-day."

"The experiment—what was it exactly?" inquired Lattimer, while Toogood surreptitiously made notes on his rather dirty cuff.

Imson shrugged his shoulders very slightly.

"Some of it came to me in sleep," he mentioned, producing a paper from his pocket and beginning to read it aloud before anyone could stop him.

"When the sun was younger, and moon and stars
        Were thrilled with my human birth,
And the winds fled shouting the wondrous news
        As they circled the sea and the earth,

"From the fight for money and worldly fame
        I drew one magical soul
Who came to me over the star-lit sea
        As the needle turns to the Pole.

"Conceived in the hour the stars foretold,
        This son of the winds I bore,
And I taught him the secrets of—"

"Yes," interrupted Povey audaciously, "but the experiment you were telling us about—?"

A murmur of approving voices helped him.

"Oh, the experiment, yes, well—all I know is," he went on with conviction, calmly replacing the poem in his pocket, "that it concerned an old rite, involving the evocation of some elemental being or nature-spirit the three of them had already evoked millions of years before, but had not banished again. The experiment they made to-day was to restore it to its proper sphere. In order to do so, they had to evoke it again, and, of course—he glanced round, as though all present were familiar with the formula of magical practices—" it could come only through the channel of a human system."

"Of course, yes," murmured a dozen voices, while eyes grew bigger and a pin dropping must have been audible.

"Well"—Imson spoke very slowly now, each word clear as a bell—"the father, who was officiating, failed. He could not stand the strain. His heart stopped beating. He died—just when *it* was there, he dropped dead."

"What happened to *it*?" asked Povey, too interested to care that he no longer led the room. "You said it could only use a human system as channel—"

"It did so," explained Imson.

The information produced a pause of several seconds. Some of the members, like Toogood, though openly, were making pencil notes upon cuffs or backs of envelopes.

"But the channel was neither Mason nor the woman." The effect of this negative information was as nothing compared to the startling interest produced by the speaker's next words: "It took the easiest channel, the line of least resistance—the unborn body of the child."

Povey, seizing his opportunity, leaped into the silence:

"Whose body, now full grown, and named LeVallon, came to the Studio!" he exclaimed, looking round at the group, as though he had himself given the explanation all had just listened to. "A human body tenanted by a nature-spirit, one of the form-builders—a *Deva*...."

CHAPTER XVIII

For all the wildness of the talk, this group of the Unstable was a coherent and consistent entity, using a language each item in it understood. They knew what they were after. Alcohol, coffee, tobacco, underfeeding, these helped or hindered, respectively, the expression of an ideal that, nevertheless, was common to them all; and if the minds represented were unbalanced, or merely speculative, poetic, one genuine quest and sympathy bound all together into a coherent, and who shall say unintelligent or valueless, unit. The unstable enjoyed an extreme sensitiveness to varied experience, with flexible adaptability to all possible new conditions, whereas the stable, with their rigid mental organizations, remained uninformed, stagnant, even fossilized.

In other rooms about the great lamp-lit city sat, doubtless, other similar groups at the very same moment, discussing the shibboleths of other faiths, of other dreams, of other ideas, systems, notions, philosophies, all interpretative of the earth in which little humanity dwells, cut off and isolated, apparently, from the rest of the stupendous universe. A listener, screened from view, a listener not in sympathy with the particular group he observed, and puzzled, therefore,

by the language used, must have deemed he listened to harmless, if boring, madness. For each group uses its own language, and the lowest common denomi-
nator, though plainly printed in the world's old scriptures, has not yet become
adopted by the world at large.

Into this particular group, a little later in the evening, and when the wings
of imagination had increased their sweep a trifle dangerously perhaps—into the
room, like the arrival of a policeman rather, dropped Father Collins. He came
rarely to the Prometheans' restaurant. There was a general sense of drawing
breath as he appeared. A pause followed. Something of the cold street air came
with him. He wore his big black felt hat, his shabby opera cloak, and clutched
firmly—he had no gloves on—the heavy gnarled stick he had cut for his collection in a Cingalese forest years ago, when he was studying with a Buddhist
priest. The folds of his voluminous cloak, as he took it off, sent the hanging
smoke-clouds in a whirl. His personality stirred the mental atmosphere as well.
The women looked up and stared, respectful welcome in their eyes; several of
the men rose to shake hands; there was a general shuffling of chairs.

"Bring another *moulin á vent* and a clean glass," Povey said at once to the hovering waiter.

"It's raw and bitter in the street and a fog coming down thickly," mentioned
Father Collins. He exhaled noisily and with comfortable relief, as he squeezed
himself towards the chair Povey placed for him and looked round genially, nod-
ding and shaking hands with those he knew. "But you're warm and cosy
enough in here"—he sat down with unexpected heaviness, and smiled at everybody—"and well fed, too, I'll be bound."

"'The body must be comfortable before the mind can enjoy itself,'" said
Phillipps, an untidy member who disliked asceticism. "Starvation produces hallucination, not vision." His glance took in the unused glasses. His qualification
was a vision of an uncle at the moment of death, and the uncle had left him
money. He had written a wordy pamphlet describing it.

"I'll have an omelette, then, I think," Father Collins told the waiter, as the
red wine arrived. "And some fried potatoes. A bit of cheese to follow, and coffee, yes." He filled his glass. He had not come to argue or to preach, and
Phillipps's challenge passed unnoticed. Phillipps, who had been leading the talk
of late, resented the new arrival, but felt his annoyance modify as he saw his own
glass generously filled. Povey, too, accepted a glass, while saying with a false vehemence, "No, no," his finger against the rim.

A change stole over the room, for the new personality was not negligible; he
brought his atmosphere with him. The wild talk, it was felt now, would not be
quite suitable. Father Collins had the reputation of being something of a scholar;
they were not quite sure of him; none knew him very intimately; he had a rumoured past as well that lent a flavour of respect. One story had it that "dab-
bling in magic" had lost him his position in the Church. Yet he was deemed an
asset to the Society.

Whatever it was, the key changed sharply. Imson's eyes and ears grew
wider, the hand of Miss Lance went instinctively to her hair and combs, Miss

Milligan sought through her mind for a remark at once instructive and uncommon, Mrs. Towzer looked past him searchingly lest his aura escape her before she caught its colour, and Kempster, smoothing his immaculate coat, had an air of being in his present surroundings merely by chance. Toogood, quickly scanning his notes, wondered whether, if called upon, he was to be Pharaoh or Cleopatra. One and all, that is, took on a soberer gait. This semi-clerical visit complicated. The presence of Father Collins was a compliment. What he had to say—about LeVallon and the Studio scene—was, anyhow, assured of breathless interest.

Povey led off. "We were just talking over the other night," he observed, "the night at the Studio, you remember. The storm and so on. It was a singular occurrence, though, of course, we needn't, we *mustn't* exaggerate it." And while he thus, as Secretary, set the note, Father Collins sipped his wine and beamed upon the group. He made no comment. "You were there, weren't you?" continued Povey, sipping his own comforting glass. "I think I saw you. Fillery, you may have noticed," he added, "brought—a friend."

"LeVallon, yes," said the other in a tone that startled them. "A most unusual fellow, wasn't he?" He was attacking the omelette now. "A Greek God, if ever I saw one," he added. And the silence in the crowded room became abruptly noticeable. Miss Milligan, feeling her zodiacal garter slipping, waited to pull it up. Imson's brown eyes grew wider. Kempster held his breath. Toogood borrowed a cigar and waited for someone to offer him a match before he lit it.

"Delicious," added Father Collins. "Cooked to a turn." The omelette slid about his plate.

But the silence continued, and he realized the position suddenly. Emptying his glass and casually refilling it, he turned and faced the eager group about him.

"You want to know what I thought about it all," he said. "You've been discussing LeVallon, Nayan and the rest, I see." He looked round as though he were in the lost pulpit that was his right. After a pause he asked point blank: "And what do *you* all think of it? How did it strike you all? For myself, I confess—", he took another sip and paused—"I am full of wonder and question," he finished abruptly.

It was Imson, the fearless, wondering Pat Imson, who first found his tongue.

"We think," he ventured, "LeVallon is probably of *Deva* origin."

The others, while admiring his courage, seemed unsympathetic suddenly. Such phraseology, probably meaningless to the respected guest, was out of place. Eyes were cast down, or looked generally elsewhere. Povey, remembering that the Society was not solely Eastern, glared at the speaker. Father Collins, however, was not perturbed.

"Possibly," he remarked with a courteous smile. "The origin of us all is doubtful and confused. We know not whence we come, of course, and all that. Nor can we ever tell exactly who our neighbour is, or what. LeVallon," he went on, "since you all ask me"—he looked round again—"is—for me—an undecipherable being. I am," he added, his words falling into open mouths and extended eyes and ears, "somewhat puzzled. But more—I am enormously stimulated and intrigued."

All gazed at him. Father Collins was in his element. The rapt silence that met him was precisely what he had a right to expect from his lost pulpit. He had come, probably, merely to listen and to watch. The opportunity provided by a respectful audience was too much for him. An inspiration tempted him.

"I am inclined to believe," he resumed suddenly in a simple tone, "that he is— a Messenger."

The sentence might have dropped from Sirius upon a listening planet. The babble that followed must, to an ordinary man, have seemed confusion. Every-one spoke with a rush into his neighbour's ear. All bubbled. "I always thought so, I told you so, that was exactly what I meant just now"—and so on. All found their tongues, at any rate, if Povey, as Secretary, led the turmoil:

"Something outside our normal evolution, you mean?" he asked judiciously. "Such a conception is possible, of course."

"A Messenger!" ran on the babel of male and female voices.

It was here that Father Collins failed. The "unstable" in him came suddenly uppermost. The "ecstatic" in his being took the reins. The wondering and ex-pectant audience suited him. The red wine helped as well. When he said "Mes-senger " he had meant merely someone who brought a message. The expression of nobility merged more and more in the slovenly aspect. Like a priest in the pul-pit, whom none can answer and to whom all must listen, he had his text, though that text had been suggested actually by the conversation he had just heard. He had not brought it with him. It occurred to him merely then and there. His mind reflected, in a word, the collective idea that was in the air about him, and he pro-ceeded to sum it up and give expression to it. This was his gift, his fatal gift— a ready sensitiveness, a plausible exposition. He caught the prevailing mood, the collective notion, then dramatized it. Before he left the pulpit he invariably, how-ever, convinced himself that what he had said in it was true, inspired, a revela-tion—for that moment.

"A Messenger," he announced, thrusting his glass aside with an impatient ges-ture as though noticing for the first time that it was there. "A Messenger," he repeated, the automatic emphasis in his voice already persuading him that he be-lieved what he was about to say, "sent among us from who knows what distant sphere"—he drew himself up and looked about him—"and for who can guess on what mysterious and splendid mission."

His eye swept his audience, his hand removed the glass yet farther lest it im-pede free gesture. It was, however, as Povey noticed, empty now. "We, of course," he went on impressively, lowering his voice, "*we*, a mere handful in the world, but alert and watchful, all of us—we know that some great new teach-ing is expected"—he threw out another challenging glance—" but none of us can know whence it may come nor in what way it shall manifest." His voice dropped dramatically. "Whether as a thief in the night, or with a blare of trum-pets, none of us can tell. But—we expect it and are ready. To *us*, therefore, per-haps, as to the twelve fishermen of old, may be entrusted the privilege of ac-cepting it, the work of spreading it among a hostile and unbelieving world, even perhaps the final sacrifice of—of suffering for it."

He paused, quickly took in the general effect of his words, picked up here and there a hint of question, and realized that he had begun on too exalted a note. Detecting this breath of caution in the collective mind that was his inspiration, he instantly shifted his key.

"LeVallon," he resumed, instinctively emphasizing the conviction in his voice so that the change of key might be less noticeable, "undoubtedly—believes himself to be—some such divine Messenger..." It was consummate hedging.

The sermon needs no full report. The audience, without realizing it, witnessed what is known as an "inspirational address," where a speaker, naturally gifted with a certain facile eloquence, gathers his inspiration, takes his changing cues as well, from the collective mind that listens to him. Father Collins, quite honestly doubtless, altered his key automatically. He no longer said that LeVallon *was* a Messenger, but that he "believed himself " to be one. Like Balaam, he said things he had not at first thought of saying. He talked for some ten minutes without stopping. He said "all sorts of things," according to the expression of critical doubt, of wonder, of question, of rejection or acceptance, on the particular face he gazed at. At regular intervals he inserted, with considerable effect, his favourite sentence: "A man in his *own* place is the Ruler of his Fate."

He developed his idea that LeVallon "believed himself to be such and such..." but declared that the conception had been put into the youth during his life of exile in the mountains—the Society had already acquired this information and extended it—and had "*felt himself into*" the rôle until he had become its actual embodiment.

"He does not think, he does not reason," he explained. "He feels—he *feels with*. Now, to 'feel with' anything is to become it in the end. It is the only way of true knowledge, of course, of true understanding. If I want to understand, say, an Arab, I must *feel with* that Arab to the point—for the moment—of actually becoming him. And this strange youth has spent his time, his best years, mark you—his creative years, *feeling with* the elemental forces of Nature until he has actually become—at moments—one with them."

He paused again and stared about him. He saw faces shocked, astonished, startled, but not hostile. He continued rapidly: "There lies the danger. One may get caught, get stuck. Lose the desire to return to one's normal self. Which means, of course, remaining out of relation with one's environment—mad. Only a man in his *own* place is the ruler of his luck...."

He noticed suddenly the look of disappointment on several faces. He swiftly hedged.

"On the other hand," he went on, making his voice and manner more impressive than before, "it may be—who can say indeed?—it may be that he is in relation with another environment altogether, a much vaster environment, an extended environment of which the rest of humanity is unaware. The privilege of tasting something of an extended environment some of us here already enjoy. What we all know as *human* activities are doubtless but a fragment of life—the conscious phenomena merely of some larger whole of which we are aware in fleeting seconds only—by mood, by hint, by suggestive hauntings, so to speak—by faint shadows of unfamiliar, nameless shape cast across our daily life from some intenser sun we normally cannot see! LeVallon may be, as some of us think and hope, a Messenger to show us the way into a yet farther field of consciousness....

"It is a fine, a noble, an inspiring hope, at any rate," he assured the room. "Unless some such Messenger comes into the world, showing us how to extend our knowledge, we can get no farther; we shall never know more than we know now; we shall only go on multiplying our channels for observing the same old things...."

He closed his little address finally on a word as to what attitude should be adopted to any new experience of amazing and incredible kind. To a Society such as the one he had the honour of belonging to was left the guidance of the perverse and ignorant generations outside of it, "the lethargic and unresponsive majority," as he styled them.

"We must not resist," he declared bravely. "We must accept with confidence, above all without fear." He leaned back in his chair, somewhat exhausted, for the source of his inspiration was evidently weakening. His words came less spontaneously, less easily; he hesitated, sighed, looked from face to face for help he did not find. His glass was empty. "We're here," he concluded lamely, "without being consulted, and we may safely leave to the Powers that brought us here the results of such acceptance."

"Quite so," agreed Povey, sighing audibly. "Denial will get us nowhere." He filled up Father Collins's glass and his own. "I think most of us are ready enough to accept any new experience that comes, and to accept it without fear." He drained his own glass and looked about him. "But the point is—how did LeVallon produce the effect upon us all—the effect he did produce? He may be non-human, or he may be merely mad. He may, as Imson says, come to us by some godless chance from another evolutionary system—of which, mind you, we have as yet no positive knowledge—or he may be a Messenger, as Father Collins suggests, from some divine source, bringing new teaching. But, in the name of Magic, how did he manage it? In other words—what is he?"

For Povey could be very ruthless when he chose. It was this ruthlessness, perhaps, that made him such an efficient secretary. The note of extravagance in his language had possibly another inspiration.

An awkward pause, at any rate, followed his remarks. Father Collins had comforted and blessed the group. Povey introduced cold water rather.

"There's this—and there's that," remarked Miss Mulligan, tactfully.

"Those among us," added Miss Lance with sympathy, "who have The Sight, know at least what they have seen. Still, I think we are indebted to Father Collins for—his guidance."

"If we knew exactly what he is," mentioned Mrs. Towzer, referring to LeVallon, "we should know exactly where we are."

They got up to go. There was a fumbling among crowded hat-pegs.

"What is he?" offered Kempster. "He certainly made us all sit up and take notice."

"No mere earthly figure," suggested Imson, "could have produced the effect *he* did. In my poem—it came to me in sleep—"

Father Collins held his glass unsteadily to the light. "A Messenger," he interrupted with authority, "would affect us all differently, remember."

The talk continued in this fashion for a considerable time, while all searched for wraps and coats. The waiter brought the bill amid general confusion, but no one noticed him. All were otherwise engaged. Povey paid it finally, putting it down to the Entertainment Account.

"Remember," he said, as they stood in a group on the restaurant steps, each wondering who would provide a lift home, "remember, we have all got to write out an account of what we saw and heard at the Studio. These reports will be valuable. They will appear in our 'Psychic Bulletin' first. Then I'll have them bound into a volume. And I shall try and get LeVallon to give us a lecture too. Tickets will be extra, of course, but each member can bring a friend. I'll let you all know the date in due course."

CHAPTER XIX

W hile the Prometheans thus, individually and collectively fermenting, floundered between old and new interpretations of a strange occurrence, in another part of London something was happening, of its kind so real, so interesting, that one and all would eagerly have renounced a favourite shibboleth or pet desire to witness it. Kempster would have eaten a raw beefsteak, Lattimer have agreed to rebirth as a woman, Mrs. Towzer have swallowed whisky neat, and even Toogood have written a signed confession that his "psychometry" was intelligent guesswork.

It is the destiny, however, of such students of the wonderful to receive their data invariably at second or third hand; the data may deal with genuine occurrences, but the student seems never himself present at the time. From books, from reports, from accounts of someone who knew an actual witness, the student generally receives the version he then proceeds to study and elaborate.

In this particular instance, moreover, no version ever reached their ears at all, either at second or third hand, because the only witness of what happened was Edward Fillery, and he mentioned it to no one. Its reality, its interpretation likewise, remained authoritative only for that expert, if unstable, mind that experienced the one and divined the other.

His conversation with Devonham over, and the latter having retired to his room, Fillery paid a last visit to the patient who was now his private care, instead of merely an inmate of the institution that was half a Home and half a Spiritual Clinique. The figure lay sleeping quietly, the lean, muscular body bare to the wind that blew upon it from the open window. Graceful, motionless, both pillow and coverings rejected, "N. H." breathed the calm, regular breath of deepest slumber. The light from the door just touched the face and folded hands, the features wore no expression of any kind, the hair, drawn back from the forehead and temples, almost seemed to shine.

Through the window came the rustle of the tossing branches, but the night air, though damp, was neither raw nor biting, and Fillery did not replace the sheets upon the great sleeping body. He withdrew as softly as he entered. Knowing he would not close an eye that night, he left the house silently and walked out into the deserted streets....

The rain had ceased, but the wet wind rushed in gusts against him, the soft blows and heavy moisture acting as balm to his somewhat tired nerves. As with great elemental hands, the windy darkness stroked him, soothing away the intense excitement he had felt, muting a thousand eager questions. They stroked his brain into a gentler silence gradually. "Don't think, don't think," night whispered all about him, "but feel, feel, feel. What you want to know will come to you by feeling now." He obeyed instinctively. Down the long, empty streets he passed, swinging his stick, tapping the lampposts, noting how steady their light held in the wind, noting the tossing trees in little gardens, noting occasional rifts of moonlight between the racing clouds, but relinquishing all attempt to think.

He counted the steps between the lamp-posts as he swung along, leaving the kerb at each crossing with his left foot, taking the new one with his right, planting each boot safely in the centre of each paving stone, establishing, in a word, a sort of rhythm as he moved. He did so, however, without being consciously aware of it. He was not aware, indeed, of anything but that he swung along with this pleasant rhythmical stride that rested his body, though the exercise was vigorous.

And the night laid her deep peace upon him as he went....

The streets grew narrower, twisted, turned and ran uphill; the houses became larger, spaced farther apart, less numerous, their gardens bigger, with groups of trees instead of isolated specimens. He emerged suddenly upon the open heath, tasting a newer, sweeter air. The huge city lay below him now, but the rough, shouting wind drowned its distant roar completely. For a time he stood and watched its twinkling lights across the vapours that hung between, then turned towards the little pond. He knew it well. Its waves flew dancing happily. The familiar outline of Jack Straw's Castle loomed beyond. The square enclosure of the anti-aircraft gun rattled with a metallic sound in the wind....

He had been walking for the best part of two hours now, thinking nothing but feeling only, and his surface-consciousness, perhaps, lay still, inactive. The mind was quiescent certainly, his being subdued and lulled by the rhythmic movement which had gained upon his entire system. The sails of his ship hung idly, becalmed above the profound deeps below. It was these deeps, the mysterious and inexhaustible region below the surface, that now began to stir. There stole upon him a dim prophetic sense as of horizons lifting and letting in new light. He glanced about him. The moon was brighter certainly, the flying scud was thinning, though the dawn was still some hours away. But it was not the light of moon or sun or stars he looked for; it was no outer light.

The little waves fell splashing at his feet. He watched them for a long time, keeping very still; his heart, his mind, his nerves, his muscles, all were very still.... He became aware that new big powers were alert and close, hovering above the world, feathering the Race like wings of mighty birds. The waters were being troubled....

He turned and walked slowly, but ever with the same pleasant rhythm that was in him, to the pine trees, where he paused a minute, listening to the branches shaking and singing, then retraced his steps along the ridge, every yard of which, though blurred in darkness, he knew and recognized. Below, on his left lay London, on his right stretched the familiar country, though now invisible, past Hendon with its Welsh Harp, Wembley, and on towards Harrow, whose church steeple would catch the sunrise before very long. He reached the little pond again and heard its small waves rushing and tumbling in the southwest wind. He stood and watched them, listening to their musical wash and gurgle.

The waters, yes, were being troubled.... Despite the buffeting wind, the world lay even stiller now about him; no single human being had he seen; even stiller than before, too, lay heart and mind within him; the latter held no single picture. He was aware, yes, of horizons lifting, of great powers alert and close; the interior light increased. He felt, but he did not think. Into the empty chamber of his being, swept and garnished, flashed suddenly, then, as in picture form, the memory of "N. H." All that he knew about him came at once: Paul's notes and journey, the London scenes and talks, his own observations, deductions, questionings, his dreams, and fears and yearnings, his hope and wonder—all came in a clapping instant, complete and simultaneous. Into his opened subconscious being floated the power and the presence of that bright messenger who brought glad tidings to his life.

"N. H." stood beside him, whispering with lips that were the darkness, and with words that were the wind. It was the power and presence of "N. H." that lifted the horizon and let in light. His body lay sleeping miles away in that bed against an open window. This was his real presence. Without words, as without thought, understanding came. The appeal of "N. H." was direct to the subliminal mind; it was the hidden nine-tenths he stimulated; hence came the intensification of consciousness in all who had to do with him. And it operated now. Fillery was aware of defying time and space, as though there were no limits to his being. Faith lights fires.... Perception wandered down those dusky byways *behind* the mind that lead through trackless depths where the massed heritage of the world-soul, lit sometimes by a flashing light, reveal incredible, incalculable things. One of those flashes came now. Through the fissures, as it were, of his unstable being rose the marvellous, uncanny gleam. His eyes were opened and he saw.

The label, he realized, was incorrect, inadequate—"N. H." was a misnomer; more than human, both different to and greater than, came nearer to the truth. A being from other conditions certainly, belonging to another order; an order whose work was unremitting service rendered with joy and faithfulness; a hierarchy whose service included the entire universe, the stars and suns and nebulæ, earth with her frail humanity but an insignificant fraction of it all....

He came, of course, from that central sea of energy whence all life, pushing irresistibly outwards into form, first arises. Like human beings, he came thence undoubtedly, but more directly than they, in more intimate relations, therefore, with the elemental powers that build up form and shape the destinies of matter. One only of a mighty host of varying degrees and powers, his services lay interwoven with the very heart and processes of Nature herself. The energies of heat and air, essentials of all life everywhere, were his handmaidens; he worked with fire and wind; in the forms he helped to build he set enthusiasm and energy aglow.

From stars and fire-mist he came now into humanity, using the limited instrument of a human mechanism, a mechanism he must learn to master without breaking it. A human brain and nerves confined him. He could deal with essences only, those essential, buried, semi-elemental powers that lie ever waiting below the threshold of all human consciousness, linking men, did they but know it, direct with the sea of universal life which is inexhaustible, independent of space and time. The fraction of his nature which had manifested as a transient surface-personality—LeVallon—was gone for ever, merged in the real self below.

His origin was already forgotten; no memory of it lay in his present brain; he must suffer training, education, and he turned instinctively to those whose ideal, like his own, was one of impersonal service. To a woman he turned, and to a man. His recognition, guided by Nature, was sure and accurate. It must take time and patience, sympathy and love, faith, belief and trust, and the labour must be borne by one man chiefly—by Fillery, into whose life had come this strange bright messenger carrying glad tidings... to prove at last that man was greater than he knew, that the hope for Humanity, for the deteriorating Race, for crumbling Civilization, lay in drawing out into full practical consciousness the divine powers concealed below the threshold of every single man and woman....

But how, in what practical manner, what instrument could they use? The human mechanism, the brain, the mind, afforded inadequate means of manifestation; new wines into old skins meant disaster; knowledge, power beyond the experience of the Race needed a better instrument than the one the Race had painfully evolved for present uses. New powers of unknown kinds, as already in those rare cases when the supernormal forces emerged, could only strain the machinery and cause disorder. A new order of consciousness required another, a different equipment. And the idea flashed into him, as in the Studio when he watched "N. H." and the girl—Father Collins had divined its possibility as well—the idea of a group consciousness, a collective group-soul. What a single individual might not be able to resist at first without disaster, many—a group in harmony—two or three gathered together in unison—these might provide the way, the means, the instrument—the body.

"The personal merged in the impersonal," he exclaimed to the night about him,

already aware that words, expression, failed even at this early stage of understanding. "Beauty, Art! Where words, form, colour end, we shall construct,
while yet using these as far as they go, a new vehicle, a new—"

"Good evenin'," said a gruff voice. "Good evenin', sir," it added more respectfully, after a second's inspection. "Turned out quite fine after the storm."

Aware of the policeman suddenly, Fillery started and turned round abruptly.
Evidently he had uttered his thoughts aloud, probably had cried and shouted
them. He could think of nothing in the world to say.

"It was a terrible storm. I hardly ever see the likes of it." The man was looking at him still with doubtful curiosity.

"Extraordinary, yes." Dr. Fillery managed to find a few natural words. It was
an early hour in the morning to be out, and his position by the pond, he now
realized, might have suggested an undesirable intention. "It made sleep impossible, and I came out to—to take a walk. I'm a doctor, Dr. Fillery—the Fillery
Home."

"Yes, sir," said the man, apparently satisfied. He looked at the sky. "All blown
away again," he remarked, "and the moon that nice and bright—"

Fillery offered something in reply, then moved away. The moon, he noticed,
was indeed nice and bright now; the heavy lower vapours all had vanished, and
thin cirrus clouds at a great height moved slowly before an upper wind; the stars
shone clearly, and a faint line of colour gave a hint of dawn not far away.

He glanced at his watch. It was nearly half-past four.

"It's impossible, impossible," he thought to himself, the pictures he had
been seeing still hanging before his eyes. "It was all feeling—merely feeling. My
blood, my heritage asserting themselves upon an over-tired system! Too much
repression evidently. I must find an outlet. My Caucasian Valley again!"

He walked rapidly. His mind began to work, and thinking made an effort to
replace feeling. He watched himself. His everyday surface-consciousness partially
resumed its sway. The policeman, of course, had interrupted the flow and inrush of another state just at the moment when a flash of direct knowledge was
about to blaze. It concerned "N. H.," his new patient. In another moment he
would have known exactly what and who he was, whence he came, the purpose
and the powers that attended him. The policeman—an inner laughter ran
through him at this juxtaposition of the practical and the transcendental—had
interfered with an interesting expansion of his being. An extension of consciousness, perhaps a touch of cosmic consciousness, was on the way. The first
faint quiver of its coming, magical with wondrous joy, had touched him. Its
cause, its origin, he knew not, yet he could trace both to the effect produced
upon him by "N. H." Of that he was sure. This effect his reasoning mind, with
busy analysis and criticism, had hitherto partially suppressed, even at its first
manifestation in Charing Cross Station. Tonight, criticism silent and analysis inactive, it had found an outlet. His own deep inner stillness had been its opportunity. Then came the practical, honest, simple policeman, the censor, who received so much a week to keep people in the way they ought to follow, the safe,
broad way....

He smiled, as he walked rapidly along the deserted streets. He knew so well the method and process of these abnormal states in others. As he swung along, not tired now, but rested, rather, and invigorated, the rhythm of motion established itself again. "N. H." a Nature Spirit! A Nature Being! Another order of life entering humanity for the first time, that humanity for whose welfare it— or was it he?—had worked, with hosts of similar beings, during incalculable ages....

He smiled, remembering the policeman again. There was always a policeman, or a censor. Oh, the exits beyond safe normal states of being, the exits into extended fields of consciousness, into an outer life which the majority, led by the best minds of the day, deny with an oath—these were well guarded! His smile, as he thought of it, ran from his lips and settled in the eyes, lingering a moment there before it died away....

How quiet, yet unfamiliar, the suburb of the huge city lay about him in pale half-light. The Studio scene, how distant it seemed now in space and time; it had happened weeks ago in another city somewhere. Devonham, his cautious, experienced assistant, how far away! He belonged to another age. The Prometheans were part of a dream in childhood, a dream of pantomime or harlequinade whose extravagance yet conveyed symbolic meaning. Two figures alone retained a reality that refused to he dismissed—a mysterious, enigmatic youth, a radiant girl—with perhaps a third—a broken priest....

The rhythm, meanwhile, gained upon him, and, as it did so, thinking once more withdrew and feeling stole back softly. His being became more harmonized, more one with itself, more open to inspiration.... "N. H.," whose work was service, service everywhere, not merely in that tiny corner of the universe called Humanity.... "N. H.," who could neither age nor die.... What was the hidden link that bound them? Had they not served and played together in some lost Caucasian valley, leaped with the sun's hot fire, flown in the winds of dawn . . sung, laughed and danced at their service, with a radiant sylph-like girl who had at last enticed them into the confinement of a limited human form?... Did not that valley symbolize, indeed, another state of existence, another order of consciousness altogether that lay beyond any known present experience or description...?

The dawn, meanwhile, grew nearer and a pallid light ran down the dreadful streets.... he reached at length the foot of the hill upon whose shoulder his own house stood. The familiar sights stirred more familiar currents of feeling, and these in turn sought words...

The crowding houses, with their tight-shut windows, followed and pressed after as he climbed. They swarmed behind him. How choked and airless it all was. He thought of the heavy-footed routine of the thousands who occupied these pretentious buildings. Here lived a section of the greatest city on the planet, almost a separate little town, with marked characteristics, atmosphere, tastes and habits. How many, he wondered, behind those walls knew yearning, belief, imagination beyond the ruck and routine of familiar narrow thought? Rows upon rows, with their stunted, manufactured trees, hideous conservatories, bulging porches, ornamented windows—his wings beat against them all with the burning desire to set their inmates free. They caged themselves in deliberately. A few thousand years ago these people lived in mud huts, before that in caves, before that again in trees. Now they were "civilized." They dwelt in these cages. Oh, that he might tear away the thick dead bricks, and let in light and dew and stars, and the brave, free winds of heaven! Waken the deeper powers they carried unwittingly about with them through all their tedious sufferings! Teach them that they were greater than they knew!

The yearning was deep and true in him, as the houses followed and tried to bar his way. Many of the occupiers, he knew, would welcome help, would gaze with happy, astonished eyes at the wonder of their own greater selves set free. Not all, of course, were wingless. Yet the majority, he felt, were otherwise. They peered at him from behind thick curtains, hostile, sceptical, contented with their lot, averse to change. Mode, custom, habit chained them to the floor. He was aware of a collective obstinate grin of smug complacency, of dull resistance. Though a part of the community, of the race, of the world, of the universe itself, they denied their mighty brotherhood, and clung tenaciously to their idea of living apart, cut off and separate. They belonged to leagues, societies, clubs and circles, but the bigger oneness of the race they did not know. Of greater powers in themselves they had no faintest inkling. At the first sign of these, they would shuffle, sneer and turn away, grow frightened even.

The yearning to show them a bigger field of consciousness, to help them towards a realization of their buried powers, to let them out of their separate cages, beat through his being with a passionate sincerity.... In a hundred thousand years perhaps! Perhaps in a million! He knew the slow gait that Nature loved. The trend of an Age is not to be stemmed by one man, nor by twelve, who see over the horizon. The futility of trying pained him. Yet, if no one ever tried! Oh, for a few swift strokes of awful sacrifice—then freedom!

The words came back to him, and with them, from the same source, came others: "I sit and I weave. I sit and I weave."... Whose, then, was this divine, eternal patience?...

There could be, it seemed, no hurried growth, no instant escape, no sudden leap to heaven. Slowly, slowly, the Ages turned the wheel. "Nor can other beings help," he remembered; "they can only tell what their own part is."... And as his clear mind saw the present Civilization like all its wonderful predecessors, tottering before his very eyes, threatening in its collapse the extinction of knowledge so slowly, painfully, laboriously acquired, the deep heart in him rose as on wings of wind and fire, questing the stars above. There was this strange clash in him, as though two great divisions in his being struggled. A way of escape seemed just within his reach, only a little beyond the horizon of his actual knowledge. It fluttered marvellously; golden, alight, inviting. Its coming glory brushed his insight. It was simple, it was divine. There seemed a faint knocking against the doors of his mental and spiritual understanding....

"'N. H.'!" he cried, "Bright Messenger!"

He paused a moment and stood still. A new sound lay suddenly in the night. It came, apparently, from far away, almost from the air above him. He listened.

No, after all it was only steps. They came nearer. A pedestrian, muffled to the ears, went past, and the steps died away on the resounding pavement round the corner. Yet the sound continued, and was not the echo of the steps just gone. It was, moreover, he now felt convinced, in the air above him. It was continuous. It reminded him of the musical droning hum that a big bell leaves behind it, while a suggestion of rhythm, almost of melody, ran faintly through it too.

Somebody's lines—was it Shelley's?—ran faintly in his mind, yet it was not his mind now that surged and rose to the new great rhythm:

> "'Tis the deep music of the rolling world
> Kindling within the strings of the waved air
> Æolian modulations....
> Clear, icy, keen awakening tones
> That pierce the sense
>   And live within the soul....'"

He listened. It was a simple, natural, happy sound—simple as running water, natural as wind, happy as the song of birds....

CHAPTER XX

He became, again, vividly aware of the power and presence of "N. H."

He was not far from his house now on the shoulder of the hill. He turned his eyes upwards, where the three-quarter moon sailed above transparent cirrus clouds that scarcely dimmed her light. Like dappled sands of silver, they sifted her soft shining, moving slowly across the heavens before an upper wind. The sound continued.

For a moment or two, in the pale light of dawn, he watched and listened, then lowered his gaze, caught his breath sharply, and stood stock still. He stared in front of him. Next, turning slowly, he stared right and left. He stared behind as well.

Yes, it was true. The lines and rows of crowding houses trembled, disappeared. The heavy buildings dissolved before his very eyes. The solid walls and roofs were gone, the chimneys, railings, doors and porches vanished. There were no more conservatories. There were no lamp-posts. The streets themselves had melted. He gazed in amazement and delight. The entire hill lay bare and open to the sky.

Across the rising upland swept a keen fresh morning wind. Yet bare they were not, this rising upland and this hill. As far as he could see, the landscape flowed waist-deep in flowers, whose fragrance lay upon the air; dew trembled, shimmering on a million petals of blue and gold, of orange, purple, violet; the very atmosphere seemed painted. Flowering trees, both singly and in groves, waved in the breeze, birds sang in chorus, there was a murmur of streams and falling waters. Yet that other sound rose too, rose from the entire hill and all upon it, a continuous gentle rhythm, as though, he felt, the actual scenery poured forth its being in spontaneous, natural expression of sound as well as of form and colour. It was the simplest, happiest music he had ever heard.

Unable to deal with the rapture of delight that swept upon him, he stood stock still among the blossoms to his waist. Eyes, ears and nostrils were inadequate to report a beauty which, simple though it was, overbore nerves and senses accustomed to a lesser scale. Horizons indeed had lifted, the joy and confidence of fuller life poured in. His own being grew immense, stretched, widened, deepened, till it seemed to include all space. He was everywhere, or rather everything was happening somewhere in him all at once.... In place of the heavy suburb lay this garden of primal beauty, while yet, in a sense, the suburb itself remained as well. Only—it had flowered... revealing the subconscious soul the bricks and pavements hid.... Its potential self had blossomed into loveliness and wonder.

The sound drew nearer. He was aware of movement. Figures were approaching; they were coming in his direction, coming towards him over the crest of the hill, nearer and nearer. Concealed by the forest of tall flowers, he watched them come. Yet as Presences he perceived them, rather than as figures, already borrowing power from them, as sails borrow from a rising wind. His consciousness expanded marvellously to let them in.

Their stature was conveyed to him, chiefly, at first, by the fact that these flowers, though rising to his own waist, did not cover the feet of them, yet that the flowers in the immediate line of their advance still swayed and nodded, as though no weight had lain upon their brilliance. The footsteps were of wind, the figures light as air; they shone; their radiant presences lit the acres. Their own atmosphere, too, came with them, as though the landscape moved and travelled with and in their being, as though the flowers, the natural beauty, emanated from them. The landscape *was* their atmosphere. They created, brought it with them. It seemed that they "expressed" the landscape and "were" the scenery, with all its multitudinous forms.

They approached with a great and easy speed that was not measurable. Over the crest of the living, sunlit hill they poured, with their bulk, their speed, their majesty, their sweet brimming joy. Fillery stood motionless watching them, his own joy touched with awed confusion, till wonder and worship mastered the final trace of fear.

Though he perceived these figures first as they topped the skyline, he was aware that great space also stretched behind them, and that this immense perspective was in some way appropriate to their appearance. Born of a greater space than his "mind" could understand, they flowed towards him across that windy crest and at the same time from infinitely far beyond it. Above the continuous humming sound, he heard their music too, faint but mighty, filling the air with deep vibrations that seemed the natural expression of their joyful beings. Each figure was a chord, yet all combining in a single harmony that had volume without loudness. It seemed to him that their sound and colour and movement wove a new pattern upon space, a new outline, form or growth, perhaps a flower, a tree, perhaps a planet.... They were creative. They expressed themselves naturally in a million forms.

He heard, he saw. He knew no other words to use. But the "hearing" was, rather, some kind of intimate possession so that his whole being filled and overbrimmed; and the "sight" was greater than the customary little irritation of the optic nerve—it involved another term of space. He could describe the sight more readily than the hearing. The apparent contradiction of distance and proximity, of vast size yet intimacy, made him tremble in his hiding-place.

His "sight," at any rate, perceived the approaching figures all round, all over, all at once, as they poured like a wave across the hill from far beyond its visible crest. For into this space below the horizon he saw as well, though, normally speaking, it was out of sight. Nor did he see one side only; he saw the backs of the towering forms as easily as the portion facing him; he saw behind them. It was not as with ordinary objects refracting light, the back and underneath and further edges invisible. All sides were visible at once. The space beyond, moreover, whence the mighty outlines issued, was of such immensity that he could think only of interstellar regions. Not to the little planet, then, did these magnificent shapes belong. They were of the Universe. The symbol of his valley, he knew suddenly, belonged here too.

Silent with wonder, motionless with worship, he watched the singing flood of what he felt to be immense, non-human nature-life pour past him. The procession lasted for hours, yet was over in a minute's flash. All categories his mind knew hitherto were useless. The faces, in their power, their majesty, the splendour even of their extent, were both appalling, yet infinitely tender. They were filled with stars, blue distance, flowers, spirals of fire, space and air, interwoven too, with shining geometrical designs whose intricate patterns merged in a central harmony. They brought their own winds with them.

Yet of features precisely, he was not aware. Each face was, rather, an immense expression, but an expression that was permanent and could not change. These were immutable, eternal faces. He borrowed from human terms the only words that offered, while aware that he falsely introduced the personal into that which was essentially impersonal.

There stole over him a strange certainty that what he worshipped was the grandeur of joyful service working through unalterable law—the great compassion of some untiring service that was deathless.... He stood *within* the Universe, face to face with its elemental builders, guardians, its constructive artizans, the impersonal angelic powers.... the region, the state, he now felt convinced, to which "N. H." belonged, and whence, by some inexplicable chance, he had come to occupy a human body.... And the sounds—the flash came to him with lightning conviction—were those essential rhythms which are the kernels of all visible, manifested forms....

He was not aware that he was moving, that he had left the spot where he had stood—so long, yet for a single second only—and had now reached the corner of a street again. The flowers were gone, and the trees and groves gone with them; no waters rippled past; there was no shining hill. The moon, the stars, the breaking dawn remained, but he saw windows, walls and villas once again, while his feet echoed on dead stone pavements....

Yet the figures had not wholly gone. Before a house, where he now paused a moment, the towering, flowing outlines were still faintly visible. Their singing still audible, their shapes still gently luminous, they stood grouped about an open window of the second story. In the front garden a big plane tree stirred its leaf-less branches; the tree and figures interpenetrated. Slowly then, the outlines grew dim and shadowy, indistinguishable almost from the objects in the twi-light near them. Chimneys, walls and roofs stole in upon the great shapes with foreign, grosser details that obscured their harmony, confused their proportion, as with two sets of values. The eye refused to focus both at once. A roof, a chim-ney obtruded, while sight struggled, fluttered, then ended in confusion. The fig-ures faded and melted out. They merged with the tree, the reddening sky, the murky air close to the house which a street lamp made visible. Suddenly they were lost—they were no longer there.

But the rhythmical sound, though fainter, still continued—and Fillery looked up.

It was a sound, he realized in a flash, evocative and summoning. Type called to type, brother to brother, across the universe. The house before him was his own, and the open window through which the music issued was the bedroom of "N. H."

He stood transfixed. Both sides of his complex nature operated simultaneously. His mind worked more clearly—the entire history of the "case" in that upstairs room passed through it: he was a doctor. But his speculative, emotional aspect, the dreamer in him, so greatly daring, all that poetic, transcendental, half-mys-tical part which classed him, he well knew, with the unstable; all this, long and dangerously repressed, worked with opposite, if equal pressure. From the sub-conscious rose violent hands as of wind and fire, lovely, fashioning, divine, tear-ing away the lid of the reasoning surface-consciousness that confined, confused them.

To disentangle, to define these separate functions, were a difficult problem even for the most competent psychiatrist. Creative imaginative powers, hitherto merely fumbling, half denied as well, now stretched their wings and soared. With them came a blinding clarity of sight that enabled him to focus a vast field of detail with extraordinary rapidity. Horizons had lifted, perspective deepened and lit up. In a few brief seconds, before his front door opened, a hundred de-tails flashed towards a focus and shone concentrated

The Vision, of course—the Figures had now melted into the night—had no objective reality. Suppressed passion had created them, forbidden yearnings had passed the Censor and dramatized a dream, set aside yet never explained, that heredity was responsible for. Both were born of his lost radiant valley. His Note Books held a thousand similar cases....

But the speculative dreamer flashed coloured lights against this common white. The prism blazed. From the interstellar spaces came these radiant figures, from Sirius, immense and splendid sun, from Aldebaran among the happy Hyades, from awful Betelgeuse, whose volume fills a Martian orbit. Their dazzling, giant grandeur was of stellar origin. Yet, equally, they came from the dreadful back gardens of those sordid houses. Nature was Nature everywhere, in the nebulæ as in the stifled plane tree of a city court. That he saw them as "figures" ,was but his own private, personal interpretation of a prophecy the whole Universe announced. They were not figures necessarily; they were Powers. And "N. H." was of their kind.

He suddenly remembered the small, troubled earth whereon he lived—a neglected corner of the universe that was in distress and cried frantically for help.... Alcyone caught it in her golden arms perhaps; Sirius thundered against its little ears...

He found his latchkey and fumblingly inserted it, but, even while he did so, the state of the planet at the moment poured into his mind with swift, concentrated detail: he remembered the wireless excitement of the instant—and smiled. Not that way would it come. The new order was of a spiritual kind. It would steal into men's hearts, not splutter along the waves of ether, as the "dead" are said to splutter to the "living." The great impulse, the mighty invitation Nature sent out to return to simple, natural life, would come, without "phenomena" from *within*.... He remembered Relativity—that space is local, space and time not separate entities. He understood. He had just experienced it. Another, a fourth dimension! Space as a whole was annihilated! He smiled.

His latchkey turned.

The transmutation of metals flashed past him—all substance one. His latchkey was upside down. He turned it round and reinserted it, and the results of advanced psychology rushed at him, as though the sun rushed over the horizon of some Eastern clime, covering all with the light of a new, fair dawn.

In a few seconds this accumulation of recent knowledge and discovery flooded his state of singular receptiveness—as thinker and as poet. The Age was crumbling, civilization passing like its predecessors. The little planet lay certainly in distress. No true help lay within it; its reservoirs were empty. No adequate constructive men or powers were anywhere in sight. It was exhausted, dying. Unless new help, powers from a new, an inexhaustible source, came quickly... a new vehicle for their expression...

And wonder took him by the throat... as the key turned in the lock with its familiar grating sound, and the door, without actual pressure on his part, swung open.

Paul Devonham, a look of bright terror in his eyes, stood on the threshold.

The expression, not only of the face but of the whole person, he had seen once only in another human countenance—a climber, who had slipped by his very side and dropped backward into empty space. The look of helpless bewilderment as hands and feet lost final touch with solidity, the air of terrible yet childlike amazement with which he began his descent of a thousand feet through a gulf of air—the shock marked the face in a single second with what he now saw in his colleague's eyes. Only, with Devonham—Fillery felt sure of his diagnosis—the lost hold was mental.

His outward control, however, was admirable. Devonham's voice, apart from a certain tenseness in it, was quiet enough: "I've been telephoning everywhere…. There's been a—a crisis—"

"Violence?"

But the other shook his head. "It's all beyond me quite," he said, with a wry smile. "The first outbreak was nothing—nothing compared to this." The continuous sound of humming which filled the hall, making the air vibrate oddly, grew louder. Devonham seized his friend's arm.

"Listen!" he whispered. "You hear that?"

"I heard it outside in the street," Fillery said. "What is it?"

Devonham glared at him. "God knows," he said, "I don't. He's been doing it, on and off, for a couple of hours. It began the moment you left, it seems. They're all about him—these vibrations, I mean. He does it with his whole body somehow. And"—he hesitated—"there's meaning in it of some kind. Results, I mean," he jerked out with an effort.

"Visible?" came the gentle question.

Devonham started. "How did you know?" There was a thrust of intense curiosity in the eyes.

"I've had a similar experience myself, Paul. You opened the front door in the middle of it. The figures—"

"You saw figures?" Devonham looked thunderstruck. In his heart was obviously a touch of panic.

As the two men stood gazing into each other's eyes a moment silently, the sound about them increased again, rising and falling, its great separate rhythmical waves almost distinguishable. In Fillery's mind rose patterns, outlines, forms of flowers, spirals, circles…

"He knows you're in the house," said Devonham in a curious voice, relieved apparently no answer came to his question. "Better come upstairs at once and see him." But he did not turn to lead the way. "That's not auditory hallucination, Edward, whatever else it is!" He was still clinging to the rock, but the rock was crumbling beneath his desperate touch. Space yawned below him.

"Visual," suggested Fillery, as though he held out a feeble hand to the man whose whole weight already hung unsupported before the plunge. His friend spoke no word; but his expression made words unnecessary "We must face the facts," it said plainly, "wherever these may lead. No shirking, no prejudice of mine or yours must interfere. There must be no faltering now."

So plainly was this passion for truth and knowledge legible in the expression of the shocked but honest mind, that Fillery felt compassion overpower the first attitude of privacy he had meant to take. This time he must share. The honesty of the other won his confidence too fully for him to hold back anything. There was no doubt in his mind that he read his colleague's state aright.

"A moment, Paul," he said in a low voice, "before we go upstairs," and he put his hand out, oddly enough meeting Devonham's hand already stretched to meet it. He drew him aside into a corner of the hall, while the waves of sound surged round and over them like a sea. "Let me first tell you," he went on, his voice trembling slightly, "my own experience." It seemed to him that any moment he must see the birth of a new form, an outline, a "body" dance across before his very eyes.

"Neither auditory nor visual," murmured Devonham, burning to hear what was coming, yet at the same time shrinking from it by the laws of his personality. "Hallucination of any kind, there is absolutely none. There's nothing transferred from your mind to his. This thing is real—original."

Fillery tightened his grip a second on the hand he held.

"Paul," he said gravely, yet unable to hide the joy of recent ecstasy in his eyes, "it is also—new!"

The low syllables seemed borne away and lifted beyond their reach by an immense vibration that swept softly past them. And so actual was this invisible wave that behind it lay the trough, the ebb, that awaits, as in the sea, the next advancing crest. Into this ebb, as it were, both men dropped simultaneously the same significant syllables: their lips uttered it together:

"N. H." The wave of sound seemed to take their voices and increase them. It was the older man who added: "Coming into full possession."

The two stood waiting, listening, their heads turned sideways, their bodies motionless, while the soft rhythmical uproar rose and fell about them. No sign escaped them for some minutes; no words, it seemed, occurred to either of them.

Through the transom over the front door stole the grey light of the late autumn dawn; the hall furniture was visible, chairs, hat-rack, wooden chests that held the motor rugs. A china bowl filled with visiting cards gleamed white beside it. Soon the milkman, uttering his comic earthly cry, would clatter down the area staircase, and the servants would be up. As yet, however, but for the big soft sound, the house was perfectly still. This part of it, almost a separate wing, was completely cut off from the main building. No one had been disturbed.

Fillery moved his head and looked at his companion. The expression of both face and figure arrested him. He had taken off his dinner jacket, and the old loose golfing coat he wore hung askew; he had one hand in a pocket of it, the other thrust deep into his trousers. His glasses hung down across his crumpled shirt-front, his black tie made an untidy cross. He looked, thought Fillery, whose sense of the ludicrous became always specially alert in his gravest moments, like an unhappy curate who had presided over some strenuous and worrying social gathering in the local town hall. Only one detail denied this picture—the expression of something mysterious and awed in the sheet-white face. He was listening with sharp dislike yet eager interest. His repugnance betrayed itself in the tightened lips, the set of the angular shoulders; the panic was written in the glistening eyes. There were things in his face he could never, never tell. The struggle in him was natural to his type of mind: he had experienced something himself, and a personal

experience opens new vistas in sympathy and understanding. But—the experience ran contrary to every tenet of theory and practice he had ever known.
The moment of new birth was painful. This was his colleague's diagnosis.

Fillery then suddenly realized that the gulf between them was without a
bridge. To tell his own experience became at once utterly impossible. He saw
this clearly. He could not speak of it to his assistant. It was, after all, incommunicable. The bridge of terms, language, feeling, did not exist between them.
And, again, up flashed for a second his sense of the comic, this time in an odd
touch of memory—Povey's favourite sentence: "Never argue with the once-
born!" Only to older souls was expression possible.

For the first time then his diagnosis wavered oddly. Why, for instance, did
Paul persist in that curious, watchful stare…?

Devonham, conscious of his chief's eyes and mind upon him, looked up. Somewhere in his expression was a glare, but nothing revealed his state of mind better than the fact that he stupidly contradicted himself:

"You're putting all this into him, Edward," a touch of anger, perhaps of fear,
in the intense whispering voice. "The hysteria of the studio upset him, of course.
If you'd left him alone, as you promised, he'd have always stayed LeVallon. He'd
be cured by now." Then, as Fillery made no reply or comment, he added, but
this time only the anxiety of the doctor in his tone: "Hadn't you better go up
to him at once? He's your patient, not mine, remember!"

The other took his arm. "Not yet," he said quietly. "He's best alone for the
moment." He smiled, and it was the smile that invariably won him the confidence of even the most obstinate and difficult patient. He was completely master of himself again. "Besides, Paul," he went on gently. "I want to hear what
you have to tell me. Some of it—if not all. I want your Report. It is of value. I
must have that first, you know."

They sat on the bottom stair together, while Devonham told briefly what had
happened. He was glad to tell it, too. It was a relief to become the mere accurate observer again.

"I can summarize it for you in two words," he said: "light and sound. The
sound, at first, seemed wind—wind rising, wind outside. With the light, was
perceptible heat. The two seemed correlated. When the sound increased, the
heat increased too. Then the sound became methodical, rhythmical—it became
almost musical. As it did so the light became coloured. Both"—he looked across
at the ghostly hat-rack in the hall-"were produced—by him."

"Items, please, Paul. I want an itemized account."

Devonham fumbled in the big pockets of his coat and eventually lit a cigarette,
though he did not in the least want to smoke. That watchful, penetrating stare
persisted, none the less. Amid the anxiety were items of carelessness that almost
seemed assumed.

"Mrs. Soames sent Nurse Robbins to fetch me," he resumed, his voice
harshly, as it seemed, cutting across the waves of pleasant sound that poured
down the empty stairs behind them and filled the hall with resonant vibrations.
"I went in, turned them both out, and closed the door. The room was filled with

a soft, white light, rather pale in tint, that seemed to emanate from nowhere. I could trace it to no source. It was equally diffused, I mean, yet a kind of wave—like vibration ran through it in faint curves and circles. There was a sound, a sound like wind. A wind was in the room, moaning and sighing inside the walls—a perfectly natural and ordinary sound, if it had been outside. The light moved and quivered. It lay in sheets. Its movement, I noticed, was in direct relation to the wind: the louder the volume of sound, the greater the movement of the air—the brighter became the light, and vice versa. I could not take notes at the actual moment, but my memory"—a slight grimace by way of a smile indicated that forgetting was impossible—"is accurate, as you know."

Fillery did not interrupt, either by word or gesture.

"The increase of light was accompanied by colour, and the increase of sound led into a measure—not actual bars, and never melody, but a distinct measure that involved rhythm. It was musical, as I said. The colour—I'm coming to that—then took on a very faint tinge of gold or orange, a little red in it sometimes, flame colour almost. The air was luminous—it was radiant. At one time I half expected to see fire. For there was heat as well. Not an unpleasant heat, but a comforting, stimulating, agreeable heat like—I was going to say, like the heat of a bright coal fire on a winter's day, but I think the better term is sunlight. I had an impression this heat must burst presently into actual flame. It never did so. The sheets of coloured light rose and fell with the volume of the sound. There were curves and waves and rising columns like spirals, but anything approaching a definite outline, form, or shape"—he broke off for a second—"figures," he announced abruptly, almost challengingly, staring at the white china bowl in front of him, "I could *not* swear to."

He turned suddenly and stared at his chief with an expression half of question, half of challenge; then seemed to change his mind, shrugging his shoulders a very little. But Fillery made no sign. He did not answer. He laid one hand, however, upon the banisters, as though preliminary to getting to his feet. The sound about them had been gradually growing less, the vibrations were smaller, its waves perceptibly decreasing.

Devonham finished his account in a lower voice, speaking rapidly, as though the words burnt his tongue:

"The sound, I had already discovered, issued from himself. He was lying on his back, the eyes wide open, the expression peaceful, even happy. The lips were closed. He was humming, continuously humming. Yet the sound came in some way I cannot describe, and could not examine or ascertain, from his whole body. I detected no vibration of the body. It lay half naked, only a corner of the sheet upon it. It lay quite still. The cause of the light and heat, the cause of the movement of air I have called wind—I could not ascertain. They came *through* him, as it were." A slight shiver ran across his body, noticed by his companion, but eliciting no comment from him. "I—I took his pulse," concluded Devonham, sinking his voice now to a whisper, though a very clear one; "it was very rapid and extraordinarily strong. He seemed entirely unconscious of my presence. I also"—again the faint shiver was perceptible—"felt his heart. It was—I have

never felt such perfect action, such power—it was beating like an engine, like an engine. And the sense of vitality, of life in the room everywhere was—electrical. I could have sworn it was packed to the walls with—with others."
Devonham never ceased to watch his companion keenly while he spoke.

Fillery then put his first question.

"And the effect upon yourself?" he asked quietly. "I mean—any emotional disturbance? Anything, for instance, like what you saw in the Jura forests?" He did not look at his colleague; he stood up; the sound about them had now ceased almost entirely and only faint, dying fragments of it reached them. "Roughly speaking," he added, making a half movement to go upstairs. He understood the inner struggle going on; he wished to make it easy for him. For the complete account he did not press him.

Devonham rose too; he walked over to the china bowl, took up a card, read it and let it fall again. The sun was over the horizon now, and a pallid light showed objects clearly. It showed the whiteness of the thin, tired face. He turned and walked slowly back across the hall. The first cart went clattering noisily down the street. At the same moment a final sound from the room upstairs came floating down into the chill early air.

"My interest, of course," began Devonham, his hands in his pockets, his body rigid, as he looked up into his companion's eyes, "was very concentrated, my mind intensely active." He paused, then added cautiously: "I may confess, however—I must admit, that is, a certain increase of—of—well, a general sense of well-being, let me call it. The heat, you see. A feeling of peace, if you like it better—beyond the—fear," he blurted out finally, changing his hands from his coat to his trouser pockets, as though the new position protected him better from attack. "Also—I somehow expected—any moment—to see outlines, forms, something new!" He stared frankly into the eyes of the man who, from the step above him, returned his gaze with equal frankness. "And *you*—Edward?" he asked with great suddenness.

"Joy? Could you describe it as joy?" His companion ignored the reference to new forms. He also ignored the sudden question. "Any increase of—?"

"Vitality, you want to say. The word joy is meaningless, as you know."

"An intensification of consciousness in any way?"

But Devonham had reached his limit of possible confession. He did not reply for a moment. He took a step forward and stood beside Fillery on the stairs. His manner had abruptly changed. It was as though he had come to a conclusion suddenly. His reply, when it came, was no reply at all:

"Heat and light are favourable, of course, to life," he remarked. "You remember Joaquin Mueller: 'the optic nerve, under the action of light, acts as a stimulus to the organs of the imagination and fancy.'"

Fillery smiled as he took his arm and they went quietly upstairs together. The quoting was a sign of returning confidence. He said something to himself about the absence of light, but so low it was under his breath almost, and even if his companion heard it, he made no comment: "There was no moon at all to-night till well past three, and even then her light was of the faintest...."

No sound was now audible. They entered a room that was filled with silence and with peace. A faint ray of morning sunlight showed the form of the patient sleeping calmly, the body entirely uncovered. There was an expression of quiet happiness upon the face whose perfect health suggested perhaps radiance. But there was a change as well, though indescribable—there was power. He did not stir as they approached the bed. The breathing was regular and very deep.

Standing beside him a moment, Fillery sniffed the air, then smiled. There was a perfume of wild flowers. There was, in spite of the cool morning air, a pleas-ant warmth.

"You notice—anything?" he whispered, turning to his colleague.

Devonham likewise sniffed the air. "The window's wide open," was the low rejoinder. "There are conservatories at the back of every house all down the row."

And they left the room on tiptoe, closing the door behind them very softly. Upon Devonham's face lay a curious expression, half anxiety, half pain.

CHAPTER XXI

D r. Fillery, lying on a couch in his patient's bedroom, snatched some four to five hours' sleep, though, if "snatched," it was certainly enjoyed—a deep, dreamless, reposeful slumber. He woke, refreshed in mind and body, and the first thing he saw, even before he had time to stretch a limb or move his head, was two great blue eyes gazing into his own across the room. They belonged, it first struck him, to some strange being that had followed him out of sleep—he had not yet recovered full consciousness and the effects of sleep still hovered; then an earlier phrase recurred: to some divine great animal.

"N. H.," in his bed in the opposite corner, lay gazing at him. He returned the gaze. Into the blue eyes came at once a look of happy recognition, of content-ment, almost a smile. Then they closed again in sleep.

The room was full of morning sunshine. Fillery rose quietly, and performed his toilet in his own quarters, but on returning after a hurried breakfast, the pa-tient still slept soundly. He slept on for hours, he slept the morning through; but for the obvious evidences of perfect normal health, it might have been a state of coma. The body did not even change its position once.

He left Devonham in charge, and was on his way to visit some of the other cases, when Nurse Robbins stood before him. Miss Khilkoff had "called to in-quire after Mr. LeVallon," and was waiting downstairs in case Dr. Fillery could also see her.

He glanced at her pretty slim figure and delicate complexion, her hair, fine, plentiful and shiny, her dark eyes with a twinkle in them. She was an attrac-tive, intelligent, experienced, voting woman, tactful too, and of great use with extra sensitive patients. She was, of course, already hopelessly in love with her present "case." His "singing," so she called it to Mrs. Soames, had excited her "like a glass of wine—some music makes you feel like that—so that you could love everybody in the world." She already called him Master.

"Please say I will be down at once," said Dr. Fillery, watching her for the first time with interest as he remembered these details Paul had told him. The girl, it now struck him, was intensely alive. There was a gain, an increase, in her appearance somewhere. He recalled also the matron's remark—she was not usually loquacious with her nurses—that "he's no ordinary case, and I've seen a good few, haven't I? The way he understands animals and flowers alone proves that!"

Dr. Fillery went downstairs.

His first rapid survey of the girl, exhaustive for all its quickness—he knew her so well—showed him that no outward signs of excitement were visible. Calm, poised, gentle as ever, the same generous tenderness in the eyes, the same sweet firmness in the mouth, the familiar steadiness that was the result of an inner surety—all were there as though the wild scene of the night before had never been. Yet all these were heightened. Her beauty had curiously increased.

"Come into my study," he said, taking her hand and leading the way. "We shan't be disturbed there. Besides, it's ours, isn't it? We mustn't forget that you are a member of the Firm."

He was aware of her soft beauty invading, penetrating him, aware, too, somehow, that she was in her most impersonal mood. But for all that, her nature could not hide itself, nor could signs of a certain, subtle change she had undergone fail to obtrude themselves. In a single night, it seemed, she had blossomed into a wondrous ripe maturity; like some strange flower that opens to the darkness, the bud had burst suddenly into full, sweet bloom, whose coming only moon and stars had witnessed. There was moonlight now in her dark mysterious eyes as she glanced at him; there was the gold of stars in her tender, yet curious smile, as she answered in her low voice—"Of course, I always was a partner in the Firm"—there was the grace and rhythm of a wild flower swaying in the wind, as she passed before him into the quiet room and sank into his own swinging armchair at the desk. But there was something else as well.

A detail of his recent Vision slid past his inner sight again while he watched her.... "I thought—I felt sure—you would come," he said. He looked at her admiringly, but peace strong in his heart. "The ordeal," he went on in a curious voice, "would have been too much for most women, but you"—he smiled, and the sympathy in his voice increased—"you, I see, have only gained from it. You've mastered, conquered it. I wonder"—looking away from her almost as if speaking to himself—"have you wholly understood it?"

He realized vividly in that moment what she, as a young, unmarried girl, had suffered before the eyes of all those prying eyes and gossiping tongues. His admiration deepened.

She did not take up his words, however. "I've come to inquire," she said simply in an even voice, "for father and myself. He wanted to know if you got home all right, and how Julian LeVallon is." The tone, the heightened colour in the cheek, as she spoke the name no one had yet used, explained, partly at least, to the experienced man who listened, the secret of her sudden blossoming. Also she used her father, though unconsciously, perhaps. "He was afraid the electricity—the lightning even—had"—she hesitated, smiled a little, then added, as though she herself knew otherwise—"done something to him."

Fillery laughed with her then. "As it has done to you," he thought, but did not speak the words. The need of formula was past. He thanked her, adding that it was sweet yet right that she had come herself, instead of writing or telephoning. "And you may set your—your father's mind at rest, for all goes well. The electricity, of course," he added, on his own behalf as well as hers, "was—more than most of us could manage. Electricity explains everything except itself, doesn't it?"

He was inwardly examining her with an intense and accurate observation. She seemed the same, yet different. The sudden flowering into beauty was simply enough explained. It was another change he now became more and more aware of. In this way a ship, grown familiar during the long voyage, changes on coming into port. The decks and staircases look different when the vessel lies motionless at the dock. It becomes half recognizable, half strange. Gone is the old familiarity, gone also one's own former angle of vision. It is difficult to find one's way about her. Soon she will set sail again, but in another direction, and with new passengers using her decks, her corners, hatch-ways... telling their secrets of love and hate with that recklessness the open sea and sky make easy.... And now with the girl before him—he couldn't quite find his way about her as of old... it was the same familiar ship, yet it was otherwise, and he, a new passenger, acknowledged the freedom of sea and sky.

"And you—Iraida?" he asked. "It was brave of you to come."

She liked evidently the use of her real name, for she smiled, aware all the time of his intent observation, aware probably also of his hidden pain, yet no sign of awkwardness in her; to this man she could talk openly, or, on the contrary, conceal her thoughts, sure of his tact and judgment. He would never intrude unwisely.

"It was natural, Edward," she observed frankly in return.

"Yes, I suppose it was. Natural is exactly the right word. You have perhaps found yourself at last," and again he used her real name, "Iraida."

"It feels like that," she replied slowly. She paused. "I have found, at least, something definite that I have to do. I feel that I—must care for him." Her eyes, as she said it, were untroubled.

The well-known Nayan flashed back a moment in the words; he recognized—to, use his simile—a familiar corner of the deck where he had sat and talked for hours beneath the quiet stars—to someone who understood, yet remained ever impersonal. And the person he talked with came over suddenly and stood beside him and took his hand between her own soft gloved ones:

"You told me, Edward, he would need a woman to help him. That's what you mean by 'natural'—isn't it? And I am she, perhaps."

"I think you are," came in a level tone.

"I know it," she said suddenly, both her eyes looking down upon his face. "Yes,

I suppose I know it."

"Because *you*—need him," his voice, equally secure, made answer.

Still keeping his hand tight between her own, her dark eyes still searching his, she made no sign that his blunt statement was accepted, much less admitted. Instead she asked a question he was not prepared for: "You would like that, Edward? You wish it?"

She was so close against his chair that her fur-trimmed coat brushed his shoulder; yet, though with eyes and touch and physical presence she was so near, he felt that she herself had gone far, far away into some other place. He drew his hand free. "Iraida," he said quietly, "I wish. the best—for him—and for you. And I believe this is the best—for him and you." He put his patient first. He was aware that the girl, for all her outer calmness, trembled.

"It is," she said, her voice as quiet as his own; and after a moment's hesitation, she went back to her seat again. "If you think I can be of use," she added. "I'm ready."

A little pause fell between them, during which Dr. Fillery touched an electric bell beside his chair. Nurse Robbins appeared with what seemed miraculous swiftness. "Still sleeping quietly, sir, and pulse normal again," she replied in answer to a question, then vanished as suddenly as she had come. He looked into the girl's eyes across the room. "A competent, reliable nurse," he remarked, "and, as you saw, a pretty woman." He glanced out of the window. "She is unmarried." He mentioned it apparently to the sky.

The quick mind took in his meaning instantly. "All women will be drawn to him irresistibly, of course," she said. "But it is not *that*."

"No, no, of course it is not that," he agreed at once. "I should like you to see him, though not, however, just yet—" He went on after a moment's reflection, and speaking, slowly: "I should like you to wait a little. It's best. There *has* been a—a certain disturbance in his being—"

"It's his first experience," she began, "of beauty—"

"Of beauty in women, yes," he finished for her. "It is. We must avoid anything in the nature of a violent shock—"

"He has asked for me?" she interrupted again, in her quiet way.

He shook his head. "And we cannot be sure that it was you—as *you*—he sought and is affected by. The call he hears is, perhaps, hardly the call that sounds in most men's ears, I mean."

The hint of warning guidance was audible in his voice, as well as visible in his eyes and manner. The laughter they both betrayed, a grave and curious laughter perhaps, was brief, yet enough to conceal stranger emotions that rose like dumb, gazing figures almost before their eyes. Yet if she knew inner turmoil, emotion of any troubling sort, she concealed it perfectly.

"I am glad," the girl said presently. "Oh, I am really glad. I think I understand, Edward." And, even while he sat silent for a bit, watching her with an ever-growing admiration that at the same time marvelled, he saw the wonder of great questions riding through her face. The recollection of what she had suffered publicly in the Studio a few hours before came into his mind again. In these questions, perhaps, lay the only signs of the hidden storm below the surface.

"Are there—are there such things as Nature-Beings, Edward?" she asked abruptly. "We know this is his first experience. Are there then—?"

He was prepared a little for this kind of question by her eyes. "We have no evidence, of course," he replied; "not a scrap of evidence for anything of the sort. There are people, however, so close to Nature, so intimate with her, that we may say they are—strangely, inexplicably akin."

"Has he a soul—a human soul like ours?" she asked point blank.

"He is perhaps—not-quite—like us. That may be your task, Iraida," he added enigmatically. He watched her more closely than she knew.

She appeared to ponder his words for a few minutes; then she asked abruptly: "And when do you think I ought to come and see him? You will let me know?"

"I will let you know. A few days perhaps, perhaps a week, perhaps longer. Some education, I think, is necessary first." He gazed at her thoughtfully, and she returned his look, her dark eyes filled with the wonder that was both of a child and of a woman, and yet with a security of something that was of neither. "It will be a—a great effort to you," he ventured with significant and sympathetic understanding, "after—what happened. It is brave and generous of you—" He broke off.

She nodded, but at once afterwards shook her head. She rose then to go, but Dr. Fillery stopped her. He rose too.

"Nayan, I now want *your* help," he said with more emotion than he had yet shown. "My responsibility, as you may guess, is not light—and—"

"And he is in your sole charge, you mean." She had willingly resumed her seat, and made herself comfortable with a cushion he arranged for her. He was aware chiefly of her eyes, for in them glowed light and fire he had never seen there before—but still in their depths.

"Well—yes, partly," he replied, lighting a cigarette, "though Paul is ready with help and sympathy whenever needed. But the charge, as you call it, is not mine alone: it is ours."

"Ours!" She started, though almost imperceptibly, as she repeated his word.

"Subconsciously," he said in a firm voice, "we three are similar. We are together. We obey half instinctively the unknown laws of"—he hesitated a moment—"of some unknown state of being." He added then a singular sentence, though so low it seemed almost to himself: "Had we been man and wife, Iraida, our child must have been—like him."

"Yes," she said, leaning forward a little in her chair, increased warmth, yet no blush, upon her skin. "Yes, Edward, we three are somehow together in this, aren't we? Oh, I feel it. It pours over me like a great wind, a wind with heat in it." Her hands clasped her knee, as they gazed at one another for a moment's silence. "I feel it," she repeated presently. "I'm sure of it, quite sure."

She stretched out a spirit hand, as it were, for an instant across the impersonal barrier between them, but he did not take it, pretending he did not see it.

"Ours, Nayan," he emphasized, again using the name that belonged to everyone. "Therefore, you see, I want you to tell me—if you will—what you felt, experienced, perceived—in the Studio last night." After watching her a little, he qualified: "Another day, if you would like to think it over. But some time, without fail. For my part, I will confess—though I think you already know it— that I brought him there on purpose—"

"To see my effect upon him, Edward."

"But in *his* interest, and in the interest of my possible future treatment. His effect upon yourself was not my motive. You believe that."

"I know, I know. And I will tell you gladly. Indeed, I want to."

He was aware, as she said it, that it would be a satisfaction to her to talk; she would welcome the relief of confession; she could speak to him as doctor now, as professional man, as healer, and this, too, without betraying the impersonal attitude she evidently wore and had adopted possibly—he wondered?—in self-protection. "Tell me exactly what it is you would like to know, please, Edward," she added, and instinctively moved to the sofa, so that he might occupy the professional swinging chair at the desk.

"What you saw, Nayan," he began, accepting the change of position without comment, because he knew it helped her. "What you saw is of value, I think, first."

He had all his usual self-control again, for he was now on his throne, his seat of power; his inner attitude changed subtly; he was examining two patients— the girl and himself. She sat before him demure, obedient, honest, very sweet but very strong; if her perfume reached him he did not notice it, the appeal of her loveliness went past him, he did not see her eyes. He had a very comely and intelligent young woman facing him, and the glow, as it were, of an intense inner activity, strongly suppressed, was the chief quality in her that he noted. But his new attitude made other things, too, stand out sharply: he realized there was confusion in her own mind and heart. Her being was not wholly at one with itself. This impersonal rôle meant safety until she was sure of herself; and so far she had been entirely and admirably non-committal. No girl, he remembered, could look back upon what she had experienced in the Studio, upon what she had herself said and done, before a crowd of onlookers too, without deep feelings of a mixed and even violent kind. That scene with a young man she had never seen before must bring painful memories; if it was love at first sight the memories must be more painful still. But was it a case of this sudden, rapturous love? What, indeed, were her feelings? What at any rate was her dominant feeling? She had felt his appeal beyond all question, but was it as Nayan or as Iraida that she felt it?

She was non-committal and impersonal, conscious that therein safety lay—until, having become one with herself, harmonious, she could feel absolutely sure. One hint only had she dropped—it was Nayan speaking—that her mothering, maternal instinct was needed and that she must obey its prompting. She must "care" for him....

Dr. Fillery, meanwhile, though he might easily have probed and made discoveries without her knowing that he did so, was not the man to use his powers now. Unless she gave of her own free will, he would not ask. He would close eyes and ears even to any chance betrayal or unconscious revelation.

"When you first looked in, for instance? You had just come in from the street, I think. You opened the door on your way upstairs. Do you remember?"

She remembered perfectly. "I wanted to see who was there. You, I think, were chiefly in my thoughts—I was wondering if you had come." Her voice was even, her eyes quite steady; she chose her next words slowly: "I saw—to my intense surprise—a figure of light."

"Shining, you mean? A shining figure?"

She nodded her head, as one little hand put back a straying wisp of dark hair from her forehead. "A figure like flame," she agreed. "I saw it quite clearly. I saw everything else quite clearly too—the inner room, various people standing about, the piano, the thick smoke, everything as usual. I saw you. You were in the big outer room beyond, but your face was very distinct. You were staring—staring straight at me."

"True," put in Dr. Fillery; "I saw you in the doorway plainly."

"In the foreground, by itself apart somehow, though surrounded by people, was this shining, radiant outline. I thought it was a Vision—the first thing of that sort I had ever seen in my life."

"That was your very first impression—even before you had time to think?"

"Yes."

"It struck you as unusual?"

"I cannot say more than that. I knew by the light it was unusual. Then it moved—talking to Povey or Kempster or someone—and I realized in a flash who it was. I knew it must be your friend, the man you had promised to bring—Ju—"

"And then—?" he asked quickly, before she could pronounce the name.

"And then—"

She stopped, and her eyes looked away from him, not in the sense that they moved but that their focus changed as though she looked at something else, at something within herself, no longer, therefore, at the face in front of her. He waited; he understood that she was searching among deep, strange, seething memories; he let her search; and, watching closely, he presently saw the sight return into her eyes from its inward plunge.

"And when you knew who it was," he asked very quietly, "were you still surprised? Did he look as you expected him to look, for instance?"

"I had expected nothing, you see, Edward, because I had not been consciously thinking about his coming. No mental picture was present in me at all. But the moment I realized who it was, the light seemed to go—I just saw a young man standing there, with his head turned sideways to me. The light, I suppose, lasted for a second only—that first second. As to how he looked? Well, he looked, not only bigger—he is bigger than most men," she went on, "but he looked "—her voice hushed instinctively a little on the adjective—"different."

Her companion made a gesture of agreement, waiting in silence for what was to follow.

"He looked so extraordinary, so wonderful," she resumed, gazing steadily into his eyes, "that I—I can hardly put it into words, Edward, unless I use childish language." She broke off and sighed, and something, he fancied, in her wavered for a second, though it was certainly neither the voice nor the eyes. A faint trembling again perhaps ran through her body. Her account was so deliberately truthful that it impressed him more than he quite understood. He was aware of pathos in her, of some vague trouble very poignant yet inexplicable. A breath of awe, it seemed, entered the room and moved between them.

"The childish words are probably the best, the right ones," he told her gently.

"An angel," she said instantly in a hushed tone, "I thought of an angel. There is no other word I can find. But somehow a helpless one. An angel—out of place."

He looked hard at her, his manner encouraging though grave; he said no word; he did not smile.

"Someone not of this earth quite," she added. "Not a man, at any rate."

Still more gently, he then asked her what she felt.

"At first I couldn't move," she went on, her voice normal again. "I must have stood there ten minutes fully, perhaps longer"—her listener did not correct the statement—"when I suddenly recovered and looked about for you, Edward, but could not see you. I needed you, but could not find you. I remember feeling somehow that I had lost you. I tried to call for you—in my heart. There was no answer.... Then—then I closed the door quietly and went upstairs to change from my street clothes."

She paused and passed a hand slowly across her forehead. Dr. Fillery asked casually a curious question:

"Do you remember *how* you got upstairs, Nayan?"

Her hand dropped instantly; she started. "It's very odd you should ask me that, Edward," she said, gazing at him with a slightly rising colour in her face, an increase of fire glowing in her eyes; "very odd indeed. I was just trying to think how I could describe it to you. No. Actually I do not remember how I got upstairs. All I know is—I was suddenly in my room." A new intensity appeared in voice and manner. "It seemed to me I flew—or that—something— carried me."

"Yes, Nayan, yes. It's quite natural you should have felt like that."

"Is it? I remember so little of what I actually felt. I wonder—I wonder," she went on softly, with an air almost of talking to herself, "if it will ever come back again—what I felt then—" _____

"Such moments of subliminal excitement," Dr. Fillery reminded her gently, "have the effect of obliterating memory sometimes—"

"Excitement," she caught him up. "Yes, I suppose it was excitement. But it was more, much more, than that. Stimulated—I think that's the word really. I felt caught away somewhere, caught away, caught up—as if into the rest of myself— into the whole of myself. I became vast"—she smiled curiously—"if you know what I mean—in several places at once, perhaps, is better. It was an immense feeling—no, I mean a feeling of immensity—"

"Happy?" His voice was low.

Her eyes answered even before her words, as the memory came back a little in response to his cautious suggestion.

"A new feeling altogether," she replied, returning his clear gaze with her frank, innocent eyes that had grown still more brilliant. "A feeling I have never known before." She talked more rapidly now, leaning forward a little in her chair. "I felt in the open air somehow, with flowers, trees, hot burning sunshine and sweet winds rushing to and fro. It was something bigger than happiness—a sort of intoxicating joy, I think. It was liberty, but of an enormous spiritual kind. I wanted to dance—I believe I did dance—yes, I'm sure I did, and with hardly anything on my body. I wanted to sing—I sang downstairs, of course—"

"I heard," he put in briefly. He did not add that she had never sung like that before.

"The moment I came into the room, yes, I remember I went straight to the piano without a word to anyone." She reflected a moment. "I suppose I had to. There was something new in me I could only express by music—rhythm, that is, not language."

"It was natural," Dr. Fillery said again. "Quite natural, I think."

"Yes, Edward, I suppose it was," she answered, then sank back in her chair, as though she had told him all there was to tell.

Dr. Fillery smoked in silence for a few minutes, then rose and touched the bell as before, and, as before, Nurse Robbins appeared with the same miraculous speed. There was a brief colloquy at the door; the woman was gone again, and the doctor turned back into the room with a look of satisfaction on his face. All, apparently, was going well upstairs. He did not sit down, however; he stood looking out of the window at the drab wintry sky of motionless clouds, his back to his companion. It was midday, but the light, while making all things visible, was not light; there was no shine, no touch of radiance, no hint of sparkle beneath the canopy of sullen cloud. The English winter's day was visible, no more than that. Yet it was not the English day, nor the clouds, nor the bleak dead atmosphere he looked at. In a single second his sight travelled far, far away, covering an enormous interval in space and time, in condition too. He saw a radiant world of sun-drenched flowers "tossing with random airs of an unearthly wind"; he saw a foam of forest leaves shaking and dancing against a deep blue sky; he saw a valley whose streams and emerald turf knew not the touch of human feet.... The familiar symbols he saw, but inflamed with new meaning.

"Thank you, Edward, thank you"—she was just behind him, her hands upon his shoulders. "You understand everything in the world!" she added, "and out of it," but too low for him to hear.

He came back with an effort, turning towards her. They were standing level now and very close, eyes looking into eyes. He felt her breath upon his face, her perfume rose about him, her lips were moving just in front of him—yet, for a second, he did not know who she was. It was as though *she* had not come with him out of that valley, not come back with him.... An insatiable longing seized him—to return and find her, stay with her. The ache of an intolerable yearning was in his heart, yet a sudden flash of understanding that brought a bigger, almost an unearthly joy in its train. At the call of some service, some duty, some help to be rendered to humanity, the three of them together—he, "N. H.," the girl—were in temporary exile from their rightful home. The scent of wild flowers rose about him. He suddenly remembered, recognized, and gave a little start. He had left her behind in the valley—Iraida; it was Nayan who now stood before him.

He uttered a dry little laugh. "You startled me, Nayan. I was thinking. I didn't hear you." She had just thanked him for something—oh, yes—because he had left her alone for a moment, giving her time to collect herself after the long cross-examination.

He took both her hands in his.

"*Our* patient then—isn't it? " he asked in a firm voice, looking deep into her luminous eyes. He saw no fire in them now.

"I'll do all I can, Edward."

She returned the pressure of his hands. His keen insight, operating in spite of himself, had read her clearly. It was mother, child and woman he had always known. The three, however, were already in process of disentanglement. For the first time during their long acquaintance, what now stood so close before him was—the woman. Yet behind the woman like an enveloping shadow stood the mother too. And behind both, again, stood another wild, gigantic, lovely possibility. Was it, then, the child that he had left playing in the radiant valley?... The child, he knew, was his always, always, even if the woman was another's.... He laughed softly. These, after all, were but transitory states in human, earthly evolution, concerned with play, with a production of bodies and so forth....

He had lost himself in her deep eyes. Her gaze lay all over him, over his entire being, like a warm soft covering that blessed and healed. She was so close that it seemed he drew her breath in with his own. She made a movement then, a tiny gesture. He let go the hands his own had held so long. He turned from the window and from her. He was trembling.

"What came later," he resumed in his calm, almost in his professional voice, "you probably do not remember?" He went towards his desk. "We need not talk about that. No doubt, in your mind, it all remains a blurred impression—"

She interrupted, following him across the room.

"What happened, Edward," she said very quietly in her lowest tone, "I know. It was all told to me. But my memory, as you say, is so faint as to be worthless really. What I do remember is this"—she tapped her open palm with two fingers slowly, as she spoke the words—"light, heat, a smell of flowers and a rushing wind that lifted me into some kind of exhilarating liberty where I felt—the intense joy of knowing myself somehow free—and greater, oh, far greater—than I am—now." Then she suddenly whispered again too low for him to catch— "angelic." A smile, as of glory, rippled across her face.

His voice, coming quickly, was cool, its tone measured:

"And you will come to see him the moment I let you know," he interrupted

abruptly. "It may be a few days, it may be a week. The instant it seems wise—
" He was entirely practical again.

She went to the door with him. "I'll come, of course," she answered, as he opened the door.

"I'll let myself out, Edward—please. I know the way. There's no good being a partner if one doesn't know the way out—" She laughed.

"And in, remember!" he called down the little passage after her, as, with a smile and a wave of the hand, she was gone.

He went back to his desk, drew a piece of paper towards him, and jotted a few notes down in briefest fashion. The expression on his rugged face was enigmatical perhaps, but the sternness at least was clear to read, and it was this, combining with an extraordinary tenderness, that drew out its nobility:

"Intensification of consciousness, involving increased activity of every centre; hearing, sight, touch and smell, all affected. Slight exteriorization of consciousness also took place. No signs of split or divided personality, but an increase of coherence rather. The central self active—aware of greater powers in time and space, hence sense of joy, heat, light, sound, motion. Distinct subliminal uprush, followed by customary loss of memory later. Her *whole* being, together with neglected tracts as yet untouched by experience—her *entire* being—reached simultaneously. Knew herself for the first time a woman—but something more as well. Unearthly complex, visible.

"Appeal made direct to subconscious self. Unfavourable reactions—none. Favourable reactions—increased physical and mental strength...."

He laid down his pencil as with a gesture of impatience at its uselessness, and sat back in the chair, thinking.

The effect "N. H." had upon other people was here again confirmed. That, at least, seemed reasonably clear. Vitality was increased; heart and mind caught up an extra gear; thought leaped, if extravagantly, towards speculation; emotion deepened, if ecstatically, towards belief. All the normal reactions of the system were speeded up and strengthened. Consciousness was intensified.

More than this—with some it was extended, and subliminal powers were set free. In his own experience this had been the case; sight, hearing, even a mild degree of divination, had opened in his being. It had, similarly, taken place with Devonham, an unlikely subject, who fought against acknowledging it. Father Collins, too, he suspected—he recalled his behaviour and strange language—had known also a temporary extension of faculty outside the normal field. He remembered, again, the Customs official, Charing Cross Station, and a dozen other minor instances.... Indications as yet were slight, he realized, but they were valuable.

Such abnormal experiences, moreover, each one interpreted, respectively, in the terms of his own individual being, of his own temperament, his own personal shibboleths. The law governing unusual experience operated invariably.

Was not his own particular "vision" easily explained? It might indeed, had it happened earlier, have found a place in his own book of Advanced Psychology. He reflected rapidly: He believed the industrial system lay at the root of Civilization's crumbling, and that man must return to Nature—therefore his yearnings dramatized themselves in personified representations of the beauty of Nature.

He could trace every detail of his Vision to some intense but unrealized yearning, to some deep hope, desire, dream, as yet unfulfilled. Always these yearnings and wishes unfulfilled!

Colour, form and sound again—he used them one and all in his treatment of special cases, and felt hurt by the ignorant scoffing and denial of his brother doctors. Hence their present dramatization.

His immense belief, again, in the results upon the Race when once the subliminal powers should have reached the stage where they could be used at will for practical purposes—this, in its turn, led him to hope, perhaps to believe, that his strange "Case" might prove to be some fabulous bright messenger who brought glad tidings.... All, all was explicable enough!

A smile stole over his face; he began to laugh quietly to himself....

Yes, he could explain all, trace all to something or other in his being, yet—he knew that the real explanation... well—his cleverest intellectual explanation and analysis were worthless after all. For here lay something utterly beyond his knowledge and experience. ...

The note of another searcher recurred to him:

Each human being has within himself that restless creative phantasy which is ever engaged in assuaging the harshness of reality.... Whoever gives himself unsparingly and carefully to self-observation will realize that there dwells within him something which would gladly hide up and cover all that is difficult and questionable in life, and thus procure an easy and free path. Insanity grants the upper hand to this something. When once it is uppermost, reality is more or less quickly driven out."

But he knew quite well that although he belonged to what he called the "Unstable," the "something" which Jung referred to had by no means obtained "the upper hand." The vista opening to his inner sight led towards a new reality.... Ah! If he could only persuade Paul Devonham to see what *he* saw...!

CHAPTER XXII

L ady Gleeson had heard from a Promethean what had transpired in the studio after she had left, and her interest was immensely stimulated. These details she had not known when she had driven her hero home, and had felt so strangely drawn to him that she had kissed him in front of Dr. Fillery as though she caressed a prisoner under the eyes of the warder.

She made her little plans accordingly. It was some days, however, before they bore fruit. The telephone at last rang. It was Dr. Fillery. The nerves in her quivered with anticipation.

Devonham, it appeared, had been away, and her "kind letters and presents," he regretted to find, had remained unanswered and unacknowledged. Mr. LeVallon had been in the country, too, with his colleague, and letters had not been forwarded. Oh, it would "do him good to see people." It would be delightful if she could spare a moment to look in. Perhaps for a cup of tea to-morrow? No, to-morrow she was engaged. The next day then. The next day it was. In the morning arrived a brief letter from Mr. LeVallon himself: "You will come to tea to-morrow. I thank you.—JULIAN LEVALLON."

Yet there was something both in Dr. Fillery's voice, as in this enigmatic letter, that she did not like. She felt puzzled somewhere. The excitement of a novel intrigue with this unusual youth, none the less, was stimulating. She decided to go to tea. She put off a couple of engagements in order to be free.

A servant let her in. She went upstairs. There was no sign of Dr. Fillery nor, thank heaven, of Devonham either. Tea, she saw, was laid for two in the private sitting-room. LeVallon, seated in an arm-chair by the open window, looked "magnificent and overpowering," as she called it. He rose at once to greet her. "Thank you," he said in his great voice. "I am glad to see you." He said it perfectly, as though it had been taught him. He took her hand. Her ravishing smile, perhaps, he did not notice. His face, at any rate, was grave.

His height, his broad shoulders, his inexperienced eyes and manner again delighted Lady Gleeson.

The effect upon her receptive temperament, at any rate, was instantaneous. That he showed no cordiality, did not smile, and that his manner was constrained, meant nothing to her—or meant what she wished it to mean. He was somewhat overcome, of course, she reflected, that she was here at all. She began at once. Sitting composedly on the edge of the table, so that her pretty silk stockings were visible to the extent she thought just right, she dangled her slim legs and looked him straight in the eyes. She was full of confidence. Her attitude said plainly: "I'm taking a lot of trouble, but you're worth it."

"Mr. LeVallon," she purred in a teasing yet determined voice, "why do you ignore me?" There was an air of finality about the words. She meant to know.

LeVallon met her eyes with a look of puzzled surprise, but did not answer. He stood in front of her. He looked really magnificent, a perfect study of the athlete in repose. He might have been a fine Greek statue.

"Why," she repeated, her lip quivering slightly, "do you ignore me? I want the truth," she added. She was delighted to see how taken aback he was. "You don't dislike me." It was not a question.

Into his eyes stole an expression she could not exactly fathom. She judged, however, that he felt awkward, foolish. Her interest doubtless robbed him of any *savoir faire* he might possess. This talk face to face was a little too much for any young man, but for a simple country youth it was, of course, more than disconcerting.

"I'm Lady Gleeson," she informed him, smiling precisely in the way she knew had troubled so many other men. "Angela," she added softly. "You've had my books and flowers and letters. Yet you continue to ignore me. Why, please?" With a different smile and a pathetic, childish, voice: "Have I offended you somehow? Do I displease you?"

LeVallon stared at her as though he was not quite certain who she actually was, yet as though he ought to know, and that her words now reminded him. He stared at her with what she called his "awkward and confused" expression, but which Fillery, had he been present, would have recognized as due to his desire to help a pitiful and hungry creature—that, in a word, his instinct for service had been a little stirred.

The scene was certainly curious and unusual.

LeVallon, with his great strength and dignity, yet something tender, pathetic in his bearing, stood staring at her. Lady Gleeson, brimming with a sense of easy victory, sat on the table-edge, her pretty legs well forward, knowing herself divinely gowned. She had her victim, surely, at a disadvantage. She felt at the same time a faint uneasiness she could not understand. She concealed it, however.

"I suffer here," he said suddenly in a quiet tone.

She gave a start. It was the phrase he had used before. She thrilled. She hitched her skirt a fraction higher.

"Julian, poor boy," she said—then stared at him. "How innocent you are!" She said it with apparent impulse, though her little frenzied mind was busy calculating. There came a pause. He said nothing. He was, apparently, quite innocent, extraordinarily, exasperatingly innocent.

In a low voice, smiling shyly, she added—as though it cost her a great effort: "You do not recognize what is yours."

"You are sacred!" he replied with startling directness, as though he suddenly understood, yet was stupidly perplexed. "You already have your man."

Lady Gleeson gulped down a spasm of laughter. How slow these countrymen could be! Yet she must not shock him. He was suffering, besides. This yokel from the woods and mountains needed a little coaxing. It was natural enough. She must explain and teach, it seemed. Well—he was worth the trouble. His beauty was mastering her already. She loved, in particular, his innocence, his shyness, his obvious respect. She almost felt herself a magnanimous woman.

"My man!" she mentioned. "Oh, he's finished with me long ago. He's bored. He has gone elsewhere. I am alone"—she added with an impromptu inspiration—"and free to choose."

"It must be pain and loneliness to you."

LeVallon looked, she thought, embarrassed. He was struggling with himself, of course. She left the table and came up close to him. She stood on tiptoe, so that her breath might touch his face. Her eyes shone with fire. Her voice trembled a little. It was very low.

"I choose—you," she whispered. She cast down her shining eyes. Her lips took on a prim, inviting turn. She knew she was irresistible like that. She stood back a step, as if expecting some tumultuous onslaught. She waited.

But the onslaught did not come. LeVallon, towering above her, merely stared. His arms hung motionless. There was, indeed, expression in his face, but it was not the expression that she expected, longed for, deemed her due. It puzzled her, as something entirely new.

"Me!" he repeated, in an even tone. He gazed at her in a peculiar way. Was it appraisement? Was it halting wonder at his marvellous good fortune? Was it that he hesitated, judging her? He seemed, she thought once for an instant, curiously indifferent. Something in his voice startled her.

The moment's pause, at any rate, was afflicting. Her spirit burned within her. Only her supreme belief in herself prevented a premature explosion. Yet something troubled her as well. A tremor ran through her. LeVallon, she remembered, was—LeVallon.

His own thought and feeling lay hidden from her blunt perception since she read no signs unless they were painfully obvious. But in his mind—in his feeling, rather, since he did not think—ran evidently the sudden knowledge of what her meaning was. He understood. But also, perhaps he remembered what Fillery had told him.

For a long time he kept silent, the emotions in him apparently at grips. Was he suddenly going to carry her away as he had done to that "little Russian poseuse"?

She watched him. He was intensely busy with what occupied his mind, for though he did not speak, his lips were moving. She watched him, impatience and wonder in her, impatience at his slowness, wonder as to what he would do and say when at last his simple mind had decided. And again the odd touch of fear stole over her. Something warned her. This young man thrilled her, but he certainly was strange. This was, indeed, a new experience. Whatever was he thinking about? What in the world was he going to say? His lips were still moving. There was a light in his face. She imagined the very words, could almost read them, hear them. There! Then she heard them, heard some at any rate distinctly: "You are an animal. Yet you walk upright...."

The scene that followed went like lightning.

Before Lady Gleeson could move or speak, however, he had also said another thing that for one pulsing second, and for the first time in her life, made her own utter worthlessness become appallingly clear to her. It explained the touch of fear. Even her one true thing, her animal passion, was a trumpery affair:

"There is nothing in you I can work with," he said with gentle, pitying sympathy. "Nothing I can use."

Then Lady Gleeson blazed. Vanity instantly restored self-confidence. It seemed impossible to believe her ears.

What had he done? What had he said that caused the explosion? He watched her abrupt, spasmodic movements with amazement. They were so ugly, so unrhythmical. Their violence was so wasteful.

"You insult me!" she cried, making these violent movements of her whole body that, to him, were unintelligible. "How dare you? You—" The breath choked her.

"Cad," he helped her, so suddenly that another mind not far away might almost have dropped the word purposely into his own. "I am so pained," he added, "so pained." He gazed at her as though he longed to help. "For you, I know, are valuable to him who holds you sacred—to—your husband."

Lady Gleeson simply could not credit her ears. This neat, though unintentional, way of transferring the epithet to her who deserved it, left her speechless. Her fury increased with her inability to express it. She could have struck him, killed him on the spot. Her face changed from white to crimson like some toy with a trick of light inside it. She seemed to emit sparks. She was transfixed. And the shiver that ran through her was, perhaps, for once, both sexual and spiritual at once.

"You insult me," she cried again helplessly. "You insult me!"

"If there was something in you I could work with—help—" he began, his face showing a tender sympathy that enraged her even more. He started suddenly, looking closer into her blazing eyes. "Ah," he said quickly below his breath, "the fire—the little fire!" His expression altered. But Lady Gleeson, full of her grievance, did not catch the words, it seemed.

"—In my tenderest, my most woman feelings," she choked on, yet noticing the altered expression on his face. "How *dare* you?" Her voice became shrill and staccato. Then suddenly—mistaking the look in his eyes for shame—she added: "You shall apologize. You shall apologize at once!" She screamed the words. They were the only ones that her outraged feelings found.

"You show yourself, my fire," he was saying softly in his deep resonant voice. "Oh, I see and worship now; I understand a little."

His look astonished her even in the middle of her anger—the pity, kindness, gentleness in it. The bewilderment she did not notice. It was the evident desire to be of service to her, to help and comfort, that infuriated her. The superiority was more than she could stand.

"And on your knees," she yelped; "on your knees, too!"

Drawing herself up, she pointed to the carpet with an air of some tragedy queen to whom a lost self-respect came slowly back. "Down there!" she added, as the gleaming buckle on her shoe indicated the spot. She did not forget to show her pretty stockings as well.

The picture was comic in the extreme, yet with a pathetic twist about it that, had she possessed a single grain of humour, must have made her feel foolish and shamed until she died, for his kneeling position rendered her insignificance so obvious it was painful in the extreme. LeVallon clasped his hands; his face, wearing a dignity and tenderness that emphasized its singular innocence and beauty, gazed up into her trivial prettiness, as she sat on the edge of the table behind her, glaring down at him with angry but still hungry eyes.

"I should have helped and worshipped," his deep voice thrilled. "I am ashamed. Always—you are sacred, wonderful. I did not recognize your presence calling me. I did not hear nor understand. I am ashamed."

The strange words she did not comprehend, even if she heard them properly. For one moment she knew a dreadful feeling that they were not addressed to her at all, but the sense of returning triumph, the burning desire to extract from him the last ounce of humiliation, to make him suffer as much as in her power lay, these emotions deadened any perceptions of a subtler kind. He was kneeling at her feet, stammering his abject apology, and the sight was wine and food to her. Though she could have crushed him with her foot, she could equally have flung herself in utter abandonment before his glorious crouching strength. She adored the scene. He looked magnificent on his knees. He was. She believed she, too, looked magnificent.

"You apologize to me," she said in a trembling voice, tense with mingled passions.

"Oh, with what sadness for my mistake you cannot know," was his strange reply. His voice rang with sincerity, his eyes held a yearning that almost lent him radiance. Yet it was the sense of power he gave that thrilled Lady Gleeson most. For she could not understand it. Again a passing hint of something remote, incalculable, touched her sense of awe. She shivered slightly. LeVallon did not move.

Appeased, yet puzzled, she lowered her face, now pale and intense with eagerness, towards his own, hardly conscious that she did so, while the faint idea again went past her that he addressed his astonishing words elsewhere. Blind vanity at once dismissed the notion, though the shock of its brief disthroning had been painful. She found satisfaction for her wounded soul. A man who had scorned her, now squirmed before her beauty on his knees, desiring her—but too late.

"You have *some* manhood, after all!" she exclaimed, still fierce, the upper lip just revealing the shining little teeth. Her power at last had touched him. He suffered. And she was glad.

"I worship," he repeated, looking through her this time, if not actually past her. "You are sacred, the source of all my life and power." His pain, his worship, the aching passion in him made her forget the insult. Upon that face upturned so close to hers, she now breathed softly.

"I'll try," she said more calmly. "I'll try and forgive you—just this once." The suffering in his eyes, so close against her own, dawned more and more on her. "There, now," she added impulsively, "perhaps I will forgive you—altogether!"

It was a moment of immense and queenly generosity. She felt sublime.

LeVallon, however, made no rejoinder; one might have thought he had not heard; only his head sank lower a little before her.

She had him at her mercy now: the rapt and wonderful expression in his eyes delighted her. She bent slightly nearer and made as though to kiss him, when a new idea flashed suddenly through her mind. This forgiveness was a shade too quick, too easy. Oh, she knew men. She was not without experience.

She acted with instant decision upon her new idea, as though delay might tempt her to yield too soon. She straightened up with a sudden jerk, touched his cheek with her hand, then, with a swinging swish of her skirts, but without a single further word, she swept across the room. She went out, throwing him a last glance just before she closed the door. At his kneeling figure and upturned face she flung this last glance of murderous fascination.

But LeVallon did not move or turn his head; he made no sign; his attitude remained precisely as before, face upturned, hands clasped, his expression rapt and grave as ever. His voice continued:

"I worship you for ever. I did not know you in that little shape. O wondrous central fire, teach me to be aware of you with awe, with joy, with love, even in the smallest things. O perfect flame behind all form....

For a long time his deep tones poured their resonant vibration through the room. There came an answering music, low, faint, continuous, a long, deep rhythm running in it. There was a scent of flowers, of open space, a fragrance of a mountain top. The sounds, the perfume, the touch of cool refreshing wind rose round him, increasing with every minute, till it seemed as though some energy informed them. At the centre he knelt steadily, light glowing faintly in his face and on his skin. A vortex of energy swept round him. He drew upon it. His own energy was increased and multiplied. He seemed to grow more radiant....

A few minutes later the door opened softly and Dr. Fillery looked in, hesitated for a second, then advanced into the room. He paused before the kneeling figure. It was noticeable that he was not startled and that his face wore no expression of surprise. A smile indeed lay on his lips. He noticed the scent of flowers, a sweetness in the air as after rain; he felt the immense vitality, the exhilaration, the peace and power too. He had made no sound, but the other, aware of his presence, rose to his feet.

"I disturbed you," said Fillery. "I'm sorry. Shall I go?"

"I was worshipping," replied "N. H." "No, do not go. There was a little flash"—he looked about him for an instant as if slightly bewildered—"a little sign—something I might have helped—but it has gone again. Then I worshipped, asking for more power. *You* notice it?" he asked, with a radiant smile.

"I notice it," said Fillery, smiling back. He paused a moment. His eye took in the tea-things and saw they were untouched; he felt the tea-pot. It was still warm. "Come," he said happily; "we'll have some tea together. I'll send for a fresh brew." He rang the bell, then arranged the chairs a little differently. "Your visitor?" he asked. "You are expecting someone?"

"N. H." looked round him suddenly. "Oh!" he exclaimed, "but—she has gone!"

His surprise was comical, but the expression on the face changed in his rapid way at once. "I remember now. Your Lade Gleeson came," he added, a touch of gentle sadness in his voice, "I gave her pain. You had told me. I forgot—"

"You did well," Fillery commented with smiling approval as though the entire scene was known to him, "you did very well. It is a pity, only, that she left too soon. If she had stayed for your worship—your wind and fire might have helped—"

"N. H." shook his head. "There is nothing I can work with," he replied. "She is empty. She destroys only. Why," he added, "does she walk upright?"

But Lady Gleeson held very different views upon the recent scene. This magnificent young male she had put in his place, but she had not finished with him. No such being had entered her life before. She was woman enough to see he was unusual. But he was magnificent as well, and, secretly, she loved his grand indifference.

She left the house, however, with but an uncertain feeling that the honours were with her. Two days without a word, a sign, from her would bring him begging to her little feet.

But the "begging" did not come. The bell was silent, the post brought no humble, passionate, abandoned letter. She fumed. She waited. Her husband, recently returned to London and immensely preoccupied with his concessions, her maid, too, were aware that Lady Gleeson was impatient. The third, the fourth day came, but still no letter.

Whereupon it occurred to her that she had possibly gone too far. Having left him on his knees, he was, perhaps, still kneeling in his heart, even prostrate with shame and disappointment. Afraid to write, afraid to call, he knew not what to do. She had evidently administered too severe a lesson. Her callers, meanwhile, convinced her that she was irresistible. There was no woman like her in the world. She had, of course, been too harsh and cruel with this magnificent and innocent youth from the woods and mountains....

Thus it was that, on the fourth day, feeling magnanimous and generous, big-hearted too, she wrote to him. It would be foolish, in any case, to lose him altogether merely for a moment's pride:

"DEAR MR. LEVALLON,— I feel I must send you a tiny word to let you know that I really have forgiven you. You behaved, you know, in a way that no man of my acquaintance has ever done before. But I feel sure now you did not really mean it. Your forest and mountain gods have not taught you to understand civilized women. So—I forgive.

"Please forget it all, as I have forgotten it.—Yours,
                    "ANGELA GLEESON.
"P.S.—And you may come and see me soon."

To which, two days later, came the reply:

"DEAR LADY GLEESON,—I thank you.
                    "JULIAN LEVALLON."

Within an hour of its receipt, she wrote:

"DEAR JULIAN,—I am so glad you understand. I knew you would. You may come and see me. I will prove to you that you are really forgiven. There is no need to feel embarrassed. I am interested in you and can help you. Believe me, you need a woman's guidance. All—*all* I have, is yours.

"I shall be at home this afternoon—alone—from 4 to 7 o'clock. I shall expect you. My love to you and your grand wild gods!—Yours, "ANGELA.

" P.S.—I want you to tell me more about your gods. Will you?"

She sent it by special messenger, "Reply " underlined on the envelope. He did not appear at the appointed hour, but the next morning she received his letter.

It came by ordinary post. The writing on the envelope was not his. Either Devonham or Fillery had addressed it. And a twinge of unaccustomed emotion troubled her. Intuition, it seems, survives even in the coarsest, most degraded feminine nature, ruins of some divine prerogative perhaps. Lady Gleeson, at any rate, flinched uneasily before she opened the long expected missive:

DEAR LADY GLEESON,—Be sure that you are always under the protection of the gods even if you do not know them. They are impersonal. They come to you through passion but not through that love of the naked body which is lust. I can work with passion because it is creative, but not with lust, for it is destructive only. Your suffering is the youth and ignorance of the young uncreative animal. I can strive with young animals and can help them. But I cannot work with them. I beg you, listen. I love in you the fire, though it is faint and pitiful. "JULIAN."

Lady Gleeson read this letter in front of the looking-glass, then stared at her reflection in the mirror.

She was dazed. But in spite of the language she thought "silly," she caught the blunt refusal of her generous offer. She understood. Yet, unable to believe it, she looked at her reflection again—then, impulsively, went downstairs to see her husband.

It really was more than she could bear. The man was mad, but that did not excuse him.

"He is a beast," she informed her husband, tearing up the letter angrily before his eyes in the library, while he watched her with a slavish admiration that increased her fury. "He is nothing but an animal," she added. "He's a—a— "

"Who?" came the question, as though it had been asked before. For Sir George wore a stolid and a patient expression on his kindly face.

"That man LeVallon," she told him. "One of Dr. Fillery's cases I tried to—to help. Now he's written to me—!"

George looked up with infinite patience and desire in his kindly gaze.

"Cut him out," he said dryly, as though he was accustomed to such scenes. "Let him rip. Why bother, anyway, with 'patients'?"

And he crossed the room to comfort her, knowing that presently the reaction must make him seem more desirable than he really was....

"Never in my house again," she sighed, as he approached her lovingly, his fingers in his close brown beard. "He is simply a beast—an animal!"

CHAPTER XXIII

It was, perhaps, some cosmic humour in the silent, beautiful stars which planned that Nayan's visit should follow upon the very heels of Lady Glee son's call. Those vast Intelligences who note the fall of even a feather, watching and guarding the Race so closely that they may be said in human terms to love it, arranged the details possibly, enjoying the result with their careless, sunny laughter. At any rate, Dr. Fillery quickly sent her word, and she came. To lust "N. H." had not reacted. How would it be with love?

The beautiful girl entered the room slowly, shyly, as though, certain of her self, she was not quite certain what she was about to meet. Fillery had told her she could help, that she was needed; therefore she came. There was no thought of self in her. Her first visit to Julian LeVallon after his behaviour in the Stu dio had no selfish motive in it. Her self-confidence, however, went only to a cer tain point; in the interview with Fillery she had easily controlled herself; she was not so sure that her self-control would be adequate now. Though calm out wardly, an inexpressible turmoil surged within.

She remembered his strength, virility and admiration—as a woman; his in genuous, childlike innocence, an odd appealing helplessness in it somewhere, touched the mother in her. That she divined this latter was, perhaps, the secret of her power over men. Independent of all they had to offer, she touched the highest in them by making them feel they had need of the highest in herself. She obtained thus, without desiring it, the influence that Lady Gleeson, her an tithesis, lacked. They called her Nayan the Impersonal. The impersonal in her, nevertheless, that which had withstood the cunning onslaught of every type of male successfully, had received a fundamental shock. Both her modesty and dig nity had been assailed, and in public. Others, women among them, had wit nessed her apparent yielding to LeVallon's violence and seen her carried in his arms; they had noted her obvious willingness, had heard her sympathetic cry. She knew quite well what the women thought—Lady Gleeson had written a little note of sympathy—the men as well, and yet she came at Fillery's call to visit, perhaps to help, the offender who had caused it all.

As she opened the door every nerve she possessed was tingling. The mother in her yearned, but the woman in her sent the blood rushing from her heart in pride, in resentment, in something of anger as well. How had he dared to seize her in that awful way? The outrage and the love both tore at her. Yet Nayan was not the kind to shirk self-revelation when it came. She brought some hidden se cret with her, although as yet herself uncertain what that secret was.

Fillery met her on the threshold with his sweet tact and sympathy as usual. He had an authoritative and paternal air that helped and comforted her, and, as she took his hand at once, the look she gave him was more kind and tender than she knew. The last trace of self, at any rate, went out of her as she felt his touch.

"Here I am," she said, "you sent for me. I promised you."

He replied in a low tone: "There's no need to refer to anything, of course. Assume—I suggest—that he has forgotten all that happened, and you—have forgotten too."

He was aware of nothing but her eyes. The softness. the delicate perfume, the perfect voice, even the fur and flowers—all were summed up in her eyes alone. In those eyes he could have lost himself perhaps for ever.

He led her into the room, a certain abruptness in his manner.

"I shall leave you alone," he whispered, using his professional voice. "It is best that he should see you quite alone. I shall not be far away, but you will find him perfectly quiet. He understands that you are"—his tone changed upon the adjective—"sacred."

"Sacred," she murmured to herself, repeating the word, "sacred."

They smiled. And the door closed behind her. Across the room rose the tall figure of the man she had come to see, dressed in dark blue, a low white shirt open at the neck, a blue tie that matched the strong, clear eyes, the wondrous hair crowning the whole like a flame. The slant of wintry sunlight by chance just caught the great figure as it rose, lightly, easily, as though it floated up out of the floor before her.

And, as by magic, the last uncertainty in her disappeared; she knew herself akin to this radiant shape of blue and gold; knew also—mysteriously—in a way entirely beyond her to explain—knew why Edward Fillery was dear to her. Was it that something in the three of them pertained to a common origin? The conviction, half thought, half feeling, rose in her as she looked into the blue eyes facing her and took the outstretched hand.

"You strange lost being! No one will understand you—here...."

The words flashed through her mind of their own accord, instantly, spontaneously, yet were almost forgotten the same second in the surge of more commonplace feeling that rose after. Only the "here" proved their origin not entirely forgotten. It was the selfless, mothering instinct that now dominated, but the division in her being had, none the less, been indicated as by a white piercing light that searched her inmost nature. That added "here" laid bare, she felt, some part of her which, with all other men, was clothed and covered away.

Realized though dimly, this troubled her clear mind, as she took the chair he offered, the conviction that she must tend and care for, even love this strange youth, as though he were in exile and none but herself could understand him. She heard the deep resonant voice in the air close in front of her:

"I am not lost now," he said, with his radiant smile, and as if he perceived her thought from the expression in her face. " I wished to take you away—to take you back. I wish it still."

He stood gazing down at her. The deep tones, the shining eyes, the towering stature with its quiet strength—these, added to the directness of the language, confused her for a moment. The words were so entirely, unexpected. Fillery had led her to suppose otherwise. Yet before the blazing innocence in his face and manner, her composure at once returned. She found no words at first. She smiled up into his eyes, then pointed to a chair. Seated he would be more manageable, she felt. His upright stature was so overpowering.

"You had forgotten—" he went on, obeying her wish and sitting down, "but I could not know that you had forgotten. I apologize"—the word sounded oddly on his lips, as though learned recently—"for making you suffer."

"Forgotten!"

A swift intuition, due to some as yet undecipherable kinship, told her that the word bore no reference to the Studio scene. Some larger meaning, scaled to an immenser map, came with it. An unrealized emotion stirred faintly in her as she heard. Her first sight of him as a figure of light returned.

"But that is all forgiven now," she replied calmly in her firm, gentle voice. "We need not speak of it. You understand now"—she ended lamely—"that it is not possible—"

He listened intently, gravely, as though with a certain effort, his head bent forward to catch every syllable. And as he bent, peering, listening, he might have been some other-worldly being staring down through a window in the sky into the small confusions of earth's affairs.

"Yes," he said, the moment she stopped speaking, "I understand now. I shall never make you suffer again. Only—I could not know that you had forgotten— so completely."

"Forgotten?" she again repeated in spite of herself, for the way he uttered the word again stirred that nameless, deep emotion in her. Their attitudes respectively were changing. She no longer felt that she could "mother" this great figure before her.

"Where we belong," he answered in his great quiet voice. "*There*," he added, in a way that made it the counterpart of her own spontaneous and intuitive "here." "It is so easy. I had forgotten too. But Fillery, dear Fillery, helps me to remember, and the stars and flowers and wind, these help me too. And then you—when I saw *you* I suddenly remembered more. I was so happy. I remembered what I had left to come among men and women. I knew that Fillery and you belonged 'there' with me. You, both, had come down for a little time, come down 'here,' but had remained too long. You had become almost as men and women are. I remembered everything when I saw your eyes. I was so happy in a moment, as I looked at you, that I felt I must go back, go home. The central fire called me, called us all three. I wanted to escape and take you with me. I knew by your eyes that you were ready. You called to Fillery. We were off."

He paused a moment, while she listened in breathless silence.

"Then, suddenly, you refused. You resisted. Something prevented. The Messengers were there when suddenly"—an expression of yearning pain clouded his great eyes a moment—"you forgot again. I forgot too, forgot everything. The darkness came. It was cold. My enemy, the water, caught me."

He stopped, and passed his hand across his forehead, sighing, his eyes fixed upon vacancy as with an intense effort to recover something. "And I still forget," he went on, the yearning now transferred from the eyes to the lowered voice. "I can remember nothing again. All, all is gone from me." The light in his face actually grew dimmer as he slowly uttered the words. He leaned back in his big arm-chair. Again, it occurred to her, it was as if he drew back from that window in the sky.

A curious hollow, empty of life, seemed to drop into the room between them as his voice ceased.

While he had been speaking, the girl watched and listened with intense interest and curiosity. She remembered he was a "patient," yet no touch of uneasiness or nervousness was in her. His strange words, meaningless as they might seem, woke deep echoes of some dim buried recognition in her. It amazed and troubled her. This young man, this sinner against the conventions whom she had come to comfort and forgive, held the reins already. What had happened, what was happening, and how did he contrive it? She was aware of a clear, divining knowledge in him, a power, a directness she could not fathom. He seemed to read her inside out. It was more than uncanny; it was spiritual. It mastered her.

During his speech he remained very still, without gesture, without change of expression in his face; he made no movement; only his voice deepened and grew rhythmical. And a power emanated from him she hardly dared resist, much less deny. His voice, his words, reached depths in her she scarcely knew herself. He was so strong, so humble, so simple, yet so strangely peaceful. And—suddenly she realized it—so far beyond her, yet akin. She became aware that the figure seated in the chair, watching her, talking, was but a fraction of his whole self. He was—the word occurred to her—immense. Was she, too, immense?

More than troubled, she was profoundly stimulated. The mothering instinct in her for the first time seemed to fail a little. The woman in her trembled, not quite sure of itself. But, besides these two, there was another part of her that listened and felt joy—a white, radiant joy which, if she allowed, must become ecstasy. Whence came this hint of unearthly rapture? Again there rose before her the two significant words: "There" and "Here."

"I do not quite understand," she replied, after a moment's pause, looking into his eyes steadily, her voice firm, her young face very sweet; "I do not fully understand, perhaps. But I sympathize." Then she added suddenly, with a little smile: "But, at any rate, I did not come to make you apologize—Julian. Please be sure of that. I came to see if I might be of any use if there was anything I might do to make—"

His quick interruption transfixed her.

"You came," he said in a distinct, low tone, "because you love me and wish me to love you. But we do love already, you, dear Fillery, and I—only our love is in that great Service where we all three belong. It is not of this—it is not *here*—" making an impatient gesture with his hand to indicate his general surroundings.

He broke off instantly, noticing the expression in her face.

She had realized suddenly, as he spoke, the blind fury of reproduction that sweeps helpless men and women everywhere into union, then flings them aside exhausted, useless, its purpose accomplished. Though herself never yet caught

by it, the vivid realization made her turn from life with pity and revulsion. Yet—
were these thoughts her own? Whence did they come, if not? And what was
this new blind thing straining in her mind for utterance, bursting upwards like
a flame, threatening to split it asunder even in its efforts to escape? "What are
these words we use?" darted across her. "What do they mean? What is it we're
talking about *really*? I don't know quite. Yet it's real, yes, real and true. Only
it's beyond our words. It's something I know, but have forgotten.... " That was
his word again: "Forgotten"! While they used words together, something in her
went stumbling, groping, thrusting towards a great shining revelation for
which no words existed. And a strange, deep anguish seized her suddenly.

"Oh!" he cried, "I make you suffer again. The fire leaves you. You are white.
I—I will apologize"—he slipped on to his knees before her—"but you do not
understand. It was not your sacredness I spoke of." Already on his knees before
her, but level with her face owing to his great stature, gazing into her eyes with
an expression of deep tenderness, humility, almost suffering, he added: "It was
our other love, I meant, our great happy service, the thing we have forgotten.
You came, I thought, to help me to remember *that*. The way home—I saw you
knew." The light streamed back into his face and eyes.

The tumult and confusion in the girl were natural enough. Her resourceful-
ness, however, did not fail her at this curious and awkward moment. His
words, his conduct were more than she could fathom, yet behind both she divined a source of remote inspiration she had never known before in any "man."
The beauty and innocence on the face arrested her faculties for a second. That
nameless emotion stirred again. A glimmer of some faint, distant light, whose
origin she could not guess, passed flickering across her inner tumult. Some faculty she could not name, at any rate, blew suddenly to white heat in her. This
youth on his knees before her had spoken truth. Without knowing it even herself, she had given him her love, a virgin love, a woman's love hitherto unawakened in her by any other man, but a love not of this earth quite—because
of him who summoned it into sudden flower.

Yet at the same time he denied the need of it! He spoke of some marvellous
great shining Service that was different from the love of man and woman.

This too, as some forgotten, lost ideal, she knew was also true.

Her mind, her heart, her experience, her deepest womanly nature, these, she
realized in a glowing instant of extraordinary divination, were at variance in her.
She trembled; she knew not what to do or say or think. And again, it came to
her, that the visible shape before her was but the insignificant fraction of a being whose true life spread actively and unconfined through infinite space.

She then did something that was prompted, though she did not know it thus,
by her singleness of heart, her purity of soul and body, her unique and natural
instinct to be of use, of service, to others—the accumulated practice and effort
of her entire life provided the action along a natural line of least resistance: she
bent down and put her arm and hand round his great shoulder. She lowered her
face. She kissed him most tenderly, with a mother's love, a woman's secret passion perhaps, but yet with something else as well she could not name—an un-

earthly yearning for a greater Ideal than anything she had yet known on earth among humanity.... It was the invisible she kissed.

And LeVallon, she realized with immense relief, justified her action, for he did not return the kiss. At the same time she had known quite well it would be thus. That kiss trembled, echoed, in her own greater unrealized self as well.

"What is it," she whispered, a mysterious passion surging up in her as she raised him to his feet, "that you remember and wish to recover—for us all? Can you tell me? What is this great, happy, deathless service that we have forgotten?" Her voice trembled a little. An immense sense of joy, of liberty, shook out its sunlit wings.

His expression, as he rose, was something between that of a child and a faithful yearning animal, but of a "divine animal," though she did not know the phrase. Its purity, its sweetness, its power—it was the power she noticed chiefly—were superb.

"I cannot tell, I cannot remember," his voice said softly, for all its resonant, virile depth. "It is some state we all have come from—into this. We are strangers here. This brain and intellect, this coarse, thick feeling, this selfishness, this want of harmony and working together—all this is new and strange to us. It is of blind and clumsy children. This love of one single person for one other single person—it is so pitiful. We three have come into this for a time, a little time. It is pain and misery. It is prison. Each one works only for himself. There is no joy. They know nothing of our great Service. We cannot show them. Let us go back—"

Another pause fell between them, another of those singular hollows she had felt before. But this time the hollow was not empty. It was brimmed with surging life. The gulf between her earthly state and another that was nameless, a gulf usually unbridgeable, the fixed gulf, as an old book has it, which may not be crossed without danger to the Race, for whose protection it exists—this childhood simile occurred to her. And a sense of awe stirred in her being. It was the realization that this gulf or hollow now brimmed with life, that it could be crossed, that she might step over into another place—the sense of awe rose thence, yet came certainly neither from the woman nor the mother in her.

"I am of another place," LeVallon went on, plucking the thought naked from her inmost being. "For I am come here recently, and the purpose of my coming is hidden from me, and memory is dark. But it is not entirely dark. Sometimes I half remember. Stars, flowers, fire, wind, women—here and there—bring light into the darkness. Oh," he cried suddenly, "how wonderful they are—how wonderful you are—on that account to me!"

The voice held a strange, evoking power perhaps. A thousand yearnings she had all her life suppressed (because they interfered with her duty—as she conceived it—here and now) fluttered like rising flames within her as she listened. His voice now increased in volume and rhythm, though still quiet and low-pitched; it was as if a great wind poured behind it with tremendous vibrations, through it, lifting her out of a limited, cramped, everyday self. A delicious warmth of happy comfort, of acceptance, of enthusiasm glowed in her. And LeVallon's face, she saw, had become radiant, almost as though it emanated light. This light entered her being and brought joy again.

"Joy! " he said, reading her thought and feeling. "Joy!"

"Joy! Another place!" she heard herself repeating, her eves now fixed upon his own.

She felt lighter, caught up and away a little, lifted above the solid earth; as if it was heat that lightened, and wind that bore her upwards. Everything in her became intensified.

"Another state, another place"—her voice seemed to borrow something of the rhythm in his own, though she did not notice it—"but not away from earth, this beautiful earth?" With a happy smile she added, "I love the dear kind earth, I love it."

The light on his face increased:

"The earth we love and serve," he said, "is beautiful, but here"—he looked about him round the roost, at the trees waving through the window, at the misty sky above draping the pale light of the sun—"here I am on the surface only. There is confusion and struggle. Everything quarrels against everything else. It is discord and disorder. There is no harmony. Here, on the surface, everything is separate. There is no working together. It is all pain, each little part fighting for itself. Here—I am outside—there is no joy."

It was the phrase "I am outside" that flashed something more of his meaning into her. His full meaning lay beyond actual words perhaps; but this phrase fell like a shock into that inmost self which she had deliberately put away.

"*You are from inside*, yes," she exclaimed, marveling afterwards that she had said it; "within—nearer to the centre—!"

And he took the abrupt interruption as though they both understood and spoke of the same one thing together, having found a language born of similar great yearnings and of forgotten knowledge, times, states, conditions, places.

"I come," he said, his voice, his bright smile alive with the pressure of untold desire, "from another place that is—yes—inside, nearer to the centre. I have forgotten almost everything. I remember only that there was harmony, love, work and happiness all combined in the perfect liberty of our great service. We served the earth. We helped the life upon it. There was no end, no broken fragments, no failure." The voice touched chanting. "There was no death."

He rose suddenly and came over to her side, and instinctively the girl stood up. What she felt and thought as she heard the strange language he used, she hardly knew herself. She only knew in that moment an immense desire to help her kind, an intensification of that great ideal of impersonal service which had always been the keynote of her life. This became vividly stimulated in her. It rose like a dominating, overmastering passion. The sense of ineffectual impotence, of inability to accomplish anything of value against the stolid odds life set against her, the uselessness of her efforts with the majority, in a word, seemed brushed away, as though greater powers of limitless extent were now at last within her reach. This blazed in her like fire. It shone in her big dark eyes that looked straight into his as they stood facing one another.

"And that service," he went on in his deep vibrating, half-singing tone, "I see in dear Fillery and in you. I know my own kind. We three, at least, belong. I know my own." The voice seemed to shake her like a wind.

At the last two words her soul leaped within her. It seemed quite natural that his great arm should take her breast and shoulder and that his lips should touch her cheek and hair. For there was worship in both gestures. "Our greater service," she whispered, trembling, "tell me of that. What is it?" His touch against her was like the breath of fire.

Her womanly instincts, so-called, her maternal love, her feminine impulses deserted her. She was aware solely at that moment of the proximity of a being who called her to a higher, to, at any rate, a different state, to something beyond the impoverished conditions of humanity as she had hitherto experienced it, to something she had ever yearned and longed for without knowing what it was. An extraordinary sense of enormous liberty swept over her again.

His voice broke and the rhythm failed.

"I cannot tell you," he replied mournfully, the light fading a little from his eyes and face. "I have forgotten. That other place is hidden from me. I am in exile," he added slowly, "but with you and—Fillery." His blue eyes filled with moisture; the expression of troubled loneliness was one she had never seen before on any human face. "I suffer," he added gently. "We all suffer."

And, at the sight of it, the yearning to help, to comfort, to fulfill her rôle as mother, returned confusingly, and rose in her like a tide. He was so big and strong and splendid. He was so helpless. It was, perhaps, the innocence in the great blue eyes that conquered her—for the first time in her life.

But behind, beside the mother in her, stirred also the natural woman. And beyond this again, rose the accumulated power of the entire Race. The instinct of all the women of the planet since the world began drove at her. Not easily may an individual escape the deep slavery of the herd.

The young girl wavered and hesitated. Caught by so many emotions that whirled her as in a vortex, the direction of the resultant impetus hung doubtful for some time. During the half hour's talk, she had entered deeper water than she had ever dared or known before. Life hitherto, so far as men were concerned, had been a simple and an easy thing that she had mastered without difficulty. Her real self lay still unscarred within her. Freely she had given the mothering care and sympathy that were so strong in her, the more freely because the men who asked of her were children, one and all, children who needed her, but from whom she asked nothing in return. If they fell in love, as they usually did, she knew exactly how to lift their emotion in a way that saved them pain while it left herself untouched. None reached her real being, which thus remained unscathed, for none offered the lifting glory that she craved.

Here, for the first time facing her, stood a being of another type; and that unscathed self in her went trembling at the knowledge. Here was a power she could not play with, could not dominate, but a power that could play with her as easily as the hurricane with the flying leaf. It was not his words, his strange beauty, his great strength that mastered her, though these brought their contribution doubtless. The power she felt emanated unconsciously from him, and was used unconsciously. It was all about him. She realized herself a child before him, and this realization sweetened, though it confused her being. He so easily touched depths in her she had hardly recognized herself. He could so easily lift her to terrific heights.... Various sides of her became dominant in turn....

The inmost tumult of a good woman's heart is not given to men to read, perhaps, but the final impetus resulting from the whirlpool tossed her at length in a very definite direction. She found her feet again. The determining factor that decided the issue of the struggle was a small and very human one. He appealed to the woman in her, yet what stirred the woman was the vital and afflicting factor that—he did not need her.

He wished to help, to lift her towards some impersonal ideal that remained his secret. He wished to give—he could give—while she, for her part, had nothing that he needed. Indeed, he asked for nothing. He was as independent of her as she was independent of these other men.

And the woman, now faced for the first time with this entirely new situation, decided automatically—that he should learn to need her. He must. Though she had nothing that he wanted from her, she must on that very account give all. The sacrifice which stands ready for the fire in every true feminine heart was lighted there and then. She had found her master and her god. Half measures were not possible to her. She stood naked at the altar. But in her sacrifice he, too, the priest, the deity, the master, he also should find love.

Such is the woman's power, however, to conceal from herself the truth, that she did not recognize at first what this decision was. She disguised it from her own heart, yet quite honestly. She loved him and gave him all she had to give for ever and ever: even though he did not ask nor need her love. This she grasped. Her rôle must be one of selfless sacrifice. But the deliberate purpose behind her real decision she disguised from herself with complete success. It lay there none the less, strong, vital, very simple. She would teach him love.

Alone of all men, Edward Fillery could have drawn up this motive from its inmost hiding place in her deep subconscious being, and have made it clear to her. Dr. Fillery, had he been present, would have discerned it in her, as, indeed, he did discern it later. He had, for that matter, already felt its prophecy with a sinking heart when he planned bringing them together: Iraida might suffer at LeVallon's hands.

But Fillery, apparently, was not present, and Nayan Khilkoff remained unaware of self-deception. LeVallon "needs your care and sympathy; you can help him," she remembered. This she believed, and Love did the rest.

So intricate, so complex were the emotions in her that she realized one thing only—she must give all without thought of self. "When half gods go the gods arrive " sang in her heart. She was a woman, one of a mighty and innumerable multitude, and collective instinct urged her irresistibly. But it hid at the same time with lovely care the imperishable desire and intention that the arriving god should—must—love her in return.

The youth stood facing her while this tumult surged within her heart and mind. Outwardly calm, she still gazed into the clear blue eyes that shone with moisture as he repeated, half to himself and half to her:

"We are in exile here; we suffer. We have forgotten."

His hands were stretched towards her, and she took them in her own and held them a moment. "But you and I," he went on, "you and I and Fillery—shall remember again—soon. We shall know why we are here. We shall do our happy work together here. We shall then return—escape."

His deep tones filled the air. At the sound of the other name a breath of sadness, of disappointment, touched her coldly. The familiar name had faded. It was, as always, dear. But its potency had dimmed....

The sun was down and a soft dusk covered all. A faint wind rustled in the garden trees through the open window.

"Fillery," she murmured, "Edward Fillery!—He loved me. He has loved me always."

The little words—they sounded little for the first time—she uttered almost in a whisper that went lost against the figure of LeVallon towering above her through the twilight.

"We are together," his great voice caught her whisper in the immense vibration, drowning it. "The love of our happy impersonal service brings us all together. We have forgotten, but we shall remember soon."

It seemed to her that he shone now in the dusky air. Light came about his face and shoulders. An immense vitality poured into her through his hands. The sense of strange kinship was overpowering. She felt, though not in terms of size or physical strength, a pigmy before him, while yet another thing rose in gigantic and limitless glory as from some inner heart he quickened in her. This sense of exaltation, of delirious joy that tempted sweetly, came upon her. He must love her, need her in the end....

"Julian," she murmured softly, drawn irresistibly closer. "The gods have brought you to me." Her feet went nearer of their own accord, but there was no movement, no answering pressure, in the hands she held. "You shall never know loneliness again, never while I am here. The gods—your gods—have brought us together."

"Our gods," she heard his answer, "are the same." The words trembled against her actual breast, so close she was now leaning against him. "Even if lost, it is they who sent us here. I know their messengers—"

He broke off, standing back from her, dropping her hands, or, rather, drawing his own away.

"Hark!" he cried. The voice deep and full, yet without loudness, thrilled her. She watched him with terror and amazement, as he turned to the open window, throwing his arms out suddenly to the darkening sky against which the trees loomed still and shapeless. His figure was wrapped in a faint radiance as of silvery moonlight. She was aware of heat about her, a comforting, inspiring warmth that pervaded her whole being, as from within. The same moment the bulk of the big tree shook and trembled, and a steady wind came pouring into the room. It seemed to her the wind, the heat, poured through that tree.

And the inner heart in her grew clear an instant. This wind, this heat, increased her being marvellously. The exaltation in her swept out and free. She saw him, dropped from alien skies upon the little teeming earth. The sense of his remoteness from the life about them, of her own remoteness too, flashed over her like wind and fire. An immense ideal blazed, then vanished. It flamed beyond her grasp. It beckoned with imperishable loveliness, then faded instantly. Wind caught it up once more. With the fire an overpowering joy rose in her.

"Julian!" she cried aloud. "Son of Wind and Fire!"

At the words, which had come to her instinctively, he turned with a sudden gesture she could not quite interpret, while there broke upon his face a smile, strange and lovely, that caught up the effect of light about him and seemed to focus in his brilliant eyes. His happiness was beyond all question, his admiration, wonder too; yet the quality she chiefly looked and expected—was not there.

She chilled. The joy, she was acutely conscious, was not a personal joy.

"You," he said gently, happily, emphasizing the word, "you are not pitiful," and the rustle of the shaking trees outside the window merged their voice in his and carried it outward into space. It was as if the wind itself had spoken. Across the garden dusk there shot a sudden effect of light, as though a flame had flickered somewhere in the sky, then passed back into the growing night. There was a scent of flowers in the air. "You," he cried, with an exultation that carried her again beyond herself. "You are not pitiful."

"Julian!" she stammered, longing for his arms. She half drew away. The blood flowed down and back in her. "Not pitiful!" she repeated faintly.

For it was to her suddenly as if that sighing wind that entered the room from the outer sky had borne him away from her. That wind was a messenger. It came from that distant state, that other region where he belonged, a state, a region compared to which the beings of earth were trumpery and tinsel-dressed. It came to remind him of his home and origin. The little earth, the myriad confused figures struggling together on its surface, he saw as "pitiful." From that window in the sky whence he looked down he watched them...!

She knew the feeling in him, knew it, because some part of her, though faint and deeply hidden, was akin. Yet she was not wholly "pitiful." He had discerned in her this faint, hidden strain of vaster life, had stirred and strengthened it by his words, his presence. Yet it was not vital enough in her to stand alone. When wind and fire, his elements, breathed forth from it, she was afraid.

"You are not pitiful," he had said, yet pitiful, for all that, she knew herself to be. On that breath of sighing wind he swept away from her, far, far away where, as yet, she could not follow. And her dream of personal love swept with it. Some ineffable hint of a divine, impersonal glory she had known went with him from her heart. The personal was too strong in her. It was human love she desired both to give and ask.

Unspoken words flared through her heart and being: "Julian, you have no soul, no human soul. But I will give you one, for I will teach you love—"

He turned upon her like a hurricane of windy fire.

"Soul!" he cried, catching the word out of her naked heart. "Oh, be not caught with that pitiful delusion. It is this idea of soul that binds you hopelessly to self-ish ends and broken purposes. This thing you call soul is but the dream of human vanity and egoism. It is worse than love. Both bind you endlessly to limited desires and blind ambitions. They are of children."

He rose, like some pillar of whirling flame and wind, beside her.

"Come out with me," he cried, "come back! You teach me to remember! Our elemental home calls sweetly to us, our elemental service waits. We belong to those vast Powers. They are eternal. They know no binding and they have no death. Their only law is service, that mighty service which builds up the universe. The stars are with us, the nebulæ and the central fires are their throne and altar. The soul you dream of in your little circle is but an idle dream of the Race that ties your feet lest you should fly and soar. The personal has bandaged all your eyes. Nayan, come back with me. You once worked with me there—you, I and Fillery together."

His voice, though low, had that which was terrific in it. The volume of its sound appalled her. Its low vibrations shook her heart.

"Soul," she said very softly, courage sure in her, but tears close in her burning eyes, "is my only hope. I live for it. I am ready to die for it. It is my life!"

He gazed at her a moment with a tenderness and sympathy she hardly understood, for their origin lay hidden beyond her comprehension. She knew one thing only—that he looked adorable and glorious, a being brought by the wise powers of life, whatever these might be, into the keeping of her love and care. The mother and the woman merged in her. His redemption lay within her gentle hands, if it lay at the same time upon an altar that was her awful sacrifice.

"Son of wind and fire!" she cried, though emotion made her voice dwindle to a breathless whisper. "You called to my love, yet my love is personal. I have nothing else to give you. Julian, come back! O stay with me. Your wind and fire frighten, for they take you away. Service I know, but your service—O what is it? For it leaves the bed, the hearthstone cold—"

She stopped abruptly, wondering suddenly at her own words. What was this rhythm that had caught her mind and heart into an unknown, a daring form of speech?

But the wind ran again through the open window, fluttering the curtains and the skirts about her feet. It sighed and whispered. It was no earthly wind. She saw him once again go from her on its quiet wings. He left her side, he left her heart. And an icy realization of his loneliness, his exile, stirred in her.... For a moment, as she looked up into his shining face silhouetted in the dusk against the window, there rose tumultuously in her that maternal feeling which had held all men safely at a distance hitherto. Like a wave, it mastered her. She longed to take him in her arms, to shield him from a world that was not his, to bless and comfort him with all she had to give, to have the right to brush that wondrous hair, to open those lids at dawn and close them with a kiss at night. This ancient passion rose in her, bringing, though she did not recognize it, the great woman in its train. She walked up to him with both hands outstretched:

"All my nights," she said, with no reddening of the cheek, "are as our wedding night!"

He heard, he saw, but the words held no meaning for him.

"Julian! Stay with me—stay here!" She put her arms about him.

"And forget!" he cried, an inexpressible longing in his voice. He bent, none the less, beneath the pressure of her clinging arms; he lowered his face to hers.

"I will teach you love," she murmured, her cheek against his own. "You do not know how sweet, how wonderful it is. All your strange wisdom you shall show me, and I will learn willingly, if only I may teach you—love."

"You would teach me to forget," he said in a voice of curious pain, "just as you—are forgetting now."

He gently unclasped her hands from about his neck, and went over to the open window, while she sank into a chair, watching him. She again heard the wind, but again no common, earthly wind, go singing past the walls.

"But I will teach you to remember," he said, his great figure half turning towards her again, his voice sounding as though it were in that sighing breath of wind that passed and died away into the silence of the sky.

The strange difficulty, the immensity, of her self-appointed task, grew suddenly crystal clear in her mind. Amid the whirling, aching pain and yearning that she felt, it stood forth sharp and definite. It was imperious. She loved, and she must teach him love. This was the one thing needful in his case. Her own deep, selfless heart would guide her.

There was pain in her, but there was no fear. Above the conventions she felt herself, naked and unashamed. The sense of a new immense liberty he had brought lifted her into a region where she could be natural without offence. He had flung wide the gates of life, setting free those strange, ultimate powers which had lain hidden and unrealized hitherto, and with them was quickened, too, that mysterious and awful hint which, beckoning ever towards some vaster life, had made the world as she found it unsatisfactory, pale, of meagre value.

As the strange drift of wind passed off into the sky, she moved across the room and stood beside him, its dying chant still humming in her ears. That song of the wind, she understood, was symbolic of what she had to fight, for his being, though linked to a divine service she could not understand, lay in Nature and apart from human things:

"Think, Julian," she murmured, her face against his shoulder so that the sweet perfume as of flowers he exhaled came over her intoxicatingly, "think what we could do together for the world—for all these little striving ignorant troubled people in it—for everybody! You and I together working, helping, lifting them all up—!"

He made no movement, and she took his great arm and drew it round her neck, placing the hand against her cheek. He looked down at her then, his eyes peering into her face.

"That," he said in a deep, gentle voice that vibrated through her whole body, "yes, that we will do. It is the service—the service of our gods. It is why I called you. From the first I saw it in you, and in—"

Before he could speak the name she kissed his lips, pulling his head lower in order to reach them: "Think, Julian," she whispered, his eyes so close to hers that they seemed to burn them, "think what our child might be!"

The wind came back across the tossing trees with a rush of singing. Her hair fluttered across their two faces, as it entered the room, drove round the inner walls, then, with a cry, flew out again into the empty sky. She felt as if the wind had answered her, for other answer there came none. Far away in the spaces of that darkening sky the wind rushed sailing, sailing with its impersonal song of power and of triumph.... She did not remember any further spoken words. She remembered only, as she went homewards down the street, that Julian had opened the door upon some unspoken understanding that she had lost him because she dared not follow recklessly where he led, and that the steady draught, it seemed, had driven forcibly behind her—as though the wind had blown her out.

It was only much later she realized that the figure who had then overtaken her, supported, comforted with kind ordinary words she hardly understood at the moment and yet vaguely welcomed, finally leaving her at the door of her father's house in Chelsea, was the figure of Edward Fillery.

CHAPTER XXIV

As upon a former occasion some twenty-four hours before, "N. H." seemed hardly aware that his visitor had left, though this time there was the vital difference—that what was of value had not gone at all. The essence of the girl, it seemed, was still with him. It remained. The physical presence was to him apparently the least of all.

He returned to his place at the open window of the darkening room, while night, with her cooler airs, passed over the world on tiptoe. He drew deep breaths, opened his arms, and seemed to shake himself, as though glad to be free of recent little awkward and unnatural gestures that had irked him. There was happiness in his face. "She is a builder, though she has forgotten," ran his thought with pleasure, "and I can work with her. Like Fillery, she builds up, constructs; we are all three in the same service, and the gods are glad. I love her . . . yes... but she"—his thoughts grew troubled and confused—"she speaks of another love that is a tight and binding little thing... that catches and confines. It is for one person only... one person for one other.... For two... only for two persons!... What is its meaning then?"

Of her words and acts he had understood evidently a small part only; much that she had said and done he had not comprehended, although in it somewhere there had certainly lain a sweet, faint, troubling pleasure that was new to him. His thought wavered, flickered out and vanished. For a long time he leaned against the window with his images, thinking with his heart, for when alone and not stirred by the thinking of others close to him, he became of a curious childlike innocence, knowing nothing. His "thinking" with others present

seemed but a reflection of *their* thinking. The way he caught up the racial thinking, appearing swiftly intelligent at the time (as with Fillery's mind), passed the
instant he was alone. He became open, then, to bigger rhythms that the little
busy thinkers checked and interrupted. But this greater flow of images, of
rhythms, this thinking with the heart—what was it, and with what things did
it deal? He did not know. He had forgotten. To his present brain it was alien.
He grasped only that it was concerned with the rhythms of fire and wind apparently, though hardly, perhaps, of that crude form in which men know
them, but of an inner, subtler, more vital heat and air which lie in and behind
all forms and help to shape them—and of Intelligences which use these as their
vehicles, their instruments, their bodies.

In his "images" he was aware of these Intelligences, perceived them with his
entire being, shared their activities and nature: behind all so-called forms and
shapes, whether of people, flowers, minerals, of insects or of stars, of a bird, a
butterfly or a nebula, but also of those *mental* shapes which are born of thought
and mood and heart—this host of Intelligences, great and small, all delving together, building, constructing, involved in a vast impersonal service which was
deathless. This seemed the mighty call that thundered through him, fire and
wind merely the agencies with which he, in particular, knew instinctively his
duties lay.

For his work, these images taught him, was to increase life by making the
"body" it used as perfect as he could. The more perfect the form, the instrument,
the greater the power manifesting through it. A poor, imperfect form stopped
the flow of this manifesting life, as though a current were held up and delayed.
For instance, his own form, his present body, now irked, delayed and hampered
him, although he knew not how or why or whence he had come to be using it
at this moment on the earth. The instinctive desire to escape from it lay in him,
and also the instinctive recognition that two others, similarly caught and imprisoned, must escape with him....

The images, the rhythms, poured through him in a mighty flood, as he leaned
by the open window, his great figure, his whole nature too, merging in the space,
the wind, the darkness of the soft-moving night beyond.... Yet darkness troubled him too; it always seemed unfamiliar, new, something he had never been
accustomed to. In darkness he became quiet, very gentle, feeling his way, as it
were, uneasily.

He was aware, however, that Fillery was near, though not, perhaps, that he
was actually in the room, seated somewhere among the shadows, watching him.
He felt him close in the same way he felt the girl still close, whether distance
between them in space was actually great or small. The essential in all three was
similar, their yearnings, hopes, intentions, purposes were akin; their longing for
some service, immense, satisfying, it seemed, connected them. The voice, however, did not startle when it sounded behind him from an apparently empty
room

"The love she spoke of you do not understand, of course. Perhaps you do not
need it...."

The voice, as well as the feeling that lay behind, hardly disturbed the images and rhythms in their wondrous flow. Rather, they seemed a part of them. "N. H." turned. He saw Dr. Fillery distinctly, sitting motionless among the shadows by the wall.

"It is, for you, a new relationship, and seems small, cramping and unnecessary—"

"What is it?" "N. H." asked. "What is this love she seeks to hold me with, saying that I need it? Dear Fillery," he added, moving nearer, "will you tell me what it is? I found it sweet and pleasant, yet I fear it."

"It is," was the reply, "in its best form, the highest quality *we* know—"

"Ah! I felt the fire in it," interrupted "N. H." smiling. "I smelt the flowers." His smile seemed faintly luminous across the gloom.

"Because it was the best," replied the other gently. "In its best form it means, sometimes, the complete sacrifice of one being for the welfare of another. There is no self in it at all." He felt the eyes of his companion fixed upon him in the darkness of the quiet room; he felt likewise that he was bewildered and perplexed. "As, for instance, the mother for her child," he went on. "That is the purest form of it we know."

"One being feels it for *one* other only," "N. H." repeated, apparently ignoring the reference to maternal love. "Each wants the other for himself alone! Each lives for the other only, the rest excluded! It is always two and two. Is that what she means?"

"She would not like it if you had the same feeling for another—woman," Fillery explained. "She would feel jealousy—which means she would grudge sharing you with another. She would resent it, afraid of losing you."

"Two and two, and two and two," the words floated through the shadows. The ideal seemed to shock and hurt him; he could not understand it. "She asks for the whole of me—all to herself. It is lower than insects, flowers even. It is against Nature. So small, so separate—"

"But Nature," interrupted Dr. Fillery, after an interval of silence between them, "is not concerned with what we call love. She is indifferent to it. Her purpose is merely the continuance of the Race, and she accomplishes this by making men and women attractive to one another. This, too," he explained, "we call love, though it is love in its weakest, least enduring form."

"That," replied "N. H.," "I know and understand. She builds the best form she can."

"And once the form is built," agreed the other, "and Nature's aim fulfilled, this kind of love usually fades out and dies. It is a physical thing entirely, like the two atoms we read about together a few days ago which rush together automatically to produce a third thing." He lowered his voice suddenly. "There was a great teacher once," he went on, "who told us that we should love everybody, everybody, and that in the real life there was no marriage, as we call it, nor giving in marriage."

It seemed that, as he said the words, the darkness lifted, and a faint perfume of flowers floated through the air.

"N. H." made no comment or reply. He sat still, listening.

"I love her," he whispered suddenly. "I love her in *that* way—because I want everybody else to love her too—as I do, and as you do. But I do not want her for myself alone. Do you? You do not, of course. I feel you are as I am. You are happy that I love her."

"There is morality," said Fillery presently in a low voice, glad at that moment of the darkness. "There is what we call morality."

"Tell me, dear Fillery, what that is. Is it bigger than your 'love'?"

Dr. Fillery explained briefly, while his companion listened intently, making no comment. It was evidently as strange and new to him as human love. "We have invented it," he added at the end, "to protect ourselves, our mothers, our families, our children. It is, you see, a set of rules devised for the welfare of the Race. For though a few among us do not need such rules, the majority do. It is, in a word, the acknowledgment of the rights of others."

"It had to be invented!" exclaimed "N. H.," with a sigh that seemed to trouble the darkness as with the sadness of something he could scarcely believe. "And these rules are needed still! Is the Race at that stage only? It does not move, then?"

Into the atmosphere, as the low-spoken words were audible, stole again that mysterious sense of the insignificance of earth and all its manifold activities, human and otherwise, and with it, too, a remarkable breath of some larger reality, starry-bright, that lay shining just beyond all known horizons. Fillery shivered in spite of himself. It seemed to him for an instant that the great figure looming opposite through the darkness extended, spread, gathering into its increased proportions the sky, the trees, the darkened space outside; that it no longer sat there quite alone. He recalled his colleague's startling admission—the touch of panic terror.

"Slowly, if at all," he said louder, though wondering why he raised his voice. "Yet there is *some* progress."

He had the feeling it would be better to turn on the light, as though this conversation and the strange sensations it produced in him would be impossible in a full blaze. He made a movement, indeed, to find the switch. It was the sound of his companion's voice that made him pause, for the words came at him as though a wave of heat moved through the air. He knew intuitively that the other's intense inner activity had increased. He let his hand drop. He listened. Their thoughts, he was convinced, had mingled and been mutually shared again. There was a faint sound like music behind it.

"We have worked such a little time as yet," fell the words into the silence. "if only—oh! if only I could remember more!"

"A little time!" thought Fillery to himself, knowing that the other meant the millions of years Nature had used to evoke her myriad forms. "Try to remember," he added in a whisper.

"What I do remember, I cannot even tell," was the reply, the voice strangely deepening. "No words come to me." He paused a moment, then went on: "I am of the first, the oldest. I know that. The earth was hot and burning—burning,

burning still. It was soft with heat when I was summoned from—from other work just completed. With a vast host I came. Our Service summoned us. We began at the beginning. I am of the oldest. The earth was still hot—burning, burning—"

The voice failed suddenly.

"I cannot remember. Dear Fillery, I cannot remember. It hurts me. My head pains. Our work—our service—yes, there is progress. The ages, as you call them—but it is such a little time as yet—" The voice trailed off, the figure lost its suggestion of sudden vastness, the darkness emptied. "I am of the oldest— that I remember only..." It ceased as though it drifted out upon the passing wind outside.

"Then you have been working," said Fillery, his voice still almost a whisper, "you and your great host, for thousands of years—in the service of this planet— " He broke off, unable to find his words, it seemed.

"Since the beginning," came the steady answer. "Years I do not know. Since the beginning. Yet we have only just begun—oh!" he cried, "I cannot remem- ber! It is impossible! It all goes lost among my words, and in this darkness I am confused and entangled with your own little thinking. I suffer with it." Then suddenly: "My eyes are hot and wet, dear Fillery. What happens to them?" He stood up, putting both hands to his face. Fillery stood up too. He trembled.

"Don't try," he said soothingly; "do not try to remember any more. It will come back to you soon, but it won't come back by any deliberate effort."

He comforted him as best he could, realizing that the curious dialogue had lasted long enough. But he did not produce a disconcerting blaze by turning the light on suddenly; he led his companion gently to the door, so that the darkness might pass more gradually. The lights in the corridor were shaded and inof- fensive. It was only in the bedroom that he noticed the bright tears, as "N. H.," examining them with curious interest in the mirror, exclaimed more to himself than to Fillery: "She had them too. I saw them in her eyes when she spoke to me of love, the love she will teach me because she said I needed it."

"Tears," said Fillery, his voice shaking. "They come from feeling pain."

"It is a little thing," returned "N. H.," smiling at himself, then turning to his friend, his great blue eyes shining wonderfully through their moisture. "Then she felt what I felt—we felt together. When she comes to-morrow I will show her these tears and she will be glad I love. And she will bring tears of her own, and you will have some too, and we shall all love together. It is not difficult, is it?"

"Not very," agreed Fillery, smiling in his turn; "it is not very difficult." He was again trembling.

"She will be happy that we all love."

"I—hope so."

It was curious how easily tears came to the eyes of this strange being, and for causes so different that they were not easy to explain. He did not cry; it was merely that the hot tears welled up.

Even with Devonham once it happened too. The lesson in natural history was over. Devonham had just sketched the outline of the various kingdoms, with the animal kingdom and man's position in it, according to present evolutionary knowledge, and had then said something about the earth's place in the solar system, and the probable relation of this system to the universe at large—an admirable bird's-eye view, as it were, without a hint of speculative imagination in it anywhere—when "N. H.," after intent listening in irresponsive silence, asked abruptly:

"What does it believe?" Then, as Devonham stared at him, a little puzzled at first, he repeated: "That is what the Race *knows*. But what does it *believe?*"

"Believe," said Devonham, "believe. Ah! you mean what is its religion, its faith, its speculations!"—and proceeded to give the briefest possible answer he felt consistent with his duty. The less his pupil's mind was troubled with such matters, the better, in his opinion.

"And their God?" the young man inquired abruptly, as soon as the recital was over. He had listened closely, as he always did, but without a sign of interest, merely waiting for the end, much as a child who is bored by a poor fairy tale, yet wishes to know exactly how it is all going to finish. "They *know* Him?" He leaned forward.

Devonham, not quite liking the form of the question, nor the more eager manner accompanying it, hesitated a moment, thinking perhaps what he ought to say. He did not want this mind, now opening, to be filled with ideas that could be of no use to it, nor help in its formation; least of all did he desire it to be choked and troubled with the dead theology of man-made notions concerning a tumbling personal Deity. Creeds, moreover, were a matter of faith, of auto-suggestion as he called it, being obviously divorced from any process of reason. He had, nevertheless, a question to answer and a duty to perform. His hesitation passed in compromise. He was, as has been seen, too sincere, too honest, to possess much sense of humour.

"The Race," he said, "or rather that portion of it into which you have been born, believes—on paper"—he emphasized the qualification—"in a paternal god; but its real god, the god it worships, is Knowledge. Not a Knowledge that exists for its own sake," he went on blandly, "but that brings possessions, power, comfort and a million needless accessories into life. That god it worships, as you see, with energy and zeal. Knowledge and work that shall result in acquisition, in pleasure, that is the god of the Race on this side of the planet where you find yourself."

"And the God on paper?" asked "N. H.," making no comment, though he had listened attentively and had understood. "The God that is written about on paper, and believed in on paper?"

"The printed account of this god," replied Devonham, "describes an omnipotent and perfect Being who has existed always. He created the planet and everything upon it, but created it so imperfectly that he had to send later a smaller god to show how much better he *might* have created us. In doing this, he offered us an extremely difficult and laborious method of improvement, a method of escaping from his own mistake, but a method so painful and unrealizable that it is contrary to our very natures—as he made them first." He almost smacked his lips as he said it.

"The big God, the first one," asked "N. H." at once. "Have they seen and known Him? Have they complained?"

"No," said Devonham, "they have not. Those who believe in him accept things as he made them."

"And the smaller lesser God—how did He arrive?" came the odd question.

"He was born like you and me, but without a father. No male had his mother ever known."

"He was recognized as a god?" The pupil showed interest, but no emotion, much less excitement.

"By a few. The rest, afraid because he told them their possessions were worthless, killed him quickly."

"And the few?"

"They obeyed his teaching, or tried to, and believed that they would live afterwards for ever and ever in happiness—"

"And the others? The many?"

"The others, according to the few, would live afterwards for ever and ever—in pain."

"It is a demon story," said "N. H.," smiling.

"It is printed, believed, taught," replied Devonham, "by an immense organization to millions of people—"

"Free?" inquired his pupil.

"The teachers are paid, but very little—"

"The teachers believe it, though?"

"Y-yes—at least some of them—probably," replied Devonham, after brief consideration.

"And the millions—do they worship this God?"

"They do, on paper, yes. They worship the first big God. They go once or twice a week into special buildings, dressed in their best clothes as for a party, and pray and sing and tell him he is wonderful and they themselves are miserable and worthless, and then ask him in abject humility for all sorts of things they want."

"Do they get them?"

"They ask for different things, you see. One wants fine weather for his holidays, another wants rain for his crops. The prayers in which they ask are printed by the Government."

"They ask for this planet only?"

"This planet conceives itself alone inhabited. There are no other living beings anywhere. The Earth is the centre of the universe, the only globe worth consideration."

Although "N. H." asked these quick questions, his interest was obviously not much engaged, the first sharp attention having passed. Then he looked fixedly at Devonham and said, with a sudden curious smile: "What you say is always dead. I understand the sounds you use, but the meaning cannot get into me—inside, I mean. But I thank you for the sound."

There was a moment's pause, during which Devonham, accustomed to strange remarks and comments from his pupil, betrayed no sign of annoyance or displeasure. He waited to see if any further questions would be forthcoming. He was observing a phenomenon; his attitude was scientific.

"But, in sending this lesser God," resumed "N. H." presently, "how did the big One excuse himself?"

"He didn't. He told the Race it was so worthless that nothing else could save it. He looked on while the lesser God was killed. He is very proud about it, and claims the thanks and worship of the Race because of it."

"The lesser God—poor lesser God!"observed "N. H." "He was bigger than the other." He thought a moment. "How pitiful," he added.

"Much bigger," agreed Devonham, pleased with his pupil's acumen, his voice, even his manner, changing a little as he continued. "For then came the wonder of it all. The lesser God's teachings were so new and beautiful that the position of the other became untenable. The Race disowned him. It worshipped the lesser one in his place."

"Tell me, tell me, please," said "N. H.," as though he noticed and understood the change of tone at once. "I listen. The dear Fillery spoke to me of a great Teacher. I feel a kind, deep joy move in me. Tell me, please."

Again Devonham hesitated a moment, for he recognized signs that made him ill at ease a little, because he did not understand them. Following a scientific textbook with his pupil was well and good, but he had no desire to trespass on what he considered as Fillery's territory. "N. H." was his pupil, not his patient. He had already gone too far, he realized. After a moment's reflection, however, he decided it was wiser to let the talk run out its natural course, instead of ending it abruptly. He was as thorough as he was sincere, and whatever his own theories and prejudices might be in this particular case, he would not shirk an issue, nor treat it with the smallest dishonesty. He put the glasses straight on his big nose.

"The new teachings," he said, "were so beautiful that, if faithfully practised by everybody, the world would soon become a very different place to what it is."

"Did the Race practise them?" came the question in a voice that held a note of softness, almost of wonder.

"No."

"Why not?"

"They were too difficult and painful and uncomfortable. The new God, moreover, only came here 2,000 years ago, whereas men have existed on earth for at least 400,000."

"N. H." asked abruptly what the teachings were, and Devonham, growing more and more uneasy as he noted the signs of increasing intensity and disturbance in his pupil, recited, if somewhat imperfectly, the main points of the Sermon on the Mount. As he did so "N. H." began to murmur quietly to himself,

his eyes grew large and bright, his face lit up, his whole body trembled. He began that deep, rhythmical breathing which seemed to affect the atmosphere
about him so that his physical appearance increased and spread. The skin took
on something of radiance, as though an intense inner happiness shone through
it. Then, suddenly, to Devonham's horror, he began to hum.

Though a normal, ordinary sound enough, it reminded him of that other sound
he had once shared with Fillery, when he sat on the stairs, staring at a china bowl
filled with visiting cards, while the dawn broke after a night of exhaustion and
bewilderment. That sound, of course, he had long since explained and argued
away—it was an auditory hallucination conveyed to his mind by LeVallon, who
originated it. Interesting and curious, it was far from inexplicable. It was disquieting, however, for it touched in him a vague sense of alarm, as though it
paved the way for that odd panic terror he had been amazed to discover hidden
away deeply in some unrealized corner of his being.

This humming he now listened to, though normal and ordinary enough—
there were no big vibrations with it, for one thing—was too suggestive of that
other sound for him to approve of it. His mind rapidly sought some way of stopping it. A command, above all an impatient, harsh command, was out of the
question, yet a request seemed equally not the right way. He fumbled in his mind
to find the wise, proper words. He stretched his hand out, as though to lay it
quietly upon his companion's shoulder—but realized suddenly he could not—
almost he dared not—touch him.

The same instant " N. H." rose. He pushed his chair back and stood up.

Devonham, justly proud of his equable temperament and steady nerves, ad-
mits that only a great effort of self-control enabled him to sit quietly and listen.
He listened, watched, and made mental notes to the best of his ability, hut he
was frightened a little. The outburst was so sudden. He is not sure that his report of what he heard, made later to Fillery, was a verbatim, accurate one:

"Justice we know," cried "N. H." in his half-chanting voice that seemed to
boom with resonance, "but this—this mercy, gentle kindness, beauty—this unknown loveliness—we did not know it!" He went to the open window, and
threw his arms wide, as though he invoked the sun. "Dimly we heard of it. We
strive, we strive, we weave and build and fashion while the whirl of centuries
flies on. This lesser God—he came among us, too, making our service sweeter,
though we did not understand. Our work grew wiser and more careful, we built
lovelier forms, and knew not why we did so. His mighty rhythms touched us
with their power and happy light. Oh, my great messengers of wind and fire,
bring me the memory I have lost! Oh, where, where—?"

He shook himself, as though his clothes, perhaps his body even, irked him. It
was a curious coincidence, thought Devonham, as he watched and listened, too
surprised and puzzled to interfere either by word or act, that a cloud, at that very
moment, passed from the face of the sun, and a gust of wind shook all the
branches of the lime trees in the garden. "N. H." stood drenched in the white
clear sunshine. His flaming hair was lifted by the wind.

"Behind, beyond the Suns He dwells and burns for ever. Oh, the mercy, kind-

ness, the strange beauty of this personal love—what is it? These have been promised to *us* too—!"

He broke off abruptly, bowed his great head and shoulders, and sank upon his
knees in an attitude of worship. Then, stretching his arms out to the sky, the
face raised into the flood of sunlight, while his voice became lower, softer, almost hushed, he spoke again:

"Our faithful service, while the circles swallow the suns, shall lift us too! You,
who sent me here to help this little, dying Race, oh, help me to remember—!"

His passion was a moving sight; the words, broken through with fragments
of his chanting, singing, had the blood of some infinite, intolerable yearning in
them.

Devonham, meanwhile, having heard outbursts of this strange kind before
with others, had recovered something of his equanimity. He felt more sure of
himself again. The touch of fear had left him. He went over to the window. The
attack, as he deemed it, was passing. A thick cloud hid the sun again. "There,
there," he said soothingly, laying both hands upon the other's shoulders, then
taking the arms to help him rise. "I told you His teachings were very beautiful—
that the world would become a kind of heaven if people lived them." His voice
seemed not his own; beside the volume and music of the other's it had a thin,
rasping, ugly sound.

"N. H." was on his feet, gazing down into his face; to Devonham's amazement
there were tears in the eyes that met his own.

"And many people *do* live them—try to, rather," he added gently. "There are
thousands who really worship this lesser God to-day. You can't go far wrong
yourself if you take Him as your model and—"

"How He must have suffered!" came the astonishing interruption, the voice
quiet and more natural again. "There was no way of telling what he knew. He
had no words, of course. You are all so difficult, so caged, so—dead!"

Devonham smiled. "He used parables." He paused a moment, then went on:
"Men have existed on the planet, science tells us, for at least 400,000 years,
whereas *He* came here only 2,000 years ago—"

"Came *here*," interrupted the pupil, as though the earth were but one of a
thousand places visited, a hint of contempt and pity somewhere in his tone and
gesture. "We made His way ready then! We prepared, we built! It was for that
our work went on and on so faithfully."

He broke off...

Devonham experienced a curious sensation as he heard. In that instant it
seemed to him that he was conscious of the movement of the earth through
space. He was aware that the planet on which he stood was rushing forward at
eighteen miles a second through the sky. He felt himself carried forward with
it.

"What was His name?" he heard "N. H." asking. It was as though he was
aware of the enormous interval in space traversed by the rolling earth between
the first and last words of the sudden question. It trailed through an immense
distance towards him, after him, yet at the same time ever with him.

"His name—oh—Jesus Christ, we call him," wondering at the same moment why he used the pronoun we."

"Jesus—Christ!"

"N. H." repeated the name with such intensity and power that the sound, borne by deep vibrations, seemed to surge and circle forth into space while the earth rushed irresistibly onwards. A faintly imaginative idea occurred to Devonham for the first time in his life—it was as though the earth herself had opened her green lips and uttered the great name. With this came also the amazing and disconcerting conviction that Nature and humans were expressions of one and the same big simple energy, and that while their forms, their bodies, differed, the life manifesting through them was identical, though its degree might vary. For an instant this was of such overpowering conviction as to be merely obvious.

It passed as quickly as it came, though he still was dimly conscious that he had travelled with the earth through another huge stretch of space. Then this sense of movement also passed. He looked up. "N. H." was in his chair again at the table, reading quietly his book on natural history. But in his eyes the moisture of tears was still visible.

Devonham adjusted his glasses, blew his nose, went quickly to another room to jot down his notes of the talk, the reactions, the general description, and in doing so dismissed from his mind the slight uneasy effects of what had been a "curious hallucination," caused evidently by an "unexplained stimulation" of the motor centres in the brain.

CHAPTER XXV

T he full account of "N. H.," with all he said and did, his effect upon others, his general activities in a word, it is impossible to compress intelligibly into the compass of these notes. A complete report Edward Fillery indeed accumulated, but its publication, he realized, must await that leisure for which his busy life provided little opportunity. His eyes, mental and physical, were never off his "patient," and "N. H.," aware of it, leaped out to meet the observant sympathy, giving all he could, concealing nothing, yet debarred, it seemed, by the rigid limitations of his own mental and physical machinery, as similarly by that of his hearers, from contributing more than suggestive and tantalizing hints. Of the use of parable he, obviously, had no knowledge.

His relations with others, perhaps, offered the most significant comments on his personality. Fillery was at some pains to collect these. The reactions were various, yet one and all showed this in common, a curious verdict but unanimous: that his effect, namely, was greatest when he was not there. Not in his actual presence, which promised rather than fulfilled, was his power so dominating upon mind and imagination as after the door was closed and he was gone.

The withdrawal of his physical self, its absence—as Fillery had himself experienced one night on Hampstead Heath as well as on other occasions—brought his real presence closer.

It was Nayan who first drew attention to this remarkable characteristic. She spoke about him often now with Dr. Fillery, for as the weeks passed and she realized the uselessness, the impossibility, of the plan she had proposed to herself, she found relief in talking frankly about him to her older friend.

"Always, always after I leave him," she confessed, "a profound and searching melancholy gets hold of me, poignant as death, yet an extraordinary unrealized beauty behind it somewhere. It steals into my very blood and bones. I feel an intense dissatisfaction with the world, with people as they are, and a burning scorn for all that is small, unworthy, petty, mean—and yet a hopelessness of ever attaining to that something which he knows and lives so easily." She sighed, gazing into his eyes a moment. "Or of ever making others see it," she added.

"And that 'something,'" he asked, "can you define it?"

She shook her head. "It's in me, within reach even, but—the word he used is the only one—forgotten."

"Perhaps—has it ever occurred to you?—that he simply cannot describe it. There are no words, no means at his disposal—no human terms?"

"Perhaps," she murmured.

"Desirable, though?" he urged her gently.

She clasped her hands, smiling. "Heavenly," she murmured, closing her eyes a moment as though to try and recall it. "Yet when I'm with him," she went on, "he never *quite* realizes for me the state of wonder and delight his presence promises. His personality suggests rather than fulfils." She paused, a wistful, pained expression in her dark eyes. "The failure," she added quickly, lest she seem to belittle him of whom she spoke, "of course lies in myself. I refuse, you see—I can't say why, though I feel it's wise—to let myself be dominated by that strange, lost part of me he stimulates."

"True," interposed Dr. Fillery. "I understand. Yet to have felt this even is a sign—"

"That he stirs the deepest, highest in me? This hint of divine beauty in the unrealized under-self?"

He nodded. There was an odd touch of sadness in their talk. "I've watched him with many types of people," he went on thoughtfully, almost as though thinking aloud in his rapid way, "I've talked with him on many subjects. The meanness, jealousy, insignificance of the Race shocks and amazes him. He cannot understand it. He asked me once 'But is no one *born* noble? To be splendid is such an effort with them!' Splendour of conduct, he noticed, is a calculated, rarely a spontaneous splendour. The general resistance to new ideas also puzzles him. 'They fear a rhythm they have never felt before,' as he put it. 'To adopt a new rhythm, they think, must somehow injure them.' That the Race respects a man because he possesses much equally bewilders him. 'No one serves willingly or naturally,' he observed, 'or unless someone else receives money for drawing attention loudly to it.' Any notion of reward, of advertisement, in its widest meaning, is foreign to his nature."

He broke off. Another pause fell between them, the girl the first to break it: "He suffers," she said in a low voice. "Here—he suffers," and her face yearned with the love and help she longed to pour out beyond all thought of self or compensation, and at the same time with the pain of its inevitable frustration; and, watching her, Dr. Fillery understood that this very yearning was another proof of the curious impetus, the intensification of being, that "N. H." caused in everyone. Yet he winced, as though anticipating the question she at once then put to him:

"You are afraid for him, Edward?" her eyes calmly, searchingly on his. "His future troubles you?"

He turned to her with abrupt intensity. "If you, Iraida, could not enchain him— He broke off. He shrugged his shoulders.

"I have no power," she confessed. "An insatiable longing burns like a fire in him. Nothing he finds here on earth, among men and women, can satisfy it." A faint blush stole up her neck and touched her cheeks. "He is different. I have no power to keep him here." Her voice sank suddenly to a whisper, as though a breath of awe passed into her. "He is here now at this very moment, I believe. He is with us as we talk together. I feel him." Almost a visible thrill passed through her. "And close, so very close—to *you*."

Dr. Fillery made no sign by word or gesture, but something in his very silence gave assent.

"And not alone," she added, still under her breath. It seemed she looked about her, though she did not actually move or turn her head. "Others—of his kind, Edward—come with him. They are always with him—I think sometimes." Her whisper was fainter still.

"You feel that too!" He said it abruptly, his voice louder and almost challenging. Then he added incongruously, as though saying it to himself this time, "That's what I mean. I've known it for a long time—"

He looked at the girl sharply with unconcealed admiration. "It does not frighten you?" he asked, and in reply she said the very thing he felt sure she would say, hoping for it even while he shrank:

"Escape," he heard in a low, clear voice, half a question, half an exclamation, and saw the blood leave her face.

The instinctive "Hush!" that rose to his lips he did not utter. The sense of loss, of searching pain, the word implied he did not show. Instead, he spoke in his natural, everyday tone again:

"The body irks him, of course, and he may try to rid himself of it. Its limitations to him are a prison, for his true consciousness he finds outside it. The explanation," he added to himself, "of many a case of suicidal mania probably. I've often wondered—"

He took her hand, aware by the pallor of her face what her feelings were. "Death, you see, Nayan, has no meaning for him, as it has for us who think consciousness out of the body impossible, and he is puzzled by our dread of it. 'We,' he said once, 'have nothing that decays. We may be stationary, or advance, or retreat, but we can never end.' He derives—oh, I'm convinced of it—from another order. Here—amongst us—he is inarticulate, unable to express himself, hopeless, helpless, in prison. Oh, if only—"

"He loves you," she said quickly, releasing her hand. "I suppose he realizes the eternal part of you and identifies himself with that. In you, Edward, lies something very close to what he is, akin—he needs it terribly, just as you—" She became confused.

"Love, as we understand it," he interrupted, his voice shaking a little, "he does not, cannot know, for he serves another law, another order of being."

"That's how I feel it too."

She shivered slightly, but she did not turn away, and her eyes kept all their frankness.

"Our humanity," she murmured, "writes upon his heart in ink that quickly fades—"

"And leaves no trace," he caught her up hurriedly. "His one idea is to help, to render service. It is as natural to him as for water to run down hill. He seeks instinctively to become one with the person he seeks to aid. As with us an embrace is an attempt at union, so he seeks, by some law of his own being, to become identified with those whom he would help. And he helps by intensifying their consciousness—somewhat as heat and air increase ordinary physical vitality. Only, first there must be something for him to work on. Energy, even bad, vicious, wrongly used, he can work on. Mere emptiness prevents him. You remember Lady Gleeson—"

"We—most of us—are too empty," she put in with quiet resignation. "Our sense of that divine beauty is too faint—"

"Rather," came the quick correction, "he stands too close to us. His effect is too concentrated. The power at such close quarters disturbs and overbalances."

"That's why, then, I always feel it strongest when he's left."

He glanced at her keenly.

"In his presence," she explained, "it's always as though I saw only a part of him, even of his physical appearance, out of the corner of my eye, as it were, and sometimes—" She hesitated. He did not help her this time. "As if those others, many others, similar to himself, but invisible, crowding space about us, were intensely active." Her voice hushed again. "He brings them with him—as now. I feel it, Edward, now. I feel them close." She looked round the empty room, peering through the window into the quiet evening sky. Dr. Fillery also turned away. He sighed again. "Have you noticed, too," he went on presently, yet half as if following his own thoughts, and a trifle incongruously, "the speed and lightness his very movements convey, and how he goes down the street with that curious air of drawing things after him, along with him, as trains and motors draw the loose leaves and dust—"

"Whirling," her quick whisper startled him a little, as she turned abruptly from the window and gazed straight at him. He smiled, instantly recovering himself. "A good word, yes—whirling—but in the plural. As though there were vortices about him."

It was her turn to smile. "That might one day carry him away," she exclaimed. They smiled together then, they even laughed, but somewhere in their laughter, like the lengthening shadows of the spring day outside, lay an incommunicable sadness neither of them could wholly understand.

"Yet the craving for beauty," she said suddenly, "that he leaves behind in me"—her voice wavered—"an intolerable yearning that nothing can satisfy—nothing—here. An infinite desire, it seems, for—for—"

Dr. Fillery took her hand again gently, looking down steadily into the clear eyes that sought his own, and the light glistening in their moisture was similar, he fancied for a moment, to the fire in another pair of shining eyes that never failed to stir the unearthly dreams in him.

"It lies beyond any words of ours," he said softly. "Don't struggle to express it, Iraida. To the flower, the star, we are wise to leave their own expression in their own particular field, for we cannot better it."

A sound of rising wind, distant yet ominous, went past the window, as for a moment then the girl came closer till she was almost in his arms, and though he did not accept her, equally he did not shrink from the idea of acceptance—for the first time since they had known one another. There was a smell of flowers; almost in that wailing wind he was aware of music.

"Together," he heard her whisper, while a faint shiver—was it of joy or terror?—ran through her nerves. "All of us—when the time comes—together." She made an abrupt movement. "Just as we are together now! Listen!" she exclaimed.

"We call it wind," she whispered. "But of course—really—it's behind—beyond—inside—isn't it?"

Dr. Fillery, holding her closely, made no answer. Then he laughed, let go her hands, and said in his natural tone again, breaking an undesirable spell intentionally, though with a strong effort: "We are in space and time, remember, Iraida. Let us obey them happily until another certain and practical thing is shown us."

The faint sound that had been rising about them in the air died down again.

They looked into each other's eyes, then drew apart, though with a movement so slight it was scarcely perceptible. It was Nayan and Dr. Fillery once more, but not before the former had apparently picked out the very thought that had lain, though unexpressed, in the latter's deepest mind—its sudden rising the cause of his deliberate change of attitude. For she had phrased it, given expression to it, though from an angle very different to his own. And her own word, "escape," used earlier in the conversation, had deliberately linked on with it, as of intentional purpose.

"He must go back. The time is coming when he must go back. We are not ready for him here—not yet."

Somewhat in this fashion, though without any actual words, had the idea appeared in letters of fire that leaped and flickered through a mist of anguish, of loss, of loneliness, rising out of the depths within him. He knew whence they came, he divined their origin at once, and the sound, though faint and distant at first, confirmed him. Swiftly behind them, moreover, born of no discoverable antecedents, it seemed, rose simultaneously the phrase that Father Collins loved: "A Being in his own place is the ruler of his fate." Father Collins, for all his faults and strangeness, was a personality, a consciousness, that might prove of value. His extraordinarily swift receptiveness, his undoubted telepathic powers, his fluid, sensitive, protean comprehension of possibilities outside the human walls, above the earthly ceiling, so to speak.... Value suddenly attached itself to Father Collins, as though the name had been dropped purposely into his mind by someone. He was surprised to find this thought in him. It was not for the first time, however, Dr. Fillery remembered.

In Nayan's father, again, an artist, though not a particularly subtle one per-haps, lay a deep admiration, almost a love, he could not explain. "There's some-thing about him in a sense immeasurable, something not only untamed but un-tamable," he phrased it. "His gentleness conceals it as a summer's day conceals a thunderstorm. To me it's almost like an incarnation of the primal forces at work in the hearts of my own people"—he grew sad—"and as dangerous probably." He was speaking to his daughter, who repeated the words later to Dr. Fillery. The study of Fire in the elemental group had failed. "He's too big, too vast, too formless, to get into any shape or outline my tools can manage, even by sug-gestion. He dominates the others—Earth, Air, Water—and dwarfs them."

"But fire ought to," she put in. "It's the most powerful and splendid, the most terrific of them all. Isn't it? It regenerates. It purifies. I love fire—"

Her father smiled in his beard, noticing the softness in her manner, rather than in her voice. The awakening in her he had long since understood sympathetically, if more profoundly than she knew, and welcomed.

"He won't hurt you, child. He won't harm Nayushka any more than a sum-mer's day can hurt her. I see him thus sometimes," he mumbled on half to him-self, though she heard and stored the words in her memory; "as an entire day, a landscape even, I often see him. A stretch of being rather than a point: a rush-ing stream rather than a single isolated wave harnessed and confined in definite form—as we understand being here," he added curiously. "No, he'll neither harm nor help you," he went on; "nor any of us for that matter. A dozen na-tions, a planet, a star he might help or harm"—he laughed aloud suddenly in a startled way at his own language—"but an individual never!" And he abruptly took her in his arms and kissed her, drying her tears with his own rough hand-kerchief. "Not even a fire-worshipper," he added with gruff tenderness, "like you!"

"There's more of divinity in fire than in any other earthly thing we know," she replied as he held her, "for it takes into itself the sweetest essence of all it touches." She looked up at him with a smile. "That's why you can't get it into your marble perhaps." To which her father made the significant rejoinder: "And because none of us has the least conception what 'divine' and 'divinity' really mean, though we're always using the words! It's odd, anyhow," he fin-ished reflectively, "that I can model the fellow better from memory than when he's standing there before my eyes. At close quarters he confuses me with too many terrific unanswerable questions."

To multiply the verdicts and impressions Fillery jotted down is unnecessary. In his own way he collected; in his own way he wrote them down. About "N. H.," all agreed in their various ways of expressing it, was that vital suggestion of agelessness, of deathlessness, of what men call eternal youth: the vigorous grace of limbs and movements, the deep simple joy of confidence and power. None could picture him tired, or even wearing out, yet ever with a faint hint of painful conflict due to immense potentialities—"a day compressed into a single minute," as Khilkoff phrased it—straining, but vainly, to express themselves through a limited form that was inadequate to their use. A storm of passionate hope and wonder seemed ever ready to tear forth from behind the calm of the great quiet eyes, those green-blue changing eyes, which none could imagine lightless or unlamping; and about his whole presentment a surplus of easy, overflowing energy from an inexhaustible source pressing its gifts down into him spontaneously, fire and wind its messengers; yet that the human machinery using these—mind, body, nerves—was ill adapted to their full expression. To every individual having to do with him was given a push, a drive, an impetus that stimulated that individual's chief characteristic, intensifying it.

This to imaginative and discerning sight. But even upon ordinary folk, aware only of the surface things that deliberately hit them, was left a startling impression as of someone waving a strange, unaccustomed banner that made them halt and stare before passing on—uncomfortably. He had that nameless quality, apart from looks or voice or manner, which arrested attention and drew the eyes of the soul, wonderingly, perhaps uneasily, upon itself. He left a mark. Something defined him from all others, leaving him silhouetted in the mind, and those who had looked into his eyes could not forget that they had done so. Up rose at once the great unanswerable questions that, lying ever at the back of daily life, the majority find it most comfortable to leave undisturbed—but rose in red ink or italics. He startled into an awareness of greater life. And the effect remained, was greatest even, after he had passed on.

It was, of course, Father Collins, a frequent caller now at the Home, betraying his vehement interest in long talks with Dr. Fillery and in what interviews with "N. H." the latter permitted him—it was this protean being whose mind, amid wildest speculations, formed the most positive conclusions. The Prometheans, he believed, were not far wrong in their instinctive collective judgment. "N. H." was not a human being; the occupant of that magnificent body was not a human spirit like the rest of us.

"Nor is he the only one walking the streets to-day," he affirmed mysteriously. "In shops and theatres, trains and buses, tucked in among the best families," he laughed, although in earnest, "and even in suburbia I have come across other human bodies similarly inhabited. What they are and where they come from exactly, we cannot know, but their presence among us is indubitable."

"You mean you recognize them?" inquired Dr. Fillery calmly.

"One unmistakable sign they possess in common—they are invariably inar-ticulate, helpless, lost. The brain, the five senses, the human organs—all they have to work through—are useless to express the knowledge and powers nat-ural to them. Electricity might as well try to manifest itself through a gas-pipe, or music through a stone. One and all, too, possess strange glimmerings of an-other state where they are happy and at home, something of the glory a la Wordsworth, a Golden Age idea almost, a state compared to which humanity seems a tin-pot business, yet a state of which no single descriptive terms occur to them."

"Of which, however, they can tell us nothing?"

"Memory, of course, is lost. Their present brain can have no records, can it? Only those of us who have perhaps at some time, in some earlier existence pos-sibly, shared such a state can have any idea of what they're driving at."

He glanced at Fillery with a significant raising of his bushy eyebrows.

"There have been no phenomena, I'm glad to say," put in the doctor, aware some comment was due from him, "no physical phenomena, I mean."

"Nor could there be," pursued the other, delighted. "He has not got the ap-paratus. With all such beings, their power, rather than perceived, is *felt*. Sex, as with us, they also cannot know, for they are neither male nor female." He paused, as the other did not help him. "Enigmas they must always be to us. We may borrow from the East and call them *devas*, or class them among nature spir-its of legend and the rest, but we can, at any rate, welcome them, and perhaps even learn from them."

"Learn from them?" echoed Fillery sharply.

"They are essentially *natural*, you see, whereas we are artificial, and becom-ing more so with every century, though we call it civilization. If we lived closer to nature we might get better results, I mean. Primitive man, I'm convinced, did get certain results, but he was a poor instrument. Modern man, in some ways, is a better, finer instrument to work through, only he is blind to the existence of any beings but himself. A bridge, however, might be built, I feel. 'N. H.' seems to me in close touch with these curious beings, if"—he lowered his voice—"he is not actually one of them. The wind and fire he talks about are, of course, not what *we* mean. It is heat and rhythm, in some more essential form, he refers to. If 'N. H.' is some sort of nature spirit, or nature-being, he is of a hum-ble type, concerned with humble duties in the universe—"

"There are, you think, then, higher, bigger kinds?" inquired the listener, his face and manner showing neither approval nor disapproval.

Father Collins raised his hands and face and shoulders, even his eyebrows. His spirits rose as well.

"If they exist at all—and the assumption explains plausibly the amazing in-telligence behind all natural phenomena—they include every grade, of course, from the insignificant fairies, so called, builders of simple forms, to the immense planetary spirits and vast Intelligencies who guide and guard the welfare of the greater happenings." His eyes shone, his tone matched in enthusiasm his gestures. "A stupendous and magnificent hierarchy," he cried, "but all, all under God, of course, who maketh his angels spirits and his ministers a flaming fire. Ah, think of it," he went on, becoming lyrical almost as wonder fired him, "think of it now especially in the spring! The vast abundance and insurgence of life pouring up on all sides into forms and bodies, and all led, directed, fashioned by this host of invisible, yet not unknowable, Intelligences! Think of the prolific architecture, the delicacy, the grandeur, the inspiring beauty that are involved...!"

"You said just now a bridge might be built," Dr. Fillery interrupted, while the other paused a second for breath.

Father Collins, nailed down to a positive statement, hesitated and looked about him. But the hesitation passed at once.

"It is the question merely," he went on more composedly, "of providing the apparatus, the means of manifestation, the instrument, the—body. Isn't it? Our evolution and theirs are two separate—different things."

"I suppose so. No force can express itself without a proper apparatus."

"Certain of these Intelligences are so immense that only a series of events, long centuries, a period of history, as we call it, can provide the means, the body indeed, through which they can express themselves. An entire civilization may be the 'body' used by an archetypal power. Others, again—like 'N. H.' probably—since I notice that it is usually the artist, the artistic temperament *he* affects most—require beauty for their expression—beauty of form and outline, of sound, of colour."

He paused for effect, but no comment came.

"Our response to beauty, our thrill, our lift of delight and wonder before any manifestation of beauty—these are due only to our perception, though usually unrecognized except by artists, of the particular Intelligence thus trying to express itself—"

Dr. Fillery suddenly leaned forward, listening with a new expression on his face. He betrayed, however, no sign of what he thought of his voluble visitor. An idea, none the less, had struck him like a flash between the eyes of the mind.

"You mean," he interposed patiently, "that just as your fairies use form and colour to express themselves in nature, we might use beauty of a mental order to—to—"

"To build a body of expression, yes, an instrument in a collective sense, through which 'N. H.' might express whatever of knowledge, wisdom and power he has—"

"Will you explain yourself a little more definitely?"

Father Collins beamed. He continued with an air of intense conviction:

"The Artist is ever an instrument merely, and for the most part an unconscious one; only the greatest artist is a conscious instrument. No man is an artist at all until he transcends both nature and himself; that is, until he interprets both nature and himself in the unknown terms of that greater Power whence himself and nature emanate. He is aware of the majestic source, aware that the universe, in bulk and in detail, is an expression of it, itself a limited instrument; but aware, further—and here he proves himself great artist—of the stupendous, lovely, central Power whose message stammers, broken and partial, through the inadequate instruments of ephemeral appearances.

"He creates, using beauty in form, sound, colour, a better and more perfect instrument, provides this central Power with a means of fuller expression.

"The message no longer stammers, halts, suggests; it flows, it pours, it sings. He has fashioned a vehicle for its passage. His art has created a body it can use. He has transcended both nature and himself. The picture, poem, harmony that has become the body for this revelation is alone great art."

"Exactly," came the patient comment that was asked for.

"One thing is certain: only human knowledge, expressed in human terms, can come through a human brain. No mind, no intellect, can convey a message that transcends human experience and reason. Art, however, can. It can supply the vehicle, the body. But, even here, the great artist cannot communicate the secret of his Vision; he cannot talk about it, tell it to others. He can only *show* the result."

"Results," interrupted Dr. Fillery in a curious tone; "what results, exactly, would you look for?" There was a burning in his eyes. His skin was tingling.

"What else but a widening, deepening, heightening of our present consciousness," came the instant reply. "An extension of faculty, of course, making entirely new knowledge available. A group of great artists, each contributing his special vision, respectively, of form, colour, words, proportion, could together create a 'body' to express a Power transcending the accumulated wisdom of the world. The race could be uplifted, taught, redeemed."

"You have already given some attention to this strange idea?" suggested his listener, watching closely the working of the other's face. "You have perhaps even experimented— A ceremonial of some sort, you mean? A performance, a ritual—or what?"

Father Collins lowered his voice, becoming more earnest, more impressive: "Beauty, the arts," he whispered, "can alone provide a vehicle for the expression of those Intelligences which are the cosmic powers. A performance of some sort—possibly—since there must be sound and movement. A bridge between us, between our evolution and their own, might, I believe, be thus constructed. Art is only great when it provides a true form for the expression of an eternal cosmic power. By combining—we might provide a means for their manifestation—"

"A body of thought, as it were, through which our 'N. H.' might become articulate? Is that your idea?"

Behind the question lay something new, it seemed, as though, while listening to the exposition of an odd mystical conception, his mind had been busy with a preoccupation, privately but simultaneously, of his own. "In what way precisely do you suggest the arts might combine to provide this 'body'?" he asked, a faint tremor noticeable in the lowered voice.

"That," replied Father Collins promptly, never at a loss, "we should have to think about. Inspiration will come to us—probably through *him*. Ceremonial, of course, has always been an attempt in this direction, only it has left the world

so long that people no longer know how to construct a real one. The ceremo-
nials of to-day are ugly, vulgar, false. The words, music, colour, gestures—
everything must combine in perfect harmony and proportion to be efficacious.
It is a forgotten method."

"And results—how would they come?"

"The new wisdom and knowledge that result are suddenly there in the members of the group. The Power has expressed itself. Not through the brain, of
course, but, rather, that the new ideas, having been *acted* out, are suddenly there.
There has been an extension of consciousness. A group consciousness has been
formed, and—"

"And there you are!" Dr. Fillery, moving his foot unperceived, had touched
a bell beneath the table. The foot, however, groped and fumbled, as though unsure of itself.

"You learn to swim—by swimming, not by talking about it." Father Collins was
prepared to talk on for another hour. "If we can devise the means—and I feel
sure we can—we shall have formed a bridge between the two evolutions—"

Nurse Robbins entered with apologies. A case upstairs demanded the doctor's
instant attendance. Dr. Devonham was engaged.

"One thing," insisted Father Collins, as they shook hands and he got up to
go, "one thing only you would have to fear." He was very earnest. Evidently
the signs of struggle, of fierce conflict in the other's face he did not notice.

"And that is?" A hand was on the door.

" If successful—if we provide this means of expression for him—we provide
also the means of losing him."

"Death?" He opened the door with rough, unnecessary violence.

"Escape. He would no longer need the body he now uses. He would *remember*—
and be gone. In his place you would have—LeVallon again only. I'm afraid,"
he added, "that he already is remembering—!"

His final words, as Nurse Robbins deftly hastened his departure in the hall,
were a promise to communicate the results of his further reflections, and a suggestion that his cottage by the river would be a quiet spot in which to talk the
matter over again.

But Dr. Fillery, having thanked Nurse Robbins for her prompt attendance to
his bell, returned to the room and sat for some time in a strange confusion of anxious thoughts. A singular idea took shape in him—that Father Collins had again
robbed his mind of its unspoken content. That sensitive receptive nature had
first perceived, then given form to the vague, incoherent dreams that lurked in
the innermost recesses of his hidden self.

Yet, if that were so—and if "N. H." already was "remembering"—!

A wave of shadow crept upon him, darkening his hope, his enthusiasm, his
very life. For another part of him knew quite well the value to be attributed to
what Father Collins had said.

Instinctively his mind sought for Devonham. But it did not occur to him at
the moment to wonder why this was so.

CHAPTER XXVI

S pring had come with her sweet torment of delight, her promises, her passion, and London lay washed and perfumed beneath April's eager sun. An
immense, persuasive glamour was in the sky. The whole earth caught up
a swifter gear, as the magic of rich creative life poured out of "dead" soil into
flower, insect, bird and animal. The prodigious stream omitted no single form;
every "body " pulsed and blossomed at full strength. The hidden powers in each
seed emerged. And it was from the inanimate body of the earth this flood of increased vitality rose.

Into Edward Fillery, strolling before breakfast over the wet lawn of the enclosed garden, the tide of new life rose likewise. It was very early, the flush of
dawn still near enough for the freshness of the new day to be everywhere. The
greater part of the huge city was asleep. He was alone with the first birds, the
dew, the pearl and gold of the sun's slanting rays. He saw the slates and chimneys glisten. Spring, like a visible presence, was passing across the town, bringing the amazing message that all obey yet no man understands.

> "This is its touch upon the blossomed rose,
>   The fashion of its hand shaped lotus-leaves;
> In dark soil and the silence of the seeds
>   The robe of spring it weaves.
>
> "It maketh and unmaketh, mending all;
>   What it hath wrought is better than had been;
> Slow grows the splendid pattern that it plans,
>   Its wistful hands between."

The lines came to his memory, while upon his mind fell lovely and wonderful impressions. It was as though the subconsciousness of the earth herself
emerged with the spring, producing new life, new splendour everywhere. Out
of a single patch of soil the various roots drew material they then fashioned into
such different and complicated outlines as daisy, lily, rose, and a hundred types
of tree. From the same bit of soil emerged these intricate patterns and designs,
these different forms. At this very moment, while his feet left dark tracks across
the silvery lawn, the process was going steadily forward all over England. Beneath those very feet up rushed the power into all conceivable bodies. Colour,
music, form, marvellously organized, making no mistakes, were turning the
world into a vast, delicious garden.

Form, colour, sound! From his own hidden region rose again the flaming hope
and prophecy. He stooped and picked a daisy, examining with rapt attention its
perfect little body. Who, what made this astonishing thing, that was yet among
the humbler forms? What intelligence devised its elaborate outline, guarded,

cared for, tended it, ensured its growth and welfare? He gazed at its white rays tipped with crimson, its several hundred florets, its composite design. The spring life had been pouring through it until he picked it. Through the huge mass of earth's body its tiny roots had drawn the life it needed. This power was now cut off. It would die. The process, as with everything else, was "automatic and unintelligent!" It seemed an incredible explanation. The old familiar question troubled him, but he saw it abruptly now from a new angle.

"We built it," came a voice so close that it seemed behind him, for when at first he turned, startled, and yet not startled, he saw no figure standing; "we who work in darkness, yet who never die, the Hidden Ones who build and weave inside and out of sight. You have destroyed our work of ages...."

A pang of sudden regret and anguish seized him. He stood still and stared in the direction whence he thought the voice had come, but no form, no outline, no body that could have produced a sound, a voice, was visible. A blackbird flew with its shrill whistle over the enclosing wall, and the gardener, up unusually early, was now moving slowly past the elms at the far end, some two hundred yards away. The old man, he remembered, had been telling him only the day before that the life in his plants this year had been prodigious and successful beyond his whole experience. It puzzled him. Something of reverence, of superstition almost, had lain in the man's voice and eyes.

"Who are you?" whispered Fillery, still holding the "dead" broken flower in his hand and staring about him. He was aware that the sound from which the voice had come, detaching itself, as it were, into articulate syllables out of a general continuous volume, had not ceased. It was all about him, softly murmuring. Was it in himself perhaps? An intense inner activity, like the pressure of an enveloping tide, that was also in space, in the soil, the body of the planet, rose in him too. And it seemed to him that his mind was suddenly in process of being shaped and fashioned into a new "body of understanding"; a new instrument of understanding.

" This is its work upon the things ye see:
    The unseen things are more; men's hearts and minds,
  The thoughts of peoples and their ways and wills,
    These, too, the great Law binds."

"I know," he exclaimed, this time with acceptance that omitted the doubt he had first felt. "I know who you are"... and even as he said the words, there dropped into him, it seemed, some knowledge, some hint, some wonder that lay, he well knew, outside all human experience. It was as though some cosmic power brushed gently against and through his being, but a power so alien to known human categories that to attempt its expression in human terms—language, reason, imagination even—were to mutilate it. Yet, even for its partial, broken manifestation, human terms were alone available, since without these it must remain unperceived, he himself unaware of its existence.

He *was*, however, aware of its presence, its existence. All that was left to him therefore was his own personal interpretation. Herein, evidently, lay the truth for him; this was the meaning of his "acceptance." It was, in some way, a renewal of that other vision he called the Flower Hill and Flower Music experience.

"I know you," he repeated, his voice merging curiously in the general under' lying murmur of the morning. "You belong to the bodiless, the deathless ones who work and build and weave eternally. Form, sound, colour are your in' struments, the elements your tools. You wove this flower," he fingered the dy' ing daisy, "as you also shaped this body"—he tapped his breast—"and—you built as well this mind—"

He stopped dead. Two things arrested him: the feeling that the ideas were not primarily his own, but derived from a source outside himself; and a sudden in' tensification of the flaming hope and prophecy that burst up as with new mean' ing into the words "mind" and "body."

The broken body of the flower slipped from his fingers and fell upon the body of the earth. He looked down at its now empty form through which no life flowed, and his eye passed then to his own body beating with intense activity, and thence to the bodies of the trees, the darting birds, the gigantic sun now peering magnificently along the heavens. Body! A body was a form through which life expressed itself, a vehicle of expression by means of which life man' ifested, an instrument it used. But a body of thought was a true phrase too. And with the words, shaped automatically in his brain, a new light flashed and flooded him with its waves.

"A body of thought, a mental body"—the phrase went humming and flow' ing strangely through him. A body of thought! Father Collins, he remembered, had used some such wild language, only it had seemed empty words without intelligible meaning. Whence came the intense new meaning that so suddenly attached itself to the familiar phrase? Whence came the thrilling deep convic' tion that new, greater knowledge was hovering near, and that for its expression a new body must be devised? And what was this new knowledge, this new power? Whence came the amazing certainty in him that a new way was being shown to him, a means of progress for humanity that must otherwise flounder always to its average level of growth, development, then invariably collapse again?

"We built it," ran past him through the air again, or rose perhaps from the stirred depths of his own subconscious being, or again, dropped from a hidden rushing star. "The more perfect and adequate the form, the greater the flow of life, of knowledge, of power it can express. No mind, no intellect, can convey a message that transcends human experience. Yet there is a way."

The new knowledge was there, if only the new vehicle suited to its expres' sion could be devised....

The stream of life pouring through him became more and more intense; some power of perception seemed growing into white heat within him; transcending the limited senses; becoming incandescent. This tide of sound, inaudible to or' dinary ears, was the music which is inseparable from the rhythm that underlies all forms, the music of the earth's manifold activities now pouring in vibrations huge and tiny all round and through him. He turned instinctively.

"You...!" exclaimed the doctor in him, as though rebuke, reproval stirred. "You here...!"

It seemed to him that the figure of "N. H.," embodying as it were a ray of sunlight, stood beside him.

"We," came the answer, with a smile that took the sparkling sunlight through the very face. "We are all about you," added the voice with a rhythm that swamped all denial, all objection, bringing an exultant exhilaration in their place. "We come from what always seems to you a Valley of sun and flowers, where we work and play behind the appearances you call the world."

"The world," repeated Fillery. "The universe as well!"

The voice, the illusion of actual words, both died away, merging in some perplexing fashion into another appearance, perhaps equally an illusion so far as the senses were concerned—the phenomenon men call sight. Instead of hearing, that is, he now suddenly saw. Something in the arrangement of light caught his attention, holding it. The deep, central self in him, that which interprets and decodes the reports the senses bring, employed another mode.

The figure of "N. H." still was definite enough in form indeed, yet at the same time taking the rays into itself as though it were a body of light. There was no transparency, of course, nor was this clear radiance seen by Fillery for the first time, but rather that his natural shining was caught up and intensified by the morning sunshine. A body of light, none the less, seemed a true description of what Fillery now saw. This sunshine filled the air, the space all round him, the entire lawn and garden shone in a sparkling flood of dancing brilliance. It blazed. The figure of "N. H." was merely a portion of this blazing. As a focus, but one of many, he now thought of it. And about each focus was the toss and fling of lovely, ever-rising spirals.

Across the main stream came then another pulsing movement, hardly discernible at first, and similar to an under-swell that moves the sea against the waves—so that the eye perceives it only when not looking for it. This contrary motion, it soon became apparent, went in numerous, almost countless directions, so that, within and below its complicated wave-tracery, he was aware of yet other motions, crossing and interlacing at various speeds, until the space about him seemed to whirl with myriad rhythms, yet without the least confusion. These rhythms were of a hundred different magnitudes, from the very tiny to the gigantic, and while the smallest were of a radiant brilliance that made the sunshine pale, the larger ones seemed distant, their light of an intenser quality, though of a quality he had never seen before. These were strangely diffused, these bigger ones—"distant" was the word that occurred to him, although that inner brilliance which occurs in dreams, in imaginative moments, the nameless glow that colours mental vision, described them better. Moreover they wore colours the human eye had never seen, while the smallest rhythms were lit with the familiar colours of the prism.

He stood absorbed, fascinated, drinking in the amazing spectacle, as though the glowing spirals of fire communicated to his inmost being a heat and glory of creative power. He was aware of the creative stream of spring in his own heart, pouring from the body of the earth on which he stood, drenching mind, nerves and even muscles with concentrated life. His subconscious being rose and stretched its wings. All, all was possible. A sensation of divine deathlessness possessed him. The limitations of his ordinary human faculties and powers were overborne, so that he felt he could never again face the mournful prison that caged him in. The meaning of escape became plain to him.

He saw the invisible building Intelligences at work.

He was aware then suddenly of purpose, of intention. The seeming welter of the waves of coloured light, of the immense and tiny rhythms, the intricate streams of vibrating, pulsing, throbbing movements were, he now perceived, marvellously co-ordinated. There was a focus, a vortex, towards which all rushed with a power so prodigious that a sense of terror touched him. He suddenly became conscious of a pattern forming before his eyes, hanging in empty space, shining, soft with light and beauty. It became, he saw, a geometric design. An idea of crystals, frost-forms, a spider's web hung with glistening dewdrops shot across his memory. The spirals whirled and sang about it.

This outline, he next perceived, was the focus to which the light, heat, colour all contributed their particular touch and quality. It glowed now in the centre of the vortex. So overwhelming, however, was the sense of the stupendous power involved that, as he phrased it afterwards, it seemed he watched the formation of some mighty sun. It was the whirling of those billion-miled sheets of incandescent fires that attend the birth of a nebula he watched. The power, at any rate, was gigantic.

He stood trembling before a revelation that left him lost, shelterless, bereft of any help that his little self might summon—when, suddenly, with an emotion of strange tenderness, he saw the great rhythms become completely dominated by the very smallest of all. The same instant the pattern grew sharply outlined, perfect in every detail, as though the focus of powerful glasses cleared—and the pattern hung a moment exquisitely fashioned in space beneath his eyes before it sank slowly to the ground. It remained in an upright position on the grass at his feet—a daisy, growing in the earth, alive, its tiny delicate face taking the sunlight and the morning wind.

With a shock he then realized another thing: it was the very daisy he had broken, uprooted, killed a few minutes before.

He stooped, one hand outstretched as though to finger its wee white petals, but found instead that he was listening—listening to a sweet faint music that rose from the surface of the lawn, from grass and flowers, running in waves and circles, like the vibrations of gentle wind across a thousand strings. It was similar, though less in volume, to the sound he had heard in the presence of "N. H." He rose slowly to an upright position, dazed, bewildered, yet rapt with the wonder of the whole experience.

"N. H.!" he heard his voice exclaim, its sound merging in the growing volume of music all about him. "N. H.!" he cried again. "This is your work, your service...!"

But he could not see him; his figure was no longer differentiated from the ever-moving sea of light that filled space wherever he looked. The same play of brilliance shone and glistened everywhere, whirling, ever shifting as in vortices of intricate geometrical designs, dancing, interpenetrating, and with a magnificence of colour that caught his breath away. There were remarkable flashings, and two of these flashings blazed suddenly together, forming an immense physiognomy, an expression, rather, as of a mighty face. The same instant there were a hundred of these mighty brilliant visages that pierced through the sea of whirling colour and gazed upon him, close, terrific, with a power and beauty that left thought without even a ghost of language to describe them. Their glory lay beyond all earthly terms. He recognized them. These mighty outlines he had seen before.

His mind then made an effort; he tried to think; memory and reason strove with emotion and sensation. The forms, the faces, the powers at once grew fainter. They faded slowly. The whirling vortices withdrew in some extraordinary way, the colour paled, the sound grew thinner, ever more distant, the great weaving designs dissolved. The lovely spirals all were gone. He saw the garden trees again, the flower beds. Space emptied, showing the morning sunshine on roofs and chimney-pots.

"We have rebuilt, remade it," he heard faintly, but he heard also the roar and boom of the gigantic rhythms as they withdrew, not spatially, so much as from his consciousness that was now contracting once more, till only the fainter sounds of the smaller singing patterns, the Flower Music as he had come to call it, reached his ears. Words and music, like voices known in dreams, seemed interwoven. He remembered the huge faces, with their bright confidence and glory, rising through the sunlight, peering as through a mirror at him, radiant and of imperishable beauty. The words, perhaps, he attached himself, his own interpretations of their ringing motions.

The sounds died away. He reeled. The expansion and subsequent contraction of consciousness had been too rapid, the whole experience too intense. He swayed, unsure of his own identity. He remembered vaguely that tears filled his eyes and rolled down his cheeks, that the destruction of a lovely form had caused him a peculiar anguish, and that its recreation produced an intolerable joy, bringing tears of happiness. An arm caught him as he swayed. The accents of a voice he knew were audible close beside him. But at first he did not understand the words, feeling only a dull pain they caused.

"Their imperishable beauty! Their divine loveliness!" he stammered, recognizing the face and voice. He flung his arms wide, gazing into the now empty air above the London garden. "The great service they eternally fulfil—oh, that we all might—" He made a gesture towards the other houses with their sightless, shuttered windows.

"I know, I know," came in the familiar tones. "But come in now, come in, Edward, with me. I beg you—before it is too late." Paul Devonham's voice shook so that it was hardly recognizable. The skin of his face was white. He wore a haggard look.

"Too late!" repeated the other; "it is always too late. The world will never see. Their eyes are blinded." An intolerable emotion swept him. He stared suddenly at his colleague, an immense surprise in him. "But you, Paul!" he exclaimed. "You understand! Even you—!"

Devonham led him slowly into the house. There was protection in his manner, in voice and gesture there was deep affection, respect as well, but behind and through these flickered the signs of another unmistakable emotion that Fillery at first could hardly credit—of pity, was it? Of something at any rate he dared not contemplate.

"Even I," came in quick, low tones, "even I, Edward, understand. You forget. I was once alone with him"—the voice sank to a rapid whisper—"in the mountain valley." Devonham's expression was curious. He raised his tone again. "But—not now, not now, I beg of you. Not yet, at any rate. You will be cast out, judged insane, your work destroyed, your career ruined, your reputation—" His excitement betrayed itself in his bright eyes and unusual gestures. He was shaken to the core. Fillery turned upon him. They were in the corridor now. He flung his arm free of the restraining hand.

"You know!" he cried, "yet would keep silent!" His voice choked. "You saw what I saw: new sources open, the offer made, the channels accessible at our very door, yet you would refuse—"

"Not one in ten million," came the hard rejoinder, "would believe." The voice trembled. "We have no proof. Their laws of manifestation are unknown to us, and such glimpses are but glimpses—useless and dangerous." He whispered suddenly: "Besides—what are they? What, after all, are we dealing with?"

"We can experiment," interrupted his companion quickly.

"How? Of what possible value?"

"You felt what I felt? In your own being you experienced the revelation too, and yet you use such words! New forces, new faculties, Beings from another order of incalculable powers to ennoble, to bless, to inspire! The creation of higher forms through which new, greater life and knowledge, shall manifest!"

He could hardly find the words he sought, so bright was the hope and wonder in his heart still. "Think—at a time like this—what humanity might gain. *Creative* powers, Paul, creative! Acting directly on the subconscious selves of everybody, intensifying every individual, whether he understands and believes or not! The gods, Paul—and nothing less— You saw the daisy—"

Devonham seized both of his companion's hands, as he heard the torrent of wild, incoherent words: "You'll have the entire world against you," he interrupted. "Why seek crucifixion for a dream?" Then, as his hands were again flung off, he turned, a finger suddenly on his lips. "Hush, hush, Edward!" he whispered. "The house is sleeping still. You'll wake them all."

There was a new, strange authority about him. Dr. Fillery controlled himself. They went upstairs on tiptoe.

"Listen!" murmured Devonham, as they reached the first-floor landing. "That's what woke me first and led me to his room, but only to find it empty. He was already gone. I saw him join you on the lawn. I watched from the open window. Then—I lost him.... Listen!" He was trembling like a child.

The sound still echoed faintly, distant, rising and falling, sweet and very lovely, and hardly to be distinguished from the musical hum of wind that sighs and whispers across the strings of an æolian harp. To one man came incredible sensations as they paused a moment. Dim though the landing was, there still seemed a tender luminous glow pervading it.

"They're everywhere," murmured Fillery, "everywhere and always about us, though in different space. Through and behind and inside everything that happens, helping, building, constructing ceaselessly. Oh, Paul, how can you doubt and question value? Behind every single form and body, physical or mental, they operate divinely—"

"Mental! Edward, for God's sake—"

Devonham stepped nearer to him with such abruptness that his companion stopped. The pallor of the assistant's face so close arrested his words a moment. They held their breath, listening together side by side. The sounds grew fainter, died away in the stillness of the early morning, then ceased altogether. It was not the first time they had listened thus to the strange music, nor was it the first time that Fillery entered the room alone. As once before, his colleague remained outside, watching, waiting, half seduced, it seemed, yet vehemently against a sympathetic attitude. He watched his chief go in, he saw the expression on his face. Upon his own, behind a mild expectancy, lay a look of pain.

"Empty!" He heard the startled exclamation.

And instantly Devonham was at his side, a firm hand upon his arm, his eyes taking in an unused bed, a window opened wide, a glow of light and heat the early sunshine could not possibly explain. The perfume, as of flowers in the air, he noted too, and a sense of lightness, freshness, sweetness about the atmosphere that produced happiness, exhilaration. The room throbbed, as it were, with invisible waves of some communicable power even he could not deny. But of "N. H.," the recent occupant, there was no sign.

"In the garden still. I lost sight of him somehow. I told you."

Fillery crossed quickly to the window, his colleague with him, looking out upon a lawn and paths that held no figure anywhere. The gardener was not in sight. Only the birds were visible among the daisies. The quiet sunlight lay as usual upon leaves and flowers waving in the breeze. "He came in," Fillery went on rapidly under his breath. "He must have slipped back when—"

The sound of steps and voices behind them in the corridor brought both men round with a quick movement, as Nurse Robbins, her arm linked in that of "N. H.," stood in the open doorway. Her face was radiant, her eyes alight, her breath came unevenly, and one might have thought her caught midway in some ecstatic dance that still left its joy and bliss stamped on her pretty face. Only she looked more than pretty; there was beauty, a fairy loveliness about her that betrayed an intense experience of some inner kind.

At the sight of the two doctors she rapidly composed herself, leading her companion quietly into the room. "He was upstairs, sir," she said respectfully but breathlessly somewhat, and addressing herself, Fillery noticed, to Devonham and not to himself. "He was going from room to room, talking to the patients—er—singing to them. It was the singing woke me—"

"Upstairs!" exclaimed Devonham. "He has been up there!"

She broke off as Fillery came forward and took "N. H." by the hands, dismissing her with a gesture she was quick to understand. Devonham went with her hurriedly, intent upon a personal inspection at once.

"Your service called you," said Fillery quietly, the moment they were alone. "I understand!" Through the contact of the hands waves of power entered him, it seemed. About the face was light, as though fire glowed behind the very skin and eyes, producing the effect almost of a halo.

"They came for me, and I must go." The voice was deep and wonderful, with prolonged vibrations. "I have found my own. I must return where my service needs me, for here I can do so little."

"To your own place where you are ruler of your fate," the other said slowly. "Here you—"

"Here," came the quick interruption, while the voice lost its resonance, fading as it were in sadness, "here I—die." Even the radiance of his face, although he smiled, dimmed a little on that final word. "I can help where I belong—not here." The light returned, the music came back into the amazing voice.

"The daisy," whispered Fillery, joy rising in him strangely.

"Nature," floated through the air like music, "is my place. With human beings I cannot work. It is too much, and I only should destroy. They are not ready yet, for our great rhythms injure them, and they cannot understand."

Trembling with emotions he could neither define nor control, Fillery led him to the window.

"Even in this little back-garden of a London house," he murmured, "among, so to speak, the humble buttercups and daisies of our life! The creative Intelligence at work, building, ever building the best forms they can. You re-make a broken daisy"—his voice rose, as the great shining face so close lit with its flaming smile—"you re-make as well our broken minds. In the subconscious hides our creative power that you stimulate. It is with that and that alone you work. It hides in all of us, though the artist alone perceives or can use it. It is with that you work—"

"With you, dear Fillery, I can work, for you help me to remember. You feel the big rhythms that we bring."

Dr. Fillery started, peered about him, listened hard. Was it the trees, shaking in the morning wind, that rustled? Was it a voice? The dancing leaves reflected the sunshine from a thousand facets. The sound accompanied, rather than interrupted, his own speech. He turned back to "N. H." with passionate enthusiasm.

"Using beauty—the artists—the creative powers of the Race," he went on, "we shall create together a new body, a new vehicle, through which your powers can express themselves. The intellect cannot serve you... it is the creative imagination of those who know beauty that you seek. You are inarticulate in this wretched body. We shall make a new one—"

"They have come for me and I must go—"

"We will work together. Oh, stay—stay with me—!"

"I have found the way. I have remembered. I must go back—"

The wind died down, the leaves stopped rustling, the sunshine seemed to pale as though a cloud passed over the sky. The words he had heard resolved themselves into the morning sounds, the singing of the birds. Had they been words at all? Bewilderment, like a pain, rushed over him. He knew himself suddenly imprisoned, caught.

"I have remembered," he heard in quiet tones, but the voice dead, no resonance, no music in it. And across the room he saw suddenly Paul Devonham just inside the door, returned from his inspection. Beside him stood—LeVallon.

An extraordinary reaction instantly took place in him. A lid was raised, a shutter lifted, a wall fell flat. He hardly knew how to describe it. Was it due to the look of anxiety, of tenderness, of affectionate, of protective care he saw plainly upon his colleague's face? He could not say. He only knew for certain in that instant that Paul Devonham's main preoccupation was with—himself; that the latter regarded him exactly as he regarded any other—yes, that was the only word—any other patient; that he looked after him, tended, guarded, cared for him—and that this watchful, experienced observation had been going on now for a long, long time.

The authority in his manner became abruptly clear as day. Devonham watched over him; also he watched him. For days, for weeks, this had been his attitude. For the first time, in this instant, as he saw him lead away LeVallon into his own room and close the door, Fillery now perceived this. He experienced a violent revulsion of mind. In a flash a hundred details of the recent past occurred to him, chief among them the fact that, more and more, the control of the Home and its occupants had been taken over, Fillery himself only too willing, by his assistant. A moment of appalling doubt rose like a black cloud....

He heard Paul telling LeVallon to begin his breakfast, just as the door closed, and he noted the authoritative tone of voice. The next minute he and his colleague were alone together.

"Paul," said the chief quickly, but with a calm assurance that anticipated a favourable answer, "*they*, at any rate, are all right?"

Devonham nodded his head. "No harm done," he replied briefly. "In fact, as you know, he rather stimulates them than otherwise."

"I know."

He felt, for the first time in their years of close relationship, a breath of suspicion enter him. There was a look upon his colleague's face he could not quite define. It baffled him.

"Of course, I know—"

He stopped, for the undecipherable look had strengthened suddenly. He thought of a gaoler.

"Paul," he said quickly, "what's the matter? What's wrong with you?"

He drew back a pace or two and watched him.

"With me—nothing, Edward. Nothing at all." The tone was grave with anxiety, yet had this new authority in it.

A feeling of intolerable insecurity came upon him, a sensation as though he balanced on air, yet its cause, its origin, easily explained: the support of his colleague's mind was taken from him. Paul's attitude was clear as day to him. He was a gaoler.... He recalled again the recent detail, brightly significant—that Nurse Robbins had turned to Paul, rather than to himself.

"With—me, then—you think?" His voice hardly sounded like his own. He looked about him for support, found an arm-chair, sat down in it. "You're strange, Paul, very strange," he whispered. "What do you mean by 'there's something wrong with me'?"

Devonham's expression cleared slightly and a kindly, sympathetic smile appeared, then vanished. The grave look that Fillery disliked reappeared.

"What d'you mean, Paul Devonham?" came the repetition, in a louder, more challenging voice. "You're watching me—as though I were"—he laughed without a trace of mirth—"a patient." He leaned forward. "Paul, you've been watching me for a long time. Out with it, now. What is it?"

Devonham, who had kept silent, drew some papers from his pocket, a bundle of rolled sheets.

"Of course," he said gently, "I always watch you. For that's how I learn. I learn from you, Edward, more than from anybody I know."

But Dr. Fillery, his eyes fixed upon the sheaf of papers, had recognized them. His own writing was visible along the uneven edges. They were the description he had set down of his adventure on Flower Hill, of the scenes between "N. H." and Lady Gleeson, between "N. H." and Nayan, the autobiographical description with "N. H." and Nurse Robbins soon after his arrival, when Fillery had so amazingly found his own mind—as he believed—identified with his patient's.

Devonham snapped off the elastic band that held the sheaf together. "Edward, I've read them. We have no secrets, of course. I've read them carefully. Every word—my dear fellow."

"Yes, yes," replied the other, while something in him wavered horribly. "I'm glad. They were meant for you to read, for of course we have no secrets. I—I do not expect you to agree. We have never quite seen eye to eye—have we?" His voice shook. "You terrible iconoclast," he added, betraying thus the nature of the fear that changed his voice, then recognizing with vexation that he had done so. "You believe nothing. You never will believe anything. You cannot understand. With joy you would destroy what I and others believe—wouldn't you, Paul—?"

The deep sadness, the gravity on the face in front of him stopped the tirade.

"I would save you, Edward," came the earnest, gentle words, "from yourself. The powers of autosuggestion, as we know in our practice—don't we?—are limitless. If you call that destroying—"

From the adjoining room the clatter of knives and forks was audible. Dr. Fillery listened a moment with a smile.

"Paul," he asked, his voice firm and sure again, "is your chief patient in that room," indicating the door with his head, "or—in this?"

"In this," was the reply. "A wise man is always his own patient and 'Physician, heal thyself' his motto." He sat down beside his chief. His manner changed; there was affection, deep solicitude, something of passionate entreaty even in voice and eyes and gestures. "There are features here," he said in lowered tones, "Edward, we have not understood, perhaps even we can never understand; but we have not, I think, sufficiently guarded against one thing—auto-suggestion. The role it plays in life is immense, incalculable; it is in everything we do and think, above all in everything we believe. It is peculiarly powerful and active in—er—unusual things—"

"The sound—the sounds—you've heard them yourself," broke in his companion.

Devonham shrugged his thin shoulders. "He sings—in a peculiar way." As an aside, he said it, returning to his main sermon instantly. "Let us leave details out," he cried; "it is the principle that concerns us. Edward, your complex against humanity lies hard and rigid in you still. It has never found that full recognition by yourself which can resolve it. Your work, your noble work, is but a partial expression. The kernel of this old complex in you remains unrelieved, undischarged—because still unrecognized. And, further, you are continually adding to the repression which"—even Devonham paused a second before using such a word to such a man—"is poisoning you, Edward, poisoning you, I repeat."

"You saw—you saw the rebuilding of—the daisy"—an odd whisper of insecurity ran through the quiet words, a statement rather than a question—"you realize, at any rate, that chance has brought us into contact with Powers, creative Powers, of a new order—"

"Let us omit all details just now," interrupted the other, a troubled, indecipherable look on his face. "The undoubted telepathy between your mind and mine nullifies any such—"

"—powers of which we all have some faint counterpart, at any rate, in our subliminal selves." Fillery had not heard the interruption. "Powers by means of which we may build for the Race new forms, new mental bodies, new vehicles for life, for God, to manifest through—more perfect, more receptive—"

Devonham had suddenly seized both his hands and was leaning closer to him. Something compelling, authoritative, peculiarly convincing for a moment had its undeniable effect, again stopping the flow of hurried, passionate, eager words.

"There is one new form, new body," and the intensity in voice and eyes drove the meaning deep, deep into his listener's mind and heart, "I wish to see you build. One, and one only—physical, mental, spiritual. But you cannot build it, Edward—alone!"

"Paul!" The other held up a warning hand; the expression in his eyes was warning too. Their effect upon Devonham, however, was nil. He was talking with a purpose nothing could alter.

"She is still waiting for you," he went on with determination, "and already you have kept her waiting—overlong." In the tone, in the hard clear eyes as well, lay a suggestion almost of tears.

He opened the door into the breakfast-room, but Fillery caught his arm and stopped him. They could hear Nurse Robbins speaking, as she attended as usual to her patient's wants. Coffee was being poured out. There was a sound of knives and plates and cups.

"One minute, Paul, one minute before we go in." He drew him aside. "And what, *Doctor* Devonham, may I ask, would you prescribe?" There was a curious mixture of gentle sarcasm, of pity, of patient tolerance, yet at the same time of sincere, even anxious, interest in the question. The face and manner betrayed that he waited for the answer with something more than curiosity.

There was no hesitancy in Devonham. He judged the moment ripe, perhaps; he was aware that his words would be listened to, appreciated, understood certainly, and, possibly, obeyed.

"Expression," he said convincingly, but in a lowered voice. "The fullest expression, everywhere and always. Let it all come. Accept the lot, believe the lot, welcome the lot, and thus"—he could not conceal the note of passionate entreaty, of deep affection—"avoid every atom of *repression*. In the end—in the long run—your own best judgment *must* prevail."

They smiled into each other's eyes for a moment in silence, while, instinctively and automatically, their hands joined in a steady clasp.

"Bless you, old fellow," murmured the chief. "As if I didn't know! It's the treatment you've been trying on me for weeks and months. As if I hadn't noticed!"

As they entered the breakfast-room, Nurse Robbins, with flushed face and sparkling eyes, was pouring out the coffee, leaning close over her patient's shoulder as she did so. Fresh roses were in her cheeks as well as on the table.

"This is its touch upon the blossomed maid," whispered Fillery, with the quick hint of humour that belongs only to the sane. At the same time the light remark was produced, he well knew, by a part of himself that sought to remain veiled from recognition. Any other triviality would have done as well to cloak the sharp pain that swept him, and to lead his listener astray. For in that instant, as they entered, he saw at the table not "N. H.," but LeVallon—the backward, ignorant, commonplace LeVallon, an empty, untaught personality, yet so receptive that anything—anything!—could he transferred to him by a strong, vivid mind, a mind, for instance, like his own....

The sight, for a swift instant, was intolerable and devastating. He balanced again on air that gave him no support. He wavered, almost swayed. "N. H.," in that horrible and painful second, did not exist, and never had existed. The unstable mind, he comforted himself, experiences dislocating extremes of attitude... for, at the same time as he saw himself shaking and wavering without solid support, he saw the figure of Paul Devonham, big, important, authoritative, dominating the uncertainties of life with calm, steady power.

In a fraction of a second all this came and went. He sat down beside LeVallon, his eyes still twinkling with his trivial little joke.

"'N. H.,'" he whispered to Devonham quickly, "has—escaped at last."

"LeVallon," came the whispered reply as quickly, "is cured at last." And, to conceal an intolerable rush of pain, of loss, of loneliness that threatened tears, he pointed to the dropped eyes and blushing checks of the pretty nurse across the table.

CHAPTER XXVII

To Edward Fillery, the deep pain of frustration baffling all his mental processes, the end had come with a strange, bewildering swiftness. He knew there had been a prolonged dislocation of his being, possibly, even a partial loss of memory with regard to much that went on about him, but he could not, did not, admit that no value or reality had attached to his experiences. The central self in him had projected a limb, an arm, that, feeling its way across the confining wall of the prison house, groping towards an unbelievably wonderful revelation of new possibilities, had abruptly now withdrawn again. The dissociation in his personality was over. He was, in other words, no longer aware of "N. H." Like Devonham, he now did not "perceive" "N. H.," but only LeVallon. But, unlike Devonham, he *had* perceived him....

He had met half-way a mighty and magnificent Vision. Its truth and beauty remained for him enduring. The revelation had come and gone. That its close was sudden, simple, undramatic, above all untheatrical, satisfied him. "N. H." had "escaped," leaving the commonplace LeVallon in his place. But, at least, he had known "N. H."

His whole being, an odd, sweet, happy pain in him, yearned ever to the glorious memory of it all. The melancholy, the peculiar shyness he felt, were not without an indefinite pleasure. His nature still vibrated to those haunting and inspiring rhythms, but his normal, earthly faculties, he flattered himself, were in no sense permanently disorganized. Professionally, he still cared for LeVallon, disenchanted dust though he might be, compared to "N. H."... He approved of Devonham's proposal to take him for a few days to the sea. He also approved of Paul's advice that he should accept Father Collins' invitation to spend a day or two at his country cottage. The Khilkoffs would be there, father and daughter. The Home, in charge of an assistant, could be reached in a few hours in case of need. The magic of Devonham's wise, controlling touch lay in every detail, it seemed. .

He saw the trio—for Nurse Robbins was of the party—off to Seaford. "The final touches to his cure," Paul mentioned slyly, with a smile, as the guard whistled. But of whose cure he did not explain. "He'll bathe in the sea," he added, the reference obvious this time. "And—when we return—I shall be best man. I've already promised!" There was a triumph of skilled wisdom in both sentences.

"The time isn't ripe yet, Edward, for too magnificent ideas. And your ideas have been a shade too magnificent, perhaps." He talked on lightly, even care-

lessly. And, as usual, there was purpose, meaning, "treatment"—his friend easily discerned it now—in every detail of his attitude.

Fillery laughed. Through his mind ran Povey's sentence, "Never argue with
the once-born!" but aloud he said, "At any rate, I've no idea that I'm Emperor
of Japan or—or the Archangel Gabriel!" And the other, pleased and satisfied
that a touch of humour showed itself, shook hands firmly, affectionately,
through the window as the train moved off. LeVallon raised his hat to his chief
and smiled—an ordinary smile....

With the speed and incongruity of a dream these few days slipped by, their
happenings vivid enough, yet all set to a curiously small scale, a cramped perspective, blurred a little as by a fading light. Only one thing retained its brilliance, its intense reality, its place in the bigger scale, its vast perspective remaining unchanged. The same immense sweet rhythm swept Iraida and himself
inevitably together. Some deep obsession that hitherto prevented had been withdrawn.

She had called that very morning—Paul's touch visible here again, he believed,
though he had not asked. He looked on and smiled. After the ordeal of breakfast with Devonham and LeVallon her visit was announced. It was Paul, after
a little talk downstairs, who showed her in. With the radiance of a spring wild-
flower opening to the early sunshine, her unexpected visit to his study seemed
clothed. Unexpected, yes, but surely inevitable as well. With the sweet morning wind through the open window, it seemed, she came to him, the letter of
invitation from Father Collins in her hand. His own lay among his correspondence, still untouched. Her perfume rose about him as she explained something
he hardly heard or followed.

"You'll come, Edward, won't you? You'll come too."

"Of course," he answered. But it was a song he heard, and no dull spoken
words. She ran dancing towards him through a million flowers; her hair flew
loose along the scented winds; her white limbs glowed with fire. He danced to
meet her. It was in the Valley that he caught her hands and met her eyes. "It's
happened," he heard himself saying. "It's happened at last—just as you said it
must. *Escape!* He has escaped!"

"But we shall follow after—when the time comes, Edward."

"Where the wild bee never flew!"...

"When the time comes," she repeated.

Her voice, her smile, her eyes brought him back sharply into the little room.
The furniture showed up again. The Valley faded. He noticed suddenly that for
the first time she wore no flowers in her dress as usual.

"Iraida!" he exclaimed. "Then—you knew!"

She bent her head, smiling divinely. She took both his hands in hers. At her
touch every obstacle between them melted. His own private, personal inhibi-
tion he saw as the trivial barriers a little child might raise. His complex against
humanity, as Paul called it, had disappeared. Their minds, their beings, their natures became most strangely one, he felt, and yet quite naturally. There was

nothing they did not share.

"With the first dawn," he heard her say in a low voice. "Never—never again," he seemed to hear, " shall we destroy his—their—work of ages."

"A flower," he whispered, "has no need to wear a flower!"

He was convinced that she too had shared an experience similar to his own, perhaps had even seen the bright, marvellous Deva faces peering, shining.... He did not ask. She said no more. Life flowed between them in an untroubled stream....

Like the flow of a stream, indeed, things went past him, yet with incidents and bits of conversation thus picked out with vivid sharpness. The dissociation of his being was still noticeable here and there, he supposed. The swell after the storm took time to settle down. Slowly, however, the waves that had been projected, leaping to heaven, returned to the safe, quiet dead level of the normal calm.... The depths lay still once more. And his melancholy passed a little, lifted. He knew, at any rate, those depths were now accessible.

"I've seen over the wall a moment," he said to himself. "Paul is both right and wrong. What I've seen lies too far ahead of the Race to be intelligible or of use. I should be cast out, crucified, my other, simpler work destroyed. To control rhythms so powerful, so different to anything we now know, is not yet possible. They would shatter, rather than construct." He smiled sadly yet with resignation. There was pain and humour in his eyes. "I should be regarded as a Promethean merely, an extremist Promethean, and probably be locked up for contravening some County Council bye-law or offending Church and State. That's where he, perhaps, is right—Paul!" He thought of him with affection and pity, with understanding love. "How wise and faithful, how patient and how skilled—within his limits. The stable are the useful; the stable are the leaders; the stable rule the world. People with steady if unvisioned eyes like Paul, with money like Lady Gleeson.... But, oh!"—he sighed—"how slow, ye gods! how slow!"...

The visit was a strange one. Nayan sat between him and her father in the motor. It was not far from London, the ancient little house among the trees where Father Collins secreted himself from time to time upon occasional "retreats."

Within the grounds it might have been the centre of the New Forest, but for the sound of tramcar bells that sometimes came jangling faintly through the thick screen of leaves. There were old-world paved courtyards with sweet playing fountains, miniature lawns, tangles of flowers, small sunken gardens with birds of cut box and yew, stone nymphs, and a shaggy, moss-grown Pan, whose hand that once held the pipes had broken off. Suburbia lay outside, yet, by walking wisely, it was possible to move among these delights for half an hour, great trees ever rustling overhead, and a clear small stream winding peacefully in and out with gentle lapping murmurs. Nature here lay undisturbed as it had lain for centuries.

The little ancient house, moreover, seemed to have grown up with the green

things out of the soil, so naturally it all belonged together. The garden ran indoors, it seemed, through open doors and windows. Butterflies floated from
courtyard into drawing-room and out again, leaves blew through dining-room
windows, scurrying to another little bit of lawn; the sun and wind, even the
fountains' spray, found the walls no obstacle as though unaware of them. Bees
murmured, swallows hung below the eaves. It was, indeed, a healing spot, a natural retreat...

"I really believe the river rises in your library," exclaimed Fillery, after a tour
of inspection with his host, "and my bedroom is in the heart of that big chest-
nut across the lawn. Do my feet touch carpet, grass, or bark when I get out of
bed in the morning?"

"I've learnt more here," began Father Collins, "than at all the conferences and
learned meetings I ever attended...."

The group of four stood in the twilight by the playing fountain where the dignified stone Pan watched the paved little court, listening to the splash of the water and the wind droning among the leaves. The lap of the winding stream came
faintly to them. The stillness cast a spell about them, dropping a screen against
the outer world.

"Hark!" said Father Collins, holding a curved hand to his ear. "You hear the
music...?"

> "'Why, in the leafy greenwood lone
> Sit you, rustic Pan, and drone
> On a dulcet resonant reed?'"

He paused, peering across to the stone figure as for an answer. All stood listening, waiting, only wind and water breaking the silence. The bats were now
flitting; overhead hung the saffron arch of fading sunset. In a deep ringing voice,
very gruff and very low, Father Collins gave the answer:

> "'So that yonder cows may feed
> Up the dewy mountain passes,
> Gathering the feathered grasses.'

"That's Pan's work," he said, laughing pleasantly, "Pan and all his splendid hierarchy. Always at work, though invisibly, with music, colour, beauty!..."

It was scraps like this that stood out in Fillery's memory, adding to his conviction that Paul had enlisted even this strange priest in his deep-laid plan...

"Each man is saturated with certain ideas, thoughts, phrases in a line of his
own. These constitute his groove. To go outside it makes him feel homeless and
uncomfortable. Accustomed to its measurements and safe within them, he interprets all he hears, reads, observes according to his particular familiar shibboleths, to which, as to a standard of infallible criticism, he brings slavishly all
that is offered for the consideration of his judgment. A new Idea stands little
chance of being comprehended, much less adopted. Tell him new things about

the stars, the Stock Exchange, the Stigmata—up crops his Standard of approval or disapproval. He cannot help himself. His judgment, based upon the limited content of his groove, operates automatically. He condemns. An entirely new idea is barely glanced at before it is rejected for the rubbish heap. How, then, can progress come swiftly to a Race composed of such individuals? Mass-judg-ment, herd-opinion governs everything. He who has original ideas is outcast, and dwells lonely as the moon. How slow, ye Gods! How slow!"...

Only Fillery could not remember, could not be certain, whether it was his host or himself that used the words. Father Collins, as usual, was saying "all sorts of things," but addressed himself, surely, to old Khilkoff most of the time, the Russ-ian, half angry, half amused, growling out his comments and replies as he sat smoking heavily and enjoying the peaceful night scene in his own fashion....

It was odd, none the less, how much that the wild priest gabbled coincided with his own, with Fillery's, thoughts at the moment. A peculiar melancholy, a mood of shyness never known before, lay still upon him. The beauty of the silent girl beside him overpowered him a little; too wonderful to hold, to own, she seemed. Yet they were deliciously, uncannily akin. All his former self-cre-ated denials and suppressions, hesitations and refusals had vanished. "N. H."—he wondered?—had provided him with the fullest expression he had ever known. A boundless relief poured over him. He was aware of wholesome de-sire rising behind his old high admiration and respect....

He watched her once standing close to Pan's broken outline among the shad-ows, touching the mossy arm with white fingers, and he imagined for an instant that she held the vanished pipes.

"After an experience with Other Beings," Father Collins's endless drone floated to him, "shyness, they say, is felt. Silence descends upon the whole na-ture"... to which, a little later, came the growling comment with its foreign ac-cent: "Talk may be pleasurable—sometimes—but it is profitable rarely..."

The talk flowed past and over him, occasional phrases, like islands rising out of a stream, inviting his attention momentarily to land and listen.... The girl, he now saw, no longer stood beside the broken stone figure. She was wandering idly towards the farther garden and the trees.

He burned to rise and go to her, but something held him. What was it? What could it be? Some strange hard little obstacle prevented. Then, suddenly, he knew what it was that stopped him: he was waiting for that familiar pet sen-tence. Once he heard that, the impetus to move, the power to overcome his strange shyness, the certainty that his whole being was at last one with itself again, would come to him. It made him laugh inwardly, while he recognized the validity of the detail—final symptoms of the obstructing inhibitions, of the ob-stinate original complex.

The outline of the girl was lost now, merged in the shadows beyond. He stirred, but could not get up to go. A fury of impatience burned in him. Father Collins, he felt, dawdled outrageously. He was talking—jawing, Fillery called it—about extraordinary experiences. "Gradually, as consciousness more and more often extends, the organs to record such extensions will be formed, you see.... If our inventive faculties were turned inwards, instead of outwards for gain and comfort as they now are, we might know the gods...."

The sculptor's growl, though the words were this time inaudible, had a bite in them. The other voice poured on like thick, slow oil:

"What, anyhow, is it, then, that urges us on in spite of all obstacles, denials, failures...?"

Then came something that seemed leading up to the pet sentence that was the signal he waited for—nearer to it, at any rate:

"...It's childish, surely, to go on merely seeking more of what we have already. We should seek something *new*...."

A call, it seemed, came to him on the wind from the dark trees. But still he could not move.

But, at last, out of a prolonged jumble of the two voices, one growling, the other high pitched, came the signal he somehow waited for. Even now, however, the speaker delayed it as long as possible. He was doing it, of course, on purpose. This was intentional, obviously.

"...Yes, but a thing out of its right place is without power, life, means of expression—robbed of its context which alone gives it meaning—robbed, so to speak, of its arms and legs—*without a body*...."

There, at least, was the definite proof that Father Collins was doing this of deliberate, set purpose!

"Go on! Yes, but, for God's sake, say it! I want to be off!" Fillery believed he shrieked the words, but apparently they were inaudible. They remained unnoticed, at any rate.

"...Hence the value of order, tidyness, you see. Often a misplaced thing is invisible until replaced where it belongs. It is, as we say, lost. No movement is meaningless, no walk without purpose. All your movements tend towards your proper place...."

A breeze blew the fountain spray aside so that its splashing ceased for a brief second. From the rustling leaves beyond came a faint murmur as of distant piping. But—into the second's pause had leaped the pet sentence:

"Only a being in his own place is the ruler of his fate."

The signal! He was aware that the Russian cleared his throat and spat unmusically, aware also that Father Collins, a queer smile just discernible on his face in the gloom, turned his head with a gesture that might well have been an understanding nod. Both sound and gesture, however, were already behind him. He was released. He was across the paved courtyard, past the fountain, past the stone figure of the silent old rough god—and off!

And as he went, finding his way instinctively among the dark trees, that pet sentence went with him like a clarion call, as though sweet piping music played it everywhere about him. A thousand memories shut down with a final snap. In the stage of his mind came a black-out upon a host of inhibitions. There was an immense and glorious sense of relief as though bitter knots were suddenly disentangled, and some iron kernel of resistance that had weighted him for years flowed freely at last in a stream of happy molten gold....

He found her easily. Where the trees thinned at the farther edge he saw her figure, long before he came up with her, outlined against the fading saffron. He saw her turn. He saw her arms outstretched. He came up with her the same minute, and they stood in silence for a long time, watching the darkness bend and sink upon the landscape.

For, here, at this one edge of the tiny estate, the real open country showed. Beyond them, in the twilight, lay the silent fields like a gigantic brown and yellow carpet whose shaken folds still seemed to tremble and run on beneath the growing moon. Along a farther ridge the trees and hedges passed in a ragged procession of strange figures, defined sharply against the sky—witches, queens and goblins on the prowl, the ancient fairyland of the English countryside.

They still stood silent, side by side, touching almost, their heat and perfume and atmosphere intermingling, looking out across the quiet scene. He was aware that her mind stole into his most sweetly, and that without knowing it his hand had found her own, and that, presently, she leaned a little against him. Their eyes, their mental sight as well, saw the same things, he knew. The first stars peeped out, and they looked up at them as one being looks, together.

"The wonder that you saw—in him," he heard himself saying. It was a statement, not a question.

"Was yourself, of course," her voice, like his own, in the rustle of the leaves, came softly. It continued his own thought rather than replied to it. "The part you've held down and hidden away all these years."

Her divination came to him with staggering effect. "You always knew then?"

"Always. The first day we met you took me into the firm."

He was aware that everything about him pulsed and throbbed with life, intelligence in every stick and stone. Angelic beings marched on their wondrous business through the sky. A mighty host pursued their endless service with a network of huge and tiny rhythms. The spirals of creative fire soared and danced....

The moon emerged, sailing, sailing, as though no wind could stop her lovely flight. She fled the stars themselves. The clouds turned round to look at her, as, clearing their hair, she passed onwards with her radiant smile. Heading into the bare bosom of the sky, she blazed in her triumph of loneliness, her icy prow set towards some far, unknown, unearthly goal, which is the reason why men love her so.

"And my theories—our theories?" he murmured into the ear against his lips. "The way that has been shown to us?"

Both arms were now about her, and he held her so close that her words were but a warm perfumed breath to cover his face as her hair was covering his eyes.

"We shall follow it together... dear."

It was as if some angel, stepping down from the sky, came near enough to fold them in a great rhythm of fire and wind. Bright, mighty faces in a crowd rose round them, and, through her hair, he saw familiar visible outlines of all the common things melt out, showing for one gorgeous instant the flashings and whirlings that was the workshop of Their deathless service.

"Look! Look!" he whispered, pointing from the darkening earth to the stars and sailing moon above. "They're everywhere! You can see them too? The bright messengers?"

For answer, she came yet closer against his side, holding him more tightly to her, lifting her lips to his, so that in her very eyes he saw the marvellous fire shine and flash. "We shall build together, you and I," she whispered very softly, "and with Their help, the sweetest and most perfect body ever known...."

But behind the magic of her words and voice, behind their meaning and the steadying, understanding sympathy he easily divined, he heard another sound, familiar as a dream, yet fraught with some haunting significance he already was forgetting—almost *had* entirely forgotten. From the centre of the earth it seemed to rise, a magnificent, deep, stupendous rhythm that created, at least, the impression of a voice:

"I weave and I weave...!" rolled forth, as though the planet uttered. He stood waiting, transfixed, listening intently.

"You heard?" he whispered.

"Everything," she said, tight in his arms at once again, her lips on his. "The very beating of your heart—your inmost thoughts as well."

THE END

Printed in the USA
CPSIA information can be obtained
at www.ICGtesting.com
LVHW010000190923
758524LV00002B/44